THE EXTENDED <u>AGE</u>
OMNIBUS

Copyright © 2020 by Ty'Ron W. C. Robinson II. All rights reserved.

Published by Dark Titan Entertainment.

The Legendary Warslinger, Redemption of the Lost, Lost in Shadows: Remastered, Accounts of The Dead Days Hod, Symbolum Venatores: The Gabriel Kane Collection, and *The Book of The Elect are* available separately in hardcover and paperback respectfully.

Battle For Astolat is a Kobo e-book Exclusive.

The Pleasured Killing and *The Passover* are separate short stories.

Dark Titan Extended is a branch of Dark Titan Entertainment.

First Printing 2020.

ISBN: 978-1-7343300-6-9

darktitanentertainment.com

WORKS BY TY'RON W. C. ROBINSON II

<u>BOOKS</u>

DARK TITAN UNIVERSE SAGA

MAIN SERIES

Dark Titan Knights
The Resistance Protocol
Tales of the Scattered
Tales of the Numinous
Day of Octagon
Crossbreed (Forthcoming)
Heaven's Called (Forthcoming)

SPIN-OFFS

In A Glass of Dawn: The Casebook of Travis Vail
Maveth: Bloodsport (Forthcoming)
The Curse of The Mutant-Thing (Forthcoming)
Trail of Vengeance (Forthcoming)
War of The Thunder Gods (Forthcoming)

COLLECTED EDITIONS

Dark Titan Omnibus: Volume. 1 Dark Titan One-Shot Collection
The Swordman Collection
The Commander Norland Collection The Chosen Son Collection
The Nano Man Collection
The Unstoppable Beast Collection

THE HAUNTED CITY SAGA

The Legendary Warslinger: The Haunted City I
Battle of Astolat: A Haunted City Prequel (KOBO Exclusive)
Redemption of the Lost: The Haunted City II
Consequences of the Suffering: The Haunted City III (Forthcoming)

OTHER BOOKS

Lost in Shadows: A Novel
Lost in Shadows: Remastered
Accounts of The Dead Days
The Book of The Elect
Hod
Hallow Sword: Cursed(KOBO Exclusive)
Symbolum Venatores: The Gabriel Kane Collection

THE EXTENDED AGE

OMNIBUS

TY'RON W. C. ROBINSON II

CONTENTS

THE WORLD OF THE HAUNTED CITY

THE LEGENDARY WARSLINGER: THE HAUNTED CITY I

REDEMPTION OF THE LOST: THE HAUNTED CITY II

NEW HAVEN'S INSTINCTS

LOST IN SHADOWS: REMASTERED

<u>**_THE BOOK OF THE ELECT_**</u>

BATTLE FOR ASTOLAT

A CONFLICT OF THE HAUNTED CITY

I

The city of Astolat stood tall amongst its neighboring regions. Astolat is the city of Elaine and her father, Bernard. The city was ravaged by an army. An unseen army, who appeared from the air. The Astolat army combated the strange and ghostly force. The ghostly army overtook the soldiers, killing them within an instant. Bernard took Elaine and they both went into hiding. Having no other choice, but to escape the city as the ghostly army sacked their home and their leader appeared before them. Dressed in a dark violet cloak with his face rarely seen, although his eyes appeared to reveal themselves. The eyes looked dead, but there was another force living through them.

Residing at a secondary home, far into the wilderness, away from Astolat. Elaine writes a letter, detailing the event of Astolat's invasion and sacking by the unknown force. Bernard entered the room, seeing her writing the letter. He's intrigued.

"What are you up to, my daughter?"

"I'm sending word for help."

"Help?"

"Yes. I know of some men who can aid us in taking back Astolat."

"What kind of me are these that are capable of doing such a matter?"

"A set-apart kind." Elaine said. "They know justice."

She finished writing the letter. Walking outside toward the pigeon cage. Placing the letter, the bird flew in the air with Elaine watching. Bernard approached Elaine from the side, also seeing the pigeon flying away.

"Hope you're right on this cause."

The pigeon flew several miles, until it reached the city of Old Jerusalem. The city was the home base to the Warslingers of the Heptad. The pigeon reached the Temple of the Heptad. Sitting outside the temple was Joshua of Ephraim. The pigeon flew to him, landing in front of him. Joshua sees the rolled letter. He grabbed the letter and the pigeon flies off, returning to Elaine. Joshua entered the temple, seeing the other Warslingers.

"Brothers, this was just delivered to us." Joshua said, handing them the letter.

Moses The Leader grabbed the letter. He opened it and read. The Warslingers stood around him, waiting for him to speak. Moses read the letter to himself and rolled it back up. Nodding, he turned to his brethren.

"It appears we have work to do. First, we make way for Old Camelot. Inform Knight Arthur Pendragon of these details. He must come along with us. For he is also our brother in this walk."

"Moses." Joshua said. "What did the letter inform?"

"It informed of some danger that has been committed. Now, it is our task to rid this malevolency from this place."

The Warslingers make ready to travel to Old Camelot, leaving Old Jerusalem on horseback. In the matter of time, Elaine awaits an answer from the Warslingers as des her father, who worries for Astolat's remains. Believing the ghostly army will turn their city into rubble and ashes.

Entering Old Camelot, Knight Arthur Pendragon was there at the gate to greet his brothers-in-arms. Standing by his sides were Maiden Guinevere and Knight Lancelot. Moses stepped from his horse and walked towards the king of Old Camelot. Extending arms, the two hugged.

"Wasn't expecting to see you this soon." Arthur said.

"Wouldn't be here if it wasn't of importance."

"What's happened?"

"We can talk inside."

"Of course."

Walking inside the castle, they reached the Great Hall, where the Spherical Table sat. the Warslingers all sat at the table while Lancelot guarded the doors. Guinevere left their presence as they started to discuss their matters.

"Now, what's taken place?"

"We've received a letter of distress from the land of Astolat. It appears something has been ongoing in the land for a while and under our sight."

"Invasion from Old Egypt?"

"We won't know until we reach Astolat. We came because we'll need you with us."

Arthur nodded.

"I'll go along. Of course, being a Warslinger myself, it is my duty."

"Believe me, I can see you have plenty to deal with. Ruling a kingdom and being a Warslinger. Only few souls can achieve both titles and become a master at them."

"Speaking of such, how's Old Jerusalem?"

"Peaceful. *El* is there with us. Always."

Arthur nodded with a smile as they headed out of Old Camelot, traveling toward Astolat.

II

Making their entrance in Astolat, the common folk watched in awe and fear as the Warslingers came in on their horses. They made their presence known. Moses turned to Joshua, Daniel, Henrich, and Charlton as they settled their horses near the station.

"The four of you will remain here." Moses commanded. "Keep this place guarded and the people safe."

"Where are you heading?" Charlton asked.

"Myself, Noah, and Arthur will be speaking to King Bernard at their second estate. They refuse to return here until the task is done."

Moses, Noah, and Arthur rode off, leaving the other four Warslingers to settle into the city. They looked toward one another before going separate ways throughout the city, finding a spot and keeping guard. Due to the lack of protection from the Astolatians.

"They carry no weapons." Charlton observed.

"They leave the fighting to the soldiers." Daniel replied. "They don't join in on the battles."

"But, we're supposed to protect them?"

"I know it irks you, Darrain. But, just this once, don't let it bother you."

Far from Astolat, the three Warslingers arrived at the second estate. Seeing two Astolat Knights keeping guard. They approached the door and it opened with Elaine standing in their presence. She ran out and hugged each of them with tears in her eyes. Relieved they received the letter and took the call. Bernard stepped foot outside, seeing the Warslingers. He nodded with great respect.

"It's an honor to have you here, Moses."

"We'll do anything to rid your city of the malevolency which circles it. May we come in and discuss this?"

"Of course."

They entered the home, sitting at the table near the kitchen. Elaine brought them some hot tea, due to the wintry weather occurring. Bernard sat with them while Elaine stood back.

"Tell us what's been happening."

"They appeared out of nowhere." Bernard said. "They showed up and started ransacking the city. Killing some of the people."

"What did they look like?" Arthur asked. "Were they possible adversaries to Old Camelot?"

"No. They didn't seem to be from our world. Nor any of the Worlds."

"You're saying they possessed some mystical power?"

"They must have. To do the things they've done. Levitation, portal binding, teleportation. They had to have been very precise in their arts."

Moses nodded. He looked over to Noah, who also nodded.

'This sounds eerily familiar."

"Do tell." Arthur noted.

"Myself and Noah in the early days dealt with a small army which did such feats. This was when the Heptad was yet to be formed and the Warslingers were few in number. This was during the early stages of the Eastern World War. Those who didn't possess weapons of any kind chose magic as their arsenal. Some we trusted, turned on us, doing the same as Bernard spoke."

"So, will you help us in taking back our city?" Bernard asked.

"I must ask." Noah said. "We just came from your city and only the people are present. No signs of any threats."

"You mean they left?"

"Did they leave after the ambush?"

"Me and Elaine left before we could tell."

Moses stood up from the table. Noah and Arthur followed his movement. A Warslinger custom. Elaine walked to the table and Bernard stood up.

"We will aid you in finding the source of this mystic power. Once it is done, you may return to your city."

"Thank you." Elaine said.

"We're just doing what we must."

The Warslingers exited the home with Bernard behind them. As they sat atop their horses, Bernard approached them.

"You can stay here for the night. We have plenty of room."

"Much thanks is obliged." Moses said. "However, it is best we return to Astolat. To keep guard. We already have four Warslingers present. I will return to you once the job is done."

"I wish you the best." Elaine said.

"Take care of yourselves." Arthur said.

The Warslingers rode off.

Later in Astolat, the four Warslingers have received accommodations in the castle chambers. One to each of them. Henrich sat in his chamber, counting the hours. A knock came from the door, catching the young Warslinger's attention.

"Door's open." Henrich said.

The door opened and Charlton entered. He shut the door behind him and approached Henrich, sitting across from him at the table.

"What is it?" Henrich asked.

"You know me. You know how this all goes. What do you think's happening here?"

"Some magic wielders probably causing a ruckus. We've dealt with such before."

"Indeed." Charlton nodded. "But, have you ever considered the cost of us doing the work of another? I mean, this King Bernard has knights of his own. Why are we here doing their bidding?"

"I'm not getting what you're speaking."

Charlton sighed.

"We're supposed to protect the ones from evil. Those who can't protect themselves."

"Yes."

"This city already has protection in the form of these knights. We're not needed here. For all *El* knows, we could be needed in Old Egypt or Old Rome."

"I get your point."

"Do you? Because from what I've seen today, you've been blindly obeying every command given."

"I'm not in authority, Charlton." Henrich proclaimed. "Neither are you. We all have our place in the Heptad. In *El*."

"Yes, we do." Charlton nodded in agreement.

He stood up and walked toward the door. Henrich watched him.

"Just remember." Charlton said. "Think about why we're here and not elsewhere. They're something going on and we need to be careful."

"I'll take your word for it." Henrich replied.

Charlton left the room and Henrich laid down on the bed, falling asleep.

Later in the night, Moses, Noah, and Arthur returned to the city and entered their own chambers. All the Warslingers were asleep for the night.

<u>III</u>

The following morning, the Warslingers gathered the Astolatian Knights to the court of the castle. Moses sat before them, giving them instructions on how to prepare for the returning army and the attacks in which will be operated. As Moses continued giving the instructions, a fellow soldier bolted through the doors, his face showing minor scars compared to his damaged armor.

"They're back!" The soldier yelled before falling on the floor.

The soldiers all stood up and ran outside. Moses and the Warslingers held back as the remaining soldiers left the room. Joshua took a step forward, yet stopped by Moses.

"We need to help them."

"And we will." Moses said. "Give it a second."

"A second?"

"This army doesn't know of our presence. Therefore, we have the alterative surprise."

Moses turned to the other Warslingers and nodded.

"You know what to do. Go now."

The Warslingers went their ways outside the castle. Moses walked on and Joshua followed him. Eventually heading outside to see the battle in front of the city and on the castle grounds. They saw the army clearly. Dark armor, scaly and sharp. Their faces covered by their burnt helmets. Moses recognized such a garment.

"This isn't new." Moses said.

"What do you mean, my Leader?" Joshua asked.

"I know who's leading them. And he's close."

The Warslingers appeared from their corners around the castle, catching the army off guard. Henrich and Charlton used their

7

arkshooters, firing rounds in the heads and chests of the mystical soldiers. The rounds from the shooters piercing through their armor like a nail through a leaf. Daniel, Noah, and Arthur swiping through the battlefield. Arthur wielding *Excalibur* while Daniel held the *Faithsword* and Noah carried the *Arkaxe*. The army was quickly being defeated with the Astolat knights cheering on the skills and fighting styles of the Heptad. Through their cheering, Moses and Joshua stepped out into the field as Henrich fired another round at the mystic soldier. The battleground set still with only the cheers of the Astolat knights. The Warslingers came over, standing next to their leader.

"This is not over." Moses uttered.

"Then, where is their leader?" Charlton asked.

"Right there." Henrich said, pointing toward the east, near the entry point of the castle grounds.

Standing before them was indeed a man, covered in scaly armor. Appeared burned, but with a violet and reddish hue. His face was with a helmet, giving him the appearance of having six eyes with a hood and cloak. The Astolat knights attempted to rush him, however, he raised his arms, lifting them off the ground and tossing them across the grounds of Astolat. He was strong in the mystic arts. Moses stepped forward.

"I know him."

"You do?" Arthur said. "How?"

"Because, he was once one of us."

"*Mosheh*." The figure spoke. "We have met once more."

"Yes, we have, Azotus Vorr."

IV

Moses and Azotus stood facing each other. Moses held his staff tightly as the sapphire began to glow.

"It has been some time." Azotus said.

"Not long enough." Moses replied. "You're the leader of this army."

"I am. They came to me after our last encounter."

"Those who sided with you became endowed with mystical abilities?"

"As did I."

Azotus held his arm out and from the thin air appeared a staff. Similar to Moses' own, yet darker, burnt, and glowing wih a violet and reddish hue of energy. The staff was endowed with the same mystical power as Azotus.

"Why don't we settle this like warriors." Azotus said.

"So be it."

The two staves collided, giving off a shockwave of energy. From there, the Warslingers aided the remaining Astolat knights against Azotus' army. The entire area of Astolat was now a battleground with Moses and Azotus standing in the middle, staves colliding and blasting energy. Henrich and Charlton stayed together, firing rounds toward the soldiers.

"What about Moses?" Charlton asked.

"He can take care of himself." Henrich replied. "We need to deal with these soldiers."

The Warslingers take the fight to the soldiers, wiping them out with some of the Astolat knights finishing them off. Moses and Azotus continued their bout, with Moses swiping the staff against Azotus' chest, knocking him across the field. Azotus arose and slammed the ground with his staff, causing a minor tremor. Stumbling Moses.

"Never did like the ground quake." Azotus said.

Azotus rushed toward Moses with staff in hand. In came closer, yet, Moses turned to him with the sapphire staff facing him. Once Azotus was in touching distance, the staff emitted a bright flash of light. The light pushed Azotus from Moses and in doing so, the soldiers of Vorr vanished due to the light.

"What kind of power is this?" Azotus questioned.

"The power you walked away from." Moses replied. "Now, go and never return."

Azotus took steps forward, trying to breach the light's power. But he could not, for the light was far stronger than the mystic power he possessed. The light did come from the staff, but its source was not in the staff nor was it the staff itself. Azotus knew this and vanished before their eyes. The Warslingers looked around and the knights appeared with them. The battle was over. Astolat had won.

Some days later, Bernard and Elaine returned to Astolat and started the reconstruction of the city. Bernard had thanked Moses and the Warslingers for their aid and effort. However, Moses did inform Bernard Azotus would not be returning to his city anymore, but he will return one day to exact payment on the lost battle. Bernard understood the Warslinger's words and chose to assist the Heptad against Vorr once the time arises. Elaine hugged Moses and thanked the Warslingers for their help. They had left the city, returning to Old Jerusalem.

On the path back, Arthur turned to Moses, thinking of Vorr and the battle. He knew the answer to his question and Moses knew it as well.

"Was he who I think he was?" Arthur said.

"He was." Moses replied. "A man once one of us. A Warslinger gone to the malevolency."

CHAPTER ONE

THE LEGENDARY WARSLINGER

I

"There I came and there I saw. The place where the ghouls dwelled until their own final breaths. A city that's rich with minerals and treasures of times past. Many have tried to discover the dark place, but those have all failed. The closest ones to come have only made it to the City's gates and have yet and never went through them. I figured that one day I will take up that boast and find The Haunted City myself."

Randolph Henrich–member of a group of holy warriors who combat the dark forces of the Worlds, took a stroll through the deserts of the Western World. The deserts were filled with dark sand, rarely any cactuses standing upright, most were laid down in the dirt, dehydrated by the new sun's rays. Randolph walked through the desert, kicking the dirt with the footsteps of his brown leather boots. He gazed up at the sun, placing his hand in the air to avoid the sun's rays from contacting with his eyes.

"Whatever designed you sure must be a mouthful of pain."

Henrich continued to walk, seeing what he believed to be a small town up ahead. He nodded, continuing to walk and barely able to keep standing since he hasn't taken a rest stop in hours.

"I can keep going. There's a town up ahead. I can keep going. I can keep going."

Henrich continued to walk through the heat of the middle of the day. While he kept walking, he heard a stumble from behind. Slowly turning around to see what caused the stumble. Henrich looked and seen a strander staring at him, dressed in raggedy clothing with a dirty gray duster coat and a dirty gray hat. His face looked like it hasn't been washed in weeks, mostly covered up by his facial hair and his long hair coming down from his hat. carrying a bag that appeared to be full of many things. From a small opening, Henrich could see a bottle of water. The bag caught Henrich's eyes immediately.

"Looks like I've found myself another strander, huh?" The strander said. "Tell me what you're doing out here in the deserts of this Western World here?"

"None of your concern. Carry on about your business, strander."

"Whoa, whoa, whoa. First off, my business was to head to the town up ahead and deliver these goods here. But, now my business concerns you, strander."

"Listen, I've been through much. I suggest you go about your business."

"I don't think so, strander."

Henrich gazed toward the bag. Intrigued to know what may be sitting within it. Possible survival gear? Food? Water? Medicine? Henrich wanted to know.

"Tell me what's in the bag you're meant to deliver?"

"I'm not telling you a damn thing as to what is laying inside this bag right here. If you really want to know, you'll drag your ass onto the town and wait till I deliver it. Then, you'll see what's in this bag."

"That's not the way I see this going."

"You look like you seem to be some kind of "slinger." Hell, I doubt your one of those ancient slingers still kicking after most of them died out. Couldn't bare the heat of the sun nor the battle against the evil."

"What I am is nothing compared to what I can do to you. I suggest you move along about your business, but if you don't go about your business keep to yourself, you'll end up in some possible trouble."

"Don't tell me what to do, boy!"

The strander put down his bag and approached Henrich with his flintlock pistol up. He placed the pistol into Henrich's chest.

Laughing and smirking in Henrich's face. His breath had the stench of a corpse in the heat. His teeth were dirtier than the sands of the desert.

"Seems to me that I'm the one in charge here because I have you locked on. Dead enter in your chest, boy."

"You believe that? You believe your own foolish words of folly?"

"Folly? No. No. You're the one who's folly. Walking around this empty field of dirt with no supplies on you. Hell, I don't even see a shooter on your waist."

"I don't place a shooter on my waist."

"Humor me for this moment before I put you in the dirt, where do you keep your shooters?"

"In plain sight."

Henrich fired the revolver through his coat, the shot penetrates the chest of the strander. The strander took steps back, holding his chest as the blood began to pour out. The strander raised his pistol up to get at least one shot on Henrich. Henrich kicked the pistol out of the strander's hand and punched him in his face. The strander fell to the ground as Henrich placed his boot against his throat.

"You're bleeding, and you won't make it to town in this condition. So, this is where you'll crossover into the After-World and greet all the other bastards that have tried such a move upon me."

"Be that as it may. I sure as hell hope to see your ass there very, very soon. That way, I can beat your ass for eternity."

"Take your time and count your numbers, strander. I'll come when He says come."

Henrich looked over, seeing the strander's gear. He walked over and grabbed the bag. Searching and digging through it, finding canned food, bottled water, bullet rounds, a shotgun, another flintlock pistol, and several knifes. Henrich smirked.

"A motherlode of savers. You came prepared didn't you, strander."

"Better to be prepared than not to be prepared. Like your sorry ass. I was sent to deliver those goods to the rightful owner. From the description I read, you're not the owner."

"I'll take your bag to the town and meet with the owner myself."

"Go to Sheol, boy."

Henrich pulled out his revolver, aiming it right into the strander's forehead. The strander looked at the pistol, intrigued at its design.

"I recognize that shooter."

"You do huh?"

"Those were seen in painting with the ancient Warslingers of the past. Only they possessed such weapons. Weapons of great power."

"You know what's funny about our whole confrontation, strander?"

"What? You're one of those damn Warslinger guys?" The strander said with a laugh following. "You could never be one of them because they were all weak and now because of their weakness, they're dead."

Henrich smiled. "Yeah. You claim they're all dead. But, you've missed the point of my question. What's funny about this whole matter is you're looking at one."

Henrich fired the shot, killing the strander. Henrich grabbed the bag, ate a can of corn, he drank two flagons of water, reloaded his pistol, placed the other pistol into his left holster inside his coat, pulled out the blastshooter, loaded it up, placing it on a sling on his back. Henrich continued his walk toward the small town. He sees the town up ahead and tips his hat, walking forward.

II

Henrich walked in a mile of an inched closer to the small town. He could see the small structures that stood before him in the town and could also spot a saloon in the middle of the town, even people walking around the buildings. Henrich kept walking in the last mile before entering the town mark. The town was called Hevoc, around the town appeared to be only a small group of people who lived there. Henrich entered the town, passing its entry line as the residents turned and stared at him. The residents themselves, dressed in duster coats and hats while the women wore dresses and headscarf, stared at Henrich walking in the town toward the saloon.

"Who is this man?" a resident wondered curiously.

"Looks like one of those slingers to me."

"He can't be one of them. They're all dead and gone from this world."

"Anything is possible. He very well could be one in disguise."

Henrich approached the saloon and entered therein. The inside of the saloon was packed with men drinking and playing cards with each other. Some stood against the saloon walls and lean against them. Others sat at the saloon bar drinking. The sound of the saloon door opening gathered their attention as they turned and seen Henrich enter the place, carrying the bag with him.

"What's in the bag, strander?" said a man at the table.

"You're about to find that out." Henrich said.

Henrich walked and stood in the middle of the saloon where everyone could see him. He placed the bag down on the floor in front of him as he gazed around the saloon. Seeing the men slowly, but surely preparing themselves, reaching to their holsters.

"No need to reach for your shooters. Not just yet." said Henrich. "I am here to see the owner of this bag here. I believe that some form of a discussion could be made to what lies inside of it. Very valuable items and a good agreement between me and the owner could make this very better for all of you here."

A man walked from down the stairs of the saloon. Henrich turned and looked at him, seeing his black suit with a top hat. His moustache stood out from beside his attire. The man looked at Henrich and saw the bag on the floor in front of his feet. The man smirked.

"You're not the man that was sent to bring me that bag."

"No. I'm not. I dealt with him out in the desert fields. He wanted to do business and we did. Now, I come here to do the business that he failed to do."

The man put his hands up, shaking his head.

"You don't have to repeat what you've already said to the entire saloon here. I overheard everything from up the stairs."

"So, you know what I recommend about what's inside this bag, here?"

"I certainly do. May I have a look see?"

"Sure."

Henrich kneeled and zipped open the bag, revealing the food, water, and gear that laid inside of it. Some of the men also looked and the items peaked their interest as well.

"Sure, a lot of firepower in that there bag." said a man at the bar.

"Good you can see it."

"Now, what is the deal you're proposing to me about these items and the bag?"

"Half and half. Half the food and water stay with me. Along with half of the weapons."

"I am aware that I was supposed to gain possession of everything inside that bag for the people of Hevoc."

"Things change in this world. Either take the deal or reject it. Your decision."

The man looked out at the men and women inside the saloon. Their faces show slight concern for themselves and the man. The man turned back to Henrich and sighed.

"Well, what's your answer?"

"My answer sadly is no. I will not let you take half of everything that is inside this bag right here. The people of this town need it more than you do. See, allow me to say this to you and maybe you'll understand clearly what I am telling you. A town of people is more important to save than one man trying to save himself."

"You know how to put your words in order."

"You can say that. I mean, who else controls everything that goes on here in Hevoc. Me of course."

Henrich nodded and looked around the saloon again. Feeling the tension in the air. The man raised up his hands, looking around the saloon at the men and women inside.

"Rally up my people. We have a choice to make this day and this hour."

"You're sure you want to do this?" said Henrich.

"I have no choice, strander. It's for the people of Hevoc."

The man rallied up the men and women inside the saloon as they all begin to surround Henrich, their pistols out in the open, all pointing at Henrich. Henrich stood still, with only his eyes following the people and his arms crossed with the bag still on the floor at his feet. The man stood in front of Henrich, smiling.

"You really think we're going to let you leave after the words you've brought in here?"

"Doesn't appear that you have a choice as to who leaves or stays." The man nodded.

"Strander. I'm going to tell you this right now and I hope to the Father Above this sinks into your cranium. You're going to die here by the people of Hevoc and after they kill you, we're going to spread out the goods in this here bag right here across the town. That way everyone will have something to continue going forward in this life."

Henrich grinned.

"For the good of the people huh. That's why you're doing all of this, right?"

"That's the purpose of this here scene."

Henrich nodded slightly. No emotion showing on his face nor in his eyes.

"Might as well get this thing started."

"You know what? You're right for a change."

The man waved his hand in the air, counting down for the people to shoot Henrich from all corners of the saloon. As the man was counting, Henrich's hands were inside his coat, locked tight onto his shooter and the flintlock. His eyes were locked on the man, still counting down.

"Seven, six five four three..." The man counted. "Two, one..."

Henrich pulled out the pistol and flintlock and fired the shot through the man's head. He fell to the ground as Henrich turned to the people and started shooting at them. Henrich's ability to shoot was very impressive that his speed was unmatched by anyone inside the saloon. The people outside of the saloon ran into their homes and nearby buildings to avoid being shot at. Henrich looked and spotted two men coming at him with machetes. Henrich nodded as he reached to his back and pulled out the shotgun, shooting the two men through their stomachs. Henrich turned and continued the shooting with his shotguns toward the ones remaining inside the saloon. Henrich stood as the last person walked in front of him, with a revolver in hand, aimed for Henrich's head.

"You're not leaving this place for all the shit that you've done!"

'I am leaving." said Henrich. "With the bag."

Henrich fired the blastshooter against the person. He grabbed the bag and walked out of the saloon, leaving it full of dead, shot up bodies.

<h1 style="text-align:center">III</h1>

Walking out of the saloon, Henrich found himself leaving, but caught the sound of a woman's screeching scream not far from the saloon. Coming close by, Henrich turned the corner, walking behind the saloon to find the woman yelling for help as she is being harassed by a group of sexual predators.

"Stop what you're doing." said Henrich.

The predators turned to Henrich, dirty as the dirt could possibly get. Their clothing worn out, tearing at the edges. Their faces are dirty as the sand, appear dehydrated as well. There were four of them and they all wanted the woman for themselves. Now, seeing Henrich gives them other opportunities.

"Look what we have here, my boys! Some strander has come into our territory."

"You know how we deal with stranders, boy? We do with them as we please."

Henrich stood still, facing the predators as they began to circle him. Measuring him from the top of his hat to the bottom of his boot. Laughing and scoffing at Henrich while showing signs of a deeper interest. One predator started licking his lips.

"You know what we should do about this strander, here?"

"What should we do?"

"After we finish with the virgin over there, we can have ourselves a strander. What do you guys think?"

"I've been wanting to get a release for weeks."

"Now, you have an opportunity my friend. Two for the taking."

"I suggest you back away from me and leave the woman alone." said Henrich.

"Or what's going to happen?"

"You heard the commotion taking place inside the saloon. What do you think will happen once that similar circumstance comes to your outside doors?"

"I think he's threatening us."

"He is. Trying to frighten us away from him and the virgin. No. It will take more than threats and trembles to move us away from what we're about to do to you and this virgin."

Henrich looked over at the woman, who's crying with tears streaming down her face. The lead predator began to unbuckle his belt, staring at Henrich. The other predators started to do the same.

"I figure we'll take you first, strander. Then, when we're finished up with you, we can enjoy this virgin over here. Corrupt her soul as they put it."

"Go ahead." Henrich said. "Make a move and you'll wish you didn't have."

"Strander still spitting out threats at us fellows. Told you it will take a lot more to frighten us to move."

Henrich blew the predator's head off with the shotgun and fired rounds at the ones remaining through the chest and heads. Their bodies fell to the ground with the echoes of the firing weapons flowing across the air. Henrich sighed as he picked up his bag from the ground and walked over toward the virgin woman. The woman showed a sign of relief as Henrich approached her and helped her up from the ground.

"Are you well?" Henrich asked.

"I will live."

"Good. That's good."

"Come on. You're coming with me."

"Why? There's nothing out there in the World for me. Nothing."

"You've never had the chance to look and see, have you?"

"I've never left this town. I was born here."

Henrich nodded.

"I can see that through your eyes. Come along with me to the outskirts and maybe you'll find a place out there that will suit you better than this lousy town."

Hesitant and fearful about her own safety, the woman followed Henrich to the exit of Hevoc and back into the desert once more, only this time, Henrich considered the woman as they entered the desert. He gave her a bottle of water from his bag. She drank the entire bottle as if she hasn't had anything to drink in days.

IV

"You never told me your name." Henrich said. "I would like to know your name."

"My name is Cara."

"Just Cara. No middle or last name to add?"

"I've only been called Cara. Nothing else besides Cara and the Virgin Woman."

"I take it, they call you virgin because you've never become one with a man. Am I right?"

"You are correct. There isn't a man around here that deems themselves to be a suitable companion to me."

"Maybe you'll find that man when you see the other places this Western World has to offer. Hell, maybe you'll travel across the Ethiopic into the Eastern World and find a suitable man of your needs there."

"You think so? You think I can find a man like that in this World?"

"I am positive that you will. Only give it some time of course."

"What of you, sir?"

"What about me?"

"You never told me your name either. I just thought that we would exchange names."

"Randolph Henrich."

Cara looked at Henrich and noticed the two pistols in his coat holster. She recognized the other one with its unique design.

"That shooter you have in your coat. I noticed the design of it.

That's not one of the shooters that belonged to the Warslingers is it?"

"You know of them?"

"Everyone I believe knows of them. They protected people from the darkness of this world. A darkness that most humans have no idea even exists. I was only a little girl when I met a demon, two of the Warslingers came in and saved me from the demon. Killed it with holy bullets as they called them."

"What would you believe if I told you that not all of the Warslingers are dead. That, the few remaining are scattered across the world. Continuing their duties on their new soil grounds. Looking for a way to reunite when it's time."

"I would say I hope that they can unite and save all of us from the evil that exists out here. Be it demons, ghouls, or humans themselves. We need to be protected and I hope that the Warslingers return and prove the doubters and mockers wrong."

"They will, Cara. One day, they will."

Henrich and Cara continue to walk through the desert. Fighting against the heat of the sun's rays as clouds began to come over the desert and slowly cooling off the area. Giving Henrich and Cara some sort of comfort.

"Where did those clouds come from?" said Cara. "They just appeared out of nowhere."

"Maybe we're being watched." Henrich said with a smile.

"Perhaps we are."

Henrich continued his smile before looking toward into the desert, seeing nothing but dirt and dead cactuses. The clouds above them had cooled them off immensely. The sweat that was coming from both of their foreheads had suddenly disappeared and evaporated into the air.

"So, where would you go if you had your choice?" Henrich said.

"I do not know. There's so many places that I have yet to visit, but I'm not sure which of them would be best suited for someone like me. Where would you go, if you had the choice?"

"The Haunted City. That's where I would go."

"Why there? You know of its legends and its feats. So, why would you make the attempt to travel there? What would be there for you to receive?"

"That city has power within it that's unheard of in our World. The evidence and receiving that someone would possess while inside of the City would give them all the answers that they sought after and could even give them knowledge unknown to others in this World."

"But, what of the one that guards the gate to the City?"

"What guardian?" Henrich said quickly. "I've never heard of someone guarding the entrance into the City."

"There is a guardian at the gate to The Haunted City. People call him many names. Such as the Dark King, the Troublesome One, Lord of the Shadows. He's truly known throughout the Worlds as the Tubal King."

"The meaning of his name would be considered as 'King of the Earth'. in the Old Speech."

"They say he knows about everyone in the World. He knows about me and my past, my present, and my future. He also knows of you, Randolph. Your past, your present, and your future."

"How can he really know?"

"Because he's King of the Worlds. He knows all that takes place on this soil."

"I don't consider him as a threat to me. As anyone ever seen this Tubal King?"

"No one apparently. They say he uses his invisible power to watch over the Worlds, seeing what everyone is doing."

"Be that as it may be, I will see to it when I come across The Haunted City that I may see this Tubal King. Hell, he can open the gate for me."

Cara smiled with a hint of fear for Henrich's well-being. Seeing him not tremble at the name of the Tubal King and what he can do.

"I'm sensing you're not afraid of him."

"Afraid?! I haven't even met the man. I'm just now learning about him after what you've told me."

"You should be afraid of him, Randolph. Be cautious for yourself and those that may travel amongst you. For they might not be aware of the Tubal King's power as you're now aware."

They walked until they saw a standing sign, pointing in two

different directions. They read the signs, rubbing the dirt from them to get a better look at what the arrows are pointing towards the directions. The left sign points toward 'the dark woods' while the right sign points to a place called Mega City, a large metropolitan city covered with darkness and clouds. A gothic looking place. Cara moved to the right, standing on Henrich's right side.

"You're going that way?" Henrich pointed. "To Mega City?"

"I figure I could get a better start there. I've heard about what happens to those that walk through the dark woods before and I am not about to make the same mistakes they've made by walking right up in there. So many monsters dwell within that forest I hear. Terrifying monsters."

"I understand your concern, Cara." Henrich said slightly. "Make your next step to Mega City. I will enter the dark woods and see what I can come up with on the other side."

"You've been through the forest before?"

"Darling, I've been through many places and I have seen so much in this life. Things that would make a bold man tremble in his boots."

Henrich handed Cara three flagons of water and three cans of food. He also gave her a knife and a small shooter with a few bullets. She thanked him for the supplies. Henrich began walking past the sign, going left as he watched Cara wave to him as she walked to the right.

"Take care of yourself, you hear?" Henrich said.

"I will." said Cara. "Remember what I told you about the Tubal King. He's watching us all."

"I shall keep that in mind."

Henrich nodded to Cara as they both walked their separate ways through the desert as the clouds above them began to spread out between the two. One cloud following Henrich and the other following Cara.

Henrich continued to make his walk through the desert. After several miles of traveling on foot with almost little to no supplies left inside the bag except for a couple of shooters, bullets, and knives. He continued walking and could see the dark woods in the horizon. Only several more miles were needed before he could enter the forest.

Henrich walked and walked, seemly getting tired and restless from the walking. The cloud continued to stay over him, keeping him cool from the sun and the intense heat of the desert. He drank from one of his flagons of water. He decided to take a slight break as he sat down next to a boulder and a dead cactus. He ate from another can of food thereof and finish the bottle of water.

"What will it take. What shall it take."

An hour had passed. Henrich had moved on from his resting place and continued walking forward to the forest that he could still see in the horizon in front of him. He kept walking, his pistols still loaded as he hasn't released a single shot since saving Cara from the predators in Hevoc. Cara was on Henrich's mind, thinking as to where she could be right now.

"Did she make it to Mega City safety? Has she made it to Mega City?" Henrich did not know and was well understood that whatever happened with Cara was on her hands and her decisions. Henrich walked, noticing his clothes being covered with the dirt of the desert. The dirt began to present itself onto his face. His facial hair covered with the desert dirt.

Walking, he realized someone was watching him from a distance in the desert. He could feel the presence there, behind him and on the side of him. Henrich took several looks from behind and to his sides. Seeing nothing but the clear desert around him, he continued to walk forward.

While he walked, he noticed there were skeletal remains lying around in the dirt. He looked at the bones and could tell they were not from ancient ones of the past times. He knew they were recent and very recent. Henrich slowly took his steps forward, inching closer to his pistols with his right hand almost to the handle of the pistol. He walked and instantly as if a flash of light had appeared, Henrich was surrounded by six individuals covered in black shrouds and cloaks. Their faces unseen by the hoods they wore. They didn't appear dirty from the desert, which triggered Henrich's interest in them. Where did they come from, Henrich asked himself. They were not dirty by any means. They appeared clean as if they were washed completely.

"What is this?" Henrich asked. "Who are the six of you meant to be? Druids? Don't look like a pair of hags."

"We are not druids, good sir." One answered slowly. "We are simply a means to advance your journey toward the dark woods."

"How did you know for certain that I was heading in that direction?"

"Because you're on the trail. Everyone that's been this way has always taken this trail. Nothing new over here."

Henrich chuckled. The hooded figure stood silent. Not even making a move.

"Am I supposed to find this funny?"

"This is not intended to be an act of humor, my good sir. We only want to advance your journey is all."

"If that is your main concern, move the hell out of my way would you."

"I'm afraid we cannot do that. See, we are here to advance your journey. Only, not in the way you're expecting it to go."

The hooded figure raised his right arm up toward Henrich, who's right hand is still on the pistol. The figure's skin was revealed as his arm was being raised with the sleeve pulling back with the cloak. Henrich looked at the skin and noticed it was pale. Almost as white as the clouds, bur with a hint of blue to them. The hooded figure opened his hand, showing Henrich a letter. Henrich paused for a moment, gazing at the small scroll in the hooded figure's hand.

"This letter is for you." The hooded figure said. "Once you read it, you'll understand everything that is happening here."

"Is that right."

Henrich grabbed the scroll and opened it. He read what was

written upon the scroll and spotted his name being mentioned. The scroll had called him, *'Randolph Henrich of the Warslingers, the Heptad'.* He stood quiet, moving his eyes, following the hooded figures around him. He noticed on the letter as well that it called for his assassination and murder by the hands of anyone, which the one who succeeded in doing so would have to meet with someone called the Mercenary Man and would be granted a great reward.

"What is the meaning of this?"

"The meaning of the scroll is simple to understand, Randolph Henrich of the Warslingers. The Legendary Heptad. We six have come here to murder the great and legendary Warslinger."

"Where's your shooter if you've come to murder me out here in the heat of the desert?"

"We don't need a shooter nor any sort of armory to kill you."

"Then, I'm not aware as to how you're going to complete the task given to you. Hell, this looks like your last day in this World you hear."

"I hear you clearly, Warslinger. So, do my other brothers around you. We're not exactly your kind. We're something much more than human beings."

The hooded figure reached toward his hood. He slowly pulled it back, showing his face to Henrich. The other hooded ones also removed their hoods from their heads. Henrich took looks at them, spotting their eyes, they appeared dead, yet alive. Henrich also noticed their jaws, as if they had extra teeth inside of their mouths. The lead hooded figure stood in front of Henrich and smiled, showing his sharp fangs. Rotten fangs at best. Henrich knew what they were, pulling out his pistol.

"We're different." The lead hooded figure said.

"Damn vrylolakas!" Henrich said as he took fire at them.

The vampires moved around Henrich, he continued to take shots at them. One vampire ran up toward him, Henrich kicked the vampire in the face and stomp his face into the dirt. The vampires tried to latch onto Henrich, but his movements were too quickly for them to keep up, even at vampire speed. Henrich later used the shotgun, blowing the heads off the vampires. The lead vampire stood and watched his fellow brethren fight Henrich, studying his move set. Henrich grabbed one vampire and squeezed his neck, afterwards shooting him in the head with his pistol.

Only two vampires remained for Henrich to kill. The leader and his brother. The brother vampire went first at Henrich, but was unable to grab Henrich by his shoulders. Henrich kicked the brother and pulled the shotgun to his face. Henrich smiled as he blew the head completely off the brother vampire, only scraps of brain tissue remained. Henrich stood and stared at the lead vampire, who was smiling, showing off his fangs.

"I am amazed how you guys managed to come out in broad daylight." Henrich said. "I've always known the ones of many that manage to come out in the shadows of the night. What makes you guys different from the rest?"

"We submit to the Tubal King. He gave us the power to walk amongst the sunlight of the day and the moonlight of the night. He knows what we need as of what he needs. We are different as I have said to you."

"Different you are, but soon you'll all be the same as the ones I've come across before in my time. Dead and gone."

"Not until you manage to kill me as you've killed my brethren. Then your words may show some valor to them."

"What in the hell would you know about valor, creature?"

Henrich pulled out his pistol, aimed it at the vampire, reloading the gun directly in front of the vampire. The vampire stood out in the open.

"Go ahead and take the shot, Warslinger. Take it now before I bite your neck right in."

"The only thing you'll be biting this day, vrylolakas, is the bullet coming from this shooter right here and the dirt beneath our feet."

"Let's see if you're telling the absolute truth, Warslinger. Will I eat the bullet from your ancient shooter and taste the dirt beneath our feet or will I have the pleasure of tasting the flesh of the legendary Henrich and drinking the blood of a Warslinger?"

"Test me and see if which scenario will deem itself to be so in truth."

"I will do what you have said, Warslinger."

The vampire snarled and ran. Jumping up in the air, lunging itself at Henrich, who pulled the trigger back and the bullet went flying in the air. The bullet flew through the dirt filled air, inching closer to the lunging vampire and went completely straight through the vampire's mouth and exited through the back of his head. The vampire fell to the ground quickly while Henrich stood and stared at the vampire's body lying on top of the dirt.

"As I said. The bullet you'll eat as the dirt you shall."

Henrich placed the pistol back into its coat holster and looked at the scroll again. Staring at the name of the Mercenary Man. He looked forward and could see the dark woods up ahead.

"I should tend to find this Mercenary Man. See what he wants of me being blotted out from existence. Another one of many that has tried to test me in the heat of battle."

While Henrich walked away from the dead bodies of the vampires, a brown horse approached Henrich from the direction in front of him. The horse was large, greater in size than Henrich was familiar to when it comes to horses.

"Where did you come from?"

Henrich approached the horse and tamed it. Placing his bag to the side of the horse's saddle. Henrich sat atop the horse and went forward to the dark woods.

VI

Henrich rode atop the large brown horse that came to him toward the dark woods in the desert. While he rode through, in the near sight of his distance, Henrich spotted an abandoned gas station. He found no one around the station and decided to stop for a moment. The station had the appearance of once being active to left deserted. Age had covered even the crevice of the station. Henrich jumped off the horse and entered the station building. Inside laid nothing but dirt and dust. Spiders residing in the cracks and corners of the station. The station was hot from the sun's rays.

"Looks like we'll be staying here for the night." Henrich said to the horse.

He tied the horse to the station, giving the horse a bowl that he found from inside the station and poured water into it. The horse started to drink the water. Henrich ate another can of food, giving the horse some of the food as well. The horse stayed at the post while Henrich entered the inside of the station. He took a curtain from the windows and a small box he laid them on the ground as the sun began to set and the moon had shown herself. The air turned from a blazing heat to a chilly wind within seconds. Henrich watched the sun set and the moon rise in the sky. Henrich understood the differences between the sun and the moon. The two opposite spheres of light that sit still in the sky above him. Henrich looked around in the sky, seeing few sets of clouds.

"I doubt it will snow here. Not in this desert."

Henrich slept inside the station while the horse was tied to the post near the station's doorway entrance. Both Henrich and the horse was chilly from the cold wind through the light of the moon. A full moon. Henrich went ahead and gathered more curtains from the windows and wall to warm himself and the horse. The curtains had no effect in warming them. Neither did his coat.

"That was worth a shot at least."

Henrich later felt a small sense of heat coming from outside the station. He gazed over to the window and looked outside, seeing a cloud hovering above the station, a cloud of fire. Henrich was amazed. He looked over to the horse and it immediately went to sleep as the cloud of fire made itself known. Henrich nodded and the warmth from the cloud kept him and the horse protected from the frozen cold of the moon's light.

"Thank you." Henrich said, placing his hat over his face to sleep.

From that moment, Henrich slept the entire night and woke up the next morning from the heating rays of the sun. while getting up from the ground, Henrich could hear his horse outside kicking. Henrich ran out to see what was disturbing the horse and in the distance, Henrich spotted a large object heading toward them. The object was running and Henrich could see the tusks of whatever was coming toward them.

"A choiros. Never seen one of them this far out in the desert."

The choiros was a mutated hog with large tusks coming from its mouth and the hog was about the size of a small beetle car. The fur that laid upon the beast was dark and dirty. The stench of the creature could be smelled out from miles away. The hog snarled with rage and lust for hunger with its red reflecting eyes. Henrich pulled out his shotgun and aimed it toward the creature.

"Disgusting animal you are."

The choiros ran toward Henrich and the horse. The horse struggled to get from the post, but it wasn't afraid of the mutated hog. It wanted to attack the mutated hog itself. Henrich could feel the intensity coming from the horse and recognized its intention toward the swine ant. Henrich smiled as he untied the rope from the post.

"Go ahead and kill the creature if that's what you desire."

The horse neighed and ran after the mutated hog. Henrich followed the horse on foot with his shotgun in hand. The choiros ran toward the horse. Henrich stopped and aimed the shotgun, the horse continued running toward the mutated hog.

The hog turned from the horse and went straight after Henrich. The closer the hog came, Henrich started firing shots from the shotgun. The rounds hitting the hog in the sides and legs, but the creature continued to run after him. Henrich sighed while firing countless shots at the hog. The hog screeched as it ran into Henrich with its tusks, cutting his left leg. Henrich grunted when he fell to the ground from the choiros' ram. The hog snarled at Henrich, its eyes showing a look of intense hunger. The hog ran again toward a down and injured Henrich, but this time the horse of Henrich jumped into the way, between Henrich and the choiros.

"What do you know." Henrich said.

The hog snarled at the horse as it ran toward the horse with its tusks in front. The horse jumped over the hog's head. Turning around from behind it and ramming it into the ground. The hog laid on the ground as the horse began to stomp on its body. Henrich looked in awe at what he was witnessing. The horse kicked the hog in its head, the blood form the creature started to pour out from its body, coloring the dirt of the desert darker. Henrich stood up, holding his left leg.

"Seize yourself."

The horse stopped stomping on the hog and walked away from the creature. The hog squealed from the pain as Henrich approached its beaten body. The hog's eyes turned to Henrich and the hog desperately tried to stand up to kill Henrich. Sighing from the pain in his leg, Henrich placed the blastshooter onto the head of the hog.

"Unclean beast." Henrich muttered as he shot the choiros.

Henrich returned to the station alongside the horse. There, Henrich took some rags that were inside his coat pocket and used them to wrap up the cut on his leg from the hog's tusks ramming. Henrich looked at the horse and it didn't have as much as a scratch or injury upon it. Henrich nodded with a slight smirk. The horse neighed at him.

"I hear you."

Henrich gathered his gear and got atop the horse. Looking out forward toward the dark woods. He rode along in the heat of the desert, leaving the station abounded once more and the corpse of the choiros for the hovering vultures to feast upon.

<u>VII</u>

Riding out in the heat of the desert and the dark woods not far in the distance from his current location, Henrich rode along the trail that continued to follow. While on the trail, Henrich stopped to rest himself and the horse. While they rested, Henrich pulled out the scroll he received from the hooded vampire. He read the scroll again, memorizing every word that was written onto the scroll.

"I, the Mercenary Man, hereby call for the assassination and murder of the one, Randolph Henrich of the Warslingers, the Heptad of the Holy Knights. The one who succeeds in doing this quest will be confronted by myself and the Tubal King to receive a great reward unheard of in this World."

Henrich smirked, rolling up the scroll and placing it within his coat. He nodded in silence, only hearing the wind of the desert blow past him and the sounds of the scowls in the air.

"It's me they want, I see. They will receive me, that they want. In the due time."

CHAPTER TWO

A FRIEND COMETH

I

Henrich continued his journey toward the dark woods of the desert. The sun still shining down upon the land and the heat continued to be extraordinary. While Henrich continued his journey down the trail lines, he noticed a small and steady outlander post. Intrigued by its landmark and position so outside of urban and civilized locations, Henrich decided to look around the post. He circled the post atop the horse, the post only looked to be similar like a subway station. Henrich spotted the doors to the post were unlocked from a small crack in the door.

"What do you know."

Henrich removed himself from the horse and approached the door. He went to open it slightly after taking a small, but steady peek through the post's dirty windows. Smeared up with dirt from the desert and old drops of rainfall from past nights. Henrich went to open the door and from the other side came a young man, whom burst through the doors as if he was thrown out of the post. Henrich didn't startle at the young man's appearance from the doors, though he did take several steps back toward the horse.

"Who are you?" Henrich said.

"I… I am… Cody Landon."

"What were you doing inside this old post here?"

"I was looking for resources to carry on my journey back home. I couldn't find any in there before I was ambushed."

"Ambushed by what exactly?"

"Those beasts. They're vicious creatures."

"What kind of beasts?"

The doors bolted open, shoving Henrich and Landon back into the dirt. While Henrich stood up, he could see three wild beasts come from the post doors. One looked like a bull, but with the legs of a lion. The second appeared to be a wolf, but had the wings of a hawk and the talons of an eagle. The third and last beast was a horse, but with the legs of a spider. Randolph stood in front of them, facing them with his shooters in hand, blastshooter on his back ready to be of use at any moment. Landon sat on the ground, scared and intimidated of the beasts and Henrich.

"Get up, boy."

"I can't fight them."

"Why is that?"

"I don't have any weapons on me."

"You mean to tell me you brought yourself out here in this wild desert and you don't even have a shooter on you? Much less a blade upon your belt?"

"I was taught that using weapons was wrong."

"Who in the hell taught you such folly?"

"My parents, sir."

"Your parents were damn fools. They practically sent you to your own death."

Henrich took one of the shooters from his holster and tossed it to Landon. He caught it and stared for a moment, not sure what to do with the weapon. Scared and confused at his current place in the moment of life and death.

"Use the shooter on the beasts, boy!"

Henrich started shooting at the three wild beasts, which were running toward them at a faster speed than what they knew beasts could run. Landon stood up from the ground, shaking in fear, the sweat covering his face and his palms slipping away from the shooter. Henrich looked at him for a moment and kicked him in his side.

"Why are you just standing there like a shivering statue?!"

"I'm scared."

"Gird up your loins and help me kill these beasts!"

Henrich fired up his shooters. The bullets of the shooter helped slow down the beasts for seconds, until they regained their regular speed. He reached to his back, pulling up the blastshooter as he started blasting the beasts with the blastshooter. The spider legs of the horse beasts were being blown off its body, screeching in the pain of losing its legs. Landon slowly pulled the trigger, firing the shooter toward the wolf beast, shooting it in its left eye. Henrich nodded.

"There you go, boy. Keep going!"

The bull-lion came at Henrich with hits horns, but Henrich's horse rammed into the bull-lion's side, knocking it over onto the ground. Henrich ran over toward the beasts and blasted the creature's head right through with the blastshooter. The blast frightened Landon and shook him up. Henrich looked over toward Landon, seeing him shaking. Henrich shook his head in shame for the young boy.

"You need to grow yourself a pair, son."

"I'm just afraid. I've never encountered things like this before."

"You are now. So, get used to it. Two more beasts left to kill, and you'll be on your way."

Henrich fired the blastshooter at the Wolf-Hawk, seeing it can only see out of one eye thanks to the shot from Landon. The Horse-Spider tried crawling quickly toward Landon. Landon backed away from the Horse-Spider, Henrich fired a shot at the Wolf-Hawk and kicked the Horse-Spider over, blasting it in its head with his blastshooter.

"Use the damn shooter, then they'll stop trying to kill you."

Henrich stared at the Wolf-Hawk, he smiled as he walked toward the wild beasts. His horse walked behind him as well toward the beast. Landon only started at Henrich and his horse, unable to make up what's he witnessed so far after meeting the man. Landon nodded to himself and follow behind Henrich.

"The last one, huh." Henrich said to the Wolf-Hawk.

The Wolf-Hawk howled at Henrich. Its teeth sharp and the growling was deep. The Wolf-Hawk's remaining eye was locked on Henrich and staring at his neck. Henrich held the blastshooter facing the Wolf-Hawk as it could barely move from the previous shots it's taken.

"What are you going to do now." said Henrich.

"Are you going to kill it, sir?" Landon said.

Henrich turned to Landon and looked at the Wolf-Hawk. Henrich nodded and handed the blastshooter toward Landon. Uncertain as of how to use a blastshooter, Landon stared at Henrich with uncertainty in his eyes. Henrich could see it, but it didn't faze him to take the blastshooter back from him. He only pressed it closer to Landon much more.

"Use this blastshooter and kill this fowl beast where it will remain. In the dirt of the desert."

"I don't know how to use one of these, sir."

"Learn. You have right now to do it."

Henrich stared at Landon as he aimed the blastshooter toward the Wolf-Hawk, which snarled at him with saliva coming from its mouth.

"This kind of beast shouldn't even be in existence. But, with all this World has been through over the course of the eons, things alter themselves and become even more corrupt than they were before."

"I'm not fully comprehending what you're telling me."

"Shoot the damn creature. Right now. Kill it before I allow it to kill you."

"You wouldn't allow it to kill me while you're standing right here."

"Boy, you don't know who I am and what I've been through in this life. I will leave you here to die by this beast's hands if you do not kill it right here. Do you understand what I am telling you?"

"I am."

"Then take your shot. Kill it now."

Landon pressed the blastshooter closer to the Wolf-Hawk, which made the attempt to rise and snatch the hand off Landon, Henrich kicked the beast back to the ground, snatched the blastshooter from Landon and finished off the Wolf-Hawk by shooting its head completely off its shoulders. The echo of the shot went through the air, sounding off after Henrich placed the blastshooter back to his back.

"I'm sorry." Landon said. "I'm just afraid. I've never seen things like this before."

"You better learn, and you better learn fast. Because in this World, this Western World, there are only those that survive and those that die."

Henrich took the shooter back from Landon, placing it into its coat holster. He opened the post doors and scanned the interior, seeing nothing living inside. Only seeing a bag, he knew it belonged to Landon.

"Go get your stuff, boy."

"Yes sir."

"I'm giving you a choice to make right now. Either you can come along with me until you've found yourself a safe place to reside or you can go on your own path and try to find a place yourself with no skills of defense against a World of monsters and disasters waiting to consume you."

Landon stared. Quiet to Henrich and to himself.

"Make a choice now. Before I end up far out of your reach."

Henrich got himself atop his horse and rode away back on the trail to the dark woods. Landon stood by himself, quiet, looking at the dead bodies of the three wild beasts. He sighed and re-entered the post, grabbing the bag of his possessions that he had, exiting the post, Landon ran as fast as he could after Henrich, following him down the trail to the dark woods of the desert.

II

Landon ran quickly after Henrich, who rode atop his horse down the trail to the dark woods. Henrich looked back as he could hear Landon's pacing footsteps approaching him.

"I'm coming with you, sir." Landon said.

"At least you've made yourself a choice. I hope you're ready for the things you're about to witness. Maybe with me, you'll get some proper training and become a skillful warrior."

"Like one of those Warslingers."

"What makes you say that?"

"Because they're an inspiration to me. The way they protected people from dark matters in this World. Those things are unheard of today and possibly can never be replicated. If it's possible to do so."

"So, you know of them and what their purpose is in the World?"

"I've read so many scrolls and tablets that speak of their presence and their accomplishments. I even know their names."

"Do you now?"

"I certainly do."

"Why don't you share them with me. Enlighten me on them if you could."

"Their names were Charlton Darrain of the Ark, Knight Arthur Pendragon, Joshua of Ephraim, Moses the Leader, Daniel of Judah, Noah of Lamech, and Randolph Henrich. They are the *Warslingers of the Heptad*. Protected us from great evils. They were called holy warriors by many who witnessed their strength and courage. Their faith also prevailed in perilous times."

"I take it you've done some studying in your alone time. Before you decided to roam this dead desert."

"I did a lot of studying. I needed to know the history of the lands and how these Worlds were formed."

"So, are you from this Western World or the Eastern World?"

"Neither. I come from the Northern World."

"The Northern World? I thought that land was desolate with ice. No living person could sustain such frigid weather."

"I lived in an area that we could keep the surroundings warm from the frozen rainfalls and strong winds that could freeze objects within reach."

"How did you survive the snow bears or frost lions?"

"We did what we could. Some of us died fighting against them. Others froze to death hiding from them."

"It must've been hard for you to live in such circumstances. Fighting for your life day and night. Trying to survive not only against the beasts of the cold, but the cold itself. The Northern World is unstable in all of its ways."

"I was the only one who apparently had common sense and I left the Northern World to come down to the Western World. Hoping to find something worthwhile to live for."

"You will have to look harder and fight as hard if you're searching for something to live for that's considered worthwhile."

"If I may ask you, why are you out here by yourself? What are you searching for?"

"Me. I'm searching for a place that many consider a legend. A folklore tale told to us as children to make us dream of bigger possibilities to live for."

"What kind of place?"

"It's called The Haunted City. A place where the ghouls reside and die. In their ways. Hell, I even hear the place can give those who enter its gates eternal life and will grant entrance to other worlds that exist within our universe."

"Sounds like a scary place to visit."

"I wouldn't call the place scary as far as fear is concerned. I would say, it's a place that many seek after and die not finding. I intend on becoming the one who finds the City and lives afterwards. That is my current mission and goal in this World."

"So, The Haunted City is somewhere here in the Western World?"

"No. The City itself dwells in a place called the Outer-World."

"I've never heard of an Outer-World."

"Because its kept secret by those who know of its location. Keeps the petty people and strangers from reaching its gates. Basically, saving their lives in the process."

"But, how do you know of all these things? You seem to me like an old regular guy."

"I'm not just some regular guy, boy. I'm part of something much more than the average life of Man."

"How would that be? I'm just curious."

Henrich sighed and pulled out his shooter and tossed it to Landon, who caught the shooter with little ease.

"Be careful with it. Look at the handle of the shooter. Tell me what you recognize."

"I don't know what I'm supposed to look at. it's a unique design for a shooter handle."

"Look closer. The symbolism of the handle. The colors of the handle. You should know this. You've studied as you said."

"I'm looking at it closely."

Landon's eyes stayed at the designs chiseled into the shooter handle. He gazed his eyes to the symbols, analyzing them to his memory. He could spot a small menorah in the middle of the design, surrounded by swords and a crown. He knew what the emblem meant and looked at Henrich with awe.

"You're one of them, aren't you? You're one of the Warslingers?!"

"I am one of them. Yes."

"Which one are you?!"

"Randolph Henrich. The Legendary Warslinger."

Landon held the shooter tightly with his emotions running wild. He rubbed his head and eyes, even pinched himself to see if all he heard and witnessed were true. Henrich stared at him, seeing Landon trying to consume himself of the shock of meeting and talking with a Warslinger.

"You'll get used to it. It happens to many people when they find things like this out."

Henrich handed the shooter back to Henrich, placing it into his coat holster. Landon slowly breathe his way back to regular status, putting his emotions down and cooling off himself.

"So, what happened with the other Warslingers?"

"We were scattered abroad. To find each other near the end of these Worlds."

"Why were all of you scattered? What did you do?"

"We lost a battle."

"Wait, you guys lost a battle?! Against who?!"

"The Evil One. We had a betrayer in the Heptad."

"No way."

"Yes. To this day, I hope to find him and make him pay for all the misery he has created for us all."

"Which one was it?"

"I won't tell you."

"Why not?"

"Because if I did, it would change your mind on the entire Hectad and how we handled things in the past."

"I'll find out, won't I? Or will you just go ahead tell me outright who betrayed you?"

"Possibly, both will come to your mind. Until then, don't give it any focus at all. It'll cause you to slip and fall."

Landon nodded as he walked behind Henrich's horse down the trail paths. Henrich gave Landon a bottle of water to drink during his walk behind him.

"I hope you're prepared for what we're about to come to once we get there."

"What's at the end of this trail?"

"The dark woods of this wild desert."

"Hold on a second. A forest in the middle of a desert? This desert?!"

"Yeah. Things are different around here than what they're told about to people."

"What's inside the dark woods?"

"Answers and unnatural creatures. Possibly people of Man as well. Traveling about on their own little journeys out here."

"What's on the other side of the dark woods?"

"A closer gateway to the Outer-World. Which means closer to The Haunted City. Makes complete sense to me to travel therein."

"Will I need to use your shooter again when we're inside the woods?"

"More than likely. Yes, you will. Hope you're set your mind on fighting instead of running."

III

Walking through the desert, Henrich caught the scent of water and flowers. Around him was nothing but dirt and stench air. Landon looked out in the distance in front of them. He looked at the ground, seeing something dark around the dirt of the desert. Landon ran toward it, causing Henrich to kick his horse to run after Landon.

"Slow down, boy!"

Landon ran fast after what he was looking at while Henrich's horse immediately caught a second wind, running through the desert behind Landon. Henrich shook his head, while he kept his eyes locked on the running Landon.

"What is he running after?"

Landon ran and ran, pacing his footsteps in the dirt of the desert. He stopped for a moment, catching his breath. As he looked up, he noticed a series of plains covering the desert grounds in front of him. Green grass across the entire desert. Landon looked back at Henrich, who was right behind him.

"Well, what do you know." said Henrich. "Plains out here."

"I thought something like this would be impossible." Landon said. "Who actually planted these plains out in the middle of the desert?"

"No one planted them. They were grown here due to the dark woods. Its power must've spread across this region. Maybe it still is spreading and hasn't grown out in other parts of the desert yet."

"We should check to see if there's any fruit or vegetables grown in them."

"I don't think we should, boy. No one knows what could be living inside these plains. You see how high the grass reaches. No telling what's around them or what could be growing inside of them."

"We should check you know."

"Boy, you need to listen to me."

Henrich looked at the tall grass, the scent of the grass blown across his nose from a gust of wind. He took in the scent of the tall grass. Landon continued to run through the plains, searching for fruits or vegetables to take with him to eat.

"I haven't found anything yet." said Landon. "What's on your end?"

"Grass. Tall, green grass."

Landon giggled. Henrich shook his head as he padded the horse's head. While looking through the grass, Landon stumbled upon a young girl, dressed in a pink skirt and a white blouse, she was dirty, and her hair was light-brown, lighter than the dirt of the desert. She appeared petite, as if she hasn't eaten in days or weeks. She was crouched down in the grass. He paused for a moment, trying to conjure up words to say to her. The young girl just sat there, seemly crying to herself.

"Ma'am, are you well?" Landon said. "It's ok."

Henrich didn't hear nor see Landon anywhere near him through the grass. Henrich looked in every direction.

"Cody, where the hell are you?"

Getting no response, Henrich rode through the tall grass, cutting it down with his machete. His horse pacing through the grass as if it was the same as the desert. Moving quickly and swiping as fast as he could through the grass, Henrich doesn't see Landon around his location.

"Where in the hell are you, boy?"

Landon stared at the young girl and crouched down toward her, looking at her face and rubbing the tears from her eyes. The young girl turned to him and stared for a bit, deciphering who Landon could be and why would he be out in the plains of the tall grass. She smiled, and Landon smiled.

"What's your name?"

"My name is Lamia."

"Well, nice to meet you, Lamia. I can take you to safety. Me and a friend are out here on a trail. You can come with us."

"Really? Thank you."

Landon helped Lamia stand up and from the grass came Henrich, bolting through with his machete.

"Henrich, good you could come over here." Landon said. "Meet Lamia."

Lamia waved at Henrich. He only stared.

"Lamia?"

"That's what she told me."

The horse paused itself. Henrich looked at Landon and stared at the young girl. Henrich noticed something strange with the young girl's eyes. Her pupils were like that of a lizard. Henrich recognized what creature possessed such eyes. He pulled out his blastshooter and fired toward her. She jumped out of the way, behind Landon.

"Boy, move!"

"But, she's just a young girl. She's lost out here."

"She's not some ordinary girl, boy."

Lamia shoved Landon to the ground of the plains. She growled at Henrich with her eyes glowing toward him. Her fingernails turn into sharp claws and her teeth sharpened up to that of a wolf. Lamia removed her skirt, revealing her lower body to be that of a serpent. Landon stared at her with fear, crawling away from her and getting behind Henrich and the horse.

"I told you not to go roaming around!"

"I'm sorry I didn't listen."

"Screwing around with a damn Lamia, while looking for some apples and tomatoes."

"She said that was her name."

"She told you the truth about that. But, you have no idea what a Lamia is do you?"

"I've never heard of one."

Henrich stared at Landon before facing Lamia with his blastshooter. He aimed the blastshooter at Lamia.

"Well, boy. Now you know."

Henrich fired the blastshooter as the Lamia dodged the round, roaming through the tall grass. Unable to be seen by Henrich or Landon. They stayed close together, circling their surroundings as they could hear the Lamia slithering through the grass around them.

"Watch your sights. She can appear anywhere."

"I'm sorry. I didn't know."

"You can do your apologizing another time. Right now, put your mind to focus on killing this creature."

The Lamia burst through the grass, swiping Henrich off his horse with her tail. Landon ran through the grass and the Lamia followed. Henrich stood up and could see the trail that Landon took. He jumped back onto his horse and followed Landon's trail. The horse plowing through the tall grass, following Landon's trail. Henrich could hear Landon hollering for help further up.

"Go faster, my boy!"

The horse ran faster as the Lamia's screech was hear from nearby, almost close to Landon's screams.

"I'm coming for you, boy!" Henrich yelled. "Hold yourself together!"

Henrich rode through the tall grass, the screeching of the Lamia continued to roll through the air along with Landon's cries for help. The screeches and screams were growing louder as Henrich came closer to their location. The horse burst through the grass and into an open field, Henrich looked over and seen Landon atop a tree as the Lamia tried to pull the tree down with her tail. Henrich jumped off the horse and walked toward the Lamia with his blastshooter and machete.

"Sex demon!" Henrich yelled. "Face me and leave the boy alone!"

The Lamia turned to Henrich and slithered her way to him. Landon looked as he slowly made his way down from the tree to the ground. The Lamia sat in the face of Henrich, who showed no ounce of fear in his expression nor in his eyes. He stared into the Lamia's own green, reptilian eyes.

"You believe that I fear you? I don't have any fear of your kind. There are things in the Worlds that I've faced that would make you shed your own hide to get away."

The Lamia screeched in Henrich's face. Yellow saliva and green mucus poured out from the Lamia's mouth. The smell covered Henrich's face and the air around him. Henrich nodded and wiped the liquid fluids from his face with a rag from his coat pocket. Placing the rag against the grass, rubbing it down to remove the saliva and mucus from it. He faced the Lamia with a smile.

"Catch."

Henrich threw the rag into the Lamia's face and as she wiped the used rag from her face to the grass, Henrich swiped at her with his machete, cutting her head clean off her body. The head rolled across the grass and stopped at the tree, where Landon was standing. Her body collapsed by its own weight to the ground.

"There." Henrich said. "That is done."

Landon walked from the head of the Lamia, its eyes still moving and her mouth opening and closing from the nerves. He walked to

Henrich who pulled out a lighter and burned the Lamia's body and head to ashes. Henrich turned to Landon and slapped him across his face. Landon fell to his knees from the impact of the slap.

"The next time you refuse to heed my words, I'll put a round in you myself."

"I… I understand." Landon said slowly. "I just wanted to know what was in the plains."

"You found out didn't you. You discovered a shadow creature waiting for her next meal. Luckily, I was here to save your scrawny ass from getting killed. Again."

"I just need a weapon of my own."

"I gave you a damn weapon and you refuse to kill. Your parents screwed that nonsense into your head. Causing you to stumble."

Landon stood up, rubbing his face from the slap. Henrich stared at him and suddenly looked beyond Landon. Landon turned around to see what Henrich was staring at and behind him was straight plains of grass. Their entire surrounds covered with grass and trees and bushes. There were even birds and insects flying around the area. Henrich looked back and looked forward.

"You see what I'm seeing, sir?" Landon said.

"I am." Henrich replied "There's no more desert."

IV

Henrich and Landon look out at the open plains around them, fields of tall grass are also present around them in different corners of the fields. Landon was astounded by the sight of butterflies and bumblebees.

"Do you see all of this?" Landon asked.

"I do. Something strange is happening here."

"What makes you say that?"

"We were just in the middle of the desert and now after killing a Lamia through some tall grass, we find ourselves in an open field with trees and living insects."

"Maybe it was a portal transference."

"There was no portal. I would've known it to be because it would've made itself known to us. Portals don't just open and close to their will. Hell, they have no will of their own."

"I thought portals come and go as they pleased."

"Where did you hear that from?"

"Some old friends up in the Northern World. Portals would appear up there nearly every day. In random locations. We never figured out where the portals led to."

"Luckily you didn't take the chance of seeing it. Could've killed yourself by transporting to a world you have no idea even exist."

"I've studied up on the possible theory of a multi-verse."

"You're saying you believe there's more than the universe that we're already in?"

"It was only a theory that I read up on. Could be a possibility."

"We'll get to that once we come across it. Besides, you're not even ready for something like that to appear on your doorpost. If you can't handle the creatures in these Worlds, how will you handle yourself against more powerful creatures that may dwell in other universes. The strength they could possess and the power that might harness."

They walked through the open field, butterflies and bees flying across from them. The birds were chirping to each other in the trees. Henrich gazed up at the trees as his horse neighed at the small critters running through the field. Landon looked up ahead and seen trees covered with fruit.

"There's fruit!" Landon said running to the fruit trees.

Landon approached the trees, seeing the trees to be covered with apples, peaches, pears, strawberries, and cherries. Henrich went over to the trees as the horse pulled an apple from the tree, eating it. Henrich smirked, he reached over and pulled off a strawberry and ate it.

"It's been a long time since I've tasted strawberries."

Landon stuffed his mouth with strawberries and started grabbing apples and eating them. Henrich stopped him from stuffing his mouth completely.

"Why don't you place some of those fruits in your bag, huh. Safekeeping."

"Oh, yeah. You're right, sir."

Landon grabbed as many apples, peaches, pears, strawberries, and cherries as he could gather and placed them inside his bag. Henrich grabbed some of the apples and peaches, putting them in his bag and the strawberries in a small pouch attached to the interior of his coat.

"Did you gather enough?" Henrich asked.

"I gathered enough so we won't starve on our journey to the dark woods."

"Speaking of the dark woods." Henrich said looking outward from the plains.

Far out from the plains stood the dark woods, Randolph and Landon stared at its dark trees and eerie appearance. Landon ate an apple and looked at the dark woods.

"What do you think lives in there, really? More creatures?"

"No telling what lies in there, boy. We'll come to that conclusion once we're inside its settings."

They walked away from the fruit trees and continued moving on forward, toward the dark woods. Other animals approached. Raccoons, hares, foxes, and among other animals that walked through the plains. The horse neighed at them to move from their trail, the animals moved with no exception, startling Landon as he looked at Henrich's horse.

"Where did you find that horse?"

"I didn't find the horse. The horse found me after I had to slay six Vrylolakas in my presence.

"Those things are out here too?!"

"Yeah. You're afraid of them or something?"

"I hear they drink blood from the people of Man. I also hear they can see in the dark and are afraid of the sun's rays."

"They are. But, the ones I ran into were not harmed by the sun's rays. They were protected with some stronger power. A power that block the sun's rays from harming them. Though, the barrier wasn't strong enough to keep me from killing them where they stood."

"The power that protected them from the sun's rays must have been a powerful force of power."

"It is a powerful force from a powerful figure."

"You know who it is or what the power could come from?"

"I may have an idea as to who possess that dark power to protect those blood-suckers from committing their own suicidal deaths."

While they were walking, Henrich started to hear critters running through the tall grass that stood next to them. Landon finished eating his apple when he started to hear the scurrying sounds coming from the grass.

"You here that?" Henrich referenced.

"Maybe it's one of those animals from the field. Could've gotten itself lost in the grass."

The scurrying continued with little faints of laughter following. Henrich knows the laughter and reached down for his shooters. Landon noticed Henrich going for his shooter and looked around, stopping in his tracks.

"Keep walking, boy." Henrich said. "I can deal with them on my own."

"Are you sure about that?"

"What can you do about them? Really?"

From the tall grass, out runs four demons. The demons stood in front of Henrich and Landon, in their way of the trail to the dark woods. Henrich nodded as he pulled out his shooters toward the demons. Landon stood still with the remains of the apple in his hand.

"What are you going to do, sir?"

"I have a way of doing this. Won't take long."

The demons stood and laughed at Henrich and Landon. The demons were dark red, covered with black lines across their slim bodies. Their claws and nails were sharp as blades and dark as the night sky. Their eyes glazed red, like a burning fire. Their scent was that of sulfur and brimstone. Looking at the demons would possibly cause someone to lose their mind and go insane, but Henrich and Landon didn't turn insane.

"Keep yourself still, boy." Henrich said. "Before they come for you first."

The demons laugh and snarl at them. The sulfur in the air causes Landon to lose his grasp on what's going on. Becoming unconscious and losing sight. Henrich looked at him and tossed him a rag, where

Landon placed the rag against his face, covering himself from the scent of the sulfur.

"Throw your apple remains at them."

"What? Why? What good will that do?"

"Throw it at them now."

"All right, sir."

Landon tossed the apple remains toward the demons, they jumped up and stared at the remains. They picked it up and sniffed it, shaking their heads with disgust. The demons formed a single-file line facing Henrich. He chuckled under his breath as he pulled the triggers of his shooters, blasting straight through the demons' chest and heads each, killing them with one shot from both his shooters.

"Holy." Landon said. "How did you--"

"I have my ways of doing things, boy." Henrich said. "Best you watch me, so you can learn and do it yourself."

Henrich placed the shooters back into the holsters and continued moving forward the trail with Landon following him.

<u>V</u>

Walking through the open fields and surpassing the tall grass of the fields, Henrich spots a small community nearby. Landon sees people standing outside in a hoard. He pointed toward the mass of people.

"You see all those people?"

"I do. Something must be taking place over there."

They proceeded to enter the small community. Henrich left his horse at the gated entrance and upon passing the gate's sign, they notice it's actually a very small town with close people. They see homes and community buildings around the area. In the distance by some of the homes, Henrich could spot children playing in the yard with one another and the parents sitting on the porches of the homes, talking and laughing. The people were dressed in what looked like 18th century to 19th century clothing. The homes and buildings around them looked to fit in with those two centuries.

"What kind of place is this?" Henrich said.

"Looks like a good place to stay."

"We'll have to see if that's the truth, don't we." said Henrich. "Let's go over there to where all the people are gathered. Maybe we can find something out about this place from them."

"All right."

They walked toward the gathering of the townspeople and immediately, Henrich noticed a structure, made of a large and wide wooden square platform and on top of it sat three guillotines, ready to be of use. He also spotted three men standing up on the side of the guillotines, wearing all black with scarlet lining and purple interior shirts. The men looked middle-aged and were known for their purpose.

"What is going on here?" Landon said.

"There's a judgment taking place. Someone is about to be judged according to these judges' rules and laws."

"I wonder what their laws are that would have them chop off people's heads. Must be something major I would guess."

"Only one way to find out. We'll need to get a little closer to the scene."

They walked up behind the townspeople as they witnessed the judges bring three men up to the guillotines and lay their heads down, preparing them for their final moments of living. One of the judges stood out in front of the crowd.

"I hereby, bring to you and to our faithful town of Savel, that we at this very moment, sentence these three men sitting on their knees before you, to their death."

The crowd cheered on for the deaths of the three men. Henrich and Landon stood in the back and were quiet the entire time. Only watching the executions take place right before their very eyes. The people were militant in their speech and in their actions, throwing vegetables at the three men and calling them out of their names.

"KILL THEM NOW!!!" The crowd screamed with boldness. "CHOP OFF THEIR DAMNED HEADS! SEND THEM TO THE FIRES BELOW!!!"

The judge signaled the guillotines as they fell and chopped off the heads of the three men. The crowd cheered the deaths of the men and ran over in hordes to their heads, which were laying on the ground. The crowd gathered the heads and committed heinous acts to them. Some kissed the heads, other proceeded to place the heads toward their genitals and behinds in gesturing movements. The judges threw the bodies down toward the crowd, which they began to tear the clothes apart from the bodies, leaving them naked in their presence. They proceed to have sexual intercourse with the dead bodies along with urinating on them bodies.

"What the hell is all of this?!" Henrich said.

"I don't know." said Landon. "But I feel we need to leave this place right now."

"The spirit of Sodom dwells over this town. I can sense it in my spirit."

"What is Sodom?"

"You have much to learn, boy. Now isn't the time for the teaching."

One of the judges looked and pointed at Henrich and Landon. He looked at them with confusion, moving his head over to the other judges that were sitting next to him.

"Have you seen those two here before?"

"No. I have not."

"They must be outsiders. Probably here to ruin our laws in this place."

"Maybe you're right. Let's make an example out of them shall we."

The judges stood up and gathered the crowd's attention with clapping and whistling. The judges smiled at the crowd, who's faces were filled with unclean lust and desires.

"It seems we have two visitors who have come to the town of Savel."

The crowd turned and looked at Henrich and Landon. Licking their lips and chanting for their executions. They stood their guard, backing away from the crowd. Some of the crowd members were lusting for Henrich and Landon. Calling for them to strip down in front of them so they could fulfill their desires.

"Tell me, what are your names and your business here in our town."

"I am Cody Landon." said Landon with his voice trembling. "This is my friend here, Mr. Henrich."

"Henrich?" The Judge said. "I only know of one Henrich and he died years ago in a great battle. Tell me, you cannot be the one I'm speaking of."

"I am more than what you deem to know based on appearances, filth."

"You dare call me filth, peasant?! You're in my town! You're surrounded by my homes and my people! Do you know what I can do to the two of you right now if I demanded it?"

"I know what you could do? You'll attempt to execute us, so your disgusting people could sodomize our dead bodies."

"The crowd does what they please with the remains of those that have died by our guillotines. Nothing I can do about that."

"There's plenty you could do about them and the actions they have committed this day before you."

"You talk as if you're an ancient man. You look like a present man, but with the tongue of an ancient. That isn't exactly possible around these parts."

"You're still looking based on physical appearances and yet, you have no idea of what's to come of you and your town full of uncleanness."

"Enough!" The Judge said. "I am growing tired of your backtalk, outsider."

The Judge sat in his chair and looked at the other two judges. Each of them nodded their heads and looked down at the crowd. Pointing to Henrich and Landon with a smile on their faces. Large smiles with their teeth shining against the sun. their teeth dirty, almost rotten completely.

"Bring the two of them up here for their executions! Let them taste the sharpness of our guillotines!"

The crowd cheered and yelled as they ran toward Henrich and Landon. Grabbing their clothes and pulling them. Some of the crowd placed their hands in the interior of their shirts and pants.

"Get off me!" Landon yelled. "Get off!"

"I WANT THE YOUNGER ONE!" A man in the crowd yelled. "LEAVE HIM TO ME!!!"

"NO! I WANT HIM AND HIS OLDER FRIEND" Yelled a woman in the crowd. "WE CAN HAVE SO MUCH FUN WITH THEM!!!"

"You people are about to take in your last breaths." Henrich said. "Hope you're ready for the next World."

"YOU TWO ARE ABOUT TO DIE!!! HOW DO YOU FEEL ABOUT THAT?!!!"

Henrich pulled out his shooter and shot two of the crowd members in the head, causing the crowd to stop in their tracks and the judges to be afraid. Henrich tossed the other shooter to Landon, who smiled.

"You know what to do now."

"I do." Landon said.

Both began firing at the crowd, whom tried to outrun the gunshots. Henrich fired one and blasted him in the head. Henrich ran toward a few of the crowd members, spearing them to the ground and shooting them to their deaths. The judges were appalled, seeing their townspeople being shot and killed by Henrich and Landon in their presence.

"Those outsiders are killing our people!"

"What should we do about them?!"

"Let's deal with them ourselves."

After firing upon firing bullets, Henrich and Landon killed everyone that stood in the crowd. All that remained were the three judges. Henrich placed the shooter back into its holster and walked up the steps atop the large structure toward the judges. The judges started backing away from Henrich as he threw them against the post of the guillotines. Each of the judges are sitting down with the guillotines above their heads.

"You can't do this to us!" The Judge said. "This is our town! Who will take charge of it if we were to die?!"

"You can leave that to the remaining townspeople that have some form of sense."

Henrich prepared the guillotines to fall upon the judges' necks. The lead Jude looked back at Henrich. Shaking his head in anger and despair.

"Tell me before you end my life, who are you really?"

"I am Randolph Henrich of the Warslingers of the Heptad."

"The Heptad. No."

Henrich pulled the lever, the guillotines fall and kill the three judges. Landon walked over toward him, looking at the dead bodies of the judges. He handed the shooter back to Henrich. Randolph looked at it and gave it back to Landon.

"You did good right there."

"Really?"

"Yeah. For right now, you can hold on to that shooter."

"I don't know how to thank you."

"You don't have to. Not now anyway."

They looked around the town of Savel. Seeing only the children running around with their parents at the homes. They left the town, returning on their trail to the dark woods.

"You think there are other places like this out there?" Landon said.

"There are many in various fields. There are many."

VI

Walking down the trail to the dark woods, Henrich and Landon decided to move forward and simply focus on the dark woods. After several miles of traveling from the wild desert to the tall grass fields to the small town of Savel, they finally make it to the entrance of the dark woods.

"This is it." Henrich said.

"We made it." Landon replied. "Do we just walk on in there?"

"It appears that is our only option."

They approached the tree field entrance of the dark woods and from out of the ground, rose up a dark cloud of smoke. The cloud was incredibly dark that Henrich and Landon were unable to see through it, nor could they even walk past it, sucking the air from the lungs when making the attempt to surpass the smoke.

"What kind of smoke is this?!" Landon said.

"I do not know." said Henrich. "But, I know it's made of magic. A shadowic magic."

They took steps back from the smoke with Henrich's horse neighing as it backed away from the smoke. Henrich noticed the horse was sensing something from the other side of the smoke and when he took a closer look at the smoke, trying to see through it, Henrich discovered three figures were standing on the other side of the smoke.

"Landon, we have company before us."

"What do you mean? Where are they?"

"Standing on the other side of the smoke cloud. They appear to be of small stature. But, from what the horse is sensing, and I can sense it too, their shadowic creatures."

Henrich pulled out the shooter and fired shots through the smoke, making the attempt to kill the three shadowic creatures standing on the other side. The bullets vanished inside the smoke, with no sound of impact following. Henrich held the shooter steady, still aimed at the smoke where he could still see the three figures.

"Why don't you lay down this smoke cloud here and face us like the creatures you are."

The smoke withered away with a gust of wind that appeared from out of nowhere. Henrich looked and found himself and Landon staring at the three figures. The three figures looked and smiled at them both.

"What do you know." Henrich said.

"What are they, sir?" said Landon. "I've never encountered women like this before. Ever."

"That's because you wouldn't find them outside of their comfort zones. The two on the sides are called Mares and the one in the middle is known throughout the Eastern World as the Cailleach."

The three women laughed at Henrich and Landon. The women on the sides appeared old in age, but nightmarish in their eyes and aura. The one in the middle stood with a staff and looked like a huge, hideous old woman. Her long white hair stood out from underneath her black and gray hood connected to her robe. The Cailleach's face appeared as a dark blue and she also wore a plaid.

"It appears that we have visitors, my ladies." The Cailleach said. "How should we make them feel comfortable?"

"Let us pass and enter the dark woods behind you." Henrich said. "That's why we're here standing in front of you anyhow."

"My dear man, why would we ever allow such a thing? You believe that you can proceed on your little journey to The Haunted City isn't it?"

Henrich stared at the Cailleach with a mere shock going across his face. Landon shivered slowly, while keeping his hand toward the shooter on his belt.

"How do you know about that?" Henrich said. "How do you know who I am?"

"We know many things, Warslinger of the *Heptad*." A Mare said.

"We know so many things." The other Mare said with a laugh.

"I am surprised that your horse caught our scent."

"This horse is nothing that you already know of in the Worlds around us."

"I can sincerely agree with you on that statement."

"Sir, what should we get ready to do?"

"Nothing yet, boy. Nothing just yet. But, we are getting past them and entering that forest there. That I can promise the both of us and these hags."

The Cailleach clapped and stomped her staff into the trail way. Smiling as the two Mares laughed, clapping their hands in excitement.

"What are you preparing to do?" Henrich said. "State your point of blocking our way inside?"

"We have a proposal for the two of you." The Cailleach said.

"What do you mean?" said Landon.

"I'm listening." Henrich said.

"If you can solve our little puzzles of threes here before you, we will grant you entrance to the dark woods behind us. If you fail to solve the puzzles of the threes, you will give us your souls."

"I'm not liking this, sir." Landon said.

"What are your puzzles of threes?" Henrich said. "Enlighten me."

The Cailleach swiped her staff in front of them and slammed it to the ground again. She stared at Henrich, who kept his hand on the shooter and finger laid tight to the trigger.

"The threes are here before you. Determine what they are and what they mean to your futures to come."

"The hell are you talking of, hag?" Henrich said.

From the sky above them, snow began to fall. Landon looked around, seeing the fields covered with snow as the entire landscape is turning a pale white. The Cailleach stood in front them along with the two Mares.

"Solve your first puzzle, scowlers." The Cailleach said. "Solve this one and the second will present itself to you."

From the Cailleach's plaid dropped rocks that started to cause a small earthquake. The land shook as the snow began to fall heavier and thunder followed. Henrich looked around as Landon tried to cover his face from the snow falling toward his eyes.

"What is happening around us, sir?!" said Landon.

"We're experiencing a shadowic snowstorm accompanied by a tremor."

Henrich continued to look at the heavy snow and the feeling of the earthquake. He gazed over at the Cailleach, who stood there, non-affected by the snow nor the earthquake.

"The puzzle is inside the weather she has formed." Henrich said. "But, what is it?"

Henrich looked around the land, jumped off his horse and started moving around in the snow-covered grounds. Landon followed him and copied what Henrich was doing, but uncertain of it at the same time.

"What are you looking for, sir?"

"The answer to her puzzle. Maybe it's buried beneath the snow she has created."

Landon looked around and stared at the Cailleach, looking at her staring down at Henrich, holding the staff down to the ground with the other Mares laughing on the event.

"Maybe it has something to do with her place of origin."

"She is from the Eastern World after all. Let's give that a chance."

The Cailleach stared at them, her patience warring out from their searching through the thundersnow storm.

"What is taking them so long, Madam?" One Mare said.

"They have no idea what to do." The Cailleach said. "They have failed the first puzzle."

While searching, Henrich stopped and looked at Landon with a confidence, possibly knowing the answer to the first puzzle.

"Sir, what is it?"

"I know what the answer is."

"You do?"

"I believe so."

Henrich stood up and looked at the Cailleach. He nodded toward her. She stared at Henrich.

"Have you discovered what is it to solve this first puzzle?"

"This weather is based off Beira, the Queen of Winter. She had the abilities to do great feats across the lands of the Eastern World. The snowstorm, the earthquake, the thunder, and the rocks that came from beneath your plaid. Those are all signs of Beira. Which implies to me that Beira is the answer to your first puzzle."

"You have done well." The Cailleach said. "I am impressed."

She raised up her staff and the snow stopped falling and the earthquake steeled down. The snow melted from the sun's rays. Landon went ahead and stopped searching through the snow-covered grounds, turning his eyes to the Cailleach, who is staring at Henrich.

"Why did you stop the storm?" Henrich said.

"Because, you speck of dirt surpassed the first puzzle, I am prepared to give to you the second puzzle. This one shouldn't be much of a troubling task since you've managed to surpass the first one."

She slammed her staff to the ground again, only this time, snow didn't fall from the sky. Henrich and Landon looked around and the sky immediately brightened, and the air turned a slight cold. The air was deeply cold that it formed small speckles of ice in the air around them. Henrich looked over at the field and noticed the grass nor the trees were frozen solid from the air.

"The trees." Henrich said. "They're not frozen."

"How could that be, sir." said Landon. "This air around us to freeze almost anything solid and the sky is so bright that it should provide some form of warmth."

The Warslinger raised his hand up toward the sky. He took another look at the trees and the grass. He nodded.

"That must be it."

"What must be it?"

Henrich looked at the Cailleach and stared into her eyes. She looked at him as if she was looking for the answer.

"Do you have what will solve this puzzle?"

"Yeah. I do."

"Speak of it, Warslinger."

"Samhain and Bealltainn. Samhain, the first day of Winter. Bealltainn, the first day of Summer."

The Cailleach stared at Henrich. She shook her head slightly. The Mares were in awe of Henrich's answer that they looked over to the Cailleach, waiting for a response. The Cailleach stomped her staff to the ground, returning the air and the sky back to its original state.

"You are indeed correct, Warslinger."

Henrich nodded. Landon stood impressed at the Warslinger's knowledge. The Mares were upset that they slightly turned their backs to Henrich and Landon. The Cailleach screeched at them to turn themselves back around.

"You have been doing well." The Cailleach said. "Are you ready for the third and final puzzle of the threes?"

"We are." Henrich said. "Bring the puzzle to us."

The Cailleach stomped the staff and within the fields formed a lake, which Henrich and Landon approached. As they approached the lake, Henrich noticed it started to grow out in feet, then miles.

"What is this?" Henrich said.

"It's a lake, sir. Water freely flowing that way."

"I can see that. But, its enlarging itself. Growing in length."

Laying on the ground in front of Henrich is a dirty gray and black plaid. The plaid is a great plaid. He picked up the plaid and analyzed it. Landon walked over to see the plaid. Unfamiliar at its purpose of lying next to the water.

"Why is this out here, sir?"

"Maybe it has something to do with this lake here. I should say gulf. It's grown out even larger than I thought."

The Cailleach watched them very closely with the plaid in Henrich's hands.

"Let's see if they know of this one." The Cailleach said. "Let us see."

Henrich took the plaid and looked around it. Landon touched the plaid and thought to himself a possible solution, which was to bury the plaid in the dirt next to the gulf. Henrich declined, stating there's something more to the plaid than just burying it next to the water.

"There's something else that we're supposed to do with this plaid and I am certain it involves the water in some capacity."

"How about laying the plaid down into the water and letting it flow away. Like the past flowing away to give room to the future."

"Maybe. But, I doubt that's the purpose of the plaid and gulf."

Henrich looked around at the gulf and the dirt surrounding it. He found a small rock and kneeled to grab it. He took the rock and the plaid toward the water. He entered the water and started scrubbing the plaid with the rock. Landon didn't know what to make of the scene.

"Why are you washing the plaid, sir?"

"Trust me on this, boy. I know what I'm doing."

Henrich continue to wash the plaid with the water of the gulf and scrubbed it with the rock. The Cailleach watched him washing the plaid. She slightly smiled as she stared at him. The two Mares stood in silence. Not understanding what was taking place.

"He knows of his Worlds." The Cailleach said. "This man knows a lot of things."

After scrubbing the plaid, Henrich dipped it underneath the water and held it there for a few seconds and scrubbed a second time. He dipped it underwater again and pulled it back up. Scrubbing a third time and placing it underwater again. The wind started to pick up around them and it started to chill down. Landon held himself tightly to keep himself warm from the cold air.

"Why is it getting cold again?"

"Because of this." Henrich said, pulling the plaid out from underneath the water.

The plaid was a solid white, pure white as snow. The Cailleach gasped at what she had seen. The ground around them was covered in snow. Henrich took the plaid and approached the Cailleach with it. He handed it to her and she held it in her hands. She looked at Henrich.

"Do you have what will solve the third and final puzzle?"

"I do. The Gulf of Korryvreckan. The place where you would bring your great plaid to wash it for three days to where the season of Winter would make itself known to you and the gust of winds would pick up."

The Cailleach nodded and slammed the staff to the ground, the great white plaid and the snow vanished in thin air. Henrich looked around as his horse walked up to him. Landon stood by the hose as they faced the Cailleach and the Mares.

"You have finished the puzzles of the threes, Warslinger and partner." The Cailleach said. "I congratulate you on your victory. You have much knowledge."

"I've been around for a very long time."

"I can sense it in your aura."

"We have completed your puzzles." Henrich said. "Now, may you let us pass and enter the dark woods?"

The Cailleach nodded and moved herself over to the side. Henrich went atop the horse as Landon stood by. They walked past the Cailleach and Mares, making their way inside the dark woods. The Cailleach stopped Henrich, calling him out. He turned around to face her, staring into her eyes as she glared into his. The Mares had vanished into a small puff of black smoke.

"Don't mind them." The Cailleach said. "They know of what their purpose is around here."

"Why did you call me out?" Henrich said. "What else do you have to say to me?"

"You have much knowledge in your memory. You are a Warslinger of the *Heptad*. But, you are not the only living one in the Worlds."

Henrich looked at The Cailleach. Landon turned around and watched the two speak to one other.

"What do you mean I'm not the only living one in the Worlds? You're telling me that the others are still walking among the Worlds this day?"

"They are in various parts of the Worlds. They are not together yet. It seemed that you were all scattered apart."

"Yeah. I already know that. I was there when it happened."

"That's not what I'm getting to."

"Then, what are you getting to? You should at least just let it out of your mouth and spare yourself the trouble of staring at me."

"You will all meet each other soon. Very soon. You'll all meet at one location in the Eastern World."

"What location in the Eastern World? Tell me."

"You will all gather together at the remains of an ancient kingdom that belonged to a king that was also a Warslinger. You know who I am speaking of, don't you?"

Henrich nodded, "I know exactly whom you're talking about."

"That is all I must tell you, Randolph Henrich of the Warslingers of the Heptad."

Henrich nodded and rode away into the dark woods with Landon following him on the side. The Cailleach started at them as she waved her hand in the air and beat her staff to the ground again, creating the thick black smoke. She walked into the smoke, vanishing.

"We shall meet again, Warslinger of the Heptad."

Henrich could hear her last words before she vanished into the smoke. He turned his head back, seeing only the black smoke. He stared for a moment.

"Maybe we will." Henrich said.

Landon looked ahead into the dark woods, seeing nothing but the darkened trees and the dark green leaves around them. The bushes within the dark woods were a dark green and the darkness of night could fit in with them and appear to be just of the same color. He looked at Henrich, who was moving past him.

"Are you ready for what's inside here, boy?" Henrich said.

"I don't have much of a choice do I."

Henrich smiled at Landon while gazing inside the dark woods, hearing hardly nothing but the sounds of insects and forest animals.

"Not really."

CHAPTER THREE

SHADOWS OF THE WILDERNESS

I

Entering the dark woods, Randolph Henrich and Cody Landon slowly made their way through a filled pathway covered in limbs and bushes. Henrich chopped down the limbs with his machete. Landon bypassed the falling limbs, shoving himself away from the bushes filled with small insects. Landon looked at the flying insects, seeing their glowing colors across their small hollow bodies.

"What kind of insects are these?"

"Those would be called the *shroudoks*. They're shadow insects. They reside wherever little light can be present."

"Really? So, light can kill them?"

"Bright light. The heat of the light, such as the sun would be even too intense for those small critters. That's why they hide out in darker areas. Such as this forest."

They continued through the dark woods, seeing and hearing more insects crawling and flying around them. From mutated butterflies with a dark hue of blue across their wings to cockroaches almost the size of small dogs running through the bushes.

While they moved through the trail, created by previous others who have entered the dark woods, Henrich began to feel a slight disoriented. Landon noticed Henrich slightly tilting his head over his left shoulder, before catching it himself.

"Sir, are you alright?"

"I'm fine, boy." Henrich said. "It's the ghouls who are in here.

They're attempting to attack with my immune system."

"Wait a second. They can do that? I've never known any kind of ghoul that could bother someone's immune system by doing nothing."

"These are a different kind of ghoul, boy. Remember, we're in their territory now. Their power is increased abundantly without the sun's rays beaming down on here brightly."

"That's something."

"You think it is. Wait until you see them in their nightmarish forms. They'll come flying toward you like a bat out of its resting place."

From the trees, bolted down a ghoul, glowing a bluish white and its eyes and mouth in complete darkness. Screeching out toward Henrich. Landon looked at the ghoul with fear in his eyes as he went to pull out the shooter. As he raised it up, the ghoul was shot and evaporated in his sight from Henrich's shooter.

"Don't worry, boy." said Henrich. "I know how to deal with these shadowic beings. Not my first time coming through a place like this."

From the shadows of the forest rained down more ghouls, all in various shades of colors. Dark blue, gray, dark violet, and white. Screeching and screaming at Henrich and Landon. They move quickly through the woods, following the trail in front of them. Landon looked back and seen the ghouls coming after them through the trees. He started shooting at them, evaporating a few of them in the process. Henrich looked back and started firing his shooter toward them.

"Keep your shooter aimed on them at all cost!"

"I will do my best, sir."

Henrich's horse rode his way through the tree limbs, crashing them down. Landon ducked from the falling limbs as the ghouls went right through them. Landon continued to shoot them. Henrich reloaded his shooter and continued firing at them. They hear scurrying coming from the bushes in front of them. Henrich looked and spotted a set of red eyes gazing at him from within the bushes. A low growl was also heard by both Henrich and Landon.

"What was that, sir?"

"There's demons here as well." Henrich said. "I'll be damned this day has become a whole lot messier than before."

From the bushes, bolted out the demons. The demons appeared to be from the same species as the demons from the tall grass. Except these were much smaller and could move at a much faster pace. Henrich's horse ran through the demons as Henrich fired at them and Landon kept the remaining ghouls at bay.

"I'm almost finished up with the ghouls." Landon said.

"Keep at them, boy!" said Henrich. "I'll handle the demons. They won't be much of a problem."

Henrich pulled out the blastshooter, firing at the demons, who scurrying around the trees and the bushes. Swinging on the limbs to sneak up on Henrich. Landon turned around and shot one of the demons off the limbs, its body fell to the ground, burning up the grass beneath it.

"I appreciate that."

"It's my job, sir." Landon said with a nod.

Henrich continued to fire at the remaining demons while Landon handled the final two ghouls hovering and circling him. Henrich jumped off the horse and walked up to the demons, shooting them one by one.

"How many times do I have to deal with your kind." Henrich said. "How many times."

The ghouls circled Landon. He nodded and tossed a blade at one and shot the shooter toward the other. The blade distracted the ghoul, but the bullet evaporated the other one. The last ghoul looked and stared at Landon with hatred piecing from its eyes and the horror could be heard from within its screeching cry. Henrich fired up the blastshooter's shots, killing the demons that were around them. He looked back, seeing Landon pull the trigger, evaporating the last ghoul.

"Seems you've improved somewhat." Henrich said. "About damn time."

"We're currently inside a dark forest with shadow creatures around us at every corner. I have no choice but to improve my fighting skills."

"I can understand that. Anyhow, it's a good thing to see how you're holding up with that shooter. Maybe in time, you'll get to have this blastshooter for yourself."

"One day. Maybe."

"Let's keep moving along, boy. Find out way through this darkness."

They moved through the woods, not confronting nor being stopped by any other shadow creatures that are lurking around within the dark woods. Throwing Henrich and Landon off for not seeing any of them, they continued to move forward. Several minutes later, they found themselves exiting the woods and entering a land surrounded by dark green grass, rugged mountains, and ridges. Henrich looked out and the land was large and massive. No end could be seen of the land by the naked eye.

"What is this place? I thought we were just inside the forest." Landon said.

"We were. This place is something else."

"Like what?"

Henrich looked around and spotted a macabre alter sitting in the forefront of the land. They went toward it and upon getting closer, the horse neighed itself suddenly, stopping its feet in its tracks. Landon stopped immediately while Henrich looked around the altar.

"What's wrong with the horse, sir?"

"He knows something we don't. I know of this place. I've seen it before in the visions of the day and the dreams of the night."

"Well, what is this place?"

"We're in the Valley of Death."

II

Looking out at the Valley of Death, Henrich and Landon noticed more forests were covering the trail that they were following

68

previously. Landon nodded and looked back at the dark woods. He looked forward at the other forests that surrounded the valley.

"I see there's more than one dark forest."

"Appears there is. We need to be careful going further into this place. Many have died here."

Henrich and the horse moved on from the altar, continuing to move forward with Landon following them. He looked around, seeing the sun's rays slightly beam down from the gray clouds above them. The air appeared a mixture of warmth and freezing. The sound of the wind could be heard if listened to very carefully.

"How many have died exactly?"

"Too many to number."

"Oh. So, what was that altar all about? Was it some shrine to a god or someone's burial grounds?"

"It was a shrine dedicated to a powerful god."

"Which god? I'm just curious to know since we're walking down this path where this god apparently resides."

"A pagan deity. A powerful one at best."

"I would guess those ghouls and demons back there were maybe its soldiers in the woods. You know, patrolling the place. Maybe those women at the entrance were like this god's gatekeepers."

"Those hags were only there to frightened those that approached the entrance and to have them fail the puzzles of threes to diminish their self-confidence and shatter their faith. Those ghouls and demons back there, were just there. We trespassed on their territory. Death is their sweet savior. They desire it."

"They desire it?"

"Just as those of Man would beg for food when his stomach began to quake on him. Same factor to the shadow creatures when it comes to death. Death is their food and substance of which they sustain on. Without death, the demons, the ghosts, the ghouls, and whatever else lies out here in these forests within this valley, would cease to exist throughout all the Worlds."

"I take it that's why the Worlds needed men like you. You know, Warslingers."

"I would take that as a small form of a compliment. Yes, we did save many from treacherous times and malevolent forces. Though, at times there were benevolent forces that turned tragic and considered the malevolency to be more seductive than remaining in their benevolent state."

"You mean to tell me that there were some that betrayed the good of these Worlds?"

"It was one of our own. A Warslinger. Couldn't take the battle much further and saw a way out of this life. By doing so, he committed us to failure as we lost the battle and we were scattered across the Worlds in a instant. I have yet to see one of my brethren since that day."

"All because he was seduced by the malevolent force of power."

"Do not underestimate the power of the malevolency. It can even change the purest man into the deadliest man. The seduction that power possesses, it can alter any man, woman, child, beast, creature, angel, demon, possibly gods. I'm not sure on that matter. But, I have seen it with my own eyes before and I know that power continues to ruin the lives of many this day."

"Do you have any idea as to where the malevolence power source may be kept?"

"It's held at the gate to the city. The Haunted City."

"That's why you're going there isn't it. To reverse the wrongs of the past and what that power has done to the ones it has affected."

"That's not why I'm going to The Haunted City. I have my own reasons for taking this daring task. Many before tried to talk me out of it. I told them that the City itself has power of its own. A power much stronger than the malevolency and the benevolency."

"If we make it through all that we might have to face on this trail way, we'll get to see this Haunted City that you're talking about?"

"We will be there. Staring at its glorious feats. Its buildings made of materials not known of the Worlds. Created and designed by an entity not of these Worlds. That City will be the place where all the answers will be revealed to anyone who dares to enter it."

"Here's hope to reaching the City in one piece."

"I wouldn't say one piece. I would speculate, few to many pieces. A lot of men have died on this journey. I intend to survive."

"The way you are, sir, I believe you will."

Henrich nodded.

'I'll see that it happens."

While moving along, from the ground arose three ghouls, like the ones from within the first dark woods. Henrich sighed as Landon pulled out his shooter.

"There's more of them." Landon said.

"Just deal with them as you dealt with the first ones." said Henrich. "They'll be out of our way soon enough."

Landon fired shots at the ghouls while Henrich loaded up the blastshooter. After loading it, a pair of ghosts came down from the gray clouds toward them. Henrich looked up, seeing the ghosts, appearing as white and gray mists with disfigured faces. He raised the blastshooter toward the two ghosts.

"Mist Ones out here as well." said Henrich. "Amazing."

Shooting the two ghosts with the blastshooter, evaporating them from eyesight. Landon eliminated the ghouls, but he noticed more coming from the dark woods in front of their trail. Henrich also spotted several more ghosts coming down from the clouds and even a few arose up from the ground.

"Appears we've stumbled ourselves to a spirit smorgasbord."

"It appears that way, sir."

Henrich and Landon continue shooting the ghouls and ghosts while making their move toward the second dark woods. Firing shot after shot, evaporating the ghosts and eliminating the ghouls. They moved with a quicker pace toward the dark woods and as soon as they made themselves near its entrance, the remaining ghouls and ghosts had vanished into the thin air, some levitating themselves up into the clouds.

"I'll be damned." Henrich said. "They left."

"Maybe they're afraid of what could be living inside this second pair of woods."

"If that is the truth, then we have much more trouble on our hands, boy."

Henrich and Landon began slowly making their way into the second set of dark woods within the Valley of Death.

<u>**III**</u>

Entering the second set of dark woods, Henrich and Landon noticed something strange about its interior. They could smell a deep stench within the woods, the smell of decay and death. It withered throughout the woods. The trees and bushes appeared to be slowly dying and the ground was covered in waste from the animals and creatures that dwell within the woods. Landon watched his steps while walking through the woods.

"This land, its covered in filth." Landon said. "It smells like corpses."

"It smells like shit." Henrich said. "You can go ahead and say it. You know it to be true."

"Ok, it does smell like shit. But, more of a corpse stench if you ask me."

"I get where you're coming from with this. No doubt there are bodies lying beneath our feet."

"Humans or animals?"

"Both. Generations of Man have come and died here."

"I wouldn't think there would be any ghosts, ghouls, or demons in this kind of woods. No matter if it's dark."

"Only way to find out is to make it through this place. Though, I am sure that we'll run into something. Its second nature for us now."

The ground began to tremble, slightly. The horse stopped walking, Landon looked around the trees and Henrich kept his head down, moving his eyes, scouting their surroundings.

"Is this a tremor?"

"Feels like one." Henrich said. "Yet, not one of earthly origin."

"What do you mean, sir?"

"It's being caused by something beneath the ground. Its rising up slowly. Whatever it may be."

The ground started to crack, breaking apart beneath their feet. The bushes and trees rose up from the ground, their roots showing up from beneath them, flying into the air. Henrich and Landon watched on and from the holes in the ground, jumped out small creatures. They looked to be demons, but also appeared to be dwarves, elves, some looked like goblins.

"What are they?"

"Something strange. We'll have to take them out anyhow."

Henrich fired his shooters at the running creatures. Landon fired shots with him toward the small creatures that were running in packs. The packs were rabid, going in many directions in front of Henrich and Landon. Both continued to shoot at the creatures. Their small stature was somewhat a threat as a few would duck down within the horde of creatures to be unseen by Henrich and Landon.

"How many of them do you think there are?" Landon asked

"By the end of this, it won't matter." Henrich said. "So, keep your shooting going."

They continued firing the shots toward the horde of creatures. Unsure of the bullets hitting the creatures, Henrich shrugged his shoulders as he reached for his blastshooter and began blasting the horde entirely. The horde suddenly ran from them like fleeing birds, though Henrich had most of them down and dead. The horde had been killed off except for a certain few that managed to escape the blast fire of Henrich. He turned to Landon, who only looked around at the dead bodies.

"Don't have pity on them, boy. They were already dead."

They continued to walk through the woods of the Valley of Death. Noticing the light of the sun was beginning to set, Henrich and Landon made a stop by a nearby tree. The tree was a tall one, where if it were to rain, the tree would be able to block the falling water from above them, to keep them dry. The cold wind blew past them as the moon arose into the sky, revealing herself once more.

"Give it a few hours and we'll be back on our feet onto the trail." said Henrich. "You understand me?"

"I understand you, sir."

Landon laid down next to the tree, going to sleep. While Henrich took watch over the campsite, he noticed the bushes in front of him to rattle. Hesitantly reaching for his shooter, from the rattling bushes came out a dog, not an ordinary dog, but a phantom dog. The dog had black fur and its eyes were red and as bright as the moon's own light. Henrich stared at the phantom dog, not making any sudden movements. He could recognize the dog had a solid body, but its body was see-through. A white mist had surrounded the dog and smoke exited from its mouth. The dog took a series of scouting around the bushes and woods, searching and turned its head and spotted Henrich, the dog stared back at him. Growling underneath its breath. The two kept their eyes locked onto each other tightly. Henrich nodded at the dog and the dog nodded back before walking away into the woods.

"Didn't expect that." Henrich said as he laid his head down to sleep, placing his hat over his eyes.

The phantom dog had walked into the bushes, which were covered in darkness and the bushes didn't make any sound as the dog walked through them. As if the dog itself had vanished into the air while walking into the dark cloaked bushes.

IV

Awaking from their sleep, Henrich and Landon continued their journey through the woods, shoving bushes and small trees out of their way. Henrich, riding atop his horse, could sense a presence deep within the woods. While making their way, Henrich could see a structure nearby, built in the middle of the woods.

"We have something ahead of us." Henrich said. "It looks big."

"What does it look like, sir?" Landon said. "Is it something that could probably assist us in our journey?"

Henrich took a closer look as the made their approach toward the structure. The large structure was large and almost towered over the trees of the woods. The outer scale of the structure appeared to be made of a solid glass with a neon texture to it. Yet, upon Henrich and Landon fully making their approach toward the structure, they happen to find out it wasn't glass that covered the outer area of the structure, but a mineral unknown to many humans. A mineral that was once used in a great war. Henrich knows of the mineral as he glances down at his shooter.

"What is it, sir?"

"I recognize this material that covers this structure. It is an ancient mineral. I've seen it during my times with the Heptad. We learned of its origin and its desire. This structure is built for a purpose and it doesn't hold something good within. This mineral was designed to keep evil from escaping their prisons."

"So, there could be something locked within the walls of this place?"

"There is something locked within. Because this isn't some ordinary prison facility in the middle of the woods."

Henrich took his hand and wiped the wall of the structure. Looking within and happens to see a set of stairs within. Though, there is more than one set of starts. Nearly over a dozen to be exact. Henrich turned to Landon and kept his eyes locked onto him.

"This is a labyrinth, boy."

"A labyrinth? So, there's something very large that is trapped within its walls?"

"Not trapped. Imprisoned for a purpose. I have heard of the tales of what lies within a labyrinth and if those tales are in fact true, we have a bigger issue facing us."

They walked through the labyrinth, trying to find their way towards the end. While they went through the labyrinth, the ground began to rumble. Landon didn't know what to make of it, but Henrich knew what was the cause of the rumbling. As it began to increase, Henrich prepared himself with his hand to his side.

"What's going on?" Landon asked.

"It's on our path."

"Our path?"

As the rumbling increased, Henrich looked behind himself and Landon to see the cause of the rumblings. Landon turned slowly and witnessed what Henrich was looking at.

"What is that?!" Landon asked, pointing toward what they're seeing.

"It's known across the Worlds as the Minotaur." Henrich answered.

The Minotaur stood on the other end of the puzzled walls, facing Henrich and Landon. The Minotaur was tall, almost over twelve feet in height. Its physique was peaked beyond human possibilities. Smoke derived from its nostrils as it stared at Henrich and Landon with its red pupil eyes.

"What should we do?!" Landon said.

"We make a way out of this place."

Henrich and Landon made a run for it and the Minotaur roared, chasing them down. The three of them ran through the labyrinth, Henrich and Landon made it their goal to find the way out while the Minotaur sought them out for slaughter and claiming them as food. While running, Henrich looked back, seeing the Minotaur chasing them. Henrich raised up his shooter and started firing at the creature.

"Is it dead yet?!" Landon yelled.

"Not now." Henrich said.

Henrich continued to shoot at the Minotaur, but the shooter wasn't having any effect on the creature. Henrich looked around at the strange interiors on the walls and knew there was something more that had to take place between them and the creature to escape the labyrinth.

"Boy." Henrich said. "Stop running."

"What do you mean stop running?!" Landon yelled. "That thing wants to kill us both!"

Henrich stood boldly before the Minotaur. Landon couldn't understand why Henrich would tell him to stop or why Henrich even stopped running himself. Henrich approached the Minotaur and faced the creature. The Minotaur glared into Henrich's eyes before letting out a loud roar in his face, blowing his hair.

"What are you doing?"

"This labyrinth isn't like the other labyrinths I've come across in my day."

"Well, what's so different about this one?"

"Usually, in labyrinths, we would have to find our way out of here. But, this one. The Minotaur is our way out."

Landon shook his head. The information given to him by Henrich isn't sinking it fully just yet. But, Landon knows he can trust

Henrich about any circumstance.

"So… how are you going to get the Minotaur to lead us out of this place?"

"Very simple."

Henrich reached to his back, raising up his blade. The Minotaur pounced around on the ground, prepared for a fight. Landon still couldn't understand what the two of them were doing. Only that they were faced off against each other in what appears to become a fight.

"If I can kill this creature, it will lead us out of this labyrinth."

"I'm not understanding how that's going to work."

"You'll see."

Henrich and the Minotaur faced off against each other in a fight. Landon stood back and watched the battle. Henrich went for several swipes of the blade, cutting the Minotaur's rough skin. The Minotaur grabbed Henrich and slammed him into the wall, later shoving him through the wall. The Minotaur prepared to ram through Henrich and the wall and Henrich knew this was his opportunity. The Minotaur roared and ran toward Henrich, the creature came closer as Henrich took his blade and jammed it into the creature's throat. The Minotaur slowed down and fell to the ground. The Minotaur is dead.

"Wait, that's it?" Landon asked.

"Yeah. It is."

"But, I thought it would take more to stop a monster like that."

'It would've. But, our circumstances don't call for it."

From the Minotaur's body arose a bluish-white fog, presumably the spirit of the Minotaur. The spirit moves across the air, going down the labyrinth. Henrich and Landon chase the spirit and as they chased the entity, it led them right toward the exit. Now on the other side of the Valley of Death. Landon shook his head.

"I guess that's how it works."

"It's not as simple as people would perceive it to be, boy."

V

Henrich and Landon exited the labyrinth and continued to make their way through the other side of the Valley of Death. Not knowing who or what they may come up against on the other side. Although, they could tell the air was slightly different and it wasn't as dreary as the previous side. In a sense, they could breathe comfortably on the other side of the valley.

"Aren't you getting a funny feeling?" Landon asked.

"What kind of feeling are you talking about?" Henrich said. "Are you speaking of this clean feeling on this side?"

"Yes. The air is just… fresh. Like if we're on the right path or something. I don't fully understand it all. But, I can sense that we're heading down a better path than what we went through before."

"We'll see about all of that when we get closer to the exit, boy."

"I hope we will."

They continued to move through the wilderness, knowing that it is completely different than the previous side of the Valley. So far, they have yet to come up against any creatures before from the other side. It calmed down Landon, he feels comfortable on this side. Though, Henrich is slightly concerned. For he knew of a place such as this with this amount of silence is something to keep a guard on.

"Something's not right around here." Henrich said with a stern look.

"What do you mean? Its peaceful on this side. We haven't run into any of those shadowic creatures or some giant half-man half-bull monster. Plus, we haven't entered another one of those labyrinths. So, what's the issue, sir?"

"Something is watching us. I can feel it."

"Are you sure?'

"I am positive about it, boy." Henrich said. "Make sure your shooter is prepared for firing."

Landon took a glare down to his side, where his shooter was placed. He checked it for ammo and there was ammo. Landon felt confident that nothing would go wrong on this side of the wilderness. Yet, Henrich was certain that something was keeping an eye on them and he knew it was only a matter of time before it showed itself to them.

"We haven't seen anything yet." Landon said. "Maybe it's just the surroundings. You know, how they look slightly like the previous side."

"That's not it, boy." Henrich said. "There's something going on here."

"I'm not getting it."

"Because you're not trained up to a level to comprehend it."

The horse turned another angle, getting both Henrich and Landon's attention. The horse could sense something was lurking in the trees.

"What's wrong with your horse?"

"Nothing's wrong. He's sensing what I'm sensing."

"Which is?"

From the nearby trees, fell long, thick branches. They moved with slow pace and from atop the branches are two women, they are naked. But, they're glowing a neon blue and their hair is glowing white as snow. Henrich looked at the women and he knew what they were. Landon was unsure as to what the women could be.

"The hell is going on?" Henrich said.

"I was about to ask you, they look like women. But, women I've never seen before. Ever."

"We are glad to see two men in our area." One of the women said. "For it has been a very long time since we've seen a man."

"Enough of this talk. I know what you are." Henrich said. "Tell me how two succubi found their way inside the Valley of Death?"

"You don't know do you?" The other succubus said with her soft voice.

"What should I know?"

"You should know that not all things are easy to understand. We've been within these trees for centuries. Looking for any man that would give us what we desire."

"Desire?" Landon asked curiously. "Like what?"

"We cannot feed off each other for the rest of the days ahead. We need others to give us the energy we seek."

"I'm not understand what they're talking about. Henrich, sir, if you may, please tell me what they're going on about?"

"They want us to have intercourse with them."

"Pardon me for a moment. You just said intercourse."

"You heard me, boy." Henrich said, looking at Landon. "They feed off sexual energy. You should've done more homework on other things that live in the Worlds rather than just the Warslingers."

"If you want to pass through this section of the wilderness, you must come into us and give us the desire that we seek."

"This stuff is crazy." Landon said. "Just crazy."

"Give me a minute here, boy." Henrich said. "Let me think on this."

The two succubi were awaiting their answers. Henrich knew the women were pleasant to look upon and their glow only enhanced their beauty and their sexual attraction. Landon was attracted to them, but was unsure of going through with the procedure.

"So, what will it be, men? Will you go into us and give us the energy we seek to desire?"

Landon shook his head. No answer could come from his mouth. For if he were to agree, he wouldn't know what to do during the procedure. For if he were to disagree, he feared what the power of the succubus could do to him. Immediately as Landon was about to speak, Henrich shut him down and faced the two women.

"I'll do it. Both of you."

"Have you lost your mind, sir?" Landon asked loudly. "How can you do two of them at the same time?"

"I didn't say at the same time, boy."

"Do you women agree to my answer?"

"We certainly do."

The two women grabbed a hold of Henrich's arms and brought him into their tree. Landon stood next to the horse and waited until Henrich came out of the tree. Landon shook his head and seen the horse doing the same. Landon nodded.

"I see you agree with what I had asked."

In the tree, Henrich went in unto the first succubus and she drained as much of his sexual energy as she could. After Henrich was finished with her, he went into the second succubus and she received a portion of his energy. Henrich continued to pleasure the two succubi as Landon waited for him. Henrich slightly enjoyed them and continued to please them even more, until Landon could hear their screams coming from the tree.

"The hell is going on in there!" Landon said.

Some few minutes after, Henrich was finished with the succubus and they were filled with energy as they began to kiss and suck on each other. Henrich looked at them and seen their actions. The succubus turned to him with a smile on their faces.

"We have to thank you for this energy. It gives us the strength to pleasure each other even more than we hoped to imagine."

Henrich smirked for a moment, he was about to tell the succubus something. Something that they weren't even aware of during the intercourses.

"The intercourses had their good shares. But, did the two of you know what would become of you both after I laid with you?"

"What do you mean?"

"What are you getting at, Man?"

"You are now my wives and now I must give you a bill of divorcement. In a different way."

Henrich pulled out his shooters and fired them into the heads of the succubus. Killing them both as their bodies fell atop each other. Their glow disappeared and the blood from their heads created a small pond for their bodies to lie in. Henrich nodded and returned to the ground. Landon looked ahead and seen Henrich approaching. Henrich came down from the tree and Landon looked back at the tree for the succubus.

"What happened to the women? I heard you guys screaming, then later I heard gunshots."

"We can move past this area, boy." Henrich said. "So, let's keep moving."

Henrich continued moving forward. Landon nodded and followed Henrich along through the remainder of the wilderness.

<u>VI</u>

"So, what really happened with those women back there?"

"I did what I had to do for us to continue further through this place."

"Did you really have intercourse with them? With both?"

Henrich sighed as he turned to face Landon. He knew the young man was curious about what had just happened. Henrich believed the boy to not have the understanding as of all that took place. He could see the innocence in Landon's eyes. Henrich's age and his experience was known throughout the research of Landon's study. But, Landon didn't know all there is to know about Henrich.

"All that you need to know is that I handled the matter."

"But, that's not really an answer, sir."

"If I were to give you all the details, you might think twice when you see a woman that you may desire."

"But, I'm not understanding, sir."

"Someday you will understand what I'm telling you and you will thank yourself for hearing it clearly."

"I guess I will."

Henrich and Landon continued moving through the Valley of Death. On their walk, they catch the jittering sounds of something running through the wilderness nearby. Both of whom are intrigued by the footsteps that are echoing throughout the valley. Henrich is unsure as to who or what it could be, though Landon is not as fearful of the footstep as he would believe himself to be.

"You think someone else is in here with us, maybe?" Landon asked.

"Could be the case. Although, I prefer that we be cautious about it."

Moving on through the valley, slowing listening to the footsteps, a young woman appeared before them, running into Henrich. She fell to the ground and slowly raised up her head, seeing Henrich and Landon. Both were unfamiliar with the young woman, as she was dressed in clothing that didn't fit in the Worlds that the two of them have come to know. The young woman moved her long blonde hair from her face as she stared at them. Henrich could sense that she didn't know why she was in the wilderness.

"Who are you?" Henrich asked. "Why are you roaming on about in these woods?"

"My name is Beth Grasslands and I don't know exactly how I got here."

"Then, where did you come from?" Landon asked.

"I'm from Washington D.C."

Henrich's expression seemed unusual, for himself and for Landon. Landon was even confused by Beth's answer as he and Henrich knew something about D.C. that Beth wasn't known to. She continued looking around the wilderness, standing still somewhat, gazing at Henrich and Landon. Seeing them carrying weapons and dressed in strange apparel.

"What do you mean Washington D.C.?" Landon asked. "I don't understand what you mean by that."

"That's where I'm from. I live in D.C."

"That cannot be possible, young lady." Henrich said. "Not to my understanding."

"Well, what do you mean by that?"

"Because Washington D.C. doesn't exist anymore. It was destroyed in a nuclear attack by enemies during the War of the West."

"Destroyed? War of the West? I'm not understanding what you're telling me. I was just in D.C. a few seconds ago."

"How so?" Landon asked. "Could you give us some details as to where you were last located?"

"I was in the middle of a paranormal investigation with my teammates and I took a turn down a corridor and suddenly I ended up here. In this forest. I've been looking for a way out ever since and that's when I ran into the two of you."

"Paranormal investigation?" Landon said confusingly. "What is that?"

"That's when you hunt spirits of the dead." Henrich said. "I've heard of such practices before in my youth."

Beth shook her head, trying to take in the information told by

Henrich. She believed that she was dreaming, but everything around her was just too real. She later thought it was all a hallucination, though the surroundings are confirming it to be one. She decided to get as much information as she possibly could to find her way back home.

"Who are you two?"

"Well, my name is Cody Landon and this is-"

"Randolph Henrich."

"He's a Warslinger."

"What is a Warslinger?" Beth asked, looking at Landon strangely.

Beth twisted her face at Landon. She didn't know what a Warslinger was. It took Landon a few seconds to realize that for himself. Henrich could tell Beth was not from their World or any of the Worlds they're familiar with. Henrich knew he had to explain as much detail as he could to Beth, otherwise she would just go crazy within the wilderness.

"A Warslinger is one of a knightly group. I am a Warslinger of the Heptad. One of the Seven."

"So, where are the other six members of this 'Heptad'?"

"They're scattered abroad. I have yet to encounter any of them for some time now. Though, we will all meet each other again."

"If I may ask you both, where are you headed?"

"We're heading towards the exit of this place." Henrich said.

"Yeah. We're going to find The Haunted City."

"The what now?"

"The-," Landon said. "Never mind me."

"If you don't mind, you should come along with us. Until you find your way back home."

"I was going to ask that, but since you've already invited me. I will take it."

"That is good to hear. Because I fear for you of what you may not know of this World or the other Worlds."

"What do you mean by other Worlds?"

"You'll soon find that out."

<u>VII</u>

After Beth decided to tag along with Henrich and Landon through the wilderness of the Valley of Death, they seemed to come upon a set of trees, though these trees are peculiar to the rest. They are bulkier and are covered in much greener. They appear to be built up of more grass than bark. Henrich approached one of the trees and placed his hand upon it. Feeling it.

"What's going on?" Beth asked.

"I don't know. He's checking the tree apparently." Landon said. "They do look strange."

"I've never seen trees like this before.

"That's why I suggested you travel with us. You almost came into this area on your own."

Henrich rubbed the tree and could feel the grass and could also feel something flowing through the trees. Like a streaming river. Henrich couldn't see any water, but he could see a greenish milky substance buried within the grass covered areas. A low-pitched moan had sounded from the tree.

"These trees aren't trees."

The tree began to burst and move. Arms grew from its sides and legs grew out from beneath. Henrich stepped back as the tree increased in height and a face was slowly forming from the spot where Henrich had previously placed his hand. The arms were made of what appeared to be strong grass mixed with bark as did its legs appear the same.

"What is that?" Beth asked with fear.

"A walking tree?" Landon said.

"No. it's a Green Man. One of many in this area."

From the Green Man's face grew out a beard, made of the grass. The remainder of its body was surrounded and covered in a composition of foliage, oak leaves, and small branches that were twisted up in the Green Man's grassy hair.

"Why have you trespassed this place?" The Green Man asked. Authority spoken through his deep-pitched voice. "Why have you come into this place uninvited?"

85

"We come to leave this place." Henrich said. "We are only on our way out of here. That is all."

"You come to escape, yet you entered into its doors. How wise are you to believe your own words? Your words speak of escape, but I sense an entry you have done."

"We just want to leave." Landon said hesitantly. "That's all we ask of you, tree-man."

Beth measured the Green Man. She was astounded, though with a sense of fear that had slowly grabbed her. Henrich looked at her for a moment and could see she was intrigued by the Green Man and how Landon had feared for his life as he tried to stand as far back from the Green Man as he could.

"How can a tree move around and talk?" Beth wondered. "What kind of forest is this?"

"One of another World." Henrich said. "There are other places just as strange to you that you have not seen."

"Tell me your names." The Green Man commanded. "First and last."

"Cody Landon, good tree-man, sir."

"Beth Grasslands."

"Randolph Henrich."

The Green Man paused and looked closer at Henrich. The name struck him, and it struck him strongly. The Green Man could recognize Henrich's attire and he could also see the shooters on his sides.

"You're one of them."

"I didn't know that your kind knew about Warslingers."

"For a time, we did. But, that was ages ago when you and your brethren walked this World together as a unit. Before the fall. Before the separation."

"So, that's it?" Landon asked. "We can get pass now since you know of the Warslingers?"

"I will allow you to pass. For you show no signs of evil."

"We appreciate it." Beth said.

"But, I must warn you. When you reach near the exit of this valley, you must watch out for the nature and shadowic creatures and scavenge these portions of the valley and you must also watch your surroundings for The Mercenary Man and his fire shots that fly across the skies and zoom through the air."

"The Mercenary Man?" Henrich said. "He came through here?"

"Very recently, he did. From what I could sense from his presence, he is waiting for you."

Henrich nodded. "It was an honor to speak to you, Green Man."

"More of an honor to converse with a Warslinger of the Heptad."

The Green Man moved aside and allowed them to continue further in the wilderness. He gave them the warnings that they would need to escape the valley in one piece.

<h1 style="text-align:center"><u>VIII</u></h1>

Walking on through the wilderness, Henrich gazed up into the air, looking toward the sky through the surrounding trees and he could tell that the sun was about to set. He thought to himself that if he kept moving continually, he would be out of the Valley of Death and closer to finding The Haunted City. The more they walked and the less disturbances that came to them, Henrich was slightly relieved, but concerned. Since there could be something following them and could attack them at any moment. He kept in his mind what the Green Man had told him. To watch out for the fire shots of The Mercenary Man and the Scavengers that are abroad.

"How far do we have before we reach the exit?" Landon asked.

"Not that far. We have just a little bit more moving to do."

"So, what's on the other side of this forest?" Beth asked. "Is there a town of some kind. Like a rest stop?"

"Truthfully, I do not know what lies on the other side of this wilderness. I only know that the trail we are on leads to The Haunted City. Which is my primary mission."

"The Haunted City?"

"It is a place unlike any other place in the Worlds. For the City has the power to grant anything of Man's desires. Only if he sees fit to use them in their proper order according to the rules of the

Worlds."

"So, what are you seeking there?"

"Truth. Some seek immortality, others seek wealth and fame. But I, I seek truth."

While they walked, Landon noticed something glowing on the ground in front of their path. He took a closer look and seen a dark rugged pot. It sat in the middle of the trail as if it was placed there, but left alone for some period. The pot was almost like a vase, but smaller and within the pot was gold. A collection of gold coins. The coins' glow had mesmerized Landon. Henrich and Beth seen Landon's attraction to the gold.

"What are you up to, boy?"

"It's gold, sir." Landon said with a stutter in his voice. He was drawn to the gold like an insect to a blinding light.

"Best you leave it be." Beth said. "Were not sure who left it there. Maybe they're on their way back to retrieve it."

"How could they be? You don't just leave a pot of gold lying around in the middle of a forest. That's idiocy."

Landon kneeled in front of the pot and raised his hand, reaching toward the gold. Henrich's horse began to act uneasy as it started to kick its legs around. Henrich looked over to Landon and immediately could tell that something wasn't right with the pot of gold.

"Boy, move!" Henrich yelled.

From two of the trees that stood on the sides of the pot, came down a large net and from underneath the dirt of the trail rose up a large net. The two nets intertwined with each other grabbed Landon and Henrich ran toward him. While Henrich ran, Beth attempted to help him, but the net also snatched them and raised them up into the air, where they sat. Henrich's horse had ran off due to the snapping sound of the falling and rising nets.

"What is your damn problem!" Henrich yelled.

"I... I didn't know that it was all a trap."

"You didn't think to wonder about that before you tried to touch the gold."

"So, what set up the trap?" Beth asked.

From one of the small bushes arose a man, short in stature, appears almost like dwarf, but dressed in green with golden buckles on his shoes and wearing a high-crowned hat. The man laughed at them, looking up to them from the ground. The man stood next to the pot of gold and took the pot, placing it underneath one of the bushes nearby.

"The hell is that?" Landon said.

"He's a leprechaun, boy." Henrich said. "Nothing to be afraid of."

"Leprechauns are real?" Beth asked. "I thought them to be only folklore story figures."

"In these Worlds, your folklore figures are real as the air you breathe."

The Leprechaun continued to laugh and giggle from the ground.

"It appears that one of you managed to steal my gold." The Leprechaun said. "Now, which of you was it?"

Landon looked at Henrich and Beth. He pointed to himself and pointed to the Leprechaun. Henrich and Beth only stared at him as they know it was his fault for their current situation.

"Do I really have to tell him."

"Tell him, boy. Or else you'll have to deal with much worse."

Landon shivered as he gazed down at the Leprechaun. The Leprechaun waived his hand to Landon, who also waived back.

"Um, good Leprechaun sir." Landon said. "It was me. I tried to steal your pot of gold."

"And could you tell me why?"

"Because it was just sitting there. Alone on the trail. It was bound to be taken by someone."

"How do you know that? How would you know that?"

"I don't know the answers."

"Yet, you continue to speak to me. Thief is what you are."

"Leprechaun." Henrich said. "Would you care to release us from this trap of yours?"

"Why would I do that? You look fine from down here."

"I beg to differ. For I do not appear to be fine up here, and I would rather like to be back on the ground."

The Leprechaun laughed again. From his side, he pulled out a staff. The Leprechaun reached up and waved the staff in the air beneath them and from them came falling down their weapons. Their weapons fell through the nets as if they were liquid, but yet they were still solid. Henrich was upset even more so, now that his weapons were in the hands of the Leprechaun.

"You little runt." Henrich said. "Let us go."

"I'm afraid I cannot do that just yet, good man. For there is much more for the three of you to do."

"What are we going to do?" Landon said.

"Do either of you have a knife on you?" Beth asked.

"I believe I do." Henrich said, slowly reaching into his boot for the small knife.

The Leprechaun danced around on the ground, coveting their weapons and rubbing them against his face. The sight disgusted Henrich. Landon was still afraid, and Beth was unsure as to what World she has now found herself living in.

"We want our weapons back you know." Landon said. "What do we have to do to get them?"

"What you must do is simple, my good boy. You must capture me in the maze of the bushes. When you do that, you will have your weapons back and you may continue on further out of this forest."

The Leprechaun picked up their weapons and tossed them into the maze of bushes, where they would be difficult to find without the Leprechaun's assistance. Seeing that site enraged Henrich a tad bit. He wasn't interested in playing some game with a leprechaun.

"How would we find you when we're still stuck up here?" Henrich said. "Isn't it unfair."

"Isn't everything unfair."

Henrich pulled out his knife and started cutting through the net. The Leprechaun noticed and started to have a panic attack. Pacing back and forth on the ground beneath them.

"No. No. No." The Leprechaun said angrily. "You're cheating!"

"Not exactly." Landon said.

"You're making a mockery of my game!"

Henrich cut through the net and the tree of them fell to the ground. The Leprechaun started backing up as Henrich looked toward him. The Leprechaun ran for his life into the bushes and Henrich followed him. Landon helped Beth up off the ground and she admonished him for doing so.

"Are you alright?" Landon asked.

"I'm fine."

Beth looked around for Henrich and the Leprechaun, but didn't see them as she turned to Landon, seeing on the two of them in the location.

"Where did Henrich go?" Beth asked.

"He went after the Leprechaun."

"Well, shouldn't we be following them."

Beth walked off, following the sounds of the Leprechaun's screaming and Henrich's yelling. Landon followed her as she followed the sounds. Henrich looked around the bushes for the Leprechaun, but couldn't find him. Henrich stared kicking the bushes to see if the Leprechaun could be hiding within them. His anger was slowly kindling, but his focus was still on his mission.

"You're wasting our time, dwarf." Henrich said. "Show yourself and give me my weapons back."

"I don't think so." The Leprechaun said from afar off. "It's not fair for the game."

"I don't give a damn about our mystery game. Give me back what belongs to me."

"Just rude you are."

"Don't play around with me any further. For your own good and for the sake of your own life."

Henrich continued moving and found himself standing in front of six small bushes. All covered with leaves and entangled with branches underneath. Henrich looked around the area and could see the Leprechauns footprints in the dirt, which disappear at the six bushes.

"If this is how you want to play your game." Henrich said, pulling out a small shooter from his back. "Then, this is how I'll play along."

Henrich fired a shot at the first bush. The shot rattled through the air and caused fear to consume the Leprechaun. In the distance behind Henrich, Landon and Beth heard the shot and they ran toward the area. Henrich fired a second shot at the second bush. Yet, no sign of the Leprechaun, though, Henrich knew he was there. Somewhere.

"You're about to exit this life if you don't show yourself." Henrich said. "I know you're in there."

Henrich fired a third shot at the third bush. Within the bushes, the Leprechaun rattled and Henrich could see the bushes rattling. The Leprechaun panted for his breath. Fear had indeed consumed him.

"Come out of there."

In the bushes, the Leprechaun looked at the weapons and closely noticed one of the shooters. He recognized it and knew it belonged to a Warslinger. The Leprechaun thought for a moment and a fourth shot fired through the fourth bush, grazing the Leprechaun's hat. Henrich fired a fifth shot at the fifth bush, where the bullet flew past the Leprechaun's chest. The Leprechaun came to the realization that Henrich was indeed a Warslinger.

Henrich aimed closely at the sixth bush, where the Leprechaun was hiding. He focused the shooter onto the bush. The shooter was ready to fire. Landon and Beth came from behind Henrich and stood by him.

"This is the last warning." Henrich said. "Come out of there or die in there. Your choice."

The Leprechaun bolted out of the sixth bush with his hands up in the air. Henrich knew that the fear has taken over him. The Leprechaun had given up and waved his hands in the air, while dropping his staff.

"Alright, alright!' The Leprechaun said. "You win the game."

"Now, give us our weapons."

The Leprechaun picked up his staff and waved it around the bushes and from out of the bushes arose their weapons. Henrich grabbed his shooters and machete. Landon also retrieved his shooter. The Leprechaun walked over to Henrich slowly.

"You're one of them."

"I am."

The Leprechaun nodded. A smile appeared on his face.

"All going well."

"What's going well?" Landon said. "What do you mean by that?"

The Leprechaun walked away from the area, allowing them to continue further. The Leprechaun stopped and turned to Henrich only. He winked at Henrich.

"In time, you'll learn why these matters are happening. In time."

The Leprechaun vanished into the air with a puff of smoke. Henrich's horse had also made its return and Henrich was relieved at the sight of it. Landon still wanted to know what the Leprechaun had meant with his words, Beth was in questioning of all she has recently seen.

"What did he mean by that, sir?" Landon asked.

"Guess we'll find out once we're out of this place."

<u>IX</u>

Almost nearing the exit of the Valley of Death, Henrich, Landon, and Beth grow tired from the walking that they have done and the chasing they've done after the Leprechaun and now it is almost sunset, and they have yet to reach the exit. Henrich kept his eyes on the sun, seeing its preparation to set. The wind blew across them and Henrich could sense the energy of the moon slowly rising in the horizon. He knew full well that they could not continue moving through the wilderness during the night, for they would be sure to get lost and perhaps lose their minds. It's an effect of the wilderness. The shadows of it can do harmful things to the minds of Man.

Walking still, from the trees come down three fairies. The fairies appeared out of nowhere and were almost a light to their path in the forest. The fairies' bodies glow a golden hue along with a bluish touch to them. Their wings were silver and glittered through the light.

Their light even touched the trees and gave them light within the wilderness. Henrich was somewhat uneasy seeing the fairies as they appeared from out of nowhere.

"Why are you three walking about in the wilderness?" One fairy said. "Don't you see the sun is preparing to set and the moon is preparing to rise."

"We can see that, fairy." Henrich said. "Why have you appeared before us? Does it concern more troubles that we may find in this valley?"

"No troubles you will receive from us, sir." The Second Fairy said. "We are only the light of the wilderness. Here to give to you a pathway toward the exit."

"How far is the exit?" Landon asked. "If I may wonder."

"The exit is not far. If you continue on foot for a matter of an hour, you will come to the exit. But, the night is almost here, and it is not good for those such as yourself to walk through this forest during the night."

"The darkness lurks at night." The first Fairy said. "It consumes those who move around in its dwelling place. It doesn't take it nicely."

"So, how are you three moving on around?" Beth asked. "How can you move through the darkness during the night?"

"We are made of light. Light that is rarely seen in these parts. But, there is something much more going on here."

"Like what?"

The first Fairy flew toward Beth. The fairy measured her from the head to the feet. The fairy glared into Beth's eyes and could instantly see where she was from and where she would be going. As if the Fairy herself possessed psychic abilities to tell he past and future of a person's life. Though, this Fairy possessed a power as such, but maybe more than expected. Beth stayed calm and still as the Fairy measured her. Henrich knew what the Fairy was doing and as for Landon, he couldn't think of anything that would make sense about the Fairy's actions.

"Why is she doing that to her, sir?" Landon asked.

"She's searching her spirit."

"How so?"

"Some fairies possess that kind of power. Others don't."

The Fairy backed away from Beth and seen the sadness in her heart. The sadness of her previous life was being buried within her spirit. The Fairy nodded to Beth with compassion in her own heart.

"I know you missed them and they miss you as well."

"I know." Beth said, tearing up a bit.

"There may be a way for you to return to your home world. But, it may come with a price."

"What are you talking about, fairy?" Henrich asked. "How can she return back to her world?"

"She will have to travel to The Haunted City. There, she can return to her home world safely and without harm."

Beth turned to Henrich and he looked at her. He thought to himself the possibilities that The Haunted City might give to her and to himself. It is his mission to reach the City, but what he may have to face between now and then is something of mystery not only to Landon and Beth, but to himself. He looked at the Fairies and could sense that they knew who he was and that he was heading to The Haunted City himself. Their energies are strange to Henrich as he's never seen Fairies such as these in his lifetime across any of the Worlds.

"We will not hold the three of you up any longer." The first Fairy said. "You may pass. But, I will suggest that you make your rest here for the night and in the morning of dawn, you may reach the exit."

Henrich nodded. "That we will do."

Henrich and Landon walked away from the Fairies. Beth followed them, but she turned back to the Fairy that spoke to her and the Fairy could see that she was saddened by the truth of her spirit, but also intrigued about going to The Haunted City to return to her own world. The Fairy nodded with a smile and waved to her.

"Go." The Fairy said. "Go with him and you will find your way back home."

"Thank you." Beth said.

"Go." The Fairy replied.

Beth caught up with Henrich and Landon as they walked near the exit. In the distance, Henrich could see the exit of the valley. The sun's light shined on the grounds and in an instant, the sun's light started to dim. The air slowly became cool. Henrich looked up past the trees and could see the shifting in the air between the sun and the moon.

"We make rest here for the night."

The three of them made their stop at the particular spot within the wilderness, a few feet from the exit and as they made their rest, the sky was darkened, and the sun was gone. Only the moon and the stars covered the sky and shined their light onto the ground. The moon's light was bright, but it wasn't bright enough to enter completely into the wilderness. Henrich looked over to Landon and Beth and they were both asleep. As was the horse. Henrich laid back against a tree and fell asleep.

In the dream Henrich had, was of a distant memory of times past. A time where the Warslingers of the Heptad roamed the Worlds and the Worlds knew them to exist among them. In the dream of Henrich, The Warslingers were facing off against a foe that appeared to hold magic in their hands. The battle amongst them took place at a castle. A castle that belonged to one of the Warslingers. Within the castle walls, Henrich fired at the foe with his shooters. Though, the foe was powerful enough to turn the bullets into dust.

"He's too strong." Henrich said to the other Warslingers.

"How can he be." said Warslinger, Joshua of Ephraim. "We can take down this mage."

While facing the mage, the castle walls begun to quake and Henrich knew something was wrong. The entire kingdom was being overthrown by a power much greater than the mage. The Warslingers made a run for it, knowing they couldn't stay at the castle, for it was being destroyed and crumbling from within. As the Warslingers run into the nearby woods, one of the Warslinger, Knight Arthur Pendragon turned back and looked at the castle, which was his and the kingdom which also belonged to him. By the castle doors, he could see a woman, a pale woman, dressed in black and violet, cheering on with soldiers of her own. Arthur knew the woman and he knew her too well. Henrich approached Arthur, seeing him spiritually destroyed as he kingdom was taken from him.

"We have to go, brother." Henrich said. "We can return another day to face them."

"But, my kingdom." Knight Arthur said. "My home. It's gone."

"You will reclaim it. In time."

Arthur turned to Henrich and nodded. He followed him and the other Warslingers into the wilderness, away from the pale woman's soldiers as she became the new ruler of the kingdom. The Queen of the Castle she became.

<u>X</u>

The sun arises in the morning and through it Henrich awakened. He prepared himself and the horse for the exit of the forest. Landon and Beth also awoke and prepared themselves. Landon approached Henrich and looked over, seeing the exit in front of them, just a few feet away.

"We're almost out of this place." Landon said. "I'm sort of thrilled about it."

"I can understand your energy." Henrich said. "Though, it is best that we be cautious as to what sits on the other side of that exit."

They gathered their gear and left for the exit. As they came closer to the exit of the wilderness, the sun's light grew brighter in front of them. Signaling a change was to come once they exited the forest.

After moving on and coming closer to the exit, the sun's light touched them individually and through that they made their exit out of the Valley of Death and its wilderness. The three of them were relieved of finally being out of the long forest. Landon was ecstatic, and Beth was calm. Henrich looked around and could see plains of green grass and rugged mountains all around. The sky was clear as the sun shined from it. In the distance, he could see what appeared to be a town of some kind. Unsure of it, he thinks about going there to see if he can gather more equipment and food.

"What do we do now?" Landon asked.

"We make way for that town up ahead." Henrich said. "It appears to be one."

Henrich turned and noticed Beth looking around at the plains and the mountains. She was in awe of its beauty and she's never seen a place like it before. She looked at Henrich as she pointed around the plains and the mountains. He knew she had never seen anything like it nor experience such a place before.

"Best you take in as much as you can." Henrich said.

"It's beautiful. I've never been in a place like this. I've never seen a place like this before."

"Don't they have plains and mountains in your world?" Landon asked.

"They do. But, not like these. These are strangely different and more colorful than the ones back on my world."

Henrich showed a faint smile to Beth. Seeing her come to grips with the World she finds herself living in. From the sky sounded a cawing sound. Henrich looked up and a bird flew past their heads. Only this bird appeared differently as it looked like a vulture, but had three legs instead of two. Henrich knows about birds of that nature and their presence isn't something to be glad over. The three-legged bird's appearance signaled trouble. A dark trouble.

From the exit of the forest appeared a silhouette of a man. He spoke clearly as Henrich turned to face him. Landon and Beth also seen the man. He was tall, almost to the height of Henrich. He was lean, but physically fit. He wore what seemed to be armor, torn and cracked armor, made of some clad material, possibly from the rocks of the mountains, though they were painted black. His eyes were a pale blue and his facial hair proved him to be at a certain age. The man applauded with he set his sights on Henrich.

"This is beautiful." The man said. "I knew you would make it out of there."

"Who are you?" Henrich asked.

"You mean you don't recognize my apparel? I think you should."

Henrich looked at the man's apparel and the Man laughed at him. Henrich's mind raced as to who could wear that type of apparel. Many faces came to his mind, but neither of them fit. He later thought of what was written on the scroll and what the Green Man had warned him about. Henrich raised up his shooter to the Man. He now knows who he is.

"You're him." Henrich said. "You're the Mercenary Man."

"Guilty."

"Wait, this is The Mercenary Man?" Landon said. "He's the guy?"

"Yeah, young man. I am that guy. But, I'm not here for you or that beautiful young woman there. I'm here for this guy and he knows why."

"So, the scroll. What was written on it was true. A bounty was placed on my head. For your Tubal King."

"You need to speak better when mentioning his name, Warslinger. The Tubal King knows who you are and has been watching you ever since you came into this life. He knows your strengths and your weaknesses. He knows the location of your brethren and their current actions."

"Can't be possible. How can one man have his eyes over all the Worlds and over everyone?"

"Because the Tubal King isn't a man. He isn't made of the same flesh and blood that you and I are made of. The Tubal King is different. He is an entity. Born in the times of the Ancients. He gained his power through deception and evil. Through that he was able to conquer The Haunted City, where he now rules over and once he enters the City, he will acquire the power to have full dominion over all the Worlds. The ones that we know and the ones that we don't know."

Henrich kept his shooter aimed at The Mercenary Man. Who only laughed at him continually. Landon and Beth were uncomfortable in his sights as he would gaze at them sinisterly and would wink at Beth, gawking at her at times and making mentions toward her breasts and legs.

"All I will tell you and all that you should know is I will kill you."

Henrich said. "And after I kill you, I will reach The Haunted City and I will kill this Tubal King of yours."

The Mercenary Man clapped his hands and scoffed at Henrich's words. He knew that Henrich had no comprehension nor understanding of The Tubal King's power. But, The Mercenary Man took Henrich's words closely, as he knows he would make the attempt to turn them into reality.

"Well then. You have your chance to kill me now, Warslinger." The Mercenary Man said scoffing. "Do it and you can reach the City and try your best to kill The Tubal King."

Henrich fired the shooter at The Mercenary Man. But, he dodged the shot and took off running. Henrich ran after him in anger while Landon and Beth made their attempt to catch up with the two men. The Mercenary Man ran into the plains, where he continued to laugh at Henrich. Henrich followed him and took another shot, this time shooting him in his right leg. The Mercenary Man fell to the ground as Henrich approached him. The Mercenary Man did not move. Not even a flinch.

"The hell is this?" Henrich said, looking at The Mercenary Man's body.

Henrich kneeled and turned his body around, face up and what Henrich saw he couldn't believe. The Mercenary Man has completely transformed into another person. When Henrich looked the Man in the face, his eyes opened, they were not human. The Man's eyes were black, and his pupils were a dark red. The Man stared to laugh as Henrich stepped back from him. The Man arose from the ground and stood face to face with Henrich. Landon and Beth stayed far back from them, seeing that The Mercenary Man has transformed into someone else. The Man appeared ageless, yet old as he was no longer dressed in the same apparel, only this time he wore a black and red cloak, with a hood that covered his head and his hands were glowing with a powerful that only fit those of evil.

"Who are you?" Henrich asked.

"I am the Malevolency Embodied." The Man said. "I am all that is evil in the Worlds. I am a force to be reckoned with."

"Give me a name."

"The Ancients knew me as the Antichrist, but you may get to know me by the name of Judas Arkdragon."

"So, you're the Mercenary Man?"

"I'm just a pawn for The Tubal King. I am here to tell you that he knows your intentions and he's not pleased with them. He wants you to cease your mission and return to your home."

"I have no home and I will not cease because of his words."

"That is fair. Anyhow, in time, I will be seeing you, your brethren, and your partners again very soon."

Henrich fired another shot, but the shot flew through Judas' body as he evaporated into a thick blanket of smoke and disappeared. Landon and Beth approached Henrich, confused as to what they've just seen. Henrich looked around and instantly, from some source, he could recognize their current location. He walked about, looking around at the plains and mountains once more and looked out further toward what appeared to be the small town. Landon approached him, trying to stop Henrich from walking constantly about.

"Sir, what's going on?"

"Things have changed for the us, boy. Things have changed."

"What do you mean by that?" Beth asked. "What has changed for us?"

Henrich looked around and focused his attention on Landon and Beth. He knew what to tell them, only if they could take it in. He looked back around the surroundings and he knew where they were. Somewhere unpleasant.

"This place. I know it now. It is trouble."

"What is this place?'

"The Land of the Survivors. Where those who scavenge survive and those who do not perish."

Henrich looked out toward the small town. He now knew it was filled with Scavengers. It is a place that many seek not to enter. A place that is deemed for only those of the strong to truly survive. Henrich's knowledge of the location came from something, but he isn't sure where it came from. Only that it appeared in his mind and now he must use it to move on further in his mission. He turned to

Landon and Beth as his horse stayed to his side.

"So, what should we do before we enter that town?" Landon asked.

"Be careful and keep to yourself." Henrich said. "Unless you want to be taken capture by the Scavengers."

"Before we enter, who are these Scavengers?" asked Beth. "I'm just wandering."

"They are a group of uncaring generations of Man. They seek what they want, and they take it from anyone who possesses it. They are dangerous people and they do not care for the young, the old, the widow, or the stranger. They only want what they desire and will do anything to get it."

"So, what will they take from us if they could?"

"Just as much as anything they want. From our weapons to ourselves for their own use and for their own pleasure. I will say that you must guard yourself while we're here. Don't make any kind of mistakes or signs of mistakes, for they will notice, and they will not hesitate to approach you."

Landon nodded. "I understand, sir. I understand."

"I understand as well." Beth said. "I will make sure to keep cautious."

Henrich nodded. He could see they were serious, but, they were afraid. Afraid of what could happen once they reach the town. Henrich looked out and he stared at the town.

"Watch yourselves. The Scavengers are abroad."

CHAPTER FOUR

SCAVENGERS ABOUND

I

Looking ahead toward the small town and knowing the location of which they stand in, Henrich prepared his mind as he, Landon, and Beth began to move toward the small town. For within that small town may very well be people of a good countenance and of a good heart. But, most of them around the area are known as the Scavengers and are not to be taken as a light-hearted gesture of words. While coming toward the small town, the face of Judas Arkdragon was seared into Henrich's mind. He tried to remember any memories that could give him some past insight on the mystical strander, but there was nothing in his mind that matched the strange energy and malevolency that was embodied in Arkdragon.

"What is our main goal in this area, sir?" Landon asked.

"We get the supplies we need, and we keep moving forward." Henrich said. "We will not stop until we've reached The Haunted City. Until then, we must guard ourselves and stand firm in the face of adversity. And a lot of adversity we are going to surely face."

Nearing the small town, the sounds of people echoed out of the town. Some of conversation and some laughter. It sounded like a place where people were good to one another. A possible place where those of evil may not dwell. Henrich tried to keep an open mind concerning the sounds he was hearing from the town, but, knew in his spirit that there was something more going on than what was seen with the naked eye.

"Those people in the town." Beth said. "It sounds as if they're not in any harm whatsoever."

"The sounds can be of deceit, young lady." Henrich said. "Although, I do have a hope that we come across some people of a good heart and mind."

They walked into the small town and there are people walking about its pathways. The people are dressed in what appeared to be casual clothing, but mostly dirty and torn in places. The people themselves appeared to be those of a quiet nature and a good heart. Henrich knew that appearances are deceiving as he continued to walk through the town's pathways as he looked ahead and seen a convenience store. Landon waved to the people with a smile on his face. Beth only nodded to them, keeping herself guarded from their possible actions. Whether their actions become verbal or physical.

"We make our way toward the store." Henrich said. "Grab some supplies and we keep moving."

"Gotcha."

"I understand." Beth said. "So, what kind of supplies will we be getting?"

"Food, water, and perhaps other things that will suit our needs of the journey ahead."

"Like ammo, right?" Landon asked. "I'm sure after all the shootouts that we've been through over these past moments, we certainty need more ammo for our shooters. I know I do."

"If we find some ammo, boy, we'll get the ammo."

"Good. Good. Because I'm sure with all of what's going on with the Mercenary Man turning into some strange man and possibly dealing with these Scavengers that lurk around here, we'll definitely need some more ammo for our shooters."

"I know that." Henrich said. "Just make sure you keep your eyes open for any signs that relate to the Scavengers."

"Umm. What are the signs of the Scavengers?"

"Fear. Dread. Terror." Henrich said, looking at Landon and Beth. "Those are the signs of the Scavengers. When you sense them, you'll know they're nearby."

"Sure." Beth said. "I got it."

"Same here. I just wonder when they'll show up is all."

Henrich tied his horse to the post in front of the convenience store. The horse stayed calm as they entered the store. The horse was protected by a force, though not many knew what kind of force it could be. Within the store, Henrich saw food, water, and other supplies suited for their needs. Landon went to grab the food, Beth went for the water, and Henrich walked toward the back counter, where the weapons and ammo were being kept. Henrich looked at the weapons clerk and pointed toward the ammunition boxes on the back shelf.

"Give me four of those." Henrich told the clerk.

"And what will you do with them?" The Clerk asked, handing Henrich the four boxes of ammunition.

"Why would you need to know about my business with them?"

"Because it is a new standard. The people of this town usually fear those who's agendas are not known to others. Secrets get these people killed and they are always killed by the Scavengers."

"So, the Scavengers have been around here."

"Yes, they have. They come and go as they please. When they come, they make an entrance for themselves and bring a posse of sorts. They come with bags, demanding that we give them our food, our water, and our weapons. They only leave when we don't have enough to meet their demands and they give us some time to reacquire what they've taken from us."

"So, you send people to their location to steal back your stuff?"

"No. We have an agreement with one of the cities nearby this region. They deliver the stuff here and we keep it here until the Scavengers make their return for it."

Henrich nodded as he placed the ammo boxes in his bag. He looked around the interior of the store, seeing only the people of the town and Landon and Beth gathering the food and water. Henrich turned to the Clerk and came in closer to him.

"When was the last time the Scavengers came here?"

"About three weeks ago."

"What is their standard waiting period?"

"Two to three weeks at best."

Henrich cocked his head as he took out one of the ammo boxes along with his shooter and began loading up the weapon. The clerk didn't know what to make of Henrich's actions, although he could sense something strange and old with Henrich, as if he's been through similar events before and he has. The clerk noticed the shooter that Henrich was loading and he could tell it was from another place.

"That shooter you have there. Where did you get it from?"

"I didn't get it from anywhere." Henrich said. "It was given to me for my sole purpose."

"But, only those ancient Warslingers carried such a weapon. It is said their shooters are made from the gold of the Outer-World."

"You're about right. They are made in the Outer-World, but are only made for those who are within the purpose."

"So, are you one of them? A Warslinger?"

Henrich stared at the clerk as he waited for an answer. Most likely an answer that would probably terrify him or give him some level of hope in the town. Seeing a Warslinger in their town would possibly enlighten the people. But, would also draw fear unto them. For they know of the legends that speak of the Warslingers and what they stood and fought for in their time.

"Make the decision for yourself." Henrich said. "You should be able to come to some conclusion."

Landon and Beth approached Henrich, showing him the food and water they've gathered. Henrich was impressed and he handed them one of the ammo boxes and Landon grabbed the box and loaded his shooter. The Clerk looked at Landon, seeing him holding the shooter.

"Isn't he a little young to be carrying open of those?"

"When you're out there, you always need some form of protection on you. He prefers a shooter."

"It's my standard now. I guess."

The sound of a loud continuous roar entered from the outside. The sound was distant form the town, but grew larger and louder. Henrich looked out toward the windows and doors. He noticed the people of the town were immediately entrenched in fear. Landon and Beth didn't know what was happening and Henrich turned to the clerk, who also appeared to be in fear.

"What's happening right now?" Henrich asked.

"They're coming." The Clerk said jolting. The Scavengers are coming."

Henrich placed his hands on his shooters as he could see what appeared to be dirt bikes riding into the front of the store. Landon looked at the bikes and was drawn to them.

"What are those?" Landon asked.

"They look like dirt bikes." Beth said. "We have them back on my world."

"Over here they're called dirt-speeders."

"I want one of those."

Two dirt-speeders were parked in front of the store as the two men who rode on them entered. The two men appeared dirty. Their clothing was dirty from sand and soil. Their countenance wasn't a pleasant sight and their energy was of evil. They looked around the store at the people, smiling at them with their rotten teeth.

"Don't be afraid of us, people!" One had said. "We're only here on our average trips."

"We're here for our stuff that you owed us weeks back and we've come to collect it."

The Scavengers started walking toward the back of the store, where the weapons Clerk stood. While they approached him, they seen Henrich, Landon, and Beth also standing in the back. Amazed at them, the two Scavengers have never seen them before in the area and it makes them feel comfortable to see what they would call new people.

"My, my. This is something to behold right about now. You folks aren't from around here are you?"

"No." Henrich said. "We're not."

"This is good. This is really good, and you want to know why it's really good that you're not from here?"

"Tell us why."

"Really simple. You're all stranders in this town and as you might not be aware of. We run this town as well as this land."

"I can tell who you two are. You're both Scavengers."

"So, you've heard of us, huh."

"I know of your people and what you do for yourselves."

The Scavengers appalled Henrich for his knowledge of the Scavenger. They gave him a small, but good form of respect. Both Scavengers turned to Landon and Beth. Seeing them, two young people. A quality fit for the Scavengers.

"This young man and woman with you?"

"They are."

"My, I've never know of the times where young men and women are taken by an older mysterious-looking man. What say of this journey of yours?"

"It is classified."

"Classified you say? Really? How can it be classified? I'm sure it is of good importance."

"It is certainly of good importance." Henrich said.

"Then you don't mind telling us what it is."

"I'm afraid I will not tell you what it is. It is none of your concern, boys."

"You don't get it, old man. You're in our town! You're in our land! You answer to us whatever questions we ask of you. You will answer us, and we will always get the truth out of you. By whatever means."

The Scavengers glared their eyes past Henrich toward the clerk. The smiled at him as he slightly waved his hand. Still in fear of them and in fear of his life. The Scavengers walked past Henrich and toward the counter.

"Do you have it ready?"

"Yes. Your stuff is prepared and ready." The clerk said with a trembling voice. "In the back. Take it."

The Scavengers clapped as they jumped over the counter and shoved the Clerk into the shelves. They grabbed two boxes, both were the size of a shoe box and in them contained food, water, and weapons such as small shooters and knives with ammunition boxes. The Scavengers had what they've come for and were prepared to leave the store with their hands full. They jumped back over the counter, grabbing their boxes and they walked away. One of them made the intention to stop and gazed back toward Beth. He measured Beth's body and he desired to have her. He approached Beth with a smile. An uneasy smile at best.

"You don't need to be hanging around these two assholes." The Scavenger gestured with a grin. "Come with me and I will show you a life worth living. A life of pleasure and a life of fun."

"I don't think I can do that." Beth said. "It's not who I am."

The Scavengers shook his head. Slightly disappointed.

"Don't be afraid of me. I know of some female friends of mine that would love to be around you and they can show you things that I can't. Things that would bring not only pleasure to themselves, but pleasure to you as well. What say you to that?"

Beth shook her head, disagreeing with the Scavenger. The other Scavenger came back around to his partner, seeing him trying to bring Beth back with them.

"What are you doing?"

"What does it look like I'm doing. I want to bring this girl back with us. She can be of use. Just look at her."

"We don't have the time for this. We only came here to get what we needed."

"Brother, she is what we need. How many of today's women would suit most of us in a daily basis. Not a one of them. But, this young woman could. She has the energy and the figure for it."

"Let's go."

"Do what your partner says." Henrich said.

"Don't talk to me. You keep your mouth shut."

The Scavengers reached into his pocket and pulled out a knife. He reached the knife to Beth's throat. Henrich was ready to fire at any moment and so was Landon. The other Scavenger stood back, with his hand on his own shooter. A shooter smaller than what Henrich and Landon have. Beth stood still as the Scavenger laughed with the knife in his hand.

"Oh, what the hell." said The Scavenger. "I guess I'm going to have to take you with me by force."

The Scavenger snatched Beth by the arm and instantly within a mere second, Henrich raised up his shooter and fired it. The bullet flew through the Scavenger's forehead as he dropped the knife and fell onto the ground. The other Scavenger jumped when seeing his partner dead on the ground. He looked up at Henrich, who kept the shooter aimed toward him. The Scavengers shook his head in anger and in rage as he raised up his shooter.

"You bastard!" The Scavenger yelled.

Landon noticed the Scavenger raising up his shooter and he took the shot, killing the second Scavengers. The two Scavengers are dead, and the entire store is in shock and awe. Seeing two Scavengers killed in their presence brought a sense of a possible hope and a possible fear as to what the other Scavengers will do to them. Henrich grabbed the box of which the Scavenger held and returned it to the Clerk.

"I don't understand." The Clerk said. "Why did you kill them?"

"Because I had no other option." Henrich said. "Keep the boxes."

"What do we do now?" Landon asked.

"We keep moving."

Landon left for the outside as Henrich approached Beth, who was slightly in fear of her life. Henrich knew that she would have to get used to the new World she finds herself in. He understands her fear and he knows in time it will pass by.

"Don't worry about it." Henrich said. "There more in these Worlds that can do far worse than what he could've done."

They exited the store and Henrich went atop the horse as did Beth. They left the store and continued moving further down the pathways. While going down the pathways, they find themselves being followed by what appeared to be more dirt-speeders. Meaning more Scavengers. Henrich turned his head around and seen them.

"Landon, we have trouble."

Landon turned to see the Scavengers chasing after them. Yelling out negative words to them and threatening them in many ways possible. Landon prepared himself to shoot them if they came closer as his hand was placed on his shooter. Henrich was the same, prepared to fire if necessary. Within minutes, a few of the Scavengers came closer to them and they started shooting them. Their dirt-speeders crashed into the mountains nearby and other flipped across the plains, setting the grass on fire.

"What do we do now, sir?!" Landon yelled.

"We take out as many of them as we can!"

Henrich and Landon continued their firing toward the Scavenges. Taking out many as they could reach according to the shooters' aiming. One Scavenger rode his dirt-speeder onto the right side of the horse. Henrich spotted him and shot him in the head. He reached over and handed Beth one of his shooters. She turned to him and gazed at the shooter.

"You use it when necessary." Henrich said.

"I will."

Moving further down the pathways, they still had to shoot own the oncoming Scavengers. It appeared to be when more we killed, more appeared and they appeared in masses with their dirt-speeders. They could not be stopped, nor could they slow themselves down if they could. The Scavengers eventually caught up to them and one took a lasso from the side of the speeder and snatched both Henrich and Beth from the horse. The horse stopped as they fell onto the ground where the Scavengers surrounded them. Landon was tackled to the ground by two Scavenger men, who laughed at him.

"He tried to shoot us! Can you believe that kind of shit!"

"I can now. Seeing he has a shooter on him and a good looking one at best."

Henrich looked around for his horse and the horse was gone. Out of the sights of the Scavengers. Henrich smiled for a moment.

"Good job." Henrich said.

He turned to see him, Landon, and Beth were surrounded by Scavengers. All of whom ranged from different ages and nationalities. They all appeared to be dirty and they carried with them an energy of fear. Henrich could see why the people of the town feared them. They feared them because of their number. Henrich, Landon, and Beth were rounded up and tied up by the Scavengers. As they prepared to leave the site, one of the Scavengers approached Henrich and stared him in the face with a smile.

"You aren't from around here."

"I am not."

The Scavenger nodded as he tapped Henrich's hat with his finger.

"Very well. Let's bring these people back to our camp. We have others who would like to see them."

The Scavengers rallied them up and brought them along, returning to their campsite. A campsite where only the Scavengers resided, and wickedness flourished.

<u>II</u>

Being captured by the Scavengers, they sit on three separate dirt-speeders, driven by one Scavenger each as they make their way to their campsite somewhere in the outskirts of the small town. The campsite of the Scavengers is only several miles away from the small town and is not a faraway area to find. Although, most of the campsite is hidden behind sets of trees from a nearby forest. Inching closer toward their campground, Henrich took looks at the surroundings, marking locations for himself to keep in memory. He made sure he knew where the Scavengers were going in their own direction. He was able to mentally measure the amount between the small town and the Scavengers' current pathway.

"What are they going to do to us?" asked Landon.

"Don't speak." The Scavenger said. "Otherwise, they'll fill your mouth up with something to keep it shut."

Landon looked at Henrich, who could tell that he was somewhat shaken up by the recent events, but he held his own. Not giving into the fear that he is feeling moving around him. But, Landon held on to confidence and patience. Henrich nodded toward him and looked at Beth, who stayed quiet during the entire way to the campsite. Henrich understood why she was silent. The dirt-speeders started to slow down and Henrich could see their campsite right in front of them.

The Scavengers entered their campsite, surrounded with even more Scavengers than Henrich, Landon, or Beth could count on their own. The campsite appeared to be covered with tents, trailers, and even some used abandoned vehicles. The Scavengers are sitting by sets of fires as they see the Three on the back of the speeders. They are intrigued, and they arose from their current sitting spot to approach them. They looked at them and some smiled with ideas and others looked with disgust as to why they would bring other people to the site.

"Who are they?" One Scavenger asked.

"They are our guests for this day. Just be patient with them and you'll see why we've brought them back with us."

The Scavengers exited their speeders, some grabbed the Three, bringing them over to a table next to a wooden pole. On the wooden pole was a light, used for the night when light would be needed. While being escorted to the table, Henrich looked and seen a pit not too far from the campsite. He wondered why they would have a pit and from the pit he could see smoke emitting from it, as if there was something within the pit burning.

"Sit yourselves down." The Scavenger said, placing Henrich, Landon, and Beth at the table.

The Scavengers leave them at the table, their hands still tied together as they looked at the Scavengers gathering together, cheering and hugging as if they haven't seen each other in ages, but, they've only seen each other last for a period of hours. Through their own actions, Henrich could tell they were of one mind and of one accord. He respected that, but, he remembered with contention between the two Scavengers that he and Landon killed back at the store. Therefore, Henrich knew that within the Scavengers, there were a few that could destroy the entire clan.

The Scavengers sat together, a few feet from Henrich, Landon, and Beth. They talked with each other and started looking around for the two Scavengers that went to the store to pick up the supplies. But, as Henrich knew, there weren't present, and neither would they be coming back. One of the Scavengers looked at Henrich and walked toward him. The Scavenger stood in front of Henrich at the table, towering over him as Henrich sat in the seat.

"What do you want?" Henrich asked.

"Just a question. When you were at the town earlier, did you happen to see two of my people there?"

"I did. They rode on dirt-speeders just like the rest of you."

"What happened to them? I would assume that you would know since you were there when they arrived."

"They're dead."

"Dead?"

"They were killed in the store while getting the supplies they came for."

"So, you would know who killed them, right?"

"I do."

"Then who did it? Was it the clerk? Was it some shopper who had a shooter on them? Anything of that nature?"

"No. It was none of those."

"Then, who killed them?"

Henrich stared into the Scavenger's eyes and he could tell that he had some care for his two partners. Henrich understood that care and gaze over to Landon, who also looked at the Scavenger. Henrich nodded to the Scavenger.

"I killed one. My friend killed the other."

"Oh. Oh. So, you and your friend killed my partners, huh."

"We did, and for a good reason."

"What good reason would you have in killing them? You didn't know them personally nor did you know them strategically."

"True, I did not know them in those manners. But, I do know of true honor, true respect, and true integrity. I was not about to allow them to disrespect me nor my friends here in any manner. Neither would I let them treat those back at the two with such disrespect. Today was their day of truth and the truth they could not accept. So, they made this day their last."

The Scavenger shook his head in anger toward Henrich and Landon. The Scavenger smiled as he punched Henrich in the face and punched Landon in the nose. Henrich nodded with a smirk as he looked at the Scavenger, seeing him fuming up with more anger.

"I understand that kind of strength. It's what is needed to survive in these parts."

"I'm sure you would." The Scavenger replied, returning to the others.

The Scavenger had approached them and told them about the

deaths of their two partners. He pointed toward Henrich and Landon and immediately, without hesitation, the other Scavengers came to them and snatched the three of them from the table and brought them forward in front of the entire clan of Scavengers, who surrounded them in a circle. Henrich, Landon, and Beth were on their knees, facing the Scavengers. All of whom were yelling and screaming at them derogatory words and utterances.

"Look at these fools!" One Scavenger said. "How could they kill one of us!"

"I like the young man." One female Scavenger said. "But, I also like that young woman."

One of the Scavengers raised his hands up, silencing the others as they stayed quiet. The Scavenger approached them and crouched to their eyelevel. The Scavengers smirked in their faces and they only stared at the Scavenger. He nodded to them.

"Well, this must be a tough day for the three of you." The Scavenger said. "Not to mention the fact that you killed two of us today and yet, how will we get our supplies from the store."

"You go there and ask for it." Henrich said. "Unless you want to die like they did."

The Scavenger laughed at Henrich and pointed with a gesture at him. Looking at his attire, somewhat strange to see in the Land of the Survivors. Yet, the Scavengers looked at all three of them as he was forming his words in his mind before speaking them out. He nodded again and pointed at the three of them several times, before rubbing his hair and walking around them in a circle and coming back in front of them, standing over them. He clapped his hands together, rubbing them.

"Well, we can start like this first. My name is Wade, and I am what you would call the leader of the Scavengers."

"The leader, huh?" Landon asked. "I would believe you all went on your own path."

"We did at one time, but that was when chaos was circling around this place. Once I came into place and showed the people that I was leader material, everything fell into order. We all had the same goals, dreams, and ambitions in our lives and we were able to have one mind. With that one mind, we developed one accord. To live as brothers and sisters together to make sure that none of us suffer as others did during the chaos of this land."

"What do you mean by suffering in this land?" Henrich asked. "What could've happened here that hasn't happened before?"

"Change, I would say. A change that shook the foundations of many cities in the Western World. Yet, I'm not sure how the other Worlds are doing in these times, but it's not my job to focus on them as it is my duty to pay attention to where I'm at today and where I'm at is here in the Western World. Living in the Land of the Survivors."

Henrich nodded.

"I can see your reasoning, slightly."

"I'm sure you can. That is why the three of you were brought here this day. We need more recruits and the three of you would be a perfect fit for us. Especially, you, young man and you, young woman. The two of you could become great being aligned with people such as ourselves."

"Why would we side with you people." Landon said. "You seem to have enough people as it is."

"You think so? Well, from where we're all sitting right now. You guys killed two of our own to begin with and from that we will need two more to take their place in our clan. People don't fall out of the sky anymore, or come out of the ground, and neither do they get thrown up from the trees of the forests either."

"This is why we're here?" Henrich asked. "To join in with you all?"

"In a matter. But, as I've already said. You killed two of our own and we'll need two in replacements. So, if I had it my way, which I will overall, I would take this young man and this young woman as the replacements and kill you, old man. You seemed to have lived a long life as it is already. You don't need any more trouble in your life, so I would spare you from it."

"You don't even know who we are. Let alone, what we're capable of doing with our own hands when it comes to survival."

Wade placed his hands on his face, his mouth dropped. He looked at the other Scavengers before placing his focus back on the three of them. He remembered something. Something he had to ask of them that was important for his cause.

"Oh, that's right. I forgot to ask of your names, occupations, and motives of life. So, I will start with… you, young man. What is your name, your occupation, and your motive of life?"

Landon stared at Wade and gazed over to Henrich, who nodded in giving Landon the opportunity to speak. Landon understood Henrich's nod and faced Wade, who was staring at him with his brown eyes and he creepy smile that was slowly growing on his face.

"My name is Cody Landon. My occupation is being a traveler of the Worlds and my motive of life is to see the Worlds return to their former state."

"Oh? You're a traveler of the Worlds? How so? You're only just a boy. A young man at best. How can you have the achievement to travel the Worlds at your age? Tell me, please. I am intrigued and interested in what you have to tell me."

"I was born and raised in the Northern World. When the opportunity came, I was able to leave and therefore travel across the Worlds."

"So, your mother and father just let you leave and travel the Worlds? All on your own? Is that right?"

"That is right. Some of the people up there died due to nature's power or meeting the beasts of the north. I chose to leave, and I came here to the Western World, looking to see what the other Worlds would offer me in my life."

"And what have they offered you so far?"

"So far? A greater understanding as to how the Worlds work and what will become of them in the future ahead."

"Who told you about this future ahead?"

"He did." Landon said, nodding his head toward Henrich.

Wade pointed at Henrich while keeping his eyes on Landon.

"And how would he know about the future and what will become of the Worlds?"

"Because he's one of the Warslingers."

Wade's smile turned into a laugh and he laughed at Landon's words along with the Scavengers that surrounded them. Landon looked at them and could tell they didn't believe the words that he had spoken out concerning Henrich being one of the Warslingers. Landon looked at Henrich, who turned to him and stayed silent. Landon understood the silence of Henrich. Beth stayed quiet, though she looked around at the Scavengers and sometimes would gaze her eyes toward Henrich. Wade clapped several times, regarding to Landon's words.

"You have some good jokes, young man." Wade said. "I will give you the benefit on that. You can make us laugh."

"It's not a joke." said Landon. "I am telling you all the truth."

"That's enough out of you." Wade said, silencing Landon with his finger. "Now, onto the second one."

Wade turned from Landon and kneeled to Beth, who looked at him with some small form of anger and disgust. Wade could fell her anger toward him and the Scavengers, but he could also tell that she was different from them all. Something with her was off with what they're used to in the Worlds. Wade stood up above her and pointed at her with another smile on his face.

"You, young woman. The same that I asked of Cody here. Your name, your occupation, and your motive of life?"

"My name is Beth Grasslands. I am or was a paranormal investigator from Washington D.C."

"Hold on a second." Wade said, stopping her from speaking. "What do you mean Washington D.C.?"

"That's where I'm from. I came from Washington D.C."

Wade shook his head. His finger waving at her in disagreement. He looked at her and could tell that her words were solid, but something was off about her answers.

"How can that be?"

"How can what be?"

"How can you be from Washington D.C. when we no longer have a Washington D.C.?"

"Well, I'm not exactly from this World."

"Then, would you please tell me and my clan where you from that has a Washington D.C.? Because it certainly isn't from the Eastern World, the Northern World, and neither the Southern

World. Plus, you can't be from the Outer-World because you're still in the flesh."

"I'm from the planet Earth and I lived in a country called the United States of America, where I resided in the capital city of Washington D.C."

"What the hell is an 'Earth' and what kind of place is called the 'United States of America'? Hell, what is an *America*'?"

"That is where I'm from. I came into this World, your World, through dimensional travel."

"I'm not understanding the big words, young lady. Can you explain all of this to me, so that I can comprehend what you're telling me?"

"I came through a dimensional wormhole that bridged Earth and your World and through that, I somehow found the wormhole and traveled through it and ended up here. Is that enough for you to understand?"

Wade nodded, proclaiming that he understood what Beth had told him about her travels. Wade understood. Somewhat.

"Fair enough, I would say. So, you're a inter-dimensional being as they would call it?"

"In this World, I am."

"My, my. Then, that explains the energy around you and the strange feelings we've been getting in our bodies since we saw you. You know we're all tingling for you and Cody of course."

"I don't understand what that means."

"That means, sooner or later. Be it today, tonight, tomorrow, or who knows when, we're going to screw Cody and you. Someday. Not sure right now, but I'll schedule it all accordingly to the day its set."

"You people are sick." Landon said. "Just disgusting."

Wade kicked Landon in the face with his boot, casing his nose to bleed more after being punched earlier at the table. Wade smiled as he let out a small sigh. A sigh of relief from the kick. He looked at Beth and wanted her to talk some more. He was very interested in her. As he reached down and had his hands go through her long blonde hair, he sniffed it, causing the other Scavengers to somewhat release a sound of awe or moan. Strangely it's what they did seeing the sight. Landon shook his head, staring at Wade in anger.

"Well, what is this paranormal investigation that you mention? You said it was your occupation?"

"That's what I am. A paranormal investigator."

"Well, I don't know what that is."

"I hunt ghosts for a living."

"Seriously? So, you get paid for hunting down ghosts, ghouls, and demons?"

"That I do."

Wade nodded with excitement. Smiling with internal joy. Rubbing his hands together.

"I want to apply for this job. It sounds interestingly good. Plus, you get paid for it and who doesn't like being paid for something they do in their lives."

Beth nodded in a way. She understood what Wade meant by his words and Wade liked how she nodded to his comments.

"And what of your motive of life? What would that be to someone such as yourself?"

"My motive in life. Is to change it for the better. To make others better than what they believe themselves to be. Even to make myself a better woman than I am today."

"I can help you with that in a hurry. Only whenever you're up for it and I know for sure that others here can help you with it as well."

Wade bowed his head before Beth, showing a sign of respect toward her. He walked over to stand in front of Henrich and as he walked he gave Landon the middle finger, to which Landon spit at Wade. Wade jumped out of the way of the spit and laughed at Landon.

"You and I are going to have some moments." Wade said. "Just you wait and see."

Wade stood in front of Henrich. Henrich raised his head up, staring into Wade's eyes and Wade stared into his. The two kept their eyes locked onto one another. Wade smiled while Henrich showed no emotion of any kind.

"You're the last one, old man. Tell me your name, your occupation, and your motive of life?"

"You're sure about that?" Henrich said.

"Either you answer them, or you die today. So, make your choice."

"Sure. I'll answer them for you."

"Excellent. Now, get on with it for me."

"My name is Randolph Henrich and I am one of the Warslingers of the Heptad."

Wade paused for a moment and shook his head. The other Scavengers stayed quiet and looked at Henrich. Wade kneeled low to Henrich's eyelevel and stared at him closer than before.

"Say that again."

"I am a Warslinger of the Heptad."

"No, you're not. You're trying to help Cody's little lie. Don't play around with me, old man."

"I am not playing around with you. I am telling you the truth."

"Is that right? Well, tell me, what is truth?"

"The truth." Henrich said slowly. "You'll never understand the truth, nor will you be able to hear it when it is spoken aloud."

"So, what of your motive of life? Is it the same as what I would believe a Warslinger to do?"

"My motive of life is to find a place hidden from the eyes and the minds of Man."

"What is that place?"

"The Haunted City."

Wade laughed and clapped his hand. The other Scavengers also laughed at Henrich's words. They did not have the belief of The Haunted City nor the belief of the Warslingers' existence. Wade nodded to Henrich.

"You're just as funny as your friend over here."

"Take it as you want." Henrich said. "But, you'll know of the truth when it manifested itself before you and your clan of Scavengers."

Wade looked closely in Henrich's eyes.

"You really believe in it?"

"Very much." Henrich declared.

"We'll see about that."

Wade walked away as the Scavengers grabbed the Three from the ground, returning them to the table where they once were. While the Scavengers sat and talked about strategy and other things of their mind during the day, Henrich gazed up toward the ski and noticed that nightfall was near. He could feel the slight chill of the night flowing through the air as the heat of the day was diminishing.

"When the time comes, let me know." Henrich said. "Let me know."

Beth noticed Henrich talking as he considered the sky. She inched over toward him, hearing what he was speaking. It was unfamiliar to her ears, but sounded like the things she's heard before in her lifetime.

"Who are you talking to?"

"A friend, Beth." Henrich said. "A very close friend of mine."

The nightfall had begun and during the night, the Scavengers would party, and they would have orgies with each other across the campsite. The Scavengers are moved the Three and placed them underneath the wooden pole, where the light would shine down upon them. As they sat on the dirty grounds, they could see the lewdness of the Scavengers. From the excessive drinking to their riotous ways.

"What in the hell are they doing?" Landon asked.

"They're living up their life." Henrich replied. "It's all that they have."

Beth watched their actions and their ways. She's seen tings familiar to those in her lifetime around people that she knew in her world.

"They're acting very similar to how people acted back on my world."

"People acted like this where you're from" Landon asked her. "Seriously? Like them?"

"It's the same. I guess people aren't different no matter what Worlds they're from."

The Scavengers continued their partying for the night hours. Henrich went to sleep underneath the pole while Landon and Beth kept watch. They looked over to Henrich, seeing him asleep as the partying is continuing. Landon started to worry for their well-being and didn't understand why Henrich would choose to sleep now in the area that they're in. Some of the Scavengers turned their sites on Landon and Beth, slowly making their way toward them. Gesturing to their private parts as well as their naked bodies. Landon and Beth tried to move, but they were tied up to the pole.

"This isn't good." Landon said.

"That I am aware of." Beth replied. "Just try to keep yourself calm."

The male Scavengers approached Beth and attempted to touch her body from all angles. She fought back with shoves and kicks while being attached to the pole. The female Scavengers approached Landon and tried to touch him. Landon fought them off as much as he could, but within his being, he desired to join them. He wanted to feel what they were feeling. His curiosity was pushing him to destroy him by joining in to their partying and orgies. Beth noticed Landon slowly fighting back and she couldn't believe it.

"What are you doing, Cody?"

"I… I'm not sure." He said. "I don't want it, but I want it."

The female Scavengers left Landon alone and approached Beth. They circled her and started breathing on her neck, touching her body. Some even placed their hands into her pants pockets, feeling her closely. She fought off the women by struggling and one of them inched over to her ear.

"You will give yourself over to us. You know that, right?"

"I will not." Beth said. "You're just a bunch of sick people. Just sick."

The female Scavenger looked Beth in the eyes and stared at her lips. Licking her own. Beth moved her head around to avoid getting closer to the woman's face.

"After I kiss you and stick my tongue in your mouth, you'll give in to me and I will have all of you. I'll placed my mouth all over your body and I will make you scream for me."

The woman inched closer to kiss Beth, but was stopped by Wade.

"Leave them be for the moment. Now isn't the time for them."

Wade nodded to Beth, signaling the other Scavengers to leave them be. Wade looked down at Henrich, who was sitting on the ground asleep. Wade laughed to himself. Seeing Henrich sleeping during a party like they're having around the campsite.

"The old man's asleep." Wade said. "How funny is that."

Wade walked away as Beth slowly sat down, trying to settle herself down and Landon slowly came to the ground, but, he was still feeling the urge to join them. He wanted to hold the women and touch their bodies. As he sat there, looking at the woman, who were partying and fooling around with each other and the men, Henrich moved his head toward Landon's direction.

"Fight the temptation." Henrich said quietly.

"How will I do that?" Landon asked. "These urges are strong."

"You're a young man. They would be strong. But, you have the option of either giving into them or tossing them away. Best you take the second option and save yourself from trouble."

Landon started to settle himself and calmed down. He looked at Beth who was calm and steady.

"What about you, sir?" Landon asked. "What do you do when you see things like this in front of you?"

"Just like I'm doing right now. Shutting my eyes and going to sleep."

"How can you go to sleep in a surrounding like this?"

"How did we sleep in the Valley of Death and in those forests? Just calm yourself and the next day, you'll be settled."

Landon nodded. He somewhat understood what Henrich told him and yet, he attempted to learn from him and understand the ways that Henrich spoke of. Henrich knew that Landon was young and that he would have these issues approaching him sooner or later.

"So, how are we going to get away from this place and keep moving?"

"In time, you'll see."

"How will I see?"

"You'll see. Just be patient."

Landon nodded and stayed quiet as the hours passed by and all three of them went to sleep as the Scavengers partied all night long until the sun arose and the moon set before the day.

<u>III</u>

In the morning after the riotous partying of the Scavengers, Henrich, Landon, and Beth are placed once again at the table from the previous day. Wade approached them with plates of food, which were of the food stolen from the store of the small town. Wade also brought them bottles of water, which also came from the store of the small town. Wade stood in front of them as he watched them eat and drink, for they haven't eaten or drunk anything since the day before the previous day.

"I hope you enjoyed the scenery of the party from last night." Wade said. "Because there's a whole lot more on the way. I'm telling you that much already."

"What happened last night was wickedness celebrating in its own lustful actions." Henrich said. "Soon, you'll all pay for what you've done to yourselves and to others."

Wade inched closer to Henrich, seeing that his words were indeed true and were of a warning. A warning that hit Wade close, seemingly to be that Wade has heard similar words before in times past.

"And who's going to deliver the payday on us? You? Cody? Beth?"

"You'll see."

"I'm hoping I will and I hope you'll be there as well to see it fail in your face."

Wade smiled and clapped his hands together, looking back at the other Scavengers, who were also eating and drinking. Wade turned back to Henrich, before gazing at Landon and Beth.

"Later on, old man, you and I will have ourselves a conversation."

"Why would I spend more time talking to you and only to you?"

"Because it concerns your current state and it will concern your possible future. That is if you and your young partners want to leave this place without any harm to be done onto you."

Henrich only stared at Wade, who continued showing off his smile.

"Later on, old man." Wade said, walking away from the table.

Landon looked at Wade and in his heart, he was disgusted by him and if he could, he would pound Wade's face into the ground with his fists. Beth only stayed quiet as she ate the food that was presented to them and Henrich kept silent and only thought to himself of the things to come in the days ahead. Henrich kept an open mind of being set free or finding a way to escape and he did not lose any faith that was within his being. His faith had only increased since they were taken by the Scavengers. Henrich kept his eye on Wade, who was speaking with some of the Scavengers and he noticed them heading towards their dirt-speeders. The Scavengers boarded up their speeders and left the campsite. Almost a dozen of them in total. Landon watched them leave the campsite.

"Where are they going?" Landon asked.

"They're going to get more supplies." Henrich said. "That's where they're going."

After a period of hours, the dozen Scavengers have not yet returned to the campsite, but Wade approached Henrich and commanded for two of the male Scavengers to bring him to Wade's trailer. The Scavengers grabbed Henrich by his arms and brought him into Wade's trailer. An old, beaten down trailer, but was good enough for Wade to sleep in during the nights. Inside the trailer was a small table with two chairs. The Scavengers placed Henrich in one and Wade sat in the other. The two Scavengers stood by the door, just in case Henrich attempted to attack Wade. Henrich stared at Wade, who only smiled at him while drinking what appeared to be some tea. Made from within the trailer.

"I told you that we would talk." Wade said. "And now we're both here."

"Talk about what?" Henrich asked. "What is there to talk about with you that would be of any importance?"

Wade placed his cup of tea down on the table and pointed to Henrich. Wade nodded as his finger shook around, while being pointed to Henrich.

"You went on about this "Haunted City". So, tell me, what is the place and how do you know of it?"

"Why should I tell you these things?"

"Because I know honestly you and your partners want to leave our campsite in one piece and not in pieces. Besides, if what you speak of is true, I would like to reach this "Haunted City" myself and claim whatever it is to claim."

"How would you claim something that you have no understanding nor comprehension of?"

"I would bring you along with me. Hell, you can be my guide and lead the way to this City and once we're both there, you can show me where this treasure of it is bound to be kept."

Henrich shook his head, gazing back to the two Scavengers before facing Wade at the table. Wade took a sip of his tea before placing the cup down once more. Wade kept his smile as Henrich didn't smile. He only stared, and he stared with a hatred. An almost perfect hatred of Wade's well-being.

"If you were to reach the City, boy, you wouldn't make it past what's there."

"So, what is there?" Wade asked. "Tell me what is there so that I will have the understanding capable of entering the place."

"It would be too much for your mind to bear. You can't even imagine the power that the City contains and yet, you want to reach it only for yourself and you want to claim what's there for yourself."

"What else would I choose to go there for? To help the Worlds and bring them peace? Hell no. The Worlds already have enough to deal with and I will not be their savior, nor will I be their protector. I would claim what's there for myself and for my clan."

"I'm not sure how, since some in your clan refuse to believe in The Haunted City. They don't believe in the Warslingers either. I remember their laughter when you questioned Cody and myself yesterday. Their laughter proved to me of how much unbelief is within them and what it will do to them in the long run of their lives."

"I have to give it to you, old man. You know a lot of things and I have never came across someone of your age who knew as much as you do. It's almost as if you've been alive for centuries. Hell, probably ages in time."

"You have no idea."

"Of course, I don't! That's why you're sitting here before me. So, we can have ourselves a conversation and get to know one another a little better than yesterday."

Henrich kept quiet and Wade drinks his tea as the two Scavengers stayed guarded at the door of the trailer.

"These Warslingers you and Cody mentioned, how could you be one of them after what is known of their existence?"

"Things aren't always what they appear to be, boy. I've seen things in my lifetime that would bring those such as yourselves to shame and to death. I've encounter enemies that the Worlds haven't seen since their time of change."

"You're telling me the Warslingers actually existed at one time or another? Seriously?"

"They still live among the Worlds. They are only scattered due to the failings that came upon them in a mission of theirs."

"Yeah. I've heard of the tale before. A Warslinger betrayed his brethren and caused them to fail at a task greater than those that came before and from that fail, the Warslingers were scattered throughout all the Worlds, until the appointed time would arrive for them to reunite with each other and extinguished the evil of malevolency from the Worlds for-ever."

Wade laughed at his own words and Henrich's words. Henrich understood that Wade and the Scavengers believed the Warslingers and the Haunted City to be only tales of myth and legends of folklore. He knew that had no belief system within their being and he could tell they were spiritually dead. Wade drank the rest of his tea and stared at Henrich, trying to think of something to say to him. Wade snapped his fingers at an idea.

"I know you're trying to intimidate with your known knowledge of ancient stories, but, they won't help you or your partners find a way to leave our campsite. Cody and Beth will soon be a part of us and you will be an old man who will die by own hands."

"You believe them to be only stories?" Henrich said. "Ancient stories from the past times?"

"I do. That's what they are. None of them are true and speak of any logical sense of reasoning."

"So be it, boy." Henrich said silently. "You have already given me your true answer."

Wade stared at Henrich.

"Before I send you out of my trailer, do you have anything that you would like to ask me?"

Henrich thought for a moment. He remembered something. Something that he seen when they brought them to the campsite to begin with. It was in his mind and it questioned him internally. Henrich looked at Wade.

"That pit." Henrich said. "It was smoking yesterday."

"Why do you ask me about the pit?" Wade wondered. "Does the sight of it bother you or something?"

"No."

"Oh. Well, I'll tell you this much and you can determine it for yourself later. What is in that pit is something that myself and my clan have built up for months while we remain out here. We found those things some time ago and we didn't know that they would be of good use to us."

"What do you mean by those things?" Henrich asked.

"You'll see soon enough, old man."

Wade nodded to Henrich and waved his hands above his head. He commanded for the Scavenger guards to toss Henrich out of the trailer, which they do, and they returned him to the table, where Landon and Beth were still being kept. Henrich sat still while Landon and Beth looked at him before seeing Wade exiting the trailer and walking over to other Scavengers.

"What happened in there, sir?" Landon asked.

"The boy's a weak one." Henrich said. "He doesn't know what he has placed himself under and neither have the rest of them."

"Did he mention of setting us free, possibly?" Beth asked.

"He did not. He wants the two of you to join him and he wants me dead. Simple as that."

Landon looked out to the Scavengers as did Beth. Landon turned his sights on Henrich and thought for a moment to himself before uttering a word to him. Landon thought about it.

"Any plan of us making an escape?" Landon asked.

"Not now." Henrich said. "But, in due time, it will show up. That I am certain of."

Across the miles from the campsite of the Scavengers, the dozen Scavengers ride down along the pathways toward several small towns. In those small towns are people who live together, and they also have supplies of their own that come from an even greater city that is not far from their locations. The Scavengers rode along in a form of a line. As if they were indeed soldiers with a clear and intended focus. They came up to the first small town and they ransacked the place. They enter one of the homes, seeing a young couple and their children sitting down, crouched into the corner.

"Clear this place out!" One Scavenger said. "I'll take a few of the spoils if they won't mind."

The Scavenger cleared many of the homes, leaving the residents of the small town screaming in fear on the outside. Some of the Scavengers raped the women and the men. Some even harmed the children to their own pleasures. The Scavengers showed the people of the town that they were in the Land of the Survivors and they were a survivor group and they took whatever they desired.

After taking the food, the water, the weapons, along with anything else they wanted, they gave the people of the tow a warning before they moved on toward the next town, where there's been word of them having even more supplies than what was known of the Land of the Survivors.

In the second town, the Scavengers noticed the buildings were taller than the previous towns. The tall buildings intrigued them to wonder what could be kept in a place like this one. Entering the town, they brought the fear of them to the people and began to do what they did in the previous town. But, this town had a large store and some of the Scavengers entered the store. They entered with a bang and had their weapons drawn on the people.

"Now, we need all of you to stay quiet or otherwise, you will all die."

The people kept silent while the Scavengers took as much as they could from them and they loved doing it. The Scavengers even provoked the people to fight with their anger and some attempted to attack them head on, but the Scavengers were too much in number for the people and they beat down some of the towns people with their weapons to death in front of the others. A few of the Scavengers entered the tall buildings and within them, they spotted strange weapons and they looked at them. The weapons were almost ancient in appearance, but modern in usage. They looked like modern shooters, but were attached to staffs and blades.

"What kind of weapons are these?" One Scavenger said.

"Let's bring them back to the camp with us and show Wade."

"Good idea. He might know what they are."

The Scavengers jumped onto their speeders and left the town. Two towns were destroyed and consumed with fear after being visited by the Scavengers. The Scavengers also left the same warning to the second town as they did with the first one. They were loaded with supplies, all stretched out around the dozens of them. The weapons were kept with the ones who were skilled with them and weapons like them in appearance and in usage.

Before the night had come, the Scavengers made their return to the campsite and delivered the supplies to Wade. Wade looked at them and cheered with a loud yell.

"You've all done well today." Wade said.

He looked at the weapons that were found in the tall buildings and he was intrigued by their design.

"These are strange." He said. "Very strange."

"We thought that we should bring them to you." One Scavenger said. "Maybe you would know what they are."

"Well, I'll tell you right now, I don't know about them. But, thanks for bringing them back anyhow."

"It is our duty."

Henrich, Landon, and Beth looked at them, celebrating their theft of the towns' goods. Henrich shook his head in the shame of seeing them.

"These people are something else, sir." Landon said. "What are we going to do about them?"

"As of right now, we wait." Henrich said.

"Wait on what?" Beth asked. "I'm not seeing the full picture here."

"Many don't see the full picture, Beth. Others see the picture in the form of a cloud or a puff of smoke. A few see the picture in full, with its bright colors and beautiful features."

Wade clapped his hands and gathered the Scavengers around. He stood in the middle of them and gazed out toward Henrich and smiled at him. Wade gave Landon another middle finger and winked toward Beth, who looked down at the ground to avoid eye contact with him. Wade only laughed at them before facing the Scavengers.

"My people, what you have done this day makes into only myself a happy man, but it makes us all happy people. For if it were not for you to go out there to those wretched towns and stand before those ignorant people, we would not have what we have today. It is because of their deeds that we have something to be proud of out here. What they have done is the same thing we did when we claimed this campsite for ourselves."

"What is he talking about, sir?" Landon asked Henrich quietly.

"He's giving them a speech to keep them in line with his order."

"How do you know that?" Beth asked.

"Because I've seen men like him before. All boast in themselves and desire everything for themselves. Greed and power consumes them and later when the time comes upon them, it destroys them."

Henrich sat back at the table, watching Wade continue to give his speech to the Scavengers.

"With all of us united. With one mind and with one accord, we can achieve anything that we set our minds and our hands to. We have the power to make our dreams and goals a reality. Unlike many people that live in the Worlds, we know what true power is and we have claimed that power for ourselves. That power gives us the right to do anything we so desire and with that, I thank all of you and tonight, we party just as much as we did last night."

The Scavengers cheered as they began their partying once more. The night had come, they grabbed Henrich, Landon, and Beth from the table and placed them in different locations around the campsite. Henrich was surrounded by some of the male Scavengers while Landon and Beth were tossed in the middle of the partying. Henrich looked at them and seen the riotous movement of the Scavengers.

"No." Henrich said. "No."

Henrich knew what they were plotting to do, and he ran toward them, but was tripped by one of the Scavengers, who laughed at him.

"Where do you think you're going, old man!" The Scavenger said, laughing.

They grabbed Henrich and pummeled him, while Landon and Beth were surrounded by the Scavengers. Wade watched on and raised up his hand, silencing the Scavengers. Wade looked at Henrich being pummeled and laughed. He pointed toward him as the other Scavengers looked on with laughter.

"The old man has finally got it." Wade said. "Beat him some more. We need entertainment tonight. Am I right!"

The Scavengers continued to beat Henrich with their fists, kicking him as he fell to the ground. They picked him up and held him, facing Landon and Beth. Henrich couldn't do much, as he was slow in movement. Landon tried to help him, but the circle of the Scavengers was too much fro him to slip through. Wade laughed, and he pointed to Landon and Beth. Wade gestured to two women Scavengers and they entered the circle, facing Landon and Beth. Wade smiled and nodded his head, excited.

"You two women." Wade said. "Have fun with them will you."

The women giggled sinisterly as they approached Landon and Beth. The Scavengers cheered on the entire event. Henrich raised his head up slowly. Bleeding from his face and his mouth. He could see through the large crowd that the women were about to molest Landon and Beth. Henrich stayed quiet, but he wanted to bolt through them to save them. But, his body didn't have the energy to do it.

"I… can't let this happen." Henrich said. "I can't."

The women Scavengers stood in front of Landon and Beth. One of the women started to grope Landon and he felt the urge rising again in his being. He shook himself to fight it off, but he couldn't. The woman grabbed his hand and placed it onto her bare breasts.

Landon felt the warmth of the woman's body and he couldn't contain the urge any longer.

"I can't control it any longer." Landon said. "I just can't."

Landon grabbed the woman by her waist and started kissing her, causing the Scavengers to cheer louder than before. Henrich could tell by their cheering that something was wrong. He looked up, raising his head slowly and could see Landon on the ground atop the woman Scavenger. Henrich shook his head in shame.

"Poor boy." Henrich said.

Beth watched as Landon began to have intercourse with the woman. Beth tried to back away from the other woman, but she was surrounded by the Scavengers. She cried out for Henrich to help her and as he made a step forward, he was beaten down again by the other Scavengers. Being beaten down, he could hear Beth's cry for help as the other woman approached her and grabbed her by force.

"Damn it." Henrich said softly as he could feel the kicks being put on him.

The woman took her own hand and placed it into Beth's pants and started to grope her. Beth tried shoving the woman away, but the woman's strength was too strong as she grabbed her, and she licked Beth's neck. She started to suck on Beth's neck. The woman used her strength to push Beth to the ground, where she started kissing her on the lips.

"Stop!" Beth yelled. "Get off me!"

Landon continued the intercourse with the woman and Beth was laid on the ground as the other woman removed her pants and pulled down her underwear, where she began to kiss her around her private parts. Beth tried to kick against the woman, but she was immediately held down by other Scavengers as the woman licked her body. Beth continued to scream, but Wade approached her and stared into her eyes. He placed his hand over her mouth, muting her scream.

"Shush." Wade said smiling. "It'll all be over soon."

Wade kept his hand over her mouth as the woman continued to lick and suck on her body roughly. He enjoyed seeing the moment as did the other Scavengers.

Henrich looked up and could see Landon having sex and Beth being molested on the ground. Henrich stayed down and in his thoughts, he knew he would bring vengeance upon the Scavengers. It was only a matter of planning and a matter of time. In his being, he knew it was the time and he was prepared for it. Afterwards, Landon and Beth were traumatized by the events and Wade approached the bloodied up Henrich, who was sitting at the table.

"What are you going to do now, old man?" Wade mocked. "We already had our fun with them and we're not done yet."

Henrich slowly raised his head up, staring into Wade's eyes.

"You and your clan…" Henrich said. "Your time is over."

"How will you go about that then?"

"I will kill every single one of you."

Wade faced Henrich and smiled. Wade punched Henrich in the face and laughed with a big grin on his face.

"I hope you will try. Because as soon as we're done with them. You're dead. Now, that is a promise that I will keep."

Wade left from the table, leaving Henrich to only stare at him and the Scavengers.

<u>IV</u>

The following day, the Scavengers sat together, reminiscing on the night before and the actions that took place in the circle. Wade brought up the events while talking of them as if they were some funny story to himself and the Scavengers. He would occasionally look over to Henrich, Landon, and Beth, seeing them not at their best. Henrich was recovering from the beatings he received, Landon felt discouraged about his actions with the woman, and Beth was in shock, due to the actions that were done to her by the woman and the other Scavengers.

"It was a moment that we will not forget, I tell you." Wade said. "Hopefully, we will have more of them in the future ahead."

The Scavengers celebrate more and more throughout the day. A few of them were seen gathering more supplies from the forests, where they kept it hidden. Henrich could see them, even though the pain that he was going through. He kept his eyes on them always, trying to figure out a plan to get himself, Landon, and Beth free from the Scavengers.

"Cody, are you well?" Henrich asked.

Landon sat still, quiet, he kept his head down and Henrich knew that he felt ashamed of his actions the previous night. Though, Landon rose up his head and looked at Henrich. Landon started to tear up a bit, remembering what he committed with the woman of the Scavengers. He felt truly ashamed of himself and of his deeds.

"I'm sorry for what I did, sir." Landon said sadly. "I didn't want to do it, but my body was telling me to. I couldn't contain it any longer. It was just too strong for me to bear and to hold in."

Henrich nodded and placed his hand on Landon's shoulder.

"I understand what it means to fall. But, that doesn't mean that it's all over and you'll be damned for your life. You have another opportunity to make things right and you will make them right. Only if you believe you have the courage and strength to do so. Otherwise, you will never recover from what you've experienced."

"Thank you for your honesty, sir. I don't know what I will do, but I will try to do better going forward. I only hope that I will not make the same mistake again and I have truly learned a lesson about not only myself, but of the internal struggle that we all fight against daily. It really is a fight."

Henrich smiled a bit, hearing those words come from Landon's own mouth. Henrich later turned to Beth, who kept silent and she was holding herself and shivering a bit. Henrich understood her motive of silence and he recognized it from others he's seen before in his lifetime.

"Beth." Henrich said. "I need you to listen to me for just a quick moment."

Beth slowly, but surely turned her sights to Henrich and in her eyes were pain, shame, and defeat. Henrich could sense it himself as eh looked into her eyes. Henrich felt somewhat responsible for what happened to both Landon and Beth. Henrich reached out to touch Beth, but she pulled away from him and he knew why she did.

"Beth, I'm sorry." Henrich said. "There was nothing I could do to stop them. They held me down and beat me while they were…."

Beth nodded in understanding Henrich.

"I know, and I can accept your apology." She said. "But, I will ask of this one favor."

"What is it?"

"When we get set free from these bonds, I will kill them all. Somehow and someway. They all must die."

Henrich smiled.

"That I can agree with you wholly possible."

Beth turned from Henrich and looked up at the sky. Landon kept to himself while Henrich sat and thought about an idea to get them free. Later, in the night, Wade rallied up the Scavengers once more, while several brought Henrich, Landon, and Beth toward him and the surrounding Scavengers. They held them still as they stood facing Wade.

"Now, I know what some of you are thinking right now. Why have I brought these three guests of ours up front. I'll tell you why. Because we need some entertainment tonight!"

The Scavengers cheered on while Henrich stared at Wade. Landon focused his attention toward Wade and the nearby Scavengers and Beth only stayed silent and still. She didn't move an inch. Wade silenced the Scavengers.

"Now, old man. This same entertainment will not be a repeat of the beautiful sight that was last night. But, this entertainment will be either life or death for the three of you."

"What are you talking about?" Henrich asked. "What do you mean this will be either death or life for one of us?"

"Because, I'm placing you three inside the Pit."

Henrich looked at Wade, who signaled for the Scavengers to bring them to the Pit. Henrich watched on, seeing a few of the Scavengers turning around from the Pit as if they were afraid of what's in it. The other Scavengers walked on with Wade towards it. Landon and Beth also gazed their sights to what could be inside the Pit. Inching closer, Henrich could feel heat coming from the Pit, which explained the smoke he seen before when being placed in the campsite.

"It's hot." Landon said.

"What is in there?" Henrich asked.

"Well, some old friends of ours." Wade answered. "But, I know that they will not harm us, but they will surely take a bite out of you three without any hesitation."

Reaching the edge of the Pit and having a few within it, Henrich could see what was conjuring the heat and the smoke. Within the Pit were Salamanders, elementals creatures of fire. Known across the Worlds as "Nature Spirits". The Scavengers cheered on as the Salamanders screeched out toward them and Wade. Henrich glanced over to Wade, seeing him smiling as if he was a child at the zoo. He waved to the Salamanders.

"Aren't they just beautiful." Wade said. "I mean look at them for crying out loud."

"Where did you get those creatures?" Henrich asked.

"None of your concern, old man. But, I will say that it took us some time to gather them all together to place them inside this hole that we dug. Besides, we originally dug the hole for any Scavengers or guests of ours that would've died here, but after we caught these creatures, we figured it was best to give this hole to them and now it is their primary habitat within our camp."

"You do not know what you're all playing with." Henrich said. "Those creatures possess power that will not only kill you all, but will destroy this entire land and make into a land of fire."

"That is not our concern right now, old man. But, if they do start to act up against us, we will put them out of their misery."

"You can't just kill these creatures with your methods of attack. They are smarter than you give them credit for."

"Tell me, how would you know all of this? Have you encountered them before in your lifetime?"

"I've seen many creatures in my life and all of them have the potential to do deadly things. Not only to Man, but to all the Worlds."

Wade waved Henrich off as he commanded the Scavengers to toss them into the fiery pit. The Scavengers shove them, and they fall into the Pit, where they are surrounded by the Salamanders. Landon and Beth stood close to Henrich in the middle of the Pit, where they were surrounded by four Salamanders. The Salamanders screeched at them and their tongues slithered with fire dripping from their mouths. The intense heat was unbearable, but Henrich stood his ground.

"Just hold yourselves and be calm." Henrich said to Landon and Beth.

"How are we going to fight these things?" Landon asked. "Because I'm concerned right now."

The Salamanders of the Pit were dry-skinned, red, and thin creatures. Wisps of flames covered their bodies and within the fires around the Pit, Henrich spotted several spiritual entities roaming around in the flames. Landon and Beth measured he creatures, seeing how the lizard creatures scaly skin was protected from the flames and how their length was about five feet.

"What can we do?" Beth mentioned. "We have no weapons to face them."

"We have no other option." Henrich said, holding up his fists against the Salamanders.

Wade stood over them and yelled out a great shout. The Scavengers stood around the Pit, holding makeshift weapons of stone. He grabbed the weapons, which were made in the images of hammers, swords, and maces. Wade tossed them into the Pit, where Henrich looked up toward him as he grabbed the hammer. Wade smiled.

"Best that you have better means to face them. Now, give us what we want. Entertainment for tonight."

Landon grabbed the mace and Beth took the sword as they stood facing the Salamanders. The Scavengers began to cheer loudly, causing the Salamanders to screech and they spit out fire toward them Henrich moved out of the flame's way and swiped the Salamander in its side with the hammer. The Salamander screech with a loud noise as its tail swiped across Henrich's chest, knocking him to the ground. Landon and Beth fought against the other three Salamanders with the sword and mace.

Henrich stood up and faced the Salamander again, this time running towards it as it spat out more fire in his direction. The flames burned through Henrich's coat and hat. He removed them, and jumped atop the Salamander. Riding it like it was a bull, Henrich took the hammer and slammed it against the Salamander's head several times. Blow after blow he slammed down the hammer. Wade kept his eyes on Henrich, looking at his fighting skills against the Salamander.

"This old man knows things that we don't." He said. "You can see it in his skills."

"Do you want us to interrogate him for you after the fight?" A Scavenger questioned.

"That is if he survives this. If he does, bring him to my trailer and I will have word with him."

"We shall do."

Henrich continued pummeling the Salamander in its head and it fell to the ground, where it began to bleed fire, a red-orange looking liquid fire in its form. Another Salamander faced Henrich and he faced it with a smile on his face. Henrich lunged toward the creature with the stone hammer in hand.

Landon took the mace and slammed it against one of the Salamander's back, though the Salamander wasn't affected by the blunt, he swiped against Landon and punched him onto the ground. Landon placed the mace in between himself and the Salamander's fiery mouth. The fire dripped onto the ground inches away from Landon's face. He grunted as he made the attempt of shoving the creature's weight off himself.

"Get off, will you!" Landon screamed, fighting against the Salamander.

Beth ran over and slashed the stone sword against the Salamanders' side, slightly cutting through its scaly skin. The Salamander backed off Landon and looked at Beth. Its eyes showed its anger toward her and she looked around at the two Salamanders.

They were prepared to pounce her and dose her with their fire. Landon stood up and attack the Salamanders with the mace. Hitting its legs and its tail.

"Take care of the other one, please." Landon told Beth.

Beth took the sword and swiped it towards the other Salamander, who backed away from the sword and spat out fire toward her. The fire touched the sword, though it did not destroy it. Beth smiled as she jumped atop the Salamander and took the stone sword, stabbing it through its back and ramming down as much as she could until the sword broke through the Salamander's stomach. The creature screamed as it fell to the ground and died. Beth pulled out the sword and jumped off the dead creature. She looked ahead and saw Landon fighting one and Henrich fighting the other.

Henrich took the hammer and destroyed the Salamander with it, until its head was flat as the ground they walked on. Landon took the mace and slammed it into the last Salamander around its body. Beth ran towards them to help as did Henrich and the three of them together slew the last Salamander. As it died, the flames that surrounded the Pit, suddenly ceased and the spirits that were within them appeared and flew into the night sky, vanishing along into the darkness. Wade stood by the edge of the Pit very still. His eyes locked on them and he began to applaud them for their victory.

"I'll be damn." He said. "They survived."

The Scavengers were silent, seeing the Salamanders killed and the Three surviving. Henrich looked toward Wade and pointed the hammer to him. Wade knew what they were about to do, he raised up his hand toward them, gesturing to them to come up the Pit and slaughter him and the Scavengers.

Beth wanted to kill them as she was covered with the Salamander's blood. All Landon wanted to do was smash Wade's head in with the mace. Henrich knew he wanted them all dead, but to try an attack on them while they're surrounded isn't a wise decision to make. Henrich picked up his hat and coat, seeing the flames on them had ceased. He put them back on, seeing Wade continuing to gesture to them.

"You have your chance to end all of us now." He said. "So, bring your asses up here and kill us all."

"I'll take the pleasure." Beth said, holding the stone sword tightly in her hands.

Henrich stopped her and she didn't know why. She looked up at them and all that was on her face was anger. Intense anger. Landon felt the same, but knew there was something wrong overall. Plus, seeing how Henrich reacted to Wade's gesture ring told Landon so much more than he already knew.

"Why are you stopping me?!" Beth yelled.

"Because if you act now, they will kill you." He replied.

"They can try."

"Beth, calm yourself." Landon said. "Listen to Henrich, please."

Beth turned to Henrich, taking in Landon's choice of words. Henrich looked her in the eyes and could see her anger. He understood her anger and why she wanted to slaughter them. Henrich held her tightly, she felt comfort with Henrich's hug. Wade watched them as the Scavengers stood quiet.

"He knows how to humble them." Wade said. "I'm starting to like this old man."

"Just wait." Henrich told Beth. "Just wait for the right moment to strike."

"Alright." She said. "I will wait for it."

Henrich released Beth and Wade signaled to the Scavengers to grab them and bring them back to the table. The Scavengers pulled them from the Pit and tied up their hands again. They took the stone weapons and placed them in a shed, where their own gear was placed. Henrich watched as they placed the weapons within the shed and shut the door. He spotted one Scavenger handing the keys to the shed to another Scavenger. He kept the Scavenger's appearance and facial details in his memory. While being brought back to the table, two of the Scavenger guards grabbed Henrich by his arms and he looked at them.

"What of me now?" Henrich asked them.

"Wade would like to speak with yon again inside his trailer."

"What for?"

"You'll hear once you're in his presence, old man."

Henrich walked with them toward the trailer and they entered it. The guards placed Henrich in the same seat as before where Wade sat in front of him. Only this time, the guard left the trailer and Wade had no tea to drink. Wade looked at how dirty Henrich was from the fights with the Salamanders. He could see the scorched burnt marks on Henrich's clothes and the blood on his face.

"I am impressed." Wade said. "Truly I am. I didn't know the three of you could fight like that."

"We did what we had to do to survive." Henrich said. "What else were you expecting?"

"I expected the three of you to be killed and eaten by the Salamanders. Who were our pets by the way and now they're dead. Thanks to you and your partners."

Henrich shook his head, looking around the trailer.

"Why am I here again?"

"Because I have something to show you."

Wade walked form the table to the back of the trailer and when he returned to Henrich, he was carrying with him the strange weapons that the other Scavengers found in the tall buildings back at the other town. Henrich stared at the weapons and he knew what they were and how they were used. Wade placed the weapons on the table between them. Wade patted them as if they were a prized dog of his.

"I was wondering if you know about these? My people found them when they scavenged a town not too far from here. They were in some tall building, just lying there. As if whoever was there left without any trace."

Henrich smirked as he looked at the weapons. Wade didn't understand the smirk, but he took it as an insult to himself. Wade slammed his hand on the table, facing Henrich. The two men looked eye to eye and not a word was said for the moment. Wade slowly backed into his chair and sighed. Henrich's smirk became nothing.

"I believe that you know what these are and what they can do."

"How would you know that?"

"Because that's why I'm asking you right now. Tell me what these weapons are and teach my people how to use them."

"And what will I get out of doing these things for you?"

"Your freedom of course."

"You promised me that a while ago and yet, look what has happened to us."

"Because you didn't accept my agreement in joining us. You declined it, so I had to teach you three a lesson in when you decline an offer that I give to you."

"Then, you'll be delighted to know that I don't accept this agreement. Neither will I teach you and your people about these weapons and how they are used."

"So, you know what these things are, and you know how to use them, don't you?"

Henrich stared for a moment, he gazed his sights down to the weapons and looked back to Wade.

"Yes. I know of these weapons."

"So, you will teach us about them. You will."

"No, I will not."

"Give a reason why you won't teach us? Why won't you teach me?"

"Truthfully, because these weapons are far beyond your understanding and comprehension. The art of these weapons would destroy your very mind and would make you into a madman."

Wade held his head down at the table. He glanced up to Henrich as he eyes turned to the weapons. He smirked at Henrich before standing up over the table and Henrich himself. Henrich only stared at him and kept silent.

"Be that as it may, old man. But, if you won't teach myself and my people the art of these weapons, then worse things will come upon you, Cody, and Beth. You think what we did you three was bad? Hell, you aren't even aware of the things that we can truly do to you. We could do things that would bring you three to utter shame. It would destroy your inner being and it will cause you to fall and to never get back up. We can do those things and we are capable of it."

Henrich nodded. Taking in every word that was spoken from Wade's mouth. He knew that Wade was speaking some truth, but most of his words were only filled with lies and attempts at drawing fear into the room. Henrich looked at Wade. A still face and a silent one.

"Do what you have to do, boy." Henrich said.

Wade didn't like Henrich's choice of words and punched him in the face. Wade punched him again and again. But, the punches didn't faze Henrich. Wade knew that as he could see Henrich kept his eyes locked on him as he was punching him. Wade walked to the trailer's door. Opening it, calling for the guards. The guards enter the trailer and stand behind Henrich.

"Take him out of here and place him at the table."

"Will do."

The guards grabbed Henrich, returning him to the table once again. While they were walking outside, Wade watched them place Henrich at the table. He stared at Henrich, Landon, and Beth with anger. He rubbed his mouth, which was beginning to foam from his anger. He entered the trailer, slamming the door shut. Henrich watched as Wade slammed the door. Landon and Beth also noticed it by the door's sound echoing through the campsite. Henrich only smirked.

"What did you say to him, sir?" Landon asked.

"I didn't say anything to him." Henrich replied. "He wanted to know how to use something and I declined."

Landon wanted to say something, but didn't know how to say. He looked at Henrich, who could see the words trying to push out of his mouth.

"What is it, boy?"

"I just wanted you to know that I repented of my actions. It was what I had to do to make myself clean again."

Henrich nodded with a smile on his face. "It was a good decision of you to make."

Henrich looked at Beth, who was still filled with anger, her fists clenched, she was ready to attack the Scavengers at any moment that she could.

"Calm yourself, Beth." Henrich said. "Just calm yourself."

"I am calm." She replied. "I will be fully calm when I get my hands on them."

"I know."

"So, do you have an idea to how we can make an escape?"

Henrich looked at the Scavenger with the shed key, who walked around the campsite continually and he glazed toward the shed itself. He turned back to Beth, showing a smirk on his face and Landon inched into the conversation.

"I might have a way out of here."

V

Randolph looked around the campsite, seeing the Scavengers walking on about their business. The night was surely coming ahead as he seen Wade speaking with other Scavengers, showing them the strange weapons. The other Scavengers wee clueless to how they worked and how they were formed. Landon looked at them and turned his head to Henrich, while gazing toward the Scavengers. Watching them as if they're about to approach them once again.

"How are we going to get out of here?" Landon questioned.

"I have an idea." Henrich said. "But, it will require to spillage of blood."

"How will that work out?" Beth asked.

"It will work out for the better. The only thing will be it must come from either one of you."

"Why one of us?"

"I've already bled for them and me bleeding again won't help out our plan. They will come and aid if it's one of you. They would leave me to bleed to death otherwise."

Landon looked around, searching for a tool that would be able to cut through their skin. He couldn't find one nearby the table.

"I don't see anything here that could cut through our skin, sir."

"Keep looking around. There has to be something capable of doing it."

Beth looked down underneath the table and found a small blade. The blade was made from glass and it wasn't sharp enough to cut through the binds of their hands, but it could slice through their skin

146

with enough force onto it. Beth handed the blade to Henrich, who looked closely at it.

"Where did you find this?"

"Under the table."

"There was a blade there the whole time?" Landon wondered.

"The worlds are stranger than you can believe, boy."

Henrich grabbed the blade.

"This will do." Henrich confirmed. "Now, who will it be?"

Landon looked over to Beth and she does the same. Landon nodded with a straight face and turned to Henrich. He held his hands open toward him.

"Give it to me." He said. "I'll do it."

"Understandable." Henrich said. "Make sure you do it slightly around your arm and not too much. Otherwise, you'll be a dead man."

"I will keep my eyes on it."

Landon took the blade and reached toward his left forearm, cutting his flesh. Landon yelled as the blade went into his skin and the blood began to arise. The yelling caused the Scavengers to look as did Wade, who seen Landon's forearm bleeding.

"The hell is going on over there?!" Wade yelled. "What are you three idiots doing?!"

Wade ran toward them as did some of the Scavengers. Henrich seen them approaching and he nodded to Landon to cease the cutting. Landon stopped cutting himself and slipped the blade over to Henrich, who placed it inside his coat pocket. Beth turned her head as Wade and the Scavengers approached them. They surrounded them as Wade looked at the wound on Landon's forearm. He could see it was cut, but not a deep cut wound. Wade gazed over to Henrich and Beth.

"The hell is this?" Wade asked. "Tell me, what is this shit? What are you fools doing over here when we're not watching you people?"

"He just cut himself by accident." Henrich said. "That's all that happened."

Wade smirked to Henrich and the smirk immediately turned into a frown. Wade was not pleased with Landon's wound and Henrich knew he wouldn't be. Wade turned to the Scavengers in a small fit of anger.

"Go get the med kit and bring it over here." He told them.

The Scavengers left to get the med kit from the trailer of Wade. Wade stood by Landon, overseeing his forearm continuing to bleed. He looked outward at the Scavengers, who were exiting his trailer with the med kit, a blue and white box. Wade waved to them to hurry themselves up.

"Come on now!" Wade yelled. "We don't have the entire night to do this mess."

They come with the kit and hand it to Wade. Wade opened the med kit and revealed bandages, patches, and other medical supplies. Wade commanded for two Scavengers to hold Landon down as he applied the bandages onto Landon's forearm with a little bit of alcohol that was within the kit. Landon yelled for a moment in pain while his forearm was being bandaged. Beth turned away from the sight and Henrich only watched on. Staring at Wade as a predator would stalk its prey in an open field.

"Almost done with your ass." Wade said. "Just be still for a short moment, will you."

Wade tightened the bandage on Landon's forearm and the Scavengers released their grip on him. Landon looked at his forearm, seeing the bandage. Wade stared at Landon. Looking him in the eye. He gazed toward Henrich, seeing him staring back with the brim's shadow covering his eyes in the night. Wade smiled back to him before facing Landon.

"Since you decided to be a fool for the day, I have something for you tonight and you're not going to like it."

"What are you going to do to me this time?" Landon asked. "Are you going to try and get one of your women to molest me again? Because it's not going to happen this time."

Wade laughed.

"You know I would. But, you've already done that whole deal. So, this time I'm going to give the Scavengers the entire night to beat you down until they're tired of beating you."

Wade looked out to the Scavengers, who grabbed Landon from

the table and brought him to their circle. In the circle were several men, who began to pummel Landon into the ground. Henrich stood up from the table, but was held down by three other Scavengers. Wade laughed at Henrich.

"You still have the fight in you. Just give up for once."

Beth looked at Wade, getting his attention. He looked at her and stared back. Seeing her anger in her eyes. Wade knew that she was not fooling around any longer. Beth slowly stood up from the table and faced Wade. Wade approached her, he held his hand up, stopping the other Scavengers from confronting her. He smirked in her face.

"What are you going to do, young lady? What can you do to me that hasn't been done before?"

Beth only stared into his eyes and she kicked him in his groin. Wade yelled as he fell to the ground. Holding his genitals tightly, screaming in pain. The other Scavengers looked at Beth and Henrich elbowed them in their faces, knocking them back. Henrich kicked them each in the head, knocking them unconscious. Landon tried to fight back, getting hits on several of the Scavengers before being crowded and jumped by many more. They yelled and screamed in his face and ears. Wade crawled on the ground, slowly standing himself up and still holding himself, trying to compress the pain. He looked at Beth and backslapped her.

"Dumb bitch." Wade said. "I should've been the one to have you myself."

Henrich kicked Wade onto the ground as he helped Beth get up from the ground. Wade looked at Henrich, who was eager to kill him where he was laying down. Wade shook his head as Henrich grabbed him by his jacket. Henrich held him up by the nearby post. Jerking him around.

"You will bring Cody back over here." Henrich said. "Do you understand what I say to you?"

"I got you, old man." Wade replied slowly. "I heard your words."

"You're going to die soon." Henrich said.

"We'll find that out won't we." Wade said with a fainting smirk.

Henrich held him and threw him to the ground, where Wade stood up and ran toward the crowd of Scavengers. He stepped into the circle, near Landon, holding his hands out to the other Scavengers.

"Cease." Wade yelled. "The boy's had his beat down for the night."

Landon stood up, wiping the blood from his nose and mouth. Wade approached him and tossed him a towel from the trailer. Landon held the towel in his hand before seeing Wade standing in front of him.

"Wipe yourself, boy." Wade said.

Landon lunged toward Wade, punching him in his face. The Scavengers came around, dragging Landon from Wade and holding him up in the air above their heads while others went to assist Wade off the ground. Wade laughed as hit spat blood from his mouth. Wade enjoyed it and stood holding his arms out toward Landon. Landon struggled against the Scavengers to approach Wade.

"Come on, boy! Come punch me again and you'll see where you will end up!"

The Scavengers dragged Landon back to the table and left him there. Wade stood by and watched. He rubbed his hands together, staring at the three of them. Henrich stood there and stared back. As did Beth and Landon. They had enough of these games and Wade knew it. He turned to one of the Scavenger guards and approached him closely.

"Tomorrow, we kill them." Wade whispered.

"By any means?" The guard asked.

"Any means necessary." Wade replied as he entered his trailer for the night.

Henrich looked at Landon, who wiped the blood from his face with the towel before throwing it to the ground. Landon has had enough of the Scavengers and ways payback. Beth wants the same as does Henrich.

"I want to beat that man down." Landon said. "I want to kill him and his friends."

"In a short time, we will." Henrich said.

"How can you be sure of that?" Beth asked. "We don't have any means to get out of these bonds right now."

Henrich reached slowly into his coat, avoiding the prying eyes of the Scavengers as they head off to sleep for the night. From his coat, Henrich pulled out a knife. Landon and Beth stood still as their eyes were locked into the knife.

"Where did you get that, sir?" Landon asked.

"I got it off the Scavenger that held me down. After I knocked him unconscious."

"So, cut us free." Beth said.

"Not right now."

Landon and Beth looked at one another. As if Henrich was crazy to hold off their chance at freedom. Beth shook her head, she didn't understand what Henrich was truly planning and neither did Landon. Henrich placed the knife back into his coat and watched as the Scavengers went to sleep. Landon and Beth noticed, and they now had the chance at being free from the Scavengers for good. But, Henrich kept the knife in his coat.

"Why aren't you cutting us free?" Landon wondered. "We have the chance now."

"We need our gear back."

"So, where is it?"

Henrich pointed to the shed across from them. Not too far from Wade's trailer. They looked ahead and noticed the lock pad on the shed's door.

"Which one of them has the key?" Beth asked.

"The one that went inside the other trailer behind Wade's."

"I'm starting to get it now." Landon said. "You're waiting till you're closer to the one with the key before cutting us loose."

"In the morning, he will walk over here and when he does. I will stab him in his neck and take the key from him. After that, we will get our weapons back and them will we kill these people."

Landon and Beth nodded to Henrich.

"Well then, I'll wait till the morning." Beth said.

Later that night, Henrich had a vision. The vision was a future that was very near. In the vision of Henrich, was a chaotic event taking place at the campsite of the Scavengers. In the vision, the Scavengers were running to save their lives. They were running from gunshots that came from the campsite and standing in the campsite were Henrich, Landon, and Beth. The three of them were all holding shooters and firing at the Scavengers. They killed many of them as others ran into the wilderness. The vision later warped itself to a field, where Henrich stood over Wade, with the shooter pointed at him.

"This is where you die." Henrich told Wade before killing him.

From the shooting, Henrich awoken from the vision and looked up at the sky, it was morning. Henrich woke Landon and Beth up from their slumber.

"Huh? What's going on?" Landon said muffled in his sleep.

"I had a vision." Henrich said. "I know how we're going to get ourselves free."

"How?" Beth asked softly.

Henrich looked up and he faced ahead, toward the shed. From the shed came the Scavenger with the key and he was approaching their location. Landon and Beth looked on seeing the Scavenger coming toward them.

"Here he comes." Henrich said.

The Scavenger with the shed key stopped at the table and gazed at the three of them. He kneeled in front of them. Dangling the key in their faces. Showing them that he is in full possession of their gear.

"How does it feel to know that I own all of your shit?" The Scavenger said.

"It feels quite well." Henrich said.

"What does that mean?"

"It means-"

Henrich quickly took the knife and stabbed it in the Scavenger's throat. He gargled on his own blood as Landon snatched the key from his dying hands. Henrich grabbed the Scavenger and tossed him behind the post, where he rolled down into a ditch nearby the campsite. Landon tossed Henrich the keys to the shed. Henrich took the knife and cut himself loose of the bonds. He then cut loose Landon and Beth. Henrich looked down at the keys and seeing how many of the Scavengers were slowly walking up for the morning. They stood up from the table, overlooking the campsite as far as their eyes could see.

"What now?" Landon said, filled with energy.

"It's time." Henrich said as they walked toward the shed.

<u>VI</u>

Henrich ran toward the shed and unlocked it with the key. Slowly, opening the shed to avoid causing the Scavengers to et up from their sleep. Henrich, Landon, and Beth entered the shed and sitting against the wall of the shed was their gear. All of it. From their shooters, their knives, and other supplies they brought along with them. They take their gear and equip themselves with it as they were before being captured by the Scavengers. Beth placed the shooter that was given to her on her hip. Landon kept his shooter and knife close by and Henrich stood there with his shooters in their holsters, the blast shooter on his back and the machete within the interior of the coat.

"Are you ready, sir?" Landon asked Henrich.

"I am." He replied. "Let's make a clean sweep of these people."

As the Scavengers awoke in the morning, Wade exited his trailer and looked over to the table. Not seeing either one of the Three there, Wade started to panic and approached the Scavengers that were walking about on the campiest.

"Where did they go?" Wade asked. "Have you seen them anywhere?"

"I have not, sir." The Scavenger replied. "I haven't seen them since last night."

"Damn it!" Wade yelled. "Where are they?!"

From the shed, Henrich kicked the door down, seeing the Scavengers standing right in front of him. Henrich fired his shooter at any of the Scavengers who were in his sights. So, did Landon and Beth. The Scavenger yelled in fear and ran off from the campsite to avoid being killed by them. Wade looked on, seeing them coming from the shed. His heart had dropped in his chest and he was at a loss for words.

"No." He said to himself.

Some Scavengers attempted to take down Henrich, Landon, and Beth. Although, they underestimated their skill set with the shooters and weapons they carried on them. Henrich pulled out the machete and began slashing Scavengers left and right. Landon took his knife and stabbed many of them in their chests and their neck. Beth took her shooter and fired it, aiming for their heads. Henrich later pulled out the blast shooter and fired it. The bullet of the blast shooter went through the backs of three Scavengers at once.

"Now, you all know who we are!" Henrich yelled.

Wade stood still with his hands on his head. He gazed around the campsite, seeing it being destroyed by them. Most of the Scavengers ran into the forests that stood near the campsite. Beth watched many of them enter the wilderness. She fired several shots toward it, not knowing if she managed to take some of them down with her aiming.

"Most of them ran into the woods!" Beth said. "What are we going to do about them, Henrich?"

Henrich blasted one Scavenger in his head with the blast shooter and turned to Beth as the blast shooter's barrel was smoking.

"We go after them." Henrich said. "And we kill them all."

Beth nodded as she and Landon went for the wilderness. Henrich killed the remaining Scavengers that stayed in the campsite and he looked up toward the trailer, seeing Wade standing there. Henrich took the blast shooter and fired it toward him. Wade ran out of the fire and went into the wilderness himself. Henrich shook his head as he watched Wade run. He never seen him with that much fear in his being.

"The woods won't save you." Henrich said.

Henrich entered the woods himself and within the tall trees, echoes of screams and gunshots could be heard. Henrich knew that Landon and Beth were killing as many Scavengers that they could find. Henrich, meanwhile, searched the forest for Wade, who was hiding within the trees of the wilderness.

"Wade." Henrich said. "Show yourself. I don't recall you being this afraid of me before and yet, you ran from me."

Further into the forest, Landon shot one of the Scavengers in the leg, causing them to fall. The Scavenger he shot was the woman he had sex with the nights ago. She looked at him as he stood over her, his shooter aimed at her head. She panted for air as she was in fear of Landon.

"You remember that night?"

The woman nodded her head quickly as she could. Landon cocked his head.

"I do too." He said, taking the shot and killing her.

Beth fired as many rounds as she could with the shooter she had. Shooting Scavengers in their backs, legs, and head. She aimed as much as she could to get the perfect shots to fire. From behind, Beth was tackled to the ground by the same woman who had her way with her that night. She jumped atop of Beth, holding her down with her own weight.

"What are you going to do now, pretty girl?!" The woman yelled. "You can't get up from me. I own your ass remember!"

She went to kiss Beth and Beth spat in her face. The woman wiped the spit from her face and Beth grabbed her shooter, firing it directly into the woman's face. Beth shoved her body off her own and continued moving through the forest, killing more of the Scavengers.

Henrich continued to search for Wade, while he was killing Scavengers that he encountered. Henrich killed many of them with the blastshooter and the machete. Wade could hear the screams and cries of his clan and he didn't know what to do. He kept himself hidden from Henrich's sight as well as Landon's and Beth's if they were to come across him in the woods.

"Show yourself, Wade." Henrich yelled. "Why are you suddenly afraid of us?"

Wade kept himself silent, as his voice would give away his location in the trees. Henrich knew he would keep silent and continued walking through the wilderness, killing all the Scavengers that remained and from the numbers, there were many of them roaming through the wilderness. They ran with fear as they were hunted down by Henrich, Landon, and Beth. Some of the Scavengers knew this day would come and they weren't prepared for its arrival.

<h1 style="text-align:center"><u>VII</u></h1>

Henrich continued killing the Scavengers that fled with Landon and Beth. Their shooters were being reloaded every time they came closer to being out. The Scavengers had no other means to fight back besides their own bodies and the branches of the forest. Wade moved silently through the wilderness, trying his hardest to be unseen by Henrich, Landon, and Beth. He continued to hear his people's cries for help and Wade shook his head in shame of himself and in shame of his people.

"I thought they were stronger than this." Wade said to himself concerning his clan. "I thought they had the heart to stay strong and overcome. But, I was wrong. I was so wrong."

Landon and Beth continued killing the Scavengers that they came across. One Scavenger grabbed a branch from the ground and swung at Landon, who moved out of the branches' path and he kicked the Scavenger's knee from behind. The Scavenger fell to one knee and as the Scavenger turned his head, he only seen the barrel of Landon's shooter and the shooter fired. The Scavenger's body fell to the ground.

"Now stand up." Landon said.

Beth fired countless rounds at the Scavengers. She followed their cries for Wade's help and she could hear footsteps coming from behind her. She turned around and was grabbed by two male Scavengers. They held her tightly and yelled in her ear. They tried to snatch the shooter from her hand, but she held onto the weapon. One decided if he couldn't get the shooter, he would get something else as he tried to place his hand inside of her pants. She kicked him and bit his arm.

"Get off!" She screamed.

"Scream for me!" One Scavenger yelled. "I have all day!"

"Listen to him!" The other Scavenger said. "Scream for him and after that, you're going to yell for me!"

They knocked Beth to the ground with their own strength. But, they didn't pay much attention to her hands as she aimed the shooter as quickly as she could and started firing it several times toward them.

The rounds went through the Scavengers' chests and abdomen. The Scavengers died as they fell. Beth stood up from the ground, wiping the dirt and leaves from her clothing. She took a moment to breathe before following the cries of the Scavengers. While she ran, she could also her the gunshots from Henrich and Landon, learning how to point out their locations in the wilderness.

Deeper in the wilderness, Landon fired shots at two Scavengers and after he fired the next shot. His shooter was out, and he had to reload. Yet, surrounding him were the two Scavengers as well as another one that appeared from behind him. They screamed at Landon as he tried to reload the shooter as fast as he could. One of the Scavengers ran toward him and tackled him to the ground. They stood over him, taunting him to stand back on his feet. Landon nodded and stood up. He placed the shooter on his side and faced the three Scavengers. They were impressed with his stance and they lunged toward him.

"You see this!" One of the Scavengers said. "He's not afraid of us anymore!"

"Look at this boy!" Another Scavenger said.

"You wanted a fight." Landon said. "So, let's fight like men."

The Scavengers nodded and approached Landon, who quickly knocked one of them down with a haymaker and the second one, Landon kicked in the abdomen and kneed him in his face, pushing him down onto the ground.

The third Scavenger swung at Landon, who ducked and punched the Scavenger several times before elbowing him in his forehead. The Scavengers laid on the ground, slowly moving and trying to regain their concentration. As they were doing so, Landon reloaded the shooter and killed them before they could stand themselves back up.

Henrich continued with his machete, slicing away at the Scavengers. Henrich stopped for a second and listened closely to the screams and cries that consumed the forest. He listened as closely as he could, realizing there were less screams than before. Henrich knew that they were almost done with the Scavengers and he kept moving, killing the rest of them that were in his sights.

Around the trees, Wade moved around slowly. He managed his

steps on the ground, avoiding the down branches and the leaves that sat atop the dirt.

"WADE!" A Scavenger yelled out through the wilderness. "Where are you?!"

"He's running around her somewhere!" Henrich yelled. "Don't worry about him. I'll take care of him when I find him."

Henrich moved forward, killing the Scavengers he could see through the trees. Wade followed him very slowly. Though, he was filled with both anger and sadness and he could not decide what to do. He couldn't decide to try to save his clan or to let them die and leave only himself to survive to rotationally rebuild the Scavengers in some way.

Landon and Beth ran through the wilderness, looking for anymore Scavengers that they could find and through their running, they concluded they've killed most of the Scavengers. They each understood why they've done what they did and went back to find each other while still hearing a few Scavengers within the forest and the gunshots from Henrich's blastshooter.

"He's not that far away." Landon said. "Just a few more feet."

As they ran through the wilderness, Henrich's blast shooter became louder as did the screams of the remaining Scavengers. Landon and Beth both ran toward the sounds. Passing by the trees around them, inching closer to the noise. While they ran, Wade watched them from afar, seeing the two of them running through the woods. Wade didn't know what to do anymore. He remained silent and looked around for any remaining Scavengers within the area. He would jump slight every time Henrich fired his blastshooter.

VIII

Running through the wilderness, Landon bumped into Henrich, who fired the blast shooter at a fleeing scavenger. Landon looked ahead, seeing the Scavenger lying on the ground with the hole in his back. Henrich reloaded the blast shooter as Landon looked around.

"Where's Beth?" Landon asked.

"She's out here somewhere." Henrich replied. "She can handle herself. No need to concern yourself about her whereabouts."

"That I can understand."

Henrich and Landon ran further out together, looking for the last Scavengers. Beth, running through the forest looked ahead, seeing them running in front of her. She nodded as she followed them through the wilderness. As she followed them, Wade followed her, moving quietly in the wilderness. He knew he lost many of his people and he couldn't do anything about it, but he kept following them. Somewhat intrigued by their actions and their way of using the weapons.

Henrich tossed Landon another box of ammo for his shooter and while Landon placed the box in his pocket, they stopped in front of the two male Scavenger Guards from Wade's trailer. Big in size according to muscle and height to Landon's eyesight. The two men weren't afraid of Henrich and Landon nor were they afraid of the weapons they carried on them. The men beat on their chests while staring at them.

"How do we take these two down?"

"Simple." Henrich said, firing his blast shooter at one of the Scavengers. Blowing his head clean off.

The other Scavenger watched as his partner's head was blown from his body and he ran toward Henrich and Landon in anger. While he ran, a shooter sounded through the forest and killed the Scavenger from the side. Henrich and Landon looked over to the side where the shot came from and there was Beth, standing next to one of the trees with the shooter in her hands. Henrich nodded toward her as she waved to him and Landon. She approached them.

"I would guess you've done your best to get revenge." Henrich told her.

"I did what I had to do to survive." She replied. "How many do you think are left remaining out here?"

"Not that many. Wade is still around. So, we can count him."

Not too far from where Henrich, Landon, and Beth are talking, a Scavenger moved stealthy through the wilderness and as he ran from their location, The Scavenger ran directly into Wade. The Scavenger paused and hugged Wade, hoping to find some relief. Wave hugged him back. They were both in fear of the Three.

"What can we do, boss?" The Scavenger said.

"Nothing we can do now, my brother." Wade replied. "Only thing we can do is stick together."

"I hear you, sir."

Wade looked around for the Three, not seeing them anywhere near his location in the forests. He looked at the Scavenger, seeing him in constant fear for his life as he would turn around to look. He would turn constantly and would not stop. He looked as if he was in shock, but free to move around.

"So, where are the remaining brethren?" Wade asked.

"Most of them are dead." The Scavenger said. "There's probably only three of us left out here besides you, boss."

Wade nodded. Taking in the information that he knows. He patted the Scavenger on his right shoulder, trying to relax him.

"Just stay quiet and follow me."

The Scavenger nodded and after he nodded, his brains splattered onto Wade. Wade wiped the blood from his face and looked ahead. Seeing the Scavenger on the ground, dead by a shooter. In front of Wade, stood Henrich, with his shooter in hand.

"I've finally found you, boy." Henrich said.

Wade ran for his life and Henrich followed him as did Landon and Beth.

IX

Henrich, Landon, and Beth chased down Wade, who ran from them within the wilderness. Wade ran out of the wilderness and returned to the campsite. He looked around the site, searching for anymore Scavengers. There were none. Within the woods, Henrich spotted two Scavengers. He pointed Landon and Beth to their direction.

"Go after those two." Henrich said. "I'll deal with Wade."

Landon nodded and went after them. Beth stopped Henrich,

before looking at Landon running.

"Leave some of Wade for me." She said.

"Fair." He replied.

Beth ran behind Landon. Henrich continued chasing down Wade and discovered he reentered the campsite. Henrich shook his head at Wade's choice of decision.

"Boy. You haven't learned anything in this short time." He said. "You are on your last hour."

Landon and Beth chased down the last two Scavengers. They fired shots at them, causing the Scavengers to run even faster. While they ran, they exited the forest and appeared on the pathways. The Scavengers looked around at the dusty road and from the other side of the pathways appeared Henrich's horse, which stampeded one of the Scavengers, killing him from his stomping. The other Scavenger watched on and took off running. He has lost hope in surviving. Landon and Beth appeared, seeing Henrich's horse sanding over a dead Scavenger and seeing the one Scavenger running down the pathways. Landon raised up his shooter, aimed for the Scavenger. He gazed over to Beth and lowered his shooter. He turned to Beth.

"Your shot."

Beth smiled as she aimed her shooter and fired, killing the Scavenger in the middle of the pathways. She sighed as she, Landon, and Henrich's horse went back to the forest to find Henrich. At the campsite, Henrich fired at the trailers and the tents that stood. He used the blastshooter to shoot at the vehicles that surrounded the campsite. Wade hid himself around the camp.

"Just do yourself a favor and end all of this." Henrich said. "You're wasting precious time here."

Wade stayed quiet, only hearing the shots from Henrich's shooters and blastshooter. He moved slowly behind his trailer. From the forest, Landon and Beth return to the campsite with Henrich's horse. Henrich looked behind himself, seeing the horse, which ran toward him. Henrich embraced the horse.

"I knew you would be back son." Henrich said.

Landon and Beth approached Henrich and the horse. He seen them standing there and pointed around the campsite. They looked on.

"He's here somewhere." Henrich said.

"Where could he be?" Beth asked.

"I am not sure about that. But, he's here and he won't leave this place."

"Why won't he leave?" Landon asked. "There's no one else here with him anymore."

Henrich looked at Landon and pointed around the campsite again.

"It's his home. It's all he's had and it will be his burial ground."

The horse gallop toward the trailer and they followed the horse. The horse circled the trailer. Giving Henrich a hint. Henrich nodded and kicked the trailer door open. He entered the trailer, but there was no sign of Wade. From the outside, Wade took off running. The horse galloped again as Landon and Beth turned around, seeing Wade running away.

"He's running off!" Beth yelled.

Henrich exited the trailer, seeing Wade running away from the campsite. Henrich looked at Beth. Seeing the shooter in her hand and her fingers twitching toward the trigger.

"Beth, you have your opportunity." Henrich said. "Take the shot."

"Yes sir." She said, aiming at Wade.

Beth pulled the trigger of the shooter and fired it. The bullet flew toward Wade and went right through his leg. Wade yelled as he fell to the ground, holding his leg. Beth placed the shooter to her side, Henrich and Landon stood by her, seeing Wade yelling and holding his leg in pain.

"You did good." Henrich said.

"Thank you." She replied. "What of him now?"

"I'll finish him off."

Henrich approached the down Wade and Landon and Beth followed him. Wade looked on as they approached him. He did what he could to back away from them as much as possible. But, his body was in so much pain, he couldn't not move from them. Henrich stood in front of him and Wade was in fear.

<u>X</u>

Henrich stood over Wade. Landon and Beth watched on while the Warslinger's horse stood still next to Henrich. Wade looked at the horse and looked at Henrich. He looked at the two of them again. He gazed to Beth and Landon.

"Where did that horse come from?" Wade asked.

"It belongs to me." Henrich said. "The horse is always close to my locations."

"That can't be possible."

"How come?"

"Because horses of this nature only belonged to Warslingers." Landon said.

"I told you I was one of them as did Cody."

"How? They're all supposed to be dead according to the stories told."

"The stories never tell all the details." Henrich said. "We are scattered across the Worlds, but in time, we will come together once again and bring a balance to the Worlds."

Wade nodded.

"Good luck with that." He said.

Henrich reached to his right holster, where he pulled out the shooter with the Heptad engraving marks. Wade looked at the shooter and he finally believed Henrich to be a Warslinger.

"Now, do you believe?" Henrich asked.

"I guess I do." Wade replied. "So, what of me now? Warslinger of the Heptad?"

"It's very simple, boy. Your life is over. Time for you to enter the Outer-World."

Henrich pulled the trigger of the Heptad shooter, killing Wade right in his campsite. While Wade's body laid on the dirt, Henrich, Landon, and Beth set fire to the Scavengers' campsite. Destroying all that belonged to them.

"Now, we can continue forward." Henrich said, getting atop his horse.

While the camp was burning, Landon spotted one of the dirt-speeders and took it. He rode on the speeders while Beth rode on the horse with Henrich. They left he campsite, which was set ablaze. Returning on the trail of the pathways, they went on about the journey toward The Haunted City.

"Do you know what else lies out here?" Beth asked.

"We'll find that out once we get far enough." Henrich replied.

<u>XI</u>

Leaving the destroyed campsite and the dead body of Wade behind and on the other side of its mighty structure, Henrich, feeling slightly relieved, traveled on horseback along with Landon and Beth. Traveling several miles from where they were, nearby the wilderness and Scavengers' site. They traveled further, on their way toward a place to gather more supplies for the long journey. While on the pathways, they came to a halt when bystanders approached them. Two of them, both were men, dressed in torn clothing. They carried wooden sticks in their hands, yelling and screaming for help.

"We need help!" One screamed.

"What is your problem?" Henrich asked.

"We just need to warn those who are traveling on this pathway to turn around. It's not safe down there."

"What is down there that makes the two of you afraid?"

"It's not safe down there." The second one said. "So, do yourselves a favor and turn around."

"Back there is only a destroyed campsite and a lot of dead bodies." Henrich said. "Nothing more and nothing else."

"Better a mountain of dead bodies and a demolished campsite than what's down there. I'll tell you that for sure."

Henrich nodded. Landon and Beth stayed quiet, seeing the bystanders walking themselves around them in a circle. They kept their hands to their side, next to their shooters. The bystanders continued to circle them, waving their sticks in their air like they were signs at a protest.

"Gentlemen, if you don't mind, we're on a journey and we do not want to be halted any longer."

Henrich went to move forward ahead and one of the bystanders decided to stand in the way of the horse. The horse shook its head, its mane flying around as Henrich stared at him, who stared back. Henrich nodded as he jumped off the horse and approached him. The bystander kept his ground, looking at the approaching Warslinger. Henrich wasn't intimidated by either one of the men and neither was he intimidated. Though, he appeared to be.

"Why won't you move out of the way?" Henrich said.

"Because you're not going down that pathway."

"Why not?"

"Because you shouldn't."

"That's not an answer, boy. Now, move out of our way or we'll make you move."

"Is that a threat? Are you threatening us right now?"

"Take it however you see it." Henrich said, getting atop the horse.

The two bystanders stood in front of them. They didn't; move, holding their sticks out in the way. Henrich nodded to them and he gazed to Landon and Beth. Landon looked at the bystanders, so did Beth. They turned their sights to Henrich, who looked back at the bystanders. The bystanders stood boldly in front of them. Their faces showed no emotion as it did previously. That confirmed to Henrich that they were playing a trick on them the entire time.

"What now." One bystander said.

"You're going to have to move us out of your way."

Henrich nodded to them, taking in their words.

"That's fine." Henrich said. "That's fine."

Henrich pulled out his shooter and fired it at the two bystanders. Killing them each with shots to the head. Their bodies fell to the ground. Henrich looked over to Landon and Beth.

"We keep moving." Henrich said, as they went pass the dead bystanders and down the pathways to continue their journey toward The Haunted City.

XII

Continuing from the bystanders they've met. They discover there to be a small village up ahead. Henrich noticed the small buildings that slightly resembled tents and hovels. They moved forward and while they came closer to the village, they could see the people that dwelled there, and they were immediately in fear of the Three. One child looked up at Henrich and ran off into the village, hiding from his sights.

"That child surely feared you." Beth said.

"I take that as a compliment." Henrich replied. "Most of these people might fear all of us. They know that we're different from them."

They decided to enter the village. Upon their entry, the inhabitants stared at them as if they are spirits to be opposed to the ones unseen. Henrich stopped as Landon and Beth seen a man approaching them. He was dressed in a mixture of sackcloth and animal skin clothing. His face was painted with red and black coloring and his hair was long, down past his shoulders, reaching his elbows. The man bowed his head before Henrich.

"It is an honor to see one of you." The man said.

"What do you mean by that?" Henrich asked.

"It doesn't take a strander or a knowledgeable man to know who you are and what you do."

The man knew Henrich to be a Warslinger of the Heptad as he looked past Henrich to Landon and Beth. He bowed to them. Showing his respect toward them as they were in allegiance with Henrich. The Warslinger looked at the village and seen its people. Young and old, men and women, ranging from all nationalities known to the Generations of Man.

"Before we came here, we ran into two men who were warning us of a city ahead." Henrich said. "What of this city they spoke of?"

"Come with men and settle yourselves down." The man said. "I can tell that you three have been through some rough times as of late. It shows within your eyes."

They listened to the man and followed him in the village. Moving

166

past the others that lived there, they nodded and waved to them. The man led them to his base of operations within the village, which was a small shack. The shack was made of bark from the trees of the wilderness. Henrich could sense a power coming from the shack. It was familiar to him.

"What is of this structure?" Henrich asked. "I can sense something here and its embedded in the wood."

"This shack was built with the wood of the wilderness that sits in the Valley of Death. I had some of my people come along with me and we took down some of the trees. Though, we had to fight out way out of the forest against those shadowic beings that lurk about. We overcame and returned here to build many of these homes for the people."

"Most of the homes are built with the same wood from the Valley of Death?"

"Yes. We could've gone into the wilderness nearby. But, whenever we made the attempt. We were harassed and sometimes ambushed by a group that called themselves the Scavengers. They gave us no other choice but to travel down toward the Valley of Death and take some of the wood from there."

Henrich looked at the man and gazed around the village once again. Landon only stared at the man, taking in the words he spoke to them. Beth stood there, silent, but listening closely. Her ears were wide open to the conversation.

"Maybe the Scavengers are the reason why I can feel your pains." The man said. "Even your clothing bears the mark of their touch."

"You won't have to worry about them anymore." Henrich said. "They've been taken care of. All of them."

"Is that correct that I hear." The man said. "You killed them all. Every Scavenger that there is? They're all gone now?"

Henrich nodded.

"That is the case." Henrich said. "We took care of them before coming down the pathways and finding your village. We killed their leader and burned down their campsite. Leaving nothing of theirs to remain standing."

The man nodded and clapped his hands. He was happy to hear

the news of the Scavengers' destructive end. He rallied up his people, telling them of the news of the Scavengers. The people of the village turned to Henrich, Landon, and Beth and began cheering them. Thanking them for saving them from any more harm. They only nodded and held their hands up to the cheering. The man stood there, smiling as he watched his people be happy and cheer.

"Please, come with me. For I know you will stay for the night as the sun is already showing signs of its setting phase."

Henrich looked up at the sky and saw that the sun was showing signs of setting. Unusual to him, knowing that only several hours have passed since the previous night. Henrich agreed to stay at the village for the night. The man led them to a empty shack, where Henrich, Landon, and Beth will stay for the night. Inside the shack were several cots and a table for eating. Henrich looked at the place and nodded. He felt comfortable within the shack.

"How will this do for you, Warslinger?" The man asked.

"It will do just fine for me. We have to thank you for this."

"There is no need. You have done enough for us in eliminating our enemy of the land. This is the best that we can do for your service."

The man left them inside the shack as they prepared themselves for the night.

As the sun set and the moon arose, the inhabitants of the village partied for the night and the party was unlike those of the Scavengers. The village's party was one of praising and thanking. They continued to thank the Three for killing the Scavengers and sparring them anymore trouble ahead. The people danced with each other and they were happy. Landon and Beth watched them dance with smiles on their faces. Signs of joy.

"They seem like much better people, don't you think?" Landon said.

"They appear to be." Beth said. "I haven't seen any problems with them as all since we've been here."

As the party was going on, Henrich walked with the man

throughout the village. Speaking with one another concerning the Scavengers, their leader Wade, and other events that prelude their current conversation. The man spoke of historical events that Henrich knew of, but didn't know that had traveled across the Worlds, hitting the ears of all who would listen. The history that contained information of the Warslingers and their legendary activities.

"I take it that you haven't come across your brethren yet?" The man asked.

"I haven't seen any of them in ages." Henrich replied. "I can only wonder when we will cross paths again.

"When you all do, you will know why you've been brought back together again. In time, it will all come to you as it did to those who came before you. It is something that happens in the Worlds. The universe itself binds these events together and most of the time, repeats itself. Many of the generations of Man believe it all to be a fairy tale of sorts. Though, I have concluded it all exists. All that we know is true."

"May I ask, where did you encounter this historical information?"

'I spoke with someone who lived ages ago and traveled the Worlds for thousands of years. The one who taught me how to survive out here in this land. He taught me how to build these shacks and homes for the people, he taught me wisdom and how to apply it and he taught me of the times before and the times to come."

"The times to come?"

"Yes. He told me some small details concerning the future the Worlds have ahead of them."

"So, what is of their future?"

The man smiled, and he placed his hand on Henrich's shoulder. He looked at Henrich, knowing him to be seeking answer and yet, he knew that the answers were already on their way to him. Just not at the precise moment. The man nodded to Henrich, while looking around the village, seeing the people continuing to dance and praise.

"This is not the time for you to know, Warslinger. Though, that time is not too far from you. It is coming closer than you think."

"Sorry to ask of this. But, I never got your name."

"My name is Necuametl. Many only call me sir, master, friend, brother, or father."

"Your name sounds familiar to my ears. Is it your birth name?"

"It was. Yet, eons of time have erased it from the minds and records of Man. When I became the leader of this village, the people only referred to me as the titles I have previously told you."

Necuametl looked up at the moon, seeing its bright feature above them in the sky. Henrich also looked up toward the moon. Necuametl smiled.

"Something isn't it. How that large object was placed there to have its ruling during the darkness and how the sun is in place when we are in the morning of the light."

Henrich nodded. Acknowledging the lights of the orbit.

"It is something to behold. In a way of matters."

"Why are you out here, Warslinger? Where are you heading?"

"I am going to The Haunted City?"

"The Haunted City? Why would you choose to do that?"

"I need answers."

"What sort of answers are you seeking from the mystical place?"

"Answers that contain details on eternal life and all of existence."

"You sure you're prepared for it when you enter into the City? Are you prepared to face those that lurk around the Kingdom of the Gate and who has dominion over the place within the Outer-World?"

"I have no other choice but to head there and find the answers that I surely seek."

Necuametl nodded. He understood Henrich's drive and ambition to reach the City. He once had the same energy and vigor as Henrich does. Though, that was a very long time ago. Henrich could tell that Necuametl was somewhat ageless. Maybe immortal. But, who could know by his physical appearance. As that of a man in his middle ages of life.

"Time for me to sleep." Necuametl said. "It was a pleasure to speak words with you, Warslinger of the Heptad."

"Same here, sir." Henrich said. "It was truly an honor to speak with one who knows much about the Worlds."

"I've traveled much. Therefore, I know much."

They shook hands and walked separate ways within the village. The partying had settled down and everyone entered their homes and shacks to sleep for the night. During the night in the late hours, Henrich arose from the bed, seeing both Landon and Beth sleeping. He walked outside of the shack and sat down in one of the chairs that stood out by the shack on the side. Henrich sat down. Outside by himself as he thought about all that he has been through on his journey toward the City. He remembered the words of Necuametl and what he had told him. Henrich kept believing in his mission and he had faith to back him up.

Henrich closed his eyes and as they closed a scream could be heard not far from the village. Henrich's eyes opened, hearing the scream. He stood up from the chair and walked out of the village, following the screaming. Henrich came to the end of the village, where a small field was located. In the field, Henrich could see three men of the village standing around a pillar of fire. The screams were coming from the pillar. Henrich was hid behind a tree and looked closer, seeing a man, being burned alive on the pillar. He screamed for his life, but his throat was damage to lower his voice. The three men of the village however were chopping off parts of his body that were being burnt up and they began to eat them.

"I'll be damn." Henrich said to himself.

Henrich now knows that the people of the village are in fact cannibals. Henrich makes a run for it, returning to the shack to awaken Landon and Beth. One of the men turned around and spotted Henrich running. Necuametl yelled as he and the other two ran after him. Henrich, returning to the shack finds himself surrounded by the people of the village and standing by them was Necuametl. Henrich looked and saw the door of the shack being kicked open and out of the shack bolted Landon and Beth, who were being held by two of the men. Henrich stared at Necuametl, shaking his head.

"What in the hell is going on?" Henrich said. "Why are you burning up and eating people of your own village?"

"Warslinger, we need what we need. There isn't much meat to be found out here in this land. So, what I have done is set up a lottery of sorts. Whoever's name is chosen from the barrel will be tied down to the pillar and they will be burnt. As they're being burnt, we will cut off the limbs of their body and eat them. For we need to eat if we seek to survive."

Henrich looked around at the people. He was in shock and he was angry. Staying in a place he thought could've been comfortable and peaceful turned into a place of hell and evil. Landon and Beth stared at Henrich, who looked toward them. Nothing he could say to them due to himself being in a small form of shock. Necuametl looked at Henrich and nodded his head to him.

"You're angry and I understand why. If I were to tell you of this when you arrived, you would've killed us all and I couldn't allow that action to be taken. Besides, you killed all the Scavengers. Even though they were our enemies, you killed them, therefore, making us starve to death. Until now."

"What are you planning to do with us?"

"Yeah." Landon said. "You could at least give us a hint as to what you're about to do with us."

"We're going to place the three of you onto the pillar of fire. You're outsiders and outsiders have a different flavor to them as opposed to those who live out here. Trust me, my people have told me a lot about how they taste."

Necuametl signaled to the men, who held Landon and Beth to take them to the pillar of fire. More of the men grabbed a hold of the Warslinger and brought him along. Necuametl walked with Henrich. His countenance didn't change, and he was still the same man who Henrich spoke to hours earlier during the partying and praising.

"All of your praise for us, it was for show? A mockery?"

"No. It was sincere. We were truly thanking you for what you did to the Scavengers. We needed them gone. Even though, we would've eaten them all into extinction. But, due to your actions, we no longer have that luxury to accomplish. Therefore, we must eat your flesh."

"There's no need for all of this." Henrich said. "Listen to me and know there is no need for this to happen."

"There is a reason for why we must do this, Warslinger. We must eat if we want to survive and eat we shall do."

Walking through the trees as they see the pillar standing before them, still ablaze from the recent kill, whose body was decimated by the people pf the village as they ran for it, pulling the body apart and eating anything they could get their hands on. The people ate as if they haven't eaten in days. Henrich could tell by the way they were munching own on the meat of the person. Necuametl stood by and watched as the people ate one of their own. It didn't bother him. For as he said, they must eat if they want to survive.

"I hope you're ready for this, Warslinger. You're all next in line to burn."

<u>**XIII**</u>

They stood out in front of the pillar of fire. Which smoked continually as they increased the flames by tossing in more of the wood from the trees. The same trees that came from the Valley of Death. Henrich looked and could hear screeching coming from the fire. The screeches were those of the shadowic entities that were trapped within the wood. Henrich thought to himself of the wood and of the people. Only a spirit of their kind would transform people to eat one another. The Warslinger has come across those kinds of spirits in his past. Necuametl kept his eyes on the three, seeing them struggling to get free from the hands of the people of the village.

"Tell me, how long has this been going for? How many days or weeks or months or years?"

"This has been going on since the inception of our village. After we built the homes and shacks, we suddenly had the urge to eat the flesh of other generations of Man. It consumed us like a fire consumes the wood. It burned in our bodies to taste the flesh of another human being and we listed after it like animals."

"You people are all sick!" Beth said. "Just sick."

"Maybe we are, madam. But, we must eat to survive."

"Enough of that." Henrich said. "You have a decision to make right now."

"And what is this decision that I must make?"

"Either you can set us free and let us be on our way or you can all meet your ends by my hands and theirs."

"So, you're threatening to kill us all? Is that what I'm getting from you, Warslinger of the Heptad? You're saying you're going to kill us if we don't let the three of you live. Then, if we let you go, where will we get our food for the days ahead?!"

"I do not know. But, I am sure that you'll stumble across some dead bodies along your searches and maybe you'll see an animal around here that you can feast on instead of feasting on other humans."

"I will not take in hand your decisions of choice, Warslinger. For this day, one of you will first be burned and after that the rest will follow. Enjoy your final moments, Warslinger of the Heptad because it is your last."

"We'll see about that." Henrich said.

Necuametl gathered the people of the village together and they surrounded the Three as they inched closer toward the pillar of fire. The pillar burned with black smoke and the wood that was burning, within the smoke and fire could been seen the shadowic entities levitating into the sky, they were being burnt alive themselves and could feel the heat. Necuametl pointed toward them and pointed to the pillar of fire. The people of the village cheered on the event.

"This is your final day! Say your goodbyes to one another as you each will become food for our stomachs."

Necuametl's hand gestured toward Landon, who the men brought forward.

"Enough of this!" Henrich said.

Henrich jerked himself from the other men, kicking them and punching them. He pulled out his shooters and blasted them each in their heads, killing them. Henrich turned to Beth and shot the shooter behind her, killing him as well. The people of the village took off and ran, leaving only a few of them remaining with Necuametl. Landon was set free and he ran toward Henrich and Beth stood by him. Each of them with their shooters in hand, facing down Necuametl and those who remained with him.

"What will you do now, Warslinger of the Heptad? Kill us or be killed?"

"I'll take your second choice of words." Henrich said. "Sorry about what I am about to do. But, you caused it to happen on your own."

"Take the shot. End my life and those of my own."

Henrich nodded and fired the shooter. The bullet went through the air, but stopped in midair by Necuametl, who held the bullet by a form a levitation. Henrich slowly lowered his shooter, seeing him holding the bullet.

"You possess such power." Henrich said. "How?"

"I told you earlier, I have traveled much. Therefore, I know much."

Necuametl waved the bullet back to Henrich, who moved out of the bullet's path. The bullet flew and ended up inside of a tree. Henrich looked and shot more shots toward him, who caught each of them and held them in the air. Henrich shook his head. Staring up at Necuametl and seeing the twirling, levitating bullets above him.

"This can't be happening right now."

"I'm afraid it is happening, Warslinger. Now, you will learn what it means to be one within my shoes."

Necuametl threw the bullet toward Henrich and he moved out of their way once again, but this time, Necuametl lunged toward Henrich, spearing him into the tree, holding his throat tightly. Henrich attempted to fight Necuametl's force, even if he was too powerful. Powerful enough that he had to have something on him that gave him the enhanced strength. Across the field, Landon and Beth fought against the men that remained. The men were unlike the Scavengers in terms of fighting. The men moved around like animals. They were faster than usual. Their attacks much stronger than the beating from the Scavengers.

"There's something with these people!" Landon said. "Something isn't right with them at all!"

"Maybe they're connected with something!" Beth said. "Something that has to do with this pillar of theirs!"

"You want to try and knock the thing down or something?" Landon asked.

"We could give it a shot." Beth said. "If you're in for it."

"I am."

Landon shot the shooter at one of them, Necuametl entered and dodged the bullet by jumping into the air like a panther and coming back down on the ground. Others climbed the trees and sat above them. Silent as the nocturnal creatures. They searched for them and they gazed up toward the sky and could see the men in the trees as their eyes only glowed in the darkness of the night. The men came down from the trees and lunged toward Landon and Beth. Trying to bite them on their necks. They held them off as much as they could and the Warslinger was still fighting Necuametl, who was unharmed by any punch or kick that Henrich delivered to him. Necuametl was in a way, invincible.

"What did you do to yourself to gain this strength?" Henrich asked.

"I was taught how to harness such power and yet, you've never managed to do the same thing. You and your Warslinger brothers only used the weapons that were given to you that you never thought of the possibilities of other ways to combat your enemies. Such a shame."

"Maybe it is a shame. At least I am still capable of standing up when I'm knocked down. Therefore, I have yet to give up and I will not cease myself in doing so."

"That's good to hear. That way, you will die a fighting man and a honest man. Only a few in the generations of Man can speak those words and remain a memory in the minds of Man."

Henrich kicked him and there was no harm done. Necuametl punched Henrich and knocked him to the ground. Necuametl kicked Henrich in the side, causing him to fly in the air and impact into one of the standing trees. Necuametl shook his head.

"This is a sight to see. A Warslinger being destroyed by my hands. Hands that aren't even worthy to touch your garments, let alone clean them."

Landon and Beth continued to fire at the roaming men, who ran around them. Landon approached the pillar and went to touch it. But, backed away from the pillar as it was still on fire and its heat was intense. Landon also noticed the blood and some flesh that were left lying on the pillar. The smell was terrible, and it stunk up the area in only a matter of minutes. The closer one approached the pillar, the stronger the stench became, and it was one to avoid at any cost.

"We can't get close to it!" Landon said. "It's too hot to touch and it is covered with blood."

"What else do you have in mind?" Beth asked. "Come up with something and let me know about it."

"Sure thing."

Henrich reached over to his back, raising up the blastshooter. He fired it at Necuametl, who backed up a bit from the impact. Henrich looked and noticed Necuametl's movements after the blast. He nodded.

"It's a start." Henrich said, firing another blast to Necuametl.

Henrich stood up, firing several more blasts from the blast shooter at Necuametl, he continued to back up as he was being hit by the blasts. Necuametl waved the smoke from the blasts away from his eyes and he could see Henrich running toward him and in Henrich's hands were the blast shooter in his right hand and the machete in his left hand. Henrich lunged toward Necuametl with both weapons. Shooting the peashooter and swiping the machete. Necuametl stepped back and looked at his chest, which was cut from the machete.

"I see that I've breached your strength." Henrich said.

"For the moment, you have." Necuametl said. "But, that doesn't give you the sign of a possible victory."

"No. It does not. What it gives me is a chance to prove to you that I can, and I will kill you."

Henrich continued his attacks against Necuametl while Landon and Beth had started to kill some of the men with their shooters. Aiming for their heads, they killed them as they could get a good aim. They still haven't come up with a plan of what to do with the pillar of fire, which was still burning, and the stench still covered the area. The stench had grown to where Landon had covered his face with his shirt and Beth did the same, using both her shirt and her hair. The stench had approached the Warslinger and Necuametl. Henrich covered his face and Necuametl did not. Necuametl breathed in the stench as it made him feel empowered.

"Continue with your attacks, Warslinger. Face me and see what becomes of you."

"As if I have a choice." Henrich said.

Henrich fired the blast shooter again and swiped the machete across Necuametl's body. Cutting his chest and neck. Henrich later took the blastshooter and slammed it into Necuametl's face. Necuametl dropped to one knee, where Henrich stood over him with the blastshooter pressed down on the back of his head. Necuametl only applauded Henrich for his actions.

"Very good." Necuametl said. "You have proven what you are capable of and what you must do in a situation of this sort."

"What do you mean by all of this?" Henrich said. "Why not be honest with us when we arrived here?"

"As I told you before, you would've done the same to us as you did to the Scavengers. You needed to be led in like an animal towards its food."

"I'm truly sorry for what I am about to do." Henrich said, with his finger on the blastshooter's trigger.

"I know you are, Warslinger of the Heptad." Necuametl said quietly. "I know you are."

Henrich took the shot and blew Necuametl's head off his body. The people of the village were watching, and they were in silence. Their leader is dead and Henrich stood over his body. Henrich looked at the people and shook his head. He was disgusted with them as he looked over, seeing Landon and Beth trying to take down the last man. Necuametl went to lunge at them and from behind Henrich took the shot, killing Necuametl. His body fell to the ground, blown in half. Henrich approached the pillar with the machete and started chopping it down. The pillar of fire trembled and shook until Henrich used the blastshooter and shot it. The blast caused the pillar to fall and once it hit the ground, the fire within it ceased and the stench was evaporating from the air.

Henrich faced the people of the village and stared at them. They looked at the Three and were more fearful of them than before.

Landon and Beth looked at the children that stood by and were sad for them as opposed to those who were adults that stood by. They now had no leader and were left stranded in the Land of the Survivors.

"What will you people do now that your leader is dead?" Henrich said. "How will you survive in this land now with no one to give you the way to move forward?"

Henrich stood in the middle of the village with the people surrounding him, Landon, and Beth. He pointed the blastshooter at them and they were not as afraid as before. It intrigued Henrich and he noticed that something was taking place within the people.

"I will leave you all here to handle this matter yourself." He said, walking away from the village. "For I will not be here to see your decision be made."

Henrich approached his horse, which was standing by the entrance to the village. He went atop the horse with Beth, Landon rode on the speeder and the Three left the village, leaving the people of the village to decide their fates. As they left and went back on the pathways, they could hear screams of many. Henrich didn't look back as he already knew what decision the people of the village made. From the village itself arouse a fire. The fire was great in size and it engulfed the entire village. The fire lit up the areas nearby in the night. Henrich, Landon, or Beth never looked back to see the flames. They moved on as the village was destroyed by the fire that came from the people of the village and all of them died in the fire.

<u>XIV</u>

They rode along the pathways as the sun began to rise. Traveling miles and miles from the Scavengers' campsite and the village of the cannibals. Coming to a field nearby a mountain. Further down the pathway during the day, they could see someone standing in the middle of the pathway. The horse ceased. Landon stopped the speeder. Henrich looked at the strange man, who was dressed in little armor and a lot of black leather. He carried with him a shooter of his own. Made of black metal.

"Who is that?" Beth asked.

Henrich jumped onto the ground, slowly walking towards the strander. He recognized him from somewhere before. Somewhere very, very recent according to the locations. Henrich pointed toward him with a confused look on his face. Henrich looked as if time has reversed itself while they were on the pathways.

"This can't be possible." Henrich said. "We saw you earlier."

The strange man who stood in the middle of the pathway is the real Mercenary Man. Known as Marco Desthain and he smiled at Henrich.

<u>CHAPTER FIVE</u>

THE WARSLINGER vs. THE MERCENARY

<u>I</u>

The Warslinger stared and he stood silently toward the real Mercenary Man, Marco Desthain. Desthain looked at Henrich with a smile on his face. He turned his sights toward both Landon and Beth and waved. They didn't wave back, but they were in fear. A small amount of fear. Henrich only shook his head.

"I know what you're about to say to me, Warslinger." Desthain said.

"And what am I about to say?"

"You're about to ask me am I Judas Arkdragon from the field near the Valley of Death."

"How do you know about that?" Henrich asked.

"I keep tracks of things regarding the incidents of the Worlds. I've been keeping tabs on you across every turn you've made under the direction of my master."

"Your master? He's this Tubal King that I keep hearing about."

"Yes. The Tubal King is my master and I am his servant. I live and breathe to do whatsoever he commands me to do. That's why I'm standing in your presence at this very moment, Warslinger. The Tubal King has been watching you ever since you became one of the Heptad and he's seen your successes and your failures."

"The scroll which was given to me by those vampires back in the desert lands? It's all true? There's a bounty on my head after all?"

"In a manner of speaking, there is. Again, I'm the Mercenary

Man and my job is to take bounties and complete them under the orders of The Tubal King. Which led me to you. If my master never spoke of you, I wouldn't be out here in your way this day."

Henrich didn't move, but his hands were close to his holsters. He was ready to fire at Desthain at any moment possible. Landon and Beth stood back from the two, giving them both the space that they needed. Desthain kept his smirk on his face and his hands were laid close to his holsters. They stared each other down like animals.

"Now, look, Warslinger. I understand that seeing me, the real me, right here is kind of shocking, but what Arkdragon did, it was all a test."

"Why a test? Why not it could've been you that I saw and that I shot."

"Because, The Tubal King wants to know more about your feats and your skills. He sent Arkdragon to confront you in my own image. Surely, I don't like it when someone decides to dress like me or even shift themselves into myself completely. But, it was what the master required of Arkdragon and he delivered and proved a lot about you that even you have yet to understand."

"You believe me to expect that you, this Arkdragon, and your Tubal King know more about me than I know of myself?"

"Exactly." Desthain replied quickly. "Because, after your Heptad were separated and scattered across the Worlds, each of you lost something that you once had. Now, all of you are slowly regaining that lost art and you don't even know what to do with it. Do you?"

Landon approached Henrich from the side, his eye locked on Desthain who stared at him. Desthain pointed out to Landon.

"That young fella right there." Desthain yelled. "Is he this Cody Landon guy that I keep hearing about?"

Landon looked at Desthain and stood facing him.

"That is my name." Landon said.

Desthain smiled at him.

"Tell me this, boy, do you really want to throw your entire life away?"

"How am I doing that?"

"By hanging around that man. He's a Warslinger and they get

people killed or they have people being seduced by the malevolency of the Worlds and of the Worlds not known."

"I will not go to that side of life." Landon said. "I will remain good in my days."

"You can say that now. But, when tragedy comes your way and more calamity and destruction is shown due to your actions, then you'll know if you're on the good side of things. But, I already know your future, boy. You will be utterly destroyed by what is to come in your lifetime and that event will turn you toward the malevolency, where you will become another servant in a long ass line to The Tubal King."

Landon disagreed. Shaking his head at Desthain. Desthain expected Landon to tear up for the moment, but there were no tears in Landon's eyes. There was only anger and a mission. Desthain looked at Landon and liked how he didn't cry. He nodded to him in respect.

"See, you're already on that path, son."

Henrich pushed Landon aside and faced Desthain. The two men locked eyes and they've had enough of the talking. Each of them were ready to start firing at each other and they were counting down the seconds that came before and the seconds that followed.

"I'm going to kill you." Henrich said. "Then, I'm going to reach The Haunted City and I will kill your Tubal King."

Desthain smiled back at Henrich, pointing toward him in a gesture.

"You know, I figured you would say something of that nature. Which reminds me of why I'm here this day. Randolph Henrich of the Warslingers of the Heptad, you have a choice to make this day. Either you can live and bow to The Tubal King and work in his service or you can die and go into the Outer-World as a man who never finished his mission to begin with. Make your decision."

Henrich looked at Landon and he looked at Beth. They nodded to him with a smile on their faces, seeing that he's already made his decision. Desthain awaited Henrich's answer, holding his shooter in his hand. Desthain waved the shooter around, counting down the time.

"I'm waiting for your answer." Desthain said. "Give it to me right now."

Henrich nodded and stared into Desthain's eyes from where he stood. The horse slowly backed away from the spot, causing Landon and Beth to follow. Desthain watched how they were moving away from Henrich and seen that he was only standing there, still and not moving an inch of his body. Desthain laughed and pointed his shooter toward Henrich.

"Your answer?" Desthain asked.

"My answer." Henrich said. "One of us shall live and one of us shall die."

"You expect that to be an answer to my question?"

"It is my answer."

Henrich pulled out his shooter and began firing at Desthain. Desthain ran from the area, into the field, where Henrich ran after him. Landon and Beth watched the two men enter the field and they followed as did Henrich's horse. While they ran, they could see Desthain firing back at Henrich as he continued to shoot. The two men were trying to kill one another and that was their only goal.

II

Henrich ran after Desthain as fast as his legs were able to move at the running speed. Desthain kept his pace up, while continuing to shoot at Henrich. Henrich would dodge the rounds and fire back at Desthain, who's armor had protected him from the bullets. A few feet behind them, Landon, Beth, and the Horse made their way to catch up to them as they ran through the field. The field was vast in its length and thee only thing that was seen across the field was a mountain and the mountain was astounding in its size and structure. Above the mountain were clouds of darkness and clouds of light. They emitted off a strange energy that came down to the field and the closer they were by the mountain, the more powerful the energy became.

"You won't be able to catch me, Warslinger!" Desthain yelled loudly. "Because once I vanish from this place, you won't be able to know where I'll be coming next. Either way, I will find you again. Somewhere and sometime!"

"Why wait then, when you have the opportunity right now!" Henrich replied. "Stop running and face me like a man!"

"I like your kind of speech, Warslinger of the Heptad. You sound like those bastards that came before. All talk and no show."

"I have the ability to show you what I can do, Mercenary. But, it appears to me that you refuse to see what I can do since you're running afar from me and from my shooters."

"Listen, Warslinger. Did it ever occur to your ass that I don't want to get shot? Maybe I don't want to die this day or any other day."

"You've fired back at me!"

"True. Very true." Desthain said.

Desthain continued firing at Henrich, who kept firing back as they both ran through the field, stepping over the tall growing green grass. Some of the grass in the field were dead or dying as their color was fading away. Mostly due to the mountain ahead of them and the energy that comes from it. Henrich pulled out his second shooter and fired it toward Desthain. Desthain looked back, seeing Henrich with two shooters.

"That's called cheating you know!" Desthain yelled. "But, I like your style, Warslinger!"

Desthain smirked and continued firing himself. Landon and Beth kept up with them, watching them shoot their shooters at each other. They didn't want to interfere in the shootout between the Warslinger and the Mercenary. Although, they wondered how much running they could keep up out in a vast field.

"How do they do that?"

"They're both skilled at what they do." Beth said. "Otherwise, one of them would be dead already."

"They can't continue running like this for the entire day. They'll tire out."

"Leaving only for one of them to take the shot and end all of this."

Beth stopped as did Landon, both watching Henrich and Desthain from afar off. They looked at one another as the Horse galloped from behind them. Beth shook her head, rubbing her hair back from her face as the wind began to pick up. Landon thought to himself within his mind. There was something they could do to assist Henrich, but what they could do was uncertain within their own selves. Landon turned to Beth and she looked at him. Both with questions concerning their current situation and yet, neither one of them had an answer to speak to the other.

"What do we do?" Landon asked. "What can we do?"

"There must be a way to stop Desthain from running."

"How do we stop him from running? I'm not getting all the corners here."

"There has to be something lying around out here that could stop him for a moment. Something that will temporary cease him from running away even further out."

Landon looked ahead to the mountain, seeing the clouds above it and seeing the lightning flashing within them. He pointed to the mountain, seeing Desthain running towards it as the shooter shots continued to echo throughout the field. Low rumbles of thunder roamed across the sky. Landon kept his finger pointed to the mountain, Beth looked at him, then gazed toward the mountain.

"Appears Desthain is heading for that mountain."

"Why would he go there?"

"He probably has some stuff there that he intends on using against Henrich and us."

Beth looked at Henrich. She smiled, and he just stood there. Unsure of what to say as he didn't know why Beth was smiling. He shook his head at her confusingly and waved his arms out.

"Why are you smiling?" Landon asked. "Is there something funny about all of this that I should be aware of?"

"No, but I have an idea." Beth said. "Come on."

They ran after Henrich and Desthain as the thunder grew louder in sound and the lightning started to increase in its surroundings. The field wasn't as safe as it was before as the lightning has caused some parts of the field to set themselves on fire. Now, they all were running in a field that was burning. Burning slowly, as the fires themselves spread out quickly.

III

The shooting continued with Landon and Beth following them. The lightning increased in its appearances and in its strikes as the field slowly became a blazing field of fire. The thunder rumbled in the sky, louder than it previously roared before. The clouds that sat atop the mountain have overtaken the field and the mountain. Something taking place between the Warslinger and the Mercenary, other things were being handled according to both of their deeds. While he chased down the Mercenary Man, Henrich would occasionally look up to the sky, seeing the lightning and hearing the thundering that was going on around him. He looked back behind him, seeing Landon, Beth, and his horse behind him as well as the growing fire of the field.

"If I don't take you down, Desthain, the flames of this field will do so!" Henrich said. "They are growing quicker than I would imagine a flame to grow out in a place like this!"

"I wouldn't be worrying about the fire, Warslinger!" Desthain yelled. "I would be concerned with surviving against me in a shootout. Remember, one of us will die this day and one of us will live. I believe that I will have the second option!"

"Only if your Tubal King finds a way to help you out here! Though, I don't that he, himself would show up to face me. He already knows of his fate when I have it in my hands!"

"You're a complete and utter fool to believe that The Tubal King is in fear of you! you're only a man and he is something much more!"

"I've heard that before!"

Desthain made a turn, and in front of him stood several sets of trees and the lightning bolts were striking the trees, setting them ablaze, but the trees entirety would not burn. The trees stood tall themselves, taking the strikes of the lightning. Only burnt branches fell from the trees. Desthain ducked from the falling branches and

Henrich done the same. Landon and Beth watched as the tree limbs were burning.

"What is this plan of yours, Beth?" Landon asked. "Because I'm wondering how it will works concerning where we're standing right now."

"I have it in the works, Cody." Beth said. "Don't worry yourself about it. I have it all under control."

"We'll see about all of that."

They continued to follow Henrich and Desthain. Running toward the mountain, Desthain looked back, dodging another bullet from Henrich's shooters. Desthain spotted Landon and Beth not too far behind them. He smirked and closed his eyes while running, mumbling something to himself.

"I need assistance." Desthain said. "Send them to assist me, please."

From around Landon and Beth, the ground started to quake, ceasing them from running forward. They looked around themselves and the surroundings, seeing the dirt fly up in the air and from the ground arose six being wearing black cloaks and hoods. Their skin was pale, and they appeared to be hungry. Henrich turned his head around and gazed out to the field and could see the hooded figures standing in the field, in a circle. Within the circle, Henrich could see the hooded figures all surrounding both Landon and Beth.

"Again." Henrich said.

"How are they out here, Desthain?!" Henrich yelled.

"My master sent them to help me!" Desthain said. "Not too worry, you are my only true goal now. Your allies will be just fine being food to The Tubal King's vrylolakas."

The vrylolakas snarled at Landon and Beth. They stood together aside Henrich's horse, surrounded by the hooded vampires. They could see the fire in the field was increasing and there was no way out of the circle for them to make an escape. Their rotten teeth were shown to them. Beth looked at them, remembering information from Earth. She continued to stare and knew they were vampires.

"Wait, these are real vampires." She said. "I didn't know they existed."

"So, they don't have these things on your World, do they?" Landon asked. "Because if they don't, I'm moving over there when I find a portal."

"People dress up as them. But, not in the manner as these."

The vrylolakas screeched their voices out toward them, causing them to cover their ears from the siren-like sound of their screams. The vampires moved around them, they pulled out their shooters and stared to take shots at them. One of the vampires ran up toward Landon in the circle, Landon seen the vampire coming and shot the vampire in the face as its body fell to the field. The vampires tried to latch onto them, but their strategy of alignment was too smart for the vampires to keep up with, even at vampire speed. They looked at each other after taking more shots toward the vampires.

"We're pretty good at this." Landon said.

"For the moment."

Henrich used the blastshooter, blowing the heads off of the vampires. The vampires didn't hesitate to stand by and watched. Each of them lunged out toward Landon and Beth. Henrich's horse stomped some of them into the ground to where their bones were shattering from the weight of the horse and the strength of the ground.

Henrich paused for a moment and looked back to Landon and Beth. He stood, seeing Desthain running for the mountain and watched Landon and Beth fight the vampires with their weapons. He seen how they were studying his own move set in a way. Henrich pulled out the blastshooter from his back and fired it outward, the round from the blastshooter traveled across the field, leading to a hit in the back of one vampire. The vampire fell and turned into ashes. Landon and Beth witnessed it and looked up, seeing Henrich standing afar off from them.

"Take them out!" Henrich yelled.

"Yes sir!" Landon replied, shooting the vampires.

They continued killing the vampires one by one. Afterwards, the horse stomped onto one of the vampires, leading to Beth to shoot it in the head. Only two vampires remained for them to kill off. The vampires weren't afraid of them and didn't bother to count the dead ones that laid around them on the field. The flames increased on the field to where Landon and Beth could feel its intense heat coming near them. One of the vampires went first at Landon, but was unable to grab him by his shoulders as Beth shot the vampire first. Landon raised his leg and kicked the vampire on the ground and shot him in his head. They stared their sights on the last vampire. They smiled as Landon blew the head completely off the last vampire, with only scraps of its brain and other remains laying on the ground.

"That's all of them." Beth said. "What's next?"

Landon turned, seeing the horse running to Henrich as the fire of the field started to grow and it headed right where they were standing. Beth noticed the flames and she started backing away. Landon could see the flames were already on their trail, growing fast and consuming all the field.

"We have to go!" Landon said, seeing the flames coming.

They ran from the sight as the fire consumed the remains of the vampires to where only ashes laid. Henrich stood and seen Landon and Beth coming his way, both were smiling, looking out to Henrich. Henrich turned back and could see Desthain near the foot of the mountain. He nodded.

"You're not that far from me, Mercenary." Henrich said.

Desthain stopped to catch his breath from the running. The running had somewhat made him slow and the heat of the flames were not helping him in any sort of way. He understood that and kept going. While he made his short stop, Desthain wiped his forehead of the sweat and his looked out behind him. Seeing Henrich with Landon, Beth, and the horse. Desthain laughed and raised his hands up to where they could see him. He waved them in the air, getting their attention.

"Did you believe the vrylolakas were all he had to offer me?! There's something else that I was given to cease you from stopping me!"

Henrich, Landon, and Beth stood still listening to Desthain's words and from behind them came a loud nose. They turned to see a choiros. Henrich shook his head as did Landon.

"Not another one of these damn things." Henrich said.

The mutated pig screeched at them as it ran toward them with its large tusks. They fired at it with their shooters, leaving Desthain only to smile at the sight of it as he continued moving forward to the mountain. Henrich kept firing and raised the blastshooter, shooting the rounds toward the mutated pig. The blastshooter blew off one of the pig's tusks, causing the estranged creature to stumble for a moment. Henrich gazed back, seeing Desthain at the mountain.

"He's at the mountain." Henrich said. 'I will go after him."

"What about us? What are we supposed to do?"

Henrich pointed to the choiros, which regained its movement. It shook its head as blood poured out from the broken tusk and blood covered its face and the fur of its body. The smell of the creature increased due to the amount of blood that was coming from the broken tusk. Henrich nodded to Landon and Beth.

"Finish that unclean creature off."

Henrich took off, leaving them to finish off the choiros. They fired several more shots toward the creature as it screeched in pain. The mutated pig ran toward them with force. They moved out of its way and continued firing at the creature from the ground.

"It's not working!" Landon yelled.

"Go for its eyes!" Beth said. "We can blind it."

They aimed for the eyes and took the shots. Landon's shot missed, but hit the creature in its side and Beth's shot went through he pig's right eye. The pig stopped running and tumbled itself over onto the ground, covering it in its blood and fur. The pig kicked around a bit, trying to stand back up. From behind Landon and Beth came Henrich's horse, which stomped the pig until the pig was dead. The horse did not hesitate to stop as it ran toward the mountain. Landon and Beth looked at each other, wondering if the horse knows something that the two of them aren't aware of.

Henrich continued to chase down Desthain, who has already climbing the mountain. Henrich shook his head, seeing the

Mercenary Man climbing up the mountain. Henrich climbed the mountain himself with Landon and Beth following them. They stopped and gazed to the mountain, which was unlike the field, silent. There wasn't any noise coming from the mountain. The only noise that could be heard was of the thunder and the flames behind them around the field. The clouds still covered the mountain, but there was no thunder roaring from above the mountain. Beth looked to the top of the mountain, staring at the dark clouds. Some parts of the clouds were white, and others were a dark gray. But within the middle was a dark blue and black.

"What do you think is up there?" Beth asked.

"We can only know if we reach the top." Landon said. "Probably where they're headed anyway."

"What of the horse? How will it reach to the top?"

Landon looked at the horse.

"Trust me, there's something with this horse that is not as natural as many people would believe."

"What do you mean by that? I don't see anything unusual with the horse."

"You haven't been around it or Henrich long enough. I know, it will take some time for you to see what this horse is truly capable of. Should've been enough when it stomped those vrylolakas and that choiros back there."

"I'll figure it out somehow." She said, walking to the mountain.

Landon nodded.

"I'm positive you will figure it out. Not sure how though."

IV

Climbing the mountain, both Henrich and Desthain, they come to the realization that something sits atop the mountain. Desthain laughed as he climbed the mountain, gazing down to the field, which was consumed by the fire. The thunder continued to roar, lightning flashed throughout the sky. Henrich followed up the mountain. Far below them were Landon and Beth, who climbed the mountain.

Slower than both Henrich and Desthain, but they were sure of themselves to reach the mountain just as the Warslinger and the Mercenary were sure to reach the top.

"We can make it up there." Landon said. "We have no choice but to."

"Basically, we shouldn't look down." Beth said.

"Now, why would you do that anyway. Unless you wanted to see how far a fall that would be. I would suggest that you keep your eyes upward and focus on climbing this rock."

Beth gazed down, seeing that Henrich's horse was gone. Landon looked at her as if she was crazy. He shook his head, seeing her looking down at the field.

"Are you going to jump or what?" Landon said.

"I'm not going to jump, alright. I just wanted to see if the horse was still down there."

"Tell me, then. Is the horse down there or not?"

"It's not down there."

"Then, let's make our way to the top. No telling what the two of them will do to each other once they reach it."

Several more feet to climb and Desthain could see Henrich below him on the mountain. He laughed to himself, pulling out his shooter and firing it at Henrich. Henrich hid beneath a nearby cliff to avoid the shots from Desthain's shooter, which was continually firing. Henrich decided to fire back, hitting the tocks on the side of Desthain.

"Good one, Warslinger!" Desthain yelled. "Good one indeed!"

Desthain climbed and reached the top of the mountain. Henrich followed and after climbing a few feet himself, he also reached the top. Henrich stopped and seen Desthain standing in front him. They were surrounded and covered underneath the clouds, seeing only a form of light and darkness. Sitting atop the mountain was a mirror, made of crystal. The mirror glittered from the light emitting from the clouds around it.

"You don't know what this is do you?" Desthain gestured. "This is far beyond your means, Warslinger of the Heptad and you know it to be the truth."

Henrich pointed at the mirror with his shooter, monitoring Desthain's movements as he looked at the crystal structure that stood with marble sides.

"What mirror is that?"

"One for only the few of Man to see. Not everyone in existence is capable of seeing what the mirror can show."

"What can this mirror show to those who approach it?"

"It can show the past, the present, and the future. Along with alternate realities and other Worlds that are not known to the generations of Man."

"How do you know about all of this, Mercenary Man? Who taught you these ways of knowledge and handed them to you to keep? Who gave you the time to learn all these things?"

"The Tubal King taught me, Warslinger. He taught me of the mirror, he taught me of the knowledge of the Worlds, and he taught me how to use this mirror to see not only my past, present, and future. But, his own timeline as well. He wanted to know about the alternate realities and Worlds that are not known. So, with this mirror, he was able to know about them and through it, he learned much. The Tubal King possesses so much knowledge that he passed some of it down to his servants. Myself included as I know a lot about the mirror and of the times to come."

"How am I to believe the words you are speaking to me?"

"Because I know them to be the truth, as you only know them to be lies because you haven't seen everything that you're meant to see. There are times ahead for you, Warslinger, where you will come across places and people who are not like those of your past."

The Warslinger stared deeply at the mirror. His shooter still raised up in his hand, pointed at Desthain. Desthain took his shooter and aimed it directly at Henrich, who noticed Desthain's movements. The two had themselves at odds. Both with their shooters pointed toward the other. They stood across from each other several feet away. The wind blew across them as the clouds rotated above them while the light fought its way to escape from the darkness in the sky. Landon and Beth reached the top and stood still, seeing the two aiming their shooters at each other.

"We should help him." Landon said.

Beth stopped him by grabbing his arm. He looked at Beth and she nodded to Henrich. Landon looked forward, seeing the mirror.

"Let Henrich deal with this himself. He knows what he's doing."

Desthain's smile grew bigger on his face and on Henrich's face was no emotion. His eyes were locked on Desthain's own eyes. Their shooters didn't flinch in their hands and they were still as the mountain itself. Desthain had to laugh, seeing himself and Henrich standing atop the mountain next to a crystal mirror. It was something he had yet to behold the sight. But, seeing the Warslinger standing in front of him, Desthain felt that he truly lived up to his name of being the Mercenary Man.

"When are you going to take the shot, Warslinger?! Take it now!"

"I will take the shot when I'm ready." Henrich said. "The time is almost here, Mercenary Man."

"I'm sure it is. Because, after I kill you and your partners and your damn horse, I will take your carcass to The Tubal King, who will rejoice at your death and then you will know that The Tubal King is one of his word and the King of the Worlds."

"How about I tell you of another alternative. I will kill you. Then, I will see what this mirror must show me. Then, I will travel across the Worlds to enter the Outer-World. Once I enter and approach the Kingdom of the Gate, I will slay your Tubal King and enter The Haunted City, where I will get the answers that I seek."

Desthain nodded and shook his head to Henrich. Taking in his words of the decision. Desthain waved his shooter around, though it's still aimed toward Henrich's chest.

"May the best man live."

"As I will." Henrich replied. "Take the shot, Desthain."

Both men pull the triggers of their shooters and shots fired across the mountaintop. The sound echoed through the clouds, blending in with the thunder from above. Landon and Beth could only watch from a distance as they couldn't even tell who was shot as both men were standing still, their shooters were aimed at one another.

<u>V</u>

The Warslinger and the Mercenary stood with their eyes locked onto one another. Landon and Beth looked on, seeing the two men standing still with their shooters drawn onto each other. Neither one of them made any movements after firing the shots at each other. Desthain smiled and from his chest, blood slowly began to drip. He looked down at his chest, seeing that the round from Henrich's Warslinger shooter went straight through his armor, pierced his chest and went through his heart.

"Wow." Desthain said, as he slowly fell to his knees on the mountain.

Henrich placed his shooters in their holsters as he walked toward the downed Desthain. He kneeled low to his face and stared at him. Desthain continued to laugh as he was in pain. A pain that was increasing growing in his chest as more blood began to come from the bullet wound. Desthain couldn't take the pain internally, but he tried to keep himself up. Although, his body thought it best for him to lie down on the ground, He stayed on his knees, holding his chest.

"You never cease to amaze those, Warslinger. I didn't know you had it in you to do such a task. I should've known because of the actions you've done in your past. Now, those things are worth seeing again, aren't they? You can be honest with me since I'm about to pass over into Outer-World."

"It was between either you or me and it seems that I came out the victor."

"For the moment, maybe. But, you should look ahead and see what your future will bring to you."

"Through using the mirror."

"By using the mirror. Yeah. Go ahead and do it. See what is in store for you and those who follow you in your footsteps."

Desthain fell to the ground, losing his breath and feeling the cold of the mountaintop. Henrich walked over his dying body to the mirror. He faced it, only seeing his own reflection. He looked back at Desthain.

"How does this work, Mercenary Man?"

"You speak the word."

'Tell me the word."

"Why should I? You already know the word."

Henrich looked and thought for a second. A word, what could be the word, Henrich thought. He searched through his mind for the word and nothing was coming through for him. He approached Desthain, who was already near-death.

"What is the word?!"

"You… already… know…it." Desthain said, losing his consciousness.

Henrich watched as Desthain died atop the mountain from the shooter. Henrich looked around, searching for anything that might have the word Desthain was speaking to him about.

Finding nothing, Henrich becomes enraged. Not only at the deceased Desthain, but himself as well.

"Damn it!" Henrich said.

Landon and Beth approached the angry Henrich. He looked at them, shaking his head and gazing to the mirror. Landon looked at the mirror and looked at Henrich. He looked at them again and took another look at the two. His mind was racing, but at a decent pace than Henrich's mind. Beth didn't understand what Desthain meant by a word, though, she was capable of tagging along with them to figure out the word that was needed to start up the mirror.

"What about Heptad, sir?"

Henrich spoke the word to the mirror and the mirror was still and silent. That word didn't work. They took the time to think again. Landon thought for a second, searching his mind for words that he's heard since tagging along with Henrich. Beth even searched her mind for words that she could remember in her head. She approached Henrich with a word on the edge of her tongue.

"What about Warslinger." Landon said. "Or you could try Tubal King or something like that."

"What do you have?" Henrich asked Beth.

"Why don't you try, *genesis*." She said. "Try genesis."

Henrich nodded and stepped forward to the mirror. He stood completely still and looked directly into the mirror. He took a breath and he spoke the word, "Genesis" and from the mountain arose a light. The light flew around them several times before entering the mirror itself. The mirror began glowing a bluish purple and a wormhole appeared within the mirror. They gazed at the mirror, seeing its light shining upon them.

"What the hell is going on?" Landon wondered.

"It worked." Henrich said. "Beth, it worked."

"The word was just there for a second." She said. "I guess I picked the right one."

From the mirror arose a voice. A voice with the sound of a woman in a mature age. The voice echoed over the mountain and it was unheard of in their ears as neither of them have heard a voice like the one of the mirror. The mirror started groaning as it became brighter than it was before. They used their arms to block the blinding light from their eyes.

"Speak your name." The mirror commanded.

"Randolph Henrich. Warslinger of the Heptad."

"Randolph Henrich of the Warslinger of the Heptad, what do you seek to know on this day?"

"I seek to know the future and my place in finding The Haunted City."

"Is that all you seek from me?"

"That is all that I seek from you."

"Very well, Randolph Henrich of the Warslingers of the Heptad. What you seek, you may not see. For what you will see is what you will find."

Henrich nodded.

"Show me the visions of the future, mirror."

"As you command."

The mirror busted open and through it brought about images which surrounded Henrich, Landon, and Beth. The three of them could see the images and they were sights of the future to come. They looked at them as they came across their eyes. One image that appeared first was of a town. The town was in the middle of nowhere and standing on the field were people.

An amount of people that was unseen in the location. The people were dressed in all black and standing in front of them was a man wearing both black and white garments. Henrich didn't know who they were, but he knew they were a part of his future toward The Haunted City. In the image, the man standing before the people spoke and they could hear his words.

"From this day forward, those who oppose us will learn why those who disobey later disappear from The Secret World!"

The image later showed the leader of the people, beheading others with an axe and the people stoning others against a stone wall. The leader stood out in front of his people, who praised him as if he was their savior in the Worlds. The image faded away as another image appeared before them. This image was of a city. The city was a large metropolitan city. Within the city walked around people, but they were enhanced with robotics arms, legs, chests, and heads. The city was Mega City and the people who lived there were in fact transhumanists. Further into the image appeared a woman. Henrich knew her.

"Cara?" He said. Seeing her walking on the sidewalk of Mega City as large autonomous vehicles passed by down the streets.

"You know of her?" Beth asked.

"I met her some time back." He said. "Before I met Cody. I met her. She said she was going to Mega City. I wondered if she was on good terms."

"Well, now you know."

The image of Mega City faded out and the third image appeared before them. Showing them the lands of the Eastern World. Walking about on the land that appeared to be made of stone and wood, they could see a pair of people crouched down together. The people were suffering, suffering of their current condition.

The image shifted to two individuals, a young woman and a young man. Both were dressed in unusual attire. Different from those that Henrich is familiar with. They carried with them katanas and other blades while they approached several men who were dressed up as samurais and slaughtered them where they stood.

"What happened there?" Landon asked.

"It hasn't happened yet, boy." Henrich said. "But, it will. Soon."

The image of the assassins faded and came the fourth image. This image showed an old castle and Henrich knew that castle. He's been there in the past. He walked forward near the image, getting a closer look. He shook his head, seeing the castle again and in the image, he could see an army standing outside of the castle being led by a man, who was known to be close with a certain Warslinger in the past, who was led by a woman dressed in a black and red dress. The woman wore a crown on her head as the army embraced her and worshipped her.

"She couldn't have." Henrich said. "Not her."

"What's wrong?" Beth asked. "Do you know her?"

"I do. I see what she's done to my brother's castle."

In the image, standing next to the woman, who took a seat is another man. Only, this man is dressed in the exactly same attire as Henrich. Equipped with the trench coat and hat. Henrich knew the man, because he was a Warslinger of the Heptad. Henrich balled up his fist and he was in anger once again.

"How could he betray us like this!" Henrich said. "How could he do such a thing to his brethren? Those who were there by his side! Who protected him against all the obstacles that we came across and this is what he does to us!"

The image shifted again, showing Warslinger Knight Arthur Pendragon speaking with a man only known as The One from Albion. They were speaking about a certain area as they each pointed toward the direction of the land they stood on. Henrich noticed the location and knew it by heart. They were pointing toward the west.

"He's still alive." Henrich said. "I knew he could survive the attack."

"Who is he, sir?" Landon asked. "The older man?"

"He is one of a trustworthy ally." Henrich said. "Good to know that he still lives.

The image disappeared, and the fifth image appeared, showing a pair of witches and warlocks sitting together and the image shifted to where the witches were altering all of reality and they were destroying all the Worlds. Henrich knew that the witches were powerful, but they couldn't contain that much power to alter the Worlds. The witches were laughing amongst each other. In the image appeared a werewolf, which lunged out onto people in a valley, killing them with its claws and gnawing on them with its fangs. The image shifted to a sight where a witch sat at a table, in her hand she held a tarot card. On the card were the Warslingers. She took the card and tossed it into a fireplace.

"I didn't know that witches and warlocks truly existed." Beth said. "I had some belief that they did exist among people, but I've never seen one before."

"Now, you have." Landon said. "In a way."

"They know of us and they know we're still alive in the Worlds."

The image evaporated, and the sixth image appeared and within this image were all the Warslingers of the Heptad with others and in front of them stood The Haunted City itself. But, in between the Warslingers and the City, was an enemy to come, who was shrouded in a dark fog. The fog was black as the night sky and within the fog, the enemy knew all the Warslingers and it desired to see them dead at the gates to the City. The image turned into a war, where the Warslingers and those who came to help battled the forces of the malevolency and the dark fog in front of The Haunted City.

The battle was intense to the point that beings of the *benevolency* appeared from the sky to assist the Warslingers and those who allied with them. The fight ended with raining fire.

"I will make it to the City." Henrich said.

"It looks that way, sir." Landon said. "Must be something to witness."

"For the time being. Until we get there, it's another story all in of itself."

All the images come together in a ball of light and banished into the mirror. The mirror's light slowly dimmed out. Henrich approached them mirror, looking at the images that he witnessed. Landon and Beth also looked at the mirror and seen the images within. The images still held them in its grasps. The images were of the future to come and even though, they were of the future, they can be altered be certain actions that could take place.

"This is your future, Randolph Henrich of the Warslingers of the

Heptad." The Mirror declared. "You have seen what is to come."

Henrich, Landon, and Beth backed away from the mirror, seeing the images faded away. The mirror sat quietly.

"So, what now, sir" Landon asked.

"Now, you all sleep." The mirror spoken.

A loud gong sounded from the mirror, causing a drift to come upon them as they fell to the ground and were in a deep sleep. The mirror itself evaporated as it entered a portal. The portal looked as if it was heading into another realm of existence and the mirror fell into the portal, to which the portal was closed afterwards. Only thing that remained on the mountaintop was silence and silence was surely needed.

<u>VI</u>

Henrich awoken from the deep sleep and he looked up toward the sky. The clouds were gone and only the dawning sun was there. He stood up and gazed over to the field, where the flames were and there were no flames. The fire had ceased, and the grass was green as if it never was set ablaze. He looked down, seeing Landon and Beth asleep and the body of the Mercenary Man gone from the mountaintop as was the mirror itself. He understood that the mirror had to be removed to another location to avoid others coming to the mountain. Henrich turned around, seeing his horse. He nodded to the horse to which the horse gallop to him.

"How did you get up here." He said.

On the cold grounds of the mountaintop, Landon and Beth also awoke from the deep sleep. They stood up slowly, looking at Henrich who was looking at them. Landon rubbed his head.

"What happened?" Landon asked.

"I am not sure. But, we've been granted the energy we needed."

"That and some silence." Beth noticed. "Finally."

Henrich nodded as he looked outward toward the direction that they needed to go, which was on the other side of the mountain. While Henrich looked toward the direction, he could see something far ahead of them. What Henrich was seeing was a structure of a city. Though, the city seemed strange to be where Henrich was looking. Landon also seen the city, pointing out to it.

"What is that place, sir?" He asked.

"I know that city." Henrich said. "Though it isn't a city that dwells in the Worlds of Man."

Beth approached them and seen the city herself. The city didn't have a modern looking appearance as there were no skyscrapers known as they are of the modern world. She looked at its buildings and they were of a gothic nature. They appeared to her as a city in the time of the Victorian Era back on Earth. She was amazed by it. Though, she could feel an uneasy feeling continuing to look at the city.

"Why does the city give me the chills? I don't know why."

Henrich turned to her and pointed out toward the city that sat in their eyesight. He knew what the city was and where it was. His heart could feel the city and what was sitting inside of it. Landon believed it to be a city that sat in their direction where they would have to gather up some more supplies for the journey.

"That city." Henrich pointed. "Is where we are going."

"What do you mean that's the city we're going, sir? I thought we were heading to The Haunted City?"

"We are." Henrich said, looking back at the city. He pointed toward it and kept his finger in the air.

"That is The Haunted City."

Landon and Beth looked at one another. Both were confused as they stared at Henrich. They shook their heads and shrugged their shoulders.

"What do you mean that's The Haunted City?" Beth asked.

"Because it is and we're getting a preview of it." He said. "Best to take it all in."

They stood together atop the mountain as the horses stood next to Henrich. The Three looked out to The Haunted City. The place where they were heading. Knowing after seeing the visions of the images, they each know there is a long journey to be had before stepping foot on the grounds of The Haunted City.

CHAPTER ONE
MYSTERIOUS WAYS

I

Moving on across the Western World, leaving the mystical mountains, the Warslinger led his new allies into the deeper parts of the revelations. Moving on from their previous encounters with foes and otherworldly scenarios. Calm and collective. More of a unit. Cody and Beth have agreed to align themselves with the Warslinger on his quest to reach The Haunted City. After seeing a glimpse of the fabled location atop the mountain. The mountain is now known as the Mount of Divination.

While they walked down the straightened path, which they knew was a road due to the tire tracks and horse prints in the dirt. Cody could see something in the horizon further out. Objects near reaching the clouds. He pointed it toward them.

"Sir, what are those?"

Henrich glanced up and saw the objects in the sky. From his eyesight, they appeared as sharp needles standing above the ground, almost touching the first heaven. Beth took a step forward, shading her eyes from the sun with her hand.

"Are those buildings?"

"Yes." Henrich said. "They are."

"What place is further down?" Cody wondered. "Is that where we're heading next?"

"If it's in our path, then yes. If not, we continue moving on."

After miles of walking, they came to a stop. Taking a moment to relax and rest, Henrich turned to his right and saw the city closer. He could see the buildings which stood tall. Cody glanced at them, looking at their height.

"I've never seen such structures before."

"Seriously?" Beth said. "You've never seen skyscrapers"

"No. What are these skyscrapers?"

"They're buildings, boy." Henrich said. "Just buildings. Although, they're not called skyscrapers anymore. Hell, they haven't been called that in almost four hundred years."

"What do they call them now?"

"Breachers of the Heavens in the Western World. Domebreakers in the Eastern World."

They continued their move toward the city ahead. Very familiar, yet old. Old due to the amount of years which have gone by since its inception. Henrich was there when the city was founded as he stood there now at its end. Or so it may seem to be. Finally, their walk had ceased as they stood in the entrance to the city.

"What was the name of this place?" Cody asked.

"Now, Old Los Angeles." Henrich declared. "A place once called a city of angels. Now, it's a resting place for the lost, the weary, and mostly, the wicked."

II

Walking through the dirty and trash-filled street of Old Los Angeles, the city has become a rest stop and a salvage point for nearby everyone who can survive the time within. Building have crumbled into rubble. Others stand tall as their once attractive appearance has faded into a plain dusty tower.

"What is that stench?" Cody looked around, covering his face.

"It's the river." Henrich replied. "It's dead."

"What's happened here." Beth wondered, looking at the city's destruction. She continued looking and saw cracks throughout the ground of the city.

"What are all these cracks?"

'A great *worldquake* came through here during the time of the War of the West." Henrich stated. "Destroyed much of whatever was in its way. People evacuated without notice. Many died. Few managed to survive and fled to the nearest region."

"And what of the rest of this place?" Cody asked. "The buildings and such?"

"Time." Henrich said. "The movement of time has transformed this place into what it's become. During my youth, this city was a prosperous place. Yet, that was all before the War of the West."

"Where I'm from, Los Angeles thrives. It's a big city. Resembles this one, but fully functioning."

"Must be pleasant." Henrich said.

"I wouldn't call it pleasant. But, it's lively."

"How many wars have there been?"

"Too many to count. I was in most of them."

"You fought in the Shooter War?" Cody asked.

"I was a front liner in that war. Very young. Eager to do the killing when it was necessary."

"And what are you now?" Beth wondered. "Are you still that same young man or are you more mature?"

Henrich sighed and shrugged.

"Little bit of both I presume."

Upon walking, Henrich caught the wind of several men scattered through the area. Five of them, dressed in ragged clothing. Torn pants and worn-out boots. They smelled of the old city. The stench of oil and must covered the area. Henrich slowly moved his hands toward his shooters. Landon spotted the hand motions and signaled toward Beth as the men inched closer.

"Well, what do we have here." One man gestured. "A couple of stranders."

"We're just passing through." Henrich said. "We desire no trouble."

"Sorry to hear your plea, good sir." Another man said, approaching Henrich. "But, you're in our city and here, we make the rules."

"And what rules to you imply to stranders?"

"We take what they have and, usually, kill them. Very simple."

Henrich nodded, looking at the men surrounded. Landon gave Henrich a nod and so did Beth. Henrich nodded back before turning toward the man in front of him.

"Now, what do you three have to offer? Water, food, herbs?"

"Perhaps, they can lend us the young woman." One man spoke from the distance. "We haven't had a new woman come through these lands in months."

"That will not happen." Beth said.

"Oh, she speaks."

"Don't take her lightly." Henrich said. "Don't take any of us as such."

"Nobody's taking anyone lightly. Just give us something of yours and you can pass."

"Not giving any of you anything. Except for one word of advice."

"A word of advice?" the man shrugged. "What advice?"

"You reap what you sow."

"I wh-"

Before the man could finish, Henrich fired a shot at the man's head. Landon and Beth turned to the men behind them and fired shots of their own. Henrich turned toward the others and let out blasts, killing the small gang. After the shotfire, silence stilled the air.

"This was on them." Henrich proclaimed. "Not us."

The three continued on their journey as the vultures appeared from the air and covered the bodies of the dead men.

III

Walking further through the city, something caught Henrich and he grabbed quickly to what it is. He moved with more speed; a vigilant look covered his face. There was no expression. Only focus. Cody and Beth paced themselves to keep up with the Warslinger.

"Sir, what is it?" Landon asked. "Why are you moving at this pace?"

'There's something here. Something in the city."

"Like what?" Beth wondered. "A portal out of here?"

"No." Henrich stated. "Something more. I haven't sensed it since the Battle of Astolat."

"Astolat?" Landon said. "It's fine and well."

"Now it is."

"I don't know what either of you are speaking of. But, what is Astolat."

"A place." Henrich said. "A tale for another time."

The Three made their move through the city. Not one stop was made nor was a break. They each moved with focus and speed. Unified in their mission to find whatever it is which has caught the attention of the Warslinger. They passed by more gangs, prostitutes, beaten-down shelters which stood empty, apart from a few homeless remaining in its shadows.

Still moving, a man indivertibly bumped into Henrich. He neither flinched nor hid himself. He stood bold, just as the Three. However, his focus was on the Warslinger and it was unsettling to Cody and Beth. Henrich has been through these situations' countless times. It was nothing to him.

"Pardon me, sir." The man said, raising his head.

"Your eyes." Cody said.

The man was elderly and blind. He stood before them, dressed in what would assume rags and a coat. His unkempt hair flowed with the sudden gusts of the air. Henrich stared at the man and the man did the same to the Warslinger.

"Your essence." The man said of Henrich. "It is familiar. Ancient-like."

"And you can tell from?"

"On your sides, the shooters. Their power can be felt."

"Wait, you can sense the shooters?" Landon said. "How's that possible?"

"Appears this man has seen many things in his life." Henrich said. "Tell me, sir, how you've come to learn of a Warslinger's arkshooters?"

"I used to travel a lot in my prime years. I've seen the wonders of the Eastern World. The structures of Old Egypt and the Temple of Old Jerusalem. I lived in Old London before it became New London. I'm sure you're understanding my words well."

"I am" Henrich said. "But, we're not here to hear stories. We're tracking something down and it is of great importance we discover the source."

"You sense it as well." The man said with a smile. "Good. I am not the only one."

"Do you know what it may be?"

"I have a clue. I am not sure it is direct."

"How about this. Where were you when you felt it as its strongest?"

"Almost out of the downtown area. Near the outside points of the city."

Henrich nodded.

"Great." Cody said. "Let's get a move on."

"As we should." Henrich said. "Thank you for your aid, elder."

The elderly man bowed before Henrich. His hands and face flat on the concrete grounds. Cody and Beth stood still, confused. Henrich kneeled and help the man to his feet. The man seemed to have been crying as he was on the ground. Not of sorrow or sadness, but of hope.

"Why bow before me?" Henrich wondered.

"It has been a long time since I've encountered a servant of El. Forgive me if my behavior was out of place."

"No need. Only do not bow before me or any other Warslinger. We're just servants as you said. If you choose to worship El, worship him in spirit and in truth."

The man nodded as the Three went their way.

IV

Walking along their projected path, tracking the source of the aura, Henrich started to notice their sudden exit of the downtown region. Due to the fact of staring at a deserted road ahead. In the distance, there were no tall buildings. Skyscrapers only stood behind them. Quiet and motionless. They could only see fields of half-dead grass and withered trees. A combination of light sand and soil covered the ground.

"Where does this road lead?" Cody wondered.

"We'll have to find out." Henrich replied. "The source is coming from along this path."

"I have to ask, what is this source?" Beth questioned. "Is it some kind of paranormal thing or something larger?"

"Where you're from, they would call it a paranormal occurrence. Here, it's a spiritual matter. One of a dire need."

"How dire are you talking?"

"A serious matter." Henrich professed. "Plus, it reminds me of things I've felt in my youth. Training and growing in this life. Sources like this were always around. A constant hesitation to all who served the benevolency of the universe."

"You know, you're going to have to tell me more about your world." Beth gestured. "It's very, mystique compared to where I'm from. Yet, very similar in a lot of ways. Almost as if this world is my world's future or vice versa."

Henrich turned to Beth. A sudden urge to speak something in his mind. He looked down at the sandy soil and back up toward Cody and Beth.

"Better you wait for the day to come and be prepared, rather than the day comes and you're not ready. Besides, this could all be a test for you. Or a purpose."

"What purpose is it for someone or something to take me from my home?"

"A higher purpose. For good or for evil. Only you'll know when the test is complete."

"And you know this how?"

"I've seen many like you before. Mindset-wise. Never have I ever encountered someone from a world you've spoken about. A place where there's paranormal investigators and go looking for trouble with the malevolency."

"There's a lot of things the people should know about the world they live in."

"And yet, how many of them disagree with that statement?" Henrich asked. "Many. Only a few can manage this knowledge. Seeing as how you've not gone crazy proves you're one of the few."

Beth nodded with respect. A calmness came over her.

"I appreciate that."

"I'm only being honest." Henrich replied. "Come on, we need to keep moving."

They continued their journey, following the aura. Ironically, Cody and Beth could not see what the Warslinger was keeping his focus on. A strange, violet trail of mist covered the air above them. His eyes were focused on it and marked it for an easy track to the source.

V

The deserted road is well, deserted. No sign of life seemed to be around the area as Henrich tracked the source. The surrounding areas were still. Not a sound nor a chirp of a bird, nor a bark of a dog, a screech of a cat. Nothing. Only complete quietness except for the wind bristling against the trees and grass.

"The breeze is nice." Beth said.

"It's to keep us cooled down." Henrich said. "Felt the same breeze when I was in the desert on this journey."

"I'm just curious as to where they come from." Cody said. "Like where a breeze starts and where does it end?"

"A question for another time, eh." Henrich grinned.

After walking several miles, not distant from downtown Old Los Angeles, they come across a sign. The sign detailed a location covered with people and life. Written in *Old Tongue*, yet Beth approached the sign.

"You can read that?" Cody asked.

"Yeah. It's English."

"It's what?" Cody said.

"One of the past languages of this World." Henrich professed. "I can read it as well."

"Wow. You have to teach me."

"I will." Henrich said.

Beth read the sign. She looked ahead, her eyes on the deserted road and what's ahead.

"The sign says there's a church down this path."

"Might explain the source." Henrich said. "then, we'll go there. See what's ongoing."

"Didn't that mirror warn you of some kind of church." Cody referenced. "It all sounds familiar."

"That's why we must go. To confirm the mirror's prophetic words."

"I understand. I guess."

They passed the sign and continued further, seeking to reach the church of the sign.

CHAPTER TWO

FINDING THE CHURCH

I

Following the trail and the aura source above, the surroundings increasing with trees. While they walk, Henrich showed a peculiar expression, taking notice of the area. It seemed to appear somewhat familiar to his memory.

"What is it, sir?" Cody asked.

"This place. This area, it's appearing familiar to me. I've been here before. Long ago."

"Then, you know where we're headed." Beth said.

"We're reaching the San Fernando Valley."

"The Valley?" Beth said. "It's still a dwelling place in this World?"

"Not sure. But, this trail and the source are coming from that direction."

As they walked, a bright flash of light appeared before them. Nearly blinding them of the path. Henrich raised his arm to avoid the light and just as quickly as it appeared it vanished. They each looked and saw someone standing before them. A young man. Wearing the clothes of a vagabond with a weathered fedora the colors of dried bark. Cody and Beth were unaware as to who the young man could be. Henrich, however kept his gaze keen.

"I've heard of you." Henrich said. "The Jumper."

"That's what they call me nowadays? Man, I would've preferred something more creative."

"Who are you?" Cody asked.

"Pardon my manners, I am the Kroger Kid."

"Kroger Kid?" Beth said. "Like from a grocery store?"

"What?" The Kroger Kid gestured. "No, I travel between worlds."

"Really." Cody said.

"He travels across the Four Worlds." Henrich added. "It's how he gets from place to place within seconds."

"Hold on, Warslinger. I can also travel to worlds outside of the Four."

"Then, let me ask this question. Have you traveled to the Outer-World? Have you seen the City?"

"Have I? It's a place of great spiritual power. But, it isn't designed for me."

"How come?" Beth wondered. "I'm sure there's a reason."

"I'm the kind of guy who does things on his own terms."

"Why bother us to begin with?" Henrich asked.

"Because I heard about a Warslinger who went through the towns of Savel and Hevoc. I noticed the Cailleach was no longer doing her little tests near the Valley of Death. Those dirty Scavengers are all dead and the Mercenary Man's body was found in another dimension."

"You've seen all of this?"

"I might have been hiding behind corners and suchlike. Maybe."

Henrich shook his head. "Why are you here now?"

"Because I know what you're seeking and where you're heading. That source does take you somewhere. But, it's best you do not do what you did to Savel or Hevoc."

"I had no choice."

"We all have choices, Warslinger."

"And yours is to stop my journey to reaching the City?"

"Why yes." The Kroger Kid giggled. "I can't let you pass."

"I wasn't asking for a pass."

Henrich pulled out his shooter without hesitation and fired. The Kroger Kid illuminated himself, vanishing in a blast of light. The three looked around and unnoticeably, the Kroger Kid returned behind them,

"I have to lure you away in one shape or another!" The Kroger Kid yelled with excitement.

Henrich looked to his left and spotted his other shooter was gone. He stared at the Kroger Kid, who was waving his shooter in the air after snatching it from Henrich's side. The Kid took off into the woods, laughing maniacally.

"Seriously." Beth said.

"He took your shooter, sir." Cody said. "What are we going to do?"

"Get it back." Henrich replied as he ran after the Kroger Kid into the wilderness.

"Ah, man." Cody said, following the Warslinger and Beth.

II

Henrich ran through the forest after the Kroger Kid, who would appear and reappear in certain locations. Cody and Beth followed fast on their feet. Henrich fired a shot every time the Kroger Kid appeared. While he continued to vanish with a quick flash of light, Henrich moved faster with every step. Shooter firing. Cody did the same as did Beth.

"I've never seen him move that fast." Cody mentioned.

"He wants his gun back." Beth replied. "What would do think he'll be doing?"

"Wait. Gun? You mean his shooter."

"Yes, that's what I mean."

The Warslinger continued firing shots at the appearing Kroger Kid, who proceeded to mock him as they moved through the trees.

"It might take you all night to catch up!" The Kroger Kid yelled.

"You're a nuisance!" Henrich said. "A pain!"

"I've heard worse!"

The Kid vanished once more and appeared before Cody, tripping him onto the ground and teleporting behind Beth, shoving her against the nearby tree. The Kid vanished with only a laugh echoing through the forest. Henrich caught up to the two, helping them up.

"He tripped me." Cody said.

"You'll be fine." Henrich replied. "Beth, how are you?"

"Just a scratch. It's nothing."

While they spoke, the Kid appeared above them, sitting in the tree. Giggling.

"Here's the thing, stranders." The Kid said, getting their attention.

"Not again." Henrich said, raising up his shooter and firing.

The Kid snatched the bullet from the air and returned it to Henrich's shooter. Right in the chamber.

"Did he just give you the bullet back?" Cody said. "And put it back in the shooter?"

"I have skills, my boy!" The Kid said.

"Give me back my other shooter and let us on our way."

"I'm sorry, Warslinger. As much as I respect you and your kind, I cannot let you bother the World beyond this forest. For the Valley has seen better days since their union."

"What union?" Henrich wondered. "Who's waiting on the other end of this forest? Who's dwelling in the ruins of the Valley?"

"Ah, now that is a conversation for another time."

The Kid raised his right index finger and Henrich's shooter was returned to his side. Henrich looked and grabbed it, holding now both shooters aimed at the Kid. Cody held the blast shooter and Beth grabbed the machete from Henrich's coat. The Kid applauded the team.

"Looks like a new Heptad is resurging from my point of view."

"You will let us pass." Henrich proclaimed. "Or else, you'll wish you could teleport to a place of peace permanently."

"More threats." The Kid laughed. "As long as you're in this region, near the Valley, I will not cease to stop you."

The Kid gazed up toward the afternoon sky, seeing the sun. He pointed toward the sky.

"Appears the sun will be going down soon, you're in this forest, and I will not let you pass. Therefore, you have two options before you. Return to where you came from or spend the night in these woods and wish for a better morrow."

Henrich stared at the Kid with intensity. Cody and Beth remained still. The Kid didn't take his eyes off the Warslinger and neither did he. Henrich took the shot with both shooters and the Kid disappeared once more. Henrich placed the shooters to his side, turning to Cody and Beth.

"Looks like we're camping here for the night."

Later in the night, after setting up camp with the equipment they carried in Henrich's bag, the three sat together under the dark sky and stars above. The silence of the wilderness and the still wind. A fire was kindled for heat as the surroundings gravely dropped.

"This world is strange." Beth said. "Very."

"So, it doesn't get cold where you're from?" Cody asked.

"It does. But, not on a day like this. It's usually warm. Somewhat cool."

"Your world isn't that different from ours." Henrich said.

"Then, let me in on it. Tell me about this place. Your Worlds."

Henrich nodded and drew closer toward the flame. Holding his hands over the fire.

"At the beginning of time, our sense of time, the Master known as El created everything from our world to yours and others beyond. Here, He created *Adamah* and it combines the Four Worlds. Afterwards, he created the stars, the heavens and the five seas. Four surround the Four Worlds and one sits in the center of them all; *Tsaphon* is the sea of the north, *Teman* is the sea of the south, *Qedem* is the sea of the east, and *Maarab* is the sea of the west. Together, they form *Tehomayim*, the great sea of the Worlds. The center sea is called the *Sea of Tabbur*, which signifies the connection of the Four Worlds. The Worlds themselves are as follows; *Yaphean*, the Northern World. A place of sheer winter and diverse kingdoms. From Anchor Bay to Old Camelot and what is now New London. Then, He created *Khamain*, the Southern World. A land filled with kingdoms and lush landscapes. The home of Old Egypt and the Amazon City. A place of beauty. Next was *Shemia*, the Eastern World. The land where El placed His name. The home of Old Jerusalem, my home and Mount Sinai. The land which is the birthplace of the Warslingers of the Heptad."

"I didn't know you were from Old Jerusalem." Cody said. "You've seen its fall."

"I was there when it fell. The moment where we lost. The defeat of the Heptad. The end of the Warslingers. Betrayal and unjust ones claimed the land soon after. That day was named the Fall of Old Jerusalem."

"And what of the other World?" Beth asked. "The Western one?"

"You speak of *Arzareth*, the Western World. Which we are currently placed. The land where the Warslingers were dispersed. A place of prophecy. Yet, there is one more world. The realm where the spirits dwell and judgment is set. The realm where The Haunted City itself sits amongst the Gate of the City and the Kingdom of Order. That place is called *Ruachayim*, the Outer-World."

"Then, what happened next?" Cody asked curiously.

"After the Worlds were formed, to keep the seas from overtaking them, El created a boundary made of steel-like ice and called the place *Qeramah*. Then, before Man walked upon the worlds, the animals were formed. Yet, there were also those above. The Sons of El, a group of spiritual beings. We know them as the Seraph."

"You mean like angels." Beth said.

"Yes. One deemed himself worthy of ruler ship. A war broke out in the Outer-World and he was defeated. Upon his downfall, his essence and dark spirit spread throughout the Four Worlds and the Malevolency was born, eventually consuming the generations of Man which came after. An opposition to El's Benevolency. That is why the Warslingers of the Heptad were created. To combat the forces made from the spread of the Malevolency."

"So, you've seen a lot during your years." Beth said. "Which brings me to a question. How old are you?"

"How old you do perceive me to be?"

"You look as if you're in your mid-forties. Perhaps early forties."

"There's no way he's in his forties." Cody said. "Impossible."

"What do you mean? He looks forty to me."

"Because I'm in my mid-twenties."

"No, you're not." Beth said. "You're at least sixteen. Maybe seventeen."

"He's in his twenties." Henrich said. "I'm certain."

"I don't understand. People in my world look much older in their mid-twenties. Then, how old are you if you're not in your forties?"

"I've been around for over five hundred years." Henrich said. "Humans age much slower in the Four Worlds than yours I'm assuming?"

"Very much so."

Henrich looked up, still seeing the aura trail in the air glowing in the night hour. He also sensed the magic of the Kroger Kid lurking around the trees.

"Best we get some sleep."

"What of that Kid?" Beth wondered.

"We'll deal with him in the morning."

The Warslinger put out the fire and sleep fell upon the three.

III

They awoke right at the brink of dawn. Henrich stood tall, gazing toward the morning sky and looking around the trees for the Kroger Kid. Beth and Cody rose up from their slumber, seeing Henrich gazing around the area.

'What is it?"

"Seeing if he's around." Henrich said. "He's watching us. I'm sure of it."

"Well, he can't possibly keep us in this forest for long." Cody added. "I mean, what's the worse he could do to us?"

While talking, the sound of a breaking branch echoed through the forest. Henrich caught the sound quickly while Cody and Beth talked. Henrich approached them, waving his hand.

"Something's out here." Henrich said steadily.

The Warslinger reached and raised up his shooter. He looked around and the sound increased. Moving closer. Cody and Beth stood up, holding weapons of their own. Henrich turned back around, following the sound and could see what it was. It was approaching them fast.

"There it is." Henrich said.

"There's what?" Cody asked, turning around to see what Henrich saw. "Oh no."

"What is it?" Beth asked.

They found themselves staring at three scorpions. Larger than Beth had ever seen. A dark brown with a hint of gold in their shelled bodies. Their eyes burning violet and the tips of their tails sharp as blades. Henrich and Cody took steps forward with their shooters. The scorpions hissed with fury and their tails slammed against the ground, tossing dirt and leaves into the air.

"What are those?!" Beth asked.

"Dire Scorpions." Henrich said.

"Like the wolves?!"

"Yes."

Henrich fired several shots toward the scorpions, but their hollow hide was too dense for the bullets to penetrate. Cody turned to Beth with haste, dropping his weapon.

"Hand me the blastshooter!"

Beth tossed him the shooter and he fired a round toward the first scorpion. The blastshooter proved effective as it burst the shell on the top of the scorpion. The shell slid off with pus. Cody fired rounds toward the other two, blowing one's claw and the other's tail off. The scorpions screeched with agony.

"What's next?" Cody asked. "We keep shooting?"

"We'll have to get closer." Henrich said.

Henrich pulled out his machete and ran toward the first scorpion. He jumped up as the claws reached out to snatch him. Henrich raised the machete and impaled it into the creature, killing it with the blow. The scorpion fell to the ground as the other two ambushed Henrich. Cody ran after him and fired another round from the blastshooter into the scorpion's face, blowing it off as it slid from the body. Henrich grabbed the remaining one's tail and used it to impale the scorpion itself. The Warslinger stepped back as the scorpion fell dead by its own tail.

"That's it." Cody said. "We won."

"It seems." Henrich replied.

"Are those things native to this place?" Beth asked, looking at the bodies in awe.

"Dire Scorpions don't belong here. They're mostly found in the Eastern World. In Old Egypt."

"Then, how did you three end up here?" Cody asked.

"The Kroger Kid." Henrich replied. "He brought them here. To distract us. To cause us to stumble from our mission."

"You're telling me there's more of these and other creatures as big as this?" Beth asked.

"A lot more." Henrich said. "You would be amazed at the creatures within the Four Worlds."

Cody looked around the trees and approached Henrich.

"Do you think he's watching?"

"I know he is."

Henrich stepped forward and looked around.

"Kroger Kid!" Henrich yelled. "I know you're watching us, and you saw what we did and what we're capable of. Either you return to me my shooter and let us pass. Or, you will suffer the same fate, if not worse like your pets from Shemia!"

The burst of light reappeared in the trees above them, Henrich looked, spotting the Kroger Kid moving through them as if he was running on air. Henrich pressed forward, grabbing his gear and ran after the Kid. Cody and Beth followed.

IV

Chasing the Kroger Kid through the forest, the eyes of the Warslinger were locked onto the young man. The Kid raised his hands and threw energy balls of light toward the three, stumbling them from the chase. No matter, Henrich proceeded past the light, for his eyes were not shaken nor blinded by the brightness. Beth had to pause, and Cody stumbled in his running, nearly tripping himself.

"We need to keep up!" Henrich yelled.

The Kid threw more energy balls and once they were in the air, Henrich raised up his shooter, firing rounds into the balls, causing them to explode and spreading the brightness of the light.

"That's not possible." The Kid said to himself, still running and teleporting.

"I can hear you." Henrich responded. "This game of yours is over."

The Kid moved and vanished into a tree in the midst of the forest. This tree was larger, thicker in size. The branches were nearly long as the tress standing around them. Cody and Beth caught up to the Warslinger, staring in awe at the massive tree.

"What is this?" Cody wondered.

"The Kid went inside the tree." Henrich said. "He's not leaving."

"How can you be sure?" Beth asked. "I mean he did show us he can teleport."

"Because this tree is his home. He dwells in it."

"I don't understand."

"The outer layer appears as a mammoth tree. But, the interior, is like a home. A mansion for his kind."

Henrich kicked the tree, causing it to rattle. He kicked it again, shaking the tree. Henrich backed up and ran shoulder first into the tree and the door opened in front of them with a creak.

"How did you know the door was there?" Cody asked with confusion. "I mean, I didn't know trees have doors."

"Only these trees, my boy." Henrich answered. "Kroger Kid! Come on out! Let's finish this!"

The three stood guard, weapons in hand as the Kid stepped foot from the tree. His hands up in the air, a grin on his face. Not one of a humorous nature.

"This game of yours is finished," Henrich said. "it's over. Return to me my shooter and let us pass."

"I can't let you pass. You'll ruin what they have!"

"That is not your place to decide what happens and what doesn't. The aura is strange and unusual to this place."

"They're seeking to help people. They have faith."

"And it is my duty as a Warslinger of the Heptad to search such places and discover what truly lies within those walls."

"I know. But, they seem happy."

"Seeming happy isn't a sure answer to peace."

The Kid nodded, showing respect with a hint of resistance in his body. Cody gripped the blastshooter as Beth held the handle of the machete tightly. The Kid snapped his fingers.

"There, you have your shooter back."

Henrich reached down and pulled out the shooter, he began searching it for rounds. The Kid held his hand up in a pause.

"Don't fret, Warslinger. I didn't take any of your rounds."

Henrich gazed with a nod, placing the shooter back into its holster.

"May we now pass?" Henrich asked.

The Kid sighed. "Fair enough."

The Kid waved his hand and the aura presented itself within the forest, however its appearance was greater, and the energy was stronger. Henrich looked up and saw the location of its origin.

"Don't worry, Kid, we won't harm anyone." Henrich said. "Anyone innocent."

"I know you won't, Warslinger. I know your kind."

Henrich signaled for Cody and Beth to leave the forest with him. They walked away as the Kid watched them leave.

"One more thing, Warslinger." The Kid said.

Henrich turned around to face the Kid.

"This isn't our last meeting. We will meet again. Someday."

"That, I am certain of." Henrich replied. "Peaceful nights and blissful days, Kid."

"May you prosper in years." The Kid replied, returning into the tree. The door shut and the tree itself vanished into the light. Leaving an open space in the forest.

The three continued following the aura, until they could hear voices, multiple voices talking to each other and once they exit the forest, they saw the source of the energy. Henrich took a step forward, Cody looked ahead and approached the Warslinger.

"Sir, what is this place?"

"It's a church community." Beth said. "I'm familiar with these places."

"A community, you're right." Henrich said. "But, this one, with the aura, there's something very spiritual happening here."

CHAPTER THREE
THE SECRET WORLD

I

The three stood in front of a gated community. Filled with people of diverse appearances and sizes. Cody had never seen the likes of such unification. Beth, on the other hand has, yet, not as it's portraying right before her face. Henrich stared, looking at the people. He found no arguing, no selfish nature, no signs of betrayal. All he saw was love. A love of humans coming together in a world lost to itself.

"This place is incredible." Cody said. "And we haven't even entered it yet."

"Are we even sure we want to go in?" Beth added.

"The source of the aura is coming from this place." Henrich said. "best we find out what it is and continue on our way."

While they stood in awe, the gates opened. Upon their opening, a man approached the three. Dressed in the clothing of a Catholic priest. He was a middle-aged man. He stood facing the Warslinger, gazed him down and up and nodded.

"I see we have new members."

"I wouldn't call us members of your community." Henrich said. "What is this place, truly?"

"Why follow me and I'll explain everything in the form of a tour."

Henrich turned, giving Cody and Beth a look. They nodded as the Warslinger turned back to the priest. He nodded with a hand gesture.

"We will follow."

"Wonderful." The priest said. "By the way, my name is Father Naillain."

"Father?" Henrich said. "There is only one father."

"I know what you're going to say and please, I will explain everything in the tour."

"I will be listening closely."

Naillain nodded. He walked before them as they entered the community and the gates closed soon after.

II

Passing through the gates, they startled and somewhat marveled at the scenery around them. The amount of people staggered Cody, never seeing such since their incident with the Scavengers, however, these seemed more benevolent. Beth respected their hospitality and greetings. Henrich walked beside Naillain.

"How did all of this begin?" Henrich asked.

"Began right around the time the air changed and the Worlds shook."

"I'm aware many places fell. I assume this one right after the worldquake?"

"Yes. I lived not far out of the limits of the city. I saw many of the towers fall upon the streets. Taking away the lives of the scattered. There was nothing I could do but pray."

"And did you receive your answer?"

"I did. But, at the cost of some relatives. They didn't take heed to my warnings of the quake's coming. I told them something was happening across the Worlds. They ignored me. Despised me. Until the day the quake shook."

"How do you know they're gone?"

"I went to their homes. Found them under trees and swallowed by the ground. I knew then, I was on the right path."

"And this path led you here? Being a preacher to those who seek answers?"

"Yes.

They continued to follow Naillain through the community. Seeing gardens, homes, trailers, and facilities. People were living together in what some would call true harmony and prosperity.

"Is there a place here for all these people?" Beth asked.

"Everyone you see here has a roof over their heads and food in their homes." Naillain replied. "No one is of need of anything."

"And you guys grow your own food?" Cody asked. "I saw the cattle over by the gates. Figured they're your meat source."

"Your right. Although, there are some here who live the life of vegetation, no discrimination here."

"I'm not surprised at that." The Warslinger said. "Many sought after food once the tragedies ceased. Vegetation was all that was left in most places."

"We found the cattle trapped in an old farm far from here. We picked them up and brought them here. They breed and bring forth more cattle."

Bleating sounds come from nearby, Henrich turned, seeing a pair of goats passing by. Cody laughed.

"You have goats too?!"

"We do."

Cody went over and petted the passing goats, laughing. They continued walking and stopped in front of the church. A large building with a steeple on top.

"This is where we worship."

"Worship who?" The Warslinger asked.

"The God of the Worlds." Naillain answered. "He's the one who answered my prayers. Gave me this land and brought these people to me. He has a great purpose for my life."

Henrich nodded.

"Good of you to keep in tune with the spiritual."

"It's what we all need in this World."

"I see."

Naillain opened the doors and gestured for his guests to enter.

"After you." Naillain said.

They entered the church, but there was something off in the air. Henrich looked up and the aura was gone. A peculiar nature of such.

III

Inside the church itself were dozens of people. Some were praying, others were fellowshipping, and a few were talking amongst each other. Naillain escorted Henrich, Cody, and Beth inside. Walking down the aisle, greeting the people around them with kind words.

"Everyone seems generous." Henrich said.

"Because they are." Naillain replied. "This is the perfect place for such a harmony."

Upon the greetings, they are brought by Naillain toward a woman, who was tending a family. Naillain stood firm, as did those around him.

"Brandi." Naillain said.

The woman turned around to see him. She smiled and nodded.

"Yes sir?"

"I would like to meet our new guests."

She approached them and extended her hand with a smile on her face.

"Hi. My name is Brandi Bush."

"Beth Grasslands."

"Cody Landon."

"Randolph Henrich."

Brandi looked at him and a quickening came into her spirit. Her smile grew as she looked into the eyes of a Warslinger.

"You're one of them?"

"One of what?" Henrich asked.

"A warrior from the East. The ones who helped in the Battle of Astolat all those years ago?"

"I was involved in that event. It was during my younger years."

Brandi looked at Cody and Beth. Measuring them.

"Now, you." Brandi said to Cody. "You're not from the Western World, are you?"

"Not exactly. I come from the Northern World. It's where I was born."

"I can tell by the way of your speech."

Brandi turned to Beth and turned her head.

"You… you're not from around here either are you?"

"I'm not from any of these places you're all familiar with."

"What does she mean?" Naillain asked the Warslinger.

"She come from another world. Not one of the Four."

"Can't be." Naillain replied. "That would mean…"

"There are other Worlds out there besides our own."

"It goes against our word of law. Our history."

"It doesn't go against them. It confirms them."

"So, where are you from?" Brandi asked.

"I'm from a world called Earth. From a city known as Washington D.C."

"D.C.?" Brandi said. "You have an operating D.C. in your world?"

"Yes."

As they spoke with her, Henrich looked over toward the right of the church and saw an older man, wearing clothing which resembled the Eastern World. Henrich knew there was something peculiar with the man and proceeded to approach him.

IV

The Warslinger approached the older man, greeting him with a handshake. The man stared and hugged Henrich.

"It is time I've gazed upon another." The man said.

"Another what?" Henrich asked.

"One of you. From Old Jerusalem."

Henrich nodded slowly.

"I didn't get your name."

"My name is Abraham."

Cody and Beth approached Henrich and Abraham. The older man greeted them with the same hug he gave the Warslinger. They themselves, weren't sure of what to make of it.

"You're very affectionate." Cody said.

"It's gentle." Beth added. "A sense of love and peace."

"I see you're with the Warslinger."

"We are…" Cody said, looking at Henrich.

"Don't be afraid." Abraham said. "I know of many things. But, if you don't mind, I would like to speak with the Warslinger myself."

"Of course." Beth replied, nodding to Henrich and walking away with Cody.

"Why do you need to speak with me?"

"Because there's a lot to discuss. Follow me."

Henrich followed Abraham to a secure and quiet area. Cody and Beth spoke with others within the church. Abraham brought Henrich to a quiet spot in a corridor of the church and the two sat down in the chairs near a window.

"First off, let me say how it is a true privilege to speak with a Warslinger again."

"Again?"

"I, myself as you can tell, come from the same landmass the Warslingers dwelled."

"Why are you here in Arzareth?"

"I came across the sea sometime after the Fall."

Henrich nodded and sighed. He looked up toward Abraham, seeing the story in his eyes. The words echoing through his ears.

"You were there when it happened."

"I was. Seen everything that transpired."

"You saw the Fall of the city. The end of our tribes and the desolation of our purpose."

"Your purpose was not destroyed. You know this better than the common folk."

"What I know is after the fall, all the Warslingers were scattered. Dispersed across the Four Worlds. I ended up in the desertlands. Traveled through some small towns, came across some peculiar creatures and humans. That trail led me here."

"I can see this isn't the destination. Only a crossroads in your journey."

"It is."

"What are you seeking? Where are you headed?"

"To the Haunted City."

"The Haunted City? Why seek such a place? After all the things you've seen. The blessings you've been given, why go there?"

"Because I need answers."

"You already have that access."

"I've tried. It seems after the fall and our dispersion; everything has gone silent. The City is outside the Four Worlds. It's the perfect place to uncover everything. Why the city fell and why we failed."

Abraham sighed.

"Perhaps, when you reach the City, will you be content with the answers you'll be given?"

"Do I even have a choice."

"You do. You can accept the answers given or decline them and walk away."

"It's a start to a conclusion."

"And yet, how do you intend on reaching the City? The Outer-World at least?"

"There are portals. Gateways throughout the Four Worlds. I intend on finding one and gaining my entry into the City."

"What of the Gate?"

"The Gate of the City will not be a problem for me."

"And this Tubal King?"

The Warslinger stared at Abraham. A knowing.

"How do you know of that name?"

"Because it's an ancient one. Far past the time before you became a Warslinger."

"Then you are aware of his lieutenant?"

"Arkdragon? I am aware."

"How?"

"I lived in the same areas as you did. I was there when you were but a boy and became a man. I am here now, speaking to you as I did my own sons in times past."

"I don't know what to make of all this."

"Make of this in what form?"

"Speaking to you concerning these things. I haven't spoken to anyone in this manner since before the Fall."

Abraham nodded with a smile.

"Then, it is time your journey begins."

Abraham stood up from his seat and Henrich followed.

"I do know what is truly happening here, as do you."

"There's something off about the Priest and this place. The energy around here seems benevolent, but dark."

"You will have those answers soon. But, for right now, see what you can learn and when the time comes, you will know what to do and I will be there by your side."

The Warslinger agreed with a nod.

"Good. Let's return to the others."

"I wonder what they're all up to?" Henrich wondered.

"Naillain is about to perform an exorcism."

"Exorcism?"

"You will see."

V

Abraham and Henrich returned to the congregation, finding them sitting down upon the pews while Naillain stood at the podium. The Warslinger spotted Landon and Beth, he walked toward them and sat down, Abraham sat behind them as they looked on.

"My family, we have been brought into this tabernacle to cast out a particular spirit from one of our own. Now, I will not point out who this individual is, but as I speak and proclaim the powers of the true god, this spirit will show itself and it will be cast out.”

Abraham leaned in toward Henrich.

“You’re familiar with all of this, aren’t you?”

“I am.” The Warslinger replied. “But, in a different way.”

Naillain continued, “Now, we have three visitors who have come from the outside and this is the perfect time for them to see what truly dwells in the Four Worlds.”

Without a notice, Naillain began yelling out with a loud voice for the spirit to come out and show itself. He screamed it further and continued speaking the phrase. Right after the first minute, a young girl arose from the pews, screaming and shouting from her lungs. Cursing out Naillain, although he continued speaking his words as the spirit moved with the young girl, trying to reach the podium, but was held down by others in the congregation. Cody was sheer afraid, Beth was startled.

“I see you have not budge.” Henrich said to Beth.

“I’ve had my fair share of these things. Frightened me when I first saw it. Now, I know it’s only part of the greater battle.”

“What is happening to that girl?!” Cody asked.

“That’s not the girl.” Henrich said. “What you’re seeing is a spirit, a demon who was masquerading and dwelling within the girl.”

“And it’s upset?”

“Upset for the fact it has to leave her.” The Warslinger confirmed. “She is being delivered and set free.”

Naillain walked down from the podium and toward the girl. He yelled with a loud voice for the spirit to be cast out and to leave the area. The spirit put up a fight with Naillain and those around him. However, when the spirit caught a glance of Henrich. It froze.”

“Come out of her!” Naillain yelled.

The spirit screamed and went silent. The girl fell to the floor. The room was quiet. Yet, above them, the spirit roamed and moved through the air, making its way toward Old Los Angeles, still screaming and enraged. Inside the tabernacle, the girl arose, and the congregation cheered.

“She has been set free!” Naillain cheered.

“Where has the demon gone?” Cody asked.

“It’s moving through dry places.” Henrich replied. “Seeking rest.”

“Will it ever try to return?”

Henrich sighed, looking at Cody.

“They always will.”

Sometime later, Henrich remained in the tabernacle with Abraham. The older man could sense something was going on with the Warslinger.

"Why have you chosen to remain in here?"

"The Priest." Henrich said. "Naillain, what god does he speak of?"

"Well, from what I've learned, he believes he serves El, the God of Salvation."

"And does he?"

Abraham shook his head.

"I don't think so. He does serve a god. Only thing is, I haven't been able to discover which one."

Henrich nodded.

"Give it time. It'll reveal itself to us."

"And what will you do when that time comes?" Abraham wondered.

"As I've always done. Finish the work and proclaim El as the true god."

CHAPTER FOUR
CONVERGENCE

I

Abraham gathered the Warslinger, Cody, and Beth into a room separated from the congregation. Abraham sat them down as he sat in front of them. Looking at the door and taking in a breath.

"What Naillain is about to do may frighten you."

"Frighten us how?" Beth asked.

"He's seeking to convert the three of you into this congregation."

"What's wrong with that?" Cody wondered. "Everyone here seems happy. At peace."

"This place is an illusion." Henrich said. "I noticed it before the gates opened. The aura in the air brought us here. Because the energy isn't a part of the benevolency."

Beth turned to Abraham. A keen look on her face.

"Then, why are you here?"

"Because it is part of a greater plan." Abraham replied. "Far greater than I can speak of."

"And Randolph is a part of this plan?"

"Indeed. He's always known. Yet, he didn't suspect it would bring him to a place like this. Nor meet someone such as myself. Yet, this reality brings people to many peculiar places. To meet peculiar people."

"But, Naillain's way of doing things, appears to be off." Henrich said. "Deeply, I know he means well. Yet, I can only wonder where he received such a message."

"Ask him when he has some time to himself." Abraham replied. "I'm sure he will give you the answer you're hoping."

"I will. Don't worry, I won't cause a disturbance of any kind."

"I know you won't." Abraham smiled. "You're not that kind of man."

II

Naillain stood before his congregation. Speaking on the great things and miracles which have occurred since their fellowship began. Henrich, Cody, and Beth sat in the back of the tabernacle with Abraham.

"The things of which the Worlds have suffered, will no longer matter in the end." Naillain proclaimed. "Because, what's about to come, will shake the foundations of the Four Worlds and they will never be the same."

"He speaks with eloquent words." Henrich uttered.

"You know the types." Abraham replied. "Very talkative."

"Eventually, we will all be caught up together in the Outer-World of Ruachayim and we will remain as one for all eternity."

Naillain looked toward the back of the room, seeing the three visitors. He extended his hand out to them for all the congregation to see. The people turned to glance at the visitors, Cody waved. Beth nodded. Henrich grinned.

"It is with great honor for us to have these three guests in our tabernacle. Fellowshipping with all of us. For they have come from the outside and have seen the tragedies thereof."

Henrich leaned in toward Abraham, keeping his gaze upon Naillain, who's now walking back and forth in front of the congregation.

"The words he's using, I've heard them in such manner before."

"Because he took them from the ancients. Naillain is only following what he learned while out there in Shemia."

"He's been to the Eastern World?"

"Of course, it explains why he knows much about the spiritual differences and the quickening of the Four Worlds."

The Warslinger sat back. Uneasy feeling within him. Abraham could feel it as well. Cody and Beth were unaware of the circumstances taking place. When Naillain would speak, the energy of his words went out to the congregation. Entering their minds and altering their motives without ease. Henrich waved his hand in front of Cody and Beth.

"What was that for?" Cody asked.

"Protection." Henrich replied.

"Protection from what?"

"You'll soon know."

III

Naillain walked down the aisle of the congregation, making a stop at Henrich, Cody, and Beth. He smiled. They grinned. Abraham sat back and watched.

"I believe it's time you three become official members of this family."

"Wow." Cody said. "Already?"

"I have a general feeling you were destined for a place like this. The Worlds only dream of it."

Naillain extended his and out toward Cody. Cody went for a reach and quickly sat back. Naillain nodded with a stern look. Uncertainty crept upon him. He shook himself and focused on Beth. Speaking to her the same words he spoke to Cody. Beth nodded.

"Do you accept?" Naillain asked.

"This place is special. One of the best places I've come across in this world of yours. But, with all due respect, I must decline. I must return to my world. It's where I belong."

"Naillain stepped back. Nodding slowly.

"That I see." Naillain said. "Much respect to your wishes."

Naillain moved over and stood before the Warslinger. Their eyes locked on one another. Naillain searched Henrich's spirit and was unaware of the Warslinger doing the same. Naillain nodded.

"Do you accept?"

Henrich was silent. He looked over to Cody, Beth, to Abraham, and out toward the congregation. All were awaiting a response from the Warslinger of the Heptad.

"No." Henrich replied. "I do not accept."

The congregation let out a loud gasp and Naillain turned to them, signaling them to be silent. They obeyed their shepherd as he turned back to Henrich. He looked at Cody and Beth. He couldn't understand the true purpose of their decline.

"Why?"

"We're on a mission." Henrich said.

"A mission? It must certainly cannot be higher than what we're doing here."

"It goes forward. Answers must be found for everything that has happened. Everything that has took place across the Four Worlds."

"That a genuine fact?"

"It's a reality."

Naillain nodded. A grin showed upon his face. He pointed toward the Warslinger. While glancing gat the window, seeing its past dark.

"Tomorrow, the two of us shall speak. One-on-one."

"What do you wish to speak on?" Henrich asked.

"Your purpose in the Worlds. My purpose. To see if they are intertwined."

"And if they are?"

"Then, my theory is correct, and the balance is near set."

Naillain turned away and took one step forward. He stopped and turned back to Henrich. He scouted Cody and Beth before focusing on the Warslinger. He could sense something around them.

"There's a barrier around the three of you. Its power is highly strong. I've never come across such a power before."

"Means we're in good company."

"Company with whom?"

"I'll tell you in our talk on the morrow."

Naillain nodded.

"I'm looking forward to it."

The congregation cleared out, leaving on Henrich and Abraham inside. Cody and Beth returned to their rooms.

"What will you tell him?" Abraham asked.

"Everything." Henrich replied.

CHAPTER FIVE
KNOWING THE TRUTH FROM THE LIE

I

A gunshot rattled across the plains, the arkshooter was held still. Holding it was Henrich. His eyes focused, his mind clear. He took another shot across the plains, eventually hitting his target. A scarecrow. Henrich showed a smile of gratitude, placing the shooter back into its holster. He turned around, finding himself standing before his master. Wearing his dark red robe, carrying his sapphire staff. His grey beard gave off a presence of the ancients. A presence of a master.

"Young Randolph, I see you've improved your range."

"Yes, Master Moses. I managed to hit the target this time."

"That I am aware."

Moses escorted Henrich from the plains, toward the small temple. Inside were others, dressed in garb familiar to Henrich's own duster and hat. Some wore leather vests, robes, and diadems. Henrich sat with Moses at the table to eat. Two plates were placed before them by a handmaiden. She was fair to look at. She carried within her a meek and quiet spirit. This pleased Henrich dearly. For there were hardly any in the region which they sat.

"Don't let your eyes wander, boy." Moses said. "For at best, you'll slip and fall."

Henrich caught himself. "Yes sir."

The two ate their bread and meat as another figure approached the table and sat with them. Henrich looked up at the visitor, raising his head from his plate. Seeing another one of his masters. He nodded his head in respect.

"Didn't expect to see me here, did you?"

"No, Master Noah." Henrich said. "I thought you were still in Old Jerusalem."

"I had to come here for duty. It is why yourself and Moses are here as well."

Henrich paused himself, wiping his mouth.

"How's Arthur and Charlton?" Moses asked.

"Being kept occupied with Joshua and Daniel. They've been sent out toward Damascus. Signs of an estranged sphinx were found. Troubling the villagers. They can't sleep nor leave their homes."

"They'll clean out the area." Moses said. "Send the spirit away."

"A sphinx in Damascus?" Young Randolph uttered.

Moses turned toward the young Warslinger. Seeing his enthusiasm in the others' mission. Yet, Moses knew he had to keep him focused.

"You remember why we're here don't you?"

"We're here on a mission?"

"Yes." Moses answered. "Take a look over there."

Henrich looked out in the distance. What he saw was a city. A large one. Standing around the city were three pyramids. One higher and larger than the other.

"What do you see?" Noah asked.

"I see a city of marvelous wonders. I see the pyramids of old. The one our ancestor constructed."

"What else do you see?" Moses asked. "Look closer."

Henrich gazed his eyes closer and what he saw was a shadow looming over the city. The skies above the pyramids seemed clear to the natural eye, but in the spiritual realm, there was a darkness. A malevolent darkness.

"Evil." Henrich said. "I see evil."

Moses nodded.

"That is why we're here in Old Egypt. To uncover what this evil is and destroy it before it spreads further out into the Four Worlds."

"I understand."

"So, is the boy ready?" Noah asked Moses.

Moses turned toward Henrich. He smiled and nodded.

"He's proven himself to me and to El. The boy's ready."

II

Henrich arose from his bed, raising up and looking around the room. Sunlight shining through the windows. Reflecting against his duster and hat. Only seeing Cody and Beth still asleep. He sat up and rested on the side of the bed, reflecting on the dream. He smiled at the memories. His mind warped from the past and to the present, remembering where he is. He stood up and dressed himself. He left the room. Outside waiting was Abraham.

"What are you doing here?" Henrich wondered.

"Figured I would escort you to Naillain's office. He's waiting for you."

"This early in the morning?"

"Indeed. He said he couldn't sleep. His mind was set on the discussion between you two. He has theories and demands answers."

"Demands?"

"I know it sounds forceful. But, they are his wishes."

"And what if he doesn't like the answers I give him?"

Abraham sighed with a gestured expression. He already knew the outcome and the results which would follow.

"Then, he may kick the three of you out or even try to kill you. For being trespassers who seek to do this place harm."

"And what are your thoughts on all of this?"

"I know the truth. When the time comes, I will be standing on the side of justice and victory. Defeat will be on the other end, hoping for a spot."

Henrich nodded with a grin. He extended his hand toward Abraham. He looked down at the Warslinger's hand and instead hugged him.

"Everything is going according to plan."

"We'll see." Henrich said.

Henrich walked down the hall, making a left turn, finding himself facing the office of Naillain. Henrich took a moment and exhaled. He approached the door calmly and as he went to knock, the door opened. As it opened, he saw Naillain sitting at his desk, staring.

"Come on in." Naillain said.

Henrich entered the office and closed the door behind him. The office was silent. Not a sound. The two stared at one another. Naillain stood up from his desk and approached the Warslinger. Looking him down and up.

"It seems the two of us have something to discuss."

"I'm all ears."

Naillain nodded.

"Good. Good." Naillain said. "Let me first begin by acknowledging your rank as a Warslinger of the Heptad."

"So, you're aware?"

"I've been aware before you even approached our gates. You see, I have a keen eye and a traveling spirit."

"Do tell."

Naillain sat at his desk. He gestured toward Henrich to sit and the Warslinger sat down, facing Naillain at his desk.

"You're not the only one here who's had the pleasure of traveling across the Four Worlds. Seeing their wonders and their marks."

"You call it a pleasure?"

"Oh, yes."

"Is seeing the lives of many perishing and suffering considered a pleasure in your field?"

"Depends on who are the perished and suffered. I can only aid those who are like myself. Like-minded and serve the same god."

"You believe you serve *El*?"

"I serve the God of the Worlds. He brought me to this land. This Silicon Valley that once was. He gave me the tools to reconstruct its foundations and in doing so, I have gained a following, a congregation. A family."

"And the exorcism you performed? Was that of your god's power?"

"Yes. Who else can cast demons out of human beings besides him."

"Yet, a foul spirit cannot cast out demons."

Naillain paused. His face became stern. His intent had changed. This is what Henrich was expecting.

"It appears we serve two different gods." Henrich added. "For the God of the Worlds is the ruler of the Malevolency."

"That so?" Naillain questioned. "And where did you learn of this?"

"From my mentors."

"You speak of the originals?"

"They taught me in their ways. It's how I became a Warslinger. A member of the Heptad."

Naillain cocked his head, standing up once more from his desk. Henrich moved and Naillain paused him with caution. No harm. No sense of attack. Henrich understood and kept still. Naillain approached

the closet and opened its doors. Upon the opening, Naillain pulled
something from the shelves, something large. He turned toward the
Warslinger to reveal a weapon. Henrich recognized it well. By its
design most importantly.

"Do you know what this is?"

"I do." Henrich replied. "Where did you get it?"

Naillain placed the weapon on the desk, wiping the sheath clean.
He removed it, unveiling a sword. The blade was forged in pure gold,
the hilt made of carbuncle with a small emerald set in the middle of the
hilt and a sapphire placed at the bottom of the handle. The blade itself
was thin, with a small thickness in its core. The tip pointed and the
sides sharpened. Henrich knew what kind of sword he was looking at
and was astonished in his spirit.

"I retrieved this during some excavations over in Old Egypt. I
figured someone of your stature would recognize such a weapon."

"It's a *purgesword.*"

"Ah." Naillain uttered with a smile. "And what is a purgesword?"

"A blade not from the Worlds. Made for the Seraph."

"This blade belongs to them who are not like us. This explains a lot.
The detail. The forging. The stones within. Tell me, how much power
do you believe rests inside this sword?"

"Too much for one of our own."

"I don't believe that."

"Doesn't matter what you believe."

"I think it does. I now have the sword. Therefore, I should be able
to use it when necessary. For example, I could use it now and kill you.
Then kill your two other friends."

"You wouldn't get the opportunity."

"You're willing to test that boast?"

"The test was proven when we first met. I've seen your kind before.
Come off benevolent. Seeking friendship, trust, and love. But in reality,
you desire control, dominance, and severity."

"I'm not like those you've met before."

"You're all the same." Henrich confirmed. "It's in your nature to
repeat the actions of your ancestors."

Naillain slammed the sword onto the desk. His temper grew, yet,
he stood back and took in a breath. Relaxing. Henrich kept his eyes
focused.

"My congregation cannot see me like this."

"Then, tell them the truth. Tell them what they need to know about you. About this place."

"I will tell them what I choose to." Naillain rebuffed. "They're under my guidance. Not yours. They will do as I say. As I command. In a sense, I am God here."

Henrich cocked his head. Staring at Naillain, while glancing at the purgesword.

"You know something, 'Father' Naillain? You talk of those in the past. Same demeanor and stature. Such like yourself tried to end the Warslingers, to erase them from the Worlds. Yet, I can speak on the opposite. For the Warslingers have always triumphed over their adversaries. For that reason, I can say, the Warslingers will be gathered again. The Heptad will be restored. All will be done at the sound of the last trump."

"And where did you here this fable?" Naillain questioned. "From one of the books in Old Jerusalem?"

"Moses, my Leader told me." The Warslinger replied. "Proclaimed it from the mouth of El."

Naillain took in the words of the Warslinger, he approached the door, opening it. Henrich stood up.

"Best you leave while I get my thoughts together."

Henrich walked toward the door to exit. After taking one foot forward, Naillain placed his hand on the Warslinger's shoulder. Holding him steady. The Warslinger was prepared to retaliate, for his left hand was already set upon his shooter.

"Best to tell your friends of our discussion, for I fear neither of you will remain here for long."

"Is that a threat?" Henrich said.

"Take it however you please."

Henrich stepped away as Naillain slammed the office door.

III

Henrich walked down the hallway, seeing Abraham, Cody, and Beth waiting for him. From their expression, they knew something was off. By the way Henrich walked toward them, they knew something had happened. Something dark.

"Take it didn't go well." Abraham said.

"It went as we expected." Henrich replied. "We have to warn these people."

"You saw it didn't you?"

"How did he retrieve the sword?"

"He did tell you of his excavation days, did he not?"

"He mentioned it."

Abraham nodded. "We both know the sword doesn't belong to him. Nor to this place."

"It belongs to the Seraph who wielded it."

"What happened?" Beth asked.

"Naillain isn't the man his people believe him to be. He's using them to gain his own purpose."

"That's not good." Cody said.

"He turned the truth into a lie." Henrich said. "That is all I needed to know from him."

"How are we going to warn them?" Beth wondered. "We can't just bombard them with words about their leader going mad."

"There's a way it can be done." Henrich said. "Just give me a little bit of time."

"And what should we do until then?" Cody asked.

"Prepare." Abraham said, nodding to Henrich. "Prepare for what is to come."

Henrich nodded back, walking away from the three and to the outside.

IV

Stepping foot on the outside, Henrich saw the congregation. How the people seemed happy and content in their current state. Yet, the Warslinger gazed up toward the sky and above him, he saw what had brought him to this place. The aura had returned and was set over the entire congregation. Over the community landscape. Its energy was dark. It was and is malevolent. As the aura slowly descended onto the people, their faces were shaped and formed differently. The life which was present in their eyes had faded away. The peace from within had vanished.

"Their will is lost." Henrich said to himself. "Their minds erased. Gone."

The people turned their focus toward the Warslinger, who was standing amid them. The congregation began to form a circle around Henrich. He was aware of their motives and their potential goal. He knew Naillain had done this. More than likely praying to the God of the Worlds to send destruction upon Henrich, Cody, and Beth. Slowly, reaching to his shooters, Henrich was prepared to protect himself at all cost. As his hand gripped the handle on the shooter, his head was jolted up toward the heavens. His eyes became clear white. The people stopped in their movement. The Warslinger was frozen still. After several seconds, Henrich regained control of himself. Shaking himself back to steadiness.

"It is time." He uttered, moving with quick pace to find Cody, Beth, and Abraham.

CHAPTER SIX
SALVATION OR DAMNATION

I

The Warslinger bolted through the door, startling Cody and Beth. Henrich looked around for Abraham and he wasn't there.

"He went off to find someone." Beth said. "What is going on?"

"We have to leave this place."

"Why?" Cody asked.

"It is not what it seems."

Henrich grabbed the rest of his gear. He commanded Beth and Cody to get their stuff immediately. As they made the moves, the doors shattered. They looked back, seeing the congregation. No longer their peaceful selves. Just energized bodies. No life was set in their eyes.

"What's happened to them?" Beth wondered.

"The aura we followed here returned and fell upon them. Taking away all we once saw."

"Then, where's Father Naillain?" Cody asked.

"He's responsible for this. He's not the man he claimed himself to be."

"Then, let's stop him and save these people."

Henrich shrugged. He knew he wanted to, yet, knew it wasn't the determined call.

"Can't. we have to leave now."

"Why in a hurry?"

"Death is coming to this place. From the sky, death will rain over this community. All that will be left is the remains of the dead and the rubble of a fevered dream."

Cody looked over to Beth. She turned to him in response.

"He's right." Cody said. "We need to leave."

Beth sighed.

"Look, I know I'm not from around here. But, I need to understand what you mean by death coming from the sky."

"Fire." Henrich proclaimed. "Fire will rain upon this place. Scorching everything and everyone."

"Then, how will we know it's close?"

"Start by watching the animals. Then, watch your steps as you exit this place."

Beth nodded. Henrich nodded back.

"Good. Let's get going."

Meanwhile, Naillain hears the rumblings of thunder in the distance. He rushed over to the window in his office, gazing outside to see dark clouds making their way toward the area. Red lightning flashing within them.

"This cannot be!"

Naillain ran out of his office and toward the cellar. Opening the hatch, he dove in and rushed toward what sat beneath the congregation grounds. A large statue. An idol of the God of the Worlds. A large figure made in gold, standing at near thirteen feet in height with the physique and facial appearance of a man, yet with the wings of an eagle and the eyes of a lion. Naillain bowed before the statue. Paying obeisance.

"I've done all you asked of me. Why is that storm headed here? What is the cause of all this?"

The statue gave off the sudden appearance of smoke. Naillain keened his eyes to get a better look and what was standing in the smoke was a shrouded figure. Cloaked in a black hood and robe.

"It is you." Naillain said with joy. "Please, help me."

"I cannot interfere with such events." The shrouded one spoke. "However, I can give you the source of this circumstance."

"Tell me."

"The visitors. They are the cause."

"The Warslinger and his fellow travelers?"

"They are not the visitors you seek. They desire to destroy all you have built here. Everything. From the buildings, the homes, the livestock, the plants, and even your precious and faithful congregation."

"I cannot let that happen. Tell me what I must do to spare all that I have built under your name?"

"Rid your land of them by any means and the storm will clear."

"And that is all I must do to keep this place protected by your great power and mercy?”

“That shall be all. You have my word.”

The shrouded one evaporated with the smoke. Naillain nodded continually, sweating profusely. He wiped the sweat from his forehead and contained himself.

“Rid of them. Yes. I can do that. Yes. I know a way.”

Henrich, Cody, and Beth were nearly out of the main building. On a quick turn down a hall, they ran into Abraham and Brandi, who were in a way waiting on them to arrive.

“I was hoping to see you.” Henrich said. “We have to go.”

“I know.”

“You know?”

“I had the vision as well. Same as yours.”

“Then you know what’s about to happen to this place.”

“Indeed. Which is why I must come with you. Brandi and I.”

“Why?”

“This path you walk on, it includes the both of us. Trust me, Warslinger.”

The Warslinger gave a nod to Brandi. She nodded back. Henrich shook his head, putting on his hat, reaching for his shooters.

“Then we need to get going.”

“Yet, you’re forgetting something.” Abraham gestured.

The Warslinger thought and remembered. He turned toward Cody and Beth, telling them he will return. Abraham kept watch over the group as Henrich returned to Naillain’s office. Kicking in the door like it was nothing, he was surprised to find Naillain not inside. Henrich looked around on the desk, it wasn’t there. He knew, approaching the closet. He opened the doors and grabbed what he came for.

“You do not belong here.” Henrich uttered, putting on the sheath of the purgesword. He walked out of the office, returning to the group with the sword’s handle seen over his right shoulder. Abraham nodded with a smile.

“It is coming to pass.”

“Let’s go.” Henrich said.

Reaching the outside of the community, the congregation bolted from all corners. Henrich fired off some shots. He continued firing rounds, until from the ground, black hands and claws came up from the ground. The stench of sulfur engulfed the community. Demons arose.

“Demons!” Brandi yelled.

He paused and reached for the sword. Pulling it from its sheath. The sunlight sparked the golden blade. The congregation and the demons came rushing at him and the Warslinger did what he had to do. Swiping and slashing his way out of the Secret World. Demons clawed against the blade, cutting themselves in the process. Henrich was amazed and continued killing the demons which came toward him in rage. Cody and Beth fired off some shots as well with Abraham and Brandi reaching the community gates.

II

The five make it to the main gate. Yet, the gate is locked and stood strong.

"What are we going to do?" Cody asked.

The Warslinger looked around and from the sky, the thunder roared, and the dark clouds had arrived over the Secret World. Immediately after the thunder, a red lightning bolt came down, striking the church of the community. Setting it ablaze.

"It is happening." Henrich said.

Naillain appeared from the main building, witnessing the church building on fire. Burning down faster at a rate unnatural. The flames had a strange roar to them. As if they themselves were alive and eating the church. Naillain ran toward the front entrance to the church, the doors blew opened by the strong flames, letting out a hollowed screech. Sounds very familiar to a woman's scream in fear.

"No. No. No!" Naillain screamed in anger. "You said you would preserve this place! You gave your word!"

The five watched on, seeing Naillain in a venting rage. Slamming his fists into the dirt.

"What's he going to do?" Beth asked.

"Watch." Abraham said.

Naillain fell to his knees. Nothing left. Nothing to live for. This is what he thought of himself. What had become of his community, he became himself. For if the church was burning, he had to burn with it. In doing so, Naillain arose on his feet and walked into the burning church. Not a thought nor a motion of retreat. Naillain was hopeless. He had nothing else to live for in the Four Worlds. He stepped into the fire. Disappearing into the flames, some of his congregation had caught sight of him and followed along.

"They're killing themselves." Brandi said.

"They chose to die with their leader." Henrich added. "Nothing more."

The rest of the congregation ran amok throughout the community grounds. The sounds of scorching screams echoed from the burning church. Mixed in with the crying howls of the those who remained. Beth looked around and noticed all the animals were gone. Every last one of them.

"They're gone." Beth said. "Just like that."

Henrich felt a peculiar presence of calming in the air. He looked up and made a move on. Abraham also felt it and looked over to the Warslinger. He knew what was to come and turned back to the gate, seeking a way out.

"Then, you know what's about to happen." Henrich said.

A heavy gust of wind came from the east, knocking over the gate, pushing it into the ground, the five ran over the gate remains and stood outside of the grounds. They continued moving further away from the area While doing so, a large whirlwind appeared from the sky and slammed into the grounds directly. Destroying everything and everyone. Due to this, the fire and the whirlwind mixed as one and once the five made it to a stopping point, they saw a flaming whirlwind and people flying into the air, some burning in flames, other not. Cody was astonished, Brandi was in terror, Beth was amazed. Henrich and Abraham paid respect.

"So, everything that was there… the people, the homes… they're all gone?" Beth asked.

"Yes." Abraham said. "Everything. There's nothing left."

"That's a lot of things gone." Cody added. "Just in mere seconds."

Brandi sighed. She approached Abraham and hugged him.

"Thank you for telling me the truth."

"It was only my duty."

Brandi walked toward Henrich and hugged him as well. He hugged back.

"I'll be willing to tag along. If you'll allow."

"You're on the other end of the grounds." Henrich replied. "You're already with us."

"The whirlwinds are the favorite tools of El." The Warslinger proclaimed. "When the darkness comes and calmness covers the air, it is time."

III

After moving miles away from the ruins of the Secret World, the five continued on their journey. The Warslinger was back to focus on his mission, to reach The Haunted City. During their short travel, they encountered some minor remains from the community grounds. Two brown horses and one dirt-speeder. Cody took the speeder. Abraham and Brandi took one of the horses while Beth took the other. From the wilderness appeared Henrich's horse. The same one from time past.

"Where has that horse been?" Beth questioned.

"He comes when needed." Henrich replied with a smile.

Cody approached Henrich, starring hard at the purgesword.

"I have to ask. What kind of sword is that?"

"It belonged to the Seraph. I guess now, this one belongs to me. Which reminds me."

Henrich pulled the machete from within his duster and handed to Cody. Cody grabbed the machete.

"You're giving it to me?"

"I no longer need it." Henrich said. "Besides, you need something else to wield when in a fight. Something extra."

Cody nodded, looking at the machete.

"I appreciate this."

"Where are we off to, Warslinger?" Abraham asked.

"Back on course. I need to reach the City. I need my questions answered and my fate determined.

They all rode off from the Silicon Valley that once was. Yet, in the trees, watch on the Kroger Kid. Rubbing his hands together with a grin covering his face.

Later during the day and the travels, Henrich remembered all the mirror had spoken to him. He was sure to believe what it told him, and he would encounter all it said. While traveling, a rushing sound came from above, they stopped and looked to the sky, seeing a large craft flying overhead. With two large wings spanning feet apart. Its body oval-shaped with a circle in the front and back. No windows on either side, only in the front. Glowing neon lights on both its sides and on the wings. The sound it gave off was close to the beat of a humming drum mixed with a horn. With speed that surpasses anything they've met. Cody stood off the bike.

"The hell was that?!"

"A techno-craft." Henrich said. "This far out? Strange."

"You've seen one of those before?" Beth said.

"I have in my travels."

"Then, you know where they're from." Cody said. "We need one, man."

"That's a difficult task." Abraham said.

"How come?"

"Because the location isn't a friendly one." Henrich said. "Yet, it would make our travels from the valleys, ruined cities, and religious communities look like a child's tale. A shepherd's walk across strait pastures in narrow corners."

"What is this place?" Beth asked.

"They call it Mega City. A metropolis built and filled with cybernetic and technological marvels, and, it's where we're headed."

1

New Haven Detective and U.S. Marshal Preston Maddox drives down a pair of narrow streets as he's on the search for Jonny Cartel, one of the top drug lords of New Haven, Connecticut. Preston, who's wearing his casual suit attire, drives through the quiet streets of New Haven. He turns a corner that heads toward Orange Avenue, around the West River.

"I take it he's around this area. Somewhere."

He turned a corner, which was leading him into a dark pathway. On the other side of the street is a small warehouse covered in rusted panels. Preston drove closer to the warehouse and spotted a white van on the left side. Preston noticed a group of guys standing by the van, wearing all black with their faces barely covered, stacking what appears to be bags of marijuana and cocaine in the back. Preston also noticed a black SUV beside the van with one man coming out, wearing a white suit with slick hair.

"There's the son of a bitch." Preston said as he sees Jonny Cartel.

Preston slowly put the car in park and turned off the vehicle. He exited out of the car and began walking toward the scene. As he walked closer, one of the men spotted him and started yelling. The other men looked up and see Preston. Jonny turned and stared at Preston. Preston does the same.

"Well, looks like the Instinct has found me." Jonny said. "What's the next step, Detective? I hope you're not here for a license plate or sticker check on my SUV here."

"I'm here to take your worthless self to prison. Unless you have another option of a location you'll like to take you?"

Jonny laughed as he looked toward his men. They laughed

along with him, until Preston glared at them. Jonny turned back to Preston, looking at his clothes before keeping his attention focused on Preston.

"Look here, I got an hour before I leave for Miami. So, do me a favor, Maddox. Get a change in style of clothes for once. This whole intimidation approach isn't quite working for you when you're wearing only slacks and a casual jacket."

"I appreciate your generosity in the apparel department, Cartel. Though, I can care less on how you perceive someone's clothing. Anyway, that's not why I'm here and you know why I'm here standing before you and your pack of goons."

"OK, so what can I do to change your mind? Hmm? Give you some profit on the side? Hand you one of my nice fine women to keep you company for the time being?"

"I can care less about your greenbacks or your filthy whores you have stashed back at your place."

Preston held his ground quietly.

"I'm giving you a few choices to make. Either you can come with me, get in my car and I'll ship you off to prison or we can have ourselves a classic standoff where you and most of your men here are killed on the spot. Your decision, not mine."

Jonny stood quietly, not making a sound. Only staring at Preston. Preston kept his eyes locked on Cartel, not making any facial expressions of any kind.

"Tongue turned to lead, Cartel?"

Jonny walked toward the van. He tells his men to pack up whatever they had in their hands and told them to leave the area. The men toss whatever they have into the van and they drive it off into the darkness of street. Preston and Jonny are the only two men at the warehouse.

"Alright, Maddox. Now you have a choice to make and make it right for yourself."

"OK. What are these choices you have in mind for myself that would make me accept them and leave you here to continue your pathetic way?'

Jonny moved his right hand to his side, revealing a revolver under the side of his jacket. Preston noticed it and looked up at Jonny.

"You sure you want to play this little round? I told you already. You want to go that route, you'll end up dead and possibly some of your men too."

"There is no other way around all of this. Now, you can choose your choice. Either you can go ahead and leave this area and don't make a second thought or I could just shoot you on the spot and leave your body to rot."

"So, if I choose the first one, I assume I'll live. If I take the second option, you're going to put one in me. Is that how this is going here?"

"You're smarter than how you dress yourself, Marshal."

"Funny. The decisions you've just gave me are similar to the choices that you gave to that woman I suppose."

Jonny stood frozen still, having what appeared to be a confused and worried look on his face. He shook his head before staying still.

"I'm afraid I don't know what you're talking about, Marshal."

"The woman, whose body was found in the river a few weeks ago. I know you're aware of the case. Only her torso was found floating in the water. Her lower body was discovered across town at some cannibal site where they were partially eating off of it. They eat mostly the thighs and some of the calves. Other than that, they still left some over for anyone to share."

"Holy shit Holy shit! God damn it! If you knew how she behaved and how she acted, you would know deep down that she deserved it, *Instinct!*."

"No, I don't know why. Probably will never figure out why you had her killed and fed to cannibals. But, overall, why did she deserve it? Is it because she didn't have enough federal reserve notes to pay her remaining price off?"

"She was nothing but a traitorous whore. Sneaking behind my back, working for that Ray Colby guy from Jersey since he just opened ship down here in my town. My town! That kind of shit doesn't play fair in my world of business, Maddox and you understand that don't you."

"I do. But, its none of my concern how you run your business. My concern is stopping your business and putting you in a cell or maybe six feet under."

Jonny started to shake, he held up the revolver, pointed at Preston. Preston stood still, starting at Cartel.

"You know what, I've just had enough of this! I have a plane to catch, Marshal. Big business meeting tomorrow. So, if you'll excuse me."

Jonny started walking toward the SUV. Preston stood his ground, with his right hand to his side. Jonny, still pointing the revolver, gets to the driver's seat of the SUV. Preston stared at Jonny with his hand still to his side. Jonny paused and shut the door as he started stomping toward Preston with the revolver.

"You take one step, you son of a bitch and I'm going to blow your fucking brains out all over this place, Instinct!"

"I wouldn't try that, Cartel. You wouldn't want to make a big mistake by killing a United States Marshal and ruining your world of business for a very long time to come. Even if you have a plane to catch for a supposed big business meeting. I'm sure your other clients and partners will understand what you've been through and will find a way for their business to continue in their eyes before they're caught on their own soil."

"I'll spell this out for you once and only this once. The only way I'll ever lose this business is OVER MY COLD, DECAYING, CORPSE!!!"

Preston pulled out his gun and fired shots toward Jonny in the chest a consecutive three times. Jonny slowly fell to the ground, dropping the revolver in the process. Preston walked toward Jonny, who's trying to reach for revolver while lying on the concrete pavement., Preston kicked it away from Jonny's hand. Jonny bled from his chest as his blood flowed around his body, soaking his suit.

"From the look of you on the ground holding your chest, you didn't listen to my warning, Cartel. I told you not to try anything like that."

"It doesn't matter, Marshal. Maybe I deserved to die. Maybe

this is where my journey ends and all. But, soon, there will come a time where you are on the opposite end of a gunshot such as this and you'll be on the ground gasping for your breath. When the day comes that it happens, you'll know what's to come afterwards."

"I highly doubt your kind and strong prophetic words." Preston said with a smile. "But, whenever that day does arrive, I'll be in this same position and the other will be in the position that you're currently lying in."

Preston reached into his pocket, pulling out his black and silver Blackberry. He dialed 9-1-1. The phone started ringing and the 9-1-1 Operator is on the other end.

"9-1-1. Please state your immediate emergency."

"This is Preston Maddox. U.S. Marshal and secondary detective over at the New Haven Detective and Marshal Agency. I've called because I'm currently standing around the West River, close to Orange Avenue at a warehouse. I need an ambulance and a coroner right away."

"An ambulance is on its way, Marshal. Should I assist backup as well?"

"No need for that ma'am. Just the ambulance and coroner will do just fine. I appreciate it and thank you."

He hung up and placed the smartphone back into his pocket. He walked over to Jonny. He kneeled in front of him as Cartel continued to gasp for his breath.

"Don't worry, Jonny. Ambulance is on its way. They'll do what they can for your sake."

"What about the coroner? Don't think I didn't hear that part."

"That's just in case you die here. Which is the most probability."

"Just go to hell, Marshal. Go to hell and burn for the rest of your eternal days."

Jonny's head cocked over as he exhaled his last breath. Jonny died on the spot as Preston only stared at his deceased body. He nodded and walked back to his car, leaving Jonny on the ground for the ambulance to find.

In a suburban neighborhood lies many homes of which families and friends live among each other. One of the homes has its lights on and inside of the home's kitchen is a forty-year old mother washing the dishes as her sixteen-year-old daughter sat in the living room in front of a fireplace watching the TV.

"What are you watching over there?"

"Just some random show. Nothing much on tonight, so I figured I would just watch something that grabbed my interest."

"Seems to me how you're pretty quiet over there that you're either in deep of the show or your bored by it."

"It's interesting so far, mom."

The daughter turned and looked toward the door. Hearing a tapping sound coming from outside. Noticing that the room is quiet except for the TV and her mother washing the dishes. She sat up from off the couch and walked slowly close to the door to see if the sound was coming from outside. The sound started again, this time alerting the mother. She looked over and turned to her daughter, who continued to approach the door.

"What was that outside?"

"I'm not sure. Sound like its right next to the door. Do you want me to go ahead and check it out?"

"Since you're already on your feet, I suggest you could. Just be cautious. There's no telling what that sound could be. Especially in a city like this."

The sound faded away as the daughter inched closer to the door. The mother continued washing the dishes as she glanced over toward her daughter and looked at what was playing on the TV. Hearing no sound, she looked at her daughter.

"Everything alright over there? You seem to be a little nervous?"

"I'm doing fine. Just taking precautions, that's all."

The daughter placed her hand on the doorknob and slowly turned the knob. Opening the door slightly, it gives a chilling creak as she opened the door. Upon seeing nothing or no one by the door, she releases a sigh of relief. The mother walked over toward the living room, seeing her daughter looking out the door and she went back to the kitchen.

"Haley, is everything alright? What are you doing?"

"I'm-"

As she responded to her mother, a hand covered by a black glove quickly reached in from the open creak on the left side of the door. The hand snatched Haley by her jaw and held her mouth shut. She tried to release a scream to gain her mother's attention. Hearing a series of bumping sounds coming from the front, the mother dried her hands and walked out of the kitchen.

"What in the hell are you doing in here?"

She stood in a frozen state as she saw Haley fighting off the black glove. Haley trued kicking out of the door at the individual's body, but the black glove held Haley tightly and slammed her head into the wall. Her mother stood covering her mouth with tears beginning to flow from her eyes.

"Oh my god. Haley, I'm coming."

As she took a step, another black glove reached out from behind her as it appeared the individual came through the back door nearby the kitchen. The intervals entered the home, their bodies appeared to be fit, wearing all black with their faces covered with solid black masks, to where even their eyes aren't revealed. The two individuals throw Haley and her mother against the walls and begin to pummel them to the floor. Both scream for help as they're being beaten.

<u>2</u>

Officers arrived at a suburb home in the New Haven neighborhoods. They are heading through, going back and forth in and out of the home. An ambulance and coroner arrived on the scene as well. The paramedics entered the home with a stretcher, as do the coroner. A black car pulled up and out came Preston. He walked toward a fellow officer. The officer turned and was immediately what some would call star struck.

"U.S. Marshal and fellow New Haven detective, Preston Maddox." The Officer said. "It's an honor to meet you."

"It's an honor to meet you as well. So, what's the situation here, officer?"

"We received a call from one of the neighbors that something suspicious was occurring late last night at this house. From what we know, there were two females, one adult, the other, teenager. It seems that they were both murdered."

"Just being curious here, but, how were they murdered."

"I'll show you.' the Officer said. 'Follow me."

Preston followed the officer into the home. Inside, the home looked like your typical standard suburb home. A nice leather couch in the living room with a flat-screen TV, a beautiful kitchen with nice shiny tiles on the floor. The home currently filled and surrounded with officers, coroner, and forensic scientists. Preston looked inside the kitchen, to the left and seen the adult woman lying on the tile floor with her head severed.

Preston turned and said to the officer, "So, this is the mother. Couldn't really tell from a distance."

"Yes sir, the teenager is in the laundry room. Follow me,

Marshal."

They walked into the laundry room, which is on the left side of the kitchen. Preston looked inside and noticed something red leaking from the dryer. He looked over to the officer and pointed to the dryer.

"Wait. Hold on a quick second. Please do not tell me that she's in there?" He asked.

"Marshal, I'm afraid she is." the officer said.

Another officer walked in and opened the dryer. The door widely opened as an arm flopped out, covered and dripping with blood. They looked inside and see that the teenage girl was shoved into the dryer and stayed inside while it was operating, in which tossed her around and killed her in the process. Preston and the officer left the laundry room, returned outside to their cars.

They walked out of the front door as Preston turned to the officer.

"What was the relationship between the adult and teenager?"

"They were mother and daughter. It was just them in the house at the time. The mother divorced a few months back and took the daughter with her."

"Should we contact the father of the daughter regarding this incident?"

The officer turned and looked toward Preston and said, "I think its best we do that after we get the bodies out of the house."

Preston walked toward his car, but the officer called him back, he walked over to him. The officer looked at little nervous, as if he's about to ask a unusual question.

"Marshal, I have a question to ask you." The officer said enthusiastically.

"Go for it, officer"

"Why do they call you "*The Instinct*" exactly? I never understood the reason for it."

Preston smiled, rubbing his chin and turning his head, looking in another direction. He exhaled slowly before turning and looked at the officer with a mild smile.

"Look at it this way, everyone has instincts in their own sense of perception. It's what makes us do what we do. I just tend to use it all the time. If not most of the time. No hesitation in place of my career. I don't second guess, unless it's confuses the living hell out of me."

"I've always been curious of why you're called that. It must be cool to have a nickname in this line of work."

"Not exactly. From my perspective, nicknames today are now overrated. Don't have any sense of meaning to them."

"Really?" said a voice from behind Preston.

Preston turned and saw his boss, Eldon Ross, the chief commissioner of the New Haven Marshal and Detective Agency. Eldon is a man in his early fifties, wearing a button-down shirt with a nice tie and slacks. Eldon looked at Preston with a glare as he turned to the officer.

"You really believe what Preston's telling you, officer? Because if you are, that just makes you nothing but a rookie in this field."

"Well, sir, he's the Instinct." The officer said without hesitation. "I meant to say, yes sir."

"The Instinct. The only thing Preston could possibly be is a hard-headed guy who doesn't listen to the instructions he's given. Instead, he makes up his own schedule of work and does what he wants whenever he wants. Try convincing me that he's using his gut to make those decisions."

"Eldon, what have I done this time for you to arrive here like this and call me out?"

"You know what you did. So, don't play those childlike games with me, Maddox. Your little incident from last night is quickly spreading around the entire agency and somewhat across the city. This isn't going to go well for you, me, or the agency."

"Eldon, let me explain the situation to you. A few weeks ago, I gave Cartel a choice to leave New Haven or he would meet us end by my hand. After those weeks had passed, I confronted him at one of his hiding spots, smuggling drugs. We talked for a bit as I gave him a short amount of time to leave and he made his decision right there. Besides, I've been on his trail for a few months now and it was getting tiresome."

Eldon shrugged his shoulders. "Yeah right. What else you have in terms of defense? Did you plan on talking him to death?"

"It was self-defense as well." Preston said. "He pulled first, and I fired the first shot. Which was the last shot before I called the police and coroner."

Eldon looked down and around the area as he rubbed his bald head. Glancing at the officers exiting the home. He looked at Preston. "Ok, once you're back at the office, we'll discuss all of this thoroughly and we'll find some way to get through your mess. alright."

"I'll see you back at the office, Eldon." Preston said as Eldon walked away from the area.

The officer walked over to Preston and said, "Jonny Cartel? The elite crime boss, Jonny Cartel."

"What about Cartel is getting you hyped up right now?"

"So, you really shot Jonny Cartel? You killed the bastard. How did it feel accomplishing it?"

Preston stared at the officer. He showed a faint smile before walking away.

"Something just had to be done about the man. That's all I can possibly say on the matter."

Preston walked to his car, gets inside and leaves the neighborhood, going to the Agency Office.

<u>3</u>

Preston arrived at the New Haven Marshal and Detective Agency. He walked into the front doors. Preston looked around and spotted everyone staring at him. Preston walked to the elevator and pressed the button. He stood waiting for the elevator door to open, so he can leave the lobby. One gentleman, wearing a grey suit walked by and looked at Preston. He does the same.

"Is there a problem, sir?" Preston said.

The gentleman turned his head and continued walking. Preston smiled as the elevator beeped and its door opened. He walked in and pressed the button for the third floor. The elevator door closed. He reached to the third floor and sees Eldon waiting for him in the head office. Preston walked toward the office as he passed by other detectives in their offices solving their own cases. Eldon sat behind his desk, surfing through the internet. He heard a knock on the door.

"Come on in, Preston."

Preston opened the door and walked in. "How did you know it was me that was walking through?"

"I can sense you from the elevator. Anyone can tell if you're in the building or not"

Preston smiled. "Funny. I'm sure you could. What did you need to talk to me about exactly?"

Eldon turned to Preston from the computer screen and looked at him with a gaze. Preston glanced his eyes a bit across the office.

"The reason why you're here Preston is because of the actions you took by killing Jonny Cartel. You know what you did was a big

261

mistake?”

“Are you sure it was a mistake. Because from my point of view, the man had to be stopped one way or another.”

“Well, this agency doesn’t go by your point of view, it goes by its Chief’s point of view. Meaning me.”

“I got that well enough.”

“So, because of your actions. With a lot of thought and right timing as well. I’ve decided that you need someone to watch what you’re doing on these cases.”

“Wait a minute. Just hold on a second. What exactly do you mean someone will be looking out for me? Are you implying a suggestion that I might have a partner?”

“Yes, Preston. That’s exactly what I’m suggesting. Look, this is how I see it. You shot Jonny Cartel out in the open with no hesitation. So, if you were to come across someone with a similar history, you would do the same to them. If not worse.”

“Of course, that’s the way I do my job. Besides, Eldon, I already told you that it was self-defense. Cartel pulled out his weapon first, he also threatened to kill me. So, what else was I supposed to do.”

“You could’ve called backup you know.”

“Call backup?” Preston said. “It wasn’t that big of a deal. We were the only two there after he commanded his guys to leave.”

Eldon leaned back in his chair, rocking in it to relax himself and feel comfortable. “So, overall, what’s the big problem about having a partner?”

“My last partner worked on both sides of the law and to make it even crazier, the guy was a snitch.”

“A snitch you say. Good thing your new partner only works on one side of the law. Our side of the law and I’ll also add that she’s very good at what she does anyway.”

“Wait. She?” Preston said with a raised voice.

“Well, of course, Preston. Your new partner is a she. There’s not a problem is there?”

Eldon looked at the door and waved his hand, signaled someone to come in. The individual walked in and stood by the door, just a few inches from where Preston sat. He hasn't looked behind him yet to see his new partner.

"Preston, here's your new partner. In the flesh I should say."

"Preston smirked. "Really. Let me get a good look at her."

Preston turned and sees his new partner. He looked at her from head to toe. She had nice straight blonde hair that reached near her shoulders and she wore a pair of blue jeans with a white buttoned-down shirt and a brown leather jacket to go with it. Preston smiled at her. She showed no emotion toward him, but only gave him a significant stare. As if she had no trust in him of any measure. Preston turned back to Eldon, smirking.

"This beautiful young woman is Emily Weston. A fellow United States Marshal and Detective from Newark in the state of New Jersey."

Preston turned again. "It's a pleasure to meet you, Ms. Weston."

"Same here." Emily said. "You look different than what I've heard."

"Do tell what you've heard about me. I'm sure the tales were pleasant enough to share to everyone, meaning me, myself, and I."

"Just that your what they call an angry man whose hell bent on claiming justice and changing the ways of civilization as we know it. Using your gun as the holy grail."

Preston laughed as Eldon chucked a bit. Emily stayed quiet with only a face with no emotion of any kind. Preston stopped laughing and noticed Emily's face. Eldon gave one more chuckle before glancing at Emily.

Emily is in her late twenties and her confidence gave her the shine of a woman who stood independent, able to get the job done. She looked toward Eldon.

"I've heard quite enough information about the murders that occurred in the neighborhood last night. I was only wondering how the investigation is currently operating?"

"The investigation is currently ongoing." said Eldon. "But, since you asked about it, you and Preston can go to the neighborhood and asks some of the neighbors about anything unusual that occurred that night."

"That's interesting enough to hear."

Preston looked at them both with a grin. Thinking to himself if he should give some words toward them. As the words near his tongue, he decides otherwise not to speak them.

"Um, pardon me, Eldon, I was planning on going over to a location where I know some answers could be currently available."

"That's Great. Even a better idea I could add to that. Since you brought it up and you apparently want some company, why don't you go ahead and take Emily with you on this."

"She can't go with me on this one." Preston said while smiling. "Besides, she's a well-established novice here in New Haven and no offense to her, but, I don't play well with others when it comes to the law and my tasks."

Emily turned to Preston and stared him in the eyes like a predator inching for a bite toward its prey.

"I could say the same about myself. In Newark, I did most of my work alone and had some help in some cases. So, look Preston, unlike some of the women that you've come across and met in your days, I'm not one of them. Nor do I fit in their caliber in any way, shape, or form. I'm just a woman that gets the job done whenever I can, however I can. With or without your assistance."

"Really?" Preston said. "You're saying you're some type of new breed of female detective. I'm sure I could dig up something from your past back in Jersey that could shake you up a bit."

"Not exactly. You'll hardly find anything on me that could lead to your gloating habits."

Emily turned to Eldon and asked for the address to the murder location. Eldon gave her the file of the location. She walked out of the office. Preston stood up and watched as Emily walked to the elevator. She turned to Eldon. Eldon is smirking at Preston.

"Listen, just try to work with her Preston." Eldon said. "Just try, please."

"Sure thing, I'll try. But, I won't like it." Preston said.

Preston left the office as Eldon goes back to the computer, still smiling about Preston's attitude toward Emily. Preston is outside as Emily waited for him at his car. Preston slowly walked towards the car. He sees Emily standing by the passenger's seat. He pointed at her and the car.

"Mind if I ask where's your car?"

"I thought I'll ride with you if you don't mind me." Emily said. "Don't want to waste gas on mine. You should be alright with that I presume."

Preston looked with a glint and said, "You have a nice valid point there."

Preston took out the keys and unlocked the car. Emily sits on the passenger's side as Preston sits into the driver's seat. He started the car and they left the office, driving to the neighborhood.

"Though, I hope you're standing next to the car when I unlock it. So, that way I won't drive off without you and you can call on a cab to pick you up and drop you off."

As they drove down the streets, Emily turned and stared outside her window at all the locations around the area that they've passed by. Preston noticed and slightly turned toward her direction and watched her as she glanced the surrounding locations. Many vehicles are passing by as Preston entered onto the freeway. The number of passing and surrounding vehicles gives Emily a questioning though.

"Looking for something out there?" Preston asked. "You seem very on point looking at these places is all."

"No. I just never knew that New Haven was this crowded." Emily said. "Though it would be much smaller than what I'm currently seeing."

"We have our moments. Some days are good while the rest are bad. We get through it all. So, what brought you here to begin with?"

"Things became quiet around Newark, so I began looking for another location to work. Later, the agency began recruiting and some of the new detectives went to Newark and I was moved here."

"By the look on your face and the tone in your voice, you don't sound to happy about your transfer. Are you happy?"

"Honestly, I didn't expect to come here." Emily said. "I'm

one of the best US Marshals in this country, so I believed they would send me to bigger places like New York, L.A., Miami, Las Vegas, Houston. Just somewhere big."

Preston smiled.

"Very soon, Ms. Weston, you'll realize that New Haven is bigger than it looks to be."

Emily looked. "Can't wait for that."

Currently at the New Haven Airport is Billy Bronson, a scruffy, scrawny, slim man who's wearing a flannel shirt with jeans and a denim jacket, also wearing a baseball cap. He walked towards the tunnel, seeing a lot of passengers walking in and out. He stood at the tunnel, scouted the area looking for someone. He caught someone from a distance and started straining his eyes to get a better look.

"Please let that be him." Billy said.

He finally sees the individual he's come to pick up. Billy walked over to him.

"There's my guy!"

The individual is known as Hoyt Bennett, a man in his late thirties, whose slim with bold features and hair that looked as if it's never been washed or combed. He's also wearing a long-sleeved buttoned shirt with jeans and black dress shoes. Hoyt walked over to Billy, smiling.

"Well, isn't it the great Billy Bronson. We meet once again in this crazy nonstop lifetime of ours."

"Hoyt Bennett. How long has it been, pal?"

They shook hands as Hoyt hugged Billy and patted him on the back. Billy decided to do the same. Hoyt picked up his bags as they walked through the airport.

"How have things been in New Haven since my little departure?"

"You know how this place works. The same old situation with the same old people. Sometimes, even new folks that comes across these ways."

"Billy, I'll say this. It's time to get things going since I'm back in town."

"How so? What do you have planned already?"

"In short words, Billy, it's time to blow some shit up."

Hoyt continued to smile as he started walking toward the exit doors of the airport Billy slowly followed him outside. Shaking his head in uncertainly as to what's being planned in Hoyt's head.

<u>4</u>

Preston and Emily arrived in the neighborhood. Preston parked the car in front of a blue and white wooden house that's across the street from the murder house. They exit out of the car and walked toward the front door, going up the short steps. Preston knocked on the door. They hear someone on the other side of the door.

"Who's there." said a voice from inside.

Emily said, "The US-" Immediately, Preston cuts her off from speaking to the individual on the other side of the door.

"The US Marshal and Detective Agency."

Preston said. "We were hoping you could speak with us about the murder that occurred across from your home."

The door opened and an African-American male is on the other side. He allowed Preston and Emily inside of his home to discuss the murder.

"We would just like to-" Preston said, before Emily cuts him off and smiled toward him.

"We would like to only speak with you, sir. About the incident."

"Come in." the man said.

Preston and Emily walked into the neighbor's home as the door closed. Preston glared at Emily.

"How's it feel to be on the other end?" Emily asked.

Emily walked into the living room as Preston stared at her.

"She's learning." Preston said as he walks inside behind her.

In the country side of New Haven, Coover and Rusty

268

Bronson, the two older brothers of Billy Bronson sit inside their small home. They are sitting around the kitchen table, counting loads of cash. Coover sniffed the cash as Rusty continued counting.

"Why are you sniffing the money?" Rusty asked. "You know how many germs and possible diseases have touch and rubbed against those dollars."

"It's a sign of good fortune, brother." Coover said. "I wouldn't give two shit loads of coke to avoid the smell of a pack of paper."

"Now, Coover, you need to make sure that no one knows what we've currently have up our sleeves." Rusty said.

"What do you mean? What's up our sleeves?"

"The plans? You remember? The plans that we're supposed to follow courtesy of our boss?" Rusty said.

"Oh, yeah. I haven't forgotten that." Coover said. "Speaking of plans, you heard about that double homicide that happened in that neighborhood area?"

"Of course. What's the big fuss about it."

"It had to be fun you know. Killing those two bitches. A mother and a daughter. It's like a double birthday gift to me."

"Yeah. You have your ways with that distorted mind of yours, little brother. Hopefully, you won't have to put it to great use when a particular time comes along."

Rusty grabbed several stacks of money and started placing half of the money into a brown leather suitcase. Coover, on the other hand, started placing some of the money in his jacket pockets.

"You can keep doing what you're doing, Coover. We need to deliver the rest of this money to the boss?" Rusty said. "He wants it as soon as possible."

"You want to deliver it now?" Coover said. "While it's still in the early hours of the day."

"Why else would we wait. Because you're too lazy to get off your ass for a change to do a proper delivery."

"I got you, brother. Lazy my ass. I can get a large amount of jobs completed whenever the situation fits perfectly."

They get up from the table and started walking towards the

front door. They walk outside towards their grey F-250 truck. Rusty placed the suitcase in the back of the truck, covering it with a black sheet made of cloth. Coover opened the door and sat in the passenger's seat. Rusty walks to the side of the truck and gets into the truck and started driving down the pathway.

Back at the neighborhood, Preston and Emily continued speaking with the African American man about the double murders across the street. They are sitting in the living room. Preston and Emily on the blue couch and the neighbor sitting in a wooden chair.

Preston told the neighbor, "We're here on business, sir and because of that we would like to ask you if you've seen or heard anything about the murders that occurred last night across from you."

"Well, officer, I came home around 11:50 and went straight into bed." the Neighbor said. "Though, I did see a black van with two individuals. They were wearing black as well, from head to toe. They came from the back of the van."

"So, is that all you saw before you went to bed?" Emily asked.

"Yes ma'am. I thought they were just stopping by or playing a trick on someone. That's what it looked like to me."

"Another question, if I may." Preston said. "Did you catch the license plate on the back of the van?"

"No, sir. It was too dark for me to see." The neighbor said.

"Are you sure it was too dark, or you just didn't want to look?" Emily asked.

"Excuse me, but, are you assuming that I knew what they were up to?" The neighbor asked.

"No, I'm just assuming that you saw something unusual and you don't want us to know about it." Emily said.

"Sir, with all due respect, she's my new partner and she's new to the town." Preston said. "She hasn't learned much since being here for a short time, so, don't mind her."

Emily gave Preston a deep glare. He sat quietly and gave her a smile. She turned her attention towards the neighbor.

"I'll tell you this, officer. You should get rid of this bitch and find yourself a much more worthy partner." The neighbor said.

Emily gets up from the couch and stood over the neighbor. Preston also stood up and started tapping her on the shoulder to get her attention. Which, he does. Emily gave him another glaring look.

"What?" Emily asked him.

"Just sit back down. We're here on business." Preston said.

Emily continued to stare at Preston. He's silent as a beeping sound is heard. It's Preston's blackberry. He pulled it out of his jacket pocket and answered it. On the other side of the phone is Eldon.

"Maddox." Preston said.

"Preston, I need you and Emily to get back to the office as soon as you can." Eldon said. "We have more things to discuss."

"We'll be there." Preston said.

Preston hung up the phone and placed it back into his pocket. He looked over at the neighbor and told him that it was nice meeting him and thanked him for his cooperation. The neighbor thanked him back and they left the house and get into the car, heading back to the office.

"Where are we going?" Emily asked.

"Eldon needs us back at the office. Something's come up I suppose."

Meanwhile, at a local bar in town, Hoyt and Billy are sitting at the bar, drinking shots of whiskey. Hoyt drinks his and puts the glass down. Billy tried to drink his glass, but can't bear the taste of it. Hoyt watches him calmly as he tried drinking the glass of whiskey.

"I sense there's a problem, Billy?" Hoyt asked. "You can't take a shot of whiskey?"

"Sorry, Hoyt. It's just too strong for me." Billy said.

Hoyt looked toward the female bartender, he gets her attention and pointed to the bottle of vodka on the shelf. She grabbed the bottle and placed it in front of Hoyt.

"Please pour my good friend here a glass of this wonderful vodka you have here." Hoyt said to the bartender. "From our he's looking, he could surely use it right now."

"I'm not sure about that, Hoyt." Billy said. "Vodka isn't my type of drink."

The bartender poured the vodka into another glass and she handed it to Hoyt. He took the glass and turned to Billy. Billy glanced at him, then glanced at the glass. Hoyt smiled.

"You are a twenty-eight-year-old man that working for the local trucking company and now, your closest friend has finally made his return home. The best thing you could do right now is have a decent drink with him."

Billy looked at Hoyt and turned his attention toward the glass. He took the glass and held it up. Hoyt kept his smile as he watched Billy with the glass in hand.

"Hoyt, if it's for your hometown return and to have you here safe and sound, I guess I'll drink to that." Billy said as he drank the vodka from the glass.

Billy's facial expression changed after drinking the vodka and looked as if Billy smelled manure close to his nose after drinking. Hoyt looked at him and smirked. Hoyt's expression showed he became proud that his friend decided to have something like vodka to drink for a change. Hoyt is now happy and turned to the bartender.

"Dear sweetheart, another round, please" Hoyt said. "My friend and I are going to have some fun around here. This is what I'm talking about."

<u>5</u>

At the city bank, Coover and Rusty parked, wearing all black with their faces covered with ski masks. Rusty gets out of the truck, while Coover stayed inside to watch the area. Rusty went ahead and walked into the bank. Once he entered the bank, seeing the people setting deposits and some even cashing their checks, Rusty started shouting in a high grumpy voice for everyone to get down. The people in the bank get down and hide under tables and around walls. Rusty is carrying a brown gym bag on his left side and a magnum gun in his right. He walks toward the counter and slams the bag onto the counter and points the gun at the banker.

"Alright, little smart boy. Start placing the money in the bag right now!" Rusty yelled. "Come on, you asshole, we don't have much time to spare with your slow packing speed."

The banker is highly afraid and started placing tons of money inside the bag. The people watched in fear. Another banker, whose hiding behind another counter, pulled out a shotgun. He placed the shotgun in gear and stood up, pointed it at Rusty. Rusty sees him and the shotgun goes off, Rusty ducked quickly to avoid the shot. Rusty ran over to the banker and shot him in the head as blood splattered across the golden-brown wall. The remaining civilians run out of the bank to avoid being shot themselves. Coover, still in the truck, sees the number of people running out of the bank. He used the door mirror to see if one of them could be Rusty.

Rusty is still inside the bank, collecting the remaining amount of money on the counter. He looked at the banker and asked him if he was done. The banker confirmed that he was finished as Rusty ran out of the bank, heading for the truck. People continue to be scattered around the entire interior and exterior of the bank. Rusty tossed the bag in the back of the truck. He turned and waved his hand toward Coover.

"Coover! Now's the time." Rusty yelled. "Load the damn thing, will you."

"Right away, brother."

He exited out of the truck, carrying a rocket launcher on his right shoulder. Coover slowly aimed the launcher toward the front of the bank and fired it. The rocket soared through the midair as it smashed itself into the bank, causing it to explode. Fire rises from the shot as they get back into the truck and drive off, leaving the bank in a sea of flames.

Preston and Emily arrived back to the agency. They walked toward Eldon's office and inside they noticed Eldon in the boardroom, speaking with a young man. The young man is wearing a red shirt with brown slacks. They walked into the boardroom and Eldon sees them.

"I see you've made it." Eldon said. "I take it there were no problems speaking with the witness."

"No problems there in that situation. So, you called. I guess there's a situation that we should know or something in that area?"

"A mighty situation. Mainly for you and your concern for New Haven. I thought you should know that your old friend is back in town." Eldon said.

"What old friend?"

"You remember that Bennett fellow, don't you?"

"Which one? The older brother or the younger brother?"

"Can't figure out which one. The two of you were friends at one point before both of you went on different paths in life."

Preston looked confused. "You mean Hoyt? Hoyt Bennett? The Hoyt that was sent to DC because of his previous actions in this town."

"Yes, apparently, Hoyt's back in town and he was last seen at the airport." Eldon said.

"What's the big deal with this Hoyt Bennett?" Emily said. "Terrible individual?"

"Hoyt is a highly-known criminal that has caused major chaos across this city. Apparently, he was caught and sent to prison in Washington D.C. But, now it seems that he's been released and he's back in town." Eldon said.

"After a while, me and Hoyt were great friends. Until I left for bigger things and he stayed and dove into obstacles that allowed himself to gain the attention of the law. After a series of events that featured banks, churches, and stores blowing up, he was arrested and sent to DC."

"So, there's no telling what he'll do next." Emily said.

"I'll visit the bar to check up." Preston told Eldon. "I have a feeling he'll be there."

"Ok. If you truly feel that's the case here."

Preston looked behind Eldon, seeing the young man. Preston pointed at him and looked toward Eldon. Eldon only glanced at Preston before centering his full attention toward him.

"While I'm at it, may I ask who's the young man over there? He looks like a kid. You're brining in kids now, Eldon?"

"He's not a kid. He's only in his early twenties. No big deal."

"Early twenties you say. To me, the boy looks like he's in his mid to late teens. You're sure you got the age correct?"

"I'm positive, Preston. Just don't bother the fellow."

Eldon turned and allowed the young man to walk forward. He walked with a sense of determination.

"Preston, Emily, this is Cody Aries. A young man who's highly trained in this field. He will be operating here from now on along with us in the agency."

"Highly trained you say?" said Preston.

"Yes sir, Marshal." Cody said toward Preston. "I'm a highly trained marksman and I've been training for years."

"Really. You're looking at the same here."

"I trained in sniper. Near and far distance from the target."

"That's an impressive feat. But, firing shots from afar is not my cup of Joe."

Emily walked forward and extended her hand to Cody. They shook hands and smiled toward one another. Emily welcomed him to the agency. Cody said it's a nice honor to meet the other marshals. Eldon walked over to Preston as Emily and Cody spoke with one another.

"So, what were you and Emily doing before you came here?" Eldon said. "If I may have the privilege of asking the two of you."

"We visited the murder neighborhood and spoke with the neighbor who lived across the street from the home." Preston said. "He spoke to us and gave some information regarding the murder victims as well as the supposed murderers."

"Ok. Get any information?" Eldon said. "On who the culprits could be?"

"Not exactly. Though, he did mention a black van with two individuals wearing black. He couldn't see any faces sense they were wearing masks. I believe ski masks for certain."

"Did you get the license plate numbers?" Eldon said. "Did he see it?"

"No. He said it was too dark for him to see." Preston said. "Only saw silhouettes of the two culprits and light reflecting off the van they got into."

"We'll be on the lookout for any black vans with two individuals." Eldon said. "Especially if they fit the size descriptions that were given to us by other neighbors in the area that spotted them."

"Sure. Speaking of looking out, it my break time." Preston said. "So, if you don't mind me."

Preston left the boardroom as Emily and Cody continued speaking with one another. Eldon prepared to leave the boardroom, but Preston walked back in. Beginning to speak to Eldon.

"Oh, one more thing while I'm standing here."

"Ok, Preston. What is it?"

Preston looked at Emily and pointed toward her. She looked at him and so does Eldon.

"Not on me or any of my own thoughts. I'll just have to say

you're going to have to do something with her. From my point of view in this field, she's a bad cause."

"I would say the same about you." Emily said. "No need of going over to Eldon to talk him into releasing me from the agency."

"Very well, Watson. It was nice meeting you, Cody."

Cody waved to Preston as he left the room. Emily looked over at Eldon. He shrugged his shoulders and left the room.

"Don't mind Preston. He loves to talk bad about others before they can get a word out about himself."

Hoyt and Billy are still at the bar, though it seems that Billy is drunk from the distorted look on his face. Hoyt smiled as he sees how happy Billy appears to be from drinking the amount of alcohol.

"Billy, how are you feeling right now?" Hoyt asked. "You look like you're feeling fine."

"Better than those murder victims from last night that's for damn sure."

The word *murder* caught Hoyt's derived attention. He wanted to hear more about the murder. So, he inched closer to Billy and turned toward him, beginning to ask more questions about more details involving the murders.

"What do you mean murders?"

"I forgot to tell you while we were leaving the airport. Probably couldn't talk about it there because the TSA and other officials would've arrested both of us as suspected terrorists. But, a mother and daughter were found murdered this morning. But, the murder occurred sometime around last night0. Possibly after midnight."

"May I ask how they were murdered? There had to have been some description on the bodies."

"You sure you want to know? Because it's very graphic in nature, the two bodies. I mean completely graphic. It could make your stomach turn circles."

"Just tell me how the bodies looked, Billy."

"Ok. Fine. The mother's head was severed completely from

the body and the daughter was found contorted inside an operating dryer."

"Good lord. Do they know who the murderers are? Are there any traces toward them? Any significant features of any kind?"

"Not, not as of now." Billy said. "Though, though, that Marshal agency group now have a hot female detective on the case along with that Preston guy."

"Preston? Sounds familiar to me. What's this Preston guy's last name?"

"Um… *Maddrops, Maddcocks, Maddtops.* Something along that category. Not sure on what it actually was."

"Madd? Its *Maddox.*"

Billy turned and looked at Hoyt with a confused gaze. Billy shook his head as Hoyt only stared.

"Ok? Its Maddox. So, what's the big deal about this guy anyway? Is he a cold case or a no-good asshole?"

"The big deal about him, Billy, my good friend is I know Maddox very well. We have a large past with each other and since he's still here, I've just conjured up an idea that will shake the foundation of New Haven as we know it. It will cause Maddox to go insane."

"What is it, this idea of yours that will shake up the city and that Maddox fellow?"

"I'll tell you once we leave. We can't risk the chance of someone hearing what we're talking about in this place. There's no telling what could happen if someone were to hear it."

"Well, let's leave now and you can tell me in the truck. If that's how you really feel about this situation."

Hoyt stood up from the barstool and handed the bartender a one-ounce silver eagle. She took it and looked at Hoyt.

"May I ask what this is?"

"Just a little something to remember me by sweetheart."

Hoyt blew her a kiss and gave her a wink. She smiled and walked to the back. Hoyt and Billy left the bar.

Back in the countryside of town, Coover and Rusty are at their home. They counted the money that was stolen from the bank. The money was scattered across a wooden table with a couple of dollars falling on the floor. Coover looked at Rusty with a concerned look. Rusty looked at Coover. "What's the look for?"

"Are we giving all the money to the boss?" Coover said. "Because, I would like to keep some it to buy someone equipment for our projects."

"No." Rusty said. "There's no way I'm doing that. The money in the suitcase will go to him. The money from the bank belongs to us."

"Good. That's good." Coover said. "Oh, you have any possible idea where "Little bro" might be?"

"He's probably handling something for mama." Rusty said. "She loved him the most you know."

"Yeah, she really cared a lot for him." Coover said. "What does that say about the two of us."

A knock on the door is heard and Coover goes to answer it. He opened the door and it's their boss, Ray Colby, a crime lord originally from New Jersey, wearing his black suit with a red shirt. Rusty comes from the kitchen to greet him.

"Mr. Colby, sir." Rusty said. "We didn't expect you to be here."

"I'm here for my money." Colby said. "Now, do you have it for me?"

"Yes sir, we do." Rusty said.

Rusty walked toward the kitchen and rolls out the suitcase. He opened the case for Colby, revealed to him the money inside. Colby smiled and looked at the two brothers. He patted them on their shoulders as he stood up and walked toward the front door.

"You boys are doing a fine job." Colby said. "Don't let that go to your heads or you won't be having a job."

"We try our best, boss." Coover said.

"Sure, you do." Colby said as he left their home.

<u>**6**</u>

Hoyt and Billy are sitting on the outskirts of town inside of a small cabin-like house surrounding by a few trees that stood up in the backyard. The front yard is covered with small bushes and short grass. Inside the house are mounted heads of deer on the walls and stuffed bears in the corners. Billy looked at the surroundings and turned to Hoyt.

"Hoyt, what's in this place if I may ask you?"

"This place, my good friend, was one of my old hideouts we had to keep ourselves from the law in any circumstance. It's just a little something I left behind before they were carried off to D.C. Fun times this place was."

"From the look of this place, it damn sure looks as if some rough-ass hunter appeared to be living in here. No offense, Hoyt, but, you're not exactly a hunter."

"I haven't hunted in quite a long time. Though, this cabin here, it belonged to my brother Darren. I guess you could consider him a rough-ass hunter. Seeing as he was always the one going out and catch us some deer, fish, elk. Hell, even one time, he brought home a total of eight squirrels for us to eat since he couldn't find any deer to track."

"Sounds like a good brother to me."

"Speaking of him, how's he been with me being absent and such?"

"From what I understand, he's still working in the mechanic areas across town. Stays to himself as usual."

"That is my brother's way of living a peaceful life. I rather not bother him in such a time we're in."

Hoyt walked toward the kitchen area, where he noticed a small closet. He walked to the closet and pulled out a key. Billy walked around the home, looking at its details left and right. Billy walked over to where Hoyt was located.

"So, the law couldn't find you here? In this little shack."

"No, they could not. The damn officials couldn't even find a trace that lead here."

They later hear a knock on the door. Before they could turn around to see who it was, they suddenly hear a voice coming from the door.

"It seems that streak has come to an end." The voice said. "If you catch that kind of clear understanding."

Hoyt and Billy turn around, seeing Preston standing in the doorway. Hoyt looked and started smirking. Billy started to shiver as if he's afraid of Preston, due to him being a US Marshal and a homicide detective.

"Of all the people who are involved with law enforcement, there would be only one of them that could possibly find me. It's been a long time hasn't it, Preston? How come you didn't show up at the airport for my arrival or should I say, my comeback to the city?"

"Didn't know you were returning to New Haven. Could care less if you didn't."

"Funny sense of humor. You should've checked your calendar, my dear friend if you really wanted to know when it was taking place. I assumed someone like you should've had the knowledge that I would return to the city that made me famous. Due to my past experiences."

"I knew you would. Just didn't think you'll be back this soon." Preston said. "So, why is it that they let you out of prison so early? Good behavior? Good assistance with the mop up crew?"

"I did my time and they released me in the right manner." Hoyt said. "Though, it did influence me of what to do with my life once I returned to the rightful place that I call home."

"The rightful place you call home? Interesting question I have and will love to ask at this peculiar time. How did your time behind bars influence you to be more of a smart-ass rather than a dumb-ass? I figured that someone who was locked up for quite a long time would have better thinking skills rather that going back into your history to what sent you into your rightful home called a prison."

Hoyt laughed as he continued the conversation by saying, "A smart-ass. Though, that's what I am, but, I thought that I could help out with the double homicide that occurred in that neighborhood last night."

"Who told you about that?" Preston asked. "I take it you've already been around the city."

"Oh, Billy here, told me about the situation."

Preston looked over to Billy and pointed at him and looked back to Hoyt. Preston turned back to Billy. Preston smiled as Billy continued to be in fear of him.

"Billy? As in Billy Bronson? Of the Bronson Brothers?"

"Yes sir, fellow Marshal detective or whatever you're supposed to be in the law enforcement. That is who I am." Billy said with a tremble in his voice.

Preston turned back to Hoyt, who said, "He told me about it while we were having a drink at the bar earlier."

"So, that explains the smell of vodka on your breath." Preston said. "I knew you were up to something. You and alcohol don't mix very well, Hoyt."

"Neither, do you and I." Hoyt said. "Though, we were friends long ago, that is until you went off to college and I just stayed here and became a crime lord."

"And after that you were caught and sent to prison in D.C." Preston said. "Yeah, we all get the back-story here."

"Yeah, we all do." Hoyt said. "But, it would seem you're here only because you have me as a suspect involving the murder case. Otherwise, why would you be here."

"I'll put it to you this way, Hoyt." Preston said. "If I find out that you had anything to do with the double homicides or you have any information regarding them, you my friend, will be in some deep shit."

Hoyt laughed and said, "Wow, still using those same old lines from high school, I see."

"Yeah, they still come in use." Preston said.

Hoyt walked back into the kitchen, going back to the closet. He looked back at Preston.

"Now, if you'll excuse us, we have some business to conduct. So, if you please leave."

Preston smiled as he walked toward the door. He opened the door and put one foot out before telling Hoyt it was nice seeing him. Hoyt said the same to Preston as he left the home. Hoyt pulled out the key once again and finally opened the closet. Billy stands behind him, watching as Hoyt pulls out a large black leather box, roughly thirty-six to forty inches.

"Whoa. What's in that box, Hoyt?"

"The solution to our new cause. Wait till you see what's in here."

Hoyt opened the box and he sees what's inside. He began to smile as Billy walked over and looked at what's lying inside of the box. Billy turned to Hoyt in shock as he asked him, "Hey, Hoyt. Is that what I think it is?"

Hoyt pulled out the object that's laying inside the box and holds it up in his hands. Billy starts backing up to avoid being hit by the object.

"Billy, it's time that we blow some shit up." Hoyt said as he looked down at his hands, revealing a grenade launcher. Hoyt looked up toward Billy and released a great smile.

<u>7</u>

It is now within the evening across New Haven as Preston headed out to eat at a seafood restaurant. He walked in and went up to the counter, where a waitress was waiting. He scouted the restaurant himself to find a perfect table for himself. He smiled at the waitress.

"How many, sir?" the Waitress said.

"Just one, ma'am." Preston said.

The waitress walked Preston to his table and he gets a glass of water and orders a Shrimp Alfredo Pasta with a salad. The waitress left the table and Preston looked around the restaurant. Seeing lots of people eating in the restaurant and talking with each other, he spotted someone in the distance. He sees a woman that looks highly familiar to him and he realized that it's his ex-wife, Karen Rogers. She turned and saw him, to which he waved at her and she done the same. Preston turned again and saw his ex-wife coming toward him.

"Karen?" Preston said.

"Hi, Preston." Karen said. "It's good to see you once again."

"Same here." Preston said. "Good to see you as well."

"So, how's life been treating you?" Karen said.

"You know, good days and bad days always come and go." Preston said. "How about you and your life so far?"

"Things have been going quite well for me and my husband."

"Hopefully its going well."

Preston looked behind Karen and saw a man approaching them, wearing a smooth grey suit with black tie. He rubbed his hand over his head as he walked toward them and looked as if he knew one of them. Karen turned and noticed him. She called him over to the table. He stopped at the table, smiling as he placed his arm around Karen's shoulders. Preston looked at him.

"From the arm trick, I take it you're the husband that she just mentioned?"

"I'm Richard, Richard Rogers." he said. "You look a little familiar. Have we met at some place?"

"Not that I can think of at the top of a hat."

"This is my husband, Preston." Karen said. "Just wanted you two to finally meet one another."

"I understand. It truly is an honor to finally meet you, honestly. So, what is your occupation exactly. If you don't mind me asking. Just curious is all."

"I run a car dealership. It keeps me in the excitement mood. One day I'll own my own dealership and potentially a car manufacturing business."

"He just loves cars. He's told me how he wants to start a vintage car collection, but, doesn't have enough of the money to afford it. Though, he's getting there. Hopefully, he'll have his collection and be proud of what he's done."

"Well, hopefully, it finds a way to get there and collect all the vehicles he wishes for."

Preston looked at Richard and introduced himself to him and they shook hands. Richard tells Karen that they have to go, to which Karen said bye to Preston, he does the same as he watched them leave the restaurant.

At a 7-Eleven, Emily stopped at a gas station, refilling the gas in her white Lincoln. Once she finished pumping the gas, she walked into the station and paid the cashier. The cashier noticed Emily's badge on the side of her hip. He glanced at her before she turned toward him.

"Something wrong?" She said.

"No ma'am. I was just looking at your badge right there. So, I take it you're a cop or something?"

"US Marshal and a homicide detective."

"Two occupations with different circumstances and outcomes. Marshals are in the big leagues compared to homicide detectives."

"I suppose you could say it that way."

She paid off the gas, nodded to the cashier and walked out of the station. As she walked back to her car, she noticed a black van parked in a shadowed area across from the gas station. She entered the car and sat for a few seconds. Trying to see if anyone will come out of the van. Though, no one did as the van stayed still and she drove off the station grounds.

During the night, Coover and Rusty arrived at a warehouse in the outskirts of New Haven. They walked inside and see four sets of steel tables merged into one with over a dozen men in suits inside.

The men sitting down at the tables are crime lords and the men standing behind them are their thugs, carrying AKs and shotguns. Rusty looked around the warehouse.

"Have any of you seen Colby around here?"

"I'm right here." said Colby walking toward them from the back entrance of the warehouse.

"Colby, we need to speak with you." Rusty said.

"About what?" Colby said. "Is it something involving the money?"

"Yes sir." Coover said. "We just need to have a word with you."

Colby walked toward the end of the table and sits. He told Coover and Rusty to sit as well. They find their sets of chairs and sit as well. The other crime lords stared at them, as if why should they be here. Rusty glared at each of them and turned his attention toward Colby.

"Me and my brother here, boss, are just wondering about our extra share with your upcoming event." Rusty said. "We're just curious about the situation is all."

"The upcoming event will be announced soon." Colby said. "As for now, you two should be concerning yourselves with the

Marshals. Since, they'll discover it was the two of you, who committed those murders."

Coover stood up, staring at Colby, "What do you mean the Marshals?! They've already got some suspects in line and we aren't any of them."

"Sure, you aren't, Coover." Colby said. "But, I do believe that you will be soon enough. Just make one mistake and they'll find you."

"I'm sure you heard that Hoyt Bennett is back in town." Rusty said.

"Hoyt Bennett has finally returned, so you say." Colby said. "Well, this is great. He can be a major asset in my event. That is unless he backs out somehow."

"What do you want us to do?" Rusty asked. "Find him and bring him in for you?"

"Or we could just kill him for you." Coover said. "Which ever one you prefer, boss."

"No need for that in this situation. Just concern yourselves about your own business this time around." Colby said. "I'll deal with Hoyt Bennett."

Coover and Rusty left the warehouse as Colby began speaking with the other crime lords in the room. His assistant closed the main door into the office area, other assistants closed the entire warehouse.

Preston headed back to his apartment during the late night. He gets there and realized that the door is unlocked. From his point of view, someone unlocked the door and went in. He pulled out his handgun and kicked in the door. He looked to his left and saw a woman sitting at his table. She is Italian, has beautiful black hair and seductive green eyes. She slowly drinks from a glass of wine from Preston's pantry.

"Carla." Preston said. "What the hell are you doing in my apartment?"

"Hello, Preston." Carla said. "It's been a very long time."

"Yes, it has." Preston said. "Again, what are you doing in my apartment? I don't recall handing you a key."

"Sit down and I will tell you how I came into entering your apartment."

Preston sat at the table and stared at Carla Garcia, his ex-girlfriend of six years. She stared at him as she continued drinking the wine. Preston only stared at her as she drank. Thinning to himself of why she's currently in his apartment.

"I told the complex owner that I lived in this apartment and forgot the key. So, he gave me one and that's how I ended up in your apartment. Funny stuff, huh."

"I don't find anything funny about someone receiving a key to an apartment that they don't live in or pay the bill for."

"You seem surprised, Preston." Carla said. "I kind of figured you would be. Seeing me here and all."

"What exactly did you think how I would react seeing you here." Preston said. "I wasn't expecting you, at all. Especially inside my apartment to which were you do not reside."

"You know I've always done unexpected things." Carla said. "You should remember all those times."

"I do remember those times." Preston said. "But, you would've learned not to do those things after the times. One of these days, it will get you killed."

"I'm sure I would survive it, if you were still by my side." Carla said. "Are you still on my side?"

Preston leaned in. "What exactly are you doing here, Carla?"

"Excuse me, is that the way to say hello, I'm only here to surprise you." Carla said. "Figured you would love this surprise."

Carla took out another glass and poured wine inside. She passed it to Preston, who took a sip out of the glass. As if a glass of wine would pull him out of concentration.

"How would you coming here, not surprise me." Preston said smiling. "As I told you, I don't recall you living here."

"Oh, I almost forgot. I did hear about the incident that occurred between you and Jonny Cartel and the double homicide." Carla said. "It's flowing all around the city. You're not too far from being considered a fugitive with all this on your record."

"I did what needed to be done." Preston said. "I gave him a warning and he didn't take it. So, I had to put him down. Besides, Cartel was a fugitive in his own right of action."

"Now, that's something I wouldn't expect from you, Preston." Carla said. "One day, it will come to pass that you'll be on the other side of the chase."

"I take it you never got to understand me very well, Carla." Preston said. "As a matter of fact, you've never known me very well."

"Oh, is that so." Carla said smiling. "Let me remind you of how you taught me some of your detective skills and some of your tricks. That was really our relationship. You're giving me free lessons on how to do the things of the law."

Preston smiled, "So, you're going to try to use my tricks against me? Is that the real reason why you're here? Some sort of information, you're trying to gain from me?"

"Not exactly, baby." Carla said. "Though, I can tell you that I plan to use them to my advantage when the right situation arises."

"Really." Preston said as he put his glass down on the table. "Because, I remember you always having to use your looks to your advantage to gain whatever you wanted."

"Which is why you're going to teach me the rest of your techniques." Carla said. "I believe I'll need them for whatever comes my way in the near future."

Preston stared at Carla as she does the same. Preston smiled and said, "I don't think so."

Carla put down her glass and gets up from the chair. Preston looked her, as she's wearing all red. She walked behind him and started massaging his shoulders. Preston doesn't do anything, though he's facial expressions shows that he's not liking it. She started rubbing him on his chest. He turned and looked at her.

"You know this isn't going to work." Preston said. "Don't even think it will in your little warped mind."

"Aw, it worked before remember." Carla said. "It worked all the time to be exact."

Carla sat on Preston's lap and begins kissing him. He starts kissing her back and he holds her in his arms tightly and lays her onto his bed. They continue kissing and go to the point of taking each other's clothes off. Now, they are only in their underwear as they continue kissing and she moans as Preston rubs his hand up Carla's thigh. They are both enjoying this moment as they continue to do so. Then, they go under the bed sheets.

Driving a small pickup truck is Hoyt with Billy in the passenger's seat. They drove toward a small building, appeared to be made of brick. it's a jailhouse. Hoyt stopped the truck and looked around the area. Billy stayed inside and began to worry. He looked over at Hoyt and said, "Why here? Why this place?"

"Billy, this is a small jailhouse, where only the minors are concerned to go." Hoyt said. "I figure its best just to put them out of their misery."

Hoyt gets out of the truck and walked toward the back. Hoyt opened the black box from the back and pulled out the grenade launcher. He walked in front of the truck and pointed the launcher towards the jailhouse. Billy noticed a small group of guards at the front door.

"Hoyt, you can't be serious about this!" Billy said. "Hoyt?!"

"These are the moments that create legends, Billy." Hoyt said. "Now, we will become the legends ourselves."

One of the guards noticed Hoyt and pointed at him. Hoyt aimed the launcher and yelled, "INCOMING CALL!" and fired the launcher. The grenade flew into a window and exploded the entire jailhouse. The guards inside are killed by falling debris and the building is up in flames, instantly killing anyone who was inside. Hoyt smiled.

"Hoyt, let's go!" Billy yelled. "Come on, Hoyt!"

"Step one, accomplished." Hoyt said.

Hoyt placed the launcher in the back of the truck and drove away from the scene as the jailhouse is consumed in flames. Hoyt laughed and smiled as he drove away from the area.

<u>8</u>

Preston woke up from the night he didn't expect. He looked around and noticed that Carla is gone. He put on his clothes and searched the room and found his notes stolen. He knew that Carla took the notes from his room. The notes contained most of Preston's skills and tricks that he's used and currently using in his field of work.

"Shit." Preston said. "Goddamn. Shit."

He grabbed his keys and left for the office.

At another location, inside a mobile home, Billy sat still until he heard a knock at the door. He opened the door and its Hoyt. Hoyt walked in to discuss the recent attack on the jailhouse. Billy is still shaken up by the event and Hoyt tries to discuss the reason for blowing up the jailhouse.

"Hoyt, I just don't understand why that location." Billy said. "Of all locations that could've been chosen."

"Look, I know that it must've freaked you out from the start." Hoyt said. But, from watching that, just imagine what else we can accomplish together. By doing this, we can set boundaries across New Haven and later beyond Connecticut itself."

"I see your point there, but, I don't think I can continue going on like this." Billy said. "Who knows what could happen next. I could be arrested or even shot at."

Hoyt looked at him, "What do you mean, Billy? You're in the business of a lifetime. For God's sake, in this line of work, you get arrested, you get shot, you get stabbed. Hell, in some occasions, you get raped, molested and mutilated. Now, we don't need to deal with your feelings and emotions on this line of work."

"I'm just saying that it's difficult for me to do these things when the Marshal guy knows who I am, and I can't imagine what could happen next." Billy said. "I could go to jail or worse."

"You shouldn't worry about my old friend, Preston." Hoyt said. "That's his instinct to search and find, from all angles. It's in his blood, but, he will never get the opportunity to catch you. That is if you're on my side."

"I'm always on your side, Hoyt." Billy said. "Always."

Hoyt smiled, "That's good to know, because I'll need you for our next task at hand."

"Which is what?" Billy asked.

"I hear from a few anonymous sources that Colby and his crime lord buddies of New Haven gather together at a warehouse on the outskirts of town."

"So, how do we find the warehouse?" Billy asked. "If that's where they are exactly?"

"I already know the warehouse's location. I used to work in there." Hoyt said. "It was once used for a trucking company, until the company closed it down and moved over to China. Now, it's the place where all drug lords hang out and talk amongst each other. The perfect opportunity to get rid of the garbage that fills this city with disgust and hatred amongst its people."

"So, when do we strike and are we using the grenade launcher again?" Billy asked.

"We will be using a launcher alright." Hoyt said smiling. "We strike within the next two days. When the building is packed."

Preston walked into the office and sees Eldon, Emily, and Cody inside of his office. He walked toward the door and went inside.

"Preston, good to see you here up and early." Eldon said. "From the look of your face and body language, you look like you have a rough night."

"Kind of." Preston said. "It was a little rough and edgy for me. What's the situation today?"

"A city bank was robbed and blown to shit yesterday." Eldon said. "Later that night, a jailhouse was blown up. So, we will be going to these two locations today to get evidence and information. We'll go ahead and start with the bank first."

"Alright. Are there any suspects involved with these cases?" Preston asked. "Or am I jumping the front gun here."

"You're jumping the gun here. Though we have no ideas right now." Eldon said. "But, there is a banker who's waiting for us at the bank scene. He could give us answers."

Preston looked. "Great, I'll meet you guys there and we'll discuss everything on the sites."

They left the office and head to their cars. Preston noticed Emily's white Lincoln. She looked at him and he smiled. Cody gets into the jeep with Eldon. They all drove down the street, making a left turn towards the City Bank. Few minutes later, they arrived at the bank scene, looked at the building covered with a black charcoal appearance. They get out of their vehicles and started walking toward the bank. Eldon looked around for Preston, yet, he's nowhere to be seen.

"Where's Preston?" Eldon said.

"He's probably running late to the sites as usual." Emily said. "As always from what I hear in the office."

Cody looked to his left and saw Preston's car heading their direction. He pointed him out.

"Preston's right there." Cody said. "I think so. That's his car isn't it."

Preston arrived at the scene and noticed Eldon and Emily staring at him. He smiled at both of them as he exited out of his car. He looked again at Emily's white Lincoln. She turned to him.

"A white Lincoln, nice." Preston said. "Surprised you had the profit to purchase one."

"It gets me around." Emily said. "And I save my money unlike others who spend it on things they don't need."

"Still, it's a very nice car." Preston said. "Though, it isn't black like mine."

Eldon turned to Preston. Shook his head as Preston only grinned slightly.

"Preston. Don't start any of this bullshit while we're here on business, please. Now let's get this going on this job."

Eldon walked around the bank's locations. Cody and Emily followed him. Preston stood and smirked before he started looking around the area. They noticed all the damage caused from the explosion. Burnt brick walls, windows blown out with huge holes on circling the entire bank. Preston continued looking around the bank for clues. They were not allowed to enter the bank, due to being cleaned out by other officials across New Haven. Cody recognized the damage and approached Eldon.

"From the look of the building, only a high-powered weapon could've caused this much damage." Cody said.

"What are you getting at, Cody?" Eldon asked. "You believe that a larger weapon was used on this place?"

"Some kind of launcher, perhaps." Cody said. "From what I can tell."

Emily walked over to Eldon. "A grenade launcher? Are you sure?"

"No, he's not sure." Preston said. "It was a rocket launcher."

Eldon walked over to Preston, who's standing next to a strap on the ground with a cap. Eldon smiled and turned to Preston.

"Excellent work, Preston." Eldon said. "I have to say I'm impressed by just little work you did finding this."

"Well, you know, I just try my best." Preston said. "Besides, it was just lying there. So, it was in my inclination to point it out for you."

Eldon walked over to Cody and he followed. Eldon told Cody to put the strap into the evidence bag for further investigation and fingerprint analysis. Cody took the strap and placed it inside the bag and walked toward the jeep. Preston turned to Emily.

"I believe it's your turn now."

"Chief, what's that over there?" Emily asked.

"Well, what is it." Eldon said. "I need some description of what's your seeing."

Emily walked over to the area and discovered a wallet. She opened the wallet and noticed it belonged to a banker who worked at the bank who possibly ran out with the civilians during the robbery. Emily waved her hand toward Cody, signaling him to come over to her.

"It's a wallet." Emily said. "Appears it belonged to one of the bankers who worked here. We could check his address and phone to see if he's still alive or dead."

"Let me have a look at it." Eldon said.

Preston walked over to them, "A wallet? You sure it isn't just a notepad or something less important?"

Eldon opened the wallet and finds the information on its owner. He smiled and turned to Emily.

"Great work, Emily." Eldon said. "Impressive work you guys are doing. It must be my lucky day."

He handed the wallet to Cody, who put it inside a plastic bag and walked to the jeep with Eldon. Emily smiled and turned to Preston, who glared at her.

"What?" Preston asked. "You've come to gloat now?"

"No." Emily said. "I'm just telling you to try a little harder if you want to impress me."

Eldon and Cody get back into the jeep as Eldon told Preston and Emily that they're heading toward the jailhouse next. They left as Emily and Preston leave.

Across the street, in a neighborhood, a burgundy Nissan. Inside are two men, one Caucasian and the other of African descent. They are wearing nice suits and ties. They sit inside the Nissan as they watched Preston and Emily leave the bank scene. The Caucasian looked at the African.

"So, what are we waiting for?" The Caucasian said. "Let's just go over there and blow them all to smithereens and be done with the job."

"As much as I would love to, we can't do that. We have to wait on Ray's word."

"I don't know about you, man. But, I'm starting to wonder if Ray has no idea what he's putting his men through. Just think about it, while we're here, watching the area, the Detective Agency have those two Marshals snooping around."

"What's your point, man?" The African asked. "You don't like what Ray has planned for them?"

"What he has planned seems to be just good and dandy. But, just think about it for a second. One of those marshals is the female from Jersey. You've heard what the guys have said about her. Telling us she's very skilled in marksmanship." the Caucasian said. "The other is that "Instincts" guy who shot Jonny Cartel not too long ago and has already cost us a lot of profit."

"You're speaking of Emily Weston and Preston Maddox. What about them makes it important for us to kill them right now?"

"I just think that Ray should look closer into this." the Caucasian said. "Just to keep a heads up on it before they come busting down his doors and taking us all to prison."

"I'll have a talk with Ray about it and see what he says." the African said. "I'll also ask him about the two marshals. From my time working with him, I know for a fact if he knows the female Marshal."

"Really. Never knew that."

"They have a long history with one another. They were the two most known people in the law area. Whenever someone talked about the law, they were both mentioned."

"That's what I'm talking about. Seems like we should be the ones to end that long feud."

"We'll wait on Ray's word to see if that will be the case."

Coover and Rusty sit inside a diner where they are having a meeting with Ray. He walked in and they sit at the table. Ray is accompanied with two bodyguards, one on his left and another on his right. He sat at the table as the bodyguards stood, guarding the area. Ray looked at Coover and Rusty.

"Glad you could make it, boys." Ray said. "It's nice to see you. So, how's everyone in your neck of the woods?"

"They're doing fine." Coover said. "Everyone's minding their own business. They have no clue to what's going on."

"No problems there, boss." Rusty said. "So, what's the situation you have for us at hand?"

"I heard about the jailhouse that was blown to pieces last night and I also heard from a reliable source that your brother, Billy was there with Hoyt Bennett."

"Seriously." Coover said. "Little young' Billy's teaming up with Hoyt now?"

"According to my knowledge, seems so." Ray said. "So, I'll let the two of you speak with your brother and find a way to tell him that he's on the wrong side of this chess board."

"We'll talk with him, boss." Rusty said. "We will. You have no worries there."

"I hope so, Rusty." Ray said. "Because, I don't want to have to kill him and later have your mother on my trails. I know for a fact what she would do if any of her sons were killed."

"You don't have to worry about our mother." Rusty said. "Once we speak with Billy and tell him about the means, he'll join our side and leave Hoyt to die alone."

"That's great to hear." Ray said. "Well, nice meeting you here."

Ray commanded his guards to leave behind him as Coover and Rusty sat at the table, plotting an idea to pull Billy away from Hoyt. They watch as Ray leaves the diner and they leave as well. Coover leaves with a mug of coffee for some odd reason.

Preston, Emily, Eldon, and Cody arrived at the jailhouse scene and see that's it much more damaged than the bank. Half of the building had completely been turned to rubble with debris covering the ground around it. Other officials are at the scene as well, including United States Marshal Darius Conway, an African-American man. Eldon walked over to him and they shake hands.

"It's good to see you again, Conway." Eldon said. "It's been a long time since you've come across the office."

"Yes sir. It has." Darius said. "Been on some business across the country and now I'm back to work here."

"So, what's the incident here?" Eldon asked. "Any leads you've gathered?"

"Well, according to one witness, they saw a truck drive up and stop in the street." Darius said. "Two men were inside, one of them got out of the truck and went to the back and pulled out a grenade launcher. He pointed it toward the building and blew the jailhouse up, killing everyone inside and the guards up front."

"Any suspects so far?" Eldon asked. "Anyone who seen the shooter and his companion?"

"None have come up yet." Darius said. "But, according to the witness I spoke with, the shooter yelled out, "Incoming Call" before he fired the launcher. So, I hope we'll receive some news very soon."

Preston looked around the area and walked over toward Eldon and Darius. Preston told Darius to excuse him and Eldon, so he could ask him about the scene.

"So, what did Darius tell you about the incident?" Preston asked.

"It seems that a grenade launcher was the cause of this." Eldon said.

"A grenade launcher?" Preston asked. "You can tell what was used on this place just by looking at it?"

"It appears so due to the amount of debris that's here." Eldon said. "First, the bank gets blown up by a rocket launcher. Now, a jailhouse is blown up by a grenade launcher. It seems that this is being done by the same individuals."

"No, not the same." Preston said. "Two different groups of individuals."

"Also, according to the witness, the shooter yelled out "*Incoming Call*" before firing." Eldon said. "You know anyone who's ever heard anyone yell that phrase out before?"

"I have." Preston said. "I have an idea who could've done this. The bank is another story."

Preston walked toward his car. Eldon looked at him and asked him where's he going. Preston told him that he's going to visit and old friend. Preston gets into his car and drove off. Emily and Cody walked toward Eldon and asked him where Preston's going.

Eldon told them that's he going on break.

<u>9</u>

Coover and Rusty drove to Billy's mobile home. They walked to the front door and knocked. The door opened and its Billy. He is surprised to see his two older brothers. He welcomed them inside. As they are inside, they notice that Hoyt is in there as well. Rusty turned to Billy.

"Billy, what's this dick doing in here?!" Rusty asked.

"I have a dick, but I'm not one." Hoyt said. "Rusty, you should ask yourself that same question. Before someone throws it back to you"

"Shut your damn mouth, Bennett." Coover said. "We already know about your deals with our brother here and we're here to tell him to turn a new leaf. Get him away from your crazy ass."

"Calling people names doesn't get you into any places anymore, Coover. So, how would the two of you have a way of taking Billy from my what I had offered him?" Hoyt asked. "You have something better in mind that what I'm offering at the moment?"

"We work for Ray Colby." Rusty said. "You remember him, don't you? The man that put you out of business after you were sent to DC."

"I surely do." Hoyt said. "The big, tall black son of a bitch that took over most of the work in this city."

"Well, how does it feel to have the knowledge of all your former employees working for him now?" Coover asked. "They left your ass high and dry and now they're working for the big man now in the big leagues."

"Overall, it feels quite refreshing, actually." Hoyt said. "Takes weight off of my shoulders from those lazy bums."

"Well, you'll have to release our brother here, since, he's coming with us to join Ray's alliance." Rusty said. "If you don't mind."

Hoyt stood up and looked in the eyes of both Coover and Rusty. Billy sat at the counter and just watched. Coover and Rusty stared a hole through Hoyt as he just gave them a grin.

"Billy, you're leaving with us." Rusty said. "So, get off your ass and come with us."

"You heard him, Billy." Hoyt said. "Go ahead and follow your worthless brothers out of the door and ruined your chance at a better life."

Billy's jaw dropped. He didn't make a move. Not even a flinch as he was stuck between a hard place at the wrong time.

"What! Are you serious, Hoyt?!"

"Indeed I am." Hoyt said. "Go on, now."

Billy stood up from behind the counter and started walking toward his brothers. But, Hoyt held him back and pulled out a magnum. Coover and Rusty begin to back off as they watch Hoyt's hand on the gun. Billy turned to Hoyt and back to his brothers.

"You really believed I would let your brother ruin his life for the sake of tagging along with his shitty brothers. I don't think so. Billy's got a bright future with me on his side."

"Billy, if you don't leave with us, you're on your own." Rusty said. "You hear me. You're on your own if you stay with this piece of trailer park shit."

"Are you coming with us, brother?" Coover asked. "Be with your family and live big."

Billy stayed quiet and finally spoke his answer., "I'm staying on Hoyt's side. We'll take over this city with or without your help."

"Goddamn it. Fine." Rusty yelled. "But, when mother finds out about your death in the paper, you'll realize what big of a mistake you've just made."

They leave the mobile home and Billy turned to Hoyt, who's still grinning, looked at Billy and said that this city will be theirs, but, they must get rid of Ray first.

Preston drove back to the hideout, continuing his constant search for Hoyt, a moment passed by that he realized Hoyt couldn't be inside. Once Preston pushed the door opened, Hoyt and Billy were nowhere in the hideout. Preston rubbed his head as he glanced around the front.

"Damn it." Preston said. "Where would you be right now, Hoyt?"

He gets into his car and headed for another location. One he believes Hoyt could surely be. Preston decided that it's getting late and he drove back toward his apartment. Preston's cell phone ringed. He answered it.

"Hello."

"It's Eldon. We just got something on our plate and I'll like you to do the job."

"What's the job if I may ask you?"

"We need to deliver around twenty-five thousand dollars to a man named Joel Green. He lives in the suburb area."

"I'll come over to the office after I pay a visit to Hoyt's apartment."

"Very well, Preston. Just make it quick."

"I will. No need to worry there."

Preston hanged up the phone and sat it down in the cup holder as he continued to drive.

Ray and his gang walked into a fancy nightclub, which Ray owns. They walked in and spot lots of women, barely wearing clothes, dancing around the club. Ray allowed his men to enjoy themselves as he walked toward the back office. He entered the office and sees Hoyt waiting for him inside.

"What the hell are you doing here?!" Ray yelled.

"Firstly, tone down your voice and I'll explain why I'm here." Hoyt said.

Hoyt asked Ray to sit and he does. They sit right in front of one another, staring each other down. Ray started balling his fist as Hoyt smirked at him.

"What are you doing here, Hoyt?" Ray asked. "You've playing a big risk standing in my presence right now."

"Be that as it may, Colby. I'm only here to speak to you about Billy, the youngest of the Bronson brothers. I'm sure you know of him."

"Yeah, I know of him. I've already spoken to his two older brothers to track him down for me and tell him to leave your sorry ass, so he could join my alliance and have a better chance of living."

"Well, that's why I'm here. His brothers had arrived at his home earlier and so I pushed them out. Told them that Billy is on my side and not yours. Figured it would grind your gears a little bit."

"I hope you realize the dangers you are putting that boy in with your narcissistic personality and you are most certainly bound to have him killed the second either of you make a mistake."

"Me narcissistic? Old Ray. Let's both face the facts here at this moment, we both know you're the only dickhead I see here who would be considered a narcissist. But, I am highly impressed that you're using big words. Truly a good job done there on your part."

Ray grinned. Staring into Hoyt's eyes. Piercing them with his anger. Hoyt stared back, showing a slight grin.

"I'll say this last word and you can get off your ass and leave my airspace."

Hoyt leaned in and smirked.

"Go ahead, friend. Say what you must speak so I can get out of your so-called airspace."

"The next time I see you, it doesn't matter where we are or who's around. When the day comes around, I will kill you on the spot. It might be tomorrow, it might be next week. But, it doesn't matter, because, soon you will be dead. Thanks to me."

Hoyt stood up and walked toward the door, he turned his head looking at Ray, Hoyt smiled.

"I can't wait for the day to arrive, friend. Because when it comes along, maybe the two of us will meet our end by our own hands."

Hoyt left the office as Ray sat at the desk, looking down at his pistol that was in his pocket to begin with. Ray thinks to himself that possibly, he could've just killed Hoyt right there on the spot. He later took his hand off his pistol and showed a slight smirk. To which he decided to wait for a better time and a better place to finally execute Hoyt.

Following the day after, Eldon and Cody are at the office, discussing the wallet that was found at the bank scene. Eldon looked at all the information regarding the wallet's owner. Cody walked into the boardroom as Eldon turned toward him.

"Chief, the owner of the wallet has been found." Cody said.

"That's some great news. So, where is the fellowman?"

"He's here waiting downstairs."

"Good. Bring him in so we can get this all set and done."

"Sure thing, sir." Cody said as he leaves the office.

Eldon put down the information sheet onto the desk and sat in the corner, awaiting the presence of the wallet's owner. Preston and Emily arrived in the office and Eldon told them about the wallet as Cody walked back in.

"While I'm here, I also have the results of the strap cap from the bank scene."

"Well, any leads?" Preston asked.

"There were no traces of DNA on the strap or the cap. I take it that whoever was utilizing it had enough intelligence to know what they were doing and how to keep their fingerprints off it."

"That's a damn shame." Preston said.

Emily turned to Preston and he does the same. She gave him a smirk. He didn't appreciate it.

"What is it this time, Emily? What's the smirk for?"

"It's a damn shame, huh."

"What else could it possibly be. No trace at all. Very clever the shooter."

Emily turned to Eldon.

"What about the wallet? Have you found anything in there that could lead to some information?"

"The wallet belongs to a Richard Ward." Cody said. "He was

one of the bankers who escaped the bank before it exploded. According to his documents, he is highly intelligent in physics.”

“Wow. That’s something.” Preston said.

“So, he must’ve dropped the wallet as he was escaping the area.” Emily said.

“Exactly.” Cody said.

Eldon walked toward Cody and said, “Is he coming up here yet?”

“He’s on his way, sir.” Cody said. “He should actually be up here any minute now.”

Preston turned to Emily and said, “Well done, Weston. Well done.”

“I appreciate your answer, but, I don’t really give a shit what you say.” Emily said.

Eldon and Cody left the office and only Preston and Emily are inside. Preston turned to Emily and said, “Watch your mouth when you’re speaking to me. You’re still a rookie in this town.”

“What’s that supposed to mean?” Emily asked. “I’m been a US Marshal for over seven years now. So, the reality is that I’m not a rookie. No matter where I go.”

Emily left the office as Preston stood at the table, watching her leave. He looked down at the information sheets and started grinning.

“She needs some work done.” Preston said.

Eldon approached him with an envelope containing the twenty-five thousand dollars. Preston took it and placed it in his jacket pocket.

“You mind if I go ahead and deliver this now?”

“I suggest you do it after we have a chat with the banker. That way it’s less on your plate.”

“Figured you would say something of that nature.”

At the warehouse, Ray is having another meeting with the crime lords of the city. He talked about how they should take out Hoyt and how many ways there are in controlling the city for their own purposes. As Ray continues speaking, one thug told him that a woman is here to see him. Ray told him to let her in and she walked in.

The room is quiet and astounded by the woman's appearance. The woman is Carla. She welcomed herself into the warehouse and Ray stood up and walked over to her.

"From your appearance, you must be Carla Garcia." Ray said. "The ex-girlfriend of the Instinct Marshal."

"You could say that." Carla said. "I'm only here to give you an offer."

"Which is?" Ray asked.

She took out a sheet and showed it to Ray. It is all of Preston's tricks and ideas regarding his position as a Marshal. Ray looked at it.

"How would this help me out?"

"Let me borrow one of your men and you'll see how it will help you in your plan." Carla said.

Ray nodded, "Very well."

He pointed toward one of his men and told him to go with Carla to work on the plans. He agreed and left the warehouse with Carla. One of the crime lords looked over at Ray, who sat back down at his seat.

"She's a fine woman, don't you think?" he asked.

"Indeed, she is." Ray said. "Hopefully, she won't let us down."

<u>**10**</u>

Preston, Emily, Eldon, and Cody sit at a table inside the boardroom waiting for the banker to arrive. The banker, Richard Ward walked into the room. He sat at the table, in front of Eldon. Eldon shook his hand and began asking questions regarding the robbery incident at the bank.

"Mr. Ward, if I may ask, what did you see at the bank during the incident?" Eldon asked.

"Well, I saw what appeared to be a male, who was dressed in all black. Wearing a ski mask." Ward said. "He was also carrying a brown bag to put the money in and he also carried a gun also."

"What else did you witness?" Emily asked.

"Well, I also witnessed when he walked up to the counter and slammed the back onto it." Ward said. "He, later, began to point the gun towards the banker, while yelling at him to place the money inside the bag."

Eldon looked at him.

"Is that all you saw during the event?"

"Well, not exactly." Ward said.

Cody leaned in.

"Can you please give us more information on the case. If you can."

"Well, as the banker was filling up the bag, the guy made everyone crouched to the ground, threatening to shoot them on the spot." Ward said. "As he was doing that, another banker reached under another counter and pulled out a shotgun. He raised it up and started blasting it towards the guy. He ducked the shots and killed the banker by shooting him directly in the forehead."

"So, you're telling us that while all this was transpiring, the individual killed a banker inside?" Eldon asked.

"Well, yes. He did" Ward said.

Preston looked over to Eldon and to Cody. He later looked over at Emily, who's listening to Ward. Preston leaned in and looked at Ward.

"Excuse me, Mr. Ward." Preston said. "But, can you do all of us a favor and stop using the word, "well". You're toning it out."

"Well, I apologize, but that's the way I speak." Ward said calmly.

"Preston, don't worry about his vocabulary right now." Eldon said. "Focus on the important things here at the moment."

"It's not the mission at hand. Is that all the information you have for us, Mr. Ward?"

"Well, yes sir it is." Ward said.

"Thank you for your cooperation and you may now leave." Eldon said.

Ward stood up from the chair and Cody handed him his wallet. He thanked them and left the office. Preston looked over at Eldon.

"You can't tell me the guy wasn't annoying."

"He was annoying." Cody said. "Very much, so."

"True, he was annoying." Eldon said. "But, he did give us information that we can use to find out who exactly pulled this stunt off."

"Of course." Cody said. "But, I have to agree with Preston on one particular thing. I just don't understand why Mr. Ward kept saying "well" before every sentence."

Preston smiled, "Tell me about it. Sounds like it's his favorite word to begin every sentence with."

"Enough about Ward's way of speech." Eldon said.

Eldon looked over at his clock and saw it was noon. He told them that they can go on break. Preston said he'll go ahead and deliver the money and afterwards he's going to visit a bar to search for Hoyt. Emily decided to go with him. Eldon allowed it as Cody decided to stay at the office and continued finishing up some research.

Carla and Ray's henchman arrive at a small diner across town and they speak about the plan.

"First off, tell me your name." Carla said. "Since, Ray didn't tell me while we were at the warehouse."

"My name's John." He said. "John Elroy."

"Well, John, are you sure you're qualified to do this task for me and for your boss?" Carla asked.

"Lady, I'm Ray's most valuable asset in his alliance." John said. "Anything that he can do, I can do. So, show me the plan."

"Sure." Carla said.

She pulled out the sheet and showed it to John. He looked at the sheet. Glancing and plotting out the sheet's plan. He squinted his eyes and looked at Carla. Carla looked at him and noticed he was slightly confused by what he saw on the sheet.

"Correct me if I'm making a mistake here. These skills and techniques look like they belong to a United States Marshal or something?" John asked.

"Indeed, they do. That's because I took them from Preston Maddox. I'm sure you heard of him in different discussions."

"This sheet belongs to the Instinct Marshal? Wait a minute, you sure you want to bring him into this? I mean, come on, Carla. You've stolen a very important item from one of the most targeted marshals in all of Connecticut."

"No need to worry of him." Carla said. "Me and him have a long history."

"How long a history?" John asked.

"Our history is long enough that we've shared a bed for years." Carla said. "So, no worries when it comes to Maddox or any of his ways of persuasion. Neither should you worry about his marshal friends."

"Oh." John said. "I need not ask any more questions regarding your history with the Marshal."

Carla goes over the plans with John as they discuss the pros and cons of the situations and begin plotting points to start with.

Arriving at a car dealership, Karen visited her husband, Richard. She walked in and sees him speaking with a customer that is screaming about wanting a eight-powered Mustang. She walked over to him and tapped him on the shoulder. He turned and smiled as he saw her. They hugged, as he commanded one of his employees to handle to loud-mouth customer.

"What are you doing here, Karen?" Richard asked. "I thought you were at work at this time of the day."

"An early lunch break brought me here. I was just curious about what's been going on around here." Karen said. "I just wanted to see how things worked is all."

"Curious about what?" Richard asked. "What have you been hearing?"

"Nothing." Karen said. "I just wanted to see you, that's all."

Richard smiled and hugged Karen. He told her to go back to her workplace and everything is fine. She agreed and left the building. Richard continued his work at the dealership.

Preston and Emily arrived at the home of Joel Green. They approached the front door and Preston knocked. The door opened, and a young man stood on the other side.

"Hello. What do I offer this pleasure?"

"I'm Preston Maddox and this is Emily Weston. We're United States Marshals and homicide detectives. We're here to meet a Mr. Joel Green. Is he here at the moment?"

"Um. No sir, he isn't. I'm watching the house for him while he's out of state. Is there something you're supposed to deliver to him? I could take it off your hands until he comes back."

"That won't be necessary, sir." Emily said. "We'll just return when Mr. Green makes it back in town."

"Are you sure about that, ma'am. Please, I can do a good service here."

Preston turned to Emily and shook his head. Emily only stared.

"This man is not Joel Green."

"Exactly. So, we'll return when he gets back."

"Point taken."

Preston turned to the man at the door.

"We'll just take it back to the office and await Mr. Green's return."

"The hell you will."

The man pulled out a Glock and pointed it toward Preston. Emily went to reach for her Glock and the man spotted her hand inching down to her side.

"I hope you placing your hand on your side to make a pose instead of reaching for that weapon of yours."

Preston held his hands up as Emily slowly raised hers above her head. She glanced over at Preston. He shook his head in confusion.

"Now, the two of you, inside now."

"Excuse me." Preston said. "We don't know what's in there."

"Just get in the goddamn house Right now!"

Preston and Emily slowly walked into the home. Seeing its neatly designed features. Preston turned his head toward the man.

"I hope we don't have to destroy this fine place all for the sake of a delivery."

"Give me whatever it is that you've come over to deliver."

"I don't think that will be necessary, sir."

"Give me the goddamn delivery. Before I shoot one of you in the forehead and leave you here to rot."

Preston reached into his jacket pocket and pulled out the envelope. The man extended his hand for the envelope. Preston handed it to him as Emily turned toward Preston with a confused look on her face as if she's about to yell.

"Preston. What the hell are you doing?" Emily said.

"Just shut your damn mouth, whore. This is between the men in the house. Women aren't allowed to speak until they are given the proper say so."

"So, are we all on the same page or what?" Preston said. "Just being the curious fellow here."

"Yeah, we are. Turn around and face the front door while I check this out."

Preston and Emily turned and faced the front door as the man opened the envelope and seen the amount of dollars that were stacked inside. He pulled them out and held them. He sniffed them and rubbed them on his face.

"I forgot how great new dollar bills smelled. They smell like the new season of a new year. This is amazing to me and you guys just don't get it."

"That's great and all. But, can we go now?" Preston said.

"No, you can't. Not until I've counted all of this. Damn this is a lot of bills. So, how much was this supposed to be anyway, Marshals?"

"Twenty-five thousand." Emily said. "I believe."

"You're shitting me right now. Twenty-five thousand dollars this is? Wow, what a load."

As the man screamed and hollered about the money, Preston and Emily looked at each other. Both conjuring up a plan of their own.

"I can't deal with this." Preston said. "How about yourself?"

"Let's just get this over with so we can continue our previous work."

The man began to kiss the pack of dollar bills when Preston turned around and reached for his gun. He raised it up and fired a shot to the man's heart. The man paused and held his chest as he fell to the ground. Preston and Emily walked over toward him and looked down at him on the floor. He began coughing as he tried to catch his breath.

"The least you could've done is let me keep the cash."

"I don't believe the dead use cash I'm afraid." Preston said.

Preston gathered up the money and placed it back into the envelope. Placing it into his jacket pocket. He and Emily leave the house as the man laid on the floor bleeding to death.

<u>**11**</u>

Preston and Emily arrive at the bar and they sit down at the bar itself. They both order a glass of water. They start having a conversation regarding New Haven and each other's lives. The bar was halfway full of customers going in and out.

"I have a quick question." Preston said. "Why did you want to come along with me? Thought, you didn't want to even speak with me. Let alone work alongside me."

Emily smiled and said, "I know I'm new to this town and that you're a pain in the ass. But, since Eldon paired us together. We are partners and we must work together on any case that comes along our way."

"You're right about that." Preston said. "Solving cases to save many lives as we possibly can."

"All of us at least try to accomplish that from time to time. Some succeed and some fail. Depends on how the job was done."

"If they were assigned the correct case to solve instead of picking and choosing what kind of case favored them."

"There's truth in that. I've worked with some who've done that before and it didn't turn out well for the victim nor the detective. But, not getting too much into your personal life. From the information that travels through the agency, I heard that you were once married."

Preston smirked and drank from his glass. He looked at Emily and then smiled.

"Eldon told you, didn't he?" Preston asked. "Can't keep that to himself."

"Yeah." Emily said smiling. "He told me that she filed for divorce and left you. Because of your anger."

"My anger they say? I can believe that to a certain extent, since, everyone believes that I have anger issues. Which I don't. I try to be as nice and polite as I can with everyone. Some take it and some don't. That's one reason why I put my job first in my life. I would guess the anger comes from whatever case I may be on or what fugitive I'm chasing during the time frame."

"That makes sense to me." Emily said as she drank her glass of water. "I've had similar ways back in Newark."

"Similar ways as in being angry most of the time."

"You could say that. There was one time where I was pursuing a sexual abuser and it came to the point that we found him raping an innocent woman. The image drove me insane and I pummeled the guy."

"You pummeled a guy? With those soft bare hands?"

"I'm sure you know how much strength you can gain with you're in a complete rage."

Preston puts his glass down and asked, "Enough about our anger and rage. Back to what you brought up about my previous marriage. What about you? Your little life story?"

"Basically, I'm not the relationship-type of woman." Emily said. "I had one boyfriend while I was in college and that went straight to shit in a heartbeat."

"By your independent attitude, I take it was you." Preston said.

"Not really." Emily said. "I discovered that was cheating on me with my roommate. Something, huh."

"I've heard that kind of story numerous amounts in my day." Preston said. "I've had friends with the same issue and never understood what they did or what they caused."

"Haven't we all been friends with people like that." Emily said smiling. "So, what's this "Instinct" thing that people say about you. I've been hearing it a lot lately and every time someone mentions it, they get uncomfortable."

"I don't know what the hell it is myself." Preston said. "I'm guessing that they mean how I react to my instincts and I follow them. Without hesitation. I just believe it's something the agency created to cause a stir in the field and to scare the fugitives and such."

"So, you just go in with your first instinct?" Emily asked.

"Pretty much." Preston said smiling. "The funny thing about it is my first instinct is always the right one. Never been wrong before and probably never will."

The sound of the bar door opening alarmed the entire establishment. Hoyt an Billy entered the bar and see Preston and Emily talking further down on the counter.

"Billy, look who's here."

"Shit. Why don't we go to another bar. There's one further down the street and it's probably not crowded."

"We're staying and we're sitting over there with them. Just for the sake of fun."

They're approaching both Preston and Emily. Preston had finally found Hoyt. Hoyt walked over to Preston and Billy has entered the bar.

"We meet again, eh' Preston." Hoyt said.

"I could say the same thing." Preston said. "Though, you've already said it. So, no point in saying it."

Hoyt smiled, "Funny. Still with the jokes I see."

"I have to add a little humor every now and then." Preston said. "I've been looking for you by the way."

"Really? You have? So, what is it that I have done this time to bring you onto my coat tails?"

"You heard about the jailhouse incident that took place. From what we received from the witness is that the shooter yelled out, "Incoming Call" and took the shot. Reason being, I only know one man in New Haven who would yell that phrase out before exploding something and the man I'm referring to is you."

"Alright. I'll come out with this one and I know Billy won't be too pleased about this. It was me. Me and Billy to be exact. It was our first task in changing the foundation of this city. Something you don't have the balls to do."

Billy jumped up from the stool and his jaw dropped as he looked at Hoyt. Billy shrugged his shoulders and shook his head.

"What the hell is your problem, Hoyt. You're giving away plot information and details."

"You want to test it out?" Preston said. "Go ahead and try it."

Hoyt looked over Preston's shoulder and sees Emily. He walked toward her and leaned on the bar to the right, staring straight into her face.

"So, who is this beautiful young lady, Preston?" Hoyt asked. "Because, she surely isn't Karen or Carla. From my perspective, she looks better than the two of them combined. If that was possible, we would have ourselves a Old West-style stand-off."

"She is Emily Weston, my new partner on the job." Preston said. "I wouldn't take her too kindly."

"It's a pleasure to meet someone of your stature, Ms. Weston." Hoyt said. "I'm sure you've done your homework and now know who I am and what I've done in this city's history. Plus, what I'm capable of doing if I'm pushed to the proper stage of behavior."

"I know as much about you that I need to know. The infamous, Hoyt Bennett. The man who caused trouble across this city and throughout the state. The one who just got released from prison in D.C. Ready to go back in your little cell over there?"

"I'll tell you one thing, sweetheart. Hoyt Bennett will never go back to DC's super max prison. The reason is simple, I'm not doing anything that's against the law." Hoyt said.

"Number one, if we're going to be speaking with each other. Don't call me sweetheart." Emily said. "You shouldn't test your luck with me."

"Oh my. You don't want me to call you sweetheart? May I ask why you prefer not? Does it make you feel good or bad about yourself in a physical mindset? Not that I care anyways about your mindset."

Preston tapped Hoyt on the shoulder and he turned toward him. Preston wasn't playing around as his face became serious as it was when he shot Cartel. Hoyt knew Preston was serious and decided to play along with him. Testing his buttons, it would seem.

"Why are you here at this time?" Preston asked. "Specifically, I might add."

"Me and Billy would always come to this place for a drink. It relaxes and sooths our bodies of what the world has done to us. In simple terms, it places us from the world and the world from us."

"It's only twelve twenty-five. Past noon." Preston said. "I knew you were a crazy man, but I don't recall you drinking alcohol at this hour."

"The timeframe doesn't matter, Preston. Funny how you said that about me but left yourself out of the picture frame. Try to remember the way you used to drink, you know that more well than us. I look at it this way and see if you can understand where I'm coming from. As long as we can drink and be separate from the world, we're doing just fine."

Hoyt turned to Billy and asked him what drink would he like. Billy, in a problematic mood said he wanted a glass of water. Hoyt looked at him and told him to order a beer and Billy decided on doing so. Billy started to shiver because he's about to drink a beer in the presence of two marshals. Hoyt sat in the seat next to Emily. He glazed at her and smiled.

"Don't mind me of where I sit. So, since you're new to this city? How has it treated you? If you don't mind me getting into that part of your life."

"Just to shut you up, I'll tell you a slight of detail. The city has treated me well. Just came in a few days ago and no problems have I had to deal with that arose from this place. Until, you popped up of course."

"Well, let me ask you this since we're on your traveling and living subject. Where do you live previously before you arrived here?"

"Excuse me, well-established fugitive and pyrotechnic. I'm not telling you where I once stayed. If you want to talk, we'll focus on the here and now. Nothing to do with the past or what happened in the past."

Hoyt leaned in toward Emily's face, getting into her personal space, causing Emily to feel highly uncomfortable and to back away from him.

"You will." Hoyt said with a straight face.

Preston stepped behind Hoyt. He looked over his left shoulder, smiling.

"I see you're watching her back." Hoyt said.

"Of course. She's my partner. Though, she can handle herself." Preston said. "But, when it comes to someone I know, a man especially, they should have some respect for women. Hoyt, last time I checked, you were already heading into some trouble with a certain group of women. May I say, prostitutes, or do you prefer hoes. Your choice."

"Preston, why have only one when you can have them all." Hoyt said. "That's the grand prize."

Billy started laughing and Preston turned to him. Once, Billy saw Preston looking at him, he placed his head down and was quiet. Preston turned back to Hoyt.

"That sounds like me when I was twenty-two." Preston said. "I'll just say this right now, Hoyt. Originally, when the double homicide occurred, I thought you had a hand in it."

"How would I have had a hand in it when I was in D.C. at the time?" Hoyt said. "Answer that for me, Preston."

"Because the murders were so unusual and strange that, since, everything unusual in this town always has a track record that somehow reverts toward you." Preston said. "Though, you were in D.C. before the incident, I thought that some of your drug lords that stayed behind might have heard from your word to cause those two murders."

"Preston, I'm afraid that my men have all gone to work for Ray Colby." Hoyt said. "I would assume a man of your stature would've had the knowledge of knowing that."

"Ray Colby, the elite crime lord?" Emily asked. "I know of Colby. We go way back during my days in Jersey. He's here?"

"Yeah, he's been in town for a few months now." Preston said. "Planning and plotting as he comes. He hasn't started anything yet that we know of."

"Speaking of Colby, Billy and I have a master plan that will soon come to light." Hoyt said.

"What are you talking about?" Preston asked.

"Soon, you will begin hearing about certain events that are occurring around the city and when the time's right, you'll see the demise of Ray Colby." Hoyt said. "It's just around the horizon."

"Hoyt!" Billy said. "You have to stop telling people about the plans! It will only make the operations worse to go by!"

"You're not doing anything, Hoyt." Preston said. "Don't even try to do anything."

"Or what?" Hoyt said. "Or what, Preston? It seems that someone's lost in shadows as to what's about to happen. Before me and Billy leave, I'll give you this only warning."

"Go ahead." Preston said. "Warn me. Give me the warning."

Hoyt smiled, "If I catch you, your sexy partner, or any of your friends from the agency, I will kill them all and that's a promise."

Hoyt told Billy that they're leaving and they leave. Preston stared him down as he leaves. Emily turned to Preston.

"What are we going to do about him?"

"Nothing." Preston said. "He'll lead us to the events."

Preston and Emily left the bar, but, on the outside are Ray's two henchman.

They are waiting in their burgundy car on a street corner. They are watching them going to their cars. The Caucasian looked and pointed.

"That's him!" the Caucasian said. "That's the "Instinct" guy."

"I see." the African said. "I'll call Ray and see what he wants us to do."

The African pulled out his cell phone and called Ray. Ray's assistant answers on the other end.

"Hey, is Ray there? Put him on for me."

"That's the female Marshal too." the Caucasian said. "She looks good as they say."

"Yes, Ray." the African said on the phone. "Sorry to bother you, but, do you remember that "Instinct" Marshal? Well, he's here at the bar. I don't know, he must be tracking Hoyt too. That's exactly what I was thinking, sir. Alright."

He ended the call as the Caucasian looked over. Waiting for

an answer.

"Well?" the Caucasian asked. "What did he say?"

"Once we take out Hoyt, we'll take out the Marshal as well."

"What about the cute female Marshal?" "We go ahead and kill her too? Just wanted to bring these things up before we had to do the tasks ourselves. Imagine what would happen if we killed them and we go back to the boss and he wanted them alive. We would be in deep trouble."

"Which is why you're not in charge nor in my position."

The African turned with an emotionless look on his face away from the Caucasian. The Caucasian kept his gaze on him.

"So, back to the previous question. Do we kill the female Marshal, or do we leave her alone?"

"What do you think. Of course, we'll kill her too."

<u>12</u>

Carla and John returned to Ray's warehouse to speak with him, regarding the plans. Ray is already inside, sitting in the same seat. Carla sat in front of Ray as John stood behind her.

"So, how did the talk go about?" Ray asked.

"Your man, John here, will be a very good asset in this plan." Carla said. "So, when do you want to start?"

"We can start as soon as you see fit." Ray said. "It's all on you, Ms. Garcia."

Carla smiled, "Well, it's good to get this going and don't worry, everything will go as smoothly as possible."

She left the warehouse when Ray spoke with John concerning her.

"How was she during the conversations?" Ray asked. "What did she bring up?"

"She's highly intelligent, boss." John said. "She knows what she's doing. Exactly what she's doing."

"That's great." Ray said. "That's very great. At least we know she's on our side for this battle and not that piece of shit fuck head, Hoyt Bennett."

Coover and Rusty returned to Billy's mobile home to give him one more chance to join Ray's alliance. They knocked on the door and Billy opened. Rusty is upset as he tried to convince his younger brother to join the alliance. Billy declined and said he's sticking with Hoyt and that they will rule over the city. Rusty walked away as Coover tried to be the oldest and convince his brother to join. Billy declined again and Coover wished him luck on his choice and walked away with Rusty. Billy closed the door and from behind, Hoyt is sitting on his couch.

"I see you declined both your brothers, Billy." Hoyt said. "Impressive skill. you're finally learning."

"I'm trying to stand on my own and make my own choices." Billy said. "I've always followed my brothers since we were kids. I never was granted attention or had any appreciation for the things I've done. Now, it seems with me on your team, I can make something of myself."

"You will make something of yourself on my side." Hoyt said. "If you were to join Ray, you'll only be his pawn. Just like your two older brothers. Apparently, they like to be sheep because they only follow, since they can't lead."

Preston and Emily come back to the office, where they told Eldon about Hoyt's upcoming events that will lead to a breath-shaking disaster across the city. Eldon decided to put the entire agency on high alert for any of these events.

"What took you two so long to return?" Eldon asked Preston and Emily.

"We had a long conversation." Preston said. "Nothing much really."

Cody walked over and said, "You guys were gone for quite a while. I was starting to wonder."

Preston turned to Eldon and said, "We saw Hoyt at the bar."

"What did he say?" Eldon asked. "Did he mention anything related to the murders or to the jailhouse attack?"

"He did say that the jailhouse attack was him." Preston said. "Him and Billy Bronson."

"Billy Bronson?" Eldon said. "Never would expect him to do something like that. His brothers though, you can definitely expect that from them."

Preston later said, "He also said that he has something planned for the city and I'm here to tell you that we must do something about it."

Afterwards, Darius arrived inside the area to speak with Eldon, regarding the double homicide. Eldon turned and walked toward him.

"Sorry to disturb you, Chief." Darius said. "But, we've finally found out who was the culprit in the double homicide."

"Who is it?" Eldon asked.

"From what we've covered up. The DNA matches both Coover and Rusty Bronson." Darius said. "We found both of their fingerprints on the kitchen stove and the dryer handle."

"Finally, we know who to look for." Eldon said. "I'll tell my two marshals to go on the search for them."

Eldon walked over to Preston and Emily and told them to search for Coover and Rusty. Preston said he knew exactly who they were, saying they all went to the same high school. Eldon told them that he and Cody are going on a search for Hoyt's plans as they look for the Bronson brothers.

"So, where do we find these Bronson brothers?" Emily asked.

"We'll head to their mother's home." Preston said. "She might know exactly where they'll be."

"You know her?" Emily asked.

"Just like her sons, we have a long history." Preston said.

Preston and Emily headed out to speak with the Bronson brothers' mother. Eldon and Cody left the office, going out to search for clues of Hoyt's plans. Eldon and Cody talked with each other about possible clues that they could find around the city.

"What are we looking for exactly?" Cody asked.

"Any areas that may have significant clues regarding Hoyt."

"So, where are we headed?"

"We'll head to the Westside. Search the areas around those spots." Eldon said. "It might give us some ideas."

Carla and John parked in front of the Marshal Agency, sitting inside a red corvette. John sits in the driver's seat as Carla sat in the passenger's seat. John is starting to become impatient for waiting and turned to Carla.

"May I ask why we're just waiting here, Carla?"

"Just be patient, John." Carla said. "This is only a part of the plan. Just relax. For my sake."

"Alright now." John said. "So, what are we doing here? You just saw the Marshal and his partner leave, so why are we here when we should be following them?"

"Because, eventually, he'll have to come back." Carla said. "Then, once he does, you'll take him out. For your alliance and for your own good."

Preston and Emily entered the New Haven County on the south-central side of Connecticut. They turned corners and Preston recognized a house on the right corner. He drove towards that direction. Emily looked around at the homes and noticed Preston heading towards a specific house.

"Do you see the house?" Emily asked.

"I do." Preston said. "It's right here. Still looks the same too."

Preston drove into the driveway and parked the car. They exit the car and walked towards the front door. Before, they get to the door, it opened and it's the Bronson brothers' mother. Barbette Bronson. She walked out and looked at both Preston and Emily.

"Oh my." Barbette said. "Is that who I think it is standing before me today."

"Yes, ma'am. It's me in the flesh."

"The well-known Preston Maddox." Barbette said. "It's been a long time since we've seen you in this neck of the woods. Around ten to fifteen years at least."

"You're correct, Ms. Bronson." Preston said. "It's been a long time indeed for most of us."

Emily walked over and shook Barbette's hand as she looked at her.

"Preston, who is this lovely young lady?" Barbette asked. "You never spread the word about you having a lady on your arm again."

"This is Emily Weston." Preston said. "She is my partner in the Marshal and Detective Service."

"Great." Barbette said. "It's nice to see there's a woman in a man's position and doing the job even better too."

"Don't start on that, please." Preston said.

"Thank you, ma'am." Emily said. "I do what I can to help."

Barbette allowed them inside the house and they walk in. Preston sees that the house hasn't changed a bit from when he was just a small child. The inside is still the same with an old couch and wooden walls.

"This place really hasn't changed." Preston said. "You must've loved the way it looked."

"I'm not going to change anything here, just to fit in with this new society we have." Barbette said. "I'm old school and I intend on staying that way."

"However you feel, Ms. Barbette." Preston said.

"You could just call me, Barb, Preston." Barbette said. "You've known me since you were a child. So, don't bother with calling me Ms. Barbette or Ms. Bronson."

Preston smiled.

"So, Barb. We're here on business to ask of your sons. The two older ones exactly, Coover and Rusty."

"What about Coover and Rusty?" Barbette said. "What kind of trouble have they caused this time?"

"They're the suspects of a double homicide." Preston said. "I'm sure you've seen it on the news. CNN had it on not too long ago. MSNBC on the other hand tried to make a joke out of it."

"I heard about the murders that transpired in that neighborhood." Barbette said. "It's very sad. Though, I wouldn't expect my sons to be the culprits. They wouldn't do such a thing."

"I believe The President made a speech about it not too long ago." Preston said. "Not really sure, but, I'll check and see once I get back to the office."

"Well, for one I didn't vote for him." Barbette said. "Do you know where they are right now?"

"No ma'am, we don't." Emily said. "That's why we're here in your presence to ask you if you've seen or heard from them since."

"Last I heard, Rusty said, that he and Coover were headed

over to Billy's home to convince him of teaming with that Ray Colby fellow."

"So, your two older sons, they're working with Colby?" Emily asked.

"It would appear so I guess." Barbette said. "They wouldn't be speaking of him unless they were."

"We saw Billy earlier at the bar with Hoyt Bennett." Preston said.

"Hoyt?" Barbette said. "Hoyt Bennett you say? That no-good son of a bitch who nearly drove this county and the city into hell with his actions. Billy should know better. That's probably the reason why Coover and Rusty went to visit him. Though, he always wanted to go on his own, but, he would never listen to anyone."

"It seems he's listening to Hoyt." Preston said. "So, what do you want us to do about your boys?"

"Do what you will with Coover and Rusty." Barbette said. "I'll take care of Billy. Show him the right way of living his life. Instead of working with that no-good bastard."

"Do what you have to do Ms. Barb." Preston said. "Well, it's time that we leave and head back to the office."

Preston and Emily left the house, returning to the office. Barbette went back into the house. She looked toward the back of the home and the back door creaked open Coover and Rusty walked in from the back and notice their mother's expression on her face. Coover whispered to Rusty, saying their mother looked pissed. Rusty looked and shrugged his shoulders. They began staggering as she stared deeply at them.

"When the hell were you going to tell me that you murdered two people?" Barbette asked. "When were you two going to tell me?!"

"Mama, we were going to tell you about it." Coover said. "But, we didn't know the right time to tell you is all."

"When?! When the fuck were you were going to tell me about it?!" Barbette yelled. "I need an answer right this minute!"

"We were going to, but, we wanted to have Billy on our side before going along with it." Rusty said. "That's all, mama."

Barbette stared and said, "It seems that the two of you are

being hunted down by the marshals and since I saved your asses this time, you better give me something in return."

"Like what?" Coover asked.

"Either you speak with Billy one more time or I will." Barbette said.

She walked toward the back of the house as Coover and Rusty leave through the front. She murmured to herself about his sons as they glanced back. Rusty tugged Coover's sleeve as the left the home.

Carla and John continue to wait outside. The two are still awaiting Preston's return to the office and now John is out of patience. He gets upset and leaves the car. Carla followed him and said to him that plans have changed. He looked at her as she tells him to go inside and wait for Preston to return on the upper floor and that she'll go in with him to distract the other officials. He agreed, and they walked in. As soon as they go inside, Eldon and Cody returned. They have no clues or information regarding Hoyt's upcoming plans.

"We couldn't find a damn thing." Eldon said. "Not one trace whatsoever at all."

"Something will come up eventually." Cody said. "I'm sure of it."

"Yeah." Eldon said. "Hopefully, Preston and Emily have something for us to follow."

They walked inside and have no idea what's about to happen in the office. Inside the office, Carla is distracting the officials as John headed to the elevator. He held the door opened as he signaled Carla to join him. She told him that she'll find her own way. He stayed inside as the door closed on the elevator, as he's heading toward the third floor. He arrived on the third floor and no one pays any attention toward him. He reached his side for his handgun, not pulling it out, but, his hand in position to do so.

Hoyt arrived at a location across town and walked into the

small building nearby. He opened the door and turned on the lights. The building, he could tell it was used as a former pawn shop before it went out of business. The building is now for sale and Hoyt is highly looking into it. Someone else comes through the door and it's the owner of the building.

"Who in the hell are you and What the hell are you doing here?" The owner asked.

"I apologize for entering without calling, even though I don't have a number to this place. But, I'm here to discuss a business proposition with the owner the price on this building." Hoyt said. "You wouldn't happen to be the owner, would you?"

"That would be who you're currently eyeballing, boy. I am the owner of this place." He said. "So, what kind of interest do you have in a building like this and why should I even bother to listen to your offer?"

"Well, my good sir, my interest in your building is quite a simple answer." Hoyt said. "I need a small place for my stash of items."

"My I know what these items are?" The owner said. "If you want to have this building, I must know some details."

"The stash is really just my items that I have back at the house." Hoyt said. "It just some things that should be kept in storage."

"I don't know about that, Mr.?" The owner asked.

"Hoyt, Hoyt Bennett." Hoyt said smiling.

"Oh, so you're the guy who caused the whole mess of things a while back and went to prison for it." The owner said. "I knew I recognized you from somewhere."

"Yes, I am he." Hoyt said. "So, do we have an agreement on this building of yours? I can take it off your hands."

"I'll think it over and speak with you tomorrow about it." The owner said. "Do we have a deal?"

Hoyt shook the owner's hand and said, "Yes, we do have a deal."

<u>13</u>

Hoyt left the building with the mindset of intending on having the building, by any means necessary. He drove down the streets and passed by a group that he noticed. He turned around and passed by the area again. He looked closely and noticed that the men standing in that spot used to work for him. He smirked as he drives away.

Preston and Emily returned to the office and walk in. But, they realize that everyone is armed and searching the building. Preston walked over to one official as Emily glanced around the entire location before approaching the officer.

"Officer, what's the hell is happening here?" Preston asked. "What is going on?"

"Some pissed off guy came in with a gun and started threatening everyone near him." The officer said. "They're saying he's up on the third floor. No one's gone up there so far. They're awaiting backup."

"No shit, pal, we're the backup." Preston said. "Emily, we have to go up there."

"I'm aware of that, smart guy. How do we get up there without being noticed by sound or anyone in general?"

"Just follow my lead and we'll get up there in a hurry."

Preston and Emily ran toward the stairs, heading to the third floor. On the third floor, the majority of everyone is either hiding or sneaking up on John, who's standing in the middle of the room, pointing the gun at all the locations around him. Carla is standing by his side, smiling and laughing at the officials.

"I'll ask again god damn it." John said. "Where's Preston Maddox?! Where's the Instinct Marshal?!"

No one responded to his question and he fired the gun to the ceiling. Sounds of harsh screaming are heard around the room as he repeated the question. But, this time Eldon stepped out of the office and Cody stood with him.

"You aren't Preston. Neither of you." John said. "So, who the fuck are you, then to stand up in front of a gun?"

"I'm Eldon Ross, the Chief Commander of this agency." Eldon said. "I'm also Preston's boss and you're trespassing on my territory and threatening my people."

Carla smiled and said, "Preston's boss. Wow, I wouldn't expect him to have a boss. I always assumed that he would go into work for himself. Not someone else."

"Listen here, woman. Either the two of you go ahead and leave this building or it's a slight possibility that the both of you might just have to die here and leave in a coroner van."

"Die here?" John said. "Really? Let me tell you something, old boy. The only motherfucker that might possibly die in this place today is either you and your little bitch standing next to you. How's that sound for a threat."

Eldon pulled out his gun and fired at John. He moved out of the way and started shooting the surroundings. Eldon and Cody hid behind the office walls as John continued to fire toward them. Preston and Emily arrived on the floor and crouched down by the entrance wall.

"Who is this guy?" Emily asked.

"Must be one of Ray's men." Preston said. 'They're probably here for us I assume."

"Didn't expect us to be on a hit list this soon."

John stopped firing the gun and looked at Carla.

"When is he coming, Carla?" John asked. "We can't wait this long for him to show up."

"Don't worry. He'll be here soon enough." Carla said. "He can't resist making a save for innocent people."

Preston and Emily ran into the room as John pointed the gun toward them. Preston spotted Carla standing by John and he's confused, yet remembers his plans were stolen back at his apartment.

"We meet again, Preston." Carla said. "So, who's your friend, there?"

"Carla. What are you doing here?" Preston asked. "What are you doing with this man?"

"We're here on a mission assigned by Ray Colby." Carla said. "We're here to kill you basically."

Preston smirked and looked at John.

"So, you're one of Ray's men." Preston said. "I knew it would have to be. Neither the Bronson brothers or Hoyt would do something like this. They would just shoot everyone they see."

"I do this shit different, Marshal." John said. "Now, since people are always saying that you have the "Instinct". Whatever that's supposed to be. I was wondering, do you know exactly when I'll decide to shoot your head off."

"If you really want to know. Just try me." Preston said. "See, where we go from there."

John laughed and glanced toward Carla.

"You sound like you aren't afraid of being killed on the spot." John said. "A man without any fear of a gun."

"No one's ever had the chance of doing it." Preston said. "I've always been the one doing the shooting and putting people down. So, what makes it different if you're on the other side of the gun this time and I'm in the same position as always."

"Alright. Let's just see how good you really are." John said.

"Oh, I like the way this is going." Carla said. "Exciting stuff we're seeing here."

Emily looked at Carla and said, "Just keep your mouth closed, alright. Before, I become the one to put a bullet through your head."

Carla laughed and said, "You have a feisty partner, Preston. I wonder what else she can do beside talking."

"You'll probably find that out sooner than you think." Preston said. "She's not one you'll like to piss off. Believe me, I know for a fact."

Eldon and Cody peeped out of the office, seeing Preston and Emily standing in front of John and Carla. Cody turned to Eldon.

"What should we do, boss?" Cody asked. "We need to help them in some way at least."

"We could create some form of a diversion for them." Eldon said. "Make it a little easier for them."

"Like shoot the guy in the leg?" Cody asked.

"We could try." Eldon said.

Just as Eldon pointed the gun, Darius snuck into the office and pointed his gun toward John. Eldon looked at him.

"How'd you get in here?" Eldon asked.

"I was already in here. Just was waiting for you, that's all." Darius said. "What should we do? Let Preston and Emily handle it, or shall we just cause a minor disturbance?"

"I have one suggestion. Why don't we just try shooting the guy in the leg." Eldon said. "Will open up some kind of chance."

"Alright, it makes sense to me." Darius said. "Let's do it."

Darius fired his gun and the bullet went through John's leg. He stumbled as Carla pulled out her pistol and pointed toward both Preston and Emily. They stood still as Carla smiled.

"Who the fuck did that?!" John said in tremendous pain. "Where the fuck did that come from?! Shit!"

"Just be lucky it wasn't aimed for your head." Preston said. "That wouldn't have been so pretty to see your brain splattered."

"You're making jokes, boy. You know something, I'm getting a little tired of being in this damn marshal joint place anyway, so I'll just put your ass down right now."

John had set up his gun stance and prepared to aim, before he can fire the gun, he is shot in the back of the head and fell to the ground. As John fell, Carla stood behind him, with the pistol up and smoke coming from the muzzle. Preston is appalled by Carla's decision and so is everyone else in the office.

"The hell just happen here?!" Eldon said.

"Why did you do that, Carla?" Preston asked. "I don't really understand what that was for?"

"You've never understood me, babe. I'm the only person

that's allowed to kill you. The *ONLY* one."

Carla smiled and looked down at John's dead body. Blood slowly begins forming a puddle around his head.

"I'll explain the news to Ray." Carla said. "Just tell him it was a accident. He'll be fine with it."

"Speaking of him. Where is Ray?" Emily asked. "Since you know where he's located?"

"You really think I'll tell you? After the threat you gave me." Carla said, "You really have a lot to learn about New Haven, sweetheart."

Carla walked toward the front door, Preston stood in front of her.

Preston stared and said, "Either you tell us where Colby is or I'm personally taking you to prison for murder. We have eye witnesses to attest to it"

"Wow. I like your options. It turns me on." Carla said. "OK. He operates at a warehouse on the outskirts of town. It was a former trucking company building. Now, may I leave?"

Carla left the office as Emily turned to Preston.

"Let me ask a question here. Why did you let her leave?" Emily asked.

"Because she'll lead us to Colby himself." Preston said. "Simple solution right in front of us."

<u>14</u>

Hoyt arrived at Billy's home. But, once he opened the door, he discovered that Billy isn't there. He walked in and searched the home.

"Billy, where the hell are you?" Hoyt said to himself.

As he prepared to leave, he turned around and was hit directly in the head with a wooden baseball bat. Hoyt fell to the ground. Being knocked out from the bat. He was completely unconscious and unaware of what had happened. The holder of the bat was Rusty. He laughed as he looked down at Hoyt. Coover walked in behind him and looked down.

"He went down quick, bro." Coover said. "The bastard couldn't take a beating. No shit, he couldn't take a swing of a bat."

"It was easy." Rusty said. "Easier than I expected it to be. Let's drag him to the truck and take him to Ray. See what he wants us to do with him."

Coover looked around the home. Searching around the area for someone or something. He walked back outside toward Rusty.

"Rusty, where's Billy?" Coover asked.

"Billy's over at mama's house." Rusty said. "She'll convince him to join us with Ray. You'll see. Mama has it all under control."

They drag Hoyt's unconscious body to their truck. They tossed him in the back and covered him up with some sheets that were lying in the back. They drove off the premises, returning to Ray's hideout.

Back at the office, officials are cleaning up the amount of blood left on the floor from John's head after being shot by Carla. Preston, Emily, Eldon, Cody, and Darius are inside the boardroom, talking about the recent event.

"Why did you let her leave, Preston?" Eldon asked. "You saw what she did. She shot another human being right there. Right outside this room."

"I let her leave, so she could lead us to Colby." Preston said. "It's a very simple plan."

"How is it simple?" Darius asked. "She killed him, but, she could've easily killed you and Emily. As well as the rest of us on this floor if it had come to that."

"I see that I somehow placed everyone in danger." Preston said. "But, me and her have a long history with one another."

"Please, don't tell me that she's an old flame?" Eldon asked. "We don't need any more of your personal details falling into business again."

"She was." Preston said. "Kind of. We met when we were very young, and I also taught her some techniques. So, that could explain how she knew how to use the gun in the first place."

"So, her with the gun is really your fault." Emily said. "Should've seen that from the start."

"Everyone just relax." Cody said. "We must have a plan to go by in case she comes back with others."

"Ok, so what's the plan, guys?" Emily asked. "If any of you have one."

Preston looked around and said, "I say that we follow Carla's trail, so that we know for sure where Colby is and how to stop him."

Darius nodded.

"I'll have to go with Preston on this one. The plan sounds good. Good enough to start from."

"Alright then." Eldon said. "We'll track down your old flame and hopefully, that leads us to Ray Colby."

As they prepared to leave the room, Cody thought and brought up Hoyt's plans. Preston looked and decided that he'll go search for Hoyt as soon as he leaves. Emily agreed to join him in doing so. They leave the boardroom.

Carla went to another one of Ray's hideouts. This time a cabin in the woods. A cabin larger than the average cabins. She walked in and Ray is sitting behind a desk. He looked up and saw Carla. But, he doesn't see John.

"Where's John?" Ray asked. "What happened out there, Carla?"

"John didn't survive the initials of the plan." Carla said. "He was shot."

Ray stood up, as he's angry about what happened with John. But, he's still concerned if the plan went the way it was supposed to go.

"Did the plan go as followed?" Ray asked.

"No." Carla said. "As soon as John was shot, I left the building and that brings me to you at this moment, standing before you and telling you this terrible news."

"You said you could get the job done." Ray said. "Apparently, you couldn't. I find out that a lost one of my soldiers and I also find out that Preston is still alive and that's gonna cause problems for me, my lady. Lots of problems. How am I supposed to explain this news to the head chief? How do I explain this?"

"I'm sure you'll find a way to do so." Carla said. "That is, if you want me to explain it to him. I could do that, if you like."

"Very well." Ray said. "Since all you seem to be used for is bringing news, go ahead and tell the chief this. I'm sure he'll love to hear it from you. Right from your mouth."

Carla left the cabin as Ray looked down at the table and slams his fists.

Preston and Emily traveled down the interstate in search of Hoyt. Emily asked him about his history with Carla and why he let her leave. He told her that because Carla looked innocent and nice, she isn't. He also told her that Carla is highly skilled with armed weapons, thanks to him training her during their past relationship. Emily wonders if Preston can stand up against her, instead of falling prey to her seductive ways.

"When was the last time you actually saw Carla in person?" Emily asked. "And I'm not talking about in the office."

"A few days ago, she was inside my apartment." Preston said.

"She must've picked the lock or something, because she doesn't have a key to it. I didn't even live here during our relationship."

"That must have been a surprise." Emily said.

"It was shocking to say the least." Preston said. "But, enough about me. What's the history between you and Ray Colby?"

"Ray was one of New Jersey's top crime lords." Emily said. "Him and I always had confrontations with one another. Later, I find out that he fled from the state and went somewhere else to hide. Now, I find out that this is the city of which he flocked to."

"It seems our past lives are coming back to us." Preston said.

"Looks that way." Emily said. "Strongly, too."

Emily then asked, "Also, at the bar, what was that phase Hoyt had said to you?"

"Which one?" Preston said. "Because, I can't fully remember what that jackass said to me. To make it even stranger, I was drinking water."

"He said something about being lost in the shadows. Something of that nature. Though, I believed it was like that or maybe it was lost shadows. Something around that I know."

"It was lost in shadows." Preston said. "It's basically a phrase used to tell people when they have no idea what's either going on around them or they have no knowledge of what's about to happen around them. To put it short, Hoyt is about to do something around this city and that's what he meant when he told me that I was lost in the shadows."

"I was just asking about it." Emily said. "In a sort of way, I kind of like it. Sounds interesting."

"I'll tell you what's interesting." Preston said. "The term *Pteronophobia*."

"*Pteronophobia*? Never heard of it. Why is it supposed to be interesting?"

"It means fear of feathers."

"That is interesting. Never knew something like that existed." Emily said.

Preston said, "I didn't either, until my cousin ran from some chickens on his parents' farm in Arkansas."

"You learn something new every day, don't you?" Emily said.

"Pretty much." Preston said smiling.

Right back at the cabin in the woods, Coover and Rusty arrived with Hoyt in the back of the truck, still unconscious, blood slowly flowing from a cut on the back of his head. They dragged his body to the front door and headed inside. Ray sat at the desk reading some files as he noticed Rusty and Coover entering and dragging Hoyt's body across the wooden floor.

"Boys, for the love of the Heavenly Father, just pick the son of a bitch up. I don't want any of his blood on my wooden floor. Especially, blood from a Bennett."

"We brought him here." Rusty said. "Just like you asked, boss."

"I should thank you, boys." Ray said. "You're doing a much better job than that slut I hired. What about your little brother? Has he decided to join my alliance?"

"We should be receiving an answer soon." Coover said. "Mama's currently speaking with him about it."

"I'm sure she'll convince him to join." Ray said. "She has that strong presence amongst us. Especially, among her sons."

They place Hoyt onto a metal table, a table that belongs to Quarles Funeral Home. Hoyt is completely unconscious.

"What do you need us to do with him?" Rusty asked.

"Leave him here and I'll send him to the funeral home." Ray said. "Since, I'm good friends with the owner, they'll know exactly what to do with Hoyt."

Preston and Emily arrived at Hoyt's hideout location and they realized that he isn't there, not seeing his truck parked at that spot. Preston decided to visit Billy's mobile home, believing that Hoyt could possibly be there.

"Are you sure he could be there?" Emily said.

"It's worth a shot to check out."

<u>**15**</u>

Billy is at his mother's home as she continued to convince him to join Ray's alliance. Billy disagreed with his mother and said that he feels better being on Hoyt's side, saying that he has full control over himself and that he's not following. Barbette continued to try and get through her son, she knew she's not getting anywhere by speaking to him.

Billy jumped up from the couch and decided to leave the home. He turned around and looked at his mother. His mother could see the sadness in his eyes for disobeying her. So, could Billy see the sadness in his mother's eye for not joining Ray and herself.

"I'm truly sorry, mom. But, whatever happens to me in this line of work, it just happens."

As Billy leaves his mother's home, she walked out the front door and watched him drive off. As he drove off, she contacted Ray and told him to do what he must, since Billy didn't listen to her.

Funeral assistants from Quarles Funeral Home arrive at Ray's cabin and they take Hoyt's unconscious body and place it in the back of one of their white hearses. The assistants thank Ray and tell him that the owner is quite pleased. They left and Ray smiled as something finally was accomplished.

At the office, Darius told Eldon and Cody that there was a fugitive on the loose in town and that they've been assign the task of capturing him. Eldon had agreed and sent Darius and Cody on the job. Cody became very excited to work on another mission as Darius turned toward him.

"Please tell me, you've done this before?" Darius asked.

"They've never sent me out to search for a fugitive." Cody said. "I've only visited case sightings, like the bank and the jailhouse."

"Hopefully, you do a great job on this one." Darius said. "Since the guy we're looking for is on the government's top ten list of fugitives."

"This is going to be fun." Cody said smiling.

Darius and Cody left the office, heading towards Darius' black Kia Forte. Cody liked the car and said, "This is a nice ride. Can I drive it once we head back?"

"You're not driving this car." Darius said. "The only thing you're driving is that head of yours on this mission. Got it?"

"Yeah." Cody said. "Sure, I do."

Preston and Emily made it to Billy's mobile home. They notice Hoyt's truck parked, but no sign of him. Preston gets out of the car and walked to the front door. He knocked. Receiving no response. He knocked again with no response. He decided to open the door and once his hand touched the doorknob, the door opened with no one inside. Preston walked back to the car.

"Find anything?" Emily asked.

"No sign of Hoyt or Billy." Preston said. "There must be a place."

Hoyt had awoken and regained a little consciousness as he saw himself lying on the table in an embalming room. He looked around and saw no one inside. He gets up from the table and walked to the back door. He opened the door as he bumped into one of the funeral assistants.

"What are you doing up?" The assistant asked.

"What am I doing here?" Hoyt asked. "That's the real question."

The funeral assistant begins to back up from Hoyt as he walked closer to him. Hoyt stared at the assistant and said, "I'll ask again. Why am I here? What is this place?"

"You're at Quarles Funeral Home." The assistant said. "You were brought here on Ray Colby's command."

"Ray Colby's command you say?" Hoyt said. "So, you're telling me that, Ray had someone to knock me out. Then, they brought me here. For what? I'm not dead."

"They probably brought you here to take your organs." The assistant said. "Possibly your kidneys or something else."

"My organs." Hoyt said. "You're telling me that this funeral home also takes organs from unsuspected people. This is a new thing."

Hoyt reached in towards his back for his gun, but, realized it isn't there. The assistant smiled and pulled out a gun from his back. Hoyt looked up and noticed that the gun the assistant was holding was his.

"Why do you have my gun?" Hoyt asked.

"I might be a dull kind of guy, but, I'm not stupid." The assistant said. "Start backing up, Bennett."

"You know my name as well, I see." Hoyt said. "Interesting. You know how to fool someone don't you. Just like how you're fooling yourself right now."

"What are you talking about?" The assistant asked.

Slowly slipping from Hoyt's right sleeve, appeared another gun. Hoyt clenched it and shot the assistant in the forehead, blowing his head and killing him. Hoyt walked over to his body and started smiling. He also took back his gun.

"I'll take that, thank you." Hoyt said, taking the gun back. "I surely appreciate you holding on to it for me."

Hoyt heard someone coming towards the front door and he exits out through the back. He sneaked around to the front and steals one of their hearses and drives off with it. As Hoyt drives away, he looks at the interior of the hearse and smiled.

"Never knew it looked so good in these things."

Hoyt reached in his pocket and found his cell phone. He

contacted Billy and told him to meet up at a local Wal-Mart on the outskirts of town. Billy agreed with a stumble in his voice as he headed toward the location.

Darius and Cody arrive at a small loan office. They walk in and speak with the lady in the front. They speak to her about a fugitive named Douglas Greene. According to the information given to Darius and Cody, Douglas used to work at the loan office, before his quit and went into a life of crime.

"We're only here to ask if you have any information regarding Mr. Greene." Darius said.

"I'm sorry, gentlemen. But, we have no information on him around here." The lady said. "All we know is that he decided to quit. We never seen him again."

Cody leaned in and said, "Do you know anyone who was good friends with Mr. Greene? Someone that used to work here?"

"There is a guy named Richard Dillon." The lady said. "He goes by the name, RJ Dillon. He lives in Hartford. If you find him, he might have the information that you're searching for."

"Thank you, Ms." Darius said. "Have a good day."

Darius and Cody leave the loan office and walked toward the vehicle. Cody looked over to Darius with a small grin on his face

"So, looks like we're heading to Hartford." Cody said. "This is starting to become one great trip."

"Keep in mind that we're here on business, Cody." Darius said. "Nothing more and nothing else."

Preston and Emily returned to Barbette's home to find any information on Hoyt and to see of Billy is there with her. They knock on the door and she opens it with mid pull, blowing a small gust from the inside of her home toward Preston and Emily.

"You've returned I see." Barbette said. "Something I never would've expected in my short wilds."

"I am truly sorry to bother you again, Ms. Bronson." Preston said. "But, we are looking for your son, Billy. Have you seen him?"

"He was here about an hour ago." Barbette said. "He left to

head back to his place. He should be there at this moment."

"We've just come from his home, ma'am." Emily said. "So, we thought that he would've came here."

"Well, he did." Barbette said. "He just left before you arrived."

"Did he mention where he was heading off to? Any particular place?" Preston said. "Just a question that I thought I could ask."

Barbette looked with a frown and said, "No. But, I believe that he was going out to meet with Hoyt Bennett someplace in town."

"That's a problem." Emily said. "Because we can't find Hoyt either."

"Hmm." Barbette said. "That's none of my concern. If you do find my Billy and that prick of a human being, you let them know for sure that Barb told you where they would be."

"We'll pass on that message. We sure will." Preston said. "Have a good day, Ms. Bronson."

Preston and Emily left Barbette's home. She watched them drive off and returned into her home and shut the door, murmuring to herself.

Hoyt is parked in a Wal-Mart parking lot, which is surrounded by cars and people. He's sitting in the hearse waiting for Billy to arrive. He looked to his right and saw Billy's truck. Billy pulled up next to him and Hoyt tells him about the events and this is the first place of where they will start. Billy walked slowly with a look of confusion.

"What the Sam hell are you doing driving a hearse?" Billy asked.
You're an undertaker now suddenly?"

"The hearse? It's a long story and I'll explain to you the details at another time." Hoyt said. "Though, I am undertaking this line of work for a short while."

"Speaking of time, what do you mean about the events starting here?" Billy said. "I'm not getting the big picture here."

"Just watch the shopping center, Billy." Hoyt said. "Just watch and watch very closely."

Billy looked and watched for about a couple of minutes. As nothing is happening. Billy turned to Hoyt with a midst of disbelief.

"Watch what, Hoyt?" Billy asked. "What's going on?"

"Billy, look inside your glove box." Hoyt said.

Billy looked inside the glove box and finds a detonator. He pulled it out and looked toward Hoyt. Billy, he starts to shiver in fear.

"Hoyt, what is this?" Billy asked in fear.

"That is a detonator, my friend." Hoyt said. "When you press the button, we will all witness an explosion that will be seen across the land and later, on the nightly news."

"I…. I can't do it, Hoyt." Billy said. "I'm sorry, but, I can't do something like this."

"Just hand it to me, my good friend." Hoyt said. "I'll take care of it."

Billy handed the detonator to Hoyt and he grabbed it. Hoyt flipped up the detonator's top and looked at Billy, smiling with intense energy running through his body. Billy shivered.

"Ladies and gentlemen. Also, you too, Billy. The events have officially begun." It's time to finally blow some shit up!"

"Oh my God!" Billy yelled. "HOYT!!!"

"*INCOMING CALL!!!!*" Hoyt yelled loudly.

Hoyt pressed the button, detonating the bomb and caused an explosion to the entire Wal-Mart store. Flames fly up into the air as they begin to engulf the entire building with people running from the doors on every corner, screaming in fear and terror. Billy is terrified completely as he looked over at Hoyt, smiling and laughing insanely.

"Let's go!" Billy yelled. "Hoyt, let's get the hell out of this place!"

"What's that, Billy?" Hoyt asked. "I can't hear you through the screams coming from the sheep running from the barn."

"Let's go!" Billy yelled again. "Right now! Let's go!"

"Right now?!" Hoyt asked. "Right now?! You mean right

now?!"

"Come on, Hoyt! Damn it!"

Hoyt puts the hearse in drive and exited the parking lot, passing by people who are scattered across the lot. Hoyt stuck his head out of the window and started hollering toward them. Screaming various words and famous quotes. They drive off the lot and head back on the main street.

<u>16</u>

At the office, Eldon tells Preston and Emily that a Wal-Mart has been blown to smithereens. Preston asked how it happened and Eldon has no answer to give him. Emily tells them they should head there to ask any questions about the incident. They leave the office, going to the Wal-Mart. Once in the jeep, Eldon calls Darius and Cody to tell them about the incident.

"Hello, Darius." Eldon said.

"Darius here." Darius said. "Eldon, what's the situation?"

"We just received a call that a Wal-Mart was blown up." Eldon said. "So, I, Preston, and Emily are heading there now to figure this all out."

"Ok. Do you need us to come along?" Darius asked.

"No, just continue what's your doing on your case and we'll deal with this one." Eldon said.

He hanged up the phone, while he drove down the street, heading to the decimated Wal-Mart building.

Ray learned of the Wal-Mart incident and he knows Hoyt is behind it. He commands his men to track down Hoyt and kill him. By any means of force. His men leave the warehouse, entering their SUVs and driving out of sight. Inside the warehouse is Barbette, who Ray didn't realize was inside with him. She sits in front of him.

"Ms. Bronson. I wasn't expecting to see you here." Ray said. "A place such as this of all the ones we have."

"I'm here to ask you about my sons. Mainly I'm here to ask about my Billy." Barbette said. "Do you have any information on him of where he is or anything in particular?"

"All I am aware of is your son being partners with Hoyt." Ray said. "I sent Coover and Rusty to speak with him, but they didn't receive an answer."

"So, you have any information on where Hoyt's whereabouts are right now?" Barbette asked. "Any information?"

"He was at Quarles Funeral Home." Ray said. "But, it seems that he escaped and blew up a Wal-Mart downtown."

"He blew up a Wal-Mart?" Barbette asked. "That's the best he's got to offer? I could give two shits on a paper plate about some goddamn Wal-Mart being blown to smithereens."

"You believe that you can do better?" Ray asked. "That's what your voice is telling me."

"Of course, I can do better!" Barbette said. "I can do a hell of a lot worse than what he's just done. I could cause panic across the entire city. Hell, I can cause panic across this entire state."

"I believe you there, Ms. Bronson." Ray said. "So, what's the plan concerning your baby boy?"

"Do what you will with him." Barbette said. "I tried speaking with him, he wouldn't listen. Coover and Rusty tried, so just do what you must to keep the alliance going."

"To keep the alliance going, we must kill Hoyt." Ray said. "I've already sent some of my men to take him out as we speak. They'll do a fine job."

"Let's hope they do." Barbette said. "Bring us a bundle of good joy and good fortune to our tables."

They shook hands and she left the warehouse. Ray gets up from the seat and leaves through the back door rubbing his head.

Hoyt and Billy are at the hideout and Hoyt is happier than a little boy during the holidays. Billy is still shaking with fear as Hoyt tried to calm him down.

"Billy, just relax, my friend. The first event is over. So, now we celebrate it."

"How can I celebrate when thousands of people were killed

right in front of my eyes. How can I live with that in my mind, just popping up continually?"

"You can get through it, friend. You just have to relax your mind and prepare for the second event."

"Ok. So, I'll ask this right now. What this second event you have planned?"

Hoyt turned and smiled.

"It's time that we take our skills to a bigger location." Hoyt said. "We'll head up to New Haven City Hall eventually and just blow that place up too. Blow it to complete shit."

"Wait and excuse me. But, City Hall." Billy said. "That's a pretty big spot to do this, Hoyt and you're going to need some heavy artillery and explosives to complete something of that status."

"That is why you call it an event. Because it's a huge location for our city and it's the only location where the entire city will actually pay attention to our needs. Once City Hall blows to shit, we will have complete control over New Haven."

"If that's how you feel, Hoyt. If you say so."

Hoyt picked up a glass of vodka and hit Billy's glass and drank it. Hoyt smiled as he believes his events are finally coming into play. Billy continues to join in, even though he's scared.

Preston, Emily, and Eldon arrive at the decimated Wal-Mart. Still with charcoal-like smoke arriving from the building. Fire trucks, ambulances, and police cars are surrounding the location. They walk toward one of the officials. He is checking each person that arrives at the scene with a clipboard.

"What's the clipboard for, officer?" Eldon asked. "Don't think we'll need one on this investigation."

"It's to check if anyone inside is either injured or dead." The officer replied. "So, I see you got the call."

"Yeah we did and while I have you in front of me. Maybe you could tell me if there are any witnesses that seen anything unusual before the explosion took place?"

"We only have one witness so far. He's over there at the

ambulance. He's being checked for injuries."

"Thanks." Eldon said.

They walk over to the ambulance and see the witness being searched for any signs of injury. He is not injured, and they release him. Before he walks away, Preston stands in front of him.

"I'm sorry, but, who the hell are you?" The witness asked.

"I'm Preston Maddox. United States Marshal and Homicide Detective. Me and my partners here just want to ask you some questions regarding the incident."

"All I saw was the explosion and nothing else after that but people running for their lives."

"What else did you see?" Eldon asked.

"Smoke, debris." The witness said. "What did you think I saw? UFOs beaming down at us?"

Preston and Eldon smiled. Emily walked toward the witness.

"Please, just tell us what else you saw and we'll be out of your way." Emily said.

"Since you put it that way, lady. There was one thing I did see."

"Well, by all means, please tell us, then." Eldon said. "For your sake I suppose."

The witness paused for a moment and uttered, "I saw these two guys, both white. They were both in trucks, parked next to each other. They stayed in there until the explosion and once that happened, they were the first ones gone."

"Did one of them yell out anything?" Preston asked. "Anything that may seem familiar to you or to this place?"

"One of them did yell out the words. Some of them I couldn't understand. But, I noticed he yelled out the phrase, *"Incoming Call"*. Don't know if that will help you or not."

"Shit!" Preston said. "It was Hoyt. It was him."

"How can you be so sure about that, Preston?" Eldon asked.

"He's the only son of a bitch that would yell out that phrase before an explosion would take place. I'll go ahead and look for him."

"We're coming with you." Eldon said. "You hear me, Preston."

Preston leaves the scene as Eldon and Emily get into the jeep and follow him. Preston stops at a red light and on the side of him arrives Eldon and Emily in the jeep. Eldon rolled down the window.

"Where are you headed?" Eldon asked.

"Going over to Hoyt's hideout in the outskirts. From my understanding, that's where he'll be currently."

<u>**17**</u>

Darius and Cody arrive at a small home in the suburbs of Hartford. They find a large brick home with a mailbox on the front lawn. The initials on the mailbox are, "RJ" Cody looked at it and turned to the house.

"Appears to be his place, Mr. D." Cody said. "What do you think?"

"Looks like it could be." Darius said. "Also, don't call me, Mr. D. Wherever you thought up that name."

"Sure, no problem." Cody said.

They walked to the front door and Darius knocked. He knocked again, no response. Cody looked over at him, believing that he's not at the house. Darius knocked one more time and the door opens. An African American male is standing on the other side.

"Excuse us, sir." Darius said. "But, we're United States Marshals from New Haven on a case concerning a man named Richard Dillon. Also known to some people as, RJ Dillon."

"Never heard of the guy." The man said.

"What's with the RJ initials on the mailbox, sir?" Cody asked. "According to that and my knowledge, it makes you appear as the guy who we're looking for."

"What has this guy done to have some marshals on his trail?" The man asked. "If I am able to know."

"RJ Dillon is a fugitive of the United States government." Darius said. "To put it in a short sentence for you, the guy's a con artist."

"A con artist you say." The man said. "From what you're saying is the guy's been giving lots of people trouble in a lot of various ways."

"A little too much trouble." Cody said. "We were given information from a loan office and the information states that RJ lives in this very house. In the end, that's why we're here and the initials on the mailbox plainly give it away for us."

"Well, I'll say this and you two can be on your way off this property. I don't know any RJ Dillon." The man said. "So, if you please leave my home, we will have no trouble."

"We can't leave this property until we receive concrete information regarding RJ Dillon and this location." Cody said. "So, if you don't mind, we'll wait here until he arrives or comes back from wherever he's currently placed."

"You'll just wait for him? Ok. If you say so." The man said as he shut the door in their faces.

Cody turned to Darius, curious.

"Did he just slam the door in our faces?" Cody asked. "Because, its looks that way."

"Yeah." Darius replied. "By that means of action, he knows something we don't know."

Darius knocked on the door again. No answer as he knocked twice as hard on the door. The door opened, and RJ Dillon walked out, facing Darius and Cody. Wearing his expensive white suit with nice black shades.

"Didn't my assistant just tell you two dickheads to leave this property." RJ said. "So, why in the blue hell are the two of you still here?"

"So, you're RJ Dillon I see." Darius said. "If you're not aware, me and my partner here are on your property to take you into custody for your con artistry."

"My ass you aren't. I'm not going anywhere in any shape or form."

He reached behind him and pulled out an RPK machine gun. Darius and Cody backed up a couple of feet with their hands in the air. Their faces show a slight fear within them. Though, they stand their guard.

"Wow, an RPK. OK. That's a nice firearm you have there,

RJ.”

"Thank you, boy." RJ said. "I won it in a poker game a few months back. Thanks to the great ace."

"Did you shoot the loser after the game was over?" Darius asked. "Just seems obvious that you would do something like that and since you're a con man, you've probably did more than just that with anyone."

"How about I just shoot the two of you, right here on the spot." RJ said. "That way I can be rid of you easily. Since you won't leave my property."

"You don't have to do that, Mr. RJ." Cody said. "We'll just leave right now if you like."

Darius and Cody start walking towards the car slowly as RJ has the machine gun pointed toward them. They get to their car and RJ commands them to get inside. They get inside and once RJ puts down the machine gun, Cody fires a gun at his knee. RJ yelled and dropped the RPK. His assistant runs out of the house, with an AK. Darius pulled out his pistol and shot the assistant in the chest. Cody runs out of the car and drags RJ with him. They place RJ in the back of the car and Darius looked at Cody.

"Didn't think you had it in you." Darius said. "Very good skill set."

"I might be a rookie Marshal in training, but I'm highly skilled in the presence of marksmanship." Cody said.

Handcuffing RJ's hands and legs, they left the area, heading to the interstate, returning to New Haven. Darius looked in the back toward RJ and glanced over to Cody, who's driving the vehicle.

"You're sure he'll be comfortable back there all cuffed up?" Darius said.

"Who gives a damn if he feels comfortable. I say he deserves it for what he's done to many innocent people."

Ray's men arrive at a small location, where they meet with Coover and Rusty about assassinating Hoyt. Coover tells the group that they must be silent on this mission and Rusty tells them that their primary target is Hoyt, but, by Ray's order and Barbette's answers, if Billy pops up on the scene, that they must shoot him as well. Rusty decides to also tell the group about the marshals. Rusty said that if any of the marshals arrive on the scene, they must take them out as well.

"We must do what we can to keep this all quiet." Rusty said. "If the marshals arrive on scene, we take them out. Completely."

"Every single one of them." Coover said. "Whether its Hoyt, our dear brother, Billy, or the marshals, we have to put them down."

"Basically, men." Rusty said. "No witnesses. No casualties. That way there won't be any traces that will lead to us, Ray, or mother."

"You're sure about all of this?"

"I'm damn sure about it."

They begin to march out with their guns and weapons. They head toward their vehicles and leave, driving to Hoyt's hideout.

Preston, Emily, and Eldon arrive at Hoyt's hideout. Eldon looked around the deserted area of grass. Emily looked around as well. Though, they spot both Hoyt's and Billy's trucks, confirming that the two of them are currently inside the hideout. Preston walked toward the front door. He knocked, and Billy opened it.

"Marshal!" Billy yelled. "Marshals!"

Preston shoved Billy out of the way, letting Eldon and Emily walk in. Hoyt arrives from the kitchen area, smiling. Preston doesn't smile, not an inch. Neither does Eldon and Emily. Preston delivered a right-hook punch to Hoyt, which knocked him to the ground. He picked him up and shoved him against the wall, knocking down one of the mounted deer heads.

"You no good son of a bitch!" Preston said. "You no good piece of shit!"

"Preston, what have I done to cause such anger from you?" Hoyt asked. "Killed someone you loved in the process or something worse than that?"

"I know, we know. Hell, everyone now knows." Preston said.

"The Wal-Mart that exploded, that was you. It's all on you, Hoyt. The witness gave you out with your "Incoming Call" battle cry."

"Preston, just relax for a minute." Eldon said. "Let the man get a breather."

"No!" Preston yelled. "There is no relaxing right now, damn it. He's killed thousands of people today and I'm not going to stand by and let him kill a thousand more! To hell with his breather!"

Preston punched Hoyt again and threw him across the counter to the kitchen. Eldon tries to calm Preston down, but, it isn't working. Billy crouches in the corner to avoid Preston. Preston continues pummeling Hoyt and Emily stopped him from doing any more damage to Hoyt as he's bleeding from nose to mouth.

"Preston, enough is enough now." Emily said. "Just calm down, please. So, we can settle this like civilized people."

Preston responded to Emily and stopped attacking Hoyt.

"I'm starting to like her even more so now." Hoyt said.

"Don't push your luck." Emily said. "Or I'll just let him continue to beat your ass to a pulp."

"Come on, Emily. There's no need for that right now." Eldon said.

Preston looked over at the corner, where Billy is and he pointed toward him, saying he's next if he tries anything that Hoyt has done. As they prepare to take Hoyt to their car, they notice headlights coming towards the house. They ducked down to avoid being seen.

"Who's that outside?" Emily asked.

"Probably someone that's come to kill Hoyt." Preston said. "For all the shit he's caused so far.'

Eldon took a peep outside the window and saw what appeared to be seven cars, all having dozens of men walk out, with weapons in their hands. Eldon ducked down and told the rest of them what's going on outside.

On the outside, Coover and Rusty are leading the pack of Ray's men toward the hideout. Coover recognizes Billy's truck and points it out to Rusty. Rusty looked at the hideout.

"Billy!" Rusty yelled. "Billy, we know you're in there, little brother. We know your good buddy, Hoyt is in there too. So, why don't the two of you do use a favor and just walk on out here nice and calm, so we can finish our business here."

"Come on little brother." Coover said. 'We're only here to talk with you. But, Hoyt, we're here to kill that no-good bastard."

Inside the house, everyone is crouched down, preparing their firearms. Hoyt looked over at Preston, still in pain from Preston's attack.

"You have to help me, just this once." Hoyt said. "Please."

"Why?" Preston said. "So, you can kill more innocent people. You've done enough. I should just let you die here."

"But, you won't." Hoyt said. "Because, we were once friends."

"We were friends a long time ago, Hoyt." Preston said. "That time has come and gone and its over for you."

The pack of men are closer to the house as they start banging on the windows and the front door. One man decides to kick the door down. But, he couldn't do it, since he hurt himself in the process. Coover and Rusty pull out their handguns and fire at the windows, knocking them out. Preston looked over to Hoyt and asked him of a back door. Hoyt pointed toward the kitchen and they all head out the back. Just as they left, Coover knocked down the door and they entered the hideout. They didn't find anyone around the area.

Just as they searched the hideout, they heard engines sound. Coover and Rusty looked at one another and walked to the outside. To which, they see Preston, Emily, Eldon, Billy, and Hoyt leaving in their vehicles. Rusty now upset, turned toward his brother. Pointing at them running off in the distance.

"Shit! They're running away, fellas!" Rusty yelled. "Grab your gear and get in your vehicles!"

They jumped into their vehicles and proceed to chase them all down. Now, on the highway, there's a chase between the two groups. Coover drives behind Hoyt's truck and Rusty begins firing at him. Hoyt ducked down as the shots came in inches closer toward his head.

"Did you hit him, bro?" Coover asked. "Did you hit him?"

"What's it look like to you, no I didn't." Rusty said. "Just keep your eyes on the damn road and just drive."

Now, Emily started to fire a couple of shots toward the pack around them. She popped out the tires on some of the men's vehicles, stopping them from the chase. She fired more shots toward Coover and Rusty, knocking out their back window. Coover started to yell as he's in a fury.

"She just knocked out our damn window, bro!" Coover said. "That isn't going by easy with me, man."

"Don't worry, mama doesn't like the bitch anyway." Rusty said. "So, we'll kill her for mama's sake."

Rusty begins firing toward the jeep as Eldon and Emily both ducked. Eldon covers his head, while continuing to drive.

"I didn't think it would be like this down here." Emily said. "I thought it would be more subtle and a little quieter."

"This is New Haven, Ms. Weston.' Eldon said. 'Not your kind of New Jersey feel of the day.'

Emily continued to fire at the pack. The intersection turns into a two-way street. Now, Coover and Rusty are driving on the side of Hoyt. Rusty fires toward Hoyt, he ducked his head and reached for his gun.

Once Rusty stopped firing, Hoyt rose up from the door and shot Rusty in the chest and also shot Coover in the right arm. Coover screams in pain, losing control of the truck. The truck drives off the interstate and dives down into a ditch on the side. The truck started flipping over around three times. Hoyt cheerfully yelled out the window.

"That's right my people!" Hoyt yelled. "That's how you handle these bastards around here!"

Coover and Rusty dragged themselves from the damaged truck. Coover helped Rusty walk his way up toward the road. Staggering and stumbling in pain, the two of them try to gain more strength as they inch closer to the road.

"Come on bro." Coover said. "I got you, don't worry."

Another one of Ray's men drive on the left lane, directly next to Preston. He looked over at them as they threat him by screaming out words. He pulled out his gun and shot their tire, causing them to turn and flip across the interstate.

"These assholes never learn." Preston said.

Emily looked over at Preston's car and he's pointing in front of them, telling them to go forward. They pass him and so does Billy and Hoyt. But, Hoyt slows down a bit next to Preston. Hoyt looked over at Preston.

"Preston." Hoyt yelled. "The next time you come into my place of business and proceed to beat me down, you won't be so lucky."

"I'll take my chances." Preston yelled. "You best be careful on this road."

"I'll be just fine and dandy. See you next time, Preston." Hoyt yelled as he drove away.

"That son of a bitch." Preston said. "He'll never get it straight through his head."

Ray, Barbette, and Carla meet at his nightclub, inside his office. Ray is pleased to see Barbette there, but he isn't pleased at all, seeing Carla.

"I have to thank you, Ms. Bronson." Ray said. "I never would expect to see you in this type of place."

"Wherever business must be settled, Colby, I'll be there." Barbette said. "So, what's the reason for us being here at such time?"

"I received a call from the chief and he's not too pleased with what's going on." Ray said. "He heard about the Wal-Mart incident and has told me take out Hoyt."

"We're all trying to take out Hoyt, Mr. Colby." Barbette said. 'The real question is how are we supposed to do that with the marshals on his trail?"

"You can leave the marshals to me." Carla said. "I can deal with them easily. Instead of killing them, I'll just use my persuasion on them."

"How can you convince me to trust you this time, Carla?" Ray asked. "You've already had one of my most allied men killed at the agency."

Barbette looked over at Carla. She took another glance before keeping her glaze locked on Carla. He raised her finger and pointed toward her.

"Wait a god damn minute now. You're the lady who lead John into that building?" Barbette asked. "You lead him in there, armed and not in the state of mind to do so?"

"He seemed like he was ready to me, Ms. Bronson." Carla said. "I just didn't know he had it in him to proceed with the mission at hand. He was a strong-minded guy."

"What happened to John isn't our main priority of the matter now." Ray said. "What currently matters to all of us is we find a way of taking out Hoyt, getting rid of these marshals, and ruling over this city."

"May that be done in a hurry." Barbette said. "Very quickly, before more shit comes into play and ruins what we already have here ongoing."

She shook Ray's hand and left the office. Ray leaned over to Carla and told her that she cannot fail him one more time or he might have to put her down himself. She laughed as she left the office.

Darius and Cody returned to the office. They've taken RJ to the downtown jailhouse and left him there, until the morning. They walk into the office and placed all of their equipment back into their locations. Cody leaves the office, heading home. Darius is doing the same. As they both head downstairs, Cody turned to Darius.

"We did a good job today." Cody said.

"I could say, yeah we did do a good job." Darius said. "A great job, really."

They walk towards their cars and they leave, heading to their homes.

Preston returns to his apartment and realizes that its unlocked again. He decides not to pull out his gun and walked in. Once he was inside, he turned on the switch and he's standing toe-to-toe with Ray Colby. Preston grunted as he saw Ray standing in front of him with a pistol pointed directly towards him.

"It seems that everyone has a key to my place." Preston said. "So, Carla gave you the heads up on my resting spot or did you just bully the owner into giving you an extra key?"

"It's the best thing Carla's done for me so far in her line of work." Ray said. "You have no need to worry if I try to kill you here. I'm only here to tell you about Hoyt's current situation and how it concerns me and my elite group."

"I could give a shit about your elite group. What's this situation have to do with Hoyt and your pals?" Preston said. "Is it about his patterned explosion attacks over the past few days or is it something that he's done to you in a way that I have no knowledge of? I assume its something more personal going on here?"

"I'm going to say this once and only once in a way that you can understand, Marshal. Either you leave Hoyt to me and I'll spare your entire agency from a total disaster. You and your marshals are invading my business. My property, you guys even ran some of my men off the road during that chase you guys had."

"Well, I'll say this, Ray." Preston said. "I'm not going to leave Hoyt alone because he is my task to accomplish. As of right now, I'm going to give you a ten-second count to leave this place, before I put a bullet through you and tell your elite friends that another one has been brought down."

Ray smiled. He nodded as he stared at Preston.

"Ten seconds, you say?" Ray said. "Sounds like a threat towards me. How should I take it from you when your weapon isn't even in your hand and mine is? Explain that to me? I can put a, what you say, bullet through you, before you even pull out your weapon."

"You'll pay to find that out." Preston said. "Just like your old buddy Cartel did. He played this game as well and you know how it ended for him don't you."

"Smooth. Ray said. "So, before I go I would want to say."

"Ten." Preston said. "And counting."

Ray laughed. He shook his finger toward Preston, who continued to stand still. Ray nodded his head.

"Funny and clever." Ray said. "You really know how to intimidate your enemies, Marshal. In ways that other marshals or detectives wouldn't even give a mere thought towards."

"Nine." Preston said. "The countdown is still on going, Colby."

Preston slowly moved his right hand to his side, almost ready to pull out his weapon. Ray doesn't even notice it. Ray placed his gun back into his back and slowly moved inches closer to the door.

"Ok." Ray said. "Alright. I'll leave. But, take my advice under serious conditions, Marshal or there will be consequences on your head."

Ray left the apartment and Preston turned around and made

sure that Ray left the area.

The next morning, Coover and Rusty are visiting the hospital to search for any injuries on their bodies due to the crazed speeding chase. They find bruised ribs on Coover, but a broken rib and a dislocated shoulder on Rusty. Barbette arrived and seen her sons in the hospital room.

"What happened?" Barbette asked. "What happened to my two babies?"

"Mama, we were ran off the road by those marshals." Coover said. "We were just trying to do the job."

"Don't talk about it in here, Coover." Rusty said with pain in his voice. "We don't need anyone hearing about our business. They might try to pull something against us, so we would have to pay more."

Leaving the hospital, walking towards their mother's partially clean brown Durango. They helped Rusty walk to the car and help him into the passenger's seat.

Coover inched closer to Barbette so he could whisper the information to her. In order to avoid confrontation with people in the hospital.

"Mama, we tried to take out Hoyt." Coover said. "But, those marshals invaded the plans. If they didn't we would've had him."

"Was Billy there as well?" Barbette asked. "Was he with Hoyt when this was taking place?"

"Yes ma'am." Coover said. "We tried to have spoken conversations with him, but, he didn't respond to us. Nor, did he come to visit us here."

"It's alright, my sons." Barbette said. "Billy has decided to leave the family that raised him. There's nothing we can do to save him now. He's on his own at this point."

At the office, Eldon speaks with Darius and Cody about their case in Hartford. Darius tells Eldon that the case when nice and they've placed RJ in custody. Eldon is impressed and thanks them both for their help in finding RJ. Preston and Emily walk into the office and Preston told Eldon that Ray was inside his apartment last night, giving him a warning not to have any marshal or law enforcement officers involved with Hoyt. Eldon tells Preston that he should take Ray's words and shove them up Ray's ass. Preston laughed.

"So, if I may ask you of this. Your anger craze, yesterday." Eldon said. "What the hell was that all about?"

"Throughout most of his adult life, Hoyt has killed thousands of people across this city and state, Eldon." Preston said. "It's about time that someone gave him a beat down and to be honest, I wasn't even quite finished with him."

"He deserved a lot more, I believe." Eldon said. "Though, you can't let your anger take control over yourself. It could cost you dearly."

"He deserved a lot more." Preston said. "A thousand times more. Since, he's killed that number of people, some innocent and some not. He deserves it."

"If Emily didn't calm you down, you've would have possibly killed the guy." Eldon said. "Imagine how that would look upon you."

"Me and Hoyt were once good friends, long ago." Preston said. "Times have changed and so have the friendships and trust."

Eldon later told Preston to head out toward the courthouse, so they can discuss RJ's case. Preston looked over at Eldon, asking if Darius and Cody should be there, since they picked the guy up in the first place. Eldon said that they will be there and so should him and Preston.

At the courthouse, the judge is sentencing RJ to four years in prison for his previous crimes such as being a con artist, he's also convicted of burglary, kidnapping, and a case of three homicides. The security handcuffed RJ and took him out of the courtroom through the back doors and towards a police car, that's parked in the front of the building.

They open the front doors and it is crowded with reporters and journalists, asking RJ questions concerning what he's done over the years. He gives them no responses as he gets into the back of the police car and it drives off. Eldon and Preston walk over to Darius and Cody and congratulate them on solving RJ's case.

"You guys did great." Eldon said. "I should tell the head office to give you guys some higher power of authority."

"I don't think you should do that, Eldon." Preston said. "Might cause their egos to take over and when the ball drops their careers would be over in a nutshell."

"I don't have that much of an ego, Preston." Darius said. "Though, I think we all know that Cody does to a certain extent."

"Not really, guys." Cody said. "When it comes to egos, you won't have to look toward him for being some kind of a narcissist.

At the warehouse, Ray finds out about what happened with the chase and that he lost a few of his men during the event. Coover and Rusty walk in with Barbette on their side.

"Coover, Rusty. Are you alright?" Ray asked.

"We're fine, boss." Rusty said. "Just some minor injuries, that's all."

"Hoyt and those damn marshal folks hurt my two sons, Colby." Barbette said. "They ran them off the road and into that foul ditch. Now their means of transportation is completely damaged."

"You shouldn't have to worry, Ms. Bronson. I'll go ahead and purchase your boys another truck. Though, we seriously need to consider the process of finding Hoyt and your youngest son." Ray said.

"It would be best if you could lead both Hoyt and that Instinct Marshal into some kind of a trap." Coover said. "You know, lead them both there, simultaneously, so that way, we can kill them both at the same time. Good plan, huh."

"The two birds and one stone play. It could work. But, how would we lead them to the same location?" Ray said.

"You let me handle that large obstacle, Ray." A female voice said from the front.

Ray looked and its Carla once again. Ray's had enough of her and commands his security to take her out. She tells Ray that she knows exactly how to lure both Preston and Hoyt into the same location to be killed. Ray asked her how and she said that she'll handle it, since she doesn't want them involved with it. Ray stood up and decided to allow Carla to go forward with the plan and that he has to leave for a trip to Newark, New Jersey.

Barbette stood up and thanks Ray for her son's new vehicle and said that they must take them all out soon. They leave and Carla leaves behind them, telling Ray not to worry. One of Ray's men walked up to him with a photo from the Caucasian and African-American men who were waiting inside the car.

"Sir, the two watchers told me to bring this picture to you." The thug said. "They suspected it would be highly useful to you."

Ray looked at the photo and it's a picture of Emily. Ray thought back to his New Jersey days and remembered who Emily was and knew she's also from Newark. He only focused on the picture as he decided to place a hit on her by hiring one hit man. He even exceeded the plan as to let the marshals know where he's headed, saying to his group that it would just to fool them and lure them into the trap.

"By doing this, they will never know what's going to hit them." Ray said. "Won't even have a clue what will be coming up on their front steps."

"You got it boss." The thug said.

The thug left the warehouse as Ray continued to read some unknown documents that were stacked on his desk.

At the office, Eldon contacts Preston and Emily to tell them that Ray has made an announcement that Ray is traveling to Newark for a business trip. Emily suggested that she'll go ahead and search around the city for Colby, since she's a native of the area. She left the office. Preston looked and turned to Eldon.

"So, as of now, I'm on my own?" Preston asked. "Due to Emily running off on her own merry goose chase."

"That appears to be the case." Eldon said. "Also, since Cody is currently partnered up with Darius, that does leave you on your own."

"Alright." Preston said. "I'll take only small portions of this to savor in."

"I almost forgot about this because of your savoring. Something did come up that I personally believe you'll be happy to solve on your own." Eldon said.

"Which is what?" Preston asked. "Picking up lunch for the agency. Or the fugitives in questioning."

Eldon leaned over his desk and pulled out a document from underneath a small pile of paper notes. He handed the document over to Preston, in which he opened it and found it containing a picture of Carla meeting with Ray at the warehouse in the outskirts of New Haven

"You have got to me shitting me. This is what you wanted to give me to do. Go around town to search for an ex and an elite crime thug."

"I figured it would do you some good. Get some of that steam off your chest at least."

"I'll manage my stream progress. So, who exactly am I searching for on this case? Can't be Colby because Emily's already on the chase."

"There have been reports of seeing your old flame circling around town. Talking and making deals with a many of people that seem to be getting paid under the radar by Colby and his elite crime friends. So, you're on this case. Since you know her very well."

"I'll go ahead and do it. But, once I am finished with this one, I'm going ahead to look for Hoyt. Some of those events haven't happened yet and we need to stop them."

"Go ahead and do that. I won't stop you there."

In the outskirts of New Haven, just around a small field near a steep hill, Hoyt and Billy are sitting in a truck, over viewing Ray's warehouse. Billy looked around at the area, searching for any of Colby's henchmen around the location.

"So, far I don't see any of Ray's guys out here." Billy said. "What are we going to do when everything is in complete order, Hoyt?"

"Good of you to ask. The last plan will involve his warehouse in a huge way. It will be an epic event for us. But, so far two of the events have happened and we can't look too far into the near future."

"Wait, I thought only one of the events had took place." Billy asked. "The two have actually happened?"

"Listen very closely. The jailhouse was the first event in the long process. The Wal-Mart explosion was only the second one and that went somewhat how I expected it to go. As of this moment, we have just two more events to go before the main course, being the warehouse here, takes its place atop the other four."

"If I may ask you, what are the next two events? I take it you're going to blow up Target next or a mall? Because, personally I don't like Target, Hoyt. They're just cheapskates over there. Don't do shit about their customers."

"Wal-Mart didn't either. I would expect you to hate nearly all of the retail stores."

"That was a good point. I never thought of it in that way."

"One thing's for sure, Billy. I'm not blowing up another shopping place. That already took its course. This time, it has to be something quieter than the last two places. Something to get people off their asses when it culminates."

"Could you give me some kind of a hint as to what place would be like that? Because, I don't know any quiet, quiet places that you could actually blow up without causing a problem."

"Believe me when I say, there's a place, Billy. There's a place around this land that's point-blank right up our noses and around the corner. But, I'm starting to think that we need more members, just to have a full overview of the entire city."

It's nightfall in New Jersey as Ray arrived in Newark. After exiting his private plane, he's escorted out of the airport approaching his vehicle. He's heavily guarded with security as they lead him towards his black SUV waiting for him out front. They walk out of the airport as Ray entered the SUV and it pulled away with three of his henchmen already inside the back of the SUV. Ray nodded at them as he reached into his jacket and pulled out his phone and started dialing a number.

"Hello, chief. This is Colby. Yeah, I'm in Newark. Everything will go as planned as we discussed. The female Marshal? She shouldn't be too far gone behind us. We'll have her in place as soon as she's in our sights. Don't worry, chief, it's all in good hands."

Ray hung up the phone and started smiling to himself.

<u>19</u>

Carla sat in a room as she was having a meeting with six of Ray's thugs and she discusses the plan to lure both Preston and Hoyt into the same location, only for them to be killed by the six thugs. As the thugs sat at a round table, looking at Carla standing up in front of them. One of the thugs stood up. He gained the attention of the other five thugs and Carla herself as he began questioning Carla's proposed plan of attack in the woods.

"So, what's your position in this plan, sweetheart?" One thug asked. "If you don't mind a man like me asking such a question."

"My plan is to be the backup." Carla said.

"Backup?" The thug said. "What kind of backup are you talking about? More guys like us or some highly trained folks that are in this for the sake of execution and a little extra profit."

"You'll just have to wait and see who they are." Carla said. "The backup will do us some good in this task."

Another thug stood up and said that she's responsible for John's death and why should they trust her on this mission. Carla said that she can be trusted, since what happened with John wasn't her fault. The six thugs look at one another and turned to Carla.

"We'll help you out on this one, Carla." The thug said. "But, don't think for a second to turn on us. By any means."

"You won't have to worry about that." Carla said. "You're all in good hands being with me."

The thugs nod as Carla left the room. Though, the first two thugs are a little uncertain about Carla's motives in the process.

Eldon contacts Darius and Cody to come to his office. They enter his office and sit at the desk. Eldon turned to them with documents in his hand.

"What's going on now, chief?" Darius asked.

"We've just received a new case that concerns a hit man." Eldon said.

"Hit man? Cool." Cody said. "Sounds like it should be great case to work on."

"Who's this hit man and what's his case of being the cause?" Darius asked.

"The hit man's name is currently unknown at this moment." Eldon said. "But, for some odd reason, his only targets are female prostitutes."

"Prostitutes? He has some obsession with prostitutes." Darius said. "I wonder why he would have that type of agenda. For whatever reason, sure doesn't sound like fun."

"That's what I'm trying to figure out." Eldon said. "Since Preston is busy with a case and Emily's out of state, I'm going to join the two of you on this one. Just to have some time out of the office."

"Where's the first place that we should look?" Darius asked.

"We'll head to a local street in the low side of town." Eldon said. "That's where most of the prostitution business takes place. If its crowded with women by tonight, we should find out hit man."

"Hopefully." Darius said.

Hoyt and Billy enter small building. Inside is a group of people playing poker. Hoyt looked at the guys and yelled to get their attention. They turned in fear and started walking towards him, pulling out their guns and knives.

"From my perspective it sure looks like a nice game of poker is being played here in the centerfolds." Hoyt said. "Mind if me and my friend here join in on the game and try to win some prizes of our own."

"Who the hell are you two boys?" One man said. "What the hell you're doing here in our place?"

"Gentlemen, gentlemen, please. No trouble has entered into your doorstep." Hoyt said. "Now just calm down and relax yourselves. I'm only here to present you fellow gentlemen an offer that you cannot possibly refuse according to how you're behaving as of this moment."

"Oh yeah. What type of offer?" The man said.

"An offer that will bring in a lot of money." Hoyt said. "As well as some control over the city."

The man looked over at his friends as they start to nod their heads in acceptance. The man turned his attention back to Hoyt. Staring him into his eyes.

"Money and control, you say? Alright." The man said. "I'll say we're all in. What do you need us to do?"

"If you and your group just follow me to my new safe haven and everything will be explained there." Hoyt said. "Please follow quickly and quietly, so we don't cause a disturbance."

Emily arrives through the interstate, entering Newark, New Jersey. Once inside the city she's already determined and going on the hunt for Ray. She drives down and travels through the downtown area to search for any evidence that will lead to him. Though, she doesn't find anything, she drives past an office building, she notices a man who looked similar to Ray physically. She slowly entered the parking lot to have a closer look. The man she was looking at wasn't Ray.

"Damn it." Emily said. "No sign of Ray here. Where could he have gone? I could check the agency. They should remember who I am."

Preston is visiting a small diner. The diner is quiet, as there aren't many people inside. He walked toward the counter, where he speaks with one of the waitresses about Carla, since that's the diner where she was located.

"Excuse me, Ms." Preston said. "I'm here to asks some questions regarding a woman who was in here a few days ago."

"Sir, you are?" The waitress asked.

"Oh, I'm Preston Maddox." Preston said smiling. "United States Marshal and Homicide Detective. I'm here to ask about a woman that was seen in this very place not too long ago."

"Marshal, huh. You can ask me anything you want, baby." The waitress said. "And I mean anything that's on your mind."

"Ok. I'm just here to ask about this certain particular woman." Preston said. "That's all there is."

"Well, do you have a picture of the woman?" The waitress said. "That way it would be easier for me to help you out, sir."

"As a matter of fact, I do." Preston said. "Here it is right here."

He showed her a picture and she looked at the photo and glanced toward Preston and back to the photo. She recognized Carla in the photo.

"I remember her and the guy she's with." The waitress said. "They sat right over in that corner, towards the window."

"Ok. You're getting somewhere now. While they were here, did you over hear their conversation or anything related?" Preston asked.

"They were talking about a plan that they were trying to do." The waitress said. "It involved something with officials and such. But, I didn't hear anything else."

"Did they mention a location of any kind?" Preston asked. "Or anything related to that matter?"

"They spoke about a warehouse across town." The waitress said. "They were saying that after they finish their plan, they'll head back there. But, they didn't mention any other locations, sir. But, you can visit an antique store across town. There's a gentleman there named Tanner. They spoke about him, so he could possibly give you some information."

"If that's the case and it seems that it is. I thank you for your honesty, sweetheart." Preston said. "I really appreciate all of the help you've given me on this task."

"You're welcome and here's my phone number." The waitress said. "You can call me if you want to know more. Whether it involves your case or just a personal call."

Preston smiled, "I'll keep the personal call in mind. Have a good day, ma'am."

Preston left the diner drove away as he continued to search around other possible locations for more information.

<u>**20**</u>

Hoyt and Billy arrived at the old pawn shop building along with the group of poker guys. They walk in and see all of the weapons that are laid out through the building. The place is also painted white and it's all clean. Billy turned to Hoyt.

"Whoa, whoa! Wait a second now?" Billy said. "Please tell me that you bought the place before you start talking with these fellows?"

"I sure did." Hoyt said. "It wasn't much. Just negotiating, really."

"Nice place, Hoyt." The man said. "We agreed to your offer. So, what you need us to do?"

"I need you and a few of your guys to head out towards the downtown area and cause a scene." Hoyt said. "A big scene."

"A big scene? What kind of big scene? A riot? A shootout? Rob drivers and steal their cars kind of big?"

"A shootout will do just fine." Hoyt said. "Though, I like the riot idea a lot, that can wait another time and you never told us your name?"

"Sorry about that, my newly found friend." The man said. "My name is Russell. Although, my guys call me Leader."

"They call you Leader, huh." Hoyt said. "Sounds good. But, you know that I'm the leader of this organization and you're the leader of your groups. So, they'll call you Leader and I'll just call you Russell. Alright."

"You got it, Hoyt." Russell said. "Whatever you say from this point on end."

Hoyt smiled and shook Russell's hand. After shaking his hand, Hoyt and Billy leave the pawn shop, letting Russell sit with his men. Thinking about Hoyt's offer.

Coover and Rusty are at a car lot with Barbette as they pick out their new vehicle. They are looking at the trucks. Coover spotted one and pointed it out.

"How about this one, Rusty." Coover said. "This one could help us out at least."

"It could work." Rusty said. "But, I don't like green. Green doesn't suit me well. As long as it's an F-250 and not a bright color, I'll be fine with it."

"How about the silver one over there?" Coover said. "That one suits you well enough. Come on, brother. It's only a vehicle we need to use."

Rusty walked over to the truck and looked at the interior. He started smiling and turned toward his mother slowly.

"Rusty, do you like this one?" Barbette asked. "You look like you do."

"Yes ma'am, I do." Rusty said. "Brother, how about you? You like this one, here?"

"I do." Coover said. "I really do."

"Let's go inside and speak with the dealer." Barbette said. "After this, the both of you should thank Mr. Colby for doing this. This is his money we're dealing with after all."

Preston had arrived at the antique store across town. He walks in and sees tons of priceless antique glasses and statues. Preston looks around toward the counter for the cashier or any employees.

"Excuse me! Anybody here?!" Preston yelled. "Hello?!"

The clerk walks from the back and looks at Preston. Preston stood still as he stared at the clerk. Who walked slowly toward the counter near Preston. The clerk took a big swallow before speaking to Preston.

"What do you want?" The clerk said. "Sir. Good sir."

The clerk had noticed Preston's badge and gun on each side of his belt. He becomes startled as he took one step back from the counter."

"Oh. A badge and a gun." The clerk said. "I take it you're a policeman, huh."

"What? No. I'm not a cop, I'm a Deputy United States Marshal and Homicide Detective." Preston said. "Since you know what I am, what's your name, slick?"

"My name's Tanner." The clerk said. "Tanner Powell."

"Well, Tanner Powell. I was told by a waitress at the diner across the block from here that you could have some possible information regarding this woman and this man."

Preston showed Tanner the photo of Carla and the thug. Tanner looked at the photo and turned back to Preston.

"No, man." Tanner said. "I have no idea who those two are. Sorry, I can't help you there, sir."

"You said your name was Tanner, huh?" Preston said. "Almost forgot after hearing you speak like that in such manner. By the look of you, I would've though your name would've been something like Troy or Steven. Hell, maybe even Freddy."

"I have some relatives named Troy and Steven." Tanner said. "Cousins on my father's side. No Freddy in my family, though I believe not to be. I really don't know everyone in my family, so I couldn't really tell you exactly."

"Yeah, great. I'm sure you'll find out sooner or later." Preston said. "And what's going on with both of your eyes? You've been smoking dope or something?"

"It's a rare form of pink eye, sir." Tanner said. "It very, very contagious, so, I would recommend that you don't touch me, sir. If you do touch me, you could get infected too and wake up the next morning with one of these or maybe something worse."

"I don't think I'll end up turning into a Dead of any sort. Though, you have no need to worry. I'm not going to touch you by any means." Preston said. "No worries there. I'm just looking for the woman on the photo. Her name is Carla Garcia by the way. The waitress told me that they spoke about you. Saying that they came by this location."

"Never heard of her in my entire life." Tanner said. "Don't

recall seeing her in this place."

"From what I understand, according to my knowledge is she operates at a warehouse not far from here." Preston said. "With that warehouse nearby this area, you're sure you didn't see her?"

"Sorry, I can't help you." Tanner said. "Truly can't."

"Ok, then." Preston said. "If that's the way you want to go on this day."

Preston walked over to the shelf and tampered with the antique glasses on the shelf. He started saying a rhyme before he tapped on one and knocked down one of the antique glasses. The glass smashed on the floor in pieces. Tanner freaked out and Preston looked at him.

"Oh shit." Preston said. "I thought it was plastic. My bad."

"Come on, man." Tanner said. "Please don't do this. Don't break anything else. I'll get in trouble over this."

Preston knocked down another glass as Tanner continues freaking out, rubbing his head and grinding his teeth. Preston picked up one of the statues from the bottom shelf. He walked toward the counter with it.

"Oh, goddamn it, man!" Tanner said. "Please!"

"Listen, Tanner Boy. All I'm trying to do is incarcerate a very bad man and the woman on the photo, Carla Garcia, may help me in completing this task. So, unless you want me to continue being a clumsy asshole in your store, why don't you tell me if she came in here. And if so, where was she headed?"

"Alright. She came in here one day with the guy on the picture. She was buying an antique to take to Quarles Funeral Home." Tanner said. "She also spoke of a hair salon. That's all I know."

"A hair salon." Preston said. "You're sure about that?

"Yes sir."

"You're positive about it?"

"Yes sir."

Preston placed down the statue and took out of his jacket pocket a one-hundred-dollar bill and laid it on the counter. Tanner looked at it while glancing at Preston.

"There you go, Tanner. I broke it, I bought it. Make sure you take care of those eyes will you."

Hoyt, Billy, Russell, and his group of men arrive in the downtown area during rush hour. Hoyt pulled Russell aside as he commanded him to bring him men towards the eastern side of the area as he and Billy decide to watch over the western side. Russell commands his men to stand still by the wall on the building next to them, which is New Haven City Hall. Billy pointed it out to Hoyt that they're standing right in front of City Hall. Hoyt's eyes lit up as he smiled.

"Oh my. This plan is proceeding excellently."

"How do you figure that, Hoyt?"

"Just watch, my good friend. Prepare to see something truly amazing in this area. City Hall is just icing on the cake for us."

Hoyt pointed toward Russell, who later commands his men to set up their gear and prepare themselves. His men reached toward the pair of duffle bags that sat in front of them, pulling out their assault weapons such as RPKs and AKs. A few of Russell's men appeared to have carried shotguns on their shoulders. The traffic later stopped, as to the light turned red. Hoyt turned to Russell and gave him the signal. Russell signaled to his men as they run out in the middle of the open road and start firing shots all around the street. Hoyt and Billy ducked behind a wall, as Hoyt laughs while watching Russell's men. Billy stared at Hoyt as he laughed.

"This isn't funny, Hoyt! What the hell is this?!" Billy said. "What have you placed them under?!"

"All of this was only a test for Russell and his men, my friend." Hoyt said. "I just wanted to see if they had the loyalty to go along with it. Besides, it was Russell's idea for this shootout. They also picked this spot and Russell gave them the signal to fire."

"Why couldn't you have just chosen the riot. It would've been so much safer compared to what we're watching. We wouldn't have to duck our heads for Christ's sake if they were just hijacking people from their cars and beating them down on the street. We could've stood by and just watched as it was happening.”

“True point you have there. Though, he did mention having a riot here instead of gunfire.” Hoyt said. “But face it Billy, this is more fun!”

Russell’s men continued firing all around the area. They’ve knocked out windows on the nearby building, even blowing out the windshields of the cars. the stoplight turned green and the cars suddenly started to move without any hesitation. They’re drove quickly to avoid the gunshots.

Russell screamed at his men to move, in which only a few had done. The drivers within the cars appear to be pissed and start to run over the remaining men on the road. Hoyt looked up and saw what was happening. Billy turned and looked as well with fear in his eyes.

“Holy fucking shit! They’re being ran over! Goddamn it, those people are running them over nonstop!”

“I didn’t think today’s society would have this sense of mind in them. Shit, Billy, we could recruit more people like these drivers here. A lot more of people like this.”

Russell’s men are jumping out of the roadway and one turned to Russell.

“Leader, what do we do?” The thug asked.

“Let me ask Hoyt.” Russell said. “He’ll tell us what we should do.”

Russell ran across the road to the other side of the street. He looked over at Hoyt, who’s still crouched down beside the stained walls.

“What in the hell shall we do, Hoyt?!”

“Head back to your cars and return to the site. Me and Billy will meet you and your remaining men up there and then we’ll regroup there and begin the process.”

“Got ya, boss.” Russell said. “Let’s go men.”

He commanded his remaining men to head back to the cars. They get in their vehicles and drive off, heading back to the site. Hoyt and Billy do the same.

“What are we going to do about him and his men?” Billy said. “Are you going to promote them in some kind of way or just get rid of them when the time is right?"

"I won't do anything to Russell or his men. They've done a great job here and have proved their loyalty to us."

Emily had arrived at the Marshal agency in Newark. The building is a five-story structure facility. Its taller and larger than the agency building in New Haven. She walked inside, and she runs into an old partner, an African American woman. She spots Emily and walked over towards her. They both hugged and greeted each other.

"My, my, Emily. What brings you back to Newark?"

"Some serious issues, Gloria. I'm here on a case that concerns Ray Colby. I'm sure you remember him, don't you?"

"Wait, he's back in town? Where the hell has he been all this time because we haven't seen a trace of him or heard about it?"

"He's been in New Haven for quite some time now. He appeared to have moved his occupation of doing some of his dirty work up there. Though, I have yet to run into him yet. I've only had recent encounters with a few of his thugs."

"Are they like any of the guys here would be?"

"Not exactly. They're worse. Much worse. Appeared to have been trained for this particular job."

They head to the fifth floor by use of the elevator. Emily recommended the stairs, but Gloria denied her entry due to the stairs repaired for some damage that occurred prior to Emily's arrival.

Once on the fifth floor, Gloria walked into her office, walking behind her desk, she pulled out a document from the drawer that contained the files of all Ray's previous and reported locations and hideouts throughout the state of New Jersey. Emily looked at the map and took a photo of it with her Samsung phone. She turned to Gloria.

"I have to say I should truly thank you for helping me with this."

"Don't mention it, Emily. Remember when you were stationed here. We were once partners. Whenever you need help, I'll always be there for you anytime you need it. So, who's your partner over at New Haven?"

"Preston Maddox. I'm sure you've heard about the guy."

"The Instinct Marshal!" Gloria said. "The guy who shot Jonny Cartel is your partner!"

"Yeah, the guy who shot Cartel and is known for using his supposed instincts to solve his cases. For those who don't know, the guy is also a huge pain in the ass. A complete narcissist."

"I thought he would be a nice one." Gloria said. "Since, he's a handsome gentleman."

"He is a nice guy." Emily said. "Only whenever he decides he wants to be."

Emily thanked Gloria again as she leaves the facility. As she enters her car, she took out her phone and looked at the photo of the map. After reading through the map's targeted locations, she decides to go for the first location, which is a construction site. As Emily leaves and drives off, there's a small black corolla sitting across the street not too far from the facility. Inside is a man, wearing a brown fedora. He watches as Emily leaves and proceeds to follow her.

<u>**21**</u>

Russell and his men return to Hoyt's site as Hoyt and Billy are already there waiting for them. Russell exited out of his truck and walked toward Hoyt, furious look on his face as he approached him.

"May I ask what in the hell just happened out there?!" Russell asked. "We were nearly hit by those damn cars, Hoyt!"

"I didn't expect that, Russell." Hoyt said. "But, you only lost about what, two, three of your men. They can be replaced very quickly. No hard feelings."

"That's not the case. They were good men." Russell said. "They put their lives on the line doing this kind of shit."

"I still say that you should've gone with the riot plan." Billy said. "Otherwise, your men would still be here."

"You have a point there." Russell said. "But, that's not the case here at the moment."

"The case is over." Hoyt said. "We now focus on what's in the next case. In which, the next one won't be so terrible as the one that's just transpired."

"Why won't it be so terrible, Hoyt?" Russell asked. "Why, is it located in a safer location?"

"Because we're going into the woods for this one." Hoyt said. "Think of it as trying out your stealth movements."

"Great. Great. Right up my alley." Russell said. "Going into the woods for what?"

"You'll find out when I tell you." Hoyt said. "You and your men may return to your homes now. You're done for the day."

Russell and his men left the site. Billy turned to Hoyt, asking him about the woods and why they're heading that direction. Hoyt decided to tell him that there is a secret cabin hidden in the woods and when the time is right, that they will have to blow that cabin into entire pieces.

Eldon, Cody, and Darius are on a street at the lower town. Cody looks around the area and tells Eldon that this is the location where the prostitution takes place. Eldon says that they'll come back later and patrol the area in search of the hit man. Eldon tells Cody to have his sniper ready for use, because he might need it. Darius asks Eldon how they're going to patrol the area. Eldon pointed across the street.

"We'll have to set up a secret location across the street there." Eldon said.

"At that abandoned building?" Darius asked. "It looks like it could help us out."

"Yeah. It could work." Eldon said. "Me and you will be on the inside, as Cody will be on the roof."

"Why the roof?" Cody asked. "I can shoot from the windows, you know."

"The roof is best for your sniper." Eldon said. "Unless it rains, then you can shoot from the windows."

"Well, hopefully it pours." Cody said.

Preston arrives at a hair salon. He walked inside, seeing all the women getting their hair done and the smell of washed hair surrounding the salon. He walked toward the counter, where the cashier was standing.

"I'm sorry to bother you." Preston said. "But, I'm Preston Maddox, United States Marshal and Homicide Detective. I'm here on business and I'll like to ask you something."

"Ok." The cashier said. "And your point?"

"I'm looking for a woman." Preston said. "Carla Garcia. Have you heard of her?"

"Do you have a picture of this Carla?" The cashier said.

"Right here, Ms." Preston said. "I just came from an antique store down the street and the clerk said that she's was headed here. So, I'm just here for some information."

He took out the photo and the cashier quickly denied seeing

her. Which through Preston off for a second before he was able to gather himself.

"Well, Ms., according to some documented information, she came in here a few days ago." Preston said. "Are you sure you didn't see her. She had to be wearing red, that's all she wears."

"Listen, in this line of work, someone like me sees a lot of different women that come into these places who wear different styles of red, sir. I'm afraid that you have the wrong location or maybe you were fooled."

"According to you, it seems I have." Preston said. "Have a good day, ma'am."

Preston leaves the salon and gets into the car. He pulled out the folder containing the documents. On the document, it mentions that Carla might have visited Quarles Funeral Home. Preston reads it and heads over to the location.

Ray sat inside a meeting at a Newark office. The meeting concerned the crime lords with their deals involving the drug shipments. One crime lord gets the attention and started asking about their shipments. Another one asked the exact same thing.

"My question is simple, gentlemen." One crime lord said. "How do we move our shipments around the country and deal with these officials and their marshal service?"

"We must create a strategy that will confuse the officials and certainly those marshals." Ray said. "I've already had to deal with two and I don't need anymore."

"How do we create this strategy?" The crime lord said. "There has to be some form of way that we could create something of that category."

"Gather your men for a meeting and hire yourself a strategist." Ray said. "That's what I've done."

"You hired a strategist?" Another crime lord said. "Never would expect you to do something like that, Mr. Colby. Thought, you plotted out your plans on your own and didn't take hardly anyone's advice. Unless it was handed to you."

"The strategist I've hired for my alliance is a former lover of a marshal." Ray said. "The Marshal that shot one of our associates, Jonny Cartel."

"The Instinct Marshal?!" The crime lord said. "You have him on your case? If he's watching you, he could possibly find the rest of us. That guy never makes a mistake. He uses his instincts for crying out loud."

"Everything will be fine." Ray said. "You won't have to worry about the Instinct Marshal. My strategist has already designed a plan that will take the marshal off the face of the earth."

"I hope so, Mr. Colby. I hope she does." The crime lord said. "If not, we'll have to tell the chief to let you go or better yet. He'll probably have us kill you if the plan doesn't go as followed."

Ray stared at the other crime lord. He grinned toward him before clearing his face of the grin.

"Anything else you'll like to say, Mr. Colby." The crime lord said. "Since, you won't join in on our little part in this situation."

"No one can get rid of me." Ray said. "I'm the best crime lord around these parts. I make things happen and I also end things. The chief will never get rid of someone who's highly intelligent and skilled as I. You can say what you want, but get this straight. You cross a line with me, I'll take the marshal's job and put you down myself."

Emily arrived at the construction site. Seeing that they're in the middle of building a new office building. She walked toward a few of the constructors to ask them about Colby. Some of the constructors look at Emily and check her out.

"Pardon me, gentlemen." Emily said. "Do any of you know the whereabouts of Ray Colby?"

"He's not here at the time." One constructor said. "Though, he frequently visits. Since this is his office that we're building at the moment."

"This is his office?" Emily said.

"Yes ma'am." The constructor said. "We don't know what it's for, but, this is commanded by him. He's paying for it. He usually comes by on Tuesdays and Thursdays just to see how it's all going. Sometimes, he'll pay some surprise visits. We all hate those."

Emily looked around as she thanked the constructors for their help and left the construction site. She looked at the photo again to search for another location. The location that she's looking at now is a shooting gallery.

From behind her is the man in the corolla. He picks up his cell phone and contacts Ray.

"Ray, sorry to bother you right now. This is Desmond. I'm on the female Marshal's trail at this moment." Desmond said. "What do you want me to do once I have her?"

"Do what I'm paying you to do." Ray said. "Kill the bitch and you'll receive your reward."

"Very well, then." Desmond said.

Desmond hung up and drove off down the street, making a left turn into the small traffic.

Eldon, Cody, and Darius returned to the street where the prostitution line takes place. Eldon decided to set up camp inside the abandoned building. The moon shines down on them during the night sky. Thunder started to rumble and the rain proceeded to pour down. Cody looked at Eldon, smiling.

"Fine, you get the window." Eldon said.

"It makes it easier for me." Cody said.

Cody reaches into the back of the SUV and pulled out a Barrett M82. Darius looked over at him, nodding his head.

"That's a nice one, Cody." Darius said.

"It's my favorite one." Cody said. "I've tried a bunch, but, this one stands out the most for me. Plus, its easy for me to handle. The other ones were just bulky and slow on reload in my opinion."

Eldon pulled out an array of weapons from handguns to pistols to rifles. Darius walked over to the table as Eldon set up the gear. He looked through the weapons.

"We're going to need all of these?" Darius said. "Chief, he's just one man, not an entire army."

"We're dealing with a hit man, Darius." Eldon said. "We're going to need as much as we can possibly get our hands on. Besides, we don't know where his location will be. So, just grab whichever weapon you like and mark your place."

Darius grabbed an AK and stood guard at the metallic garage door. Cody went to the upper floor, placing and pointing the sniper rifle out of the window at a minimum. Eldon stood by the windows on the first floor, looking out. On the other side of the street, a limo pulled up slowly. Eldon looked outside and sees the chauffer open the back doors. Coming out are six prostitutes, all carrying umbrellas.

"They look hot don't they, chief?" Darius said.

"They seem to be alright." Eldon said. "But I'm disease-free and I'll like to keep it that way."

The prostitutes stood on the sidewalk as an array of vehicles went back and forth on the road. Few of the cars parked over near the sidewalk, the prostitutes walk toward the cars and some leave. As Cody was looking out the window, he noticed an unusual occurrence to the left side of the building. He pulled out his communicator and contacted Eldon.

"Cody, what's the situation from your point of view?" Eldon said. "Do you have anything in your sights?"

"Something's going on to the left of the building. Appeared to have looked like a man sneaking across. Looked to me as if he was carrying a weapon of some sort."

"Me and Darius will keep watch down here and search the area. Just keep your position and stand your ground until you have a full visual of what's moving around."

Eldon and Darius noticed a few of the prostitutes were already taken by buyers as they see only three are remaining on the sidewalk. Darius shrugged shoulders as Eldon shook his head.

"It looks like they're going fast." Darius said. "They must be good or something. I mean, to go that fast, that's incredible for prostitutes. Especially in today's age."

"I don't know how this business goes and works, Darius. Though, from the way you're talking about it in such a high manner, it seems to me that you know some stuff about this line of work. But, as for me. I'm a married man with three children, so I have no idea how the prostitution business works nor, will I ever get in line at the academy of whoredom."

"I'm currently in a relationship as well." Darius said. "Though, my brother is a pimp. So, that's where I learned a lot about the prostitution business. Growing up with someone like that shows you a lot in your youth years."

Cody looked out of the left window and seen another individual, who's standing on top of the building to the left. Cody spotted a man, wearing a black fedora, black leather jacket and some black jeans, aiming at the prostitutes with a sniper rifle. Cody contacted Eldon and warned him of the hit man being on the roof of the left building. Eldon ran up the stairs and stood by Cody, looking out the window toward the hit man.

"That's him." Cody said. "The appearance, the sniper, and the stance. He's the guy we're looking for."

"Make sure you have a clear go around just in case he decides to move over an inch."

They continued to look out the window at the hit man. Cody turned his rifle and aimed the weapon out the window through a small crack. Pointing it toward the hit man, Cody goes into deep focus as he slowly prepared to fire the immediate shot. Eldon reached to his side and raised his gun, aiming out the window to the hit man.

"Do you have a clear view to gain a clean shot?" Eldon said.

"Yes I do, chief." Cody said. "Ready for the commanding order."

As Cody prepared and placed his finger on the trigger to fire, the hit man turned to the right direction and started firing toward them. Eldon and Cody ducked down as glass began to shatter all around them from the broken windows. The gunfire caused the remaining prostitutes to run away from the sidewalk. Meanwhile, downstairs, Darius began to hear the gunshots coming from the upper floor. He stood up and ran upstairs. The hit man continued firing shots from his rifle as they're still crouched on the ground.

"We now know it's him." Eldon said. "And he knows it's us that's followed him."

"What are we going to do? Are we just going to wait till he runs out of ammo and take the shot?"

"Just wait for the moment where he assumes we're dead and then you take the shot."

Darius burst through the upstairs door and crouched down on the ground to avoid being shot by the hit man. He slid over to where Eldon and Cody were hunkered down.

"Looks like whatever you did gave him some knowledge of our whereabouts. So, you found him and he found you." Darius said.

"Yeah." Eldon said. "Could you see him from downstairs? A clear view at least."

"If he were to move closer to the edge, I could get a shot at him from downstairs. we should be able to see him."

"Alright, I'll go downstairs and attempt to take the shot." Cody said. "I will need you two to cover my back by firing shots toward him for a distraction."

Cody swiftly sprinted downstairs and ran to the left side of the building, looking outside the small pair of broken windows. Once he looked out of the window, seeing only half of the hit man close to the edge of the building.

Cody aimed the rifle out the window toward the hit man and used the scope to have a closer view. He knew from then on that he had a clear shot.

"I have a clear shot, chief. What should I do now?"

"Take the damn shot."

"Yes sir."

Cody stood still and fired the shot. The round went through the hole of the window and flew through the air, inching near the hit man, who continued firing at the upstairs floor. Eldon and Darius were stilled ducked underneath the windows. The round went pass the brick wall and hit the hit man in the chest. Holding his chest, the hit man crouched down as he fell to the ground. Not hearing anymore gun fire, Eldon and Darius took a small look out the window and saw the hit man down on the ground, slowly moving.

"So, we're going to the roof to check if he's still breathing?" Darius said.

"Something like that." Eldon said. "Let's get up there."

Upon reaching the other building and making it to the rooftop, other police officers with many officials had arrived at the scene as well. They make the discovery that the hit man survived the sniper shot from Cody as the officer slowly placed the hit man in the back of the police car. Shutting the back door, they thanked Eldon and his marshals for helping out with the cause and drive off. Eldon turned and told Cody that he was good at keeping his eyes open at his surroundings, otherwise, they probably wouldn't have caught the hit man. Eldon walked over to another officer.

"Did you find the name of the hit man, officer?" Eldon said. "Because, we didn't have any sort of information on the fellow."

"We don't have any knowledge of his real name, sir." The officer said. "From what we've gathered, the name he goes by is The Jackal. Something within that category."

"What's all on his record?" Eldon said."

"According to his criminal records, The Jackal was one of the country's most primary hit men. He primarily completed jobs and tasks for certain companies who were involved with the prostitution business. He also did some small duty in the marijuana business and the crystal meth business."

"So, he was basically killing off prostitutes because he was paid by a competitor to do so." Eldon said. "Never knew a job like that ever existed."

"Though, we hope to question him as soon as he recovers. We should have more information tomorrow at noon, hopefully. We'll contact you when we've gathered enough information."

"Thank you, officer." Eldon said.

Eldon walked over to Darius and Cody, who were discussing the type of rifle The Jackal used for his assassinations. They turned toward Eldon as he approached them in a slow manner.

"What's next on the agenda now, chief?" Darius said. "Any more places we should probably be looking out for."

"I'm going to get a drink." Eldon said. "I would assume that the two of you would be coming along with me? Just to celebrate what we've just accomplished here."

“Sure.” Cody said. “I’m up for it.”

<u>22</u>

Inside his hideout, Hoyt and Billy discussed the cabin location with Russell and his men. Hoyt tells them how the cabin is hidden deep within the woods and he discovered there were a trail of tire tracks that lead to the location.

"So, how are we going to be able to head over there on foot?" Russell said. "We're going stealth mode on them or something?"

Hoyt told him that they will have to drive at a closer location, then they'll walk to the cabin on foot. Russell agreed to the decision and they start preparing themselves for the plan. Billy looked at Hoyt and leaned over toward him across the covered table.

"Now, this cabin that we're going to hit, Hoyt. Is there any chance that Colby and my brothers could be inside at the very moment we drop ship?"

"I wouldn't assume they would be, Billy. According to a reliable source of mine, Ray's currently out of state and your two brothers are currently going car shopping for a new truck. So, from adding all of that up, I doubt that they'll be inside the night we invade the place. Don't concern yourself with possible outcomes. I'll take care of those situations."

"I'm just checking, because my mama might cross paths with us and you know how she feels about you." Billy said. "I don't want anything to go down between my mother and you, Hoyt. Things could turn very ugly if that were to happen."

Hoyt smiled and patted Billy on the back.

"I'm sure your mother and I will be just fine if we were to cross paths on this task. I'm well aware that she doesn't like me at all and I'm fine and dandy about her opinion for someone such as myself. But, for right now, let's just concentrate on the plan ahead, alright."

Emily entered a small convenience store and when she glanced around the area, she noticed the same black corolla that's been following her. She walked into the store when Desmond gets out of the corolla and followed her inside. She walked down the small aisle and Desmond continued to follow her. She looked back as Desmond pulled out a magnum and started firing. She ducked and the cashier crouched behind the counter.

"Take the money! Take it!" The cashier yelled. "Please don't kill me!"

"I don't want your money and I'm not here to kill you, fool." Desmond said. "I'm only here for the female Marshal."

Emily peeked around the aisles as she began loading up her gun. She stayed quiet as Desmond walked slowly through the aisles one at a time.

"Emily." Desmond said. "Emily Weston. I know you're in here, baby girl. I suggest you just come on out and take this bullet from your good friend, Colby."

"So, Ray sent you to do his dirty work?" Emily asked. "Not a surprise there? He's always had pawns to do the work, he was afraid to do."

"He sure did." Desmond said. "He's also paying me to do it for him. Since, he's on business at the moment."

"Business, huh?" Emily said. "You sure its business and not murder?"

"I don't give a shit what Ray does with his time." Desmond said. "All that matters to me, is killing you and getting paid. So, just come on out, so we can end this."

"Sure, no problem." Emily said.

Emily slowly took a peek toward her right and saw Desmond walking through the aisle. She turned and fired at Desmond's leg. He fell to the ground as Emily ran over toward him and immediately, she kicked the magnum out of his hand and kicked him in the gut two times.

"You're good aren't you?" Desmond said. "Surprised me there

for a bit."

"Better than you think." Emily said. "I'm not your average officer."

Eldon, Cody, and Darius sat inside a bar, having a share of beers. The door opened and Preston walked in. From his slouchy appearance, it appeared he also had a rough day in searching for Carla. He sat next to Eldon and glanced over toward Cody and Darius.

"Look who else decided to join us." Eldon said. "How's your day of investigating been?"

"It went as fair as it could possibly go." Preston said. "It's been a busy day overall."

"Don't assume that its just you that's had a rough day doing your job." Eldon said. "The three of us just dealt with a hit man who only targets prostitutes and nearly took us out with a sniper."

Preston turned, "Say that again. A hit man whose only occupation was to target prostitutes and you're saying that he nearly had all three of you in his range?"

"Not exactly." Cody said.

"Me, Cody, and Darius just captured the son of a bitch who was targeting prostitutes, while we were there searching for him. Though, apparently from the brief information we had, he was hired by a competitor to take out those prostitutes. Seems like he had an easy job to live by."

"It would seem so." Preston said. "Though, killing prostitutes isn't one on my list of things to do. Nor would I ever assume that there would be such a occupation for one man to take upon himself."

"Maybe he needed to money for some major crisis."

"That is possible."

Darius looked over at Preston.

"Just imagine how that job would be like." Darius said. "Hunting down women and assassinating them."

"Just sounds like a pervert with a sniper to me." Cody said. "Though, I'm not a pervert, by any means."

Eldon took a gulp of his beer and looked at Preston.

"So, how did your search go for Carla?" Eldon said. "Did you find any information on her?"

"Not exactly as I thought it would." Preston said. "I went to the diner and the waitress told me that she was indeed there but didn't know any other information. The next location was an antique store. Freaked out the clerk and he told me to head to a hair salon. The cashier there, acted like a complete bitch, but she didn't give me any information. So, tomorrow, I'll head out to Quarles Funeral Home. Hopefully, I'll find some information there."

"You might." Eldon said. "Because, according to some sources, Ray and the owner of the funeral home are good friends. So, Carla might've visited the place and gave the funeral assistants some information regarding her plans."

"I hope so." Preston said. "Otherwise, I might just have to visit Ray's warehouse myself."

"As long as you have backup when you decide to do that." Eldon said. "We'll have your back on that one, no worries about it."

Preston smiled, "I appreciate that. A lot."

<u>**23**</u>

The next morning, Preston headed for Quarles Funeral Home. He arrived at the funeral home, seeing their white limousines and hearses parked in front, each with a license plate saying, "Quarles". Preston walked towards the front door. He opened it and went inside. Preston looked at the interior of the funeral home. Seeing the nice brown colored walls and its burgundy carpet. One of the assistants walked toward Preston.

"Nice place, it really is." Preston said. "They must be having some good business here."

"Welcome to Quarles Funeral Home, sir." The assistant said. "How may I help you here on this particular day?"

"Yes, please. Though, I'm not here to make any arrangements. But, I'm looking for a woman named Carla Garcia." Preston said. "And to be fair I'll show you a picture of her. Maybe it can refresh your memory."

The assistant looked at the picture.

"Do you recognize her?" Preston said. "Because if you do, you can say so."

"No. No sir." The assistant said. "I don't recognize this woman. Perhaps, you have this place mistaken."

"No." Preston said. "There's no mistaken identity here. I have documented proof that she was inside this building. She had spoken with someone inside this building. Whether it's you or one of your other co-workers, she spoke with someone here. Would the owner happen to be here? If he is I would love to speak with him on this matter. So, is he here?"

"He's not here, sir." The assistant said. "But, if you'll like to leave a message, I could tell him."

"I'm not going to leave any kind of message." Preston said. "Look, I'm a United States Marshal. So, you better give me some type of information now or I'll search this entire funeral home, room by room. Hell, I'll even pay a visit to the embalming room if that's what I'll have to do."

"I'm terribly sorry, sir." The assistant said. "But, there's no information here regarding who you're looking for. I can help you out with something else."

Preston squinted his face and pulled out his gun and shot it in the air. The assistant ducked down on the ground in fear, covering his head. Preston leaned down toward the assistant, holding the gun in his hand and smiling.

"I didn't want to do this." Preston said. "But, if doing this completes this case, then I'll do whatever's necessary to get the job done. Now, I'll give you one more chance to tell me what you know. Starting right now. Go."

"There's a cabin." The assistant said. "A cabin in the woods not too far from here. Its right around the interstate, sir. She came in one day and spoke with one of our directors about it. She told the director that the location is one of Ray's hideouts from you people."

"Wait, I'm sorry. Did you just say, you people?" Preston said. "You going racist here, pal? I'm very sure your family raised you to have just a little respect for people and their racial backgrounds. Didn't they?"

"No sir. I didn't mean it in a racial sense." The assistant said. "By you people, I meant the law. That's all I know. The cabin in the woods. That's it. Nothing else."

"Ok then. Thank you for cooperating with me today." Preston said. "Really, you should've told me earlier, otherwise you would've pissed your pants in front of me like a coward."

Preston leaves through the front door as the assistant realizes that he just pissed his pants. He shook his head in shame as he walked down the hall toward the restroom. Outside, Preston gets into the car and contacted Eldon on the phone.

"Eldon, its Preston." Preston said. "I found a location. A

cabin in the woods on the outskirts of town. I'm heading there now. I'll contact you if I need backup of any kind."

Preston leaves the funeral home and drives toward the interstate. He passed through the vehicles on the road as he's heading to the New Haven forest.

During the moment in which Preston headed to the forest, Emily arrived at the shooting gallery place. She gets out of her car, but, noticed the place was surrounded by thugs. She believed those men to be associates of Ray. She decided to walk in, but, the men won't allow her.

"Look honey, no one inside without an appointment with Mr. Colby." One thug said. "Not even someone who's sexy as hell such as yourself."

"Well, go inside and tell your boss that Emily Weston is out here waiting to see him." Emily said. "He knows exactly who I am. The supposedly sexy as hell woman."

"Alright." The thug said. "Wait right here, baby. Guys, please watch her."

The thug walked inside approaching Ray. He tells him that Emily is waiting for him. The thug walked back out and allowed Emily entrance to the shooting gallery. She walked in and looked to her left and she finally sees Colby. She walked toward him as he was sitting down in a chair, with a silver revolver in his hand.

"You don't want to try anything stupid, do you Watson?" Ray said. "Seems after a long search, you've come across this way and have finally found me. Though, I am impressed that you did in such short time and not your new partner."

"Preston doesn't fully understand what you're capable of." Emily said. "But, I do. I know what you've done and how you've done them. I've chased you down for years and you're still doing the same damn shit as you were once before."

"So are you, Watson." Ray said. "You're still a marshal. Going around solving cases and capturing fugitives across the country. Sometimes even going across the world to find your criminals to save countless people from trouble. So, don't come to me and tell me that I'm doing the same shit. Because you're doing it as well."

"At least all the shit I do, isn't illegal." Emily said. "Think about that for a change and maybe you'll just realize it for once that you're on the opposite side of the law."

"I realize it very well, indeed I do." Ray said. "You and I have a long history with one another. Right here in this city for exact. Though, tell me something, Watson. How come you were moved over to New Haven in the first place and left New Jersey? You seemed to be well at home over here."

"I'm not here to talk about my business life, Colby." Emily said. "I'm here to tell you that I'm taking you straight to prison. Also, I know about John Elroy, you thug. The thug that was shot by Carla."

"What do you mean, shot by Carla?" Ray said. "Not from what she's told me. She told me he was shot by one of your marshal buddies."

"He was shot in the leg by one of my partners." Emily said. "She's the one who killed him. She shot him in the back of his skull and I'm kind of surprised that you put your trust in her to use a few of your men. Seemly enough that she might kill them as well behind your back and tell you another complete lie. The woman's only trouble, Ray and since you like trouble, you just planted yourself into a lot of trouble."

"I'll tell you this, Watson." Ray said. "You let me go for only this time and this time only, just let me deal with Carla and once that's done, then I'll take my place behind the prison walls. Do we have an agreement on that?"

"No, we don't have an agreement on that." Emily said. "You leave Carla to Preston and I'll deal with you. This is our battle. Carla is Preston's problem to handle, not yours or mine. Now, you're coming with me right now. Let's get moving."

"Very well, then." Ray said. "If that's what you want. You've made your decision and so have I."

Ray looked down and smiled. He then raised up the revolver, Emily looked toward it and Ray fired it. Emily moved out of the way, quickly as she pulled out her handgun and fired a shot at Ray, hitting him in the shoulder.

"Nice try, asshole." Emily said. "You forgot I'm highly skilled in marksmanship. You know that knowledge full well."

The thugs outside could hear the shooting taking place and without hesitation, they ran inside. Emily finds a back-exit door to her left and escapes using it. Once she's outside she headed out and ran toward the front. She got into her car and drove away. The thugs ran back out and start firing at Emily in the car. The thugs helped Ray into his SUV. Where he sat with rage.

"Are you alright, sir?" A thug said.

"I'll be fine." Ray said. "Just track her down quickly."

"Yes sir." Another thug said.

<u>24</u>

Coover and Rusty test out their new truck, by driving it across town and they're loving it. They even try to impress some women they pass by during a red light. The women aren't impressed by their lack of seriousness. They drive the truck back to their location. They walked towards the house, but, Rusty smelled something that's similar to gasoline.

"What is it, Rusty?" Coover said.

"You don't smell that, Coover?" Rusty said. "It's coming from the house."

"I smell something." Coover said. "You sure it isn't mama cooking us a nice hot meal."

"Hell no it isn't mama's cooking. We need to move from the location." Rusty said. "As soon as we can. Get in the truck and let's get out of here."

They ran back towards the truck and as soon as they pull off, the house exploded and is now engulfed in flames. Coover looked back and is enraged.

"What the hell!" Coover said. "What the hell is going on! Someone just blew our home up, Rusty!"

"I think I know who done it." Rusty said. "Let's go tell mama what just happened and after that, we'll go visit Hoyt and Billy."

After they left, from the other side of the house, rises both Hoyt and Billy. Hoyt is laughing as Billy turned to Hoyt.

"You could've killed them." Billy said. "They're my brothers. My two older brothers."

"They'll be fine, Billy." Hoyt said. "You see they escaped the area. Besides, they were already going to hand your over to Ray, so you could be killed. I'm basically doing you a favor by causing them to leave. As soon as they track you down and find you, the first thing they'll do is hand you over to Colby. Now, do you want that to happen?"

"No." Billy said. "I don't want that to happen. They wouldn't do that to me. I'm their brother."

"Yes, you are. But, they take the commands and orders from Ray and your mother." Hoyt said. "Whatever your mother commands, they will do it and so will Ray."

"What's the plan now?" Billy asked. "We gather up with Russell and his group and head to the cabin? Or do we wait on something else to happen?"

"We'll gather up with Russell and head straight for that cabin." Hoyt said. "They won't know what will hit them."

Eldon received a call from Emily, stating that she's on her way coming back to New Haven and her job in Newark was done. Cody walked in the office and Eldon tells him that Emily is coming back soon. Cody nodded while implying that the judge wants them both at the courthouse to discuss The Jackal case.

"Why do they need us at the courthouse?" Eldon said.

"We're the guys who brought him into custody." Cody said. "In that sense, they would need to speak with you, me, and Darius about the case. They just want to know what went down that night."

"Oh Goodness." Eldon said. "Let me contact Darius and we'll meet up at the courthouse."

"Sure thing, sir."

Cody walked out of the office as Eldon picked up his cell phone and contacted Darius. Darius answered, Eldon tells him that they must meet up at the courthouse, commanded by the judge to discuss the case of The Jackal. Darius agreed and told Eldon that he'll show up at the courthouse.

Ray is inside of a hospital in Newark as he is being bandaged up on his shoulder. Two of his henchmen are inside the room with him. Ray looked at one and asked him if they found Emily. The thug tells him no, but, they could contact Carla and see if she knows if Emily's returned to New Haven. Ray agreed and sent his henchmen out of the room.

The doctor finished up the bandages and he leaves the room. He walked outside and turned to the left, The SUV was sitting outside, waiting for Ray. Ray gets into the SUV. Inside the SUV, one of his henchmen looked and told him the news that Emily was headed back to New Haven. Ray smiled and said that he must do something that will bring Emily to her knees.

On the outskirts, Russell showed up in the front of the woods, along with his men behind him. One of his men walked over and asked Russell if Hoyt and Billy are nearby the forest. Russell tells the guy that they should be coming soon, since Hoyt's hideout is close to the forest. Russell pulled out a set of binoculars and looked around the interstate for Hoyt and Billy's trucks. As Russell uses binoculars to look around the woods, he sees two trucks coming near them.

"I see something over there." Russell said. "It should be them I would suspect."

The trucks pull up in front of them and stopped on the side of the road. Hoyt and Billy jumped out of them. Hoyt walked in front of Russell and his men. Hoyt stopped and smiled.

"See, my men." Russell said to his men. "They wouldn't let us down."

Russell looked at Hoyt and Billy. Smiling.

"Great to see you. So, what the plan, boss?" Russell said.

"Russell, I know the shootout didn't go correctly as planned, so, I'm apologize to you and your gentlemen, regarding that incident." Hoyt said. "But, this mission right here, will go as planned. No need to worry there. First, we will head out into these woods, find that cabin and once we've done that, blow it to shit."

"Hoyt, what about bears?" Billy said. "You know that bears live in these woods. What should we do if we run into one?"

"I'm sure you've been told what to do when you encounter a

bear in the woods." Hoyt said. "Make sure if you encounter a bear. Just llie down and play dead. That whole crock of shit."

"I'm not too sure about that." Billy said. "Not too long ago, some guy said that doesn't work. They can still kill you. you're still breathing."

"Don't worry about the goddamn bears, Billy." Hoyt said. "Fellers, let's head out toward the cabin. We should at least reach the location by nightfall."

"Alright, guys." Russell said to his men. "You heard Hoyt, let's get a moving on."

They start walking through the woods, heading towards the cabin.

Eldon, Darius, and Cody are at the courthouse, where they're sitting inside the courtroom, observing The Jackal case. The judge is demanding that The Jackal be sentenced to eight years in prison. Right after the case is over, the judge calls Eldon, Cody, and Darius over to his office in the back of the courtroom. They walk in and the judge tells them to sit down in the chairs, in front of his desk. They sit in the chairs as the judge sits behind his desk, drinking a cup of coffee.

"You needed to speak with us, your honor." Eldon said. "That's the reason why we came. We didn't come to see the hit man get handcuffed."

"I called you guys here, on this wonderful day, to just ask you about your encounters with The Jackal." The judge said. "So, how was the whole thing? How did it play out?"

"It was all as well, judge." Eldon said. "We were just doing our jobs as officials of the law. That's all and nothing else."

"The whole thing was crazy at the time as well." Cody said. "Though, we got the job done. No worries."

"No worries, huh." The judge said. "Let me ask you gentlemen something. How did those prostitutes look? Were they delicious? Did they look smoking hot? Would any of you try them out just for the sake of pleasure and desire of your own hearts?"

"They looked hot, alright. I can tell you that." Darius said. "But, I wouldn't put money down to see if they're delicious in any way."

"You have a point there, Marshal." The judge said. "They might have some of those STDs out there. Just spreading their sickness across lives and ruining families. Nothing but filthy whores they are."

"You could say that again, judge." Eldon said. "But, all things go to Cody here. He's the one marksman who put the hit man down for the count."

The judge stood up and placed his cup of coffee on his desk. He walked over to Cody and extended and shook his hand.

"You don't know how you've made so many people happy by doing what you did." The judge said smiling. "Congratulations, Marshal on your fine job."

"Oh, I'm not a marshal yet, sir." Cody said. "I'm still in training for that spot. Right now, I'm only considered a Contemporary Marshal."

"Very well. Good job anyway."

The judge turned to Eldon with a smile on his face.

"The Jackal fellow is in the other room. I'm just telling you because if you want to get more information out of him. He's all yours."

"Well, thank you, Your Honor."

Eldon told Cody and Darius about The Jackal. He walked out of The Judge's office and into the room next door. Inside the room were concrete walls and only two windows on the front and back. Two chairs and one table. Sitting in one chair was The Jackal sitting at a table with his hands cuffed. Eldon looked at him through the window.

"He seems calm right now. Thought, he would be highly pissed off."

"He might be pissed when we walk in and have a chat with him." Darius said. "So, shall we piss him off."

They entered the room and The Jackal raised his head up toward them. Giving all three of them a demeaning glare of intent rage. His eyes pierced them and later they subdued. Eldon sat at the table while Cody and Darius stood behind him, on both sides of the table.

"So, we hear you'll be in federal prison for a total of eight years. How do you feel about that?"

"How do I feel about that? It's simple to be honest. Funny, you law enforcement types never understand the truth about people like me."

"Well, explain to the three of us how you're so different about you than the rest of the rotten criminals and fugitives that we've come across in this line of work?"

"I'm one of the best there is in my field and my boss knows that. So, he won't let me stay in a room with three walls and a cot with a pot to piss in. He knows he'll need me when a situation occurs."

"You're saying your boss will bail you out or something? Or will he just find a way for you to escape the cell."

"My boss is a man who has enough Federal Reserve notes to bail me out and to buy me a mansion that I could live in for the rest of my days on this Earth."

Cody leaned in, gaining Eldon's attention as the Jackal looked at him from the chair.

"Chief, you mind if I have a word with Jackal here?"

"By all means. Have a word with him. He's done me wonders today. Your turn, Cody."

Eldon stood up from the chair, allowing Cody to sit down in front of The Jackal. They have a ten second stare down before Cody smiled.

"So, tell us, what is your job exactly? Besides just going around killing innocent women for the sake of money."

"I am a hit man. Which you're already aware of. I hunt down and kill whoever I'm ordered to buy the ones who pay me the greenbacks to do it."

"So, you don't just hunt down prostitutes for the sake of paper. You're telling us that you take operations to hit anyone you're order to by the one who's paying you."

"You're smarter than you look, young one. You sure you're in the right type of fieldwork, pal?"

"I'm nowhere in comparison with you or anyone that's in your line of duty. That's all I needed to know. Thank you for your time, Jackal."

Cody leaned up from the chair. They looked over to Darius, seeing if he wanted to have a word with Jackal. Darius declined as Jackal laughed. They leave the room as Jackal continued to laugh. Eldon was last to leave as he looked back.

"Chief, I just want you to know. When I'm bailed out, I'm sure my boss will have me come for you and your two Marshal boys. Believe you me."

"If and when that day decides to take its course along our lives, me and my Marshal boys will be ready to take your sorry ass down once more, Jackal."

Eldon shut the door as Jackal smirked and looked at his handcuffs.

<u>**25**</u>

Preston reached the entrance to the forest. He gets out of his car and he looked to the right and saw a pack of F-150 trucks sitting on the side of the road by the trees. He walked over to the trucks and looked inside. He recognized two of the trucks. Preston showed a faint grin.

"I see Hoyt and Billy's trucks." Preston said. "I wonder what's their business here?"

He walked into the forest as the sun is slowly setting. The forest becomes darker as he goes deeper, he pulled out a flashlight to watch his surroundings. He looked down and noticed some tree branches, scattered across the ground. All of which were broken and smashed, as if something passed through this area. He notices human footprints within the dirt and proceeded to follow them.

While Preston headed deeper into the forest, across the street is Carla and her pack of thugs. The thugs are all armed with automatic weapons. Carla commanded them to cross the interstate to reach the forest. They crossed the interstate by running, neither of them walked across. Carla is the last to cross. She reached the other end as one thug took out a flashlight and they proceed into the forest. Carla pointed out the trail that goes straight to the cabin, which the thugs followed her.

"We should follow this trail, my men." Carla said. "This trail was made by Ray, so it will lead us straight to the cabin."

Hoyt, Billy, and Russell, and his men are now in the middle of the forest as they hear howls from coyotes and wolves. Billy, shaken in fear of being attacked by a bear of some sort of animal, turned to Hoyt.

"How far are we from the cabin, Hoyt?" Billy said. "It's getting very freaky out here."

"We're not too far from the cabin." Hoyt said. "You should see the reflections from the windows. Once you see those, you know we've made it there."

"So, once we've reached the cabin, Hoyt." Russell said. "What do we do at that point? Just blow the place straight to Shit-Ville?"

"Now that's some smart thinking there, Russell." Hoyt said. "But, I would prefer we looked around at the interior, see what we can take and then, we'll blow the place to Shit-Ville. As you like to call it."

Russell turned and saw what Hoyt was carrying over his right shoulder, which was a black metallic box. Russell, now curious, decided to ask Hoyt what's inside the black box. Hoyt stopped in his tracks and turned to Russell, showing his grin toward him.

"You'll find out once we've reached the cabin." Hoyt continues walking as Russell catches up with Billy.

"He sure is secretive about his work isn't he." Russell said.

"Don't say it to him, Russell." Billy said. "You'll only put yourself in much greater danger. Hoyt doesn't like it when people talk about him behind his back. Believe me when I tell you that."

"Why is that?" Russell said. "Something happened to the last guy he was partners with?"

"The last guy who talked about Hoyt behind his back ended up six feet under." Billy said. "That should clear your thought of mind I would assume."

Billy continued walking with Hoyt as Russell showed a worried grin upon his face.

Preston continues walking through the forest and he hears the howls of coyotes and wolves around the area. He heard something moving through the trees toward his right. He reached down for his gun and pulled it out, holding it in his hand, he slowly continued walking and he heard the sounds coming closer. Preston looked to his right and saw a average sized brown fox run past him in a pace.

"Nothing, but a fox." Preston said. "Lucky bastard has me a little freaked out."

Preston later hears something behind him, he turns and its one of Carla's thugs. He grabbed Preston by the neck, choking him. Preston delivered several elbow shots to the thug's head and punched him. The thug fell to the ground as Preston began kicking the thug and afterwards tossing a pile of leaves onto him.

"Useless asshole." Preston said. "You should never attack a marshal from behind. Doesn't do you any good."

Preston leaned down and snatched the thug by his shirt. The thug bled from his nose and mouth. Preston stared at him, grinning.

"What the hell you are doing out here at the brink of night?" Preston said. "Tell me. Tell me now before I put a bullet through you."

"I was with Carla, until I took a wrong turn and lost the group." The thug said. 'That's it. I haven't done nothing else I swear."

"That's not all I'm looking for, shit kicker." Preston said. "Why is she out here, and why is she leading a pack of Ray's thugs from his pack?"

"I'm not telling you anything else." The thug said. "You no good motherfucker!"

Preston put the gun directly on the thug's head, with his finger inches away from pulling the trigger. The thug began to panic.

"Ok. Ok!" The thug said. "We're here to kill you. That's why she brought us out here. To kill you. That's our purpose."

"Kill me?" Preston said. "Why would you want to do that? I'm only after your boss and that witch from my past. So, I would really like to know something right now and that is who assigned this operation to you?"

"It was all Carla's idea." The thug said. "She told Ray about it and he accepted it and granted her the use of his men. That's all I know, honestly."

"Well, I have to thank you for telling me the truth." Preston said. "While, you're at it, get a real job for Christ's sake. And make sure it's a legal one."

Preston leaves the thug, laying on the ground in a pile of leaves as he continued walking through the forest as he places his gun back into its holster. As he walks, he notices a reflection, coming from in front of him. He started moving faster and he saw that he reached the cabin. Preston walked around the entire cabin with his gun in his hand. He walked toward the front door, grabbing on the knob, he opens the door. He looked around and sees Ray's desk and some of his equipment scattered across the cabin. He notices that the cabin is a two-story house. As he proceeds to walk upstairs, the lights turn on. Preston stops in his tracks and hears people coming in. He turned and saw Hoyt, along with Billy, Russell and his men.

"Hoyt. Billy." Preston said. "Who's your new group of buddies here?"

"Preston, this is Russell." Hoyt said. "Known to his men as Leader."

Preston stared at Russell and smirked before turning toward Hoyt.

"I now can see why they call him 'Leader'." Preston said. "Because they're just like you. Followers. Can't lead for shit, so you decide to just follow whoever you see around you."

Hoyt smiled and said, "You know Preston. What the hell are you doing here? Would you care to tell us that?"

"Unlike you and your pack of shit, I'm here on business." Preston said. "Now, I just ran into one of Ray's thugs and he told me that his men are heading this way to assassinate me."

"Assassinate you?" Hoyt said. "This is a great day after all. I get to see a longtime friend die and I get to see something blow up. This is indeed a great day for Hoyt Bennett."

"No, it isn't, Hoyt." Preston said. "This isn't awesome. What will be awesome though, is throwing you, Billy, and your pack of followers here into prison. Where you can rot."

Russell pulled out his AK and points it at Preston. Preston doesn't move an inch and smirked at Russell.

"You really think you can put one through me?" Preston said. "Be honest here. You think you can, before I put one through you? Just give me your honest answer, *Leader*."

"You are one funny son of a bitch, Marshal." Russell said. "I should do those guys a favor and take you out myself."

Hoyt turned to Russell. Telling him to put down his AK. Russell nodded and lowers the weapon. Preston turned to Hoyt.

"See what I mean." Preston said smiling. "Followers only follow. Can't make any decisions for themselves. Tell me, Hoyt. Where do you go to find people like this, because I'll never figure that out myself."

A bullet rams through one of the front windows, hitting one of Russell's men. Everyone inside the cabin ducks down behind the walls, the desk, and even the chairs. Hoyt turned to Preston, who's crouched on the ground, reloading his handgun. Hoyt takes out his pistol. Preston looked over at Hoyt and the pistol.

"Nice firearm, Hoyt." Preston said. "Where'd you get it? Or should I say, where'd you steal it from?"

"It was a gift from my dad." Hoyt said. "You remember him, don't you? He and your father were business partners back in the day."

"Yeah, they were." Preston said. "Right now, we need to focus on the guys out in the front and not on our past."

"Let me ask you something, Preston." Hoyt said. "They say you use your instincts to solve your cases. So, tell me, what do your profound instincts tell you about the outcome of this cabin shootout event?"

Preston nodded and smirked.

"My instincts are telling me that we'll live." Preston said. "Though, you'll be heading back to prison. Not so good for you, huh."

Carla and her thugs surround the entire area of the cabin. She walked toward the front door, with two thugs behind her. She looked inside the windows, seeing all the guys inside, all of whom are still scattered and crouched down. She looked to her right and saw Preston. She smiled.

"I'll go through the back door." Carla said. "You gentlemen find a way to get those men out of the cabin. Leave the Marshal for me to handle."

Carla heads toward the back door as he thugs begin shooting out the windows of the cabin. Preston, Hoyt, Billy, Russell, and his men are still crouched behind the walls and desks. One of Russell's men comes up from behind a chair and fires his machine gun out the windows. He kills a few of the thugs, but, one thug comes across and shoots him in the chest, right over the heart, instantly killing him.

More of Russell's men begin to fire, but the thugs begin to take them all out instantly. Russell watches as he sees his men falling dead on the ground.

"No!" Russell yelled. "Goddamn it! Hoyt, we need to try another tactic, now!"

Hoyt raised up his pistol, looking at Russell.

"As you command, Russell." Hoyt said. "As you command."

Hoyt leaned up out the window and started firing at the thugs. He began taking most of them down. The other thugs begin shooting toward him. Hoyt ducked back down behind the wall and moved over toward the desk. Billy is shaking with fear and has no clue or idea of what to do.

"Hoyt!" Billy yelled. "What in the hell do I do!"

"What the hell you think, Billy." Preston said. "Shoot back at the assholes!"

Billy raises up and fires his machine gun out the windows. He ducks as the thugs continue to fire back.

"It's not working!" Billy yelled. "There's too many of them out there!"

"Just keep shooting!" Hoyt yelled. "Just keep firing! You'll take some out. It shouldn't be that many left standing!"

Preston looked out the windows and starts firing. He's taking out the thugs one by one. He ducks as they fire back. Preston moves across the cabin to the left and continues firing out the window as he moves across. The thugs fire back and continue firing. All of the windows are all knocked out. The thugs stop shooting. Preston takes a peek out of the windows. He sees only four thugs remaining, as the others are all dead. Preston looked at Hoyt.

"Hoyt, just take a shot for Christ's sake." Preston said. "There's four of us and there's four of them. Russell, Billy, I suggest you two take some shots, now."

"You heard, Preston, boys." Hoyt said. "Aim and take your

shots.”

They start taking shots out the windows at the four thugs. Billy shoots one thug in the head and starts jumping up and down in excitement. Another thug fires towards Billy and he crouches down, back against the wall. Hoyt looked down at Billy.

“What the Sam hell are you doing, Billy?!” Hoyt said. “Shoot the worthless pieces of shit kicking assholes, goddamn it! Shoot!”

Preston and Russell are firing at the remaining thugs. Preston kills one and now there’s only one more thug remaining. Preston looked at Hoyt.

“You want to take this one or shall I go ahead?” Preston said. “I’m going to need an answer now.”

“Let me take the shot, Marshal.” Russell said. “I got this motherfucker in a clean spot.”

Russell fired a shot and killed the last remaining thug. They lower their weapons and look at one another. Billy stood up from the wall, Hoyt only stares at him. Hoyt turned to Russell.

“I’m truly sorry about your men, Russell.” Hoyt said. “I truly am. They served their purpose for you and this group and have done a great service.”

“They sacrificed themselves to protect their leaders.” Russell said. “They knew what they were going into.”

Preston looked and placed his gun back into its holster and looked at Hoyt. Seeing him with the pistol in hand.

“You’re not too bad with that pistol.” Preston said. “Must’ve been training for some time.”

“Same to you with that Glock of yours.” Hoyt said. “You know how to use that weapon.”

“I was a former marksman instructor.” Preston said. “It helped out a lot.”

As they prepare to leave, they hear the back-door opening. Hoyt walked over to the door and sees Carla walk inside with two thugs. They backed up against the windows as Carla stared at them. She turned her attention toward Preston, who’s not pleased at all to see her.

“Why are you doing this, Carla?” Preston said.

Hoyt looked and started smiling.

"Carla." Hoyt said. "So, this is Carla? Wow, I didn't recognize you there. How's life been so far?"

"Life's been truly great to me, Hoyt." Carla said. "You didn't think that I would forget about you, huh?"

"There was some doubt in my mind that you would." Hoyt said. "You should've called me. We could've hung out together. Just like we did in the old times."

Preston turned to Hoyt. Showing a faint grin.

"This isn't a social visit, Hoyt." Preston said. "She's here to kill me on Ray's behalf."

"Wait. She's working with Ray?" Hoyt said. "How interesting indeed. More sheep scurrying in the field for me to slaughter."

"Why do you think she's here?" Preston said. "Didn't you see those thugs walking behind her?"

"You shouldn't have to worry, Hoyt." Carla said. "Ray can take care of you. I'm only here for Preston."

Russell raised up his AK and shoots one of the thugs, the other thug pulled out his weapon and Billy shot him in the head. Hoyt and Preston turned toward Billy.

"SHIT! Goddamn it! He shot at me!" Billy yelled.

Carla pulled out a revolver and aimed it toward Preston. He looked at the revolver and stared her in the eyes before scouting the surroundings of the cabin. Looking out for any of Carla's men.

"Meanwhile, I'm only here to kill you, honey." Carla said. "The rest of these guys are Ray's problem, not mime. So, babe, are you ready to go to heaven?"

"Depends on the time their open. Speaking of time, do you have a watch on you? Because, if you do you could tell me the exact time. Because, correct me if I'm wrong. But, I believe that the gates are closed around this time of a day."

"So funny all the time. Yet, you're only as funny as the ones who laugh at your joking and smartass remarks. Now, I suggest you close your eyes, babe. I don't want you to look at what I'm about to do to your pretty face."

"But, I want to see your face before you take the shot. Last sight of my time in the world would be looking upon you. So, I'll just keep my eyes opened if you don't mind me doing so."

"Your choice."

Hoyt ran over and backslapped Carla with his right hand. She fell to the ground as he escaped along with Billy and Russell. Preston knelt down at Carla, as she held her face.

"You shouldn't trust Hoyt. Never" Preston said. "Even in your contorted and disfigured mind, you shouldn't trust a man like him."

"I shouldn't trust anyone, Preston." Carla said. "Not even you."

"I agree with that as well." Preston said smiling. "Only to an extent."

On the outside, Billy and Russell are backing up as Hoyt opens the black box and pulls out a grenade launcher. He aims toward the building as Preston and Carla look toward him. Preston and Carla run toward the back door as Hoyt aims the launcher toward the front room. He gets to the aiming in its position and starts smiling. Hoyt turned to Russell and Billy.

"Billy, Russell, grab your pairs of socks and hold your balls in your vices. For this is it, my friends!" Hoyt yelled. "INCOMING CALL!!!"

Hoyt fires the launcher, blowing up the entire cabin. Russell and Billy duck down to avoid being hit by debris. Hoyt stood and watched at the cabin as it was engulfed into flames. Russell looked at the cabin, so does Billy. Hoyt turned to them.

"That's what I'm talking about, guys!" Hoyt yelled. "That's what we came to see! This is what we want! Now, only one more place remains, and we will have started a new era across New Haven."

They ran off the area, going into the darkness of the forest. From the right side, Preston and Carla walk out of the forest. Preston looked at Carla, both are covered in ash from the explosion and smell like burned wood

"The next time you want to try something with Hoyt being involved in the location, don't try it." Preston said.

Preston leaves the area as Carla walked toward the left of the forest. The cabin is completely engulfed in flames. The cabin now, is falling toward the ground, as its now decimated from top to bottom. The cabin is now just a pile of ashes as the smoke reaches above the trees in the forest, alarming some of the nearby residents of the area.

<u>26</u>

Emily returned to New Haven and arrived at the airport. She walked outside and sees Preston waiting for her inside his car. She walked over to the car and gets in. She looked at Preston.

"Didn't know you were picking me up." Emily said. "Should've called someone to do it instead."

"You don't worry about me." Preston said. "It's only for Eldon that's all."

"So, how's New Haven been since I was out?" Emily said. "The standard way I presume."

"Extremely crazy as usual." Preston said. "How was New Jersey? Interesting?"

"It was crazy." Emily said. "Not crazy as here. But, just crazy."

"Well, it seems you're heading back to the office." Preston said. "Since, your car is parked there for some reason. You should've parked it here, that way you could've drove yourself to the office without anyone, such as myself picking you up."

"Just drive, Preston." Emily said. "The faster you go, the quicker we'll be on the same page."

"If that's what you really want."

Preston drove off, leaves the airport.

At the office, Eldon and Cody are talking about the stock market as Darius walked inside, telling them that Emily's back in town. Eldon said he's happy and asked where she was. Darius told him that Preston and Emily are heading to the office as they speak.

"It's a good thing she's back in New Haven." Eldon said. "Some great news there. Hopefully, she solved that case of hers, so she

419

can continue her work with us."

"Looking at the time, Chief. Emily and Preston should be here any minute now it appears." Darius said.

From the front door, Preston and Emily arrived. They approached Eldon's office Eldon walked out of his office with a smile on his face as he greeted Emily back from her visit to New Jersey. Preston walked into the office behind her with his arms crossed.

"Good to have you back here in New Haven." Eldon said.

"Just doing my job, chief." Emily said. "That's all. So, what's been going on since my absence?"

"A few things, really. Me, Cody, and Darius had to settle a case involving a hit man who only targets prostitutes." Eldon said. "Cody took the guy down with one shot."

"Wow." Emily said.

"Just doing what I've been taught." Cody said.

"Wish I was on that case." Emily said.

Emily looked at Preston.

"So, I'm sure you had something to do, Preston." Emily said. "What did you go out and do for yourself?"

Preston stared and later smiled toward them.

"Nothing much, really." Preston said. "Just went to certain places to track down Carla and her devious plans."

"Speaking of her, did you find Carla?" Eldon said. "I've been meaning to ask you that? So, from what you've just said, you found her?"

"I did find her." Preston said. "Though, Hoyt and his group of followers intervened. As did some of Ray's men and afterwards, everything went to hell."

"What happened?" Emily said.

"I went into the cabin, at that moment is when I ran into Hoyt and his men." Preston said. "Afterwards, the shooting started and once I and Carla escaped, Hoyt blew the place to shit."

"He blew the cabin to shit?" Eldon said. "He's always blowing things up."

"That's what Hoyt does. That's what he always does. When he and I were kids, during the Fourth of July, Hoyt would take all the fireworks and place them in a certain location and light them up. Causing a massive explosion wherever he was. I can say he's destroyed at least ten to twenty buildings in his lifetime. It's what he's good at so he continues to do it. That's what he does."

Eldon turned to Emily.

"Did you find Colby?" Eldon said.

"I did." Emily said. "After a long search, I found him at a shooting gallery and managed to shoot him in the shoulder."

"You shot him in the shoulder?" Eldon said. "Did he survive?"

"Yeah, he survived barely." Emily said. "He's probably somewhere plotting his revenge against me."

"If that's the case, Emily. He'll be at the warehouse." Preston said. "Since his cabin has been destroyed."

Hoyt and Billy speak with Russell at his newly designed hideout location, sitting at a round wooden table, speaking about the final event. Russell says that they need more men to back them up on this final event. Hoyt tells him that the three of them will do just fine, since this one will require a bigger weapon, rather than the typical grenade launcher. Billy looked at Hoyt with a questioning look.

"Now, what do you mean when you say a bigger weapon?" Billy said. "How big are we talking here? Because, the grenade launchers will do just fine."

"Of course they do, Billy." Hoyt said. "But, since this is the final event that will change all of New Haven and its people. The event must require an even bigger weapon to do the job and the weapon will be in our hands the day that event comes."

"So, I take it specifically, you already have this weapon in your possession, boss?" Russell said.

"I already have it." Hoyt said. "I'm always prepared before the time is upon us. Keeps me on the complete balance."

Coover and Rusty are at the warehouse, seeing Ray with his

shoulder bandaged up under his coat. Rusty's face showed a slight concern for his boss as Coover had no words to conjure up from his mouth.

"What happened to you, boss?" Rusty said. "Was it Hoyt? If so, me and Coover can go now and take him out."

"It wasn't Hoyt, gentlemen." Ray said. "He had nothing to do with it. That I know of at this time. It was Weston."

"I'm sorry, boss. But, who in the blue fuck is Weston?" Rusty said. "If, you could tell us."

"The blonde female Marshal." Ray said. "She came to me and shot me in the shoulder, when I was in Jersey. I had her, but, it seemed that she knew exactly when I was going to shoot her. Like she saw it before."

"You think she also has the "Instinct"?" Coover asked. "Because it's been said it's possible she has it."

"I'm not too sure." Ray said. "During her time in Jersey, the officials, as well as the crime lords would always say that she had some sort of technique, similar to Maddox's Instinct."

"Well, boss, is there anything you need us to do for you?" Rusty said. "Since, we're not busy at the moment."

"No, I'll be just fine." Ray said. "Just contact your mother for me. We're going to have a plan for this task very quickly."

"You got it, boss." Rusty said.

They walk out of the warehouse and in comes Carla, Ray looked up at her and noticed the bruise on the right side of her face.

"What the hell happened to you?" Ray said. "One of my men didn't do it? Did they?"

"No, none of your men are responsible for the bruise on my face." Carla said. "Hoyt. He hit me in the face."

"Hmm. I see" Ray said. "Don't think that I didn't hear about my cabin in the woods. How you allowed it to be destroyed."

Carla's face showed a faint grin as Ray looked up at her with dire disappointment in his face.

"Carla, I give you one primary task to take and looked where your actions have done to my secret location." Ray said. "I know that Hoyt was there, along with his new group of vigilante buddies and the Bronson brothers' youngest blood. I suppose that's how you received that bruise upon your face. When Hoyt bitch slapped you and left you for dead."

"I had them where you wanted." Carla said. "I would've killed them if I saw what Hoyt was about to do."

Ray smirked and said, "From my point of view, you deserved that slap to the face. You were too highly focused on Maddox that you forgot the task at hand, which was to kill him without any hesitation. Only if you didn't let your emotions get in the way, he would be dead, and I would be thanking you right now. But, he's not dead and neither is that bastard, Hoyt Bennett."

"I understand that my emotions got caught in the task." Carla said. "But, I was close to finishing it completely."

"Being close enough doesn't mean shit to me, Carla." Ray said. "You had a job to do and you didn't get the job done. So, how am I supposed to feel about that? Knowing that the men I let you use for the job are now dead, because of your selfish emotional needs. The cabin, my only known secret location is now destroyed because of you. Speaking of which, I don't know what else I can use you for, Carla. I don't know anything else."

"Just give me another chance, Ray." Carla said. "Please, just give me another chance. I know I can do it this time. I can promise you that on this one."

"I have no need of you or your false promises, Carla." Ray said. "Just leave my warehouse at this moment. Leave yourself or I'll have one of my men here make you leave. Leave this earth that is. So, I suggest you make your choice right now."

Carla walked out of the warehouse as Ray's facial expression showed he's highly upset about what happened to his men and his cabin. He slammed his fist to his desk and tossed the sheets of paper to the ground.

<u>**27**</u>

Hoyt and Billy head out toward the warehouse. Russell is behind them inside his truck. They stop and get out of their vehicles and Hoyt uses the binoculars, looking in front of him. He sees the warehouse.

"There it is, my wonderful congregation. There's the warehouse, my boys." Hoyt said. "That's where Ray does most of his dirty work. Now, we've got him where we want him."

"You want to go in there right now and take him out?" Russell said. "You know we could do that for you."

"Russell, I appreciate your bravery. But, we'll save the chaos for a later time." Hoyt said. "Right now, we're only scouting the location just to make sure where we'll be once the time comes along."

Billy looked around the area, scouting out the entire area. He turned to Hoyt, thinking.

"So, when the time is accurate, Hoyt." Billy said. "How do we complete the job here? We're going be in this spot or are we going to be a little closer to the place? What if someone catches us while we're out here on this. We're going to be screwed."

"Billy, Billy. I'll say this once and only once directly to you, my friend." Hoyt said. "You focus on the plan and I'll focus on the ones that you're speaking of. Things will come into plan, I'm highly sure of it."

Coover and Rusty walked into their mother's home. She walked out across from the kitchen. She looked at them as Coover smiled. Rusty walked toward his mother.

"What in the hell are you boys doing here?" Barbette said. "You should be helping Ray out right now with his problems. You know that his cabin was destroyed last night. And we all know who did it."

"We know about the cabin, mama, but, he told us that he didn't need anything, mama." Rusty said. "He only wanted us to speak with you."

"Well, what did he say?" Barbette asked. "Not something terrible I hope."

"He said something about planning something fast." Rusty said. "He also wants to speak with you in person. About the situations concerning Hoyt and the marshal people."

"Very well, I see." Barbette said. "I'll pay a visit to Ray and see what he wants to talk about. But, I want to make sure that the both of you stay by his side. As of this moment, he'll need all the help that he can get."

Preston, Emily, and Eldon are sitting at a diner, at noon, eating lunch. Eldon speaks with Emily about her trip in Jersey. Preston turned and looked at Eldon.

"I'm highly surprised that you survived the trip, Emily." Eldon said. "I was a little worried that you wouldn't return. But, you proved me wrong."

"She can take care of herself, Eldon." Preston said. "You heard what she said about Colby. She shot the guy in the shoulder. Not too far from the chest. Good job, Emily."

"I was only doing my job." Emily said. "Though, I don't let my emotions get in the way, like Preston when he's facing Carla."

"It's not that my emotions get in the way of business." Preston said. "Just that I knew her for so long that I wouldn't think that she would be able to do something like this of this caliber."

"Preston, you should know that everyone you've either dated or slept with over the years, will eventually come back into your life one way or another." Eldon said. "You of all people should have that in mind."

"Eldon, I don't know how you conjure up all this kind of shit." Preston said. "Exactly, where do you find all of this information?"

"The library, Preston." Eldon said. "It's the sort of place that carries all kinds of books. Fiction and non-fiction. They also have books on nature and politics."

"I know what a library is, Eldon." Preston said. "I've been to one before."

"I'm sure you have." Eldon said. "Probably when you were in high school. Was that the last time you saw a library? Or you didn't even attempt to walk in a check out a book."

"Very funny, Eldon." Preston said. "Hilarious."

Emily looked at Eldon and asked him about the plan to take down Ray. Eldon said that they will have to come up with something clever to pull off, so Ray and his alliance don't figure out the marshals have in store for them. Preston said that they need to watch their surroundings. Emily asked why would they, because of Ray's crime partners? Preston nodded and told them that they need to watch out for Hoyt, Billy, and Russell. Since, Hoyt has been trying to kill Ray and take back his place as crime boss of New Haven.

"Well, no shit." Eldon said. "We'll have eyes across the entire location. Ray and his friends won't even see us on the outside"

"How is that, Eldon?" Preston said. "You're going to spread all of us out across the warehouse or have you brought in a group of interns to do the scouting."

"Not exactly, though I decided to contact the CIA and I also called in some SWAT groups to cover our backs." Eldon said. "No big deal about it."

"Did you make sure that they bring grenade launchers?" Preston said. "Because, they could come quite in handy for this one."

"Why do we need grenade launchers, Preston?" Eldon said. "We're not like Hoyt and his group of *let's blow shit up* buddies."

"I'm just saying that we should have some with us." Preston said. "Only to have an even match against them. Who knows what they'll bring with them."

"I see your point on that." Eldon said. "I'll think it over with the CIA. See what answer they'll give me, if I choose to do so."

"Very well." Preston said.

Barbette arrives at Ray's warehouse, where Ray is looking at a map of the entire city. He looked up and asks Barbette to sit. She sits in front of him and he moves the map to the side of the table.

"I'm pleased you could make it, Ms. Bronson." Ray said. "I'm sure you know our times are starting to get rough around here. Mainly on me."

"I can tell." Barbette said. "My boys came to me and told me that you wanted to discuss something you have in mind. Some sort of plan that will change the state of this city."

"I have a plan and I'm asking you to be a part of it." Ray said. "Just to see how you feel about it."

"I would like to hear it, Mr. Colby." Barbette said.

"This plan concerns all of the crime lords that surround this city." Ray said. "I'm going to have a meeting at this warehouse in a few days to speak with them about it publicly. But, I'll tell you about it right now. The plan involves taking out Hoyt and his group of explosive buddies."

"What about my son?" Barbette asked. "Specifically, Billy. What do you have in mind for him?"

"I figured that you would deal with him yourself." Ray said. "I don't want to be the cause of you losing one of your boys, even if it's one that didn't listen to his brothers or his mother's warnings."

"I see your point there. So, tell me how soon will this plan come into play?" Barbette asked. "Sooner than we hope or not to soon?"

"Once I have settled it with the other guys, the plan should begin to unfold." Ray said. "But, once the plan begins, we must take out Hoyt and afterwards, we'll deal with those marshals."

"I've heard the history between you and the blonde one." Barbette said. "I also heard that she's the one who shot you in the shoulder a few days ago. So, I figure that you'll handle her and leave the Instinct Marshal for me. My two boys will deal with those other marshals they have backing them up.”

“I’m up for that.” Ray said. “So, do we have a deal?”

Ray extended his hand and Barbette looked at it. She shook his hand in agreement. Ray smiled.

“Let the process begin.” Barbette said smiling.

In downtown, a meeting is being held at City Hall, concerning the economy and how they should increase jobs across the city. The room is entirely full, from left to right of over a dozen citizens. Every seat is taken as some extras stand in the back because of it. As one of the lead gentlemen stand in front of them, behind a podium, he talks about the cause and says that they should increase jobs across the city, therefore there won’t be any problems to cause someone to turn to a life of crime.

As he continued saying his speech, the doors opened up and everyone looked toward them. The gentlemen behind the podium looks straight and in comes Hoyt, Billy, and Russell. Hoyt, holding his arms out and hands open, smiling as he looked down at the gentlemen.

“My, my. It’s been a very long time, since I’ve stepped foot inside of a crowded location such as this.” Hoyt said. “Usually, I’m the one who brings in the big crowd. For parties of the rightful ones of course.”

“Sir.” The gentleman said. “Who are you and what concerns you about the economy? If you may ask?”

“If I may, I’m the guy that will change the foundation of this city’s economy for years to come.” Hoyt said. “Ladies and gentlemen of New Haven, Connecticut. We are all trying our hardest to find jobs and to work. Some of us have families to take care of, while some of us are only in it for ourselves just to make a buck or a name for ourselves. I am here to say that there’s something new coming to New Haven and it will bring happiness across the entire landscape of this city. Once the dark cloud that’s currently above us, passes along. A new and brighter cloud will emerge, and the sun will shine down upon us and we will have succeeded against this broken economy and its vile operators."

The audience began to clap as they started to agree with Hoyt. He walked up to the gentleman at the podium. The gentleman stared at him as Hoyt smirked toward him and extended his hand toward the podium.

"May I?" Hoyt said to the gentleman.

The gentleman moved away from the podium, letting Hoyt take his spot. Billy and Russell stood behind him, watching the gentleman and his associates.

"Don't try anything funny." Russell said. "I mean it."

"He won't." Billy said. "He's too afraid to do anything. He could barely speak when we walked in here. So, don't expect anything from him."

Hoyt grabbed the microphone and looks out toward the audience.

"Now, since I have a microphone, I don't have to raise my voice to speak the truth." Hoyt said. "Now, when the time comes when we all have jobs and this city is out of the economy's path, that will be the start of a new era for New Haven. Now, the rich folks and the crime lords that surround this city will also learn of that new era. An era that will bring them down to our level. A level that will show them that there no better than the rest of us. A level that will stand the test of time against crime in the city. Once, they feel that era upon them, they will look at us all and fully understand the true ways of life."

The audience continues to clap, as some of the civilians start to yell in joy. Hoyt smiles and looks back at Billy and Russell.

"This is going better than I hoped." Hoyt said. "Just keep your eyes on these guys right over here. I got the crowd in my hands."

Russell and Billy turn around and stare at the gentleman and his associates. They sit back and just look on at the audience, seeing how they're accepting Hoyt when he just walked into the building. Hoyt continues his speech.

"Now, I know some of you are asking yourselves, how is this man, who just walked in here a few minutes ago, knows so much about the economy and how to fix it. Well, for those of you that don't know who I am, my name is Hoyt Randall Bennett. The younger son of Ory and Loretta Bennett and the younger brother of Darren Bennett, who's currently in Hartford, obtaining his psychology doctrine. I was born and raised in this city and so, I'm currently stating that this city, with my profound help, along with my two partners, who are currently standing behind me, Billy Bronson and Russell, also known as Leader, will stand together to wipe out this depression upon our city and will restore the good inside of it and inside of us all New Haven citizens."

The audience began to clap louder. More cheers of joy began to pour out of the civilians. Russell looked out towards the audience and looked at Billy.

"Looks like he's got them." Russell said.

"Hoyt sure loves to talk." Billy said. "You can clearly see that."

Hoyt smiled and looked back at Billy and Russell. They smile as well.

Hoyt nodded toward the crowd of people and continued smiling at them.

"We got them on our side now. They won't accept or take anyone else's word except for mine."

<u>28</u>

Preston walked into Eldon's office, as Eldon reads some documents. Preston sits down in the chair. Eldon looks up at him. Preston just stays quiet.

"Something on your mind, Preston?" Eldon asked.

"May I have a word, Eldon?" Preston asked.

"Sure." Eldon said. "As long as it doesn't involve anything to do with your personal life, I'm all ears."

"Nothing to do with my personal life." Preston said. "I heard that Hoyt was present at a City Hall meeting today. Thought, you knew about that."

"I didn't know, Preston." Eldon said. "Though, if you look on the bright side of things, it seems that nothing's been blown to shit, so, what's the problem?"

"I'm only wondering what he's told the people." Preston said. "He could've said anything to them and they probably fell for it. Not knowing that they're being used as his pawns. It just aches me to see that."

Eldon gets up from the chair and walks toward Preston.

"We'll just have to see what comes up next, Preston." Eldon said. "That's the only way we'll know for sure what Hoyt and his boy band are up to with the city."

"Yeah." Preston said. "As long as he's not recruiting them just to blow their shit up, I'll have no problems. Well, its Hoyt. He's known for doing this kind of shit and later doing even worse shit."

Meanwhile, Coover and Rusty sat inside their rental house,

431

sitting on the couch watching the Outdoor Channel. They hear a knock on the door, they look at each other.

"Well, go answer the door, Coover." Rusty said. "I'm busy at the moment."

"Fine." Coover said. "But, if its Hoyt, Billy, or one of those marshals, you're dealing with them. Not I."

Coover opened the door and its Barbette. She walks inside and Coover closes the door. Barbette grabbed the TV remote from Rusty and turned off the television. Rusty looked at his mother, questioning.

"What was that for, mama?" Rusty asked. "I was watching that."

"There's something more important than watching animals get hunted down." Barbette said. "I've spoken with Ray and I'm going to tell you what he told me."

"What did he say, mama?" Coover asked. "Is it a raise? Is it about Hoyt and Billy?"

"Let me talk and I'll tell you what it's about." Barbette said sitting down in a chair. "Me and Ray have come up with a plan that will bring Hoyt and the marshals down."

"Really?" Rusty asked. "This already sounds great."

Later during the day, Karen and Richard sit in a living room, watching the TV. The doorbell rings and Richard takes a look back at the door and turns to Karen.

"Should I answer it?" Richard said.

"Yeah." Karen said. "Why wouldn't you."

Richard gets up from the couch and walks toward the front door. He opens the door and sees Preston, who's leaning against the wall, staring a hole through Richard.

"Detective." Richard said nervously. "Marshal. Detective Marshal."

"Richard." Preston said. "Richard Rogers."

Karen sees Preston standing in the doorway. She gets up and walks toward him and Richard. Preston looks behind Richard's shoulder and sees Karen approaching him.

"Preston." Karen said. "What are you doing here?"

"I'm here to speak with you." Preston said. "If you don't mind."

"Oh, I mind, Detective Marshal." Richard said.

"I was talking to Karen." Preston said.

Richard walks off to the kitchen as Karen allows Preston to enter their home. Preston walks to the living room and sits on the couch. Karen walks in and sits in the chair in the corner.

"Why are you looking at me like that?" Preston said.

"Because I find it quite strange to see you here." Karen said. "I spoke to you at the restaurant the last time we crossed paths. What more do you want?"

"I don't want anything." Preston said. "I just came by to see how you were doing with Richard."

"Why do you care?" Karen said.

"I don't care about Richard." Preston said. "I care about you and your safety."

"Don't see why you do." Karen said. "We're not together anymore. So, no feeling should be attached."

"You're telling me that you don't have feelings for me anymore?" Preston said. "Is that it?"

Karen gets up from the chair and walks toward the front door. Preston does the same, following her to the door. She opens the door, but Preston presses his hand against the door, closing it. Karen looks up at him, while Richard peeps through the kitchen.

"It's a yes or no answer." Preston said. "You seem not to tell me."

"Because it doesn't matter, Preston." Karen said. "If it did, I would not be married to Richard, nor would I be speaking to you about this matter."

Preston paused and stayed quiet for a quick second.

"Fair enough." Preston said.

He opened the door and walked out toward his car as Karen watches him. Once, Preston leaves, she shuts the door and turns back to Richard.

"Everything alright, honey?" Richard said.

"Everything's fine." Karen said. "Just something to get off his chest, that's all."

<u>**29**</u>

Hoyt, Billy, and Russell are all waiting in their trucks, looking dead ahead at the warehouse. Hoyt looked at his watch and turned toward Billy.

"It's time." Hoyt said. "Let's get this party started."

"Are you sure about this, Hoyt?" Billy said. "I'm positive that there's another way we can do this. My brothers are in there for Christ's sake!"

"Then, it's their fault." Hoyt said. "Besides, I've been waiting for this moment for a long time now."

They get out of the truck and mark their positions. Russell has his AK ready for use as Billy carries his machine gun. Hoyt goes to the back of the truck and pulls out a rocket launcher. Billy and Russell look toward Hoyt.

"Holy shit, Hoyt!" Russell said. "A rocket launcher! That will do the trick perfectly."

"That's the reason why I chose it." Hoyt said. "A grenade launcher was alright. But, a rocket launcher is even better. Gives you a greater aim as well."

Preston, Emily, Eldon, Cody, and Darius arrive at the warehouse location. Preston and Darius head toward the western side of the trees as Eldon and Emily stay at the eastern side of the trees. Cody walks up a nearby hill and sets his sniper up there. Cody looked down and was able to see the entire location. Preston looked to his right and saw two trucks, he knew for certain that those were Hoyt's and Billy's. He also knew that Russell was along with them.

"What do you see, Preston?" Darius said. "Colby and his pals?"

"No, I see Hoyt and Billy's trucks over there to the right." Preston said. "Looks like this will turn into a show for us."

Preston pulled out his communicator and contacted Eldon.

"I see Hoyt and Billy's trucks, Eldon. You want us to take them out right now or wait? Because, from the way this is all being set up and placed, we're in for a major shootout."

"I hear you clear. Just wait for now. I called the SWAT team for a little assistance. They'll give us all the help we can get on this one once they arrive on the scene."

Emily looked at the surroundings of the warehouse with all types of vehicles parked in front. From Corvettes to Chargers to even Lamborghinis. The area looked as if a party was going on. Emily turned to Eldon.

"So, what do we do once the SWAT teams arrive?" Emily said. "Go straight in and take them out?"

"That's a good plan." Eldon said. "But, let's see how Colby and his gangbanging friends handle it first. Don't want them to get too startled by our arrival."

Eldon contacts Cody through the communicator.

"Hey, Cody. How's the view from up there" Eldon said. "Is it looking great or what?"

"The view's just great up here, chief." Cody said. "I can see the entire location from this point of view. If I wasn't here for this moment, I could come out here on a good and have me some good hunting."

"I'm sure you would. Just keep us posted on anything you see that's unusual, alright." Eldon said.

"Sure thing, sir." Cody said.

Inside the warehouse, Ray is continuing a meeting with the crime lords that he spoke to while he was in Jersey. They continue speaking about their drug shipments and how they can transport them across the state and country.

"By doing the transporting on that trail, we will have no problems moving our shipments across the state and across the country." Ray said.

"If that's the case, Mr. Colby." One crime lord said. "How do we make sure that we don't get caught in the process?"

"You getting caught by the officials is not on me." Ray said. "It's on you."

"I agree with Colby on that one." Another crime lord said. "He has a point with that. If you get caught, it's your fault. You let yourself slip out for them to find and capture you."

Coover and Rusty lean forward towards Ray and the crime lords.

"That's good thinking, sir." Rusty said.

"Yeah, that's a great thought." Coover said. "But, none of us, should get caught. Unless we're either drunk or high."

"The chief has demanded that we take more and charge directly into the promise land." Ray said. "It's what he wants us all to do."

"I don't take orders from the chief, Colby." One crime lord said. "I do what is best for my alliance. Most of the chief's orders are inexplicably erratic."

"Which is why he gave me the choice of taking you gentlemen out." Ray said. "So, what will you do? Will you obey the chief's commands and live? Or will you follow your own path and die? Make a choice, pal?"

On the outside, Hoyt is slowly moving closer toward the warehouse with the rocket launcher on his right shoulder. Billy and Russell watched Hoyt as he continues getting closer.

"What are you trying to do, Hoyt?" Billy said. "You trying to get yourself caught or killed?"

"I'm only getting a closer shot, Billy." Hoyt said. "Gives me an adrenaline rush and makes for more entertainment."

"Does he know exactly what he's doing?" Russell said. "He could be seen, captured, or even killed by Colby and his gun thugs."

"I have no idea." Billy said. "He's trying to get us captured by Colby. Because, I don't want to deal with my mama at this point.

She'll kill me."

"She'll kill us before she'll get to you, Billy." Hoyt said. "Just relax and prepare to enjoy the show."

Preston looked over and sees Hoyt with the launcher. He looked at Darius, who's keen on the warehouse.

"Darius, you continue your watch on the warehouse." Preston said. "I'll be right back."

"Where are you going?" Darius asked. "Though, Eldon wanted us here?"

"I've got something to finish here." Preston said. "Won't be too long."

Preston crouched down behind the bushes as he slowly walked over toward Hoyt, Billy, and Russell.

Hoyt continued to aim the launcher and moves his hand toward the trigger. He starts to smile as Billy and Russell started backing up behind the trucks nearby. Hoyt's eyes light up.

"INCOMING CALL!!!"

"Don't think so, Hoyt." Preston said across from Hoyt.

Hoyt looked at Preston, but also fired the launcher. The rocket flies across the ground and hits one of the crime lords' vehicle. A blue and white Charger. The Charger exploded and flies into the air, covered in flames. Debris starts to fall and inside the warehouse, Ray and the others hear the explosion. They walked toward the front door and debris falls in front of them, a few of them back away from the door as others run out the door, heading toward their cars.

Hoyt looked at Preston with an angry glare. Preston stared at Hoyt, with his right hand to his side.

"What the hell have you done, Preston?" Hoyt yelled. "I had them right where I wanted them. You've just destroyed the entire event! I even gave you a warning that you should not come here, but you didn't listen to that either!"

"I lied, Hoyt." Preston said. "You, of all people, besides Eldon, should know I do that for a reason. The right reasons actually."

Billy looked up from behind the truck and seen Preston. Preston turned and saw Billy's head peeking out from the back of the truck.

"Aw shit!" Billy said. "He caught us! We're all caught! We're going to jail! We're going to jail!"

"Yeah. Aw shit is right, Billy." Preston said. "You're all headed to prison and Hoyt, you just got out of the cell. Looks like you're going back for another vacation."

"Preston, I'm not going anywhere, until those men inside that warehouse come with me and the price of their consequences." Hoyt said. "If not, I'll have to pull some drastic measures to make sure of that. Either they come to prison with me or they die here on the spot. Your call, Instinct."

Preston grinned.

"I'm sure they'll be headed to prison, along with you, Hoyt." Preston said. "You and your boys here. You'll all fit just fine, behind bars."

As they stand completely in the open, a gunshot is sounded as Preston and Hoyt duck down around the trucks. Billy decided to dive into the front of the truck, laying under the windshield. Russell laid under his truck, looking around the area. Preston pulled out his communicator and contacted Eldon.

"Eldon, what the hell's going out?!" Preston asked. "Who's doing the shooting at us?"

"It seems that the crime lords have taken matters into their own hands." Eldon said. "I suspect that they're trying to kill us."

"You think?" Preston said.

The crime lords and their thugs continue to fire at Preston and the rest of the group. Eldon and Emily are hiding under the bushes as Preston and Hoyt hide behind the trucks. Billy is still laying down inside the front of the truck, so does Russell under his truck.

"Hoyt, what the hell do we do, man?!" Russell asked.

"We'll have to fire back." Hoyt said. "Just like the cabin. But, this time, we fire until we fall."

Preston continues speaking with Eldon through the communicator.

"Eldon, what should we do?" Preston asked.

"It looks like we're going to have to fire back." Eldon said. "Straight shots, no misses."

"Now you're talking." Preston said.

Preston stood up and began shooting toward the warehouse and its front door. Hoyt does the same and fires as well. To the left of them, Darius is also firing at the warehouse, so do both Eldon and Emily. Atop of the hill, Cody is firing down and aiming with his sniper rifle. Through his aim position, he sees one thug with an AK. He fires the sniper and the bullet goes clean through the thug's chest and out through his back. The thug falls dead.

"That was very sweet." Cody said.

The warehouse door slammed open, pouring out dozens of thugs, all carrying AKs, shotguns, machine guns, and even handguns. They run out through the door and start firing back at them. Most of them shoot towards the trucks. Billy hears the bullets hitting the truck and he screams in fear. Hoyt looked at Billy inside the truck.

"Billy, get out here and shut the fuck up!" Hoyt yelled. "You're part of this too."

"I'm staying in here, Hoyt!" Billy yelled. "I'm not going out there and getting my head blown off!"

Preston and Hoyt moved from the trucks and crouch behind the metallic fence close by. They hear the bullets bouncing off the fence. Eldon, Emily, and Darius are continuing their share of firing back.

"I haven't done something like this before!" Emily said.

"As I've told you before, Emily." Eldon said. "Its New Haven. I suggest you get used to it."

They continue to shoot and duck from the incoming shots. Cody is still firing his sniper from atop the hill. He pulls out his communicator and its Eldon on the other end.

"Eldon." Cody said.

"How are things on your end?" Eldon said. "Or should I say, below you."

"Very good, actually." Cody said. "I guess they don't even know that I'm up here. You can still see me, though?"

Eldon looked up towards his left and he could still see Cody, atop the hill, firing down at the thugs.

"I can see you clearly, Cody." Eldon said.

"Appears that the thugs and their bosses aren't minding their surroundings." Cody said. "Shows their intelligence."

"Yeah." Eldon said. "Shows it alright."

Preston continued firing back and so does Hoyt. They notice that the two of them haven't missed a single shot at all. They looked at one another, impressed.

"I've always known that you were good with a weapon." Hoyt said.

"Yeah. I proved that at the cabin." Preston said. "You're not so bad yourself."

"I do what I must to survive." Hoyt said. "That's what my father always told me."

The gunshots continue to sound as the thugs continue to fire. Ray and his men leave out of the back door of the warehouse, leaving the other crime lords and their thugs to defend for themselves. As soon as they reach the outside, they hear sounds in the sky, as if something's is coming. They look up and see a SWAT helicopter flying over the area. Preston looked up and sees the helicopter. From the left, arrives a SWAT van and over six police cars. The thugs stop firing and run toward their vehicles.

SWAT members pour out of the van and tackle the thugs by the cars, knocking them to the ground. Some of the thugs run into the woods, not able to track down. One thug gets into a car and drives toward the exit, but a police car drives in the way and the thug rams into the police car, knocking himself unconscious.

Cody looked at the SWAT surrounding the scene.

"Finally, they've arrived." Cody said smiling.

Eldon looked at the scene as SWAT members run past him. Eldon smiles.

"It's about time they showed up." Eldon said. "Business has now been picked up."

Russell and Billy noticed the SWAT officers. His men run off into the woods, Russell looked back at Billy.

"If you see Hoyt, tell him we went for cover." Russell said, as he ran off into the woods with his men.

"He did not just leave me here with a SWAT team." Billy said. "Oh, the days that will come."

They walk over to the warehouse and see that the SWAT members have handcuffed all the thugs around. Preston walked over and looked to his right, seeing Ray running into the woods.

He proceeds to chase him, Hoyt looked over as well and followed Preston into the woods. Ray runs through the woods and as he dodges the trees, he runs into Hoyt, holding his pistol. Ray began slowly to back up as Hoyt walked closer.

"Now, Hoyt. Let's just talk this over." Ray said. "We can make a deal here."

"No, Colby." Hoyt said. "There's no need for talking, because I've already made my decision to take you out. You've taken my men, you've destroying the city with your corruption. So, I believe it's time for you to go, my friend."

"Not that way, Hoyt." Preston said from behind Hoyt. "Now, move away from Ray before I have to put one in your back."

Hoyt moved to the left. Smiled as he turned over toward Preston.

"You really going to shoot me, Preston?" Hoyt asked. "Because, if that's the case, I would love to see you try."

Ray stood still with his hands over his head. Quiet and not even moving an inch.

"Looks like the two of you are busy." Ray said. "So, I'll just leave you guys alone to speak among yourselves."

"You're not going anywhere." Preston and Hoyt both said.

"Don't mock me." Preston said to Hoyt.

"Mock you?" Hoyt said. "Don't mock me is what you mean."

"My point exactly." said Ray.

Ray looked to run but was stopped by Preston, who jumped in front of him. Ray slowly turned back around as Hoyt aimed directly at his head.

"Preston, I think you should just leave please." Hoyt said. "We have so much business to discuss."

"I'm not leaving him here only for you to murder." Preston

said. "He's coming back with me to the agency."

"Well, I believe we should let Colby, here decide his own fate" Hoyt said. "What will it be, Colby?"

"Would it be alright if I were to make up my own option?" Ray said. "It would be a much fair deal."

"No." Hoyt said. "Either option one, you go along with Preston to prison or option two, where he leaves you here for me to finish the job that needs finishing."

"My god, this isn't happening." Preston said.

Preston moved over quickly to Hoyt and smacked him in the head with his gun. Hoyt fell to the ground, knocked out from the collision. Preston looked down at him and turned around, where Ray is nowhere in sight.

"Shit." Preston said. "Damn it!"

<u>30</u>

Back at the warehouse site, most of Colby's crime thugs were arrested and taken to jail by the SWAT team. Preston walked back to the site from out of the woods with Hoyt in tow, handcuffed. Eldon thanked one of the SWAT officials and turned, seeing Preston with Hoyt.

"I see you have him." Eldon said. "Great news there."

"Yeah I do." Preston said. "Wasn't an easy task, you know. Had to deal with him constantly talking on the way over here"

"You keep telling your fairy tales, Preston. We'll see who's living in reality, who's waiting for his chariot to arrive."

"Could you please take him over to the SWAT van. That way we can't hear him speaking."

"I CAN TALK LOUDER IF YOU WANT, CHIEF! HOW DOES THIS SOUND TO YOU?!"

Eldon fanned his arm as the SWAT members walked over and grabbed Hoyt, dragging him to the van. Preston smiled as he turned and focused on Eldon. Eldon shook his head as he watched Hoyt being dragged off.

"From what just transpired, I'm sure it wasn't easy for you to deal with."

"I manage as much as I possibly can."

Emily walked over to Preston and Eldon. They turned toward her as she looked around to see who was being arrested and placed in police cars and SWAT vans. Her face began to change as didn't see Colby being placed or sitting in any of them. She looked at Preston with a slight concern.

"Something wrong, Weston?" Preston said.

"Have you seen Colby anywhere?" Emily said. "You can't tell me the bastard got away."

"Last saw him, he was in the woods. I caught up with him and Hoyt came in right after. It was between him or Hoyt. I couldn't risk Hoyt of escaping, so I went for him first and as I turned around, Colby was gone. He ran off as I was apprehending Hoyt. Hoyt was very close to killing him."

"So, what you're saying is Ray's still out there. Free and at large? No one to chase after him."

"Afraid so. I would believe he shouldn't be too far along from this location it would seem. I mean, the forest where he was is right behind me. Probably if you take some steps, you could find his tracks and follow them to the finish line."

"Thanks for information." Emily said. "I'll go ahead and do that."

Emily went to walk into the forest as Eldon raised his arm in front of her. She glanced over and faced him as Preston held his head down for a second before raising it up and facing Emily himself.

"Fine. I'll wait until when we have an appropriate time of doing the task. Contact me when its settled."

She walked off as Eldon looked at Preston, uneasy.

"You do realize that the emotion she's currently in that she's going to go on a hunting spree now." Eldon said.

"Yeah." Preston said. "Wasn't much I could do except to shoot him."

"Good thing you didn't. Otherwise, we would all be looking at another "Jonny Cartel event" with you killing another elite crime boss in New Haven."

"It would've given us some media attention time. That would've helped us in some way of having an advantage."

"I prefer we don't have any of those kinds of people running over to the agency, asking for a god damn interview about our jobs. When they can't even do their own damn jobs."

"I feel your pain, Eldon and it's a cold one indeed."

"You'll be feeling something of that caliber if you continue to piss me off in such a manner."

Nearby Preston and Eldon, Coover, Rusty, and Billy were all being arrested and taken to jail. As Eldon went to answer his cell phone, Preston walked over to them and placed Hoyt inside the truck. Coover and Rusty stared at Hoyt, which he does the same to them.

"You have something to say to me?" Hoyt said. "If so, I would like to hear it please."

"I've got a lot to say to your ass. You and Billy. The two of you don't know who you're dealing with here by causing all of this."

"It doesn't matter who we're dealing with. What matters is showing Colby and his group of lapdogs that Hoyt Bennett is in town and is here to stay. You understood all of that, Rusty."

"Don't play smart with me, Hoyt." Coover said. "Because, I'll show you what I can really do and it doesn't involve me using my mouth."

"Is that right. I assumed you used your mouths for countess things. Who's to tell exactly what for when you walk around with stains across your face."

Coover lunged at Hoyt, ramming his shoulders into Hoyt. Rusty and Billy tried pulling Coover off as Hoyt kicked him in the knee. Coover yelled in pain as Hoyt laughed at him. Preston walked over to the van, gaining the attention of the four men.

"I suggest to the four of you. No fighting in here guys." Preston said. "One mistake could put an extra charge on your timeslot."

"You've made a big mistake, Preston." Hoyt said. "I could've taken them all out and would have done a great service to my city."

"I have to say, you were doing a good thing." Preston said. "You just went about it the wrong way."

SWAT officer walked by and closed the back door of the truck, as Hoyt smiled at Preston when the last door was shut. Preston watched as the SWAT truck drove off from the site. Emily walked back to Preston, looking at the truck.

"It's a shame really." Preston said.

"How is that?" Emily said.

"Because Hoyt just came out of prison and now it looks like

he's going back in."

"He made his choice to do what he does." Emily said. "Nothing could've changed that."

Eldon walked toward them, placing his cell phone back into his pocket.

"I just received a phone call from the coroner's office that contained information regarding the double homicide in that neighborhood." Eldon said. "Appears they were also responsible for blowing up the bank as well."

"May we know who you're talking about here?" Preston said. "At least on a job extent."

"The DNA and witnesses' descriptions added up and lead to Coover and Rusty Bronson. The two older Bronson Brothers."

"No wonder they were the first suspects that many were expecting. It was obvious to a certain degree."

"At least they were in that truck and are heading to prison. Where they can settle their losses and find a way to move on with their lives or better yet, just rot in prison"

"You couldn't have said it any better." Preston said. "Job well done I say."

"We'll deal with the rest of this in the morning." Eldon said. "Because I'm tired and I need some sleep."

"Same here, Eldon." Preston said. "See you tomorrow then."

"I'll see you at the office tomorrow. Good and sound."

Eldon walked away as Preston approached Emily.

Preston turned to Emily.

"I figured we'll search for Colby right away, first thing in the morning." Preston said. "That way, we'll have enough energy in our systems to track him down long term."

"I very well could use the energy." Emily said. "I'm up for the task."

Late in the night, Richard and Karen are sleeping in their bed as the front door's bell ringed. Richard raised his head from his pillow, believing that the TV was still on. From his point of view, he knew for certain that the TV wasn't on. The doorbell ranged again as he got up from the bed and walked downstairs toward the door. He took a slight peek through the blinds next to the door. Seeing no one as the bell continued to ring. He opened the door and Preston stood before him.

"Jesus Christ." Richard said. "I couldn't see you through the blinds."

"You're that paranoid that someone would come over to your house and try to do what exactly."

"Never mind, Mr. Maddox. May I ask what you're doing here?"

"I need to speak with Karen. It'll be a quick word and I'll be out of your hair's reach."

"I don't know if she's awake."

"Well can you go ahead and check. Just to make sure. If she's asleep, I'll go ahead and leave. If not, I just need a word."

Richard nodded as he let Preston enter into his home. Preston looked around at the interior of the home. Glancing at his museum-like qualities and the fireplace that sat in the living room near a large flat-screen TV.

"If I may ask, how many TVs are in this home?"

"What's it to you?

"Just curious is all. I've seen one of those TV's before. Though, it was inside a store weeks before the Black Friday fiasco took place. I decide I shouldn't get one because I would have to worry about the possibility of someone coming over to my place and trying to kill me over a damn flat screen."

"I'll tell you. I was lucky to get one of those."

"Really. When did you get it?"

"Black Friday. Last year. Had to fight through an entire mob just to put my hands on it. Luckily, I checked out before the police arrived and nearly electrocuted everyone inside the store with their taser guns"

"Sounds like a crazy morning that was."

"It was around eight or nine in the evening."

"Holy shit. Stores are opening on the day of the supposed thanks."

"Yeah. These are some crazy times when you have people nearly killing each other over TVs."

"Can you imagine how'll they react when there's no food or water available for them to purchase. They'll turn into pure savages."

"When that day comes, I will be ready for certain."

"Same goes here, Richard."

Preston glanced up and saw Karen coming down the stairs. She looked at him as if he stole something from the house and returned to take even more of the items. Preston smirked a bit before Karen approached him up close.

"You can leave us here, Richard." Karen said. "I'll be just fine."

"Are you sure, sweetheart? I mean, I could join in on the little conversation you two are having."

"No need, Richard. It'll be quick and savvy."

"If I may ask you, why are you here at my house after midnight?"

"I just needed to have a word with you and like I told Richard, I'll be out of your hair. Just a word is all I need from you."

Uncertain of Preston's motives, Karen agreed to speak with him as they entered the kitchen. Preston pulled up one of the wooden stools from the counter and sat down as Karen stood on the other side of the counter. She opened the refrigerator.

"You want anything to drink while you're here?"

"No thanks. I don't want to take any of your water or soda or alcoholic beverages."

Karen closed the refrigerator as she walked over to the counter and faced Preston.

"So, what did you want to talk about? Especially at this time of night. Just unusual to me that you would do this. Well, not too unusual."

"I just came from a massive shootout in the outskirts of town and I just need some word comforting is all."

"Word comforting?"

"Yeah. That sounds about right I believe. Shouldn't be so difficult I suppose. You used to give me a lot of word comforting back when we were together."

"I did that because that was the only way to get you to relax about anything and afterwards you wanted physical comforting."

"I didn't come here for anything physical. Just some small words of advice and that would be all."

"Ok then. How about these words of advice? You just came from a shootout in which you could've been killed and currently lying down on the table in a morgue. But, you didn't die and you're not lying down on the morgue table. So, the words of advice are you're still alive and you're able to correct any mistakes you've made in your life to move forward. You know, continue saving people's lives and giving them hope for a better world or at least a better city.

"Same sort of frame I get it. I understand what you're saying"

Preston looked at his watch and his eyes grew as he stood up from the stool and tucked it beneath the counter. He walked over to Karen and hugged her. He kissed her on the cheek.

"It was nice speaking with you, Karen. It really was. The word helped in their own way."

"Glad I could help out in some sort of way."

Preston walked to the front door as Karen walked behind him. He opened the door and took a step out before turning toward her.

"Oh. Richard seems like a good man. Just try to keep him home on Black Fridays can you."

Karen laughed as Preston smiled.

"I'll manage my best on that one. it's a big task."

"I'm sure it is. Well, nice speaking with you and I'm out of your hair now."

Preston exited the home and walked toward his car. Karen watched him leave the area as she went back upstairs to bed. Richard waited for her in the bedroom, guessing to himself if she would return to bed.

Preston drove back to his apartment, he opened the door and walked in. As he laid down on his bed, placing his hands onto his chest and slowly closing his eyes, prepared to go to sleep, his cell phone began to ring. He grabbed it and answered the call.

"Hello." Preston said. "Who's this?"

The voice on the other side was mumbled. Preston couldn't understand what they were saying.

"Who is this?" Preston said. "Hello? Is anybody there?"

He hung up the phone and began thinking. He noticed that the caller sounded like a woman.

Around close to midnight, Emily arrived at her apartment. She placed her bag and other gear onto the desk nearby the counter. As she took off her leather jacket, her cell phone began to ring. She glanced over and looked at the number. Knowing it from her past, she knew it was from New Jersey, so she answered it quickly.

"Emily Weston speaking." Emily said.

"This is the Newark Marshal and Detective Agency." The caller said. "We wanted to make sure we contacted you straight ahead. Detective Gloria gave us your number, so we could speak with you on this urgent matter?"

"Yes, ma'am." Emily said. "What is it that you would need to speak with me and why is it such an urgent situation?"

"We contacted you because your father was found dead." The caller said. "We figured you were the first to call on this matter."

Emily paused as she cannot even continue to talk. She shakes a bit before placing the phone toward her ear. She tried to catch her breath and she started breathing calmly before she spoke on the phone.

"My father's dead?" Emily said. "May I ask what the cause of death was?"

"From what we understand here at this moment, it appeared he was murdered."

Three weeks total have passed since the incident that occurred at the warehouse between Ray Colby and Hoyt Bennett. Preston stayed calm and to himself as he's seemly sat in a courtroom, reviewing a case involving his old friend. The Judge is recommending that Hoyt stay in prison for a total of six months. Preston agreed with the judge to a certain extent, but insisted on visiting Hoyt at the prison.

Within a couple of days, Preston traveled to Washington D.C. to visit Hoyt and arrived at the prison to speak with him in person. Preston awaited Hoyt's presence in the calling room as took a glance to the side and spouted Hoyt, wearing an orange prison suit coming towards him being guarded by security officers of the prison. Hoyt sits in front of Preston, smiling.

"What a sight to see for myself. I am highly surprised to see you here in my presence, Preston."

"Just came to visit." Preston said. "To see how you were, really. Being back behind bars to where no harm can come from your hand."

"So, if I may ask, what's been going on in New Haven so far? What have my allies been doing in this spare time they possess? Have the people forgotten who I am or do they still remember the actions that I've taken?"

"They still remember what you've done to the city and its innocent residents." Preston said. "But, they don't want to remember you or see you, for that matter. Your line of guys are not really in the limelight these days. Seeing how they beloved and devoted leader is currently behind bars and won't be able to speak with them until his six months of jail time is officially off."

"Funny, how you speak about me directly toward myself. Good stuff you're pulling here. Though, overall, I don't blame them at all one bit for staying out of the spotlight. In time, they will return under that light with me by their side and we will continue what we started. Only this time we won't have any interferences from either side of the law."

"From the sound of your voice and how your body reacted along with it, I can tell you're being completely serious about what you just said. Least they won't have to worry anymore about you or what you've got conjuring up in that head of yours that could put the rest of them behind steel bars. I figured that your time here would give you enough hours to clear your head of that ruckus that goes around. Try thinking of happy thoughts. While you're here, you could write a book of your own or some music lyrics like other inmates have done."

"Funny. Hoyt Bennett writing a book or even a song in prison. Crazy shit and even I would say no to that kind of offer. No matter how much money were thrown in my face for such garbage that was created. While I have you here, let me ask you a question, Preston. Have you ever heard of the theory? A theory that involves someone like myself to corrupt someone such as yourself to do unspeakable things to his co-workers and loved ones."

"Can't say that I haven't." Preston said. "Does this supposed theory have a name exactly? Something that I can keep my attention toward if it ever comes across."

"Well, I'll just say this. Preston, you need to always remember flat out that I'm your equal. The Yin to your Yang." Hoyt said. "Take it how you want. But, believe it or not, I am."

"We'll see about that when or if you're released from prison once again, Hoyt."

Preston left the booth as Hoyt watched on and continued to speak. He raised his voice so Preston could hear him. Preston turned around, he stared at Hoyt, who smiled. Preston shook his head in shame for Hoyt.

"I am your equal in pure magic, Preston Maddox! Remember that phrase and keep it in your head for a long time to come. I am your equal in pure magic!"

"Maybe in pure madness."

"That one was great, Preston. Really good job on that one."

Preston turned back around toward the front entrance and walked out. Hoyt smiled as the police grabbed him by his arms and returned him to his prison cell.

"I'm his equal. It's funny." Hoyt said.

Hoyt sits inside the prison cell laughing hysterically as Preston left the premises and headed toward the airport, returning to New Haven.

THE PLEASURED KILLING

An array of marshals and police officers walk throughout the office building. Many spoke with each other. Others were in the boardroom with detectives discussing cases which culminate between Point Hope and New Haven, Connecticut. In the distance, a desk covered with files containing information on fugitives, murderers, and con artists. The phone rang, the fellow detective at the desk answered.

"This is Brant Harper. United States marshal and detective agent speaking."

Brant is a young detective. Somewhat early in the field. Sitting quietly, listening to the other individual on the phone.

"Yes ma'am. I'll look into that right away. Thank you."

He hung up the phone and looked around the office area. Few detectives and marshals pass by in the office. Brant stood up from his desk, walking toward the filing room. He entered the filing room and went into the system of files. No one else was in the room as he entered. Searching and looking through the file system labeled "*Codenames*" While searching through the files, he stopped upon one, taking the information and printing it out. He approached the printer, waiting for the papers to release. The papers were printed and Brant exited the room. Brant returned to his desk and begun reading the files. He noticed the codename listed above. "***Codename: The Pleasure Man***".

"The Pleasure Man?"

He continued reading the file before stacking it, placing it inside a manila folder and putting it in his desk drawer. He looked at his watch, packed his gear, and left his desk. Brant walked through the area until he was stopped by a fellow detective.

"Sorry to bother you before leaving, Harper. From what I understand, you weren't involved in the warehouse incident that occurred over in New Haven a week ago?"

"No I wasn't." Brant said. "Heard about the incident. Crime bosses meeting in secret. Discussing plots to shake down New Haven. The warehouse being attacked by a vigilante congregation lead by Hoyt Bennett. Last I heard of anything, the agency took care of it."

"Sure they did. The *Instinct* Marshal was one of the leading officials there along with Emily Weston."

Brant looked at his watch again before facing the detective. Time is moving.

"Why are you telling me this?"

"The Chief informed me to tell you you're needed over in New Haven in about another two weeks."

Brant shook his head in disagreement.

"What do you mean I'm needed over there? I have duties to take care of here."

"The Chief's aware of that. Which is why he placed your time slot to the next two weeks. He knows you're currently on a case here."

The Detective walked off as Brant turned his head toward him and back.

"Take care, Harper."

"Same to you."

Brant walked and exited the agency building.

In an undisclosed location elsewhere, a pair of mannequins sitting on a shelf, covered in blood that appeared to have been smeared upon them by a human hand. The sound of laughter echoes from behind. A man walked into the room, rubbing his hands together. Blood rested on his hands. Wet and warm.

"Only time will tell if they'll ever enjoy the pleasure of my wonderful work."

Brant drove down a street. Passing by homes as leaves fly off the ground as the car passed by. Brant reached over to the passenger seat, pulling up a map. He gazed at the map while driving. Glancing down the areas marked in red ink. The marks indicated locations of which the Pleasure Man was once located. The research was done due to left-behind messages and victims he murdered.

"He's been around."

Inside his home office, Brant sat at his desk, studying the map trying to decipher the Pleasure Man's next possible location. He rubbed his head as he continued staring at the map.

"Only if I could find your next move without you even noticing me. Would it go as planned."

Brant pulled some folders from the drawer. Placing them on the desk next to the map. He searched through the folders, revealing files. The files contain other information on the victims and the locations where they were killed.

He glanced over at the map and to the files and realized that the map was a definitive tool in searching for the Pleasure Man. Brant picks up the phone and contacts his Chief.

"Chief, yes, its Brant. I have discovered some information on the Pleasure Man and I would like to search these locations. If its fine with you."

A slight pause as Brant listened to the Chief.

"Thank you, Chief. I'll get to it immediately."

Brant puts the phone down as the Chief hanged up on the other line. Brant stared at the map and the files.

"If I find these spots, I'll find the Pleasure Man."

The following day, Brant entered through the door of an abandoned home. The home was one of the dotted locations on the map of where the Pleasure Man has once been spotted or sometimes located directly. The electricity of the home was shut off. Brant pulled out a flashlight to search the home, spotting for anything that could be a signal of the Pleasure Man.

Brant walked into the living room of the home. Holding the flashlight in his left hand while his right hand is holding the map and near his weapon on his side. He sees the living room completely cleaned out. No furniture, no home equipment. Just the walls and the floor.

"There has to be something here that could lead to him."

He continued searching, heading into the kitchen. Entering the kitchen, Brant saw the stove, a counter, drawers, but no table for anything to sit on. Not even a dining room table.

"I should check the upstairs area."

He left the kitchen, turning toward the staircase.

He walked up the stairs, seeing three doors. One in front of him, another to his right, and the last one down a hallway near a bathroom. He enters the room in front of him.

Upon opening the door, he saw the room is completely spotless with nothing inside. However, he did notice the room was very clean as if someone was previously inside the home.

"Someone cleaned up well."

Brant left the room and went into the second room, which was to his right.

He opened the door slightly and saw the room was filled with a wooden table and some old furniture. The room appeared to be a storage room. Brant searched the room and was unable to find anything.

He exited, staring down the hall toward the last room. Walking down the hall to the door, he caught the sound of a slight creak from the bottom floor. He decided to take a look back and didn't see anything. He focused his attention back toward the last room. Taking a small glance in the nearby bathroom. Nothing was there to indicate evidence. He opened the last room's door and Brant saw the room was set up as if someone was living there. There was a bed, clothes racked in the closet, and even a flat-screen TV rested on the wall. He scratched his head before walking to the closet. Moving the clothes in the closet and searched them. Finding nothing but old receipts and tissue paper. He searched the drawer, finding nothing but old newspapers and magazines.

"Appears this place isn't the spot."

Brant left the house.

The next location Brant arrived to was an old theater in Point Hope. Seeing no one around as he approached the doors. He enters the old abandoned theater and looks at the map. The theater is placed as the number two location to where the Pleasure Man was last seen.

"Hopefully I can find something here. This looks like his kind of place."

Brant entered, searching the theater in every spot possible. He then opened the double-door room and revealed it was an auditorium with a stage. Used for plays. He walked down the long aisle of the auditorium. Seeing only empty seats and hearing nothing but his footsteps, he approached the stage and walk up the stairs. He took a look at the seats and thought in his mind of how many people would be sitting in those seats while watching a play or a musical. He approached the back rooms. The rooms where the actors and crew would be preparing themselves for their roles in the musicals or plays.

Brant noticed the room was recently used. He's unsure of the reason due to the theater being closed. He did notice the costumes in the closets and the amount of make-up tools that were sitting on the tables along with wigs and hair brushes and combs. Brant looked at his watch.

"Almost time to return to the office. I'll take one last look."

Brant came up to another room nearby, opening the doors. The room was pitch black with only the light from the sun coming in from the other room. Brant took out his flashlight and saw a pair of mannequins atop a table. The mannequins' faces have been decorated with sinister and creepy smiles, frowns, anger, confusion. Brant pulled out his gun, aiming it toward the mannequins.

"The hell is this?" Brant questioned.

He approached the table, seeing the red coloring on the mannequins. He shined the flashlight on the mannequins, all have been decorated with a red substance. Brant pulled out a cloth, wiping some of the red materila and put it in a plastic bag. Brant caught a strange smell, which came from within the room. Tracing the odor, he realized the smell came from the mannequins themselves, particularly the red substance. Brant recognized such a stench.

"Blood."

Shining the flashlight on the rest of the mannequins and seeing that they're all covered with the blood and looked at the one with the smiling face, seeing it has a handprint on the chest made from the blood itself. He spotted a note on the table in front of the smiling mannequin.

The letter said, "*Without pleasure, there can be no true satisfaction.*" Signed, The Pleasure Man. Brant took the letter and threw it onto the table, resting in a small puddle of blood.

"I have to find him."

Brant left out of the auditorium after seeing the blood-covered mannequins. Outside, he approached his car as his cell phone rang. He looked at the ID, seeing it's the office.

"Harper." Brant said.

"We have some major news for you, Marshal."

"Does it relate to the Pleasure Man case?"

"A family of five are being held hostage in their home."

Brant stood next to his car as he listened. He unlocked his car, opening the door. He entered into the car while listening to the office over the phone.

"Where is their home located?"

"In the suburbs. Not far from where you are."

"I'll get there as soon as I can."

An electrical cracking sound came through the phone, interrupting on both ends. Brant looks at the screen, seeing it begin to warp and twist. A glitch? He continued to hear the official on the other side, cracking up.

"I can't hear you clearly through this disturbance. Hello?"

"Is this the marshal that is currently tracking my whereabouts?" Another voice said through the cracking.

"Who is this?" Brant asked. "Who's hacking through this line?"

"By now you should know full well who I am. I'm the guy you're looking for."

Brant paused.

"You're him. The Pleasure Man."

"It's about time we spoke."

"How'd you get this line?"

"I wouldn't concern myself with such pettiness. You're speaking to me, aren't you?"

"Where are you?"

"I'm currently sitting in a suburban home with a family of, about five. Two adults and three children. That's about right."

"I hope you're ready for the two of us to meet in person because I'm on my way there now."

"While, your on your way over here, let's see how fast you can get here to save this family in despair. I feel like teaching them some pleasurable techniques."

"Don't you dare place your hands on that family. If I see a scratch or a slight bruise, I will not hesitate."

"I'm counting on it, Marshal. I'll see you very soon. Don't be late."

Brant heard the screeching screams and hollers in the background.

"You better not harm them! You hear me!"

The phone clicked off with complete silence.

"Damn it!"

Brant started the car, driving at quick speed. Brant speeds down the road, heading towards the suburb home where the Pleasure Man is holding a family hostage. Passing by other vehicles and driving pass stop signs and red lights, nearby causing collisions between cars. He continued to speed up, until he saw a series of suburb homes ahead. Brant took out his phone, pressed speed dial to contact the office.

"Someone pick up." Brant clamored.

Within the office, the ringing echoes as many detectives move continuously through the office. At one desk, an officer picked up the phone.

"Yes."

"I need to speak with the Chief, please. This is Marshal Brant Harper. On pursuit of the Pleasure Man's location."

"The Pleasure Man?" The officer said. "Right away."

The office gets up from his chair and runs toward the Chief's office. The officer knocks as the Chief looks up.

"What can I help you with?" The Chief asked.

"Brant's on the pursuit of the Pleasure Man as we speak. Do you want me to call in the officials for follow?

"Wait till Brant calls back for details."

"Why?"

"Just do what I say. Brant knows how to operate in these matters."

"Are you sure, sir?"

"He's fine."

Brant drove down the road of the suburban area. Scouting the homes for the exact one, he took small glances at a map and back toward the homes. Seeing no sign, impatience brewed within him. Up to that point, he saw a man standing outside of one home waving in the air. Brant knew such a sight.

"This must be the place."

He pulled up his car and stormed out of it. Running toward the front door. He rammed through the front door, seeing a family. Husband, wife, two sons, and a daughter sitting in the living room. Their hands tied behind their back with duct tape placed on their mouths.

"I'm here to help you."

Brant moved over to them, only to be stopped by the sound of the click of a gun behind him. He froze, slowly turning around to see the Pleasure Man standing in front of him with a gun. The Pleasure Man wore a white mask. No emotion. No life present. Giving himself the appearance of a doll or a walking mannequin.

"It's about time we've come face to face. Now, remove your weapon from your side and slide it over to me."

Brant pulled out his gun from his side slowly, leaning slowly toward the floor. He slid the gun across the living room floor. The Pleasure Man picked it up and set it on the counter. Brant stood still with his hands in the air.

"Isn't this a sight to see. A marshal holding his hands up in the air in the presence of a fugitive."

"I only ask that you do not hurt the family. That's all I-"

"I believe that's the usual cliché we've always heard someone say. Wouldn't you agree, young man?"

The young boy's voice muffled in fear. The Pleasure Man nodded.

"I thought so too."

"This is only between us now." said Brant. "Not the innocent family that's sitting in their own living room tied down and taped."

"The only reason they're here is because I needed a suburb home to use and I love an audience. It gives me great pleasure."

"What would you want? Pleasure or satisfaction?"

"I prefer both." he Pleasure Man chuckled. "The more, the better."

Brant slowly reaches behind his back and pulls out another gun and aims it toward the Pleasure Man.

"Oh!" The Pleasure Man jumped. "Another weapon."

"I will ask you again. Let the family go and it will be settled between you and I."

The Pleasure Man nodded slightly, snatching Brant's other gun from the counter. Holding it up.

"I have a different agenda, Marshal."

He slid the gun back toward Brant, who slowly reached down to pick it up, watching the Pleasure Man stand still. Brant now had both his firearms and only one aimed at the Pleasure Man.

"Looks to me that you've lost this one."

"The show isn't over just yet."

The Pleasure Man reached behind his back, revealing a kitchen knife. He knelt down toward the young boy. The parents attempted to scream, they moved the bodies like tremors, but the duct tape held in their voices. Brant held his gun tightly, aiming at the Pleasure Man.

"Leave the kid alone!"

The Pleasure Man slowly slid the knife across the young boy's throat. Laughing at the scenery.

"You've seen my mannequins. The work I displaced upon them. I believe that

I will need a younger one's blood to complete my next one."

The Pleasure Man pulled back the knife, inching closer toward the boy's throat. The family trembled in horror as Brant fired a shot through the head of the Pleasure Man. He fell to the ground with blood pouring from his head.

Sometime later, the other officials arrived at the scene. Brant walked out of the home, approaching his car. The Chief came over toward him.

"How did it go in there?"

"It went into a necessary cause for action."

The Chief nodded.

"I knew you could handle matters like this."

Brant entered his car.

"So, where's the Pleasure Man?" The Chief asked.

Brant's car backed up into the street as a coroner van pulled up in the driveway. The Chief's face went still.

"Never mind."

The Chief entered the home with other officers at the scene. The coroners came out of the van, taking out the stretcher and the body bag. Brant drove down the street. He glanced at his mirror, seeing the home from behind. He focused his attention back to the road. Ending his mission of the Pleasure Man.

TOGETHER AS ONE

Running for their lives in the darkness of the night, Erica and Grady lead their group of eight into the woods near the suburbs of Denver, Colorado. They run through the woods, terrified by what they just encountered. As they continue to run, Grady looked back and noticed whatever they were running from has stopped following them. He turned to Erica and glanced at the group.

"They're not following us anymore."

"That doesn't mean they'll leave us alone. We have to keep moving."

"Erica, look around you, it's night and we have nowhere else to go. We'll stay here for the night and head off at the brink of dawn."

Erica nodded and walked toward the other members of the group, checking them for injuries or cuts. Grady looked around the area, not hearing or seeing anything that's approaching them. He sighed and walked toward the group.

At the brink of dawn, Grady leads Erica and the other members of the group out of the woods and towards a set of streets. Grady is a Caucasian male with dirty blond hair coming down to his neck as Erica is of Hispanic descent with a little Italian. Grady tells them that they must keep moving straight. As they move straight, following the street paths, they find themselves inside a suburb area. The streets abandoned by cars being left with their doors open and trash surrounding the homes. Grady spots a few homes and sees the windows broken in and doors kicked down. He walked ahead and saw five homes that looked undamaged.

"Erica, check this out."

Erica approached Grady as he pointed out the five homes, comparing them to the other seven that surrounded them. Erica looked at Grady and turned toward the group, signaling them over to their location.

"Five houses and ten of us." Grady said.

"You're thinking of searching those homes?" Erica said.

"Two to a house. We'll search for supplies and gear."

Grady began telling the other members of the group to search the homes. He pairs Danny, a scrawny Caucasian boy with Chase, his current girlfriend. Jesse, an African American male with Clyde, a close friend of Erica's. Lucy, the young girl of the group with Chloe, the spoiled girl. Tyson, the fighter of the group with Ross, the expert hunter of the group.

Sending them towards the homes, he and Erica search the house in front of them. A two-story home with a Yukon parked in the driveway. They find a spare key under the mat in front of the door. Grady used the key to open the door and enter the house. The house is quiet to the point where they could hear a pen drop on the wooden floors. They walk through the living room and enter the kitchen.

"I'll check the rooms upstairs. You'll check up here." Grady said.

Erica checked through the first floor for any supplies, weapons, or food. Grady walked up the stairs toward the second floor. He moved quietly to avoid making any kind of noises. As he stepped up on the second floor, he sees the bathroom to his right and two bedrooms, one in front of him and another to his left. He entered the bedroom on his left, seeing an array of posters and books in the room, not finding anything useful. He entered the other bedroom. He looked around the room, noticing it was a young girl's room. Not finding anything in the bedroom. He checked the bathroom and found only two boxes of bandages and a bottle of alcohol. He grabbed the bandage boxes and alcohol bottle and placed them inside his backpack.

Downstairs, Erica searched through the living room, the kitchen, and the den. While inside the den, she finds a stash of ammo rounds for a shotgun, though no shotgun is in her sights.

"Damn it." Erica said. "Where could the shotgun be."

She left the den and walked into the backyard. Seeing the patio and swimming pool in the yard with floats and pool equipment along with barbeque pits and lounge chairs. She smiles as she thinks of what the world once was. She glanced around the backyard, seeing the downtown city of Denver in front of her in the distance, with smoke in the air with a mist of fire in it. She returned inside the home, going upstairs to check on Grady.

Grady walked down the hall towards another door. As he inched closer to the door, he moved very slowly. Reaching for the doorknob, he tried not to yank or push the door open. As he slowly opened the door, he sees its a master bedroom and the floor, Grady spots two decayed bodies of a man and a woman. Flies buzzing around the bodies with maggots coming out.

"Jesus Christ."

As Grady sighed and Erica approached him.

"Anything up here?" Erica said.

"Only two boxes of bandages and a bottle of alcohol."

"Not the one you can drink, huh."

"Not even close to that one."

They laughed at the comment before they both heard a loud pitched scream come from outside in the streets. Their laughing immediately stopped as they looked at one another. The first thing coming to their minds is the other members of the group.

"The group!" Grady yelled.

"Holy shit!" Erica said.

They run down the stairs at a very quick pace and run to the outside where they see the other group members running out of the homes in panic as they're being chased by hordes of The Dead.

Grady and Erica run out of the house and see their group being chased by The Dead. As they run toward their group, Grady spotted Lucy being cornered by three of The Dead. Grady pulled out his 9mm Glock and fired three shots into the heads of The Dead.

Saving Lucy, he ran over toward her, helped her up as they began to run down the streets from The Dead.

The other members of the group run out of the homes with supplies in their grasps. Danny ran out of the home with a bag of beef jerky and eating some at the same time. He ran over towards Grady.

"What are you doing eating that?"

"I'm hungry, Grady."

"Put that up and help us get out of here!"

Danny placed the beef jerky in his backpack as he helped the other group members exit the homes safety. Grady looked around and seen the entire group with him. As he prepared the runoff, he sees Erica looking inside the Yukon back at the house. He ran over towards her as one of The Dead slowly approached her from behind.

"Erica! Behind you!"

Erica bust through the window of the car door. As Grady ran closer toward her. She turned around, facing The Dead, with a shotgun in her hands. She fired the shot, blowing The Dead's head completely off its body. Its corpse fell to the ground as Grady approached her.

"The shotgun was somewhere."

Grady smirked as they ran off along with the group down the deserted streets of the suburb. They ran as fast as they possibly could with The Dead following them at the same speed, some slower. They continued to run down the streets, before making a right turn.

"Where could we go?!" Erica said.

"There has to be someplace we can go!"

While they ran, Grady looked ahead and seen a bus. He gets an idea in his head and starts running at full speed toward the bus. Yelling at the group to follow him at his own pace. He ran toward the door of the bus. Opening it by shoving his shoulder through the middle of the door. He looked inside, checking for any bodies. Not seeing anyone inside the bus, he looked around for the keys. Erica signals to the group to get into the bus.

They rammed themselves into the bus. Erica looked behind her and saw Grady staring at the corpse of the bus driver with the keys sticking out of his pocket. Erica raised her head, seeing the Dead inching closer. Grady also saw the Dead approaching as he goes for the keys. Not seeing a head wound on the driver, he moved slowly to grab the keys. He moved slowly to grab the keys. The driver sat up, groaning at Grady. He moved back and the driver's head is shot off. Grady looked behind him, seeing Erica with the shotgun.

"Get the keys, Grady."

Grady snatched the keys and jumped into the bus. He sat in the front seat of the bus and started the engine. He backed the bus up, running over the horde behind him. He puts the bus in gear and looked ahead of him, seeing downtown Denver in the distance.

"Let's get out of here."

Grady drives the bus down the streets, escaping the horde behind him. He glanced back at the group, all sitting in the seats of the bus with Erica sitting behind him.

"Is everyone alright?!" Grady said.

The group responds in saying they're all alright. Erica looked at Grady and glanced to where he was driving.

"Where are you heading?"

"I'm heading through Denver so we can get out of this city."

Grady drives the bus down the streets, passing by a sign that reads, *"DOWNTOWN DENVER, DO NOT ENTER!!!"*

Grady continued to drive the bus at forty-five to fifty miles per hour. Passing by signs that suggest not the enter the downtown area or even get close. Ignoring the signs, he continued to inch closer to downtown. Erica stood behind Grady, looking outside the windows and seeing the abandoned, deserted streets and suburbs.

"So, how do we get pass downtown?" Erica said.

"I know a few ways through the area to get us out of the area faster. We'll have to avoid those things at all cost. We can't be risking the lives of our group, let alone our own lives."

He drove past a few streets, knowing he's about to enter the downtown area. He slowed the bus down to get past a few vehicles that were in the street. Not able to continue driving straight, he turned to his left and drove down the street.

"Looks like I'll have to find another way into the city." Grady said.

Driving straight, he noticed a large truck blocking the street. Slowly losing his patience, he turned down the street on his right. Getting closer to the city as the building became taller. He spotted what looked to be a boulder in the middle of the street. Erica looked through the window, confused.

"What is that?"

"I don't have a clue, but we're about to find out."

Getting closer to the object in the road, Grady quickly stopped the bus. The other group member stood up and looked to see what was in front of them. Erica also looked. Grady was uncomfortable with what he saw. What they saw in front of them was a massive horde of The Dead. From an estimate amount, it had to be over forty to fifty corpses standing in front of them and slowly approaching the bus. Grady is lost deciding as Erica turned to him.

"Ram through them."

"What are you talking about?"

"Just ram through them, Grady! You backed up on the others, just ram through."

The Dead was closer to the bus that previously. With the group members beginning to panic, Erica turned to Grady and kicked him on his right leg. He jumped from the impact of her kick.

"Ram through them, dammit!"

Grady looked at Erica and glanced at the group before turning back toward the front. He stared at the horde and smiled.

"Fuck this."

Grady stomped his foot on the pedal and the bus began to move at a quick speed. The bus moved faster and faster as it reached the horde. Grady yelled as the bus rammed through the horde. Body parts flew in the air and against the bus windows. Covering them with dark blood. The group members held their heads down as Erica watched Grady ram through the horde. He even honked the horn for more excitement at ramming them.

"Now, this is what I call fun!" Grady yelled.

While ramming through the horde, a tire spike strip laid in front of the bus. Not able to see the strip on the ground due to the amount of blood that's covering the windshield and windows. The bus rammed through the strip, blowing out the tires. Grady grabbed the steering wheel as he tried to gain back the control of the bus. Hearing the tires screeching and scratching across the concrete road. The bus rammed into another vehicle that was sitting in front of them. The impact of the bus hitting the vehicle caused the bus to turn over on its left side.

Getting up slowly from the impact of the fall, Grady looked at the group and seen that most of them died on the fall's impact with only a few that are still alive, although have serious injuries. He looked at Erica, who's getting up with a few cuts on her arms, face, and chest.

"You alright?" Grady asked.

"Good as I'll ever be. Yourself?"

"I'll manage it."

Grady looked through the bus's back window and seen more of The Dead approaching the bus. He grabbed whatever supplies he could get from the other group members that had died and helped Erica get to her feet. Grady kicked the bus door opened and crawled out. Helping Erica crawl out of the bus, he sees there in the city park. He looked over to his right and spotted the Denver Zoo.

"Over here, quickly!"

Erica moved as fast as she could alongside Grady as they approached the entrance to the zoo. They look back at the bus and see its surrounded by The Dead as they tear through the bodies of the group members and hearing a few of them scream in pain as they're being ripped apart from almost every limb.

They approach the front entrance of the zoo and began knocking on the doors for anyone's assistance. They scream as The Dead turn toward them and slowly approach their location. They continue to knock on the door and the door opened. They looked and seen a zookeeper standing in the doorway with a rifle in his hands.

"What are y'all just standing there for! Get in here!" The zookeeper said.

Grady and Erica ran into the zoo entrance as the zookeeper fired shots toward The Dead that were approaching the zoo. He fired a few more shots before turning around and closing the door, blocking The Dead from entering the zoo at any cost.

They entered the zoo as the zookeeper closed the door and blocked it from The Dead entering. He turned toward Grady and Erica and gave them the direction to follow him. They followed him into what appeared to be his own office space. Grady and Erica looked around the office, seeing photos of visitors and animals.

"So, I see I'm not the only survivor out here." The zookeeper said.

"True. Where are the other zookeepers?" Grady said.

They left the zoo right at the start of the outbreak. Many of them died in the front, some took their own lives. They couldn't live in a world where the dead reigned supreme."

"I'm sorry about that."

"I wouldn't be. They made their own choices during this cause."

Grady and Erica looked at each other before turning back toward the zookeeper, who stood up.

"Just follow me to my apartment complex."

They looked at each other confused as they followed the zookeeper through the zoo toward his apartment. Leaving the office, they walked through the zoo, seeing many of the animals still inside the spaces. They passed by the monkeys, the lions and tigers, the fish, and even the alligators. They arrived at the zookeeper's apartment complex, which sat towards the left end of the zoo.

Upon entering it, they noticed that it was covered with food, supplies, and weapons. Ranging from handguns to rifles. The zookeeper sat behind a table and started eating an apple. Grady approached him while looking around the apartment.

"I see you've been staying here for quite a while."

"It's the only place I can be. So, what's your names?"

"I'm Grady and she is Erica."

"Well, you can just call me Kirby. I'm the lead zookeeper here."

"Nice to meet you, Kirby."

Kirby allowed Grady and Erica to sit at the table with him as he allowed them to eat some of the fruit that was sitting on the table. As they ate the fruit, Kirby looked at Grady.

"So, could you two tell me what the hell is going on?"

"That's what we're trying to find out. Last I heard this was all over the east coast. The south and west coast I'm not too sure about. London was the last place that was talked about. The whole city is said to be a quarantine zone."

"Never thought that I would live to see the day that London would be closed down as a quarantine zone. Though, I'll probably never get the chance to visit now."

Erica glanced around at the weapons that laid on the couch and the floor of the apartment. She turned to Kirby.

"I see you have yourself an array of weapons to fight off those things."

"They were kept in the armory in case one of our fierce animals became highly aggressive to control or escaped its space."

"About those animals?" Grady said. "You're feeding them while you're here?"

"Someone has to. You can't just leave these animals here defenseless. The only way to let them loose is to open their spaces, though, I just can't let these animals go. I've grown an attraction to them."

"I see."

"So, where were you two heading? If I may ask."

"We're planning on heading north. Maybe south if the decision comes up again."

"So, I take it you'll need a vehicle to get on your way."

"We'll like one if you have a spare." Erica said.

Kirby nodded. He stood up and walked toward a closet door. He opened the door and pulled out a key. He handed the key to Grady.

"This is the key to the suburban out in the parking lot. You shouldn't have to worry, its gated up."

"Thank you."

Kirby walked over to the weapons and gave them two rifles and two handguns. He also gave them a bag of food and water with a few medicine boxes.

"I'm sure you'll need that as well for your journey."

"We don't know how to thank you." Erica said.

"Don't worry about that."

"Why don't you come with us." Grady said. "Try to find a way out of this hell."

Kirby shook his head. Disagreeing to Grady's offer.

"I belong here with the animals I love and care for. Nothing else out there matters to me anymore."

Kirby walked to the door.

"Follow me to the parking lot."

They followed Kirby to the parking lot. He pointed at the blue suburban in front of them.

"That's the suburban right there."

Grady and Erica place the weapons and gear in the back of the suburban. They get into the suburban and Grady started the engine. He drove towards the closed gate, seeing only a few of The Dead in front of them. Kirby ran over and unlocked the gate. Grady turned to him.

"You're sure about staying here?"

"I have no other option, but to stay here. I still thank you for your proposal. Now, please go."

Grady nodded as he drove through the parking lot and out of the zoo. He turned to his left and drove down the street. Kirby watched them leave and showed a slight smirk before closing the gate and returning inside the apartment.

LOST CAUSES

Running through the deserted streets, avoiding the Dead that roam throughout the entire area, breathing heavily and slowly losing his pace, Lyle finds his way toward the Denver Convention Center. Running near the building, he glanced behind himself and sees The Dead surrounding him. Moaning and screeching at him, trying to catch him.

Lyle ran to the entrance of the center and started banging on the glass and metal doors.

"Help! Anyone home, please!"

Lyle turned around seeing The Dead inching closer to him and the center. He continued banging on the door and yelling for help. As he yelled, he noticed something moving inside the center, approaching the doors. The Dead were closer and only a couple of inches away from grabbing Lyle. As their moans grew louder, the doors burst open and three men are standing in the doorway, with shotguns and handguns in their hands. The man in the middle glances at Lyle.

"Well, aren't you coming in?!"

Lyle nodded and ran inside the center. The three men began firing shots at the horde as it approached them. Firing shots to eliminate as many as possible from the entrance. Blowing the heads and upper bodies off the decayed corpses. Lyle watched the shots fire in front of him. The three men began backing up toward the doors. Once they were back inside, they closed the doors and blocked them with table counters, chairs, and trash cans.

"That was worth a shot." One man said.

They turned around and stared at Lyle, who was still standing behind them, worried about his life. One man signals to the other man to check Lyle for any bite marks or scratches. The man snatched Lyle by his left arm and pushed him against the wall.

"Just take it easy." Lyle said. "I haven't been bitten or scratched."

"We are taking you easy." The man said. "If not, you would be laying on the ground outside dead right now."

Checking Lyle for any marks or scratches. Not finding any, he turned toward the other man and nodded. He nodded back and approached Lyle.

"Looks like you're clean, pal." The man said.

"No kidding."

The three man stand in front of Lyle. They extend their hands as Lyle looked at them, uncertain about their behavior or motive.

"You don't have to be afraid of us, son." The man said. "What's your name?"

"My name's Lyle. Lyle Macken."

"Nice to meet you, Lyle."

The man turned toward the other two. Lyle looked at them and shook their hands as well as shaking the other one's hand.

"These two are Wilbur and Jett."

"Good to meet you two."

"My name is Truman. Hope you will be safe in here with us."

"Better to be safe than sorry."

Truman appears as a man who is a hunter, Wilbur seemed like a construction worker and a potential alcoholic, and Jett was a young kid who could barely survive on his own. Lyle.

"Let us walk you through." Truman said. "Show you around this merry place."

They walk through the Exhibit Hall of the convention center. Lyle looked around at its stellar structure and architect.

"This is a nice place."

"You can say that again." Truman said. "When we came into this place, there was no one else here. No employees or managers. Just us and only us."

"Do you have any exact idea as to what happened here in Denver?"

"I don't have a clue. Heard some things from the radio and the news. Hardly any information I've heard has yet to be true."

"So, those things out there, you've been around them?"

"Before the three of us found each other, we were all out there basically on our own. Jett, though lost his friend by a horde when they attacked his camp site."

"I ran as fast as I could to survive." Jett said. "When I came closer to finding a place, I ran into Truman and we were teammates ever since."

Lyle looked at Wilbur and approached him.

"If I may ask, what about yourself?"

"I was drunk before the outbreak took place. When I awoke from my nap, I seen a bunch of those motherfuckers on my yard, so I decided to blow their heads off their shoulders. I left my home and seen the entire streets covered with those things. After a while, I ran into Truman and Jett and that brings you to this place."

Lyle nodded as he continued to follow Truman through the hall and toward the Mile-High Ballroom. Truman unlocked the door and opened it, entering the ballroom. Seeing a stage in the front with over dozens of chairs standing and knocked down on the floors. The ceiling had its circular and square design structure. Lyle was in awe of the ballroom and what it had presented itself to look like.

"This is a nice-looking room."

"It is. Too bad we won't be able to see anymore performances inside this place."

Lyle looked around toward the stage and seen it covered with guns and ammo. Also, some clothes were sitting in the chairs at the front. He turned toward Truman who was walking near the stage.

"So, you guys sleep in this room?"

"We certainly do. Its big enough for the three of us. If you want to stay in a room to yourself, there's a meeting room down this hall through that door."

"Thank you."

Lyle walked through the door and down the hall before

entering one of the meeting rooms. Seeing how it was heavily designed and presented, he showed a slight smile and Truman entered the room, handing him a pillow and some bedcovers.

"I'm sure you'll need these for your rest."

"I highly appreciate it, Truman."

"Don't mention it. I'm only trying to help. Good night."

Truman closed the door as Lyle set up the covers and the pillow and went straight to sleep. Shutting his eyes and thinking about how the world once was.

Lyle suddenly jumped up out of the covers with sweat pouring down his head. What woke him up was the sounds of several shots being fired inside the ballroom. Lyle places his clothes back on and runs out of the room and down the hall toward the ballroom. Upon entering the ballroom, he sees Truman, Wilbur, and Jett firing shots at a horde of The Dead that have entered into the building somehow and have burst down the ballroom doors completely.

"Holy shit." Lyle said.

Wilbur turned and seen Lyle looking at the horde. He ran over toward the stage and grabbed one of the handguns. He approached Lyle and tossed the gun at him. Lyle caught the gun in his hands and stared at Wilbur.

"Help us that these bastards out!" Wilbur said.

Lyle started firing shots at the horde as they continued to enter. Each of the men fired as many shots as they could to take out The Dead. Reaching closer to reload their weapons as the horde is getting larger. Truman turned around and ran toward Lyle. Wilbur and Jett follow him.

"We'll have to move out of this location!" Truman said.

While running out of the ballroom, one of The Dead caught Wilbur by his left leg and bites into his calf. Wilbur grunted in massive agony and shot the Dead in its head. He ran behind Lyle in pain and slammed the door. They later regrouped inside the Four Seasons Ballroom. One of the newly set rooms inside the convention center. As they got back together. Truman started checking each of them for any marks or scratches.

"Everyone alright?" Truman said.

"I'm ok." Lyle said.

"Same here, Truman." Jett said.

"What about you, Wilbur?"

Truman turned toward Wilbur, who was standing still, with his face looking as if he's in tremendous pain. Truman looked down at Wilbur's leg and noticed blood pouring out of his pants.

"What the hell is that, Wilbur?!"

"What do you think, dumbass. I was bit."

"What the fuck!" Jett said. "What are we going to do?!"

Truman silenced Jett as he turned toward Wilbur. Cautiously looking at him and slowly reaching for his pistol on his right side.

"I'm sorry it has to come down to this, Wilbur."

"Whoa! What the fuck are you doing, Truman?! You're not going to shoot me!"

"What other option do I have?"

Wilbur looked at Jett and Lyle before reaching into his back and pulling out his gun. He aimed the gun toward Truman's head as Truman held his pistol toward Wilbur's head.

"Killing me won't save you the harm of turning into one of those things, Wilbur."

"I'm not ready to die! Not yet."

Truman started quietly at Wilbur, who did the same. Lyle and Jett stood silently against the walls of the ballroom. The room is completely silent. Truman and Wilbur continued to hold their firearms up aiming at each other.

"Sorry it has to end like this." Truman said.

"So am I." Wilbur said.

Wilbur fired a shot at Truman's chest He yelled in pain as he began to hold his chest. Wilbur began to approach him, but Truman looked up and fired the shot at Wilbur. Shooting him straight through the forehead, killing him. Wilbur's body fell to the ground with a thump to follow the impact. Truman fell to the ground and had died from the bullet, which had gone directly through his heart.

Lyle and Jett looked at the dead bodies of Truman and Wilbur. The blood draining from the body of Truman and the head and leg of Wilbur.

"Why did this have to happen?!" Jett said. "Why did this happen."

"Just calm down." Lyle said. "We're going to be alright."

"So many lost causes. How many more must I endure in this new world. How many!"

Jett panicked and ran toward the ballroom doors. Lyle yelled at Jett not to open the doors. As Jett opened the door, he was mauled by the horde that was waiting on the other side. Lyle ran out of the room through the side door as he heard Jett screaming as his body was being ripped.

Lyle found himself on the outside of the center in the parking lot. Not seeing as many of The Dead as before, due to them mainly being inside the convention center itself. Lyle searched the cars to see if they were unlocked. He finds one red Mazda and sees that the door is unlocked.

"Oh, thank God."

He gets into the car and realizes he doesn't have a key. He checks the glove box for the key and doesn't find it. He later searched the upper mirror and only a few pieces of paper fell out.

"Where the hell could a key possibly be?"

He later looked in the back of the car, not finding them key. He decided to look under the seats and found a key under the driver's seat. He looked at the key and smiled. Putting the key in, he started the car. He yelled in excitement as he drove the car out of the parking lot. Passing by The Dead.

13 DAYS

DAY 1

The sun shines down on Denver, Colorado. The streets are quiet and covered with abandoned cars and streets of trash. In other streets are covered with walking corpses that appear to be chasing a group of five out of the city and into the woods.

"Run and keep running!" Yelled Lucas toward his group as they ran out of the city of Denver, Colorado and into the woods toward the outskirts of the city. They are running from the out slew of undead corpses that have risen from the graves and morgues that are seeking to devour them completely. They are called the Dead.

"Where are we supposed to go?! You think there's such a place for us anymore?!" said Bret.

"We have to find a safe place to keep quiet and to cover us from being discovered by these things!"

"Where could we find a place like that, Lucas?" Marylyn said.

"We'll find a place soon. We just need to worry about getting out of our current circumstance with these things on our trail."

The group is a pack between Lucas, their leader. A slim guy with light skin, Marylyn, a young woman with dark hair who is paired with Lucas before the outbreak. Bret, a young guy that is a close friend to Lucas before the outbreak, Jeanette, Bret's on and off girlfriend, and Curtis, a friend of Bret's and Lucas that joined them when he escaped the Dead.

Curtis reached into his side and pulled out his gun and began firing at the Dead that surrounded them from outside the city. Lucas screamed toward Curtis to stop shooting them and continue running deep into the woods.

"I have to keep firing at them!" Curtis said. "If not, we'll be their food out here and I'm not interested in being their serving."

The group continues running further into the woods to the point where they are surrounded by the trees and bushes. They find a nice spot and they remain quiet for a few minutes. In those minutes, they could hear the Dead walking in the distance, their feet sliding across the dirt and grass, breaking downed tree branches, and their moaning that sends fear into one's body without touch.

The sun begins to set as Lucas decided that they will set a small camp in the space they currently stand in. Once nightfall approached, there was no noise or sign of the Dead. Lucas was thrilled as was the rest of the group. They each found a place to settle in the small space to where all of them were comfortable in their own space. Lucas started a fire to give them some light and heat as the night brought a cold temperature upon them. The night had settled, and the group was calm and quiet.

DAY 2

Dawn has reached the wilderness as the sunlight shined down on Lucas and Marylyn, who were already awake and sitting down near the worn-out wood from the fire. Bret and Jeanette had some time to themselves while Curtis decided to take a small walk into the woods.

"So, where do you think we could find some place that will keep us safe from those things?" Marylyn said.

"Out of all the places that have been built on this earth and in this country. I would expect there to be some place of any kind to be a safe haven for an amount of people. No matter how many."

"What about weapons? I mean we can't just keep going around with little to no ammo in our guns and we barely have any machetes and staffs to use."

"We can always search for that, but we could use some of these larger tree branches as weapons. If we can find one that is already on the ground."

"That's right, you don't want to become a disturbance and send those things near us."

"That's the reality."

They laugh at each other. Hearing the sound of kissing and look over and they see Bret and Jeanette kissing each other to the point where they were almost getting ready to have sex with each other. Lucas looked around and didn't see Curtis.

"Where did Curtis go?"

"He went out for a walk. That's what he said." Bret said.

"Out there?" Marylyn said.

"That's right. He shouldn't be too far from us. He didn't walk out that far from where we are."

Lucas stood up and knocked the dirt off his clothing. Marylyn stood up, concerned about Lucas' current train of thought.

"What are about to do?"

"I'm going out there to find him. I just need to be sure he's all right and has a weapon on him."

"I'm sure he has a weapon on him, Lucas. There's no need to go running out there like some sort of hero. Curtis will be back, and we'll continue on to our safe haven."

Lucas looked into Marylyn's eyes and released a slight sigh.

"Sorry, but I'm going out there to find him."

Lucas grabbed his handgun and a medium sized tree branch from the ground and headed out into the woods to find Curtis. Marylyn only watched on and wiped the sweat off of her forehead. Bret and Jeanette continue kissing and cuddling underneath their covers.

Curtis walked around the forest, not too far from the group's camp site. He walked around, thinking to himself how the outbreak started and could there be a possible way in finding a cure to bring back society as it previously were.

"It can't be the whole country can it?" Curtis said to himself. "I mean, it just can't be possible that the whole country was wiped out. What about the world itself?! Could the entire globe be populated by those walking corpses?! I'm starting to freak out talking about this to myself."

While walking, Curtis stepped on a downed branch. Its cracking sound traveled through the quiet wilderness and he began to hear moaning coming from deep within the woods. Curtis begins to hear steps not too far from his location. He slowly walked to see what else was walking in the woods. He moved a bush from his viewpoint and saw several of the Dead walking around and near his current spot.

"Oh shit! Oh shit!"

Curtis took a few steps back and tripped over another larger branch. The sound of his fall was heard by the Dead. All of whom began to moan louder and approach his location. Curtis began to panic quietly as he reached for his gun and placed it to his head. He hears some footsteps coming closer and a hand comes down on is shoulder.

"Dude, get up!" Lucas said.

"Oh shit! You're here. They're on their way to this spot. We have to move!"

"No kidding, Curtis."

Lucas and Curtis walk back toward the camp site as the Dead slowly enter the woods where they previously were standing.

DAY 3

The group continued walking through the wilderness in search of a haven to keep themselves protected from the Dead that walked constantly around the woods and some even in the woods. While walking in the wilderness, they see an opening and taking that opening had brought them onto a highway where they could see both ends of the streets. The streets were empty, no vehicles were laying on the streets. Lucas decided that taking the highway trail would probably help them in finding signs for a location to keep occupied.

While taking the highway trial, they come across a lone hitchhiker. The hitchhiker sees them and immediately runs toward them. Lucas tells the group to be on edge when the hitchhiker approaches them. The hitchhiker confronted them and stood in their pathway.

"Please, I need some help." The hitchhiker said. "I could help you and your people. Please?!"

"I'm sorry. We don't know who you are, and you do not know who we are." Lucas said. "There's nothing we can do for you."

"Are you sure?" Jeanette said. "He can't join us?"

"Please?! I will do anything for you and your people, and I mean absolutely anything."

Lucas took a few steps back from the hitchhiker as he reached out toward him in a lustful manner. Lucas looked over the hitchhiker's left shoulder and saw what was behind him. The group also saw what was approaching the hitchhiker from behind. Lucas and the group ran as the hitchhiker seemed confused. He hears moaning behind him and is backed by the Dead, three of them. They began to rip him apart from his abdomen and bite his neck and arms, eating the flesh thereof.

Lucas looked toward them and see the Dead eating the hitchhiker. Lucas quietly lead the group pass the Dead as they continued looking and following the highway trail. Upon finding themselves entering a small patch that lead them back into the woods, Lucas spotted something ahead, something big and tall. He ran toward the object.

"Lucas, wait!" Marylyn said.

Lucas continued running as the group tried to catch up. The group finds him standing still looking a building in front of him. They walked toward him and set their eyes on the building. Lucas and the group were appalled.

"You see what I'm seeing." Marylyn said.

"I am, Marylyn." Lucas said. "This looks like our spot."

The group were staring at an abandoned warehouse that stood at least three stories tall and was wide enough to have clear space to do anything inside of it. The warehouse didn't appear to be rusty or old in any sort of way. The warehouse appeared to be recently built and planned to be used for construction before the outbreak began. Lucas smiled as they walked toward the warehouse.

Lucas noticed the sun going down and the moon slowly rising up, indicating that nightfall was approaching. He decided that he group would set camp in the small garage area of the warehouse for the night and that they would find a way into the warehouse in the morning.

DAY 4

Lucas and Bret try to find any tools to use in order to get into the warehouse. Curtis, Marylyn, and Jeanette also searched around the outside and around the warehouse for any tools. Curtis decided to check the garage itself for any tools. He searched the desk's drawers and found a key that was laying underneath a drawer. He walked outside toward Lucas and Bret as they were trying to break the lock on the front doors.

"Guys, I found a key."

"Where did you find it?" Lucas said.

"It was underneath a drawer in the desk back in the garage. I figured it would be worth a try."

Lucas grabbed the key and placed it in the lock. He turned the key and it unlocked the lock pad on the door. Bret pulled the chain and padlock off the door. Lucas turned around and smiled at Curtis. They opened the warehouse doors and they entered the warehouse. Seeing its interior space, the area they stood in appeared to be a lobby of a sort. The warehouse was clean and filled with tools that would be used for building construction and had car parts such as engines, tires, and used doors and seats.

"This is our new dwelling place, guys." Lucas said. "As of right now, this is our new home."

"Look at the size of this place." Bret said. "We can each have our separate spots in here."

"Yeah we could." Curtis said. "I wonder what else they have

in here that could be useful."

"I would worry about that tomorrow. For right now, its best that we bring in our gear and get settled. We'll do some more searching tomorrow and that way we can search this entire place."

"Fair enough, Lucas." Curtis said. "I'm taking that spot over in the corner over there."

Marylyn walked over to Lucas as the rest of the group grabbed the gear and placed it inside of the warehouse. She patted Lucas on the back and smiled at him. He turned toward her.

"Seems like a good place to start." Marylyn said.

"This is our place until the time is necessary for us to leave. As of right now, we're staying in this place."

DAY 5

The next day, Curtis is the first one to awaken and he sets out on searching the other parts of the warehouse. After a couple of minutes pass, Lucas also awakens and sees Curtis walking up on the first set of stairs that head toward the second level of the warehouse.

"You're going to wait for me or are you in some hurry?" Lucas said.

Curtis turned around and seen Lucas looking at him from below. Curtis laughed as Lucas smiled. Lucas began walking up the stairs, following Curtis up onto the second floor of the warehouse. They reach the second floor of the warehouse and see that its nearly empty except for the wooden planks that sit at the opposite end of the floor.

"What do you think of this level?" Lucas said.

"I think it's a good start at least to have something going. I mean, we could build stuff ourselves in here. We have the tools necessary to get the jobs done."

While looking around the second floor, they began hearing slight footsteps coming from the third floor of the warehouse. Lucas grabbed his gun and slowly walked toward the staircase that lead up to the third floor. Curtis followed Lucas quietly as he held a 2x4 in his hand. They get near the staircase, until they see two men walk down the staircase and stand in front of them. The men appeared to be rugged and seemed like they've been drinking.

"Whoa. What do we have here?" One man said.

"Looks to me like there's more people living in this place with us." The other man said.

"Nah. These guys had to break the lock on the door in order to get in. Tell me who are you and what are you doing here in this warehouse?"

"My name is Lucas, and this is Curtis. We entered this warehouse yesterday with our group and we don't intend on leaving."

"Well, my name is Dreyfus and my friend over here is Kurt. We're not telling you to leave. This warehouse is big enough for us all to live in."

"Is that right?"

"Yeah. That's right. I need to see you and the rest of group in full before we can come to terms on how this kind of living will suit with us all. Remember, we were in this warehouse first. We placed the lock on that door."

Lucas nodded as he and Curtis began walking back down to the first floor with Dreyfus and Kurt behind them coming down the staircase. Marylyn, Bret, and Jeanette are all awake as they see Lucas and Curtis coming down the staircase.

"Lucas, what's going on?" Marylyn said.

"That sounded like a woman and I mean a woman!" Dreyfus said.

The group stood together as Dreyfus and Kurt stepped off the staircase and approached them. Marylyn began to have a small sense of fear, so did Jeanette. Lucas, Curtis, and Bret stood in front of them and faced Dreyfus and Kurt.

"You brought women into this place. Two of them at that." Dreyfus said. "Seems our deal has just changed a bit, Lucas."

"You're not touching them by any means." Lucas said. "We won't let you do such a thing."

"Damn straight, boys." Bret said. "Make one more toward our girls and you'll regret having made the move."

Dreyfus and Kurt laughed as Lucas and the group stood still and kept themselves in a serious fashion. Dreyfus placed his gun back in his belt and held his hand up.

"Our deal is simple. This is our warehouse, we got here first.

So, that gives me and Kurt here total leadership of you and this usage of this warehouse.”

“Is that all you’re asking for?” Lucas said.

“Our second add-on to this deal is full control of your two women.”

“I don’t think so, boy!” Bret said.

“We already said you’re not getting near them by any means.” Lucas said. “We made that statement perfectly clear.”

Dreyfus nodded as he stared into Lucas’ blue eyes. He took a step back and gave a smirk.

“You have till tomorrow to make the decision.” Dreyfus said. “We’ll be up on the third floor while you think it over with your group and by tomorrow morning, we will be back down here and if no decision is made between all for you, we’ll go ahead and make the decision for you. Very simple.”

“Oh, it’s simple all right.” Lucas said. “It’s very simple. We’ll talk with you two in the morning.”

“You surely will, Lucas. Good day and night, ladies.”

“I can’t wait to touch your skin tomorrow, ladies.” Kurt said. “It will be a pleasure worthwhile.”

Dreyfus and Kurt walk back up the staircase toward the third floor. Lucas sat with the group about their circumstance. The group believe they should leave the warehouse and go searching for another place to dwell in. Lucas believes otherwise.

“We’re not leaving this place.” Lucas said. “Not by any chance we are leaving from this place.”

“What do expect us to do when those guys come back down here in the morning?” Curtis said.

“When they come back down here and if they make any sudden movements, we kill them. Very simple.”

DAY 6

The following morning arrives as Lucas didn't sleep at all. He sat down near the staircase waiting for Dreyfus and Kurt to come down. Bret and Curtis wake up along with Marylyn and Jeanette. After a few hours near noon, Dreyfus and Kurt come down the stairs and face the group. Lucas stood firm as he stared Dreyfus in the eyes. Dreyfus laughed.

"So, we would like to hear your answer now concerning our arrangement from yesterday."

"There is no answer." Lucas said. "We're not handing over our girls and we're not leaving this place."

"Let me get this straight. You're not giving us your women and you're not leaving our warehouse? Is that what I heard come out of your mouth?"

"That's exactly what you heard."

Dreyfus nodded and swiped Lucas in the face with a punch. Lucas dropped to the ground on one knee. Dreyfus laughed as Bret rammed him into the wall and began pummeling him. Kurt grabbed Bret and punched him in the abdomen and threw him toward the ground. Dreyfus rubbed his face and walked over to Curtis and punched him.

"Your women are ours and you're under our ruler ship, boys!" Dreyfus said.

Dreyfus walked over toward Marylyn and began rubbing her from her forehead down to her breasts. He exhaled as he looked at her face.

"We are going to have so much fun, honey. Believe that."

Dreyfus stood in front of Marylyn, Kurt approached Jeanette and immediately tossed her down and tried to unzip her pants. She began kicking to shove him off her, but he kept coming.

"I'm going to show you how to use that mouth of yours, baby." Kurt said. "Now, open yourself up for me to make my entrance."

Jeanette began screaming as Bret stood up and ran over toward Kurt. Bret snatched Kurt off her and started beating him in the head with both his fists.

"I told you ass not to place your hands on her!" Bret said. "Told you, bitch!"

Curtis got back to his feet and attempted to get Dreyfus away from Marylyn, but Dreyfus punched Curtis again and shoved Marylyn against the wall and completely closed her in.

"It's time we have some fun, honey." Dreyfus said. "Trust me, you'll love it."

Lucas stood up and seen Bret pummeling Kurt on the floor. He turned and seen Dreyfus having Marylyn against the wall. He ran over toward them and grabbed Dreyfus by his scraggy hair and threw him down on the ground. Lucas started punching Dreyfus, But Dreyfus counted and smacked Lucas in the face with an open slap.

"You're one tough boy!" Dreyfus said. "Too bad you have to go now and without your women."

Dreyfus walked over toward the downed Lucas and kicked him in the gut. Dreyfus laughed as he walked over toward Marylyn. Lucas pulled out his gun from his side and shot Dreyfus in his right leg. The sound of the gun caused the entire place to echo and suddenly became silent. Kurt looked over and seen Dreyfus holding his leg. He punched Bret and shoved him off and looked toward Lucas, where he seen the gun in his hand. Kurt stood up and ran toward Lucas.

"You shot him!"

Lucas turned and shot Kurt in the chest. Kurt stopped in place as he reached over to his chest and placed both hands above the bullet wound. Lucas walked over toward him and kicked him in the chest, knocking him to the ground. Dreyfus looked and seen Kurt dead on the ground with his hands on his chest. Lucas turned toward Dreyfus.

"Remember now, it's very simple." Lucas said. "We're not leaving this place."

Lucas fired another shot at Dreyfus, going through his head with his blood splattering the wall behind him near Marylyn. Dreyfus' body collapses to the ground. The group looked on and they looked at Lucas who only stared at the two bodies of Dreyfus and Kurt. Curtis rubbed the blood from his lip onto his hand and walked around the bodies.

"We don't have to worry. This place is ours."

DAY 7

The group settled themselves to be calm. Lucas and Bret had taken the bodies of Dreyfus and Kurt to the other side of the warehouse to rot. Marylyn began to worry about how Lucas would behave after killing Dreyfus and Kurt in front of them without any means of hesitation. Bret comforted Jeanette and Curtis continued to bandage the scars on his body from the fight.

"Are you ok, Lucas." Marylyn said. "You haven't said much since you killed those two men."

"There's nothing wrong with me for you to start concerning yourself with my well-being. I did what I had to do to keep all of us safe. Those men made their choices clearly and they were given the warning not to do so."

"So, you're just going to leave their bodies to rot out there in front of this warehouse? Their stench could draw in those corpses out there and they could be on us like hounds."

"No need to worry about that. We took those bodies deep into the woods so those things out there wouldn't get near this place. I will say this again, Marylyn. We're not leaving this place. This is our home now."

"I understand you clearly."

"Thank you for doing that and I appreciate it with much gratitude."

Lucas turned away and began walking up the staircase to the second floor of the building. Marylyn grabbed some of her gear and decided to place it on the second floor where she decided she would dwell in. Bret and Jeanette made the decision to stay on the first floor to keep an extra eye out on anything that might come near the front and back doors.

Curtis had joked around that he would take the third floor and so he had done. He grabbed his backpack and went up to the third floor where he was surrounded by mechanic and engineering tools and some food and supplies left from Dreyfus and Kurt.

"Hey, Lucas. They're some very useful stuff on this floor." Curtis said. "I think you should come up here and see this for yourself.

"I'm coming on up." Lucas said.

Curtis hears the footsteps of Lucas approaching him on the floor. Lucas walked up behind him and looked around the floor, seeing the tools and the supplies of some to little food and a bunch of ammo and three handguns laying down that once belonged to Dreyfus and Kurt.

"First thing is we take those bastards' weapons and food." Lucas said.

"I figured you'll do that from the start."

"Someone has to, and we'll find some sort of way to use these tools for killing those things out there."

Curtis laughed at Lucas' words of choosing. Lucas didn't understand why Curtis was laughing.

"What's funny? What did I say?"

"You said we're going to kill those corpses out there and you didn't realize you said corpses and kill in the exact same sentence."

"They're undead corpses. So, we would have to kill, kill them. If that makes any kind of sense."

"It works for me, Lucas."

"You're taking this floor from what I heard, correct?"

"Yeah. I got this floor. No problems at all."

"I just wanted to make sure everyone knows what floor they are on so there won't be any kind of problems between us."

"No issues coming from me. I got the top floor and I'll do pretty well."

Lucas walked back down to the second floor and noticed the sun setting. He and Marylyn settled on the second floor for the night as Bret and Jeanette took the first floor. Curtis laid on the third floor by himself and fell asleep after eating the chocolate pudding that was left behind by Dreyfus and Kurt.

Later that night, Curtis walked down to the first floor, knowing he had to take a leak, he decided to use the back door to avoid waking up Bret and Jeanette. Curtis went toward the back door and pushed it open. The doors open and Curtis is staring in the eyes of the Dead. About seven of them stare at Curtis and he looked toward them in a solid manner. His body not moving an inch.

"Oh shit." Curtis said.

The Dead lunged at Curtis, taking him down on the ground. Curtis yelled loud enough for the rest of the group to hear. Bret was up and had his gun in hand. He ran toward the yelling and seen Curtis on the group, being eaten alive by the Dead.

"Shit! Shit!" Bret said.

Bret began firing the gun at the Dead, killing them with shots to their heads. Lucas ran in from behind Bret and locked his eyes on Curtis, who was continually being ripped apart by the Dead. Lucas shook his head and pulled out his handgun and walked over toward the Dead and began shooting them one by one.

"This isn't happening to us right now!" Lucas said. "This cannot be happening to us right now!"

Marylyn and Jeanette stood back as they watched the shooting take place. They also noticed Curtis' body on the ground and the large amounts of blood that poured out from his body. After they killed the Dead, Lucas kneeled at Curtis' body. Seeing Curtis is dead, Lucas took his handgun and shot Curtis in the forehead, to avoid him turning into one of the Dead.

"So long, friend."

The group remained quiet for a few minutes before more of the Dead began to approach the warehouse. The group ran and realized that the warehouse would be surrounded within a few more minutes. Lucas had wrestled with the thought of staying at the warehouse, but he knew it would potentially cause more deaths in their group. Lucas told Bret to pack their gear quickly and that they were leaving. Bret and Jeanette had their gear packed up and ready.

"Do we really have to go?!" Marylyn asked.

"I'm sorry, but we have no other option to do. We have to leave this place before we end up like Curtis."

Marylyn had her gear packed. Lucas began packing his and decided to run up the third floor and take some of Curtis' gear along as well. He also grabbed the remaining food, a crowbar, and a wrench. Lucas ran down the stairs and seen more of the Dead coming from the back, appeared to be over a dozen of them in that short time.

"You guys have all of your stuff?!"

"Yeah! We're good to go!" Bret said.

The Dead began to inch closer toward them as they stood in the front and grabbed whatever else was left that they could take along with them. Their moans and footsteps began to send a chill down their spines and fear began to consume the entire group, including Lucas in the situation.

"We have to go now!" Lucas said.

"We're on it!" Bret said.

The group ran out of the warehouse through the front door as over a dozen of the Dead had fully taken over the warehouse in hordes. Lucas decided to take one look back at the warehouse and continued running back into the wilderness where they came before.

"Damn it!" Lucas said.

DAY 8

The group walked constantly through the woods, trying to find any sort of shelter possible while also avoiding the large amounts of Dead that surrounded them from all angles of the wilderness. They're all exhausted from the running they've had to do in order to avoid the Dead from seeing them. Jeanette begins to slow down as she leans against a tree to catch her breath.

"We have to keep moving." Lucas said. "It's necessary that we do so."

"Just let me get a little breather, please." Jeanette said. "That's all I ask."

"Five minutes and we continue on moving."

Bret decided to stay with Jeanette at the tree. Lucas decided to take a small walk to see what was ahead of them. Marylyn stayed behind him as he walked through the bushes.

"Keep yourself ready for any sign of those corpses." Lucas said.

"I'm aware of my surroundings, Lucas."

Lucas moved the bushes from his viewpoint and saw what appeared to be an open field straight ahead of him. He rubbed his eyes and took another look. Lucas sees a schoolyard that is clear of any Dead nearby. He glanced over toward the right and saw the school itself sitting still with no Dead around it.

"There's our place." Lucas said.

Bret and Jeanette catch up with Lucas and Marylyn and they

also see the school and the schoolyard in front of them. Lucas turned toward them and pointed at the school.

"We can take that place and make it ours."

"I don't see any of those things around the school." Bret said. "Let's check it out to see for ourselves if its secure."

"What if some of those things found a way to get inside the school like they did back at the warehouse." Jeanette said. "We should be careful on this one."

"She has a point, Lucas." Marylyn said. "Overall, it's your decision to make."

"We're going in."

They run out of the bushes to avoid the Dead from catching up to them and they begin to jump over the gate to get into the schoolyard. After they jumped the gate, they see a door ahead of them that goes into the school.

"So, what's the plan now?" Bret said. "We just take this place for ourselves?"

"We should check the cafeteria to see if there's any food left over." Lucas said. "It can come in handy for us."

Before they could reach the door, it opened. The group takes a few steps back, but Lucas stands his guard. Coming out of the door is an middle-aged man carrying a shotgun, behind him are two young women and a young man, all of whom carrying weapons ranging from knives to handguns.

"Who are you people and why are you here?" The middle-aged man said.

"We're here to see if this place was secure from those things." Lucas replied. "We don't want any trouble at all."

The middle-aged man looked at the group from their heads to their feet. He placed his eyes back on Lucas.

"None of you were bitten, were you?"

"No bite marks or scratches on us, sir."

The middle-aged man nodded and moved over to the side, allowing Lucas and the group to enter the school. The middle-aged man shut the door and locked it from the inside.

DAY 9

After entering the school, the group decided to look around for anything they could use for survival. They enter what appears to be a large office that might have been used for conference meetings.

"You can just call me the Custodian." the middle-aged man said. "These three are Pratt, Silica, and JiJi."

They greeted the three other survivors and sat with them at one of the conference tables. They looked over to another table and saw the large amount of food sitting on the tables with some bottles of water and soda.

"You may get something to eat and drink if you want." The Custodian said.

"You sure we can?" Bret said. "Only asking to be sure."

"By all means take as much as you can get."

They agreed and began to eat some of the food on the table and took some bottles of water for themselves. Lucas grabbed a bottle of water and approached the middle-aged man.

"I have to thank you for allowing us in this place."

"It's the least I could do. None of you had any bite marks or scratches and it appeared that you all were running nonstop through the woods. The amount of dirt and broken limbs on your clothing pretty much prove that point."

Lucas smiled as he took a sip from the bottled water.

"Been a while since I had a bottle of water."

"That long you say."

"I basically lost count of the days that have gone by since we all took off and left for safety."

"Follow me."

Lucas followed the middle-aged man into the nearby office where he seen a large calendar posted on the wall. The days were marked with an X except for one where it said, "The Dead Arose". Lucas pointed toward it, thinking to himself.

"It's only been that long?"

"Yeah. The outbreak started around six days ago and I've been trying to keep track of it ever since. I figured someone should keep counting the days."

"I can somewhat agree on that."

"Why don't you and your group take the rest of the day to settle up and we can continue on with our discussion tomorrow."

"I would highly appreciate that. Thank you."

"Don't thank me, good sir. Thank yourselves for finding this place and jumping over that fence to get here."

<h1 style="text-align:center">DAY 10</h1>

Right around the start of the next day, Lucas, Bret, and the Custodian decide to go out into the woods to hunt for some deer. Pratt decided to stay with Marylyn, Jeanette, Silica, and JiJi. Outside in the woods, they formed a sort of huddle structure to see all angles of their surroundings.

"I take it you've done this before?" Bret said.

"Back in my day and at my former home, I went out and hunted deer for dinner."

"Free food." Lucas said. "Smart strategy."

"It is. Not having to worry about if I was going to eat the next day or the next week."

"I couldn't do it. I need some fast food in my life to keep going."

"Do you see any fast food around now?"

"No. They're all closed down because of this outbreak. I will tell you that chaos does indeed ruin some things in life that are useful."

"Those fast food places only wanted your money and they surely received it gently."

"You have a point there, sir." Lucas said. "So, how many deer have you encountered in these woods because while we were running through here, we didn't run into any kind of animal."

"The deer sit in the quiet places of the wilderness. It is our duty to seek out those places in order to find them. Once we find them, we'll have them in our sights and soon on our dinner table."

After walking a couple of more feet, the Custodian encounters an adult male deer sitting in the woods eating off the bushes. He smiled and let out a small laugh.

"There's our food right there. Look at that thing of beauty."

"How can we catch that thing in a time like this when those things are running loose out here?" Bret said.

"Simple."

The custodian kneeled and moved a bag over to his side and revealed a bow and a pair of wooden arrows. He raised it up as he looked toward Bret.

"Bow and arrow, buddy. Useful for quiet kills and quick takedowns, if used correctly."

The Custodian placed one of the wooden arrows bow onto the bow and aimed closely toward the deer. He stayed quiet and so do both Lucas and Bret.

"I got this one." The Custodian said.

He released the bow and the arrow flew through the woods. The arrow hit the deer in the neck, piercing its hide. The deer moved around before falling onto its side. The Custodian smiled as he placed the bow onto his back and moved the arrow set.

"We got our kill."

Back at the school, Pratt seemed a bit uncomfortable being the only man in the room with four women. He found himself attracted toward Jeanette and he approached her. She glanced at him and he gave off a small smile.

"I don't know what you're doing, but its best if you stop." Jeanette said.

"Why should I stop."

Pratt placed his hand on Jeanette's shoulders and started moving his hand lower onto her breast and even lower onto her jeans. Jeanette grabbed his hand and placed it on his head. Pratt gave off a small sigh.

"I'm sorry, but Bret is my boyfriend."

"Oh, well then I truly apologize for my act of seduction toward you. I meant no harm."

Jeanette looked over toward Marylyn, who sat at the table reading a book. She looked over in the corner to see Silica and JiJi kissing each other passionately and shoving each other on the wall and back in the corner.

"I see why you're not with one of them."

"Yeah. You know why I made the moves on you. They should take that in the other office or classroom. I mean we're in a school after all."

Lucas, Bret, and the Custodian return to the school with the deer in their possession. Pratt smiled as he looked at the deer's body. Rubbing his hands together.

"Look at how much meat we have stocked up just with this one buck."

"Don't get too carried away, Pratt." The Custodian said. "We still have to skin it and do the other assumptions."

"You're right there and I will offer my hand in helping."

"Well, thank you."

DAY 11

The group ate the deer and had most of the deer meat left over to later consumption. Lucas and Marylyn sat in the other office to talk amongst themselves. The rest of the group stayed in the main office and talked among themselves.

"What do you think of this place?" Marylyn said.

"What do you mean?"

"I mean how do you feel about this place and about these new people?"

"They're good people and this place is starting to seem like our official stopping point."

"You're sure about that?"

"The whole school and the schoolyard are completely gated, and those things can't climb over the gates, otherwise they'll just pierce themselves on the top. Luckily none of us did."

Marylyn nodded and smiled. Lucas smiled also.

"I see your point there, Lucas."

"All you need to worry about is being safe and having me at your side. That's all that should be on your mind."

"We can't try our relationship in this new world. It just doesn't appear right to me."

"Don't worry about that. Once we're officially set up in a place, like this, we can discuss all of that."

"Ok"

Lucas leaned over and hugged Marylyn. She held him tightly

as they both smiled over each other's shoulders.

DAY 12

Everybody sat in the main conference room and spoke with each other. Lucas and the Custodian made it official to everyone that they're officially staying at the school to live in and start a new life if possible.

"We're going to try this place out and see if it works to our advantage." Lucas said. "So, as of this day, we should at least have a small celebration for finding a safe haven and living this long in this apocalyptic time we currently dwell in."

"So, we shall." Pratt said. "To survival."

"TO SURVIVAL." Everyone said as they took a toast and drank the soda.

Everyone continued to talk, and they even had a small party amongst themselves. Lucas sat with Marylyn to discuss plans of their relationship. Bret and Jeanette decided to take one of the classrooms not far from the conference room for themselves to live in. Pratt stayed in the other office drinking cups of soda, and Silica and JiJi stayed in one of the nearby classrooms enjoying one another.

They continued to party for most of the day till nightfall and they still partied. Most of the group fell asleep except for Lucas, who was plotting out ideas as to how to kill the Dead with new techniques.

"This is only a plan in progress, and I will remember that." Lucas said.

In the woods behind the school, one of the gates have been

knocked down by what seemed to be a tree. Cracking sounds are heard as the Dead begin to slowly enter the schoolyard. After three head through, seven walked through. After seven walked through nine walked through and the entire field was covered with the Dead all moaning and sliding their feet through the grass. One of the school's back doors is unlocked and one of the Dead rammed his head through the door, opening it slightly. Shoving against the door and walked through, allowing more of the Dead to enter the school without anyone realizing it.

DAY 13

A loud screech is heard as the group run to a nearby classroom and see Silica and JiJi being attacked and ripped apart by the Dead. Lucas screamed for everyone to grab their stuff and head out. The Custodian grabbed his shotgun.

"What are you doing?!" Lucas said.

"I'm clearing a way out of here and I can do that with this baby here."

The Custodian began firing at the Dead, but more seemed to appear. He continued firing as the rest of the group grabbed their stuff and began to head out. Bret opened the door leading out into the schoolyard and seen it to be overloaded with the Dead. The Dead lunged at Bret, ripping his neck apart. Jeanette screamed as she tried to pull Bret from the morbid hands of the Dead. More of the Dead came up behind Jeanette and started biting her on her head, neck, back, and legs. She went down screaming next to Bret as the Dead ate them both alive.

"We have to go!" Lucas yelled. "NOW!"

"You go!" the Custodian said. "I'll hold them off!"

"They'll kill you!" Pratt said.

"Just go."

Lucas, Marylyn, and Pratt ran out of the school and onto the other side facing the gate. They jumped over the gates as they can hear the shotgun going off several times before it went silent. They knew them that the Custodian was dead. While running, Lucas stumbled upon a vehicle that sat in the yard. He ran toward it and found it was unlocked.

"Get in here!" Lucas said.

They threw their bags in the car and they entered the vehicle. Lucas noticed that they couldn't find the key. Lucas looked around the car and couldn't find the key as the Dead inched closer toward the car.

"Come on!" Marylyn said.

"Where the hell is the damn key?!" Pratt panicked. "We're about to become breakfast for those biters!"

"Not if you stop screaming."

"Sure. We'll just be a pair of flesh omelets for them. All in different shapes and sizes to enjoy a wonderful meal."

Lucas checked underneath the seat and found the key. He kissed it and placed it in the ignition. The car starts and Lucas see it apparently has a full tank of gas.

"We're out of here." Lucas said.

He slammed his foot on the pedal and the car drove off, ramming the Dead that were in front of it. Lucas turned onto the road and drove off, leaving the school behind him as he took a glance in his rear-view mirror.

SYMBOLUM VENATORES
THE GABRIEL KANE COLLECTION
THE RISE OF THE MUMMY'S TOMB

1863
EGYPT EYALET

It is the beginning of summer as the Monster Hunter and Ufologist, Gabriel Kane travels to Cairo, Egypt by ship to investigate the Pyramids of Giza and the ancient tombs of the old leaders. He also seeks on discovering if extraterrestrials had any part in the construction of the pyramids and had any influence on the pharaohs of old. Even though it is at risk from the ruling Ottoman Empire.

Upon arriving in Cairo, Kane, wearing a brown hat and trench coat, he searches for a camel to use in order to gain access toward the location of the pyramids. He ends up finding a man who is selling camels and he approaches him.

"Camel will cost you." The Camel seller said.

"I know. How much for the camel?"

"I personally accept gold or silver."

Kane smiled as he pulled out five shekels of gold and three shekels of silver from his coat pocket. The facial expression of the Camel Seller changed in an instant, showing excitement and shock.

"That will do, my good sir. That will do."

The Camel Seller accepted the shekels of gold and silver from Kane and gave him the camel. Kane mounted onto the camel and set his sights toward the pyramids that were in his eyesight within a distance.

"Move it." Kane said to the camel.

The camel began to move as Kane kept his eyes of the pyramids.

Kane continued his movement toward the pyramids as night immediately approached and covered him along with the landscape.

Kane decides to stop and allow the camel and himself some rest before arriving at the pyramids, which are within a three to six-mile radius of his location.

Waking up along with the sunrise, Kane mounted back onto the camel and moved along closer to the pyramids. Kane raises his head upon entering El Giza, seeing the Great Sphinx in the horizon as he approaches the Pyramids of Giza themselves. Astonishing in some form by their height and size, he began to wonder how the structures were built and how much strength was needed to complete a task of that size.

Kane mounts off the camel and begins his investigation on searching and studying each of the three pyramids. He begins with the smallest one, known as the Pyramid of Menkaure. Already with the knowledge of the pyramids as tombs for the pharaohs, Kane searched the smallest one for any details concerning extraterrestrials either involved with the building or with the pharaohs themselves.

"I understand and know of the legend of Herodotus." Kane said. "Believing how Menkaure was more of a benevolent Pharaoh than the ones that came before. So, it may be."

Kane entered the mortuary temple of the pyramid and discovered how the foundations of the inside were made of limestone. Kane glanced down at the floor and realized they were made from granite and had granite facing surrounding him by way of the walls.

"Judging by the minerals it took to build this thing, this must have taken a long time to complete and this is just the interior."

Kane looked and seen what appeared to be an inscription in the temple. Kane stared at it while deciphering the language. After deciphering, Kane understood the inscription stated that the temple was made as a monument for the Pharaoh's father, who was the king of upper and lower Egypt. While inside, Kane also discovered carved images of the old kingdom and understood it due to its high presence of evident details it held.

Kane continued his search of the Menkaure pyramid, before deciding that he should search the other two before the next nightfall. Kane continued his search with only a little water to drink and hardly ate anything before his investigation of the pyramids. Kane finished his search of the Menkaure pyramid. He set his sight on the second pyramid, known as the Pyramid of Khafre or Pyramid of Chephren. The second tallest of the three pyramids. Khafre is the tomb of the fourth dynasty pharaoh Khafre, who had ruled from the time of 2558 till 2532 BC.

The Khafre pyramid has the length of two hundred and fifteen point five meters leading to seven hundred and six feet. The rising height of the pyramid went from one hundred and thirty-four point four meters, equaling four hundred and forty-eight feet in height.

"Amazing are these structures."

Kane had understood that the pyramid may have been robbed ages ago and decided to head straight toward the burial chamber of the pyramid. Kane had questioned if the pyramid possessed two locations of entry, but he never figured it out to be exact. He continued walking until he had entered the subsidiary chamber. Which had opened from the west of the lower passage. Kane believes the chamber was used to store precious items that belonged to the pharaoh or anyone close to him. The passage above appeared to be made in a clad of granite, which descended into a horizontal passage that lead Kane straight toward the burial chamber. Kane followed the passage directly.

Kane found himself standing inside the burial chamber. Kane looked at the size of the chamber and noticed it was carved from the bedrock through a pit. The roof of the chamber was constructed of limestone beams that appeared to have been gabled. Kane saw how the chamber had a rectangular shape and stared at the sarcophagus of Khafre. Seeing how his coffin was carved out of complete block of solid granite and how it had sunk into the floor. Kane looked down closer to the sarcophagus and seen what appeared to be small animal bones laying close to the coffin.

"Animal bones. Hmm."

Kane looked around and decided to leave the Khafre pyramid and to finally search the third pyramid, the largest of the three and the most known one of the three pyramids. Kane exited the Khafre pyramid as he stared at the Great Pyramid of Giza, also known as the Pyramid of Khufu or the Pyramid of Cheops. The Great Pyramid is the oldest of the pyramids in the Necropolis Giza area.

Kane searched the three known chambers of the pyramid. Going through the three of them in the amount of time he had left until sundown. The lowest chamber appeared to be cut from bedrock and laid where the pyramid was built, however left unfinished. The second and third chamber were the King's and Queen's chamber. Kane noticed that the pyramid was the only one to possess ascending and descending passages. The three smaller pyramids near the Pyramid of Khufu appeared to have belonged to his wives.

While searching, a loud bang had sounded from the outside, gaining Kane's attention, he rushed out of the pyramid to the outside to see what caused the loud noise. Kane had exited the pyramid and found himself standing in the presence of an ancient Egyptian army with a living mummy in front of them.

"What is this?" Kane said.

Kane continued to stare at the Egyptian army and the living mummy that apparently led them. Kane slowly reached for his pistols on his side until the mummy took a step forward in front of him.

"Who are you and how are you even alive?" Kane said.

The mummy spoke in Egyptian and Kane could understand the ancient language the mummy had spoken. Kane gripped his pistols tightly, waiting for the mummy to strike with his army.

"You are Akhenaten." Kane said. "If that is the case, then why are you over here?"

"I am here to tell you to leave this land before the curse falls upon you and those that will follow you in the future."

"What curse will follow me into the future?"

"It appears as if you lack spirit and do not seek to understand the curses that dwell in this land. The curses that those before you in times past felt, the plagues that ran their course on this land and the curses of the ancestors that lived here in times past."

"You won't be able to fool me, Akhenaten. The curses will not affect me in any way because I know what is going on around here."

"Be that as it may, stranger. But I warn you to leave this land at once."

"So, I take it that this curse of a mummy's tomb is your doing.

You're the mummy that folks say has risen several times and placed curses on those who entered this land in search of knowledge."

"I warn you to leave. This is your final warning, stranger."

"I won't leave." Kane said as he fired his pistols toward Akhenaten and his army.

Akhenaten didn't make a flinch as the bullet flew past him without any harm. Kane continued to fire before placing the pistols back in their holsters as he pulled out his sword and ran toward Akhenaten. Akhenaten placed his left hand in front of Kane, shoving him back a few feet as lights shined down from the sky. Kane partially covered his eyes to see where the lights were coming from and seen three unidentified flying objects in disk shapes, hovering over the three pyramids of Giza.

"What is this?" Kane said. "The flying disks."

The sun had set, and the moonlight shined down upon the area. Kane looked above the disk and noticed the pyramids were in the exact alignment with Orion's belt in space.

"Interesting placement they did."

Kane turned to see Akhenaten, but he and his army had vanished without any noise being sounded. Kane turned back to the three flying disks as they began to levitate higher in the air and leave at warp speed. The sky was clear of the disks and silence filled the area. Kane nodded with his hat and turned away, seeing his camel still sitting in the same location as he left it. Kane makes the decision to leave the area as his theory had presented itself before him in the form of Akhenaten and the three flying disks.

THE UFO CRASH OF 1863

NOVEMBER 28 1863
AMERICAN CIVIL WAR

During the night, something mysterious in the sky is falling towards the ground. As it falls, it glows a reddish-green color and coming down faster and faster. It slams into the ground and is stuck there. The next day, Confederate soldiers discover the crash and take the object to one of their bases. Their leader, Robert E. Lee confirms that it was only a bombing accident but didn't tell them the description of the object. He commands his soldiers to take the object in their possession and to keep it highly secret.

On a ship, heading towards the United States, is Gabriel Kane. A monster hunter and ufologist. Kane is a man in his early twenties. Twenty-Three exactly. He's lean and gloomy, somewhat somber-looking at times for his age. His skin appears pale with his cold eyes. His face is shadowed by his hat. He is dressed entirely in black and is equipped with a weaponry that features a rapier, a dagger, a cutlass, a saber, and a pair of flintlock pistols.

He arrives in the United States to discover the crash site. As he travels across the northern lands, he runs into a group of confederate soldiers, who are weary of his presence.

"Identify yourself, sir." One soldier said.

"I am Gabriel Kane. Monster hunter and ufologist from Europe." Kane said. "I am here to visit the area of which an object crashed."

"There was no crashed object." The soldier said. "I believe you've been given wrong information. Now, return to your home."

"I don't live here." Kane said. "I came across the Ethiopic Ocean on ship. I heard directly that something fell from the sky around this area. So, that's why I'm here and my information is never wrong."

"This time it is." Another soldier said. "Now, leave this area at once, boy."

"Just tell me where the location is." Kane said.

One of the soldiers smacked Kane in the face with the butt of his rifle. Kane's head turned quickly before he wipes the blood off his mouth and turns to the soldiers, smirking.

"If that's how you want to play it." Kane said.

Kane kicked the soldier and knocked him to the ground. He looked toward the other two soldiers standing by, who ran toward him, Kane fired at them with his flintlock pistols.

Kane defeated the soldiers and continued looking for the crash site. As he continues searching the woods, he sees tracks on the ground in front of him. Kane walks over to the site and kneels, tracking the snow around the area. He looked up and spots something buried in the snow. He walks over and wipes the snow from it. It's a metallic object, a small, but heavy piece. Kane picks the object up and examines it. With his confused expression he says that this object appears not to be man-made. He puts the object in a small bag and continues walking toward the nearest town, just a few miles north.

Kane sees the town in front of him, surrounded with a few wooden buildings. He enters the town and sees the Union soldiers. Kane walks up to one of the soldiers and get his attention.

"Excuse me, but do you have any idea about the crashed object?" Kane asked.

"I'm sorry, sir. Who exactly are you?" The soldier asked.

"I am Gabriel Kane. I am a visitor from Europe."

"From Europe." The soldier said. "Why would you be in a place like this, especially during these times."

"I don't understand what you're talking about." Kane said.

"As of right now, we're in a civil war. North versus South." The soldier said. "See, me and the others you see around here are Union soldiers, the north. While the men in red are the Confederate, the south."

Another soldier in the distance calls out to the soldier speaking with Kane. He looks and tells Kane that he should look out for himself and that he might have to choose a side if he decides to stay a little longer. Kane looks on as the soldiers leave the town, heading into the forest. Kane walks through the town, looking at the buildings and certain areas. He sees both soldiers and civilians throughout the town. He decides to buy a map of the area and he looks through it. Going through the forest and heading to Adams County. Kane leaves the town and heads back into the forest, following the map.

Kane arrives west of the woods and discovers a frontier, surrounded and occupied by Confederate soldiers. Kane smiles at the sight of them, as if they're just targets to be taken down. Kane hides in the bushes to avoid any contact with the soldiers. He looks to his right and sees a group of them carrying an object of a large size, the object is covered with a blanket of sorts. The soldiers take the object into the large building in the middle of the frontier. Kane decides to sneak into the frontier, passing by soldiers swiftly. As he moves faster, he runs into a soldier.

"Who are you?" The soldier said.

The soldier took Kane's hat off and slammed it. Kane raised up and looked at the soldier. From behind Kane, more soldiers appear and eventually surround him. Kane notices that the soldiers are seriously hiding something due to their level of secrecy of hiding in the forest. The soldiers grab Kane and take him to the head center of the frontier. Inside the center building, sits Jefferson Davis. Davis sees the soldiers bringing in Kane.

"What are you doing?" Davis asked.

"We found him sneaking into the frontier, sir." The soldier said. "We caught him just in time."

The soldiers hold Kane in the center, facing Davis. Kane looks at Davis.

"What is your name?" Davis asked.

"My name is Gabriel Kane." Kane said. "I'm only here to investigate the crash that occurred in the woods."

"There was no crash." Davis said. "It was only an accident that happened out there. What could possibly crash?"

"There had to be a crash." Kane said. "I saw tracks and I found debris."

Davis stared deeply toward Kane. Staring him in his eyes with a slight confusion in his face."

"Debris? Of what?"

The soldiers let Kane go as he reached into his pocket, showing Davis the metallic piece that he found. Davis' face expression changes drastically, showing a sign of nervousness, along with an expression of anger.

"I found this piece in the woods, right around the crash site." Kane said. "The object was here in this spot."

"Ah! This doesn't prove anything!" Davis yelled. "Take him away."

The soldiers grabbed Kane by his coat and dragged him out. Once they reached the outside, Kane head butted the soldier and kicked the other one in the gut. Kane ran off into the forest as the soldiers began firing at him. Kane entered the forest and the soldiers run after him. Kane continues to run deeper into the forest as the soldiers track him by his footprints in the snow. As the soldiers follow the tracks, Kane turned left of the forest, his footprints disappear since there's little snow in the area. Kane continues moving and the soldiers lose tracks of the footprints.

"He couldn't have gone far." One soldier said.

The soldiers turn back and return to the frontier. Kane has now entered a complete grassy area, with only little snow. The sun shined down on him, as his hat have given him shade. As Kane continues walking, he looks at his map for the surrounding areas.

"Where am I?" Kane said, looking at the map. "What is this location?"

He looks at the grassy locations, not seeing nor hearing a single sign of life anywhere close. As he continues to walk forward, he spots a group of soldiers, wearing blue uniforms on horsebacks. Some are walking behind them. Kane stops and stands still as the leader of the Union soldiers comes toward him on his horse.

"Who are you, sir?" Kane asked.

"I am Abraham Lincoln." he said. "The President of The United States."

Kane is taken along with Abraham Lincoln and a group of Union soldiers to their frontier. Upon arriving at the frontier, Kane looked around the location, scouting the area for any sign of Confederate soldiers. Lincoln signaled to Kane to follow him inside the frontier. Kane followed him into the frontier.

While entering the frontier, Lincoln sat at a table and waved his arm toward the other seat which faced him. Kane looked and wondered.

"Please sit." Lincoln said. "We can talk right here."

Kane sat down at the table, facing Lincoln. Other Union soldiers walked in and out of the frontier. Many of them stayed outside guarding the location. Lincoln signaled the nearby soldiers in the frontier to stand guard outside, leaving him and Kane alone inside to discuss what's taken place. The soldiers exited the frontier leaving Kane and Lincoln inside at the table. Lincoln offered Kane some water and he took the cup. Both drank the water before speaking to each other.

"If I may ask, Mr. Kane. What were you doing out there?"

"I was running from some Confederate soldiers, sir. They were chasing me until I ran into you and your soldiers."

"When we found you out there, we didn't see any Confederate colors wandering about. So, why were they chasing you if I may ask?"

"I'm a resident from Europe. I came over here to investigate a crashed object that fell near this location. When I was searching for the object, the Confederate soldiers took me in and claimed that no object crashed, but I found evidence that goes against their words."

"Where is this evidence that you speak of? Do you possess it on you at this very moment?"

"I do."

Kane reached into his coat pocket and pulled out the metallic-like object. He handed over to Lincoln, who looked at it and rubbed his chin, questioning himself about the object. He handed back over to Kane, who placed it back into his pocket.

"I've never seen a texture like that in my lifetime. You believe the crashed object was made of that material?"

"Yes sir. I found this little fragment at the crash site. I didn't find the whole object. Someone took it and has hidden it from the eyes of many."

"I take it you believe the Confederate took the object and has hidden it from the people and mainly the Union. Might they believe the object could give them some form of extra help in this war that's taking place?"

"Whatever the case may be, sir. The object is not something to be toyed with. It possesses power of unspeakable energy. Energy that this world has yet to study and figure out."

Lincoln nodded while lying back in the chair. He took another sip of water from his cup and looked over at the door, seeing the soldiers walking about and keeping guard. He raised himself up from the chair closer to the table. He lies his arms across the table.

"I figure that you align with us and we can find this object you're speaking of. That way we will know for sure if the Confederates have taken it and are planning to use it for their own personal gain against us and the North. What do you say to that, Mr. Kane?"

Kane sat quietly, thinking to himself. He looked toward Lincoln and extended his hand. Lincoln extended his and both shook on the agreement.

"So, where do we head toward to find this object?" Lincoln said.

"We'll have to enter their domains. The only way to be sure about the whole situation."

"It's a fair start."

At a Confederate frontier, Jefferson Davis speaks with other Confederate soldiers about Kane's whereabouts. He questioned them on where he could have run off to and if he was a spy sent by the Union and Lincoln. The soldiers declined the statement and said he was only a man looking for the object. Davis walked out of the frontier and looked around the location. Giving himself some air from the inside.

"For goodness sake. We must find that man. By any cost."

Kane stood outside the frontier along with Abraham Lincoln discussing way of entering the Confederate frontiers. Lincoln gathered some soldiers to accompany them on their investigation. Gathering the soldiers, Lincoln considered the possible cost of having his men die because of a alien craft being hidden.

"I truly hope there's a craft." Lincoln said.

"There is a craft and you'll see it for yourself when we get to the destination."

"I believe your word, Mr. Kane."

Kane and Lincoln gather their supplies and head out for the Confederate base where the spacecraft is hidden. The Union soldiers follow them with their rifles in hand.

Upon leaving the base early on, Davis and a group of Confederate soldiers find a Union army base and immediately attack. Davis yells out orders to destroy anything and anyone they find within the base. The Confederate soldiers ransacked the base, destroying all that sits in the base. After the search, no Union soldiers are found by Davis and his Confederates.

"You cannot tell me that we've been made fools of." Davis said. "Where are they? Where could Lincoln be?"

Traveling a few miles from their base, Kane and Lincoln see a Confederate base in front. Kane sights no sign of Confederate soldiers nearby. He points out toward the base as Lincoln looks ahead.

"I see no bodies around the area." Kane said. "Shall we enter in?"

"Be cautious I warn." Lincoln said. "We don't know if this is a trap played by Davis and the Confederates."

They approach the Confederate base slowly, hiding behind the snow-covered trees and bushes to avoid possible sight. Kane looks around and sees no one, the area is as quiet to the point where only bird could be heard or the falling snow from the trees.

"This place is abandoned." Kane said. "We have our opportunity here, Mr. Lincoln."

"Where would they keep this craft, you speak of?"

Kane sees a large settlement ahead that sits near the back of the base. He points toward it.

"That's where it would be."

Kane mounts off the horse and runs toward the large settlement as Lincoln follows him and commands the Union soldiers to keep watch of the area in case Confederates appear to enter. Kane reaches the settlement and enters it and Lincoln looks around at the base before entering the settlement himself. Once they both entered, their eyes were locked on the craft, which sat on the ground in the middle of the settlement.

"This is it." Kane said. "This is the craft that fell from the sky."

"You were speaking the truth, Mr. Kane." Lincoln said. "Now I can see you're a man of your word and a loyal one."

"Don't give too much credit ahead of the victory."

Kane walks over to the craft and examines the encryptions and designs that are carved on the craft's surface and understands that it is an alien spacecraft. He pulls out his notes from his coat pocket and compares the drawings to the carved images on the craft. He sees that they are one in the same.

"This is an alien spacecraft indeed." Kane said. "There's more to the universe than what we know."

Kane and Lincoln immediately hear shots fired from the outside. They rush to see what's taking place and discover the Union soldiers firing at the Confederates that have appeared to the base. Lincoln looks ahead toward the entrance of the base and sees Davis with them.

"Men, we must leave at once!" Lincoln said. "We'll take this battle out into an open field!"

"You're planning on ending this now." Kane said.

"You don't have to stay with us any longer, Mr. Kane. You'll already found what you've been looking for and now you can continue on with your journey into the mysterious."

"No. You helped me and now I must aid you in your war against Davis and the Confederates."

Lincoln nods.

"Let's leave now!" Lincoln said.

The Union soldiers begin to leave the Confederate base. Davis shoves soldiers aside and sees Kane with Lincoln. He points toward them with anger in his eyes.

"There's that adventurer! He's traveling alongside Lincoln! I knew he was a Union soldier to begin with!"

The Union soldiers leave the base. Davis moves quickly to see where they're heading, and he spots an open field in front of them. He looks to his Confederate soldiers and hands them more rifles.

"We head toward that open field and we eliminate these Union soldiers for good and we take down Lincoln and this adventurer!"

The Confederate soldiers cheer as Davis leads them toward the open field. Kane looks back and sees Davis and the Confederates coming behind them near the field. He gets Lincoln's attention and points. Lincoln looks back and sees Davis coming. He smiles.

"Let them come and let them die."

Kane stands with Lincoln and the Union soldiers in the snow-covered field awaiting Davis and his Confederate soldiers to appear before them. The Union soldiers are ready for combat just as Kane and Lincoln are. In front they see Davis approaching and the Confederates at his back. Lincoln points out at Davis.

"This is the moment where this civil war will end." Lincoln said. "No more bloodshed upon this land amongst Americans battling Americans."

"Let's go ahead and finish this, Mr. Lincoln." Kane said.

The Union soldiers are ready as Davis and the Confederates face them. Both the Union and Confederate are opposing each other in the open field as it snows down above them. Davis smirks at Lincoln and Kane.

"I see you have the adventurer at your side, Abraham."

"I do and he is keen to do his work and move on from this."

"This is not his war. Its ours. The North versus The South. Nothing More. Union or Confederate and he made his decision to become a Union fool."

"We didn't want this war between us, yet you've asked for it and now you have it. For right here, it ends for good and there's no reason to continue this bloodshed on this land amongst Americans."

"Enough of your words, Lincoln. Let's get to the bloodshed."

"Suit yourself, Jefferson Davis of the Confederate."

The Confederate soldiers quickly run toward the Union, which do the same as Lincoln and Davis stand behind and watch the two armies run to each other in battle. Kane stares at Davis and glances at the armies battling it out amongst each other.

Shots are being fired and some are stabbed to death with blades. Davis looks at Kane and points at him. Kane spots Davis pointing and decides to approach him. Lincoln stops Kane as he walks toward Davis.

"What is it?" Kane said.

"Do not kill Davis. He's lost within his mind."

Davis looks ahead at Kane and Lincoln and laughs.

"Why are you holding the man back, Abraham? Afraid that he'll fail before you and give the Union a bad name on your expense?"

Lincoln looks at Kane. Concerned, yet trustworthy.

"Be careful."

Kane begins to approach Davis until the sky lights up above them and the battling armies. Kane looks up, holding his arm up to avoid the blinding light from above. What Kane sees is an alien spacecraft above the battlefield. Lincoln and Davis also spot the craft above them. Both are afraid, fear settling in their hearts at the sight of the large object.

"Oh my." Davis said. "It is real."

"What is it doing, Kane?" Lincoln said. "Why is it just sitting above us?"

"I do not know."

The craft begins to charge up as the sound of its engine begins to roar. Kane decides to get away from the battlefield. He pulls Lincoln alongside him.

"What are you doing, Kane?!"

"We have to get away from this area immediately! The craft is about to shoot down at us!"

Davis continues to stare at the craft, seeing its energy forming from beneath it. He is astonished at what he sees.

"Oh, how you can aid us in this war. The possibilities are endless."

The craft shoots down a beam of energy on the battlefield, separating the remaining Union and Confederate soldiers. Kane and Lincoln are behind a set of trees to avoid the blast. Davis is knocked to the ground at the impact of the beam. Kane looks up and sees the craft take off into the sky and it vanishes. The area is now quiet with a large burnt circle in the battlefield with melted and burned snow.

A few days later, Lincoln announces the civil war is still ongoing and the Union soldiers are preparing for more battles against Davis and the Confederates. Kane has taken the crashed craft with him on a ship as he returns to Europe to study the craft even more so than he could within the woods of a civil war going country.

THE UNDEAD AND THE EXTRATERRESTRIALS

1866
FEUDAL JAPAN

Three years after The UFO Crash of 1863, Monster Hunter and Ufologist, Gabriel Kane has now taken a trip to Japan to study of the ancient Japanese history and its culture. Now, during the final years of Feudal Japan. Kane is highly aware of its history and looks to discover more about it.

Kane, now twenty-six, three years after his involvement with the American Civil War, has learned a lot more about his occupation as a monster hunter and ufologist. Kane, wearing what appears to be a grayish-white trench coat and hat, with red Japanese markings on the coat, arrives at a small museum in downtown Edo. Inside the museum are dozens of artifacts containing amounts of history about Japan and the early years of Feudal Japan. Kane looks at one book and reads about its history.

"A very interesting history here." Kane said as he looked through the book.

Kane continues to look through the book and the museums, loud screams are heard from the outside of the museum. Kane, quickly turns and runs outside. Once outside, Kane sees a swarm of zombies. The zombies appear to be wearing ancient Japanese armor and gear. The zombies turn to Kane and run after him. Kane pulls out a sword and runs through the zombies, slicing them apart. As he slices through them, they spew out a liquid which is glowing green. One of the last zombies runs toward Kane, Kane moves toward the right and slices the head off the zombie's body.

After fighting off the zombies that surrounded the area, Kane kneels and examines the green liquid. As he gathers some in a small container for experimentation. Once, he stands up the Shogun military arrive. They stare at Kane, knowing that he's a foreigner. They walk over to him, speaking in Japanese.

"You are to come with us, sir." One soldier said.

"Very well." Kane said. "If you suggest it."

Kane holds his hands out as the soldiers handcuff him and take him onto their carriage back to their base.

Once they arrive at their base, they bring Kane, who's blindfolded, into a sort of interrogation room. They sit him down in a wooden chair and leave the room. Kane listens to see if anyone is inside the room. Hearing no sounds, he finds a way to take off the blindfold and looks around at the room. The room is completely covered with Japanese art from each wall. The room resembles a samurai dojo room to an extent. Kane looks behind him and sees the brown wooden double doors.

"Would like to speak with someone, please." Kane said, speaking in Japanese. "Anybody around here who I can speak with?"

Kane hears the double doors open, a Japanese man, wearing a white robe walks into the room with two Shogun soldiers. They stand on both sides of Kane as he looks in front of him, seeing the Japanese man.

"Do you really believe your staring will frighten me?" Kane said to the man. "I've come across worse."

The Japanese man stands silently while staring at Kane.

"For starters, where am I?" Kane said.

The Japanese man walks closer to Kane. Kane looks up at the man, seeing hardly any emotion in the man's face.

"You, sir, are in Edo Castle.' The man said.

Kane pauses as he begins to think. He looks at the man, startled.

"If we're in the Edo Castle, that makes you the Shogun." Kane said. "You're the military dictator of Japan."

"I am Shogun Yoshinobu." The man said, "The seventh son of

Tokugawa Nariaki, daimyo of Mito."

"So, you're the current Shogun." Kane said. "But you said you'll never step foot in this castle nor Edo if you were Shogun. Why are you here?"

"I had to break my vow because of your troubles." Yoshinobu said. "For that reason, you must pay gravely and by gravely, I mean dreadfully."

Kane tries to break free of the ropes tied to his hands. Yoshinobu walks around him, quietly.

"You destroyed our test drill and that is why you must pay with your life.' Yoshinobu said. 'You've come into my country and disturb my governance.'

Kane continues to sit in the chair with his hands tied together behind his back as Shogun Yoshinobu walks around him in circles and later sits in front of Kane. Yoshinobu stares in the eyes of Kane, who does the exact same.

"Why don't you just kill me while I'm here." Kane said. "Because you know, I'll be out of here immediately within seconds."

"Your courage doesn't frighten me." Yoshinobu said. "Though my creations will certainly frighten you."

"Don't even bother trying to have your inventions to frighten me." Kane said. "Like I said, I've seen much worse."

Yoshinobu stood up.

"We know who you are, boy." Yoshinobu said. "You're Gabriel Kane, that monster hunter, ufologist man."

Kane stares at Yoshinobu.

"How would you have known?" Kane said.

"We've heard about your tale of being abducted by higher beings." Yoshinobu said. "We even heard about your tale in the Americas."

"So, I'm sure you know how that ended." Kane said.

"It doesn't matter how it ended." Yoshinobu said. "What matters is why are you in Japan to begin with."

"I was only here to study to country's history, nothing more." Kane said. "Why else would I be in Japan."

"Why did you destroy our Shogun undead?' Yoshinobu said.

"Excuse me?" Kane said. "What do you mean by your Shogun undead? You created those things?"

"We have such objects that can do a lot of things." Yoshinobu said. "We created them for a future military run. Today's event was only a test run, which your actions came along and destroyed them."

"You have no reason for creating zombies." Kane said. "What more could they do for you or your military."

"We can do so much more for our military." Yoshinobu said. "We've been doing very much so."

"I hope you and your country are enjoying your time in the sun. Because as soon as I get out of here, I'm exposing your plot and your reign will fall."

Yoshinobu smirked and began walking towards the door.

"We'll see about that, Mr. Kane. If you can escape this room anyway."

Yoshinobu leaves the room and locked the door. Kane turned his head towards the door behind him. He begins to move his arms around to let them loose. After moving left and right, he releases his left arm and lowers it towards his left leg. Reaching into his boot, he pulled out a blade and cut the rope from his arms and legs. Kane stands up and walked to the door. He tried to open it, though the door wouldn't bulge. Kane shoves his shoulder into the door three times. The door does not even move. Kane decides to pull out a small sharp knife from his coat pocket and jams it into the crack of the door. After shoving it through, the door opened as Kane jumped out of the room. He sees he's in a hallway covered with red, green, and white Japanese art and paintings.

"Which way should I go?" Kane said.

Kane chooses to head left in the hallway, passing by closed doors that could be a room like the interrogation room he was previously locked into. He turned down the hallway and quickly stopped as he seen two soldiers guarding a gate that leads into the other side of the castle. Kane slowly slips through the guards and finds himself entering the Shogun army base. He scans the interior of the base, noticing all the army's weapons and armor. Passing by one of the tables of weapons, he discovers two circular blades that look like two shrunken. He sees they have handles on the back as he pulled them, the blades quickly turn with a loud buzzing sound. Kane releases the handles and smiles.

"What a great invention."

Kane takes the blades and looked forward, seeing another door. He opened the door and sees numerous dead Shogun soldiers laying on beds and laboratory tables. Kane scans the bodies and notice their veins are glowing a greenish color. Kane's eyes squint as if he's seen the liquid before. He looks on the right side of the room, seeing a blanket covering a large object. Kane yanked the cover sheet off the object, revealing it.

"It makes sense now." Kane said. "Perfect sense."

Kane paused as he stared at a destroyed and somewhat damaged alien spacecraft. He walked over to touch the object but notices the green liquid that surrounds it. He backed up and looked at the bodies again, doing the math in his head, he realizes that the spacecraft liquid was used on dead soldiers to resurrect them as zombies. Kane searches the room to find a way to release the ship from its connection to the wall as its pumping the liquid into the dozen bodies of soldiers.

"How do I release this object from this wall?"

Kane reached to his right side and pulled out his sword and tries to swipe the long cable that its connected to the spacecraft to the wall. The sword doesn't leave any sort of mark on the cable. Kane pulled out two knives and tries to stab the cable from the wall. Not making any improvement as he tried jamming the knives in between the cable and the wall, Kane finally decided to use the Edo Blades. As he swiped the cable with left and right attacks, the cable suddenly gives loose, snatching itself from the wall as the spacecraft leaned and fell to the ground, causing a great disturbance to the soldiers standing outside the base.

Kane heard the footsteps of the soldiers entering the base and heading closer to the door. He searched the room for a way out and finds a small door to the right of the room hidden by a dirty brown curtain. He leaves out through the door just as the soldiers enter. Seeing the spacecraft on the ground and the cable cut from the wall, they sound the alarm. Kane tries to escape the castle's premises as he ran faster than he could possibly think. Though, he found himself surrounded by more Shogun soldiers, with Yoshinobu behind them.

"You thought you could easily escape my grips."

"It was worth a shot. Just wanted to see what you would do."

Yoshinobu looked at his soldiers. He nodded towards them and turned back toward Kane.

"Men, bring Mr. Kane to the dojo."

The soldiers snatch Kane by his arms and pull him into the dojo arena. They toss Kane in the middle of the room, facing Yoshinobu. Kane gets to his feet and sees he's surrounded by over a dozen soldiers, standing guard with their swords in hand. He looked at Yoshinbou, who's getting out of his robe, wearing a somewhat form of militaristic-martial-arts uniform. He grabbed his sword from the wall and approached Kane.

"I'll give you a chance. If you can defeat me in battle, I will let you leave the castle grounds and you can be on your way out of Japan."

"Very well. If that's what you want."

Kane stands face to face with Shogun Yoshinobu. Both have their swords drawn, facing each other. They began to circle each other as the Shogun soldiers stood still. Yoshinobu started to smirk at Kane, causing him to question the uncertainty of the battle.

"Well, are you ready to fall?"

"Only if you make the first move."

Yoshinobu swiped a rough swing toward Kane with his sword. Kane jumped back and slowly paused while he stared into Yoshinobu's deadly eyes. Kane moved slowly as he circled Yoshinobu, who did the same. The soldiers continued to surround them without making any moves or sounds. Kane turned to one soldier, who's holding a French rifle and swiped his arm, cutting it off.

"They won't even move." Kane said.

Yoshinobu jumped toward Kane with the sword in front. Kane swiped the sword with his own. Knocking it to the ground, Yoshinobu picked it up and raised the sword in the air, coming down like a strike of lightning. Kane held his sword up, blocking the impact of Yoshinobu. Kane struggled to hold back Yoshinobu's impressive physical strength. Kane noticed he was going down toward his knees as he couldn't fight off Yoshinbou's strength. He pushed back, slowly rising above Yoshinobu. As he faced Yoshinobu in the face, he kicked him in the abdomen, knocking him back.

"You decide to use your own body?" Yoshinobu said.

"In a fight, you use all that you have."

Yoshinobu dropped his sword and kicked it toward the wall. He began to set up in a pose as Kane stared. Yoshinobu moved swiftly as he kicked Kane in the face, knocking him into the soldiers. Which the soldiers shoved Kane back towards Yoshinobu, who proceeded to pummel Kane with various martial arts techniques of punches and kicks. Yoshinobu raised his elbow up above Kane's back and slammed it down. Kane fell to the ground in massive pain. Spitting out blood, he laid on the cold and hard wooden floor as he looked at Yoshinobu standing above him with his sword.

"It would seem you're not a great fighter, Mr. Kane. To which you appear to be much weaker than what the stories have told."

Yoshinobu raised the sword above Kane's throat. As he drove the sword toward Kane, he moved and kicked Yoshinobu from behind, knocking him through the window and outside. The soldiers began to move towards the window. Jumping through it and going to the outside, Kane proceeded to follow them. While outside, Yoshinobu noticed that most of Edo's civilians were standing by, staring at their Shogun. He yelled at them in Japanese to return to their homes. Kane jumped out of the window behind Yoshinobu. The civilians were covered with fear as they stared at Kane.

"So, you want to continue this battle?" Yoshinobu said.

"I plan on defeating you in front of your own people. To show them that even a leader of a country falls."

Yoshinobu ran toward Kane. Making a variety of attacks toward him. Kane dodged the attacks and backhanded Yoshinobu, who turned around as he held the right side of his face. He rubbed his lips, seeing blood on his hand. He turned to Kane with a fire in his eyes and he ran back toward him. He continued the attacks toward Kane. Getting a few jabs and haymakers in on Kane, Kane kicked

Yoshinobu in the stomach and punched him in the face, knocking him to the pavement. Kane looked up at the civilians and turned to the soldiers.

"This is your Emperor."

As the civilians stared, an abrupt sound of distant groans began to approach their location. Civilians began to run as a horde of zombies approached the location. The Shogun soldiers ran over and began fighting off the horde. Swiping their heads and arms off with their swords and firing at them from a distance with their rifles. Other soldiers were ambushed by the zombies. Two zombies spot Kane and Yoshinobu. As they approach, Kane went back into the dojo, picked up his sword and ran back through the shattered window and began cutting off the heads of the zombies. Yoshinobu looked up and seen the horde of zombies against his soldiers, as well as Kane fighting a few of them off. He got back to his feet as Kane turned toward him.

"What are you staring at, Yoshinobu? Aren't you going to fight?"

Yoshinobu didn't say a word and walked back into the dojo. Kane shook his head as he continued to fight off the rest of the zombies. Many of the soldiers were killed by the zombies or by the green liquid that dripped from their decayed bodies. After the fight, Kane returned into Edo Castle and grabbed whatever was left of his gear and decided to leave Japan.

Upon leaving Japan, the following year, Kane discovered that Yoshinobu had retired from being the Shogun of Japan and wasn't seen by anyone of the public eye again. He also found out that it was the last and final Shogun, thus making it the end of Feudal Japan.

THE DEVILS AND THE DEMONS

1870
VICTORIAN ERA

In the middle of the year 1870, Monster Hunter and Ufologist Gabriel Kane walked into the lair to have a meeting with the Knights of the *Symbolum Venatores*, the Order of Hunters. Once inside the large conference room, covered in memorabilia of hunters throughout the ages, they sat. Kane sat with the Order as they discussed their new plan to him. The Order requested for Kane to end a group that is called The Cult. Kane asked them more about the group, figuring out how they worked and what they've done to others that have crossed their path. The Order told Kane The Cult are a group of Satan worshippers who have committed various murders across Europe and have been involved in Satanic rituals of both human and animal sacrifices.

Kane agreed to find the group and annihilate them off the earth. As he walked out of the room, they warn him to be very careful of apparent demons that follow them in the shadows as well as their strength, a gift due to their high worshipping. Kane stated he'll take his chances and headed off onto his quest.

Kane traveled to the eastern side of England, searching for The Cult. Showing no signs of the satanic group, Kane decided to travel to the northern area of England. Kane traveled almost nonstop searching for The Cult.

Nightfall caught up to Kane and the sun's light dimmed away. Kane pulled out a lamp to see where he's walking. His coat and hat stood out as his silhouette shown through the shadows and the wind was slightly blowing.

"There has to be some way of finding this group before complete darkness covers the lands."

While moving, he heard sudden sounds of footsteps are heard around Kane. He slowly reaches for his pistol and aims it around him. The footsteps are getting closer.

"Whoever you are, I suggest you reveal yourself." Kane said.

Kane continued to hear the footsteps around him as the sound appears to come closer. Kane reached to his other pistols and holds it up along with the other pistol. He circles himself around the location as he begins to see cloaked figures circling him. Dressed in all black robes with hoods covering their faces. They're not making and noises of any kind, except for their creepy footsteps. Kane glanced back at the entire crowd before one of the cloaked figures approached him directly. Kane holds the pistol towards the cloaked figure's forehead.

"State your names immediately!" Kane said. "Before I have to just rid you off before me and continue on my journey."

"We are The Cult."

"Cult of what? Wizards? Demons?"

"We are The Cult of Hastur, our Fallen Angel and Savior."

"Hastur? The Fallen demon."

"He is our Angel and our Savior! You will speak of him not. Until you become a member of his Cult."

"That will never cease to happen."

"Be that as it may. For we and Hastur know who you are. Gabriel Kane, the monster hunter and ufologist."

Kane smirked and cocked his head slightly while holding his pistols toward the Cult around him.

"So, you know who I am. I take it that Hastur sent you here to stop me from finding you and killing you all."

"Hastur warned us or a coming force that rides in the night to stop his works as well as ours. We will not stand by and let you destroy what our savior has created and built for us. For he has spoken and has declared that we vanquish you off the face of earth, so that he can continue his work for his coming rule."

"If what you're saying is true and your boss wants me dead. Why don't you and your guys take care of me now while I'm still here by myself."

"Don't worry. We're about to."

The cloaked figure turned around facing the Cult. He raised up his hand and lowered it in the direction of Kane. He turned toward Kane and revealed his eyes. A piercing red glow emits from them as Kane pointed both pistols toward him.

"What the hell are you people."

"We're worshippers of Hastur. He's given us power that many humans cease to believe in our time and later in the future generation. Until our savior returns and turns this world into his own kingdom of chaos and death."

"Not while I'm still around."

Kane fired a shot to the cloaked figure's head. The bullet goes through his head as he fell to the ground. The Cult looked down at his body and raised their heads toward Kane in complete silence.

"Anyone up for the next round?" Kane said.

The Cult ran toward Kane as he fired shots continuously around him. Blowing off heads and shooting through abdomens. The Cult reached closer as Kane placed his pistols back into their holsters and took out a sword. Kane began slicing through the Cult as they came closer toward him. One member of the Cult slapped Kane in the face. Kane smiled and cut the head off the member. Kane continued fighting off the Cult and discovered their seemly increasing in numbers.

"How are they doing this."

Kane found himself being smothered by The Cult, until a blast of light appears from behind him. The Cult look up toward the light and immediately covered their faces as the light burned them. The Cult ran off into the darkness of the nearby forests as Kane was crouched on the ground, covering his head. After a brief of silence, Kane stood up and looked around, not seeing any of the Cult in sight. He looked behind him and seen a man standing, facing him. The man wore a suit and had a moustache and short black hair. Kane took a greater look at the man as he closed a book he was holding before placing it into his pocket.

"I suggest you say something. That way I know you're not possessed and in control of your own self." The man said. "So, I won't have to kill you."

"I recognize you from somewhere. I may ask who you are?"

"We might have cross paths once, for starters. But, allow me to introduce or reintroduce myself. My name is Thomas Carnacki."

"The Thomas Carnacki. The Ghost-Finder."

"Correct, Mr. Gabriel Kane."

Kane and Carnacki stare down each other as they meet for the very first time. Kane placed his sword back into his holder as Carnacki stood still.

"How do you know my name?"

"There are so many tales that concern you, Mr. Kane. Many describe who you are and what you've done throughout your illustrious history."

"So, I take that I can ask what you are doing out here?"

"I'm looking for a being that's known as Hastur. A fallen demon of sorts. I had understood that a group called The Cult were his army or worshippers that gave him the power to do the things that he wished."

"You just ran them off with your light sorcery."

Carnacki waived his hand toward Kane while he shook his head.

"I possess no sorcery of any kind. I've trained in many ways that I've learn how to use the energy that lives around us in our everyday lives."

"Be that as you say, I'll rather use my weapons to get the job done. That way it's a clean kill."

"Seems that you do not have much faith in using the energies of this world."

"I have faith. Only not in those who decide to use other means to fight their battles for them."

"If you believe your words so. Why are you out here exactly? If I may ask. For investigation purposes."

"I'm also on the hunt for Hastur and I found The Cult. Had them in my grasp before you arrived and ran them off.

"They nearly had you on the ground to rip your body apart for the worshipping. I came along and saved your life here. So, I suggest you show someone like me a little respect and say thank you."

Kane walked up toward Carnacki and looked him in the eyes.

"You'll get your respect when I receive my respect."

Carnacki nodded with a smile.

"We'll see how you'll get your respect, Mr. Kane. Until then, we'll travel together to find Hastur. Remember, two hands are better than one."

"We'll see how your work will pay off. This isn't some ordinary ghost that you're dealing with. This is a demonic force that preys on fear and hopes on gaining control of the world as we know it."

"I know what we're dealing with and I will handle it accordingly to how I do my work. As for you, just do what you know how to do and don't get in my way when we come across Hastur and his Cult."

Carnacki walked off into the forest as Kane looked on. He reached down and picked his hat up from off the ground and placed it back onto his head.

"The suggestion is the same here, Carnacki."

Kane walked into the forest behind Carnacki. Holding his pistols in hand as Carnacki continued to carry his book throughout their walk in the forest. Carnacki looked back and nodded his head.

"So, how many things have you come across in your lifetime of being a hunter?"

"I've come across things that the world disbelieves. Many of those things include the undead, extraterrestrials, mummies, spirits, and so on."

"So, you've never come across a werewolves or vampires?"

"I have yet to encounter such creatures. I know I will in the future, but for now, my focus is on finding Hastur and stopping him and his cult of crazed mortals."

While walking through the forest, they find a spot in the middle of the forest where no trees stood tall and hardly any bushes or high grass was settled. Carnacki walked over toward the cleared spot and kneeled. He reached and rubbed the ground and sniffed his hand.

"Smells like this area was burned by something."

Kane walked over and sniffed the ground. Taking a second to think, he slowly reached for his pistols.

"It's sulfur."

Kane looked up and in front of him and spotted a horde of demons. All with sharp teeth and claws that smelled like brimstone on their darkened scaled bodies. Kane shoved Carnacki as he glanced up toward the demons.

"Oh dear." Carnacki said. "What shall we do about them?"

"What do you think. We'll fight them all off and clear this area."

Kane ran toward them as he fired shots from his pistols. Killing a few of the demons as Carnacki took out his book and began reciting rituals against the demons that threw them off of what they sought out to do. Kane took out his sword and sliced through the demons. He glanced back as Carnacki who was reading out of his book.

"Carnacki! What the hell are you doing over there!"

"Patience, Mr. Kane. For I am about to save our lives at this moment in an instant."

"We'll see who saved who."

Carnacki began reading from the book and immediately the demos started to vanish completely. Kane looked around as the demons disappeared through a thick black smoke. As they vanished by numbers, Kane looked over toward Carnacki, who held his book in the air and continued reciting the ritual. Once he completed the ritual, the demons were vanished completely from the entire area. Kane walked over toward Carnacki and took one glance at the book.

"What the hell is in that book of yours?"

"Words that will save our lives for this purpose of saving this world."

"If you say."

"Let's continue on searching for our leading quests."

Carnacki and Kane continued walking through the forest. While walking, Kane could hear something rustling around in the trees above them. The sound was intense enough to the point that Kane began firing shots into the trees. Carnacki turned and looked back at

Kane.

"What are you doing?"

"Whatever is in the trees is too big for an animal."

"For God's sake, its only animals running around in those trees. Nothing more could it be."

Carnacki took one step further, a member of the Cult jumped down from the trees in front of Carnacki and smacked him through the trees and into another large tree trunk. Kane looked and reached for his pistol before being snatched and thrown across the trees.

"You individuals will never cease to understand the power of our savior, Hastur. For he is great to us as we are to him."

"I'm tired of hearing what you believe about your demon."

Kane lunged toward the member and punched her, knocking her on the ground. Carnacki gets to his feet and approached Kane. Wiping the dirt and moss of his coat, Carnacki looked down at the member and recognized it was a woman. He looked at Kane.

"Tell me you didn't hit a woman."

"She attacked me first. She deserved it for being a worshipper of a demon."

They began to hear footsteps coming from behind them. Crushing fallen branches with each step. Kane and Carnacki turned around facing the entire Cult. All of which had glowing red eyes. Kane pulled out his pistols as Carnacki reached for his book.

"You've come too far to ruin our savior's work. Now, we have choice but to kill the two of you and sacrifice your bodies and your blood to Hastur, our savior."

"Not today." Kane said.

Kane fired shots, though the bullets went through the Cult completely. Not even leaving a mark of any kind. Kane paused as he looked over to Carnacki, who began turning pages in his book as the Cult ran toward them.

"Carnacki, they're approaching us."

"One moment, Gabriel Kane. I'm searching for something here."

"We don't have time to do this, Carnacki."

"Just have patience this once, young one."

The Cult inched closer toward them as Kane held his sword in front. He glanced at Carnacki who continued turning pages. Kane began to become enraged at Carnacki's actions.

"CARNACKI!!! DO YOUR WORK!!!"

"If you insist so greatly."

Carnacki opened the book to the point of which the book could nearly be ripped in half if it opened more. He began reading what he called the Sigsand Manuscript. The Cult had suddenly stopped and looked at their bodies. Carnacki glanced over toward Kane.

"Fire your shots, Mr. Kane. Before this ritual runs off."

"If you say."

Kane fired shots from his pistols and immediately began killing the members of the Cult. He continued firing as he thought to himself what exactly is Carnacki dealing with within that book of his. Nearly running out of ammo, Kane decided to use his sword and began cutting through the Cult completely from every angle he could possibly picture in his mind. It finally came down to the last three members of the Cult in which they ran toward Kane and Carnacki. Carnacki dodged a punch and slammed the member to the ground before stomping on his chest. Kane ducked the shots from the other two and sliced them both in half. He looked down at the other one and stabbed it in its hearts as Carnacki looked on.

"I didn't suspect you had any physical fight within you."

"I prefer to use my book to get the jobs done rather than my fists and feet."

Kane turned around and noticed a building nearby. He pointed in the direction as he and Carnacki walked over toward the area. Once they reached the area, Kane realizes it's a church. He also spots significant symbols and lettering around the church's walls and notices that a cross that sits atop the church is upside down.

"Appears we've found their worshipping site."

"Seems you are correct on that statement, Mr. Kane."

They approached the door and Kane kicked in the doors. As both walk inside the church, they discover a large amount of animal skins laying around the walls of the church and they also noticed a strong odor of blood within the church's walls.

"I take it you smell the blood." Kane said.

"I surely smell it."

"Now, we need to see what's in here to stop Hastur."

They walk near the altar before hearing a sudden rumbling sound coming from underneath them, near the altar.

"What is going on?" Carnacki said.

"It's him."

The floor blows open, knocking Kane and Carnacki to the ground in the aisle. They can only see dirt flying in the air. Kane fans his arms, moving the dirt from his sight. As the dirt and dust cleared from the air, they found themselves staring at Hastur himself. A large demon with rough burned skin, ram-like horns, and bones on his back that resembled wings.

"I've finally come to terms of seeing my Cult couldn't rid you off this decadent wasteland."

"So, you're Hastur. The fallen demon that's come to rule over the lands." Kane said.

"I am that and much more. More of which you couldn't possibly understand with your human minds."

Kane and Carnacki continued to stare at Hastur. Staring at his large physique and his towering height of which nears the height of a grizzly bear on its hind legs. Kane pulled out his sword and pointed toward Hastur, who smiled.

"I do not know what you're smiling about, demon. Your end has finally come and has come to your own doorstep."

"The two of you combined don't have the strength or willpower to defeat me all on your own."

"You have no idea what kind of power we possess, Hastur. Many will remember this night greatly as the night the fallen demon Hastur met his death."

"We shall see whose death will culminate on this very night. One thing is highly sure, it won't be my death."

Hastur rammed at great force with impressive speed into both Kane and Carnacki, shoving them into the concrete walls of the church. Both struggled to let themselves free from Hastur's rough horns.

Kane began stabbing Hastur in both his abdomen and back with his sword. Hastur roared in pain as he backed away from Kane and Carnacki. Carnacki tried to regain his breath as Kane ran over toward Hastur and continued stabbing the large demon in his abdomen. Hastur swiped his arm across Kane, who ducked and went behind him, stabbing him in his back. Hastur raised his foot up and back kicked Kane into the wall.

"Weak mortal. You believe giving me mild pain from a metal blade will end my existence."

"I'm trying what I believe has a chance to work against a being such as yourself."

"Just accept your death as a favor of my gratitude."

While Hastur started walking toward Kane as he reached onto his side, pulling out from his coat a double-barred shotgun. Hastur stopped and stared at the weapon. Preferably into the barrels.

"Guess I'll give this a try." Kane said.

Kane fired the shotgun, blasting Hastur on his chest, blowing him back a few steps. Hastur was appalled by the force of the shotgun and looked at his chest. Rubbing it before looking down at Kane. Only black and reddish ash fell from Hastur's chest. It even smelled of a greater sulfur mixed with the gunpowder. Carnacki looked on as he turned pages through his book.

"That weapon you possess has great power. Yet it fails to have the power to finish me off."

"I haven't used it to its full potential."

Kane fired another shot that blew off one of Hastur's horns. He roared in massive pain to where Kane and Carnacki covered their ears to protect them from any damage due to the loud road. Hastur shook his head and his eyes began to glow a dark red emitting smoke from them.

"I've toiled with you humans enough! Now I finish you completely."

Hastur reached down as Kane took another shot, shooting a small hole through Hastur's right hand. He smirked as he jerked Kane by his coat and held him up to the equal height of himself. Hastur stared into Kane's eyes as he began talking in an unusual way. Carnacki looked on and stopped on one page.

"He's trying to possess Kane."

Carnacki ran over toward Hastur, who spotted Carnacki and swiped him back against the wall. Hastur looked back toward Kane and smiled.

"If you shall not perish, I shall make you one of my own. Someone with your skill set will be very useful for my ruling army in the days to come."

"Your days won't be coming, Hastur." Carnacki said. "For your days are done away with as I read this ritual to send you back into your prison."

Hastur threw Kane to the wall as he ran over toward Carnacki, who read the ritual aloud. Hastur noticed that his body was degrading in front of him. He looked down at Carnacki as he continued to yell out the ritual.

"No! Stop what you're doing, mortal. Stop!"

"I now send you back into your prison for all eternity."

Hastur's body completely falls apart as he turned to black smoke before a bright light appeared out of the book and approached the smoke as it inhaled it completely as it disappeared. The church is silent as Kane gets to his feet and nodded at Carnacki.

"Great job." Kane said.

"Same goes to you, Mr. Kane."

The church began to rumble as it started to fall apart. Kane and Carnacki ran out of the church as it fell to the ground and became nothing but dust and debris. They took one last look at the demolished church before facing each other.

"Seems the job is done." Carnacki said.

"For now."

"Until we meet again in this matter."

"That's what I was thinking."

They shook hands. Ending their recent partnership as they walked their separate ways, leaving the church completely abandoned in the middle of the forest.

Several days later, Kane returned to the Order, where they

thanked him for stopping Hastur. Kane replied to them how he had assistance in his quest to which the Order stopped him from continuing and mentioned that Carnacki was given their blessings for helping. Kane stood silent as he stared at the Order.

"How did you know Carnacki was aligned with me?"

"Because we sent him. We know you're still a young man who's learning his steps in this new life, so we thought we should send someone who's well-trained in this field of the supernatural."

"You could've at least said something to the extent of him investigating the same incidents."

As they spoke with each other, Carnacki had walked through the doors as he handed the Order a scroll. They nodded to him as he glanced at Kane and nodded. Kane nodded back as Carnacki left the room. The Order placed the scroll on the table before speaking to Kane.

"Still, you've done your job and it has done us greatly."

"If there's anything out there that might need my hand involved, you know how to contact me."

Kane left the Order's lair and stood outside, watching the sun arose from behind the clouds.

THE HOWL OF THE WOLFMAN

1877
LONDON

England has been on the rough end of murders throughout the past few weeks. Witnesses have reported over a dozen killings that were apparently caused by a "Wolfman". The police have been on the series of murders for weeks and haven't found a trace. Now, they have decided to contact Gabriel Kane to investigate these Wolfman murders. After three days, Kane arrived in London, starting his search for the Wolfman.

Kane headed into the London City Police Headquarters. When he entered the building, the people turned to him, automatically knowing he's the Monster Hunter and Ufologist known across the world. Kane walked toward an officer standing by the lobby counter.

"The commissioner of your city wanted to see me." Kane said to a officer.

"Yes, Mr. Kane." The officer said. "His office is right down that hall."

Kane looked down the hall, gazing at the newspaper clippings on the walls, all focused on the Wolfman sightings and murders. Kane saw a door in front of him and entered the room. Inside is the commissioner of the police sitting at his desk. Kane knocked on the door.

"Who's there?" The commissioner asked.

"Gabriel Kane." Kane said. "The man you've contacted."

The commissioner raised his head up from the desk, covered with paper, staring at Kane. He welcomed him into the office. Kane sat in the chair facing the commissioner.

"I'm truly glad you could make it." The commissioner said.

"I go where I'm needed." Kane said.

"We needed you here because of your certain background with these types of investigations." The commissioner said. "We've received reports that the series of murders that have been caused over the past few weeks were done by a werewolf or Wolfman as the witnesses call it."

"I've heard of such a beast, but never encountered one. What location have these murders occurred?"

The commissioner revealed a map of the city from his desk drawer. He laid it out on the desk, Kane glanced over it as the commissioner pointed to the location.

"Right here, in the City Park." The commissioner said. "Most of the murders have occurred at this site. Others were in the woods and two in an alleyway just across town."

"Any traces of a suspect?" Kane asked. "Just to be sure?"

"There haven't been any signs of a suspect. Nor any traces."

"Here, I will help you on this investigation." Kane said. "Get to the bottom of it."

"I thank you for that, Mr. Kane." The commissioner said.

While Kane prepared to leave, another man entered the office. The man has curly black hair and he's wearing a black frock coat with an upturned collar shirt, a brown silk waistcoat, and black slacks with brown dress shoes. The commissioner stood up to approach the man, shaking his hand. The man later turned his attention toward Kane, who walked toward him.

"Kane, I like you to meet Mr. Sherlock Holmes." The commissioner said. "He'll also be on this investigation as well."

"The well-known Sherlock Holmes." Kane said. "An honor to meet you."

The two detectives shook hands.

"You're the great Gabriel Kane." Holmes said. "The Monster Hunter/Ufologist. Let me ask a question. What's a Ufologist, really?"

"This isn't the time for questions. We're on a serious investigation and I'll like to get to it."

Kane leaves the office as Holmes and the commissioner look back at him.

"He's got quite the temper." Holmes gestured.

"He takes his job very serious, Mr. Holmes. I hope you do the same on this case."

"Don't worry about it, Commissioner. I'm highly excited for this case. Its about a Wolfman."

Outside, Kane gets onto his horse and rode off, looking at a map of the city. He begins the investigation by heading towards London City Park. Holmes walked outside of the police headquarters, taking note of Kane riding off in the distance.

"Impatient one I'm guessing." Holmes said as he gets onto his horse and follows Kane.

Kane rode through the city of London toward the City Park, Holmes came over on the side of him. Kane took a quick glance over at him with uncertainty.

"How would someone like you be a part of this particular case?" Kane asked.

"Because, I can solve any case. Ordinary or supernatural. I can get the job done."

"I hope so." Kane remarked.

"By the way, my partner, Dr. Watson will be joining us. He should meet us at the City Park."

"I'm not a fan of being in the crowd. Much less a fan of anything."

They reached the City Park and began their search. Kane took to the eastern portion of the park while Holmes searched the western portion. Civilians stared at Kane, due to his well-known background. He approached one male civilian.

"Excuse me, sir, have you seen anything unusual in this park?"

"No. Nothing." The civilian answered.

"Thanks."

On the other side of the park, Holmes continued his search for clues as he flirted with a pair of women walking through the park. As he flirted, Dr. John H. Watson, wearing his casual slacks and vest coat with a brown coachman's hat, approached from behind.

"What exactly are you doing, Holmes?"

"What does it look like?" Holmes said. "I'm speaking with these beautiful women here. But I'm glad you've arrived to help."

"Help with what? You're flirting techniques or this Werewolf case?"

The women look at Holmes, questioning him about the Wolfman case. He grinned, enjoying and savoring the women' attention. Holmes continued speaking with the women as Kane walked up behind the women.

"This isn't the time for messing around." Kane declared with certainty.

"Just relax. Here, meet Dr. Watson."

Kane glanced at Watson and shook his hand.

"It's good to meet you."

"Indeed." Watson said. "What have you discovered so far?"

"Nothing. Haven't found a clue."

Holmes looked to Kane and Watson. Smiling.

"I think it's best we return later tonight and investigate." said Holmes. "Since the murders only occurred during the night."

"Agreed." Watson said.

"Good thinking." Kane remarked. "At least you're using your mind this once."

Kane leaves the park as Holmes looks back at Watson.

"He doesn't like me very much, does he." Holmes said.

"You can't tell, Holmes." Watson said.

Kane, Holmes, and Watson return to the City Park later that night and its completely dark and quiet. The only thing they can hear is the sound of crickets and their horses as the snow falls from the sky. They walk together, not splitting up, though that's what Kane wants to do. Holmes look at the sky, towards the moon. He sees the clouds covering it.

"They say that this 'Wolfman' always appeared when there was a full moon." Holmes said.

"That is correct." Kane said. "Why do you ask?"

Holmes pointed towards the sky, as Kane and Watson look right above them. The clouds are covering a partly of the moon. They can't tell if it's a full moon or a crescent moon.

"Can't tell.' Holmes said. 'What do you guys think? I'm just observing it right now.'

"Judging by my view, it seems to be a crescent moon.' Watson said. 'If you look just towards the right, you can see the top point of the moon.'

"Really?' Holmes said. 'I don't see it.'

Kane looked towards the direction of Watson's. He turns back to Holmes.

"Just wait for the clouds to move over.' Kane said. 'Once that happens, we'll get a good view of the moon.'

"So, Kane, what types of cases have you been on before this one?' Holmes asked.

"I've done a few exorcisms, I also encountered a living mummy controlled by aliens nine years ago.' Kane said. 'When I was twenty-three, I was involved, well rather pulled along into the American Civil War while investigating an extraterrestrial crash site. I've encountered zombies, gargoyles, warlocks, and among other things.'

"You've basically been through hell and back over your lifetime.' Watson said.

"Pretty much.' Kane replied. 'It's what keeps me going.'

Holmes and Watson discuss the moon to each other, Kane notices something in the bushes towards the left of them. He slowly walks over to the bushes, with his right hand to his side, slowly grabbing hold of his pistol. Watson notices Kane moving slowly and so does Holmes.

"He's found something.' Watson said.

"I wonder what exactly?' said Holmes. 'There has to be something around here with a clue.'

Kane reached closer to the bushes and pulls out the pistol, aiming it into the bushes. He looks around it and sees a brown cat jump from the bushes, running into the darkness. Kane looks on as Holmes and Watson come from behind him.

"It was only a cat it seems.' said Holmes.

"At least he debunked it.' Watson replied.

Kane moved toward them, looking up and noticed the clouds have moved, unveiling a full moon. He then sees something huge, standing a few feet behind Holmes and Watson. He sees it has a long snout, long high ears, the claws on its hands and feet, and its body covered completely in brown fur. Kane has finally seen the Wolfman.

"Move!" Kane yelled. "It's behind you!"

Turning around, facing the Wolfman. Howling and pouncing toward them on all fours. Holmes and Watson raised up their revolvers and begin firing at the Wolfman. Kane reached into his left side, pulling out silver bullets, reloading his pistols.

"Why aren't our shots working?" Holmes asked.

"You need silver bullets?!" Kane yelled.

Holmes turns to Watson, no sign of expression on his face. Watson looks at Holmes, while still firing at the Wolfman.

"We don't have silver bullets, do we?" Holmes wondered with confusion.

This is not the time!' Watson said.

Kane finished reloading and fires at the Wolfman. It swiftly moves side to side, avoiding the shots. It looks down and notices the silver bullets. It looks up at the three and roars, before running into the darkness of the park.

"Damn it! Where did it go?!"

Holmes takes out a flashlight and points it towards the darker area of the park. He notices something moving around. He starts running toward the darker area.

"There it is!" Holmes said. "Right down here!"

"Be careful, Holmes!" Kane yelled. "It can be a trap!"

"Don't worry yourself, Mr. Kane. I know what I'm doing."

Holmes, walked through the dark area, hearing rumbling throughout the bushes around him. He looked around, not seeing anything. Holmes turned back toward Kane and Watson. They glanced at him, questioning.

"There's nothing here." Holmes said. "It must've run off."

"You sure?" Watson asked.

"I'm positive There's nothing here."

Kane ran over to Holmes, looking both left and right for the Wolfman. He gets to Holmes and searches the area himself. Holmes only stares at Kane.

"You really had to look for yourself, I see.' Holmes said. 'I just said there's nothing over here.'

"Over here, yes. But, what about over there."

Kane points to the left of the area, facing the exit to the park. Standing by the exit is a man, whose only wearing torn pants. Kane runs over to the man, as Holmes and Watson follow. Once they reach the man, they notice that he's out of breath.

"What's his problem?"

"Have to find out."

Kane attempted to grab the man's attention, but nothing worked. Holmes knelt in front of the man, staring into his shocked eyes.

"Excuse me, sir." said Holmes. "Have you seen a Wolfman anywhere?"

The man slowly turns his head toward Holmes, facing him. The man starts to sob as if he's both sad and afraid.

"Wolfman?" The man uttered loudly. "There's no Wolfman here."

Kane's temper starts to get the better of him as he gets into the man's face, aiming his pistol towards the man's forehead, staring a hole deeply through him. Holmes looks at Kane and backs off, standing next to Watson.

"Now tell me, have you seen this creature?" Kane asked the man. "Have you seen it?"

"No!" The man yelled. "I haven't seen a Wolfman!"

Holmes looked at the moon, the clouds have shaded its light. He tapped Kane on his left shoulder, pointing up.

"If the moon's cover, does it stay a werewolf, or does it change back into a human?" Holmes questioned.

Kane gazed above him at the shrouded moon, turning back towards the man.

"Him." Kane said. "He's the Wolfman."

"Really?" Holmes asked. "Because he's looks a little slim to be a gruesome beast."

"It's him!' Kane yelled. "Watch the clouds, for when they move, he'll turn back into the werewolf."

Kane pulled out both pistols, aiming them towards the man, Holmes does the same and Watson looked up at the moon, the clouds started to fade away, revealing the full moon once again.

"The clouds are gone." Watson said.

"Cover me." Kane yelled.

They backed up, watching the man. Within seconds, they noticed him starting to twitch. He cramped up into a cradle on the ground, holding himself in his arms. As he screamed in pain, the tone in his voice decreased in pitch. Growing deeper, beast-like. He glared toward them.

"Run for your lives, gentlemen. RUN!"

The man's skin starts to peel off his body like dead shreds of hair. Beneath the shredding skin, thick brown hair starts to grow in its place. The man's head transforms painfully into a snout as he ears heighten. His eyes change from green to yellow. His nails transform into sharp razor claws as his hands and feet turn completely hairy. The man turns toward them and reveals himself to be the Wolfman. He roared at them and lunged.

"Watson!' Kane yelled. "Watch out!"

Kane fired a shot toward the Wolfman's chest, straight into the heart. The Wolfman and Watson both fell to the ground after the fire.

"John!" Holmes yelled. "Are you alright?!"

They helped Watson to his feet, dusting the dirt off his shoulders. He looks at them, holding his right side.

"I'm ok. Just a bruise will remain. Nothing dire."

"That's a good thing you didn't get bit." Kane said. "Otherwise, that could've been you later."

Placing the pistols back onto his sides, Kane approached the Wolfman's body, realizing he's transformed back into human form and dead.

"Looks like we're done here." Holmes said. "Who wants a drink? I know I do."

"Indeed. This was something I never studied for."

"Not many in your fields have study such truths." Kane said. "*Requiescat in Pace.*"

The next morning, Kane returned to the police headquarters as the entire city of London thanked him, Holmes, and Watson for finding and killing the Wolfman. They thanked the city and Kane's work was finished. His focus was set to leave London, heading off into the western side of Europe. Outside, Holmes came towards him.

"I only wanted to say that I appreciated the time we worked together."

"I have to say it's an honor to have worked with a famous detective." said Kane. "You take care and tell Watson that I said get well."

"I will." Holmes said. "Surely."

Kane rode off out of London, not even looking back to the city. Holmes prepared to leave when spotted Watson nowhere to be found. Inside a public bathroom, Watson is staring at himself in the mirror. As he removed a part of his clothing from his right side, he saw blood. When he fully removed his shirt, he knew he wasn't bumped or scratched by the Wolfman. He was bitten.

"No." This cannot be happening."

JOURNEY TO TRANSYLVANIA

1887
TRANSYLVANIA

Transylvania is a highly known location to the world. A place where people fear due to its known history of vampire tales. Now, in the mid-1800s, Gabriel Kane, a monster hunter and ufologist, highly known for his encounters with legendary beasts across the world. Kane is a man in his late forties, lean and gloomy, somewhat somber looking. His skin appeared pale with cold eyes. His face is shadowed by his hat. He is dressed entirely in black and is equipped with a weaponry that features a rapier, a dagger, a cutlass, a cross made of steel, and a pair of flintlock pistols.

The reason for Kane becoming a monster hunter and ufologist is the fact that he believes that he was abducted in his early days by extraterrestrials. Now, with that knowledge, Kane's main goal in life is to rid the world of all evil in both legendary and extraterrestrials.

Kane, who's now on the road, heading towards London. As he is heading there, he makes a stop upon Hertfordshire. Kane enters the small country town, seeing its residents and how they look at him with fear. Kane sees a small bar and enters it, leaving his bold black horse standing in front of the bar, tied to a pole. Kane walks into the bar, which is filled with mostly men and a few women. The people in the bar notice Kane and stare at him. Kane walks towards the bar and sits on a stool as the people continue to stare. Kane looks at the female bartender.

"May I have a glass of whiskey?' Kane asked the bartender.

The bartender pulls out the whiskey bottle and pours it into a glass and hands the glass to Kane. Kane takes the glass and begins drinking the whiskey. As the bartender turns to put the glass away, Kane grunts, getting her attention.

"Leave the bottle here.' Kane said. 'If you please.'

"Yes sir.' said the bartender as she leaves the bottle in front of Kane.

She leaves the bottle and from behind Kane comes two men, wearing Victorian clothing, with one wearing a hat. They each stand on both sides of Kane and they stare at him.

"So, you must be Gabriel Kane.' the Man with the hat said.' 'The monster hunter.'

"The ufologist, too.' the other man said. 'So, tell me, Kane. What actually is an ufologist?'

"Do I really need to speak with you.' Kane said.

"You do if your life depended on it.' the man in the hat said.

"Hmm.' Kane said. 'If my life depended on it.

The man in the hat taps Kane on his hat. Kane feels the vibration and quickly turns around and punches the man in the hat. Kane stands up, staring deeply at the other man. He runs outside the bar. Kane looks down at the man on the ground.

"You dropped your hat.' Kane said smiling.

Kane finishes his last glass of whisky and leaves the bar. Outside, he gets onto his horse and rides off into the forest, continuing his journey.

Kane arrives in London and heads for the church. Inside the church is the Priest, who knows Kane on a professional and personal manner. He hears a horse outside and from the door comes Kane.

"Didn't expect you so soon." The Priest said.

"When I'm on a journey, I arrive faster than expected.' Kane said. 'So, what do you have for me?"

The priest walks over into the office and leans toward the desk. On the desk is a scroll. He hands the scroll to Kane, who opens it and reads it.

"From the look of this scroll, it seems Dr. Jekyll is on the loose again.' Kane said.

"It appears so.' The priest said. 'He was last spotted here in London. Which is why I contacted you."

"You want me to catch Dr. Jekyll and bring him to justice.' Kane said. 'I can do that, no problem."

"But, there is a catch, Gabriel.' The priest said. 'Jekyll has been seen as his alter-ego, Mr. Hyde."

"That should make it more exciting for me." Kane said.

"According to the local reports, Jekyll has been using his other persona to terrorize homes." The priest said. 'He has also even killed local civilians as well as their animals, if they owned farms, of course."

"Don't worry, old friend.' Kane said. 'I can take care of Jekyll and his big ego."

Kane thanked the priest. Leaving the church.

Outside Kane looks at the scroll and heads for the first location, East London. The sun is now setting as Kane travels to East London, during that period, Kane ran into a large pack of wolves. He passes them quickly them, though they chase him and his horse. Kane pulls out his pistols and begins firing at the wolves. He only kills two as the other three run off into the nearby woods.

The sun set and the moon arose, Kane arrived in East London. As he enters the location, the streets and surrounding are all but noisy. Usually around nighttime, the location would be crowded with individuals who would go out and have a good time with one another. But, Kane believes that everyone is in their homes only to avoid Dr. Jekyll's other half. Kane continues going through the location. He then notices a poster on a brick wall.

He gets off his horse and walks to the wall. He looks at the poster and sees an illustration of Jekyll's other half, Mr. Hyde. it's a Wanted, Dead or Alive poster.

"So, that's what he looks like." Kane said.

As he read the description of Hyde and as he reads it, he hears a loud scream. He runs over to his horse to track down the scream.

Kane's horse runs quickly toward the screaming. When Kane arrives he sees a man and a woman, laying on the ground, dead. Kane looks at their bodies, searching for any bite marks or animal wounds. Instead he only finds what appears to be saliva, from an unknown creature. Kane takes a sample of it and heads off, saying a prayer to the deceased man and woman. As Kane goes around the area, he sees a man on the side of the road. Wearing what appears to be a robe, his head covered with a hood.

"Excuse me.' Kane said. 'Do you know where I can find Dr. Jekyll?"

The man continues to stand still and silent, only throwing rocks into the nearby bay.

Kane gets off his horse and walks toward the man.

"I asked you a question, sir." Kane said.

Kane grabs the man and he turns around. Kane backs up, noticing that the man has no face.

"What the hell are you?" Kane said.

The man runs to Kane and knocks him down. The man pounces on top of Kane, trying to bite his face it seems. Kane struggles to get the man off and pulls out his dagger and stabs the man in the neck. The man falls to Kane's side as Kane gets to his feet and pulls the dagger out. Kane kneels and looks at the man, checking his features. Kane's very confused.

"What are you?" Kane said.

Kane leaves the body there and continued. In front of him, he sees an old abandoned church. He leaves the horse in front of the church as he enters. Inside the church, which is very, very old. From the look of the church, it hasn't been used in decades, maybe centuries, depending on how old the building is. Kane walks slowly on the wooden floor. His footsteps can be heard throughout the entire church. He reaches the upper floor and sees a man, sitting in the corner. He's not wearing a shirt, so Kane can only see him from behind. Kane stops and looks.

"Excuse me." Kane said. "Who are you and why are you here?"

"Leave me alone." The individual said. "I have peace here."

"Doesn't seem so." Kane said. "Tell me your name."

The man stands up and turns around, facing Kane.

"I am Dr. Jekyll." The individual said. "I know who you are, Gabriel Kane."

Kane pauses.

"Well, you know why I'm here." Kane said.

"You've come to take me out." Jekyll said. "Or should I say, you've come to take my other half out."

Kane walks slowly toward Jekyll, hands above him.

"Dr. Jekyll, let's not bring your big friend in here with us." Kane said. "He would cause a lot of trouble and damage."

"Well, it's too bad, Gabriel Kane." Jekyll said smiling. "Because he's already here."

Kane grabs Jekyll's arm and Jekyll hits Kane, knocking him across the room. Kane looks up and sees Jekyll transforming into Mr. Hyde. Now, Kane is staring in the eyes of Hyde.

"It's about time that wretched doctor let me out." Hyde said.

Kane stands up, facing Hyde. Hyde looks at Kane, smiling.

"Gabriel Kane!" Hyde said. "I'm a big fan of your work. Especially that time when you were in America. Great story."

"Hyde, we don't need any trouble here." Kane said. "Just let Jekyll out and we'll call it a night."

Hyde holds his chin, thinking. He looks down at Kane, who's only staring at him.

"Well?" Kane said.

"Nope!" Hyde mocked.

Hyde backhands Kane into the wall. Kane pulls out his pistols and begins firing at Hyde. He jumps around the room, avoiding the pistol shots. Kane stops firing as he sees Hyde in front of him, standing still.

"Ran out of ammo, Kane?" Hyde said smiling.

Kane runs toward Hyde and punches him. Hyde staggers, but catches Kane's next punch and slams him on the ground. Kane looks and sees Hyde's foot above him. Kane rolls out of the way as Hyde's foot goes into the floor, breaking the wood. Hyde sees that his foot is stuck in the broken wood. He desperately tries to pull it out as Kane attacks him with his rapier and cutlass. While Kane was attacking

Hyde, he noticed that his saliva was similar to that of the deceased man and woman he previously saw. Hyde smacks Kane back and pulls his foot out of the wood. Hyde turns and sees Kane on the ground. He runs and jumps, Kane pulls out one pistol and aims it at Hyde. He fires and Hyde falls to the ground.

Kane looks and sees Hyde reverting to Jekyll. Kane turns him over on his back and sees that he shot him in the chest.

"Jekyll, I'm truly sorry." Kane said. "But, it was your doing."

"I shall thank you, Gabriel Kane." Jekyll said. "For now, I'm free."

"Yet, you are." Kane said.

"Though, I was meant to send you a message, if we ever came into contact." Jekyll said.

"Which is?"

"I've been under the control of Count Dracula. He's the reason why my alter ego has been causing havoc."

Dracula? Why tell me now?!"

"Because, if you were to kill me, he would like to see you. In fact, he's been wanting to meet you for a while now."

Kane watches as Jekyll gave up the ghost. He leaves him in the church and exits the building. He gets onto his horse, returning to the priest.

Kane returns to the priest and tells him that Dr. Jekyll is dead. The Priest looks at Kane with a little uncertainty. Kane walks toward a table, covered with a map of certain locations across Europe. Kane looks up and places his finger on one particular location. The Priest walks over and looks at the location.

"That's Transylvania, Gabriel." The Priest said.

"I am aware. Dr. Jekyll said Dracula desires to meet me. I intend on traveling to Transylvania to encounter him. Just to see what he wants."

"I do not know why Dracula would want to see you, Gabriel. Unless, he requires you to do a bidding of his."

"I do a lot of biddings, you know that for sure." Kane said with a smirk.

Kane gathers more equipment and ammo before leaving the church. As Kane walks toward the door, he turns and faces the Priest. The Priest nods as Kane smiles, leaving the church. Outside, Kane rides the horse into the clear, quiet streets, that lead to the mountains.

Kane travels through the deserted streets, he reaches the mountains. According to the map, Transylvania lies just above the mountains. Kane looks up at the dark and foggy mountains, not seeing any source of a trail or lead to Transylvania or Dracula. Kane, instead makes a left turn, entering a small forest. Kane travels through the forest. It's quiet, and foggy. As Kane travels through, he stumbles upon a cemetery. Kane looks at the cemetery, as he looked he spots what appears to be a white dress running through the cemetery. Kane stops his horse and goes to look. He pulls out his pistols, walking slowly into the foggy cemetery.

"Mmm." Kane uttered. "Anybody here? I saw you."

A white mist passes from behind Kane as quick as a light. Kane turns, not seeing anything behind him. He continues walking deeper into the cemetery. He now spots something that looks like the dress he saw, standing behind the tree, covered in shadow. Kane walks to the tree.

"Excuse me." Kane said.

Kane looks and sees a woman, who appears as mist. Her face appears reminiscent of a skull. She looks at him and shrieks loudly. Kane covers his ears, trying to block out the loud and painful scream. She flies by Kane and knocks him down. Kane rolls over and starts firing at the mist, knowing that the pistol has no effect on the apparent ghost. Kane gets back on his feet and notices that there's two more mists flying around the cemetery. He spots one and pulls out his rapier sword.

"Who's first?" Kane said.

One mist flew toward him, screaming in pain. Kane ducks and slices through the mist with his rapier. The mist screams and flies into the air. Kane spots the other two approaching him. He stands still, holding the rapier, preparing to slash them. As he raises the rapier, a bright light appears from behind him, causing the mists to fly off into the distant. The light dims and Kane turns, seeing a woman with long black hair and wearing Victorian attire. Kane looks and places his rapier by his side.

"What are you doing here?" The woman asked.

"I thought I saw someone out here.' Kane said. 'So, I went to look. Who are you?'

"My name is Victoria Gretchen. Descendant of the Gretchen Liege."

"I've heard of that name before. I'm Gabriel Kane. What are you doing out here?"

"I was traveling through the forest, until I heard that shriek. So, I came to see what the problem and the problem was just you."

"I'm not the problem, miss. I'm looking for a way to Transylvania and to Dracula."

"You're looking for Dracula?" Victoria said.

"Do you have any clue where I can reach Transylvania?" Kane asked. "I heard that it's behind these mountains. Is that the case?"

"Transylvania is indeed behind those mountains.' Victoria said. 'But, if that's where you're going, you'll need my assistance."

"I'm sorry, miss. But, I work alone. It's what I do best."

Victoria smiles as Kane looks at her weary.

"Well, now you'll have to deal with a traveling teammate. First, we need to reach the lower town. To the east."

"Why the lower town? What's there that we could use?"

"The villagers know the exact trail to Transylvania. Besides, it's where I live."

Kane and Victoria head off into the darkness toward the lower town.

It is now daylight, cloudy morning as Kane and Victoria arrive at the lower town. Villagers roam the main town area, buying food and supplies. Kane looks around the area.

"I don't see how you could live here." Kane said.

"Why is that?" Victoria said.

"Because you don't seem to fit here. By your appearance, it doesn't seem that you could be living here."

"For one, I grew up here as a child. I was born in London, but my family decided that the city wasn't their type of standards. What about yourself, Kane?"

"Never really knew my blood family. Such is a very long story."

Victoria walks toward an old building, that appears to be housed of elderly villagers. Kane walks behind her, as the villagers look and stare at him. Some appear as if they are afraid of him. Kane follows Victoria through the building.

"These people seem to fear me. I do not know why."

"The people across this land know who you are and what you've done. You might not know this, but, you're famous to them."

"I don't see how. I'm only a monster hunter and ufologist. I don't see how that's being called famous. I would suspect ridicule or distain. Some form of persecution would do nicely."

"Trust me, it's around."

Victoria finds a wooden box in the corner of the building. She walks over and pulls out a key, opening the box. Kane walks toward her and looks into the box. He sees a large amount of ammo and weapons.

"Where did these come from?" Kane said.

"They were my father's. Like yourself, my father was on a quest to find Dracula some time ago. Unfortunately, he didn't succeed in finding him."

"Sorry about that. Well, for now, we can accomplish your father's goal. You and I."

Victoria turned, staring at Kane.

"At first, you wanted to do this alone. Now, you want to do this with me. Someone had a change of heart or something?"

"No." Kane said. "It's just that since your father was on the same journey as I, it would be suiting that you can be involved as well. Achieving your father's goal."

"I see."

They look throughout the box, sounds of screams are heard from the outside. Victoria and Kane run to the front door, leading to the outside. They reach the outside and see villagers running in panic as a swarm of vampires chase them. Killing the ones that can't run as fast.

"Vampires!" Kane said. "They belong to Dracula."

"Who else could own an army of vampires." Victoria said. "Come on!"

Victoria and Kane attack the vampires. Kane fires at them with his pistol, shooting one in its wing, causing it to crash into a house. Victoria pulls out a pistol from her back and shoots one vampire in the head. She fires at the others surrounding both her and Kane. Kane reloads one pistol and a vampire lands in front of him. Kane goes for a punch, the vampire catches his fist and kicks him in the stomach, knocking him into a wall. Victoria looks and fires at the vampire, hitting it in the shoulder. Kane stands up and runs toward the vampire. Kane punches the vampire and pulls out his rapier sword, slicing the vampire in two.

"Good one." Victoria said.

They continue fighting off the remaining vampires. Kane reaches into his trench coat pocket, pulling out a small bottle of water. One vampire spot it and screeches toward the other vampires. They turn and fly off into the sky. Victoria, confused, turns to Kane. Spotting the Holy Water in his hand.

"They fled." Victoria said.

"I noticed. Probably the water.'

"One of their primary weaknesses." Victoria said. "Along with the cross."

"Not exactly. The cross is a dud. Takes a stronger force to eliminate them. Believe me, I've seen it."

Kane looks around, seeing the villagers surrounding both him and Victoria.

"It was them!" A villager yelled. 'They brought that plaque upon us!"

"No!" Victoria yelled. "We did not. You all know for a fact that vampires have always entered this location to feed. This was only one of their outings."

Kane walks toward Victoria. Looking around the area for any signs of the vampires. He also looks at the number of villagers that surround him and Victoria.

"Do you have any idea where those vampires fled?" Kane asked.

"They went east." Victoria said. "If we follow them, they should lead us to Dracula."

"Good."

After gathering the gear out of the box, Victoria and Kane left the lower town, following the trail of blood left from a few fleeing vampires. After hours of tracking, the trail leads them to a small cave. They enter the cave, its dark, damp, and cold. The only sound throughout the cave is the sound of water flowing in the darkness.

"What could possibly live in here?" Victoria said.

"Anything from rodents to dragons." Kane said.

"Dragons?" Victoria said with a stare.

"Yeah, I've ran into a few one time." Kane said.

Kane takes one step forward, he feels something rough under his boot. He stops and looks down as Victoria stops behind him.

"Kane, what is it?" Victoria said.

"This isn't rock I'm standing on. Something else."

Kane looks down and sees a scaly tail. He jumps off and the tail slithers deeper into the cave. Victoria goes to turn back to the entrance. Kane grabs her by the arm, not letting her leave the cave.

"What are you doing?!" Victoria said. "You've seen the size of that tail?!"

"I've faced worse throughout my lifetime. Come on, we need to find out what's at the end of this cave."

They walk further down into the cave. They reach an apparent dead-end, Victoria turns to Kane. He looks around not finding another way around the dead end. He looks behind Victoria and sees the scaly tail. He points to that direction and follows it. Victoria turns and runs behind Kane. Kane runs as he follows to keep track of the tail. He turns from corner to corner, following the tail. Victoria tries to keep up with him.

"Slow down, Kane."

"This tail is leading us somewhere! 'We have to find out where!"

Kane turns one final corner before facing the creature that the tail belonged to. Victoria runs behind him and stops as she sees the huge scaly creature staring at her and Kane. Kane pulls out his rapier, staring at the scaled beast. The creature roars at them with its wings flapping. Kane holds his hat as the wind is so intense.

"What is this beast?!" Victoria screamed.

"It appears to be a Basilisk with wings. Dragon wings at most." Kane said. "I've never believed in these things."

Kane raises his pistol and fires at the beast. The shot had grazed the beast's head, just above the right eye. It shakes its head and rams over into Kane, knocking him down. Victoria raises her sword and starts to stab the creature. It roars in pain as she continues diving the sword into its side. The beast swipes Victoria across the small area of the cave. Kane jumps onto the beast, trying to reach for its head. The beast shakes Kane off and tries to bite his leg, only for Victoria to run over and cut the tongue of the beast.

"Great work." Kane said.

The beast staggers as blood dripped from its mouth. It rams toward Victoria, exiting the small area of the cave. Kane walks over to her, helping her up. As she gets to her feet, she looks behind Kane, noticing a locked wooden door.

"There's a door." Victoria said.

She runs over to the door. As she notices a chained lock on the handle. Kane pulls out his pistol and shoots the lock off of the door handle. Victoria looks at him as he opens the wooden door. Behind the door is a small tunnel with light at the end. They walk towards the light and as they get closer, they can hear a man talking. They decide to run towards the light. Once they reached the end, they noticed that they were in a castle corridor. Kane looks to his left and turns to his right, he spots a male, wearing nothing but black turn the corner.

"This way." Kane said.

They follow the man in black to his location. Once they found the location, the man was standing in the middle of the room, covered in marble, with a huge window at the front, overlooking the front of the entire castle as the moon shined down upon it.

"It appears you have been looking for me, Gabriel Kane." The man said.

Kane pauses and looks at Victoria, who is speechless.

"Who are you?" Kane said.

The man turns around and stares at Kane with a smile. Victoria's facial expression shows that she knows exactly who the man in black really is.

"It's him.' Victoria said softly.

"Dracula." Kane said with a determined voice.

Kane stares directly toward Dracula. Their eyes locked on one another. Kane's hand slowly reaching for his pistol. Dracula stares deeply through Kane, smirking.

"Reaching for your pistol, Gabriel Kane." Dracula said.

"How do you know me? We've never met."

"I know everything that's needed to know. Besides, I've heard a lot about you. Your days over in the States during their Civil War, you're time against the Shogun's undead and their captive extraterrestrials."

"How do you know this?"

"I also remember you facing those demons with the Finder and taking on the Wolfman. You've been through a lot of trials at such a young age."

"All you need to know is that I've come here to kill you."

Dracula walks toward Kane, slowly. Kane raises up his pistol and aims it directly at Dracula's heart.

"Go on. Shoot me. Shoot me and you would've accomplished what you came for."

Kane holds the pistol, still aiming at Dracula's heart. Victoria looks at Dracula walking toward Kane as she turns to Kane, forcing him to shoot Dracula. Kane is caught in a daze as he doesn't understand how Dracula knows his history.

"GABRIEL!" Dracula yelled. "SHOOT ME! END MY LIFE AS YOU WISHED!"

Kane fires, shooting Dracula in the heart. Dracula stumbles as Kane and Victoria watch. Dracula stands still and rubs the wound. He turns to Kane, laughing. Kane and Victoria start to worry as

Dracula was not wounded from the shot.

"What is this? I shot you in the chest!"

"I'm not like your past adversaries, Gabriel. I am beyond what you fully understand!"

Kane pulls out his rapier and starts to slash at Dracula. He dodges every move from Kane. Dracula moves toward the left of Kane, he grabs him by his coat and slams him into the brick wall.

"Highly determined to kill me." Dracula said. "But, you don't fully understand."

Victoria pulls out her sword and stabs Dracula from behind. He stands still, laughing at Victoria. He reaches toward his back, pulling out the sword. Victoria backs up slowly as Dracula turns toward her and tosses her back the sword. She catches it and stares. Dracula bows before her.

"Impressive, my lady. Impressive indeed."

She runs toward Dracula. Delivering kicks and punches at him. He's quickly dodging them. He moves to the right and kicks her in the abdomen, knocking her into the wall behind her. As he walks toward her, behind him, Kane is staggering to get to his feet. Kane reaches into his pocket and pulls out the water. As Dracula walks slowly toward a downed Victoria, Kane lunges at Dracula. Kane opens the bottle and pours all of the water onto Dracula's face. Dracula shakes and twitches on the ground, clawing at his face and body. Victoria gets to her feet and stands on the side of Kane, watching Dracula on the ground. After a quick second, Dracula stops moving and turns his head, looking at Kane and Victoria. He smiles at them and laughs.

"Blessed Water." Dracula said. "Good choice. Too bad it doesn't work."

Kane slowly backs up, looking at Victoria.

"I thought the water would have an effect on him." Victoria uttered.

"It appears that it doesn't. We need to figure out something else."

"Agreed."

Kane runs toward Dracula and slams him into the ground. Kane gets over him and starts to pummel Dracula with punches. Victoria watches on as Kane continues beating Dracula to a pulp. Dracula doesn't even attempt to counter an attack as he only laughs as Kane pummels him.

"Why won't you die?!" Kane yelled.

"I am already dead! I would expect you to have known that before you've come to see me."

Dracula shoves Kane and kicks him into the air and watches as he falls to the ground, grunting. Dracula gets to his feet, walking slowly toward Kane on the ground. Kane reaches for his pistol, but Dracula speeds over and snatches it.

"Your guns won't do you any good. For you have already attempted its use upon me."

Dracula walks toward the windows and looks outside at the full moon rising above the clouds. He turns toward Kane as Victoria runs over to him, helping him up slowly, as he appears to be bleeding from the mouth.

"I believe that we should save this for another time, yes." Dracula said as he opens up the windows.

He looks back again at Kane and Victoria. They notice that he's transforming. Giant leathery wings span out from behind him. His head starts to change shape, as his teeth sharper and his eyes turn red as blood. Dracula has now fully transformed into a giant humanoid bat. He screeches at them and flies out the windows. Kane runs over to the windows, seeing Dracula in the sky, flying off into the distant, trailing the moonlight.

"This isn't over." Kane declared with intention. "This is definitely not over."

WEREW☉LVES AND VAMPIRES

1890
EUR☉PE

Late October of 1890, sightings of Dracula have risen to an extreme, so extreme that the Venatores have sent Gabriel Kane to follow these sightings to track Dracula down. Kane's ultimate goal is to kill Dracula and vanquish him from the earth, now he has that opportunity in searching for him and his supposedly new castle in the mountains of Europe.

Kane decided to travel through the valleys, where the first sightings surfaced. He spotted old homes and carts but saw nor heard anyone. As his horse slowly walked through the small pairs of homes. The surroundings were silent. Only the whistling of the cold. Kane knew this was uncommon, especially in the location which he moves through. Without notice, a small gang of vampires, dressed in villager clothing bolt out from the bushes around Kane and move to attack him. Kane revealed his rapier and started to slash the vampires with the silver blade. The vampires scurried away from the scene, in fear of the blade. Kane placed the blade into its sheath and continued. Moving further out of the valleys, he hears a sound in the tress nearby.

"More of them." He said, believing them to be the vampires again.

Upon moving closer, his vision went black as he was attacked from behind and dragged away.

Kane awoke from the fall from the trap. He saw Victoria and Tom to his left, all of them tied to chairs with their hands behind their backs. Kane scouted the surroundings, knowing they're inside a cabin. He saw his weapons and gear sitting on a wooden table not too far from himself. Kane pulled himself over toward the table. As he moved, he caught the sound of the cabin door opening and closing. He moved himself back, seeing a young man and woman. They walked in and stared at Kane, the young woman stared at Kane, running to him with a knife in her hand.

"What were you doing over here?!" The young woman yelled.

"Relax." The young man said. "He's not going anywhere. He's tied up."

"Why am I tied up?" Kane asked. "Who are you two?"

"We're what people like you should fear." The young woman said.

"We're called the Night Watchers." The young man said. "We scout the night to stop any monsters or creatures from causing harm to the living."

Kane nodded.

"So, you're telling me you have no idea who I am?" Kane said. "Not an ounce of a clue?"

"It doesn't matter who you or your people are." The young woman said. "What matters is why were the three of you out at this time of night."

Victoria slowly moved as she began to regain consciousness. When she began to have a clear view of the area, she saw the young man and woman and realized she's tied to the chair by her wrists.

"Where am I? Who are you people?"

"Like we told your friend over there, we're the Night Watchers." The young woman said.

"What do you want from us?" Victoria said.

"We want answers, damn it!" The young woman said. "Nothing less than that!"

Tom woke up from the young woman's yelling. She looked to him. He attempted to move as well, but couldn't because of the tied ropes.

"What the devil is this?" Tom asked. "Where am I? Kane? Victoria?"

"I'm going to ask this question again." The young woman said. "Who are you people and what were you doing out this late?"

They heard the front door open and in walked an middle-aged man, wearing a gray hat and coat. The young man and woman turn and move to the side of the cabin as the man walks over to the three. He looked at them and stopped at Kane. Squinting his eyes to get a better look.

"I know you." The man said. "You're Gabriel Kane, the monster hunter and ufologist. Word travels abroad about your achievements and adventures."

"Wait, he is?" The young woman said.

"Indeed." The man said. "Riley, please untie them."

The young man and woman untie Kane, Victoria, and Tom. Kane stands up and goes for his weapons and gear as the man walks over to him.

"It's an honor to meet a legend in our field." The man said.

"Legend?" Kane said. "I'm just doing what needs to be done."

"Sorry about them tying you and your people up." The man said. "They're very strict when it comes to trespassers."

"So, what your name?" Kane said.

"I'm Raymond Rogers." The man said. "The young girl is Riley Hazelwood and the young man is Connor Hartley."

"Sorry about yelling at you." Riley said.

"Don't bother. You were just doing what needed to be done."

Raymond watched Kane set up his gear.

"If you don't mind, Kane, where were you three headed off to?" Raymond asked.

"Looking for Dracula's new castle. Sightings have surfaced and we intend on ending them and Dracula permanently."

"Funny you say such a thing." Raymond said.

"Why is that?" Kane said.

"Because that's who we're hunting down as well." Connor said. "The big baddie himself."

"That so?" Victoria said. "You know of Dracula and his

intentions?”

“Of course, ma’am.” Raymond said. “We do what must be done. That’s the reason why we’re out here.”

“So, I take it you do it your way and I do this my way.” Kane said. “That way, neither of us will get in each other’s way.”

“The guy is smart for a change.” Riley said.

“Why don’t we all travel together.” Connor said. “The more of us there is, the easier it will be to track down Dracula and get past his army.”

“Dracula now has a pack of werewolves at his disposal.” Kane said. “By that count lots of people will be easily tracked down by them.”

“Not if we’re skilled.” Riley said. “I’m good with a sword. Some slicing would do us a service out there against his forces.”

“I have the bow and arrow to back it up.” Connor said. “Quick and quiet is my asset.”

Kane looks at them and turns to Raymond.

“What about yourself?’ Kane said. “What field are you useful in terms of weapons?”

“I’m one of the greatest gunslingers and occultist that ever lived in Europe.” Raymond said. ‘I can hold my own and then some. You‘ll see when we head out there.”

Kane nodded.

“Fair enough.” Kane said. “Let’s all go hunting.”

They grab their weapons and gear and leave the cabin. As they walk outside of the cabin, a gray werewolf lurks at them from atop a small hill and runs off into the woods.

The werewolf climbed up massive amounts of hills and reached a castle. One of old construction. Gothic in nature, yet ancient. As it climbed the castle, it reached the top floor and on top stood Dracula. The werewolf paused and stood still in front of Dracula and was intimidated by his presence.

“What do you have for me on this day.” Dracula said. “Anything useful to decipher.”

He walked over to the werewolf, glaring into its eyes. By doing such, he saw Kane, Victoria, and Tom speaking with the Night

Watchers and leaving the cabin.

"It seems Gabriel has more company. It won't matter very long."

Dracula turned to one of his assistants. Staring toward them with his glaring eyes.

"Command the herd to track them down. Make sure they kill them."

He turned back toward the werewolf. Petting it on its head.'

"You're doing a very good service for your lord. Now, go back out there to help the herd track them and bring some backup with you."

The werewolf climbed onto the wall, jumping from the roof as Dracula grinned, over viewing the valley.

Kane and the Watchers walked throughout the woods, not spotting anything that seems to be vampire or werewolf relatable. Keeping their eyes closely to their surroundings. Which were dark and only to be seen with the glimpses of moonlight.

"Haven't ran into anything yet." Connor said.

"Keep your eyes open, young one." Raymond said. "Be at your guard at all times."

From the woods, bolted out a small army of vampires. Snarling with their teeth toward them. They stood together, forming a circle in front of the vampires. Kane held his gun out in front as did the others.

"When they come for us, fire." Kane said. "Make sure to aim for their heads."

"We've done this before." Riley said. "This isn't some new thing for us."

"Show some decency, Riley." Raymond said. "Do as the man said."

The vampires lunged at them, they fired their guns toward the vampires with Riley slicing them with her sword and Connor shooting arrows into their heads and mouths.

"Take this." Connor said, firing an arrow into a vampire's mouth.

Using the techniques they know, they eliminate the vampires and nod toward each other in their small victory. Upon walking away,

Kane turned seen three werewolves staring them down from atop a hill in the distance.

"We're not finished yet." Kane said to the group as they gazed toward the three werewolves atop the hill.

"What should we do?" Victoria said.

"If they start running down and lunge, we kill them. But they seem to be of a different mission."

"What do you mean a different mission?" Riley said. "You mean they're not here to kill us?"

"They could if they wanted to. But it appears they're up to something else."

The werewolves continue to stare down at Kane, Victoria, Tom, and the Watchers. As they slowly crawl down the hill toward them, snarling with saliva dripping from their mouths and their fowl stench inching closer, Raymond turned to Kane.

"So, what do we do now?!" Raymond said.

"We fight if they run down." Kane said. "Kill them just as we did with those vampires."

The werewolves seem to prepare themselves for the attack, but immediately pause and run away, whining, as if they were startled. Catching Kane and the group off their guard, they look around for the werewolves and cannot find them anywhere.

"Where did they go?" Riley said.

"They ran off." Kane said. "But, why?"

Stomping sounds are heard coming from behind Kane and the group. To which they turn around to see and find themselves face to face with hybrid creatures. Drooling and snarling at them.

"The hell are those?!" Connor said.

"I know what they are." Kane said. "They're called the Beast Folk. Human and animal hybrid creations."

"Created by whom?" Victoria said.

"I know a guy."

The Beast Folk roar as they run toward Kane and the group, who are already prepared for the fight ahead.

Meanwhile, at the castle, Carmilla sits with Dracula inside of his main room, gazing out through the windows, overseeing the mountains with the moon above them. She slowly places her arm across Dracula's shoulders and kisses him on his cheek. He chuckled and shook his head.

"No need to try and seduce me, Carmilla. You know that I am already dead and not alive. Also, I am aware that you have no interest in the pleasures of men."

"With time, many things can change."

"Not things such as we have spoken. It appears you want to say something to me."

"I have a proposition for you, if you would like to hear it."

"I am listening."

"I thought since you're planning on ruling this world and I am here to witness it take full circle. How about we both rule the world? A dual ruler-ship?"

"Dual ruler-ship?" Dracula said. "You must be joking with me."

"I am not joking with you, Lord Dracula. I am being completely honest with you on this one."

"Very well, Carmilla. I will be completely honest with you when I say no."

"No?"

"That's right. No. This world is only meant to be ruled by one individual and that individual will be me."

Dracula turned and walked away from the windows. Tossing Carmilla's arm from his shoulders. She gazed at him with anger, but pressed it down as she wanted to see the outcome of the long-term planning.

"Carmilla, focus on your part and everything will go as planned."

In the woods near the mountains and hills, Kane and the group battle it out with the Beast Folk. Many have already been killed by the group and only two of them stand remaining. Kane tackles one and shoots it in the head, while Victoria and Raymond deal with the other Beast.

"Just kill the thing!" Kane said.

Victoria raised up her sword and chopped the head of the Beast completely off its body. Its head rolled across the dirt and the surroundings were silent.

"What person would create such abominations?" Raymond said.

"Doctor Moreau." Kane said. "He's working with Dracula."

They continued to walk through the woods, nearing the mountains in the horizon. Upon coming close to the mountains, they find themselves near a large body of water and atop the water laid an island. With a large structure upon it. Kane looked up and pointed toward the island.

"What is that up there?" Kane said.

The group looked up toward the island. Uncertain of what to make if it. Victoria looked and could recognize the structure. She turned to Kane, while looking at the large and tall structure.

"Kane, it's a castle."

"A castle?" Thomas said. "Who's castle?"

"I may have an idea as to who resides on in that castle."

"What do you mean by that?"

"That would explain why those Beast Folk came at us so easily. We were near their place of creation. That island is the Island of Moreau.

Kane and his crew reach the island. An island that's known for Doctor Moreau's creations. They walk toward the large building.

"Is this where Moreau's Beast-Folk were created?" Riley said.

"Some." Kane said. "This island appears to be the place for the other work he's had a hand in occupying."

Kane bolted through the front entrance, entering the main laboratory. Only finding old remains of surgeon tables and doctoral tools, Kane gazed the area continually, spotting two doors, both lead deeper into the building.

"He's not here?" Victoria asked.

"Doesn't appear to be." Kane replied. "However, those two doors could give us the answers we need."

"So, we'll have to split up." Riley said. "Easy tracking."

"As it may be." Raymond said.

"Very well." Kane replied. "Myself, Raymond, and Tom will check the left door. Victoria, you, Riley, and Connor will search the right door."

"And what if we don't find anything?" Conner asked.

"We all return to this spot. We'll give out details if we find any then."

The groups split and went there separate ways. Behind the left door waited a long hallway. Kane nodded as they entered. On the right, waited another hallway, yet, with doors on both sides. Unsure if they were entrances to other labs, restrooms, bedrooms, or anything else of such nature. Victoria shook her head as they entered. Riley kept his right hand on the handle of her sword. Connor had his bow ready with an arrow already in place.

Kane, Raymond, and Tom continued moving stealthy down the left hallway. Not seeing any doors or any exit points in their reach. Tom was frightened of what could happen. Raymond had his revolvers in hand, Kane was prepared for a fight. Whether it were against a vampire, werewolf, or another beast folk.

"I must ask." Tom said, gazing around. "What happens if we don't find Doctor Moreau?"

"What do you mean?" Kane asked.

"Well, if he's not here, then, where will he be?"

"He could be somewhere roaming the area for all we know." Raymond said. "I'm positive he wouldn't go too far from this place."

"Maybe he would." Kane said.

"Why is that?" Tom asked.

"He's working with Dracula. If he needed a quick place to hide or to continue his work in secrecy, Dracula's castle is the perfect hiding spot. The perfect place to create monsters of his own making."

"Yes." Raymond added. "And, if he were to create monsters under Dracula's rule, those beasts could very well form Dracula's new army."

"An army of vampires, werewolves, and beast folk?" Tom said. "This isn't going very well is it."

"It's certainly not."

Meanwhile, on the right side, Victoria, Riley, and Connor search the rooms within the hallway. Only finding them to be closet spaces for surgery tools, some restrooms, and one storage room.

"I must ask, why are the two of you with the older man?"

"Because he saved us." Riley said.

"Saved you? From what?"

"A werewolf attack." Connor said. "Our parents were ambushed by werewolves. Raymond appeared and saved us.'

"You're brother and sister?"

"No." Riley said. "We lived in the same village. The werewolf had appeared and slaughtered most of the villagers. My family was killed first before Connor's. Raymond saved us and believed we needed to be watched over. So, he took us in as one of his own."

"And the monster hunting?"

"Once we were older, Raymond told us of his profession. Hunting monsters. That explained why he appeared in the village during the attack. We've never seen him before that. So, in order to protect us, he trained us. I learned how to wield a sword. Connor grew in the skill of archery."

"I see."

"After our training, we went out with Raymond on hunts." Connor said. "Saving lives and killing monsters. We were given the name 'The Night Watchers' because of our efforts."

Victoria nodded.

"Do either of you miss the childhood days or do you wish you didn't have to live this life?"

"I've grown into this." Riley said. "I'm better off protecting others from what I suffered."

"And I loved the thrill of the hunt." Connor smirked. "Vampires, werewolves, gargoyles, anything that's a challenge makes this all worthwhile."

While walking on the checkered floors, Connor spotted another door in front of them. Directly in place, a two-door entrance to another room.

"Maybe, something's in there." Connor said.

"As always." Riley added. "We'll have to check it out."

"Agreed." Victoria replied.

Opening the double-doors, they find themselves in a large room. Not as large as the front laboratory. But, within they see tables. Long tables lined up parallel to each other. Victoria looked around and knew what the room was.

"This place is a dining hall."

"A dining hall?" Connor said. "In a dump like this."

"I'm guessing this was a place for scientists before they left it." Riley said.

"It seems so."

Checking out the beaten-down hall, a stumbling sound of glass shattered behind them. They turned with quick pace as the double-doors shut. Connor raised up the bow, Riley twirled the sword, Victoria held his blade. Each was ready for the fight. Connor looked around, not seeing anything in the darkness. Only the moon was the light source.

"Do you hear that?" Riley asked.

They listened and what they could hear were footsteps. Each step inching closer. They manage to look and standing before them was one of the beast folk, standing approximately seven-feet in height, and its skin torn and hairy, upper body was of a man. The lower was of a goat... A Satyr-Man. Victoria jolted with the blade in place, Riley held the sword still, Connor fired an arrow. The arrow pierced the Satyr-Man in the arm. It pulled the arrow from its body and shrieked. Lunging toward them. Connor moved from its path and fired another arrow while Riley ran up toward the creature, slashing it with her sword. Victoria wielded her blade and attacked the creature from behind, Riley took the front, and Connor circled the Satyr-Man. Each one delivering attacks on the creature. The Satyr-Man swiped its arm toward Riley, who ducked down and slashed the ankles of the creature. The beast folk fell to one knee, where Victoria jumped on its back, stabbing it in many places. Connor ran up and fired two arrows into the eyes of the creature. The Satyr-Man knocked Victoria from its back and ran forward, impaling itself into Riley's sword. The creature still attempted to grab Riley and eventually died due to the sword impaled through its heart and the amount of blood that had fallen.

"See." Connor said. "That was a challenge."

"What kind of creature was that?" Riley asked.

"One of Moreau's experiments." Victoria replied. "Come on, we need to tell the others."

Upon them returning to the lab, they found them already waiting on them. Now regrouped, they each told one another of their findings. Kane, Raymond, and Tom found nothing. No sign of Moreau. Victoria told Kane of their encounter with the Satyr-Man and their lack of finding Moreau. Kane took all the information in and quickly knew where the doctor was located.

"We need to go to Dracula's castle. They're all there."

"I must ask." Connor said. "What if they're waiting on us to come?"

"Then, it makes this task very easy."

The following day, word had spread to the neighboring lands of strange activities of an sudden arrival of a strange and dark castle atop Mount Elbrus.

Within the castle, Dracula waited patiently, staring out of the large open window. Carmilla approached him from behind, gazing out toward the small village and snowy range of the mountain.

"Have you done what you've offered to do?" Dracula asked.

"I have. The armies are prepared and ready for your command." Dracula nodded.

"Excellent. Because we have guests in a matter of time."

"Guests?" Carmilla questioned. "You speak of the hunter and his allies?"

"Who else do I speak of. I'm positive they visited the Doctor's island and found not him. Therefore, Gabriel Kane knows he's here with us and they're coming."

"Perhaps I can make a distraction. A diversion of sorts. Weaken them for you."

Dracula turned to Carmilla and agreed. She exited the room and right after came Moreau. Hesitant to speak with Dracula. But, it would be necessary if he did.

"You've heard the news haven't you?" Dracula asked.

"I am aware the hunters invaded my island and entered my laboratory. The signals have went off."

"And you are aware hey are headed here. To find us all and eliminate us."

"I figured such a thing would happen. It explains the vampire and werewolf armies outside at the gates.

"What of your beast folk?"

"What of them, my lord?"

"Are they ready for the fight to come?"

"Oh, yes." Moreau grinned. "They are ready."

"Then, make way."

Moreau bowed and left Dracula to himself, who continued to look outside. Patiently awaiting the arrival of Kane.

After some mere hours of travel, Kane and the group stood at the entrance to the small town. There, the townspeople rushed toward him, telling him of the strange castle that stood on Mount Elbrus. Victoria turned to Kane, while gazing up at the mountain in the distance, they could see the castle for themselves.

"He's there." Kane said. "He's in there right now. Looking down at us."

"How can you be sure he's looking at us?" Riley asked.

"I just know."

Just as Kane said, Dracula was indeed looking down toward them. Still in the same place as he was hours before. Only, this time, he felt a jolt go through his body. Dracula shrugged the pain away.

"He's here. He's down there."

Kane and the group prepared to make way toward the mountain. Knowing that the possibility of reaching it during sunup is a slight chance. More so, they estimate their arrival at the gate of the castle directly at nightfall, which will cause more trouble for them in the form of vampires and werewolves. Not to mention Moreau's beast folk.

"How do we proceed?" Tom wondered. "Do we just walk in or do we move quietly?"

"We'll manage." Kane said. "It's going to take all of us to enter the castle. Just leave Dracula to me."

"Understood." Tom replied.

"And what of the vampires, werewolves, and those other things?" Connor asked. "We'll handle them I suppose."

"We must." Raymond said. "For we can only wonder what else dwells in such a dark place."

"Very well." Kane said. "Let's get moving."

After some travel, they arrived at the base of Elbrus, looking up at the dark and gothic structure that was the castle. Kane was ready. He blood was pumping, ready to face Dracula. Victoria could sense Kane's anger searing.

"I would keep that inside until you have the opportune moment."

"I agree."

Tom looked up toward the sky and noticed something strange to himself. He pointed, giving signal to the others.

"What is that?" He asked.

Coming down from the sky above hem was Carmilla and six other vampires. Screeching loudly as they made landfall. Carmilla stood in front of them, facing the group. Her smile was beautiful and sinister. Kane pulled out his rapier as did the others.

"Who is she?" Riley asked.

"I am Carmilla, my dear. And you look so beautiful."

"I'm not taking that compliment."

"No bother. Soon, I'll be taking all of you."

"Enough." Kane said. "Where's your boss?"

"My boss?! Gabriel, if you only knew. This is the both of us combined. Our union will shake the foundations of this world and build a new one. One of monsters."

"There's too many humans to make that a possibility." Victoria said.

"Try it when they refuse to fight for themselves."

"We'll fight for them." Connor said.

Carmilla chuckled.

"How kind of you. Take them!"

The vampires went in for the attack. Swiping their clawed hands and talons across the air above them. Kane raised his rapier and slash one's leg. Victoria and Riley managed to bring down two more. Leaving the other three to Tom, Raymond, and Connor. Connor fired several arrows into one, leading it to crash into the snow. Raymond took out his revolvers and shot one in the head.

"This is a trick." Raymond said.

Tom threw a knife toward the last one, but missed.

"Oh dear." Tom uttered.

The vampire rushed toward him and as it inched closer, Kane jumped in between them, stabbing the creature before it could slash Tom's neck. The vampires were defeated. Carmilla applauded them and flew away.

"After her!" Kane yelled.

They chased Carmilla toward the castle. Moving closer and closer. As they were almost near the entrance. Several of Moreau's beast folk appeared. Halting their progress. Raymond, Riley, and Connor stood against them. Their weapons ready.

"Go!" Raymond yelled to Kane. "We'll hold them off!"

Kane nodded with respect as he, Victoria, and Tom went off to the castle gate. Behind them, they could hear the gunfire, arrows flying, and a sword slashing.

"I hope they make it." Tom said.

"They can take care of themselves." Kane added. "They'll be fine."

Right when they entered the castle, Carmilla flew up and standing before them was Moreau, twirling his hands.

"I am delighted you've come."

"Where's Dracula?" Kane asked.

"He's here. But, you'll only get to him if you can kill my most prized creation."

Walking into the open room was a tall figure. It appeared humanoid, yet, it was hairy and with it came the smell of blood and water.

"The hell is that?" Tom said.

"It is what I call a Vamp-Wolf!" Moreau yelled. "And, it is not alone."

Behind the creature came three werewolves. One grey, another black, and the last one brown. Moreau ran out of the room in a hurry. Kane was agitated to the point where it was everything or nothing. He went for the Vamp-Wolf with his rapier, swiping its chest and legs. The creature backhanded Kane and Victoria went in for the attack herself. Tom was chased around by the werewolves, leading to Kane killing one and standing before the other two. Victoria kicked the beast and the creature grabbed her, throwing her against Kane. During the fight, Dracula entered the room, hoping to gain a closer look and Kane turned to see him.

"Gabriel Kane." Dracula said. "We meet again."

"For the last time." Kane replied.

"Then come. Come and end my life as you desire."

Kane went for Dracula and was snatched by Carmilla from the air and tossed into the wall. Tom saw Dracula walking in the midst of the battles, he reached into his pocket, revealing a small dagger made of silver. Kane stood up, shaking himself. Victoria managed to kill a werewolf while dodging the claws of the Vamp-Wolf. Tom moved quietly behind Dracula, raising the dagger and as it came down, Carmilla grabbed his arm.

"No, my dear. That is not going to happen."

Tom dropped the dagger, Kane saw it fall and it gave him a opening. Possibly. Carmilla held Tom up off the ground, ripping his cloak to reveal his neck. She could feel the blood pulsing through him and it moisturized her. She opened her mouth, unveiling the sharp fangs.

"I need some help over here!" Tom yelled in panic.

Kane grabbed the dagger and Carmilla went for the bite.

However, Tom had another blade and pierced it in the heart of Carmilla. She paused with a shocking jolt. Her eyes turned from black to white. The fangs reverted. She dropped Tom and fell to the ground. Dracula watched on. He nodded.

"Impressive from a friar of such low nature."

Kane rushed toward the Vamp-Wolf, stabbing it with the dagger. Victoria jumped up and beheaded the creature. Its body fell as the one werewolf remained. Lunging toward Victoria, only to be shot by Kane's revolver. The room was paused. Dracula clapped his hands in their victory.

"You three are very skilled in the art of the kill. How can you manage such a foe as myself? I can only reveal in battle and in your deaths."

Raymond, Riley, and Connor entered the room, seeing Kane and Dracula facing off. Connor fired an arrow toward the vampire lord. Dracula caught the arrow with ease, breaking it into small shards of wood.

"You're not fit for this kind of challenge, boy."

"This is between you and me." Kane said. "Just us."

"Indeed. But, by the way you look, you're tired. Beaten. I don't want to kill you at your lowest. I want you at your best."

"What are you saying?"

"I will come to you when you are in your best shape. Then, we will battle."

"NO!" Kane went for a shot and Dracula was gone. "Dammit!"

After a bit of calming down, they returned to the small town. Connor looked up at the mountain and noticed the castle was gone. As if it had never been there. Kane knew Dracula moved it. He and Raymond shook hands.

"Are you sure you don't need us to help you in this endeavor?" Raymond asked.

"I'll find him." Kane replied. "It's fate."

Raymond nodded.

"May you kill him for the best."

The Night Watchers left. Tom approached Kane as did Victoria.
"I have to ask, besides finding Dracula, what is next?"
"Finding Dracula." Kane said. "That is all that's next."

THE SEARCH FOR DR. FRANKENSTEIN

1891
BISMARCK GERMANY

Gabriel Kane heads toward Germany after being contacted by The Knights of The Holy Order to investigate the missing Dr. Victor Frankenstein. Currently, the year is 1891 and Kane has had many encounters that would appear strange to the normal society. As Kane enters Germany on his black horse, he notices the location's areas are covered with pictures of Dr. Frankenstein, all have the word "missing" above his headshot photo.

Kane's first location to investigate is the University of Ingolstadt, the museum that Dr. Frankenstein attended during his early years of studying. Kane always heard rumors that Frankenstein was high on creating life, though it seems that he never succeeded in accomplishing it. Kane enters the university, noticing many physicists walking throughout the campus. He heads toward the front office.

"Excuse me." Kane said to the lady at the front desk. "I'm here to discuss the missing doctor. Dr. Victor Frankenstein."

"Oh, sir.' The lady said. 'We haven't seen or spoken to him in months.'

"Is there a trail that I can follow.' Kane asked. 'Did he mention anywhere he was headed?"

"Last we heard; he was living in the mountains."

"Thank you." Kane said as he left the university.

Kane now travels to the mountains, searching for the missing doctor. As he travels through the crowded forest, heading down the trail, he spots a cabin above him, towards the front of the mountains. Kane commands his black horse to run faster, moving quicker to get a closer look at the cabin. Once, he has a better view, he sees that it's a large cabin, with smoke coming from a pipe in the roof, meaning something's inside. Kane gets off his horse and walks up the pathway heading into the mountains, right at the cabin.

By nightfall, Kane reaches the top of the mountains. He walks slowly toward the large cabin. He stands by the wall, taking a look into the window. He sees nothing inside, but a lab table and some equipment. As he looks deeper into the window, he notices someone walking around. He quickly moves from the window and heads toward the front door. Kane stands by the door, with one hand on the doorknob, the other hand at his side, holding his revolver.

He quickly opens the door to the cabin and walks in. As he enters quietly, the door squeaks as it closes itself. He turns and sees no one behind him. He walks around the cabin, seeing dozens of jars containing human remains and surgeon equipment and tools.

"What was he doing in here?"

Kane continued searching the cabin and its surroundings. As he walks toward the operating table, he hears footsteps from behind. Kane quickly turns and aims his revolver at Dr. Frankenstein.

"Dr. Frankenstein." Kane said. "Where have you been? You've been declared missing by the country of Germany."

"My good sir, I've been here the entire time.' Victor said. 'You look familiar. You're Gabriel Kane, the monster hunter and ufologist.'

"I am. I've been sent by the Symbolum Venatores to find you."

"The Knights?" Victor asked. 'What would they want with me."

"They believe that your grave robberies and goal to create life is turning a little chaotic. They want to stop what you're doing."

Victor stared at Kane as he walked over to his wooden desk, surrounded with jars and paper.

"I cannot stop Mr. Kane." Victor said. "This is my life's work. I do not have anything else to live for."

"You can start a new life. A new journey."

"No. There's no possible way I'm leaving this life and moving on like the rest of you. Besides, my work has already been completed."

Kane pauses.

"What work?"

"The ability to prove that God is not the only one who can create life." Victor said. 'I've accomplished it."

"How do you know you're telling the truth and not some false lie?' Kane asked.

Victor walked over into another room and opened the doors. Kane walked behind Victor as he saw someone sitting down in a chair in the distance.

"Who is that man, Victor?"

Victor commands the man in the chair to stand up and face him as well as Kane. The man stood on his feet; his height was around eight to nine feet in length. He had long black hair that reached his shoulders, he was wearing nothing but torn cloth and what appeared to be a ripped cloak. The man looked up at Victor and pointed at Kane.

"He is my creation." Victor said. "The Adam of my labors."

"A modern Prometheus."

The man walked over to Kane, looking down at him. Kane nods with his hat as the man only growls. Victor pushes the man back away from Kane. Kane only stares at the man, looking at his greenish-grey skin, with knots and bolts in his body.

"You created a creature, Victor." Kane said. "You must get rid of it, immediately."

"Never, Mr. Kane."

Victor turned to the man, whispering something in his ear. Kane only looks on as the man turns his focus on Kane. The man runs over to Kane, knocking him through the cabin wall. Kane rolls onto the ground, reaching for his revolver, seeing the man walk out of the cabin and into the dawning sunlight. The man roars as Kane only stares.

"This is going to be very difficult."

Kane gets to his feet and fires a shot at the creature's leg. The creature stumbles and looks at its leg. It turns to Victor, who commands him to get rid of Kane. The creature runs over to Kane, knocking him into the mountain walls. Victor walks outside and stares at his creation. As it pummels onto Kane. Kane takes out a knife from his coat and swipes at the monster's arm. The monster backs up, holding its arm in pain. Groaning at its arm, it looks at Kane and rams him into the mountain wall. As Kane tries to get to his feet, Victor walks outside as he holds his hands behind his back, watching his monster attack Kane.

"What are you doing, Victor?!"

"Just standing by while my creation destroys you for trespassing." Victor said.

"Trespassing? I was sent here to look for you."

"You see that I'm doing just fine here. Now, just lay there and die."

The monster grabs Kane by his coat and throws him toward the cabin, laying right in front of Victor. Kane looks up and lunges at Victor. Now holding a pistol at Victor's head, the monster stops moving and stares at Victor.

"Tell your monster to step back." Kane said to Victor.

"Stand down, my creation."

The monster steps back as Kane shoves Victor toward it. Kane continues to hold the pistol at Victor and watches closely at the monster.

Now, you will come with me, Victor." Kane said. "That isn't a question."

"I've already said, I'm not going with you."

Kane points and shoots at the monster's leg with his pistol. The monster groans and falls to one knee while holding the injured leg. Victor screams at Kane not to kill his creation. Kane turns to Victor, demanding that he come along with him. As Victor continues to decline, Kane fires another shot at the monster, hitting him in the other leg. Victor goes down to his knees and surrenders to Kane.

"Enough!" Victor yelled. "I'll go along with you. Just please don't kill my creation."

"Fair enough."

Kane placed the pistol back into its holster and takes Victor back to his horse. Kane walks back and grabs his hat off the ground, which fell off during the fight. As Kane prepares to leave, Victor notices his monster staring at him. Victor tells the monster to go back into the cabin and that he'll be safe. The monster nods and enters the cabin. Kane looks ahead and rides off on his horse with Victor in tow.

Back at the Venatores base, Kane brings in Victor to the Order. The Order stare at Victor intensely. One knight walks up to Victor and places his hand on Victor's shoulder.

"It is a proud privilege to see you in our presence, Dr. Frankenstein." the hunter said.

"Why am I here to start with?" Victor said. "What do you want with me?"

"Your unparalleled talent, of course." A hunter said. "We know about your creation, the monster."

Why bring up my precious creation?' Victor said.

Because you have proven that God isn't the only one who can create life." The hunter said. "Which is why we would like you to join us in protecting this plane."

"Protect it from what?"

"I wouldn't expect you to know all the information, doctor. But, you live in a world where evil presents itself in pure form. No hiding, no disguises."

Kane stands up from against the wall, presenting himself in front of the Order.

"What they want is you to work for them and your monster. I'm sure they would like to use him on quests."

Victor looks dazed.

"My creation is not a weapon to be used upon. It is a living being with emotions."

"A living abomination of deceased people, doctor. Sure, it can be used as a weapon."

Victor shakes his hand in disagreement.

"I will never let my creation be used for such purposes.' Victor said.

"It seems that you do not have a choice."

The hunter waves his hand towards the door and as it opens, Victor sees his creation in a cage being rolled into the room. Kane looks and begins to reach for his pistol. The Knight notices him and raises his hand toward him.

"That won't be necessary, Gabriel. We have it under control."

"Are you sure about that?' Kane asked.

The cage is shaking as the monster roars at the Order. Victor walks over towards it, trying to calm it down. He does very little as Kane walks across to the other side of the room, hand still on his pistol.

"If I may ask, what's the main purpose of this monster being here?"

"The same purpose we just told Dr. Frankenstein here. His great creation can be used to protect the world from the evil that lurks."

"Thought that's what I was for." Kane said.

"You are. We just feel it's more suitable to have others to do the work for us as well.'

"Don't hurt my creation!" Victor yelled.

"We're not going to, doctor.' The Knight said. 'You have nothing to worry about here.'

Victor looks around and turns his attention towards the Order.

"I'll help you on your quests.' Victor said. 'As long as my creation isn't harmed in any means.'

"Fair enough." The Knight said. "Welcome, Dr. Victor Frankenstein to the Order.'

The Knight walks over and shakes Victor's hand.

"You're doing a great service for your world and its people."

Kane walks around as the Order turns to him. He realizes it and looks back.

"Kane, you've always done what was right and you have succeeded once again." The hunter said. "We thank you for helping us."

"No problem. It's what I'm here for. So, what's the next quest?"

The hunter smiles and hands Kane a piece of paper, covered with an encryption. Kane reads it and looks at the Knight, smiling.

"I'm on it."

Once outside, Kane gets onto his horse and rides off, heading on his next journey.

THE INVISIBLE MAN

1898

THE LATE ENLIGHTENMENT

In the mid-winter season of 1898, Dr. Kemp, a fellow British scientist has met with the Symbolum Venatores. He travels all the way to enter their headquarters. As he walks through their temple, seeing many artifacts and paintings from centuries past, he enters their main conference room. As he sits down inside the room, he tells them of many cases being sought out in England by a man who cannot be seen with the naked eye. Once he finishes speaking, the Order declares they will investigate the case, thus contacting Kane.

Kane arrived, entering the conference room, Kemp is nowhere in sight, since he left and returned home.

"You know why you're here, Gabriel." The lead hunter said.

"Another case I suppose. What is it this time?"

"We need you to go to an English village in West Sussex, England to find a man who cannot be seen with the naked eye."

Kane pauses.

"Wait, you're speaking of the cases that have been raising across England." Kane said.

"Of course. We need you to head over there to stop them. Only God knows what more could happen if its not stopped."

"Where's the doctor? Doctor Kemp?"

"He has returned home. You shouldn't have to speak with him. We've already done that part."

"I would like to speak with him myself. Just for my own sake at least."

"If that's what you would like to do, go ahead. You may leave." Kane nods as he walks out of the room.

Kane leaves the headquarters and heads for Port Burdock. Within a week, Kane enters Port Burdock and looks through the town for Dr. Kemp's location. Traveling through, he spots a house with the name "Kemp" on the side of the door. Kane mounts off his horse and walks toward the front door. He knocks as he hears someone walking towards.

"Who's there?" Kemp asked.

"I am Gabriel Kane. I was sent by the Venatores to speak with you about the man who can't be seen."

Kemp opens the door, smiling.

"Oh, please come on inside, sir."

Kane enters the home as Kemp closes the door. Inside the house is warm, due to the fireplace being set. Kemp allows Kane to sit in the chair facing the fireplace, Kemp sits beside him.

"I was wondering what you knew about this man?"

"His name is Griffin." Kemp said. "I worked with him on finding a way out of his troubles."

"What kind of troubles, if I may ask?"

"He discovered a way to turn objects or life forms invisible. He Didn't have much to do tests on, so he did it onto himself. Thus, becoming the man who cannot be seen."

"How are you sure that its him who's doing these attacks?"

"The reports suggest that the culprit of this cases cannot be seen. The witnesses who were at the site speak of the victims dying in the hands of an invisible force."

"Do you know where I could find him?"

"I have no idea where he could be. He burned his house and all that could lead to him."

"No evidence." Kane said. "Smart of him."

"I'm sure you'll find him, sir. He'll turn up soon enough."

While Kane and Kemp drink their coffee, they hear screams coming from outside the home. Kane gets up and opens the door, seeing a man on a horse ride through. Kane walks over and stops the man.

"What's the problem?" Kane asked.

"There's a incident in Iping." The man said. "The police are shooting at something we can't see."

"It has to be him." Kemp proclaimed.

"An Invisible Man it must be."

Kane gets onto his horse and looks back at Kemp.

"Where are you going, Mr. Kane?"

"I'm going to do what I was sent for."

Kane nods his hat at Kemp and rides off, heading for Iping.

In the streets of Iping, police are shooting at a force they cannot see. One officer walked over to the leading officer.

"What are we shooting at, sir?" The officer asked.

"The man who cannot be seen." The leading officer said.

"How do you know he's still there?"

"Enough with the questions and keep firing at that spot!"

As the officers continue to fire at the spot, the citizens run throughout the town in horror, most of them are leaving through the town as Kane enters. He mounts his horse and runs over to the officers.

"It's him." Kane said.

Kane pulls out his pistol and fires at the location. After he fires, the officers turn to him and he continues to look ahead, spotting the dirt on the ground to bounce up as he someone is running through. Kane shoves the officers out of the way as he chases the Invisible Man.

He follows the trail of dirt that's been shoved around and later finds footprints. He tracks the prints down a few streets and finally into an alleyway. Kane slowly reaches for his pistol as he follows the track, through the other end of the alley, he sees civilians running all over the place, but Kane spots a man leaning against the wall, wearing a brown trench coat and a hat.

Kane looks again and notices that the man has no legs nor a head.

The man turned toward him and Kane fired his pistol. The Invisible Man runs down the other street as Kane follows him. When Kane reaches closer to him, The Invisible Man stops and turns toward Kane.

"I suggest you leave me alone."

"I will not." Kane said. "You're coming back to the Venatores with me."

"I think not."

Kane jerks the Man's left arm. The Invisible Man turns.

"If that's the way you want this to go."

The Invisible Man punches Kane, knocking him back as he continues to run off. Kane shakes his head and looks around, spotting the tail end of the trench coat turning right. Kane runs and continues to chase him. As Kane catches up to him, he pulls out his pistol and fires, hitting the Invisible Man in the right leg. The Invisible Man is now limping at he tries to outrun Kane.

As Kane gets closer, The Invisible Man enters a large crowd of people trying to find their way through other areas of the city. Kane rams through the crowd, looking for The Invisible Man. Once through the crowd, Kane looks down and sees the hat and coat that the Invisible Man was wearing with smears of blood on them. Kane uses his blade to cut a cloth off the coat and places it inside his coat pocket. He looks around the snowy areas of the town for other footprints, he spots none.

"Damn it."

Kane returns to Port Burdock to speak with Kemp. As He arrives at Kemp's home and enters, he sits down.

"What happened in Iping?" Kemp wondered.

"I found him. Though, I lost him.'"

"Oh dear."

Kane reaches into his coat pocket and pulls out the cloth from the Invisible Man's coat and hands it over to Kemp.

"It's his blood on the cloth."

Kemp grabs his glasses and observes the cloth. Smiling.

"How did you get this?"

"I shot him in his right leg."

"Excellent work you've done here. I will examine this as soon as possible."

"I thank you for that. I should be leaving now. Most High only knows what I have next on my list."

"Good to see you again, Mr. Kane."

"Always a pleasure."

Kane leaves Port Burdock, returning to the Venatores. The next week, sightings in western Europe have been on the rise of a mysterious Invisible Man causing harm to the villages.

THE PHANTOM OF THE OPERA
1910
BELLE EPOQUE

In the late winter of January 1910, Gabriel Kane travels to Paris, France to uncover the mystery behind the apparent Opera-Ghost. It is said that the Opera-Ghost appears as a man, wearing opera clothing and a white mask. The Secret Society have told Kane that the Opera-Ghost is always sighted inside the famous Paris Opera House known as *Palais Garnier*. When Kane arrived in Paris, he notices everyone around the downtown area and throughout are wearing the similar white mask that the Opera-Ghost wears. According to the citizens, the mask is known as the Phantom Mask, referring to its appearance and color.

Kane enters a church that's not far away from the Opera House. Inside the church, he is greeted by a young man, short, with brown hair. He's a friar known only as Tom.

"You must be the Gabriel Kane? The Gabriel Kane known across the lands."

"Indeed, I am." Kane said. "You're Tom. The Knights speak heavily of you."

"The Symbolum Venatores?" "They don't even know I exist, yet I work for them."

"They know you exist." Kane said. "You're just not in their high rankings is all."

"Maybe if I could team with you and others, I could be in their sights."

"Me entering this church and meeting you means the Knights have an eye on you. They wouldn't send me here otherwise. Definitely not for a friar of any sort of the imagination."

Kane pulled out a note and handed it to Tom. He put on his glasses and read the note before glancing up at Kane with a blank stare. He held the note above his shoulders.

"You're telling me that the Knights want me to assist you in investigating the Opera-Ghost?"

"Yes. Didn't you just mention that if you could align yourself with me or any of the others, you would be in their sights."

"But that was just me talking out of my ass. I didn't think that it would happen. Not until I became a monk."

Kane takes the note back from Tom and placed it inside his leather coat pocket. Tom only stared as Kane looked at him and glanced toward the church doors.

"We need to go immediately."

"Why immediately? Why not tomorrow?"

"Because tomorrow, the Opera-Ghost could be gone and lost in my sights."

Kane and Tom head toward the opera house, they notice posters and banners covering the exterior of the house as well as other buildings throughout Paris, which represent the Opera-Ghost himself. Tom is terrified by the number of banners that are surrounding Paris for the Opera-Ghost. As more people are seen wearing the ghost masks, they finally arrive at the opera house, where they meet, Viscount Raoul, Vicomte de Chagny.

"Ah! The legendary Gabriel Kane has arrived in Paris." Raoul said. "What a pleasure it is to see you here in Paris."

"The pleasure is all mine." Kane said. "It's been a while since I've stepped foot in Italy."

"It's good to have you here in our presence. I'm sure you're not in the mindset to take a small break so we could have a conversation."

"I'm set for a conversation."

Raoul walks Kane and Tom through the house, seeing many

banners and posters that speak of the Opera-Ghost. To the people walking around inside the house, it's just an ordinary trick played by well performed actors. Raoul enters an office room where Kane and Tom follow. They sit in the chairs as Raoul closed the door. He sits by the wooden desk facing Kane.

"So, what was this conversation that you wanted to speak to me about?"

"It concerns the Opera-Ghost as well as this opera house."

"Is this place cursed because of the ghost?" Tom said.

"No. I hope not. It only seems that he's bringing people into a trance. Whenever they see a poster, a banner, or even when they wear those masks. It's like they have no control over themselves."

"You want us to look into that mystery."

"If you can. I don't want a bunch of zombies entering this opera house."

"Believe me when I say, you haven't seen what a zombie exactly is."

Raoul smirked and extended his hand toward Kane.

"Just please help the City of Paris out on this one."

Kane shook Raoul's hand and nodded.

"We'll do what we can about the trance state while we search for the Opera-Ghost."

Kane and Tom leave the office as Raoul sits behind the desk, rubbing his hands together as he looked outside the window, seeing many citizens wearing the ghost mask and staring at banners and posters.

"Please help us."

Kane and Tom walk around the downtown area of Paris. They examine the streets and the people. Kane also studies the banners and posters. He stares at the Opera-Ghost on the posters. Scratching his chin, Kane turned to Tom, who was glancing around at the Paris citizens.

"Tom, come over here and look at this."

"What have you found this time?"

Kane pointed toward the Opera-Ghost's face on the poster. Pointing toward the eyes.

"Do you see what I'm seeing?"

Tom squints his eyes and shook his head.

"I'm not seeing anything, Gabriel Kane. What are you talking about exactly?"

"These posters and banners. They're all laced with something."

Kane reached up and snatched the poster off the brick wall and onto the ground. Citizens looked on and stared at Kane and Tom. Tom looked back toward them and held his hands up.

"There's nothing to see here ladies and gentlemen. So please continue on with your sight-seeing."

"He ripped down the Opera-Ghost's poster!" A gentleman said.

"He tore it off the wall like it was hardly anything!" A lady said.

Tom backed up near Kane as the citizens slowly approached the two of them.

"Gabriel, The citizens are approaching us and they're not looking so nice."

Kane turned around, facing the crowd. He raised up his pistols toward them. The crowd stopped moving and slowly took steps back from Kane and Tom.

"If any of you want to live after this day, I suggest you back away and return to your previous occupations. Do it now I say."

The crowd raised up their hands and turned away, returning to their sight-seeing and other activities. Kane placed the pistols back into his pouches. Tom looked at him with a worried eye.

"Were you really going to shoot them if they stepped closer?"

"Would've shot at their arms and legs. Nothing more."

Kane returns to looking at the poster and grabs Tom.

"The eyes. Do you see the glow coming from them?"

Tom looked and noticed a glare coming from the Opera-Ghost's eyes. He looked at Kane and took another glance at the poster.

"What is that supposed to be exactly. Is that what's causing the trace state in these people?"

"Its magic. Someone is using magic to bring people here to see the Opera-Ghost. Once the trance is in place, the people will never leave Paris under their own power."

Kane takes out a match and burned the poster in front of the citizens. Many of them ran off from the area as Kane and Tom watched the poster burn.

"So, what's next on our agenda?"

"We'll return to the opera house tonight and find the Opera-Ghost ourselves. Once we achieve that goal, we'll end all of this."

A full moon shines bright over Paris as Kane and Tom travel toward the opera house for the investigation. Upon arriving at the house, Raoul stood outside by the front entrance as Kane and Tom approached him.

"I see the two of you are for this."

"Its why we're here."

Raoul opened the front doors and allowed Kane and Tom to enter. Raoul turned toward Kane, calling him out. Kane turned, facing Raoul.

"I wish you two the very best of luck on this."

"You won't have to worry."

Raoul leaves the opera house and only Kane and Tom are inside the house.

They walk through the house, completely silent to where they can only here their own footsteps while walking or even hearing their own heart beats while standing still. Tom carried a lamp while Kane had a pistol in hand.

"So, what area shall we search first, Gabriel?"

"I believe its best that we search the auditorium. It is where the Opera-Ghost does his work."

Once they reached the auditorium, Kane begins to feel uneasy as they enter. Tom looked around and feels as if something flew past him to where he couldn't see it.

"Something just went by, Gabriel. I don't know what it was."

"I'm having an uneasy feeling standing in here."

Kane stared at the stage and clenching his pistol. Tom looked around with the lamp. A black cloth passed by Tom, knocking the fire out of the lamp out. Tom screamed as Kane stood quiet, facing the stage.

"It just knocked the lamp out."

"It's him."

"What do you mean its him?"

"Up on the stage!"

Kane moved as he grabbed Tom from the chandelier, which fell over their heads. Slamming on the floor where they were standing. Tom looked back at the chandelier and turned to the stage, where he sees Kane aiming his pistol toward the Opera-Ghost.

"He's here, Tom. The Ghost is in our sights."

The Opera-Ghost stood still as it stared into the eyes of Kane. He pointed toward him as Kane took a shot. The Ghost jumped out of the bullet's frame and lunged over to Kane, punching him across the auditorium. Kane falls against the wall as he stared at the Ghost, which slowly approached him with no sound coming from him.

The Opera-Ghost approached Kane slowly as Tom looked around the auditorium for anything to use as a weapon. Kane got to his feet as the Ghost inched closer toward him.

"You've caused enough trouble here. Using magic to bring innocent people into your opera house to watch you perform mysticism."

"They come because they have nowhere else to go to achieve greatness or to feel greatness within them. I give them the illusion of greatness and they love it most."

"Not by my sights do they love it. They can't even leave Paris under their own willpower."

"Who would want to leave this beautiful city. There's not other place on Earth that could equal the amount of beauty and love than Paris herself. Who are you to say otherwise."

"I'm the man that come to end your reign of magic and to bring forth justice into the lands of Paris and all places throughout France. I am Gabriel Kane and I am what you fear most."

Kane lunged at the Opera-Ghost, tackling him onto the ground. Kane begins pummeling The Ghost in the face, cracking its phantom mask. The Ghost backhanded Kane and kicked him in the gun, later ramming him into the walls. Kane slides off the walls and onto the floor. The Ghost rubbed his mask, noticing the crack, his eyes begin to fill with rage as he reached over and grabbed Kane by his black leather coat and started slamming him against the wall. Tom, meanwhile, continued searching for a weapon and finds a metal rod.

"There we go."

Tom grabbed the rod and ran over toward Kane and the Ghost. Tom jumped up and hit the Ghost in his back with the rod. The Ghost stumbled before turning around, facing Tom and staring into his eyes. Tom slowly backed away with his hands in the air.

"No worries. I was just trying to help my friend out. That's all."

"You would use other means to try and fight me off. When will foreigners ever learn that Paris and this opera house are powerful in nature. They fuel me, just as I fuel the citizens."

Kane looked up at the Ghost, through his blurry vision, seeing him reaching for Tom. Kane gets up and rams into the Ghost's back and reached out toward the Ghost's face and snatched off the mask. The Ghost backed up, covering his face. He mumbled to himself as Kane and Tom watched. The Ghost stopped moving and removed his hands from his face. Holding his head down, he slowly raised it up, revealing his disfigured face.

"Oh, dear lord." Tom said.

The Ghost yelled in fury as he ran and shoved Kane into Tom, knocking them back on the floor and he began to choke them both.

"It's always those who do not fully understand. Leave me be at this moment or else suffer your sudden death."

The Ghost released his hands from Kane and Tom's throats. Tom backed away as Kane stood up. The Ghost raised up his cloak and disappeared through sudden smoke that appeared from his feet. As the Ghost vanished, Tom looked around the damaged auditorium.

"Where did he go, Gabriel Kane?"

"He vanished to another hiding spot."

"He might try and sneak up on us."

"He won't. We've just agreed on equal terms. We leave this place and he refuses to use magic in his performances."

The following day, Kane speaks to Raoul about the Opera-Ghost and gives him the great detail of their encounter and what took place inside the auditorium. Upon leaving Palais Garnier, Kane and Tom run into a woman, who suddenly stopped them.

"Please stop. I need to have a small word with you." the woman said.

"By all means, miss. Speak."

"You shouldn't worry about the Opera-Ghost anymore. He's in good hands and will do all that he can to bring good into this city."

"Excuse me, miss. Who are you exactly?" Tom said.

"My name is Christine Daae. I'm very close to the Opera-Ghost. As I said, you won't have to worry anymore about his activities. I'll take good care of him to make sure of it."

Kane stared at Christine and nodded toward her. She smiled and walked away. Tom looked back at her before turning to Kane.

"That was surreal. She's close with the Opera-Ghost."

"We'll leave the Phantom of the Opera alone. For now."

Kane and Tom ride off on their horses, returning to Rome where they'll speak once again with the Knights.

HOD

PROLOGUE - THE MURDER

The forest was cold, snowed in, and completely iced over. The atmosphere would cause a person to shiver in their footsteps to even taken the daring chance of walking through the forest covered in snow. Especially during nightfall where the forest would become silent as the outer depths of space. No sign of any animals either. Complete quietness.

Though, there was that one time during the night, when a man decided to take the daring opportunity to enter the snowy forest during a full moon. The man seemed to make an impression on his friends and possible lover. He took pleasure in taking those daring actions that many seem to do today. His dare was to enter the forest during nightfall and overcome the cold and shivering atmosphere.

Not even wearing a coat, he went out with only a short sleeve shirt and shorts. He might've had wore sandals, but we couldn't tell due to the fact that when we found him, he was halfway eaten and his feet were bare, his clothes ripped with claw marks and bite marks. His friends didn't know what to make of their friend's death and were too afraid to tell anyone of his daring feats.

We spoke to his friends concerning him and they hardly spoke a word besides the fact of him running into the forest with a smile on his face. The detectives however believed it to be a bear that attacked and killed him. But a hunter who discovered the remains believed it to be something more than a bear. Funny enough, one detective joked that it might have been an elk that killed him and used its antlers to create the claw marks.

"No elk could've done this." said the Hunter. "I can tell you exactly what killed this man. But, you'll end up locking me behind a steel door."

"Tell us what could've killed this man."

"A full moon was out on the night he entered these woods and we know the legends of this land."

"We are not buying this folklore tale of a werewolf being responsible, sir."

"Just hear me out, detectives. I know this sounds crazy, but you have to believe me and take this in."

"We prefer not to."

The detectives would laugh in the hunter's face and walk away to their vehicles, preparing to leave the forest and head back into town. The friends had already left the scene with little tears in their eyes and softness in their hearts. Without any ideas as to who or what might have killed the man in the snowy forest, the detectives were out of options. Until that Sunday, where the freezing rain had begun to come down and when he entered through the doors of the detective building that they knew something was happening in those woods.

I - THE INVESTIGATION

After a series of days had passed away, the detectives took slight heed to the warning of the hunter concerning the possibility of a werewolf as the culprit of the forest murder. Everyone within the small town kept the information of the murder to themselves, most were afraid to speak to someone about it. The hunter stayed in his cabin outside of the small town to avoid certain mockery and scrutiny. He was already the laughingstock of the town months back dealing with his hunting of deer to the point where deer figured out the shooting grounds of the hunter, thus never making a return to the field.

The hunter sat alone in his cabin, covered in snow. Placing wood into his wood stove to heat up the cabin, he sighs while sitting down in an old beaten chair. The hunter's cabin is covered with trophies he acquired in hunting games. The cabin is even packed with stuffing of his kills, ranging from deer to bears to an mountain lion. He reached over to a table nearby and grabbed a book, began to read it until a knock comes from the door. Reluctant to answer the door, believing it to be a towns person coming over to mock him or throw snowballs at him.

"Go away." said the hunter.

They knock again with the hunter's patience being tested. He refused to stand up and answer the door. Going back to reading his book, he ignored the door and the knocking.

"I am not in the mood to be playing with snowballs. Thank you."

The knocks continue and increase. Nearly out of patience, the hunter stands up and walked to the door. He took a peep outside through the peek hole, seeing a man standing there. The hunter gently sighs before placing his hand on the doorknob. He opened the door and standing there is a man dressed in amalgam of modern and Victorian era clothing. The man is wearing a black duster coat, a gray buttoned-down shirt with black slacks, black and gray leather boots, and a black hat. The man's black and gray hair strands down to his shoulders, covering his ears. The man stands still while the hunter thinks to himself as to who the man could be.

"Hello, sir" The hunter said. "How can I possibly help you?"

"I heard about the murder in these woods. I understand that it was you whom discovered the remains of the victim."

"Yes. Yes, I did. Is there something wrong?"

"I would like to talk to you about it."

"I'm not in the mood to speak on the subject, sir. If you want more information on it, go to the detectives' office and they can give you all the information that you'll need."

The hunter proceeded to close the door, but the man placed his foot in between. Frightening the hunter immediately, he opened the door wildly.

"Sir, whatever you want, just take it."

"I don't want anything of yours. I only want to speak with you."

"About what? I told you where to go about the murder."

"I'm not here about the murder. I'm here about the werewolf."

The hunter paused and slowly took the time to regain himself back to normal, he calmed down and allowed the man to enter his cabin. The man entered and looked around the interior of the cabin, sighting the stuffed animals and trophy mounts.

"You are a hunter I can see."

"I am. Do you want anything hot to drink?"

"Do you have any coffee available?"

"I do."

"I'll take some of that. Thank you."

The hunter pours a cup of coffee for the man and brought it over to him. Giving him the coffee, he sits in his chair as the man sat in the opposite chair. The man took a sip of the coffee as he looked at the hunter.

"What can you tell me of the werewolf?"

"I didn't see the creature. I only brought it up as a possible suspect in the murder. The victim had marks on his body that were made by an animal and it couldn't have been made by a bear. The marks were too detailed."

"The bite marks and claw marks were very distinctive is what you're saying?"

"They were. I tried to tell the detectives, but they tossed the idea away. Blaming it on a bear in these woods."

The man nodded as he took another sip of the coffee.

"By the way you've spoken, you know a lot about werewolves I presume."

"I've heard about the legends. The transformation of man into beast. I've had family that have told me they've seen werewolves around this forest and in town. A legend that lives this long cannot be made of folklore tales."

"No. They cannot."

The man finished his cup of coffee and stood up, walking to the door. The hunter stood up and followed him. The man opened the door, taking his steps outside.

"Thank you for the coffee. You've shown me compassion."

"Where are you headed? If I may know."

"I'm going to speak with those detectives you've said. I want more information on the victim."

The man stepped outside of the door, walking in the snowy grounds. The hunter watched and he wanted to say something, it sat on the tip of his tongue.

"Pardon me, sir. But I would like to know your name. You didn't tell me your name."

The man turned and faced the hunter. He stared at him for quite a moment.

"Hod." The man said. "You can call me Mr. Hod."

The hunter looked on as Mr. Hod walked away from the cabin and into the forest. The hunter closed the cabin door and sat back in his chair and continued the reading the book he had placed on the table.

In the small town, the residents walked around the area, buying from local shops and selling from local shops. Many of whom only spoke about business ventures and homesteading as they refused to bring up a conversation about the murder and the mentioning of the werewolf. While the residents were doing their daily business, they spotted Mr. Hod walking into the town.

All the residents stopped what they were doing and only stared at him. Hod kept to himself, avoiding eye contact with the residents. He walked through the streets. Residents began to talk amongst themselves as to who Mr. Hod could be.

"Why's he wearing those clothes?" said a man.

"He looks dirty." a female said speaking with a friend.

"He scares me." a child said.

Mr. Hod looked around the small town and found the detectives' office and proceeded to approach it. The residents would move out of his way. Avoiding contact with him period. They continued to stare at him and make comments pertaining to the way he dressed and look as far as he appearance was concerned. Hod found himself standing in front of the detectives' office. The building was entirely made up of wood and stone. He walked up the steps of the office and entered through the door as the residents walked closer to the building.

Inside the detectives turned and stared at Hod, who stood by the door looking at them. One detective approached him, shaking his shoulders with a thrust walk, trying to intimidate Hod, but he was unshakable.

"What can we do for you sir?"

"I came here to speak on the matter of the forest murder."

"Why is that? You know the animal that did it? Or did you do it?"

The detectives laughed slightly at the detective's remark.

"I know the animal that killed the person."

The detective chuckled as he walked toward his office. Hod followed him. The detectives look on at Hod, confused about his choosing of apparel, stating it looked too ancient for their time.

"So, you found the bear that did it?"

"Wasn't a bear, detective."

"A mountain lion is what you're telling me? I thought were rid of those damn things around here."

"Neither was it a mountain lion?"

"Well, what the hell could it be?"

"The victim was killed by a werewolf."

The detective slowly turns to Hod and stared.

"You haven't been around that lone hunter, have you? Because if you have, maybe his fanatics and kookiness have rubbed off on you."

"I did speak with him and no. His fanatics have not rubbed onto me. But, they have given me insight onto this town of yours."

"Listen, sir. We aren't listening nor buying into some children's horror tales. We have our own fictitious troubles to deal with around here."

"The werewolf is no fabled tale. Of course, it has its place in ancient folklore, but those folklores are based on actual events that have taken place ages before our time."

"How would you know any of this to be true? You're part of the government's secret agency or something?"

"What I know, the government would kill, rape, and slaughter anyone to find it out for themselves."

"I'm sorry. But we're not listening to any werewolf stories here."

"I have a proposition for you, detective. You and this entire town of yours."

"Which is?"

"I will find the werewolf and I will kill the creature. After which, I will leave this town and never bother to return."

The detective looked at his colleagues, who were also silent and were unable to come up with anything to say to Hod.

"So, when you kill this werewolf you're talking about, you want some reward before you leave?"

"I want and ask for nothing in return for the werewolf's kill. As of right now, I ask to see the victim's remains."

"The remains are nothing but bone and torn muscle."

"The remains have clues that contain where the werewolf has headed and will strike next. Show me where the body is."

"The body is kept at the morgue across the street. You can go there and ask for the remains. They should let you see them."

"Thank you for the talk." Hod said as he nodded with the tip of his hat.

Hod walked to the office door and exited, leaving the entire building of detectives silent. Outside of the office, Hod walked down the steps and through the crowds of residents that surrounded him and watched him approach the morgue. Before he entered through the morgue doors, a young girl approached him. He looked down at her, noticing her smiling, but could sense her fear of him from within.

"What do you want, little girl?"

"Why are you wearing those kinds of clothes?"

"Because, the clothes present what I am and where I come from."

"So, you're old?"

"You could say that."

"How old?"

"Older than you can possibly count."

"Oh…." The little girl said.

Hod showed a faint smile before entering the morgue while the residents continue their frightening stares. Hod opened the door and entered the morgue building. He glanced around the room, searching for someone inside to speak with concerning the body of the victim. He spotted no one inside the room until he took a few steps toward a door and it opened. Out of the door walked out the morgue attendant, who was frightened for a bit at the sight and presence of Mr. Hod. Slowly shivering.

"What can I help you with, sir?"

"I'm here to see the remains of the victim that was found in the forest."

"Why would you want to see that?"

"Because my purpose here requires me to take a small study of the remains to understand what committed the murder."

"So, you work with the detectives?"

"I work alone. I am not from around here."

"But, how would you get the right to come here and solve a murder that doesn't concern you. You're not even from here and you want to solve this. Why?"

"The murderer is known throughout the lands. I came to this dead house to see the remains to uncover more of what I need. I know what killed the individual in those woods."

"We all know it was a bear that killed him."

Hod stared at the morgue attendant. Silent and showing no emotion on his face.

"A bear was not responsible for the murder."

"Then what could possibly have the strength to do such a thing?"

"It was a werewolf and apparently the people here seem to keep quiet about the lore of werewolves. As if you're all trying to hide something that cannot be hidden no longer."

"We refuse to speak of such folktales around here. We don't want to frighten the children and spread fairy tales across the town."

"By lying to yourselves, you already have."

The attendant leans her head down, facing the floor as if she's in shame of Hod's words. Hod approached her and raised up her head and stared, slightly encouraging her to spread the truth about the werewolf lore.

"Show me where the remains are, and I will be out of your sight."

The attendant nodded slowly. "This way."

Hod followed the attendant through the door and walked down a quiet and cold hallway heading toward the chamber. While walking, the attendant was hesitant to bring Hod into the chamber, fearing he could kill her and run off with the remains. Hod didn't say a word. Hod continued to follow the attendant down the hall and kept to himself.

"I truly hope this is not some form of small-town trickery. Because if it is, not only will this attendant be shown the truth. Those standing outside these walls will surely know what is going on in their town. Whether they decide to believe it or not. She's walking quite slow,

The attendant reached the chamber doors and opened them as a cold breeze swiftly went out through the opening. The breeze touched Hod, gently touching him on his face. The cold had no chilling effect on him as he kept to himself and walked into the chamber. He looked around and seen the amount of bodies that were laying on the tables. Many of them appeared to have animal-like marks on their bodies.

"The remains are over here, sir."

"What happened to these people?"

"I fear they suffered from the same animal that killed the man in the forest."

"How long has this been going on for?"

"Almost three months now."

"The detectives don't do anything about this. Who's in charge around here?"

"The detectives don't like it when we bring it up. They're owned by the upper-class elite. They control most of what goes on here. The finances, the news we receive, and so on."

"Where can I find your elite class?"

"I, I do not know, sir. They keep to themselves and appear as they please. We only answer to them. Most of us here don't even question them out of the fear of death."

"Seems to me that there's been enough death going on around here to worry about your own selves."

The attendant walked over to one of the walls and pulled out the table, where the remains laid. Hod walked over and looked at them. Pulling out tools like a forensic scientist. He glanced at the remains and took deep looks at the bones, the muscles, and the skin fragments that remained. The attendant stood by and watched Hod study the remains in every detail that he possibly could. Using a magnifying glass to look closer at the bite marks within the bones. Hod looked around and didn't see the skull.

"Where's the skull?"

"This is all that remained."

"They didn't find the skull?"

"It is possible it's still out in the forest. They won't go back and check. They told us this is all they needed to start their search for the killer."

Hod pushed the table back into its closing and closed the chamber door. He walked out of the room and back down the hallway. The attendant tried to keep up by following him because of him power walking.

"Wait. Where are you going?"

"I am going into the forest to find the skull. When I do, I shall return here and deliver it to you to compete the remains. Without the skull, I won't have all the information I need."

Hod walked out of the morgue with the attendant looking nervous as to what could come up between Hod and the skull. Outside, Hod noticed the number of residents that stood outside of the morgue had increased. They stood around him, making way for him to walk by. The residents stared at him as he kept to himself.

"Who do you think you are." A man said. "Why are you here trespassing our town. We don't need foreigners like you around here."

Hod stopped and turned toward the man. The residents took a few steps back to avoid being in Hod's eyesight. He kept his attention focused on the man who appeared to be a farmer as he wore a farmer's garment.

"Trespassing your town. How could I do such a thing when I am here on duty."

"We don't know who you are. Hell, we've never even seen you before. You must be some guy from the outer borders of the forest."

"I am from the outer borders and once again, I am here on a duty. Not a vacation. As I told the attendant inside the morgue, you, townspeople live in an area of lies. You all know the truth and refuse to believe it and accept it. You'll rather live in a world of make believe than live in a world where the truth reigns. The truth of the matter is that it wasn't a bear that committed those acts of slaughter in the forest. It was a werewolf and the beast is still out there."

"You can't talk to us like that! You're not even a resident of this town. You have no right to speak to us in such a manner!"

"I have spoken. When I return from the forest, if I am to see you or any of these people again. I will speak once more. Your detectives won't solve your problems for you and now I will solve this one problem as it affects more than this measly little town."

Hod walked away, heading toward the exit of the town into the forest. The residents stood watch and looked at the farmer. The farmer looked around and glanced at his fellow towns people.

"Don't you even dare look at me like that! I was standing up for you people and what do I get? No respect, no aid, not even another voice to stand up with mine own."

Hod continued walking through the snow-covered ground as he entered the forest. The sounds of people form the town began to fade away as he went deeper into the forest. Hearing nothing but silence and a few specks of bird in the sky flying over the trees. He looked around in the snow, searching for the spot where the victim was killed.

"By the look of the snow, the victim's final place of living isn't far from this particular spot. Its closer than it appears to be."

Hod walked past the pair of trees and spotted claw marks in the wood. The claw marks were dug deep into the wood. He rubbed the wood, searching for something that could be remaining inside. Hardly finding anything, he pulled out a knife from his coat and started to slice the tree in the areas of where the claw marks were stamped. Slicing and even cutting through the wood, a small object fell out of the hole and into the snow. Hod stopped what he was doing and placed the knife back into his coat. He kneeled and searched in the snow to find what had dropped from the tree. He picked up the small object and looked closer at it with his magnifying glass.

"The object is a piece of a nail. The werewolf must've broken it off when it dug into the tree. Possibly at the moment of pouncing the victim. By the look of it, the beast is very strong and could've possibly killed the man with just the force of its lunging toward him."

Hod turned around and looked in front of him about a few feet away and seen dried blood in the snow. He walked over to it and rubbed the blood.

"This is the spot of the victim's fall. Now, where is his skull?"

Hod began digging in the snow with a pair of branches that were laying in the snow nearby a tree. He dug until he could see the dead grass underneath the snow. He continued digging in the surrounding areas and couldn't find the skull. After several minutes of digging, Hod stopped and looked around to see anything sticking up in the snow.

"Where is it?"

Hod started to walk and noticed something in the snow that laid in front of his left foot. He dug into the snow at the exact spot and instantly seen the eye socket of the skull. He reached down and pulled the skull up from the snow and wiped away the snow. He placed the skull into his bag and proceeded back into town.

II - THE BLUE MOON

While the sun was preparing itself to set away from the town and night was slowly approaching, Hod entered the town with the skull in tow. The residents returned and followed him back to the morgue. He didn't look back at the residents as they slowly followed him and were almost on his back. They noticed the bag and tried to take peeks to find out what was inside. Hod grabbed the bag and held it tightly to his chest and maintained his focus.

"I ask of you all to leave the bag alone and let me be."

"We only want to know what you have inside."

"An important object in finding the werewolf."

The residents stopped walking and stood still as they watched Hod enter the doors of the morgue. The residence kept to themselves and not even one of them spoke a word as they went back to their regular business. Hod entered back into the morgue and the attendant seen him come through the door and approached him.

"I take it you've found the skull?"

"I have."

Hod placed the bag onto the table and pulled out the skull. He handed the skull carefully to the attendant who placed it next to the remaining parts of the victim's body. She scanned the remains in full, trying to sort out the possibilities of the victim's body. Mr. Hod carefully examined the body himself. From the skull to the feet.

"What do you perceive now?" The attendant said.

"I perceive a full evaluation of the victim. There could be some werewolf venom in the bones."

"We can do a search through the bone marrow."

"Let's give it a test."

Hod and the attendant did their part of the test runs. Operating as best as they could.

"I'm sure you heard about the other cases besides the one in the woods."

"What other cases?" Hod wondered.

"There was a couple that was attacked, and a pair of bankers ambushed in the streets."

"I was not aware of such events. Were these before this recent one?"

"Yes. All the bodies had similar marks to this one here. I'm not sure what kind of animal would do such a thing so discreetly. But I'm hearing a lot about werewolves. So, I'll take what I can get."

"Believe my words, werewolves exist, and they come in all shapes, sizes, and forms. Some are just wild beasts, others intelligent creatures."

Upon the work, they discovered the venom of the werewolf indeed remained inside the bone marrow. Yet, when removed, the venom glowed a bright blue. Its hue was brighter than the lights in the room. The attendant stepped back from the table as Hod kept his gaze upon it. Before quickly covering the glow with his hand.

"What was that?"

"Spirituality." Hod said. "A powerful one."

While the attendant gathered the venom, Hod glanced toward the window and saw nightfall had arrived and the moon's light glistened upon the clear barrier between Hod and the outside.

"How are we going to tell the detectives about this?"

"Tell them." Hod said, his eyes locked on the outside.

"What will you do?"

"Find the creature. Night has come and it's out there. Lurking. Waiting."

"You said the light from the venom was spiritual."

"Which means we're dealing with a spiritual werewolf."

"I don't understand. I've never heard of such a thing."

"Spiritual werewolves are rare. Very rare."

"As in treasure rare?"

"Rare as in Eden rare." Hod proclaimed. "Either the creature came through another dimension or from worship. Doesn't matter. I will find it."

Hod left from the morgue and went outside. Walking towards the woods. A loud screech echoes through the surroundings. Hod stopped in his tracks, circling the area, listening to the scream. Tracking its whereabouts and without notice, Hod ran toward the sound and found himself running deeper into the town and as he reached the source of the scream, he stopped and could only stare.

"What is this?" Hod uttered.

Standing in front of Hod was a deceased woman and on top of her, gnawing at her throat was the werewolf. Tall, grey-haired, and brute size. The werewolf stood up, facing Hod. The werewolf let out a howl and the color of the moon transformed into a blue moon. Hod looked up, seeing the change in color.

"What are you?"

The Werewolf roared at Hod. Moving his hand to the side, pulling out a revolver and firing toward the wolf, which runs from the shots. Hod went and chased the beast into the woods. Hod stopped near the entrance and mediated. Looking at his revolver, he nodded and reloaded.

"I have to stop this."

III - THE LIGHT OF THE MOON

Hod entered the forest in search of the spiritual werewolf. Following its tracks in the snow at every turn, except for the moment where the tracks are nowhere to be found. Not even a scratch mark in the snow. Hod continued moving through the woods, hearing the faint sound of howling in the distance. Covered in the trees.

"I know you're here." Hod said.

From the distance, the werewolf lunged out at Hod. Its fangs sharp and pointed. The hair of the wolf glistened in the moonlight. Hod moved quickly and took a shot, missing as the werewolf returned to the trees in the distance. Hod breathed quietly while continuing to aim the gun.

"Just one time."

The werewolf lunged once more toward Hod, the gun was raising as it fires, hitting the wolf in the left shoulder. The werewolf slips in his steps and tumbles down to the snowy ground. Hod runs toward the beast, which swipes toward him with his right arm, Hod fires another shot as the wolf lets out a screeching howl. Hod sighs, lowering the sun slowly.

"That's it."

The moonlight looms over the wolf's body and from it rises a spirit. The spirit startles Hod without question, yet with curiosity in his cold eyes.

"What is this?"

The spirit flows higher into the air, passing over the trees and vanishing into the night sky. Later, Hod returns to the town to tell them of the news. The werewolf is dead, but the spirit still wanders.

"What must we do now?" A civilian asked.

"Take care of yourselves." Hod replied. "My work has just begun."

Hod left the small town of Rosebane. Returning to the lair of the *Symbolum Venatores*, the monster hunters within the shadows of the world.

Hod will return...

THE PASSOVER

An uproar has been ongoing in a small county concerning the event known as Easter. Two men appeared before a crowd of the county's residents, stating the truth of Easter and exposing its pagan history and roots. The two men speak to the crowd about the word Easter and how it refers back to the pagan goddess known as Astarte or Ishtar. They even went into detail of how the rabbit and eggs came into the pagan holiday.

"The rabbit is an unclean animal. Why would you people entertain such an abomination." One man said.

"The rabbit is also a symbol for fertility and the eggs deal with fertility rights as well. In the ancient days, the eggs would be colored with blood and placed on grounds concerning their worship toward their pagan goddess."

A middle-aged man in the crowd approached the two men speaking. He appeared angry at their words and couldn't hold in his emotions toward them.

"You two are just trying to ruin our traditions! We didn't ask for you to come here and talk to us about its history."

"If you are were true believers as you say, you would be partaking in the Passover. The first of the Most High's feasts and the beginning of the new year. Exiting the dead season and coming into the season of life."

"January is the beginning of the new year!" A woman yelled. "What are you talking about?!"

"To you and this world, yes. But to the Yahweh's people, Passover is the beginning of the year."

"What are you guys talking about? We praise the name of Jesus every Easter. We eat lamb every Easter. We know what we're doing and the Lord knows our hearts."

"That they're desperately wicked and who can know them but the Father." The men said.

"We know why we partake in Easter. We've been doing it since the time of our parents, grandparents, and so on! Leave us be!"

The two men turned to one another. They agreed to leave, but decided to give the crowd one last warning that concerns themselves and their partaking of Easter.

"We leave this last message. For those of you who will not be partaking in the pagan day of Easter, leave this county before dark and find shelter in the wilderness. As for those of you who will be partaking in worship your pagan goddess. You all will be slaughtered before sunrise by what we've grown to call, an Overseer. We leave you, Shalom."

The two men walked away and left the county. Only a few in the crowd took the two men's warning seriously and left the county. Most of the people stayed in the county and partook in the worship of Astarte. Later that night, a full moon shined down upon the county as the people partook in the celebration of Easter. Some even presented carved images of Astarte.

"I will say those men were telling the truth." One man said to the people. "But we love our traditions."

The people partied and drank for most of the night. They later ate a table full of lamb, swine, and even shrimp. They ate until they could not even lift a spoon or fork to put in their mouths. They were drunk off of the wine and beer they drank. Some of the men swapped wives and laid with them that night in their homes.

While they partied and worshipped Astarte, walking in the wilderness nearby was a figure that carried a hybrid weapon of a machete and axe. The figure paused as it look out to toward the county, hearing the reveling and partying of the people. The figure proceeded to enter the county. The figure looked like a human, but from its presence, through discernment of spirit, you could tell it wasn't a human being.

People ran out of their houses and into the streets, dancing and partying. Bringing the party to the outside. But, when they turned and looked, they seen the figure slowly walking toward them. Believing it to be some form of a joke being played by someone who lived in the county. They laughed it off and walked toward it.

"What are you doing dressed like that?!" A man said. "Who are you playing a joke on?"

The figure raised its arm and swiped the weapon toward the man, slashing his neck. As he falls to the ground, the figure walks over his body and proceeds to slaughter everyone else in its sights. From that night until sunrise, the figure slaughtered and killed every man, woman, and child that was dwelling in the county and even destroyed their Easter images and smashed the carved images of Astarte. Leaving most of it in the streets. As the sun began to rise, the figure vanished into the wilderness.

Within a few hours after sunrise, the residents that fled the county returned to see the streets filled with the dead and their blood flowing. The county still stood, but its Easter images and artifacts were destroyed. A man looked down and seen the smashed Astarte statue. He looked up and turned to his wife.

"Those men were right. The Overseer came and cleansed this place."

"We were warned and they were warned." His wife said.

"Yes. Honey. We have to thank God for it. Greatly."

After cleaning up the county, the remaining residents removed all the images of Easter within their homes and burned them. They later decided to partake in Passover rather than the pagan day of Easter. During the night, a young boy living in the county had a dream where he seen the two men appear to the county again, proclaiming that the Overseer would return if they continue to keep their traditions rather than converting to the Laws of Yahweh and keeping his holy feast days. In the dream were images concerning Halloween, Christmas, Valentine's Day, St. Patrick's Day, Sunday Worship, and even their birthday celebrations.

In the morning, the boy awoke and told his mother and father about the dream. They rubbed it off, saying that it was only a dream and nothing more. Within a few months, the two men returned and gave warnings concerning the other pagan holidays and declaring the Overseer would return.

THE BOOK OF THE ELECT

<u>HAND OF DOLPH</u>

From the eyes I saw nothing but darkness. The cold air rattled me by its cool touch as it swooped in from the doorway. Trying my hardest to lay back to sleep, I could not. Upon deciding to get up from the bed and take a small walk around my home, I began to wonder if I was having an unusual event in my own home. True, I did have my skepticism on the matter of ghosts or spirits. Whichever you prefer to call them. I did hesitate to do a full search of my home because of my thoughts telling me of a burglar in the home. Once that thought entered my mind, I immediately grabbed my sword and walked slowly through my home.

Upon finding nothing inside the home. I took a big exhale and walked back to bed. Few hours later I wake up to the same sight of darkness and the cold air had returned. Now, I wonder if someone really is inside my home. I hear sounds of footsteps coming from the kitchen area. I jumped up and ran toward the kitchen. While I entered it, no one was inside the kitchen. Wiping my head from this strange occurrence, I had no answers to give to these kinds of questions. I started to have a low level of panic inside of my body and rushed back to the bedroom. I later went back to sleep.

I woke up the following morning to the sense of someone in my home. I decided to get dressed and I walked into the front room of the home and I saw no one. But, I could swear I heard someone in the home beside myself and I could hear their voice. It sounded like a elderly woman's voice talking as if she wasn't the only one in the room.

After doing my labor, I returned home and prepared for bed. Though, this time when I entered the home, I saw the elderly woman standing in the hallway, looking towards the kitchen. I called out to her and she didn't make the slightest move. I called to her again and she slowly inched her way toward my sight. She stared at me with cold eyes and I stared back. She gave me a nod and walked down the hall and evaporated in thin air. From that moment on, I knew I wasn't alone in the home and my skepticism had disappeared from my mind as I had witnessed a ghost firsthand.

After witnessing the woman, I began trying to contact her spirit, so I could understand why she would be in the home and not on the Other Side as they like to call it. After a few attempts of practicing with the Ouija Board, I came into contact with the woman. She told me her name was Margaret and she was a former resident of the home during the late 18th Century. I asked her why she was still in the home and she responded by saying that the Endless Ones had kept her here due to her sacrifice of saving her own lover from being murdered by another spirit that once dwelled inside this very home.

Week after week and day after day, I continued to have conversations with Margaret and discussed possible ways to help her leave this realm. She told me that there would be possible ways to help her go into the Other Side, but I would need the tools necessary to accomplish the task. The first tool she told me was knowledge of both this world and the other and how they work and co-exist among each other. The second tool would be faith that I would come out of it alive myself and not lost in the time space as a spirit wandering the earth looking for a way out.

Upon the coming months, I immediately dove my head into many books, accounts, and historical records that contained details of the Other Side to demonology to the Occult and to faith and how it works when facing these kinds of odds. After about four months, I came to the senses that I would be ready to help Margaret enter the Other Side.

One night on sixth day, I sat by myself and began inciting a ritual that would help me conjure up Margaret and send her into the

Other Side. While saying the ritual I seen Margaret standing in front of me and as I looked up toward her I noticed a very dark shadow behind her. I felt the same cold air as before when my eyes gazed upon it.

From the shadow I could tell it was indeed the same darkness that I saw before. Margaret couldn't say anything, but I could tell that she was in fear and I didn't have a clue how to protect her from that dark shadow. But, from her eyes I could tell that she knew what the dark shadow was, and she was very still not to move away from it or it could've possibly snatched her deeper into the abyss.

From that night on, I continued to study and do a plethora of research to help save her from this house and the dark shadow. Upon doing my due diligence, I uncovered that the land of which the home is built over was once used as a place where the occult would come and perform rituals and sacrifices to a being called The Unheard-Of. Their rituals and sacrifices would first bring out the Endless Ones, which is what Margaret had told me about. After the Endless Ones come and go, they deliver the prayers of the worshippers of The Unheard-Of in hopes of him giving them their prayers and answering them in any part of their lives.

After studying and reading about the Endless Ones and The Unheard-Of, I finally managed to prepare myself physically and spiritually to perform the session. During that night, I managed to conjure up Margaret again and she appeared before me. She appeared and had a small smile on her face. As I continued the session, I once again felt the cold air touch my face and the darkness appeared in my sights. This time it stood directly in front of me. The fears and doubts of failing had started to overcome me due to the shadow in my presence. I could hear Margaret's voice, telling me to fight the shadow with my faith and understanding. I gained my strength and continued to session while the shadow stood there. Eventually, the shadow disappeared, and I witnessed Margaret glow a bright white, a white unlike anything I've seen on this earth. The light emitted from her and she slowly ascended and vanished. Afterwards, I could only feel peace and security, knowing that she is no longer trapped and has moved over onto the Other Side.

To this day, I can still remember that incident and I've also heard countless stories and accounts of others having the same incidents in their own lives. It's been about ten years since the incident and I've learned quite a lot in between those ten years concerning the Other Side, the Endless Ones, and The Unheard-Of. Though, my story isn't the only one that must be told to the world.

I am only known to the people of this world and the elect few as Dolph and I have just presented to you the story of how I became a helping hand into saving a trapped spirit from the darkness that dwells in this world and beyond.

DREAMS AND VISIONS OF LEVI

These are the dreams and visions of Levi, "*The One who Called Them*". These are the words of gratitude and faith of Levi, who prayed and kept faith in the Most High that he would deliver them from the treacherous world where elemental beings were wrecking havoc across the earth. Where no mortal man could find a way in an attempt to stop them. As many people of the earth began to lose faith, Levi held on to his faith and never thought of relinquishing it. The world was as if the tribulation had already taken effect and the world knew of its power and terror. Beings made from the earth, fire, water, air, carbon, ice, sand, and amongst many others were crossing the earth, doing much damage that could be possible to witness.

Blessed is Levi for his great faith. Levi, a young man whose eyes were indeed opened by the Most High, saw a vision of the Holy One on the throne, he saw the heavens and the angels above. Levi knew what he saw was the Messiah sitting on the throne in the future days to come where his Kingdom will come down from Shamayim and will rule for one thousand years on the earth until the Final Battle between the Lawless One and The Most High Yah. Levi had concerned himself for trying to help the earth by fighting against the Elementals, yet he knew that they were sent by the Most High to teach humanity a lesson in humility and for them to truly know their place.

Another night, Levi had fell asleep and was witnessed to another dream where he saw all the Elementals standing near the ocean coast, where he saw above a total of seven beings come down from the sky. He could see their wings and how bright they were. The beings looked as if they were made of some form of metal not known to earth or humans. Levi understood that the seven beings were a symbol of a force that will come to earth when the time is right. Levi would tell his advising Marshal about his dreams and he was mocked and ridiculed of them as the people of the earth were already giving up and waiting to die to the Elementals. Levi never gave up hope or faith as the majority of the world had given up.

Levi went asleep again and was revisited with another dream, where he saw the seven beings standing before the Elementals and all of humanity. The beings stood above the skyscrapers of the earth and fought against the Elementals, killing them without any pure force. Levi would watch as he witnessed the Elementals being destroyed by the seven beings and he knew it was a sign of good things to come upon the earth. The dreams stayed constant with Levi wherever he would go, the dreams were on his mind and his faith was increasing. Throughout the months, Levi began having visions, where he would see each of the seven beings individually and he would speak to them. He learned their names and their purpose.

In the first vision, Levi found himself in the clouds as he stood in front of the first being, who's revealed its name as Master Titan to Levi. Levi was able to see Master Titan in all of its glory. Master Titan was made of a material not suited for earth, suited for the heavens. Master Titan had told Levi to prepare himself and his allies for their coming, even though they may not listen. They are coming. Levi would tell his Marshal and allies about the dreams and visions. They perceived them to be a fairy tale that Levi was creating in his head.

The second vision had Levi find himself standing before the second being in the clouds, who told Levi its name was Covert Ghost and it told Levi its purpose and also revealed that it was also coming and warned Levi to tell his allies. Levi continued to tell his Marshal and allies about the dreams and visions, and they continued to deny him a word. Levi kept his faith strong and his hope held high towards the Father.

The third being appeared in a dream to Levi, where he saw himself standing in the clouds again facing the third being. The third beings told Levi its name was Iron Cavalier and its purpose was to aid the previous two in the first battle against the Elementals. Stating that they would win the first battle to make a statement to humanity. Levi understood Iron Cavalier very well and was told to warn his allies about their coming. Levi told Cavalier that they would not listen and yet, Cavalier repeatedly told Levi to warn them. Just to give them the warning is all he would have to do.

Levi had given his Marshal and allies the entire warning of the three beings appearing for what they called the "*first battle*". Levi was laughed at and mocked for his words, he didn't fall short and he gave them the rest of the warnings and left the area. Upon doing so, he witnessed the three beings come down from the sky for everyone to witness. The three beings were Master Titan, Covert Ghost, and Iron Cavalier. They had arrived on the earth and split up in three paths, heading towards the Elementals. Levi knew his faith was answered. The Marshal and his allies came toward him and asked for forgiveness to their ignorance. Levi forgave them as they aligned together with the beings to fight off the Elementals. Though, Levi remembered that he saw a total of seven beings in his dreams and these were only the first three of seven.

After a week, Levi had a vision where he found himself hovering in the air and encountering the fourth being who called itself Skycrush. Skycrush told Levi that he travels through the air and is coming for the "second battle". Levi warned his Marshal and allies about the second battle approaching and they believed him, but still had conjured up thoughts about giving up completely. Levi's faith was still intact, even after the "first battle" was over and won by the first three beings.

In another dream, Levi came into contact and was visited by the fifth being. Levi had seen the being's head as it appeared as a mechanical lion's head with golden eyes. The being told Levi its name was known to earth as Lion Blade and it was coming for the second battle. Levi understood its words and continued to warn the Marshal and his allies about the second battle's coming. Even though, Levi was stuck with his teammates Sheba and Felix as they were tasked with taking down Baal and Moloch for destroying the environment, the beings still ringed a bell in Levi's conscious.

Later, Levi had a vision where he seen the sixth being who called itself Red Slash, for its red coloring. Red Slash had told Levi that the second battle would be more difficult than the first battle due to the increasing power of the Elementals. Levi understood the words of Red Slash and continued to warn everyone that he came into contact with. By that time, the Elementals were stronger than before and most of humanity had completely given up, except for Levi, Sheba, Felix, and his Marshal.

As the second battle had ensured and Levi saw the beings were having a more difficult time with the Elementals than before, he continued to pray for faith and hope that the beings would overcome the Elementals' increasing strength. Levi kept his faith and hope intact as the fight for the earth was becoming more difficult as the days went by. The two men, Baal and Moloch had increased the Elementals' power by polluting most of the earth through cloud spraying and genetically modified crops.

During the days where hope seemed almost lost to many, where the Elementals were apparently winning against the beings because of their increased strength. Levi had another dream and vision where he stood in the midst of the seventh being, who was more powerful than the first six. Levi had noticed something drastically different about the seventh being. The seventh being was covered in the colors of white, gold, and red, all of which shined from its presence. The seventh being had told Levi that his name was Armega Grath and he would save the earth from the most powerful of all Elementals, known as Barawk, an elemental made of lightning. Armega told Levi that he and the six beings were called Vigils and their purpose is to watch over humanity until the time of tribulation and judgment.

"*What you see here, Levi, are the days where faith must be restored, and hope shall never be lost.*" Armega said. "*I am now coming to end this battle and bring peace to the earth.*"

Levi would question Armega Grath about the end of the battle and how the future would be. Armega would only tell him that he would end the battle and would bring peace to humanity for a limited time as there are other beings who exist and are destined to come to earth to prepare for the End Days.

"When you see me come down from the heavens, you will know this great and third fight will be over and the Elect will be protected until the time of tribulation and judgment occurs."

Levi had awoken and found himself on another mission with Sheba and Felix as they were at their final attempt to stop Baal and Moloch. While on their mission, a loud trumpet had sounded from the sky and Levi knew it was Armega Grath and he saw him coming down from sky, glowing and shining in his presence. Armega had aided the remaining Vigils in the third battle against Barawk and Esh, an elemental made of fire. After defeating and killing all of the Elementals, the Vigils revealed themselves to the world and to humanity. Armega looked down and saw Levi. He thanked him for his faith, trust, and hope and vowed that they would return when the next threat makes its presence known to humanity.

These are the dreams and visions of Levi, *"The One who Called Them"*. Blessed be his name as one of The Elect who will inherit the Kingdom of Yah in the days to come upon the earth and upon all of Creation, be it the Father's Will.

DREAM OF THE UNHEARD-OF

Legends have told about a unseen force that works in the shadows. A malevolent force. Some call this force the Devil or ha-Satan as others tend to use other names that appear lower than the previous two such as Lucifer, Mammon, accuser, adversary, Father of Lies, deceiver, old serpent, the dragon, Son of the Morning, or even Son of Perdition. One name that the ancients used was The Unheard-Of. Though, The Unheard-Of has a different description as far as appearances go, but the attitude and character remained the same.

The Unheard-Of is a legendary figure that goes throughout history in many cultures and mythologies. Only mention in a certain few and removed from many in recent memory, The Unheard-Of has a profound history of accounts in which he has been present among the earth and humanity itself. It is said that he is the one who corrupted mankind in order to have them follow in his image and laws. The Unheard-Of is also known for creating the large amounts of war and destruction that have been on the earth and are still continuing at a small, but faster rate. For those who have looked into the tale of The Endless Ones, they have discovered that The Unheard-Of does not work alone and has his soldiers known as The Endless Ones to do his biddings for him. He also has humans on is side as well, giving them promises that they can't deny, yet he delivers some and denies many, thus taking their spirit when they die on the earth and keeping them in his domain of darkness and void.

At one time, an elderly man by the name of Gaius wrote in his own chronicle book of how The Unheard-Of had appeared before him and offered him a chance at immortality and wealth, if he did what he was commanded to do. The Unheard-Of had commanded

Gaius to attack his descendants and murder them in cold blood. Gaius, a holy and earthly, but spiritual man declined the offer and rebuked The Unheard-Of, casting him out of his presence. The Unheard-Of is known for appearing before humans that he sees bold enough to take on his offering in exchange for power and wealth. There is even the story of how The Unheard-Of attempted to bride the Messiah into ruling the world and its kingdoms. The Messiah declined the offer and The Unheard-Of disappeared.

Through the numerous accounts of history, The Unheard-Of has been operating in the shadows, just as he does in modern time. If many were to look at the wars, the famines, the desolations, the violence, the purging of many cities, towns, countries, states, provinces, parishes, and even small islands, they would see the foul hands of The Unheard-Of on them. The Unheard-Of would also hand out false lies in order to cause disturbances in many groups that would seem to be untouchable and unbreakable, yet he has managed to break many up and cause grudges among them.

In claims of The Unheard-Of, it is said that he usually appears before humans in a form of the serpent or in the form of a man who appears well-dressed and speaks with flattering, kind words. Though his heart is full of evil, envy, strife, and violence as he seeks to destroy his next victim. History shows how The Unheard-Of was formed and what turned him into the entity that he is in this time. The Unheard-Of was once a servant for the Most High *YAH*, aligned as one of the primary archangels among Shamayim. His name was Abednego, which means shining and servant of light. When the day came that the Most High created the humans, known as Adam and Eve and the Most High told the angels of Shamayim to bow before them since they were created in His image. The angels bowed except for Abednego, who refused to bow due to the Most High creating mankind from dust as he and the angels were created from fire. Abednego's pride began to corrupt him and he set out to dethrone the Most High from his Kingdom and even convinced one third of the angels to aid him in doing so. When the Abednego revealed his true intentions, his allied angels stood beside him and faced the Most High and his angels.

The War in Shamayim took place for a total of seven days in human time as Michael The Archangel battle Abednego and cast him out of Shamayim along with his allied angels. After being cast out, The Most High stated that his days are numbered and there will come a time when he must face his judgment and will be sentenced for eternity. Now, Abednego is known as The Unheard-Of and the rebel angels are known as The Endless Ones, though some human spirits have become Endless Ones as well do to their dark spirit and character.

It is prophesied that in the near future, The Unheard-Of will rise up a man in the earth, a political figure, a man who will be loved by all in the world except by the believers and followers of the Most High. The Unheard-Of calls his leading man Abaddon and he will command The Endless Ones to do his biddings on earth as The Unheard-Of watches over him and applauds his actions in desolating the earth and killing the true believers of the Most High.

During the days before that terrible account, the earth will be filled with nonbelievers and followers of The Unheard-Of. Faith of the Most High will evaporate from many of humanity and will in turn go toward The Unheard-Of. Many humans will end up worshipping themselves and building temples and graven images to themselves in honor of themselves. Their birthdays will become their most celebrated day in the year. To this day, The Unheard-Of still works in his ways, more so than ever as his time is becoming short and he's gathering as many spirits as he can for the coming battle that will take place in the future.

Many say they dream of The Unheard-Of, stating that he's trying to gain their attention in seeking a deal for their spirit. Some accept and some decline, but all will have their answer when the battle occurs on the earth as the sun will be darkened and the moon will turn into blood and the stars will fall out of the sky. The heavens will be shaken, and the earth will rumble as the day is approaching for The Unheard-Of's greatest fall.

THE OLD MAN

In the distant past of mankind, during the days of iniquity and transgression, in a small cabin on the outskirts of the city lived an old man. Though, his name has been lost in history, but what he had accomplished stood the test of time. For the Old Man was a consistent man, a man who did his labor and rested on the seventh day. He was humble and to many people righteous. For people feared him because of his submission to The Most High and he feared the Most High greatly.

One day, when the king known to his land as Ahab, son of Omri arrived at the Old Man's home with his wife Jezebel, the daughter of Ethbaal king of the Zidonians by his side. He walked toward the door and proceeded to knock, but it opened, and the Old Man stood in the presence of a king and his queen.

"It is I Ahab, your king and my great wife and queen, Jezebel." said Ahab.

"For what purpose does thou intend to make by stepping onto my property, King Ahab?" the Old Man replied. "Is there something you wish to take from me? Is there a bounty on my head for a crime that I did not commit? Is there a damsel who has claimed that I laid with her when I did not? For what purpose does thou have by standing at my doorstep?"

"Calm yourself, sir. Thou are not in any trouble. I and my lovely queen here would like to speak with you about a proposal that involves my kingdom and yourself in a pact."

The Old Man stared deeply in Ahab's eyes and didn't bother

to even glance into Jezebel's. For he knew what kind of woman she was and he could see how her heart was full of rebellion, jealously, and envy. He allowed Ahab and Jezebel into his home carefully, looking back for any signs of Ahab's soldiers that could be surrounding his home without his knowledge. Though, the Old Man never showed any fear to Ahab or Jezebel. He knew The Most High was with him at all times.

Ahab and Jezebel sat down in his chairs as he approached them at the table, where he had water sitting. Jezebel began to scratch her throat as she glanced over to the water. Ahab noticed her behavior and signaled the Old Man.

"Good sir, my queen appears to be thirsty from the long journey over to your home. Could you care to give her some water."

The Old Man poured some water into a small cup and handed it over to Jezebel, who drank all the water that laid still in the cup. She sat the cup down and smiled at the Old Man, thanking him for the water. He nodded and returned his attention toward Ahab.

Jezebel continued her way of gaining attention in the room by interrupting the conversations between the Old Man and Ahab, suggesting alternative terms and agreements as to what Ahab's offer to the Old Man was about. The Old Man scratched and rubbed his forehead as Jezebel continued to interrupt the conversation. The Old Man raised his hand toward Jezebel, silencing her. Ahab noticed the situation.

"How dare thee decide to raise thou hand toward my queen! You do understand that I could have you in chains if I must be."

"Fear not, King Ahab. For I will not smite your queen. I am a patience man and I would never lay thy hand on a woman. For it is injustice to *YAH* and to His Kingdom."

Ahab shook his head and Jezebel puffed her breath and mumbled in front of the Old Man and Ahab. Ahab tried to relax Jezebel, but his couldn't as she slapped him on his face and caused Ahab to stumble in his seat. The Old Man laid down his head, seeing a woman attack a man in his presence of all in his own home.

"You would never tell me what to do!" Jezebel said. "I am

your queen for a purpose and that purpose is to fulfill what is rightfully mine. If I command you to bow down to our Lord, Baal, you would do as much. For I am your queen."

"Ahab, I suggest you get rid of your nail instantly before more harm comes your way. A saucy woman will never do a man any good unless she is fully capable of submitting toward your husband. I would never bow before any false god nor idol. For I am a believer and follower of the Most High and he will protect me."

"You accuse me of not submitting?!" Jezebel yelled. "My king only submits to me! I shall never submit to anyone who walks among this earth."

"Perhaps you do not submit to the Most High. For he is the one who gave you the breath of the spirit of life. He is the one that placed you into this land that you have gained the opportunity of becoming queen. Yet, you throw it all away for more power and destruction. Tell me it isn't so and you can rebuke me."

"I have no need to respond to thou ridiculous questions, old man. I am your queen and you will do what I command thee to do!"

Ahab leaned over toward the Old Man and whispered in his ears before standing up and leaving the home with Jezebel, who continued to rant on about her royalty and good looks. After seeing the king and queen leave his land, the Old Man walked into the center of his home and went down on both knees and prayed to the Most High for forgiveness, in allowing the two royalties into his own home of solitude and set-apart.

"Abba Father, please forgive thee for bringing the iniquity into my home of solitude and peace. Please continue to give me the courage and wisdom while I continue with my earthly life as I know that one day I will be in your presence and will look upon thou face in glory and in peace. Please protect me from the world that stands boldly outside of these walls. Please let your spirit fall onto those who will obey your laws, your statutes, and your commandments. For they will deem themselves as the worthy and Elect in your name and in this world full of evil and wrought. In your glory, AMEN."

The Old Man continued to live in his home that stayed set-apart from Ahab and Jezebel's kingdom and from the world. Many years later, after the downfall of Ahab and Jezebel, the Old Man grew even more weary as he later found himself guiding a young man and his wife. After several more years, the Old Man died, and he gave up the ghost and entered Shamayim to live and dwell among the Most High and the Heavenly Host that stood around him.

THE FAITH OF STEPHANIE

During the late days in the land of Urz, there lived a young woman named Stephanie and she was lovely, respectful, and had great fear for the Most High. Stephanie desired a life full of peace and prosperity. Though, in Urz, she could only gain that peace and prosperity through a man who was fearful of the Most High and followed his laws, statutes, and commandments. Though, there were many men that dwelled in the land of Urz and out of a thousand, not a single man was found to have been worthy of Stephanie's love.

"Oh, my Father in Shamayim, please deliver my praise to find someone who I can truly be with and live among them in your loving sight." Stephanie said.

Stephanie was twenty and two years old when she first went to search for a man who had the qualities of the righteous that lived among the earth. She continued her search throughout the entire land of Urz and still wasn't able to come to terms as to why she couldn't find a man worthy of her presence and love. One day, she left the land of Urz and traveled east toward the kingdom of Akadia and was greeted by her grandmother, Merith, who was fearful of the Most High and was greatly protected by Him.

Merith was one hundred and thirty years old when Stephanie greeted her in the kingdom of Akadia. Stephanie entered her grandmother's home and stayed with her for a number of four nights and four days as she began to learn wise words and knowledge from her grandmother. Merith stated that a man must seek a woman and not the other way around. She began to speak of another woman who was named Beth, she had lived in a land not far from Urz, who seek greatly to find a husband. Merith said that after seven years of wandering and searching, Beth finally found a man worthy of her love in the presence of the Most High. Many men had come before her and did not meet the qualities that she deserved and seek.

"What should I have to do to place myself in the right position or area for a righteous one to stand in front of me and take me as his wife?" Stephanie asked. "What must I do to achieve such a task?"

"I suggest to you, my granddaughter, that you work on yourself first and foremost before going and searching for a husband to cleave onto. I do not want you to make the mistake that many women and men have made over the centuries when it came to this type of discussion. Only a few have listened to words such as this and have succeeded in finding a husband or wife. Many decided to close their ears and ignore the wise council and ended up failing in the process."

Stephanie continued to learn from her grandmother as she stayed in her home for another three night and three days and gained even more knowledge on the discussion and began building up her faith. After the three nights and three days was due, Stephanie left her grandmother's home and left the kingdom of Akadia and returned to her home in the land of Urz, where she dwelled for seven more years, seeking and searching for a husband to cleave onto. During the seven years, she met a man, who spoke with flattering words and impressed Stephanie. They became closer as nights and days went by. Eventually, Stephanie discovered that the man she was seeing had done evil in the sight the Most High and discovered he had been killed in battle against the armies of Isabelle while aiding with Queen Zimmah in the kingdom of Zimmahiah.

Three more years had passed, and Stephanie was only holding onto her own faith in the Most High to give her a husband to cleave onto. During one night, she went down on her knees and prayed loudly for the Most High to hear. She screamed "Oh, *YAH*, I praise in your name and I hope you can hear my voice crying out for your glory. If it is not in your decision to give me a husband, I will understand. For your will be done and I will obey your will and take heed from the evils of this world."

After her prayer, she left the land of Urz and traveled into the kingdom of Dianapolis, where she met Lebbeus, a man who was of heart, praise, and confession. He also trembled in the fear of the Most High. The man had gazed his eyes upon her and could see the love pouring off through her spirit. He approached her as she did him and they set a discussion to speak amongst themselves. After several months of meeting and speaking with one another, the two eventually came to an agreement and married in the kingdom of Dianapolis in the sight of the Most High, who approved the marriage set before them.

Stephanie had finally found peace and prosperity as she submitted herself to her husband as she sold her home in the land of Urz to live with her husband in the kingdom of Dianapolis. After two years, she bares a son, naming him Luke, she said, "He will become a gentle man who will be a shining example of knowledge and wisdom amongst the kingdoms of the earth." She lived with Lebbeus and her son Luke for all the days to come in the kingdom of Dianapolis. One day, she decided to go into a quiet room and give praise to the Most High for her marriage, her son, and her peace that she found on earth. She praised Him in all of His glory. She stated that she began to know her age is catching up to her and prayed that Luke will be a fine man and a servant of the Most High in his days of growth.

She loved her husband. Lebbeus and she loved her son, Luke. But, her ultimate love was toward the Most High, for He was her One True God and her named was written in the book of eternal life as she is one of the Elect.

THE SOUND OF CLARK ZYACK

Clark Zyack was a striving musician and tried his way into becoming a sensational star through music, fame, and glory. He wanted to be praised by millions of people across the world and wanted them all to chant his name in the glory of fame. He desired all the money that he could possibly achieve from his music and hope to gain himself a large mansion where he could live the life of a rock star.

Upon an ultimate opportunity to have his own music tour, he became cocky, arrogant, and selfish. Only looking out for himself in many ways that he could barely keep track of anyone around him that took him for a colleague or a friend. Doing his tours, he became increasingly addicted to alcohol and drug substances. Many of his friends began to abandoned him when he couldn't control his behavior and his drinking habits. After months of tours and little breaks, he started losing friends one after the other. Telling himself he didn't care about them in the start, he continued his drinking and continued using numerous amounts of drugs, from cocaine to heroin to even attempting crystal meth during one of his stage shows.

One night, while he was drinking and taking cocaine, he passed out and lost consciousness. He awoke and found himself in a place consumed by darkness. No light shining in any direction, only pure darkness. The purest darkness that could possibly exist among human beings. Much darker than when the lights go out or when a person's head is fully covered. Even with the moon covered up, the darkness wouldn't equal to the pure darkness that Clark felt. He later noticed he could stand up and walk. He couldn't see where he was going, but knew every route of the mysterious location.

He continued to walk until he heard voices ahead of him. The voices were calling unto him to follow them. He told them he couldn't see them. In just a mere nanosecond, Clark's eyes were able to see the location in full detail. Clark looked around and seen that he just exited out of a small prison cell structure. He felt the intense heat burning him from all directions. Suddenly, he could hear loud screams coming from a distance.

He looked at the figures that spoke to him. They wore black cloaks and had their heads covered with hoods to where their faces couldn't be seen. There were a total of three of them that stood in front of Clark.

"Where am I?" Clark asked.

"Come with us and you'll discover it." One cloaked figure said.

The cloak figures gestured their hands toward Clark to follow them. He followed as they were walking through a dense and narrow hallway. He could overhear their conversation. They were making fun of the amount of screams that were heard and one even made fun of Clark's nakedness. Clark looked down at himself and noticed he was completely naked. Though, he had a human body and wondered how the intense heat wasn't burning his flesh. He continued to follow them through the hallway and they stopped. Clark stood behind them as they turned to face him. They each slowly reached to their heads and removed the hoods. They revealed their faces to Clark and he quickly screamed in fear. Their faces were as goblins, though burnt roughly and had very scaly skin as it looked to have been peeling off because of the burns and heat.

"What are you?! Where am I?!" Clark yelled.

"You're with us now, Clark Zyack. Welcome home." The three figures said.

The figures ran over and grabbed Clark. They began stabbing him with knives, blades, and even swords. Clark screamed as the pain was more painful than it would be on earth. As they were stabbing him, one figure grabbed Clark and raised him over their heads and walked toward a lake. The lake was made of fire and the smell of sulfur and brimstone poured off of it immensely. When Clark seen the lake and noticed the millions of people who were in it and screaming in pain, he knew he was in Hell or the Underworld, as many people call it.

"I haven't done anything wrong in my life!" Clark yelled. "Why am I here?! Why am I in this place?!"

They inched themselves closer to the lake, a tall figure emerged from a stack of boulders. The figure had a tail and its body looked as it was made from molten lava that dried. Its eyes glowed red as much as the fire glowed. The large figure stood above Clark and the three figures as if they were like small dogs to him. The figures backed away and left Clark on the ground facing the tall demon.

"Please tell me what I have done to deserve this torment?!" Clark yelled. "Please, I'm begging of you to tell me!"

"You pathetic human!" The large demon said. "You fooled around with alcohol immensely, you played around with drugs that ruined your earthly system. You laid with many damsels that you did not claim for your own and some were married to other men. You treated everyone around you like a sack of shit and you complain about doing everything right. Foolish ones never learn from their mistakes. Instead they hold on to others' mistakes without looking at their own!"

Clark yelled as the large demon snatched him by his head and walked over to the edge of the lake. He allowed Clark to stare into the lake as he saw millions of people who have died over the years burning in eternal torment for what they done with their earthly lives.

"You see all of those wretched souls down there." The large demon said. "They treated their earthly lives like it was a toy to them. They foiled their bodies with toxic chemicals and ignored the truths that were presented to them in their lifetime. Many souls that are down here and those that are yet to come are of souls that were lovers of self, lovers of money, they are boastful, arrogant, revilers, disobedient to their parents, ungrateful, unholy, unloving, irreconcilable, malicious, gossipers, without self-control, brutal, and most of all. Haters of all that was good and beautiful."

"A few of those sound like me."

"No. They are all that you are and because you decided to fool around with meth, you're down here in Gehenna with us."

"No, please. Let me return to earth. I can change my life around for the better. There has to be something that I can do to fix all of my problems."

"If you could do such a task, it will take great sacrifice and I'm not a believer in you to see such a task be accomplished."

"No please!"

"It's time for you to burn, Clark Zyack. For all eternity."

The large demon held Clark up over its giant head. Clark screamed as he tried fighting the demon, but his attacks had no damage to the demon. The demon suddenly freezes, and his body jumped back and crashed onto the boulders. Clark fell to the ground and raised his head. He saw a figure glowing in immense gold reach out toward him with its hand.

"Take my hand." The glow said.

Clark took the hand of the glowing figure and found himself going through a tunnel of light. He felt an immense amount of love and peace. He later continued through the tunnel and saw his life in the past, the present, and what the future could be. While seeing his own life, it starts to dwell on him all the tings his has done wrong in his life. From the alcohol to the fornication to the drugs to the hatred. He starts to cry as he wipes the tears from his face.

"I can change my ways. I know I can."

He continued through the tunnel, until he found himself in a hospital bed. Back in his earthly body, he saw that he was in a hospital and was brought in by some close friends after passing out from the combination of alcohol and cocaine. After a few days, they released him from the hospital and his life was completely changed from the events that he went through. He could still see the figures watching him at all times. He knew he could change his life around for the better and could help others having the same problems that he once had.

Months later, he changed his music format to a much better form of music. His new music was able to affect many people across the world in such a good way, that his new success was even better than his previous success. He was rid of the alcohol, the drugs, the fornication, and the hatred. He was married to a beautiful woman and had two sons with her.

After years of mediating on the event, he knew the glowing figure was the Messiah and had thanked him for saving him. One day, Clark walked outside of his home in his backyard and looked up in the sky. He could see a variety of angels looking down on him. He smiled and nodded as the angels ascended into the clouds. The Sound of Clark Zyack will go on to change many lives for the better for the rest of his days.

THE LOST TEMPLE

The Lost Temple is a legendary and mystical place where people can go and receive knowledge and healing. The temple was always visited by large groups of people on a daily basis. Many came over to the temple to pray and worship. Some came to cause chaos and even attempted to destroy the temple. Throughout the eras of time, many groups of people came to the temple. Those who worshipped pagan gods such as Baalim, Moloch, Tammuz, and Astarte, Queen of Heaven.

A variety of pagan god worshippers would come to the temple to receive knowledge and healing from their pagan gods, only to have caught a disease or even went insane by the vast amount of knowledge that conjured into their minds. During one night, while the worshippers of Astarte laid to rest at the temple, they were attacked and slaughtered by the Eshians or Fireans, the worshippers of the Fire Orb, powered by their god, Megazorah. They were led by Abishag, who proclaimed the temple a place of worship only for the Eshians. After the slaughtering, they took the surviving ones and made the men slaves, they raped and forced the women to be wives, and even molested the children and some even married them under the unction of Megazorah, their god.

"See this land before you, followers of Megazorah!" said Abishag. "We have taken this temple and proclaimed it the Temple of Megazorah, our god!"

The Eshians relished in their ruler ship of the temple and gained its knowledge and healing. The temple began to create witches, wizards, sorcerers, and doctors of the mystic arts. The people began to take pride in themselves with the found power and some started to proclaim themselves as gods. When they would speak of themselves being gods, Abishag would have them sealed to the ground, where he would kill them with their own sword, as they had believed they were above Megazorah and not below him.

A day came to pass when Yirmeyahu, known in modern times as Jeremiah, came across the temple and saw the Eshians bowing before it. He even seen some of his own people, Hebrew Israelites bowing down and drinking wine in front of the temple, praising Megazorah and the Fire Orb. Abishag noticed Yirmeyahu looked in the distant. He approached him and tried to bribe him in joining in. Yirmeyahu declined and said that in the latter days, they would all regret bowing down to idols and worshipping false gods. Yirmeyahu walked away, not looking back at Abishag, the worshippers, or the temple. As he worshipped and praised the Most High above all things.

Within decades, the Eshians found themselves at war with the Qerachians or Iceians, who worshipped the Ice Orb and their god, Steelzorah. The battle lasted eight days in front of the temple itself with both orbs sitting inside the temple on the pedestal. After the eight days, the Qerachians were declared the victors as the remaining Eshians took the Fire Orb and ran into the wilderness from the Qerachians. Four decades pass, until the Qerachians were dethroned from the temple by the Meads and Persians, who took the temple for themselves.

The Persians enjoyed their time with the temple, becoming great people amongst themselves. After they possessed the temple, it was overtaken by the Greeks, and later the Romans. Who completely transformed and defiled the temple. They took what they learned from the temple and its healing powers and began to use it for a sight-seeing location to merchandise the fellow Roman citizens or tourists who were passing through. The Pharisees even one time attempted to deceive the Messiah in entering the temple, which he decided to say, the temple was made of mortal hands and is bound for destruction due to its defilement and sinfulness.

Barbarians had feared the temple's power and refused to enter or even get close to it. After the Resurrection of the Messiah, people began to depart from the temple, causing the Pharisees to lose money and control over the masses. The temple was left abandoned until the 4th Century where the Roman Emperor, Constantine the Great had rediscovered the temple and used it form many of his worshipping ceremonies. He even allowed the pagans to enter the temple to worship their pagan gods. Constantine had noticed a large increase of people in Rome as the temple was the main attraction. He allowed all people to come in and worship their gods within the confinements of the temple.

Many people disapproved of Constantine's motives and ended up succumbing to death. Constantine enjoyed and relished in the celebrations that took place at the temple, from Saturnalia to the birthday worshipping to the people and to their gods. Constantine had made a law declaring that the rights to the temple will be passed down to the Roman Catholic Church, the Vatican.

After Constantine's death, the Vatican took full control of the temple and kept it for use of worship and healing. The knowledge of the temple was kept secret by the Vatican from the masses. From the 4th Century to the 21st Century, the temple is still in use. Though, not as much as it was in the past centuries. People come and go by the temple for healing and prayer, thus not knowing its grueling and profound historical accounts, since they have been kept secret from the public eye. Some information is out in the public for people to search and find the truth.

As it is told in the *Covenant of Ages*, in the Book of Deception and Salvation, the temple will be used as a massive marketing tool to lure people for profit by fooling them that the temple was used by the Messiah in ancient Rome. Many will succumb to the lie as only a few will see the truth in clear sight. The Antichrist will use the temple as the main source of worship in Rome, besides the city of Jerusalem.

When the Messiah returns, He will destroy the temple from the earth and its knowledge and healing will be lost from the unbelievers and sinners of the earth.

BEYOND THE STEEP HILL

There is this tale and legend of a hill that appears as one steep and if someone decided to cross over and through the hill, they will find ultimate happiness in the earthly realm. Many have often wondered what could possibly be lying over on the other side of that steep hill. Could it be a city of wondrous prosperity? Could it be a load of gold and silver for one to be rich in the world? Could there be a virtuous woman who happens to live on the other side of the steep hill, waiting for her true lover to come to her? Whatever the case may be, many have decided to attempt crossing the steep hill.

The earliest known event of the hill is where a young man was seeking to please his concubines as he boasted up to go beyond the steep hill and find whatever was lying on the other side. In turn, the young boy didn't cross the hill as a gust of wind had blown him back toward his concubines, where he fell in front of them and was embarrassed of their laughter towards him. He decided to try again the second day and fell again due to the gust of wind. With his temper flurrying, he determined to try again, but this time he had two of his trustworthy allies to join him. The three men climbed the hill as the gust of wind returned, this time they held on by holding close to one another. After the gust vanished, they continue to reach over and suddenly a lightning bolt came down from the heavens and slammed directly in front of the three men. Causing them to fall on their backs towards the ground. The men weren't hurt from the fall and they were so embarrassed and terrified, that they left the hill alone.

The second attempt was during the time and ruler ship of King Liam, where a group of women warriors, led by their leader Queen Zimmah were seeking on discovering a treasure beyond the hill that could be used for warfare and dethroning Liam's kingdom and the kingdom of Queen Diana, the mother of Yisabelle. Queen Zimmah craved the desire of finding a divine weapon hidden behind the hill and sent her warriors to find it. As they climbed the hill, reaching for the top, angels came down from the sky and thwarted them off from the hill. The angels' appearance gave Zimmah the ultimate impression that there was a divine weapon beyond the steep hill, which fed her craving of the hill. Zimmah later tried again, this time with both her men and women warriors. They ran like wild animals towards the hill and Zimmah sought the angels in the sky to come down and deny her of the treasure. This time no angels came down from the sky. Zimmah began to revel in her finding. As the warriors inched closer, a lightning bolt that looked like fire came down and struck the warriors. Burning their armor and flesh until they were no longer walking. Zimmah fled the bottom of the hill with her remaining warriors as they left the burned bodies of their warriors on the hill to rot.

The third attempt took place during the time of the Greeks when the armies of King Mirrannidon sought their way towards the hill on their king's demand. The soldiers in groups of five each walked up the hill. King Mirrannidon was present for the events as described in his counselor, Rilrod's writings. The soldiers took ease as they walked up on the hill. Knowing the history that has unfolded from the hill.

"Nothing can stop us from claiming what is beyond this hill." Mirrannidon said. "We control all of Lelat and we will control the world."

"What if there's something beyond the hill that might cause your kingdom to fall, my lord?" Rilrod said.

"You speak of utter nonsense like a buffoon, Rilrod." Mirrannidon said. "You know how my conquests always end."

The soldiers continued with ease as fireballs began to drop out of the sky in mass. The balls ranged in sizes, some came down small, some came down medium, and some came down large. Mirrannidon fled from the raining fireballs. Commanding his army to fall back as he left the area.

"We shall try it another day. Be it the will of the gods of Eragard!" Mirrannidon boasted. "We will succeed!"

The fourth attempt took place during the days of Rome where a Hebrew soldier known as Arah, who fought for the glory of the Most High had a tragic event. After saying goodbye to his family, he went into battle against the enemies of Yah and was struck by a blow of an arrow fired by a Roman soldier. Arah immediately fell to the ground as the battle continued. He became dazed and suddenly found himself floating in the air. He could see the entire battle taking place below him.

He knew he was in spirit form and his earthly form had died on the battlefield. He noticed that a bright glowing light was in front of him and he reached for it with great strength. After reaching the light, he saw a city made of gold with streets of transparent gold. He knew he was in the physical realm anymore. He was in the midst of Shamayim or the Third Heaven as the modern world knew. As he looked around, trying to maintain his composure, he saw a man approaching him. The man had hair like wool and it was white as snow. His skin looked like bronze that was burnt in a furnace and his eyes looked like they held fire within them. Arah knew that this man was indeed Yahshua Ha-Mashiach or as he's commonly referred to by many in the English tongue, *Jesus Christ*. Arah fell to his knees and his face hit the golden streets.

"Please forgive me of what I have done in my life." Arah said. "I repent for all I have done and sinned on the face of the earth."

Yahshua commanded Arah to stand up and face him. Arah stood up, weeping. Yahshua said that Arah's time on earth was not done and he had to return. Arah shook in his feet as he told Yahshua that he didn't want to return to earth and that he was killed in battle and died a warrior. Jesus stated that his family needed him back and his work for the Most High was not yet done. Arah asked Yahshua what the work was, and he stated that he must do the will of the Father, that he and others who listen will have eternal life. Arah listens to Yahshua's command and is immediately return to earth, where he wakes up on the battlefield with his wound healed. Upon returning home, he came across the hill and knew of its history. He went to climb the him and had reached the peak where he could see over the hill. What Arah saw was unbelievable to his eyes and gave him even more hope in glorifying the Most High. Arah returned home and told his family about the hill and what he saw on the other side.

"There are no words on this earth that can describe what is beyond the steep hill." Arah said. "Not even the thought of a word nor a word created can truly describe what lies beyond it."

Still to this present day, people who know the history of the hill have tried to see what is beyond it and have not even reached the peak as Arah had done nor did they get far enough like the armies of King Mirrannidon nor did they burn like the warriors of Queen Zimmah. Nor were they highly embarrassed as the young man and his two allies. No one living today knows for sure what truly lies beyond the steep hill.

THERE WERE GIANTS
IN THOSE DAYS

During the age when the earth was filled with violence and wickedness, there not only existed man among the earth, but giants were also present during the time of wickedness. Chanokh was one to witness the giants of renown enter the earth through the means of the Sons of Yah mingling with the Daughters of Man. Through the intermingling, came forth giants and the men of renown.

The giants fought alongside each other through the earth in those days, whereas even Chanokh knew their existence was not to be created nor to be designed. Giants began to form during the time of Queen Alyssa, whom had a giant build her castle and queendom alongside the men who allied with her, believing her false prophecies that were stated to come in the latter days. The giants were later witnessed by many others whom had come into the earth in those days and had seen the trouble that stood before them.

Harold, a man who had witnessed the galactic war between the Dark Gods and the Cosmics, witnessed the giants being used as tools for both legions against one another after Chanokh was taken from the earth to Shemayim by The Most High. The giants had picked sides, stating the winning side would rule the earth for one thousand years in their lifetime. In which, the Dark Gods won and the giants that sided with them became conquerors over the lands in the earth. Until they were overthrown and defeated by Harold, The Cosmics, and The Most High himself.

The Giants later became more corrupt than before. As they would begin to eat the flesh of man and drink their blood. It was during the days of Dore that the end of the Giants would be completed, and their death would be a civil war amongst each other before the flooding water had covered the lands of the earth. During those days, men fought back against the giants with swords, hammers, bows and arrows. The giants had overcome them in their bloody battles before The Most High spoke to Gabriel to cause them to fight each other until they were all dead.

The giants fought one another in a combat of blood and sweat. Giants slaughtering giants across the lands of the earth. For many had become witness to the great towering battles and foreknew it would be the beginning of the end of their time. The giants later rallied other giants to assist them and the civil war had begun. During the civil war, Dore and his family were preparing their vessel in preparation of the deluge that was coming after the civil war. Mankind in general had become partakers and witnesses to the battles of the giants. Some fed into the fights as a form of entertainment.

The mothers and fathers of the giants were weeping at their children killing and slaughtering each other. The fathers, which were the Sons of Yah, petitioned Chanokh to speak with The Most High in an effort of repentance. But, The Most High had rejected the petitioning and they were left to remain and witness their offspring kill each other in fights of bloodlust and rage. The giants fought for years and years. Generations of man that came before and came during were all witnesses to the war of the Giants. From Chanokh to Dore, the giants waged in a civil war.

Many of the Sons of Yah were taken and bind during the final days of the civil war. Unable to see their offspring again as they were taken into the darkness abyss. During those final years, Dore had preached to mankind, speaking of preparation of the water falling from the sky. Mankind mocked Dore as they went about their lives and continued to watch the war of the Giants as entertainment for their own sakes. Alyssa was gone from the earth, Chanokh was gone from the earth, Harold was gone from the earth, and Dore remained on the earth during the last years of the Giants' war.

Some nights, Dore could hear the roaring and smashing of

the giants as they fought night and day constantly without any rest due to the spiritual power of the Archangel Gabriel with his order from The Most High. The fallen angels bound into eternal prisons until their appointed judgments. They could still hear the sounds of their offspring fighting and dying in slaughters. Dore spoke with Methus, father of Miykael and grandfather to Dore about the coming deluge and the end of the giants' civil war. Methus foreknew that he would leave the earth and enter the spiritual realm after the giants had killed each other in order for the deluge to come across the earth. Dore's three sons, Adad, Samael, and Mordecai were also witnesses to the giants' final days of war.

In those last days of the time of the giants in the days of Dore, the giants were at their last. Constantly full of energy and rage in warfare. Dore and his family were set to enter the vessel before the deluge had come. Methus had prepared himself in entering the spirit world and leaving the natural world.

"The time is almost here, grandson." Methus said to Dore. "Once the abominations have killed themselves on the face of the earth, I will leave this world, allowing the deluge to come and wash the earth of its wickedness.

The giants fought to their last breaths as they all killed each other in warfare. The giants were all dead. Methus had passed on into the spiritual world. Dore and his family were set in the vessel as The Most High had closed the door and the deluge came and washed the earth of its wickedness. Forty nights and forty days the waters stood above the grounds of the earth with the wickedness beneath it, grasping for air.

After the waters had settled and Dore's sons had begat their own children with their own wives, a remnant of the giants was left behind. Though, these giants were in heightening size as of the giants that came before. There were giants in the days of Queen Alyssa, Chanokh, Harold, and Dore. But, the giants that came after were great in stature and powerful, but were nothing like the predecessors before them.

The predecessors however, within them were spirits of their

own. Their spirits were of evil and had proceeded from their bodies. The evil spirits of the giants afflicted, oppressed, destroyed, attacked, do battle, and work destruction upon the earth and everyone on it, causing trouble. They take no food, but have an everlasting hunger and thirst, which cause offenses.

The spirits of the giants rose up against the children of men and against the women, because they proceeded from them. The spirits of the giants are what are commonly known as demons.

CETUS

The Cetus, a rare beast that has gone throughout history as one of the world's most terrifying creatures to live underneath the deep seas. The Cetus has its rare cases of destroying ships that sail above the oceans and dragging them and their crew deep beneath the sea to drown and later to eat upon. Those who have seen the Cetus with their own eyes depict the beast as a creature of pure malevolence and evil and its presence of great fear and trembling.

The Cetus is usually associated with the Greek God known as Poseidon, who used the Cetus to attack Ethiopia during the Greek era with Cassiopiea boasted of her daughter, Andromeda's beauty above the Nerieds that lived in the deep waters. In the *Hebrew Scriptures*, the monster is depicted to be the beast who swallowed Jonah. In the *Covenant of Ages*, the individual known as Ohm came into contact with the Cetus and was also swallowed by the beast, only to be freed a few days later. The Cetus is said to have been turned to stone by Perseus during their encounter. There also is a constellation of stars named after the beast itself.

There is one tale that hasn't been spoken about the Cetus that will present itself at this very moment. The time when the battle between the Ostacrean and Magnitran armies in the land of Lelat. During the battle, a warrior who is known as Accladus saw the Cetus with his own eyes before their ships made landfall to face the Ostacrean armies. In Accladus' own words he described the Cetus as a large serpent with eyes that could rip out an individual's soul and throw it deep under the sea until the soul had entered the depths of

Hadi, where it would burn for eternity.

"The Cetus' eyes possessed so much darkness that it could suck the soul out of someone's body and throw it deep into the deep sea until it slammed into the ground where it would open, and the soul would be in the dwelling realm of Hadi, who guards the underworld."

There is also the event where the Roman army went into battle with the remaining Greeks and they used the Cetus as a tool for war. Having their soldiers ride on the back of the beast to destroy the Greeks who had ships in the nearby waters. They reveled at the sight of the beast attacking the Greeks and eating their bodies at such quick pace. It even created waves with its body to turn over their ships.

"We can use this creature for our own desires. The creature could possibly help us end this war with those lasting Greeks who continue to thwart our plans of world domination."

The Cetus had later disappeared with many ending tales to its name. People still say they've seen the monster throughout the centuries and decades that have raced over the face of the earth. From the 6th Century to the 19th Century as well into the 20th Century and the 21st Century.

There is also the legend of the Loch Ness Monster, who some believe could very well be the Cetus itself. Though, no evidence has been conclusive enough to determine of the Loch Ness Monster is indeed the Cetus of ancients' old. In the past and present hours, people cling to the idea of a colossal sea monster living beneath the seas that surround the land. People from all parts of the earth come together to tell the stories of their possible encounters with the Cetus while on a ship or near the waters of the sea. There was a quote that an individual said about the Cetus and its future place.

"We will come across the Cetus one day. I know in my heart that

we will, and the great legend will be solved once and for all."

The individual continues his search for the Cetus at all parts of the earth where the seas may touch. He seeks the beast and craves its present before his eyes. He also has some companions with him as they all travel together to find the monster and reveal its legendary presence before the modern world. Though, interesting enough, there are tales of the Cetus' return and what its purpose is of returning and its full intent.

"The Cetus will return, and its imposing threat will spread across the globe like a pandemic. People near the seas will regret having their homes placed there as the Cetus will seek to destroy all that they possess. I surely hope they've prepared themselves for the great disaster that awaits them and others who live near the seas' waters."

Some believe the Cetus will be used for good and find a way of saving people trapped at the seas. Others believe that the Cetus is only an animal that has outlived many of its ancient companions and still dwells in the seas of the earth to this day and will do so beyond our time. There are those few who believe that the Cetus will be conjured up from the oceans by an evil force, who will use the beast for its own intended purposes of causing chaos across the globe.

In many books and legends, the Cetus is said to have risen, disappeared, and to return in future days. As sightings of the creature continue to show itself across the globe, many will only wonder if the Cetus will return and cause the chaos that many believe it will or will it return and protect the human race from itself and clean the seas that were once pure of filth and decadence.

"Those of us, who have intelligence and use it wisely, we know that this creature called the Cetus is one of many legends to spread across planet earth. It is our duty and task to find this creature at once before it finds a way to discover us once again and brings about the end of our world."

"Come quickly! The beast has appeared before us in this

distressful time we live in. Send the armies to combat the creature as we are in a terrible situation, trapped here in these waters as the beast stares at us. Only the Most High himself can truly help us overcome the threat we currently face. Send your armies at whatever disposal you can. For if you do not, this monster will come to your waters and destroy them as well. For this creature is not of great miracles and spectacles, but of pure hatred and deep malevolence that it possibly cannot be stopped by mortal men. Only Yah can stop the creature, for it is Him who created the world and it is Him who created the Cetus. Praise Yah. Praise YAH!"

THE ENDLESS ONES

The Endless Ones, many do not understand who they are or where they come from. They have been around since time began and are constantly growing in numbers. Created by The Unheard-Of, the Endless Ones scatter across the universe in a variety of ways. Both physically and spiritually. There have been many reports of the Endless Ones in both modern day and history.

Historical accounts describe the Endless Ones as humanoid beings that appear to be transparent in some parts and fully physical in another. One historical account described in Hebrew mentioned the Endless Ones had once taken over the world through The Unheard-Of, when many people began to consume themselves in violence and sodomy. Upon taking over the land, The Endless Ones were worshipped as gods and granted wishes and miracles to their followers. Many of their followers were misguided spirits who were lost and couldn't find their way to the Other Side. Other human beings who opposed the Endless Ones were either tortured or put to death by them or their followers.

Throughout the latter parts of the historical accounts, it stated that their powers began to fade as many humans turned to another source of faith to guide them in the power of the Christ. Upon losing their powers, The Unheard-Of decided to make himself known and showed himself to a large crowd that surrounded the followers of the Endless Ones and gathered them all, including the followers and took them away from the Earth to never return in their physical form.

After that moment in history, there have been slightly no

signs of the Endless Ones on the Earth until the later days of the 14th Century when massive accounts of sighting took place. Many believed that the sightings were a sign that they were returning along with The Unheard-Of to destroy the world. But, that was not the case as the sighting were concluded as misguiding and falsely reported to the general population at that time. In latter centuries, sightings continued to be reported, some even by police, military, and political officials at the time. Though, none were taken seriously to consider a proper investigation and search.

In the early 1800s, there were sightings of the Endless Ones described by the witnesses and were fully detailed in drawings of them. Citing their large and strange humanoid shaped features with their rough burgundy red skin that appeared as if it was burned nearly to a crisp and their piercing and deadly glowing yellow eyes. The eyes resemble that of The Unheard-Of, citing that he has endowed them with some abilities of his own to use to their advantage. The drawings made the front page in news across Europe and later found its way across the globe.

Towards the 1900s, near the first World War, people began to assume that the war was started by the Endless Ones causing a stir in dividing countries from another, thus helping one country fight another with their supernatural help and guidance. Many believed the theory to be subtleness and ignored any possible reference or evidence of the Endless Ones aiding a country in the World War. After the war ended, sightings of the Endless Ones began to fade once again as many people moved on with their lives and their current state in faith. It wasn't until near World War II that many people began to realize that supernatural occurrence were taking place, and many believed it was in the form of Adolf Hitler and the Nazi party.

During the 1930s and 1940s, people were in constant fear of Hitler's rise to power by leading Germany into a new World War with a multitude of countries aligning and opposing each other. During one of Hitler's speeches, people said that they witnessed two humanoid beings enter the offices of the location, which is said where the Nazi party were into to discuss their plans in secret.

When Hitler gave his speeches, people reported seeing the Endless Ones standing beside him as he gave out the speeches declaring his plan to rule the world and create a new race of superhuman beings called the Aryans. Many Germans followed suit to Hitler as he led them into World War II. Many people believed that Hitler was given the idea of concentration camps by the Endless Ones to keep the ones who opposed him in line while he continued his plan of world domination.

After World War II, the Endless Ones began to fade again as the Third Reich collapsed, the Aryan race vanishing, and Hitler disappearing from public and military personnel. Afterwards was the creation of the United Nations, as many saw the opportunity of uniting the countries of the world into one singularity form of government. Some speculated that the Endless Ones were seen again near the Vietnam War and even the Cold War. Sightings of the Endless Ones disappeared with many people who believed they even existed and considered their historical accounts to be fairy tale stories passed down through generations.

Later near the 1980s and 1990s, smaller evidence that indicated the Endless Ones' existence began to give rise to their presence in the world. In the late 1990s, many continue to ignore or even declined information regarding them as they considered it official to be fairy tale stories taken too seriously. Upon the 2000s, as incidents began to occur, few people began to assume that the Endless Ones were making their return to the earth as the faith of a majority of people have died out or faded away over time. In today's time, many begin to believe that they are returning and are preparing the return of The Unheard-Of, who will make his presence known in the world and will claim it for himself.

The sunlight beams through the windows of an office. Inside the office are a young boy and an adult man, dressed in a white shirt and brown slacks, who's reading out of a book. The young boy sits in a chair with his hand on his chin, looking at the adult man reading from the book.

"You're saying that the Endless Ones are walking around us today and they're about the present The Unheard-Of to the world?" The young boy said.

"Son, I'm only reading from this particular book to give you a better way of understanding things. Though, you won't fully understand it until you get much older."

"So, when I'm older, I'll be able to see the Endless Ones and The Unheard-Of with my own eyes?"

The adult man laughed as he closed the book and placed it onto the nearby bookshelf. He walked over the boy and rubbed him on his head. He knelt toward him.

"Only time will tell, my son."

CRIES OF THUNDER IN THE SKIES

In the skies, dark clouds form and the thunder roars tremendously above the ground, striking fear and trembling in the hearts of people. The lightning mostly makes its appearance before the thunder introduces itself to the ears of the world. There are many stories that delve into the power and mystery of thunder and lightning. People would seem to disbelieve or disprove anything that could trace toward the power of thunder and lightning.

When people look up into the skies and they noticed the dark clouds forming above them, getting close together and the first small sound of thunder roars, many run into shelter for protection. The lightning had already made itself known before the thunder roared and yet the people's eyes didn't catch a blink of it. The rain would come falling down from the heavens and onto the earth like a colossal shower taking place. When it comes to rain, the differences between people around the world come together. Some love the rainfall, some hate it, and others really have no care for it other than to clean their material wealth that sits outside.

Legends in the earth tell of a large bird that flies through the air, hidden in the dark clouds causing the thunder and lightning to take place amongst the people and the land they live on. This bird is known as the Thunderbird. A colossal bird of great proportions that when it flies, the sound of thunder follows it with its roar and the lightning presents itself like a lighting show. The Thunderbird also has many names across its long and cryptic track record of existence.

The Thunderbird has been seen by many people throughout time and some say they continue to see the creature to this day. Though, none have ever had the opportunity to say if they've ever come face to face with the creature or even attempted to capture it for money or glory. Many Native Americans tell the story of the Thunderbird with great detail of its shrouded history. Historians and zoologists have also studied the Thunderbird and could never come up with a solution to its mystery.

"I for one say on this day and time, when the mysterious creature known to us as the Thunderbird makes its presence fully known to the world, that will be the day when all the mysteries of the earth be revealed unto mankind to witness." - Thomas Bradford.

Scientists would usually speculate or throw out the possibility of a Thunderbird existing, let alone flying through the sky creating the sound of thunder and producing lightning from its eyes and wings. They wouldn't believe the possibility of a creature being able to create thunderstorms out of thin air, let alone air that could be filled with dew and possible precipitation. Many of them would say that the individuals or groups that sighted the Thunderbird were only see regular sized birds in large scale due to their binoculars zoomed in or any other theory they could bring up to detest the possibility of the bird's existence.

Some would insist that the Thunderbird was only part of the dinosaur species known as the pterodactyl, due to its appearance and early reports of its sightings in the earth. People have speculated that the Thunderbird could also be an enhanced pterodactyl due to the amount of chemicals in the air or even radiation from the sun or the earth's core.

There is the other theory of there being more than only one Thunderbird living amongst the earth and they travel in various locations, but rarely come together. Many sightings have taken place in Alaska, where people would see the creature flying in the sky above the woodlands. It was usually seen during the winter as it would be searching for prey to consume. There have been other historic legends that regard the Thunderbirds as protectors of the earth that once destroyed reptilian beings that traveled and roamed across the earth.

There are many comparisons between the Thunderbird and the Roc, another colossal bird that is hidden in plain sight. Though, the only sighted Roc would be King Roc that lives not on this earth, but another planet amongst humanoid Roc beings. But, that is for another season to discuss. The Thunderbird and Roc are both large birds with incredible wingspans and able to fly at great speeds.

They can also create hurricane force winds using their wings during flight. Both of the gigantic birds could snatch an elephant or a whale to eat as food whenever they chose to. The Thunderbird is also spoken about as carrying snakes as its travels in the air.

"There will come a day when the legend of the Thunderbird will no longer be a legend, but a reality among people." - Michael Ledford.

Though, when you look at the world, it is filled and shrouded with mysteries since its inception and creation. If the Most High Yah had created the Thunderbird for its use in creating thunderstorms is mainly unknown to the human mind and far too complicated for the human mind to grasp for understanding. Many who have read the Bible know the Most High uses weather to bring humility unto humans in order for them to understand the sense of fear and trembling, in a way of understanding their place on the earth and existing on this side of glory.

It is understandable that the Most High wouldn't have to create a creature such as the Thunderbird to create thunderstorms to bring humility unto His people. If He did create the Thunderbird, as well as all the other strange and mysterious creatures that have been sighted and continue to roam the earth to this very day, He did it for his own pleasure and no argument can be created in order to combat the cause and need.

The Most High has created all things that dwell in the earth and out of the earth. Everything was created for his own pleasure and for his own glory. If the Thunderbird is a true creation of the Most High, then it is for his glory that the Thunderbird continues to live and stays shrouded in mystery unto the Age of Revelations unfold and all is revealed unto mankind.

THE BAITAL

In this world, there have been many to have encountered the creature known as the Baital. A large shaped creature that has the appearance of a human with brown skin and hair with large bat wings on its back and a goat-like tail. Its eyes frighten whosoever lays sight upon it. The Baital attacks its prey vigorously and sometimes kills them without any hesitation or thought. The creature comes from the depths of Hindu Folklore and Mythology and it said to hang itself to trees by its toes, same as the average bats across the world. The name Baital is a variation that comes from the Hindustani word known as "betal". The Baital is said to live in the country of India.

From what is spoken about of The Baital is its skin and facial features. The Baital is said to have a very thin body as if it appeared to be completely stretched across its bones, giving it the impression of an undead body. Old legends have said that its body was near the strength of iron or metal, which would imply that it could not be stopped by any ordinary weapon created by human beings. The Baital possesses either green or red eyes, depending on the area of its location. Its face appeared like a dried-up coconut as some would say. By looking into its eyes, people could tell that there was no life-force within the vessel nor did its eyes ever give off a twinkle of any kind. Within the Indian culture, the color brown is associated with fiends and witches.

The Baital has no blood of its own within its body. Instead it takes over the dead bodies of many who have died and were buried underneath the tree that The Baital possessed and marked as its own territory. Some would believe that The Baital is a vampire of anceitn times, though The Baital does not drink the blood of its victims.

The Baital is also said to tell stories of its history with a king known as King Vikram, who constantly batted with The Baital in ancient times. Vikram had made a promise to a sorcerer that he would capture The Baital. Of course, Vikram had faced many odds and challenges along the way in his process of trying to capture The Baital for the sorcerer. The Baital proved itself as a match for Vikram as tales of riddles would ensue and keep Vikram in a constant trap as The Baital was content in its present state. The countless battle between the two would last through the cycle of capture and release.

"I cannot bear this no longer." Vikram had said concerning the riddles of The Baital. "I must overcome this task of confronting the Baital. I have to."

Vikram's conquest of The Baital lasted for a total of twenty-five times as he returned to The Baital's marked tree and dealt with the riddles and questions thrown upon him to answer. After the situations that erupted during the events of Vikram and The Baital, The Baital itself vanished into the spirit realm. Some accounts have said of The Baital's whereabouts are known to those who seek it.

"If we try hard enough and focus with great concentration and strength, we can find this Baital and the realm where it hides from open eyes. We can use its power to do whatever we so desire."

How can one find The Baital without knowing the proper place and location to seek and search for it? How would one truly know The Baital's intentions in this present world as it is unlike the world of King Vikram. There are many servants of the Most High who see The Baital as an enemy and a servant to the Unheard-Of. The Baital is not of any godly consent nor will it ever be of any godly consent. Judging by its appearance, its stature, and its character, The Baital is a celestial creature that is bent on causing devastations to anyone who attempts to seek its presence.

"We must find a way to capture this creature. How can we know for certain what is taking place amongst the spiritual realm when we have no eyes inside?"

The early tales of The Baital were written in ancient Sanskrit, which is a primary language among Hinduism. The twenty-five events between Vikram and The Baital were written and captured in a book of twenty-five tales and legends, concerning the two battling it out with riddles and questions to be answered amongst each other. The time and date that The Baital had its encounters with King Vikram were recorded in the 1ˢᵗ Century BC and some recordings of the encounters continued into the 11ᵗʰ Century, where all of the recordings were compiled and put together as a complete set.

In today's times, many would wonder where The Baital could be hiding in this present world. The Baital could still be inside its country of origin, India. The Baital could be wandering across the globe, traveling to each country, seeking out a victim of its own to choose and cause madness. Though, it is not said if The Baital would return in the End Days and we do not exclude its theory, for The Baital could be used as one of the Unheard-Of's servants and warriors in the Final Battle at the Land of the Forbidden where the forces of The Unheard-Of collide with the forces of the Most High Yah in a battle that will transformation all of creation as we know it.

The Baital marks its tree of territory and continues to use the corpses that lie underneath its tree for its own purposes. Remember, The Baital is not a vampire by any means or stretch of the imagination, no matter how its outer physical presence may seem to appear in front of your eyes. To this very day, people would still say they've seen The Baital and some may have ultimate proof of their encounter with the creature. They may see an animated corpse that may have risen from The Baital's tree. Whoever shall see The Baital in person and in its full form, they must prepare themselves for an overflow of questions and riddles to be answered and solved.

THE COMING WRAITHS

The planet called earth is surrounded and covered with spiritual beings that travels throughout the universe and the spiritual plane of existence. These spiritual beings are able to shift into human beings, extraterrestrials, animals, or any other source that they can model their shift after. These spiritual beings could be angels, demons, or wraiths. The Wraths are the majority of those that shift into other beings to cause and lead others either astray or lead them to something of great ancient importance. The word Wraith arrives from the ancient Norse word, "*Vordr*", which means "*Guardian*" in the English tongue and translation.

Wraiths would usually appear to those who are near death or even after their death will appear before those who are surrounding the deceased earthly body, leaving them as just empty husks of flesh and blood. Wraiths are ghost-like entities that some would call phantoms, specters, apparitions, manifestations of the dead. Other names for them are Soul-Stealer, since they appear before one's death to enter into the eternal realm of either peace or torment. The primary trait of the Wraiths is to travel amongst the earth with a driven purpose to consume and capture the souls and spirits of humans. Look at today's people and the Wraiths are doing an excellent job in their line of duty.

Many of the Wraiths would possibly confuse the living into doing their own will instead of doing the will of the Eternal One. The Wraiths are able to transform a human spirit and soul into a wraith of its own, therefore it will become simply one of them. A member of the Wraith Clan and under the control of the Unheard-Of.

The majority of Wraiths are under the control of the

Unheard-Of. Just as the Endless Ones are under his control, as well as the Kingdoms of the Earth, so are the majority of the Wraiths.

"What you gaze before you are my Wraiths. They do my biddings to please me for bring humanity to its knees to worship me. For I will be like the Most High and I will ascend to His throne and claim it for myself. I am the Unheard-Of."

The true physical or astral appearance of the Wraiths are mainly all black or mostly a large black fog or cloud that either has a pair of eyes or doesn't have any eyes. Some have mouths and other do not have mouths. The ones with eyes are able to see and the ones without eyes aren't able to see, but are guided by the Unheard-Of through his own vision. The ones with mouths can speak words of a sweet and pleasurable nature, only used to deceive the illiterate ones. The ones without mouths are able to use telepathy to communicate with a human being through their mind and are able to read their thoughts and in near control over their conscious.

They hide in dark, deep caves and forests throughout the twelve hours of the day and rise out of the darkness to torment and to deceive during the twelve hours of the night. The demons take over the day and leave the night to the Wraiths as the demons take time to torment those in their sleep and those who aren't on the right side with the Eternal One. The Wraiths are able to release a loud screech similar to the screech of a banshee. The screech will create and build up fear in the hearts and minds of humans, both male and female.

"The screech became so intensity and unable to bear that I ran out of my home and into the nearest ditch to cover myself from its torturous yell."

The true way of knowing their presence is by the sight of dark clouds. The temperature will drop exponentially, and the Wraith will be known before whosoever is in its presence. Sure, the person might be near freezing due to the fast drop in temperature, but they will surely heat up when their gaze hits the Wraith in its eyes. For surely what would someone do if they came into contact with a Wraith. One question they should ask is why they have come into contact with a Wraith. Have they asked for something greater to seek after in this finite life or have they disobeyed the Eternal One in order to gain something for their self-will and self-indulgence?

I, Michael Ledford have yet to come into contact with a Wraith. I've encountered stupid people amongst all things and yet, I can see the demonic and wicked spirits that live among them and inside them. Once, I was like them, I lived after the manners and pleasures of this wicked world. I desired only what I wanted and what I sought after for my own self. I was all about myself, until I was hit with a spiritual awakening and found myself doing the will of the Eternal One and forsaking all that I had before me.

Now, I am truly a new creature and I no longer do what my own will suggests and throws into my mind. The spiritual awakening brought me closer to the Eternal One and I dearly and truly hope when I see the King coming down from the clouds along with the New Jerusalem out of Shemayim, will the Wraiths finally be put to rest for all eternity with their associates both on earth and in the spiritual realm, and along with their leader, the Unheard-Of when the King and His people rule the earth for one thousand years in peace.

Surely, you're thinking to yourself, this can't all be possible or you're thinking there's no Wraiths or Eternal One and yet, people like you do not bother to do the proper research and study to confirm it for yourself. Neither do you ask the Eternal One for wisdom and understanding. I'm speaking plainly to those who ask questions, but refuse the answers given to the damn questions they asked. The reprobate minded ones. There, that's what they are.

But, to those who truly seek after the will of the Eternal One and continue to do battle within the confounds of spiritual warfare, continue your worship and prayers. For the Wraiths, the Endless Ones, the stupid humans, the demons, and the Unheard-Of will try anything to get your minds off serving and worshiping the true King of the Universe with all diligently.

FORESEEN THE BUNYIP

The Bunyip is a strange creature within the realm of cryptozoology and mythology that is said to lurk within swamps, billabongs, creeks, riverbeds, and waterholes. Some claim the creature to be a water spirit, a spirit that dwells within the Murray River of Australia, its longest river within the Australian Alps. The Moorundi people that live near the Murray River have claimed to see the creature and that it can change its shape and form before the year 1847. Some have claimed the Bunyip to be an gigantic starfish that lives in the Murray River. Others have stated to be in a sense of dread that they can no longer describe its appearance to those who ask of it.

Many newspapers in the 19th Century describe the creature with a crocodile-like head, a dog's face, dark fur, walrus-like horns or tusks, depending on the witness, a duck's bill, flippers, and a horse-like tail. Reports in 1851 indicate that the Bunyip was killed by a spear after it killed an Aboriginal man. Early settlers of Australia claimed to have seen the creature during their arrivals to the continent. Many believed the Bunyip to be a creature that awaited discovery.

Hamilton Hume in 1818 stated to have found large bones. However, did not call them the bones of the Bunyip as some had suggested it to be. Hume and his partner, James Meehan described the bones relating similar to a hippopotamus or manatee. There were fossils found in the Wellington Caves in 1830 by George Rankin, a bushman. Others were later found by Thomas Mitchell. The word *Bunyip* came along in July of 1845. An Australian museum stated to possess the skull of a Bunyip in 1847. William Buckley wrote an account of the creature in his biography in the year of 1852.

In other times after 1852, the Bunyip was said to have been spotted by those who crossed the Australian Alps such as Gabriel Kane, the Monster Hunter and Ufologist during his early studies of becoming a member of the Symbolum Venatores. Kane spoke to his masters of the creature thereafter, only leaving it remaining alive near the Murray River where he witnessed it. Other hunters came across the creature during their studies. Some went to fight, yet lost in the end to the power of the creature.

Many monster hunters made it their mission between 1852 to 1886 to find the Bunyip, yet failed to do so. Others claimed to have seen the creature, but were unable to fight it themselves.

"How can we fight a creature that can change its shape and size? Its form? One minute, it shows itself as a hybrid of many animals that come across the waters of Murray River. Later it appears as if it's an enormous starfish that washed along into the River from the Sea. The next minute it turns itself into some spirit, a water demon perhaps, but not so sure on that matter. In time, Hunters, such as ourselves will confront this creature and then we will have foreseen the Bunyip for what it truly is. Rather it be a natural creature or a spiritual one."

ROAR OF THE WERETIGER

There is a beast that scatters throughout the jungles of Asia with the power and strength of a tiger and the intellect of a human being, which would be great cleverness. This hybrid creature is known to Us as the Weretiger. The Weretiger is spoken about in many ancient folklores and mythologies. They share a great similarity with werewolves and possibly werefoxes and werebears.

The Weretiger goes throughout the day looking like an average human being walking amongst other humans. It is not till nightfall, where it transforms into the Weretiger and begins a bloody massacre by killing anything that comes across its eyesight. The Weretiger has a great thirst for blood in any form possible within the jungles of Asia. Many have come across the beast and only a few have survived the encounter to tell their side of the story when it came across the Weretiger.

There are certain rituals that Asians have taken up to try to transform themselves into Weretigers and scatter the jungles of Asia. Only a few had received the terrible end of the ritual by becoming sick and thrown out into the jungles for the Weretiger to kill and consume. The Weretiger's body is set up as a brute creature with an incredible amount of strength and intelligence. The body of the Weretiger include its long sharp teeth, its slashing long claws, incredible feat of senses with its eyes, nose, ears, and mouth. With its teeth and claws, it can cause deadly bites and devastating slashes. Unlike average tigers, the Weretiger possesses in tail on its body.

The only possible way to transform into a Weretiger is to be bitten by one. Depending on the person who transformers, they either seek revenge on someone or they have an intense craving for power and violence. Maybe the craving for ruling is in there as well.

The Weretiger is said to have started in the areas of India before being spread over into the jungles of Asia, where it currently remains dormant from modern day civilizations. There were a group of explorers and people of adventure who traveled into the deep jungles of Asia to search out the Weretiger and reveal its presence to the world. They were named Gates, Laura, Kenny, Kathy, Rex, and Jude. Gates was the leader of the group as they entered into the jungles.

The jungles is covered with massive trees and slithering insects looking for food and places to rest. Gates finds a location near a large rock where he and his group set their camp for the night. The group place their bags and equipment together at the rock where Rex will stay and watch the cameras during the night with Kathy.

"Ok, Laura will be with me and Kenny, you're with Jude." Gates said.

"Alright then." Kenny said. "Let's get this mission done."

Gates, Laura, Kenny, and Jude walk into the jungles and split up. Two to Two. Gates and Laura went east, and Kenny and Jude went west. All they could see in front of them was pure darkness with the exception of the moonlight shining through the trees. Gates reached into his cargo pants pocket and pulled out some night-vision glasses. He had two in his hand and gave one to Laura.

"Put this on. It should help you watch your steps." Gates said. "The moonlight is shining and yet we can only see darkness in front of us and there's no telling where the Weretiger is at this moment."

"Who knows, Gates, we could come across the beast ourselves and hopefully not be killed."

"We'll see about that once we face the beast."

Kenny and Jude continued walking west on their side of the jungles. Jude noticed some very large footprints on the ground in the muddy dirt. She kneeled down to have a better look at the footprint.

Kenny stopped as he saw her studying the print.

"What did you find?" Kenny said.

"This footprint is larger than any known animal in this jungle. Look at the size of its paw to its nails. This isn't an ordinary tiger we're dealing with here."

"Of course not, lady. We're out here to search and find the legendary beast known as the Weretiger. Which it would be incredible to capture it and reveal it to the world."

"That's if we can capture it. It has the cunningness and intelligence as a human being."

"Sometimes, even human beings are able to be easily fooled and captured by their hunters."

Rex and Kathy sat at the campsite, where they watched on the cameras the majority of the jungles. Nothing was showing itself on the camera and it was dead silent. Rex continued to glance at all four cameras and still nothing was seen.

"Anytime now we should come across something." Rex said. "This jungle is too big not to have some form of movement."

"We still have a few hours of searching and we should come into contact with some kind of animal. Be it a tiger, a panther, or the Weretiger itself." Kathy said.

Gates and Laura kept walking through the darkness with their night-vision glasses on and their small digital cameras in hand through the jungles until they reach what appeared to be a small creek. Gates stopped walking as so did Laura. He scouted the area for any sign of life moving.

"Didn't know there was a creek out here." Gates said.

"It's no telling what you'll find out here, Gates."

They searched around their side of the creek, hearing only the slight sounds of owls hooting in the trees and fish swimming in the creek. Gates looked down and saw the same kind of footprint that Jude saw with Kenny. Laura looked down at the footprint as Gates searched for samples of hair, saliva, or blood.

"Think that's its footprint?" Laura said.

"It could be. Look at the size of it. Unless we're dealing with a fairly enlarged tiger or panther, this could possibly be the footprint of the Weretiger. Which means it's dwelling in this jungle with us tonight."

After Gates took the samples and placed them inside a plastic bag that he put into his shirt pocket, a loud shriek of a roar is heard throughout the jungle. The entire group hears the roars and knows it's not from an ordinary animal. Gates looked around himself and Laura forming a 360 degree circle.

"We have to find the location where that roar came from!" Gates said. "Let's go!"

Gates and Laura ran through the jungle, following the sound of the roar as it can still be heard. Kenny and Jude decide to also track down where the roar was coming from as Rex and Kathy at the campsite were completely glued to the cameras for any sign of movement.

"That roar should've woken up the majority of this jungle's inhabitants." Rex said. "We are about to see a lot of movement taking place."

On the cameras, Rex and Kathy spot several shapes moving past the cameras. They paused one of their cameras and looked to see that it was a pack of orangutans that ran across the camera, going through the trees, away from the roar's location. The other three cameras showed constant movement from animals such as the Silvery Gibbon, the Proboscis Monkey, a Slender Loris, and on the ground, they saw a couple of snakes that slithered past the cameras. But, no sign of the Weretiger was found on the camera.

"No Weretiger, Kathy." Rex said. "Dammit."

After a brief second of silence, they heard a thumping sound that came from nearby their campsite. Rex and Kathy each sat still as the thumping sound inched closer toward them. They sat quietly as the thumping sound turned into a large object that they could see with their own eyes. The object stood still as it stared at Rex and Kathy and gave off a small roar. Rex listened closely and noticed it wasn't the Weretiger and he squinted his eyes and saw it was only a Sumatran Rhinoceros. The Rhinoceros turned its head and continued to walk past the campsite. Rex and Kathy are relieved by the Rhinoceros' appearance.

Back in the jungle, Gates and Laura find themselves deeper in the jungle where the roar is right next to them. They hear rusting in the trees and they turn to see both Kenny and Jude. They all catch their breath.

"Looks like we ran into your zone." Kenny said.

"Just trying to find what is giving off that roar." Gates said. "We have to keep moving."

Gates' communicator sounded off as he answers it. Rex is on the other side of the talkie. Gates answers Rex's call.

"What is it, Rex?"

"We see a large number of animals scattering through the jungle and you have to watch yourselves."

"You're telling us this now instead of earlier?"

"We have a little incident of our own over here with a Sumatran Rhinoceros. We saw a rhinoceros."

"Good call, but did you see anything that could lead toward the Weretiger because that's why we're all out here?"

"No, we didn't capture footage of the Weretiger. Sorry, Gates."

Gates sighed as he turned to Laura, Kenny, and Jude. He told Rex to stay on standby just in case something else would come along. He tells them that they only have about thirty minutes left before sunrise and they have to find the Weretiger before then. Now, all four of them stay together in a group as they quickly search around the jungle for the Weretiger.

Now, with only twenty minutes remaining, the group is becoming more intolerant of the Weretiger's whereabouts. Gates is constantly fighting off the idea of calling off the mission and returning back to camp.

"We have to keep searching with whatever means we can have." Gates said to himself.

Rex communicated back with Gates again through the talkie as Gates responded to his call.

"Anything this time, Rex?"

"Yeah. We just saw something very large walk past the camera and its heading toward your direction."

"What did it look like, Rex?!"

"It looked like a fairly large brute and it didn't look like a friendly type of animal, Gates."

"Thanks, Rex."

"Watch yourselves out there, Gates and company."

They hear the roar again and it appeared to be closer than they originally imagined. Kenny pointed toward the trees in front of them as they began to rustle and shake. The branches of the trees began to break and fall to the ground where the dirt would fly up into the air at mid-range.

They saw a large beast walk out of the trees, with a stick in hand that appeared to be made from the skulls and spines of both a human being and a ram. The beast stood on its hind legs to the estimated height of twelve feet. Its teeth were sharper than any other animal that lived in the jungle and its eyes pierced the group like death on swift wings. The group could only stare in intensely and stay in complete silence as they stared at the beast and its large brute figure. The beast stated at the group and raised its head toward them and gave off a roar. The group had fully recognized that roar and Gates could only believe as the sun began to rise, and he took off his night-vision glasses.

"Guys, this is the Weretiger." Gates said. "This is the roar of the Weretiger."

<u>YAHSHUA AND THE UNHEARD-OF</u>

This is a retelling of the events that described Yahshua the *Machiyach*, Jesus The Christ's time in the wilderness. The time where He was led up by the Spirit to head into the wilderness for the test of being tempted by The Unheard-Of, the Ha-Satan. The story takes place in *Matthew Chapter Four* of the Hebrew Bible, where it describes Yahshua in the wilderness undergoing the trial of overcoming the temptation of the ha-Satan.

The story should be a lesson to anyone of where temptation comes from and how it tries to control, but its up to the individual to overcome it with strength and faith. If Yahshua, the Son of Yah, could overcome the temptation of the ha-Satan, anyone with true believing and living faith can overcome the ha-Satan's temptation and wiles.

The ha-Satan is known for tempting any true believer into doing things they would not exercise in ordinary detail. He's tempted the majority of believers and everyone else on the earth is already overtaken by his temptation and wiles, and they do not see it otherwise. The reason of that is because they are blinded to themselves and refuse to look upon it to see if it's true or false.

The story also confirms the idea of the Unheard-Of beings in control of the earth and controlling all the kingdoms that live upon it. He is called the "god of this world' because the majority of the world worship him in many deceitful ways, ways they have awoken to confront in their lives.

Yahshua had stayed in the wilderness for forty days and forty nights. He fasted thought all the days and through all the nights. He became hungry afterwards as his flesh craved food for his stomach. It was then when the Unheard-Of had brought his presence before Yahshua, to tempt him into eating.

"If you are the Son of Yah, go ahead and command those stones to be made bread for you to consume." The Unheard-Of said.

"It is written, Man shall not live by bread alone, but by every word that proceeded forth out of the mouth of Yah." Yahshua had responded.

"So, he says." The Unheard-Of had said. "Let me take you to another place and show you what you could have."

The Unheard-Of shrugged his shoulders and decided to take Yahshua up into the holy city and had him sit down on a pinnacle of the temple that was placed in the holy city. The Unheard-Of stretched his arm forth with a smile on his face as he showed Yahshua the holy city that was before him.

"If you are the Son of Yah, cast yourself down, for it is written, He shall give his angels charge concerning you and, in their hands,, they shall bear you up, lest at any time you dash your foot against a stone."

Yahshua looked at The Unheard-Of and had responded to his demands of temptation.

"It is written again, you shall not tempt Yahweh thy Elohim." Yahshua had said unto him.

"Very well then. I'll show you something far better than this city and far better than bread."

The Unheard-Of continued his smiling and shrugged his shoulders yet again as he attempted to break Yahshua with one more test of temptation. The Unheard-Of decided to take him up onto an exceeding high mountain, where he showed him all the kingdoms of the earth and the glory of them.

Yahshua looked upon the kingdoms of the earth and turned his attention back toward the Unheard-Of, knowing in full of the test he's undergoing.

"Look at this spectacle! All of these kingdoms, all these things will I give unto you. If you will fall down and worship me above all things." The Unheard-Of said boastfully.

Yahshua stared at the Unheard-Of and knew well in great

detail of what was taking place and how to overcome the temptation of the Unheard-Of.

"Get from hence, Satan, for it is written, you shall worship Yahweh thy Elohim above all things and Him only shall you serve."

"I can't take this anymore!" The Unheard-Of said. "You've proven enough."

The Unheard-Of left the presence of Yahshua as the angels of Yah came down before him and ministered unto him. For he has overcame the temptation of the Devil and his wiles. For Satan, the Created Being attempted to tempt Yahshua, the Creator and yet, the ha-Satan had failed in the process of tempting Him who created him.

HUMANITY'S
DECEPTION AND DOWNFALL

In my line of work, I am known as Michael Ledford and I am here to tell you my theory on Humanity. A species that should've never existed nor thought of. A species that proclaims itself above all things in the universe. Humans tend to have an assumption of themselves, both collectively and individually as something superior than what's already been. They say to themselves how unique they are, how perfect they will become. Only to be destroyed by the slightest event that takes place before them.

When something "good" comes their way, they profess that the Most High has given it to them, when in reality, it was only another human benevolence that pleasured them with the "good" that they were given. When something "bad" comes their way, they ball their fist and raise it above themselves while yelling at the Most High for causing the "bad" to occur when in reality, it was only their own actions that brought about the "bad".

The majority of humans profess that they believe in a Higher Being and yet their actions, works, and character follow another being of supernatural origin. Many in reality, worship themselves and see themselves as the Higher Being because they have a lot of material goods, a lot of greenbacks to fill their pockets with, unless they carry it around in briefcases or large gym bags.

The humans come together as collectives, I call them the "collective groups", because of the lack to be individuals. The individuals are no better themselves. Prancing around like boastful children who were given everything they could want. Only for honest people to see them only as spoiled ingrates who hark for attention in any aspect of reality.

The humans always talk of some action they seek to do or have done. Many profess that they will change the world, when in reality, they haven't changed anything, not even themselves or their carnal mind. Sure, when some become upset, thoughts from the spirits and the heart conjure up in their minds, but it is up to them to discern those thoughts and find themselves within them. Many accept all of their thoughts because they believe it's actually them creating the thoughts.

They build, write, sing, dance, play, teach, travel, and do other things that interest them and mostly themselves and call it the life worth living when its only what they perceive as living. They take vacations to foreign lands that they only dream of when people who live in those areas see it as only a city or town, simple and reform.; Unlike the minds of people who travel, calling it a glorious place with nice people when they haven't even spoke with the majority of a people who live in those lands.

They date, they marry, they become one, they conceive children, they raise their children, they watch their children become adults and they just go away. Who can really find a virtuous woman in today's standards of time? Who can find a godly man worthy of a woman's true love and nature? If someone knows the answer to these two questions, speak up and profess your theories and philosophy toward Us who are only asking the questions to questions unanswered by the standard world.

The one thing humans tend not to do is think ahead into the future realm, where things they have done bring about either consequences or rewards. Generously with modern humans, there's more consequences than rewards. Simply because they value their own opinions, their though patterns, they Book of the Law rather than those who have lived longer than they have aged on this earth.

The Bible states that you should not lean to your own understanding, yet ninety-nine percent of this pre-hell world leans to their understanding. It's amazing really, how the currently Unheard-Of had rebelled against Yah for creating the humans. Truly, you can't really blame him because of their flawed nature. Sure, a few will do some good in this physical realm, but the majority will do only evil and they will surely justify it and themselves in the process.

Many of these humans would take the Unheard-Of's side if they listen to him speak with his slithering tongue and flattering words of pleasure. Because they're carnal and worldly in nature. They say you can't be too spiritual, for it will make you no earthly good. Well, what kind of good can you do in these End Days.

If those few humans can balance the spiritual and earthly, maybe there will be some true good walking amongst the earth. But, where will you find them? In reality, you won't. Either you can become them or stay in your carnal mind where everything worldly and materialistic can be your master and savior. I don't use the word "lord" because for those who truly know, lord is Baal. But, that's a whole other topic to discuss on a later date.

Overall, I seriously suggest the human race think before they act and speak. Because the tongue is indeed filled with deadly poison and holds life and death in its grasp. Many do not think of the future days nor the present day they live upon. Personally, to me, this race is despicable. They cry out for handouts as in having other humans to do their duty for them and to hand it to them when the labor is completed. Yet, they desire to do no labor of any kind, only desire to sit on their asses and stare at that one-eyed monster that dwells in their living rooms and bedrooms, Yah forbid, there's one in the kitchen and bathrooms.

But, I will state this, the humans will not listen or hearken to any warning that may shout out before them. They will only huddle in their collective groups and mock and laugh at the warnings before their wrath is spread amongst the earth. A few understand that everything they see before them on this earth will soon come to pass, just like their flesh bodies. Which will return to dust as it was created from dust.

This species' deception is currently at hand. If you don't belielieve these words, look outside your dwelling places and check it out. That's correct, I said belielieve instead of "believe", so excuse my choice of words. As their deception takes its toll on them, their downfall will surely follow afterwards.

CALL OF THE REAPER

The Reaper is called upon death
For death brings his presence
As does his heaviness

The Reaper takes the souls
Of those that have left the earth
The Reaper takes the souls

To the other side of glory
Where only the Eternal King
Will be able to sentence them

To a place of peace and comfort
Or to a place of dread and torment
The Reaper knows of his calling

As does his duty in place
For the Reaper will not hinder his work
Nor will he delay on his work

His work is what began at the Garden
Wherefore Adam and Eve disobeyed the one commandment
Thus bringing death into the physical world
Of which we currently live in this day

Before the Fall of Man, death was nonexistent
Eternity ruled over all the physical universe

Until the Lawless One decided
To take matters into his own hands
Causing a civil war in Shamayim

Angels fighting angels above us
Knowing not the outcome of their warfare
Only the Eternal King foresaw the conclusion

The Lawless One is cast out
Thrown into the atmosphere of the Earth
Which is his currently dwelling place

For he persuaded Eve to take the forbidden fruit
Eve gave the fruit to Adam, doing what she done
Causing the Fall of Man in all of Creation

The Lawless One laughs at the sight
Of his mighty work for he aided death
To enter into the earth, so it may destroy

The Reaper was later born
With the power of death in his grasp
For many continue to fear him
He has no strength beyond what he was created for
That was to transfer the souls from earth into Glory
Wherefore does one fear the Reaper

Is it his gaze that troubles many?
Is it his presence that fears those?
What else could it be besides his power of death itself

For whatever the status of it may be
The Reaper continues his sole purpose
To transfer souls in the universe

Without death, the Reaper would cease to exist
Though, there are those who merchandise it
Continuing to do so this day
They say they love the Reaper
But they hate death, despise it
Would rather see life than death

That was a previous generation on the earth
For the current generation has no love
Nor do they have any hate of death

They love the sickening of many
They despise good and embrace evil
When death comes, they laugh instead of mourning

Death shown worldwide across many
They continue their humorous acts
Disrespecting others and not caring

They are this generation we see
The perverse and faithless generation
The last generation of this Age

The Reaper constantly watches
Gazing his eyes over this generation
As deaths strike constantly around us

Without any sense of care
People continue as if nothing happened
Many die and many laugh

Few witness and speak out
They are persecuted and killed
Open for the Reaper to take them

Who will wake up this generation
From their own mistakes and failures
If they do not see them, who will

Overall, we only have a short time
To prepare ourselves and to speak with others
To prepare themselves along the way

Many will laugh and attack the speaker
Plotting deceitful ways to attract the Reaper
Toward them in order to kill them

The Call of the Reaper is fairly simple
One does not completely enjoy the sight of death
Unless they know where the spirit is going afterwards

Many will be sent into eternal hell and damnation

Screaming and clawing toward the heavens
For another opportunity at life on earth

They will be declined and will continue to burn
For their iniquities and transgressions
Which they have wrought unto themselves

When the Reaper came unto them
At the end of their days
They didn't scream nor smile at him

Their faces were like stone
Hard and stiff in structure
Unable to crack or shake off

Until they were transferred into the judgment
Where they stood before the Eternal One
The One who commanded the Reaper to do the duty

They would try to plead
They would try to reason with the One
But, their earthly lives prove all that would be said
Few will be welcomed into eternal peace and loving
Singing and cheering upon one another in the glory of the
Eternal One
Where his light is the sun of all eternity

They will shout the name of the One in glory
Singing praises toward him amongst the angels
The cherubim also sing among them

Their faces will appear as light unseen
The beauty of their spiritual figures beyond human
comprehension
They are as bright as the stars of the night

The Reaper understands his purpose
And his fully aware of his coming end
When death will cease to exist

On that day, death itself will die
The Reaper along with it
Not having any use among the living

The Reaper understands his duty
As well as his takings of souls
The transferring of them fuels him

It gives him the strength he needs
To continue his purpose
The purpose of souls into Glory

The Call of The Reaper
Must be known throughout all the generations of old
Till the generations of today

Unless they decide to ignore the Reaper
And ignore his purpose
They will never understand nor receive understanding

The farther they move
The closer the Reaper comes
For they do not have much time left

There will come a day
When the Reaper himself
Will appear before all of creation

Showing his true form
Not afraid of the outcome
He himself will bow before the King

For it is of the King that created him
And allowed him his purpose in the universe
To move souls to and fro into Glory

Whether it be eternal peace
Whether it be eternal suffering
He knows where they will go

The Reaper sees his calling
As does one with his purpose
For he does not question

If he were to question
He would be in the same position
As many on the earth throughout the ages

The Reaper and death have lost a battle

Before in the ages and they will lose
Again in the coming future

Though, that lost will be their last
That loss will be their final
That loss will end the Call of the Reaper

For it is said
Death is the final one
To be defeated and to be unseen

ABADDON'S RISE TO DESTRUCTION

For the time is near
When the Witnesses of the Most High
Appear before all who live on Earth
They will preach the end days
The future Kingdom will be prophesized

The people of the World
Will grow in hatred and envy
Taking measures into their own hands
To kill and destroy the Witnesses
To end their prophesizing

The Witnesses will be shielded
By The Most High, the Creator of All
Nothing will be able to annihilate them
Nor kill them before their time.
They, themselves will exhale fire from the mouths

Supernatural talks will ensure
People will become petrified by the power
They will stand and watch the Witnesses
Prophesizing of the great things to come
Though the people of the world disbelief

For the Witnesses stand alike olive trees
That cannot be knocked down nor shaken by the might of
man
For they can shut Heaven, that it not rain in their days
Powers that can turn water into blood and smite the earth
with plagues
As often as they will during their days

Upon finishing their divine mission on earth
The Beast will ascend out of the bottomless pit
His goal to make war with them and the Most High
He will overcome the Witnesses and kill them
The people of the world will be astonished on earth

For their dead bodies will lie on the ground where they were
smitten
The people of all cultures and creeds will see their dead bodies
For three days and a half, they shall not be buried
For the people of the world will not give them the respect
Of a honorable burial, for they were smitten and suffer graves

The people of the world will rejoice and sing
They will make merry and shall send gifts to one another
Because the two Witnesses, the prophets had tormented them
That dwell on the face of the earth
For Abaddon's Rise has begun will a praise of worship
Abaddon will causeth all to receive a mark
A mark that will allow those to either buy or sell
Those who do not receive the mark are subjected to death
Abaddon's rule is made of an iron forged from the pit
Abaddon's leadership is that of the god of this world

After the three days and a half
The Spirit of life from the Most High will enter
Into the bodies of the Witnesses as they will stand upon their
feet

A great fear will fall upon those who will witness
They will tremble at their presence
A great voice will come from the heavens
Saying, come up here, for they will ascend
Into the heavens in a cloud
Their enemies will beheld them
And tremble at their presence

Within the same hour, an earthquake will shake
Trembling the earth greatly as a tenth of the city shall fall
The earthquake will slay men of seven thousand
The Remnant were affrighted
For they gave glory to the Most High

The second woe has past
For behold to the earth
The third woe cometh
Cometh quickly before the earth
To prepare for the Coming King
Abaddon knows of the time
Abaddon knows of the seasons
Abaddon knows of the Coming
He prepares his army for the time
He prepares his people for the seasons

Abaddon awaits for the Coming
The Coming that confronts his time
The Coming that stumbles his seasons
Abaddon sits for the forty-two months of the seasons

For after the seasons come Abaddon's destruction

SONS OF *YAH*

Known in the Book of Enoch. For those in the Know.

The Sons of Yah or the Sons of the Elohim as some may prefer to call them are the angels that dwell in Shamayim and that even includes the ones who fell from the divine place after the time of creation. The ones that fell are called Fallen Angels, two hundred of them after which they rebelled alongside the Unheard-Of and after the War in Shamayim, they were cast out of Shamayim and descended onto the summit of Mount Hermon during the days of Jared, the father of Chanokh. They called it Mount Hermon because they had sworn and had bound themselves upon the mountain by mutual imprecations.

The names of the leaders of Sons of Yah are as follows, Shemyaza, their leader, Azazel, Arakiba, Rameel, Kokabiel, Tamiel, Ramiel, Danel, Ezeqeel, Baraqijal, Asael, Armaros, Batarel, Ananel, Zaqiel, Samsapeel, Satarel, Turel, Jomjael, Sariel. For these are their chiefs of the tens.

The Sons of Yah had all together decided to take themselves human wives and they had chosen one for each of themselves, and they began to go in unto them and to defile themselves with them. They later taught them charms and enchantments, and the cutting of roots and had made them acquainted with plants. After a while, the human wives became pregnant and they bare great giants, whose height had reached three thousand ells. The giants had consumed all the acquisitions of men.

When men could not sustain them any longer, the giants

turned against them in pure hatred and anger and began to devour mankind. They began to sin against the birds, and beast, and reptiles, and fish, and they devoured one another's flesh and began to drink the blood of them they slaughtered and consumed. Afterwards, the earth had laid in accusation against the lawless ones.

Azazel had taught men how to make swords, and knives, and shields, and breastplates, and made known to them the metals of the earth and the art of working them in warfare. He also taught the women them how to make bracelets, and ornaments, and the use of antimony, and the beautifying of the eyelids, and all kinds of costly stones, and all coloring tinctures. Afterwards, there arose much godlessness and they began to commit fornication with one another and were led astray and became corrupt in all of their ways.

Semjaza had taught them enchantments, and root-cuttings. Armaros taught the resolving of enchantments, Baraqijal had taught them astrology, Kokabel taught the constellations, Ezeqeel taught the knowledge of the clouds, Araqiel taught the signs of the earth, Shamsiel taught the signs of the sun, and Sariel taught the course of the moon. When the men began to perish from the face of the earth, they cried loud and their cries went up to Shamayim.

Then, Michael, Uriel, Raphael, and Gabriel looked down from Shamayim and had saw much blood being shed upon the earth and all the lawlessness being wrought upon the earth. They each said to one another,

"The earth made without inhabitation cries the voice of their crying up to the gates of Shamayim."

"Now to you, the holy ones of Shamayim, the souls of men make their suit, saying, "Bring our cause before the Most High.""

They said toward the Master of the Ages,

"Master of Masters, God of gods, King of Kings, and the Elohim of the Ages, the throne of Your glory standeth unto all generations of the ages, and Your name holy and glorious and blessed unto all the ages! You have made all things and power over all things have You and all things are naked and open in Your sight and all things You see, and nothing can hide itself from You."

"You see what Azazel has done, who has taught all unrighteousness on the earth and has revealed the eternal secrets which were preserved in Shamayim, which men were striving to learn.

"And Semjaza, to whom You have given authority to bear rule over his associates. For they have gone to the daughters of men upon the earth and have slept with the women and have defiled themselves and have revealed to them all kinds of sins. The women have also borne giants and the whole earth has therefore been filled with blood and unrighteousness."

"And now, behold, the souls of those who have died are crying and making their suit to the gates of Shamayim and their lamentations have ascended and cannot cease because of the complete lawless deeds which are wrought upon the earth. And You knowest all things before they come to pass, and You see these things and You do suffer them and You do not say to us what we are able to do to them in regard to these."

Then said the Most High, the Holy and Great One had spoken, and sent Uriel to the son of Miykael, and said to him,

"Go to Dore and tell him in my name, "Hide himself", and reveal to him the end that is fast approaching. That the whole earth will be destroyed, and a deluge is about to come upon the whole earth and will destroy all that is on it. And now instruct him that he may escape, and his seed may be preserved for all the generations of the world."

Again, the Most High turned and said to Raphael, *"Bind Azazel hand and foot and cast him into the darkness, and make an opening in the desert, which is in Dudael and cast him therein. Place upon him rough and jagged rocks and cover him with darkness and let him abide there forever and cover his face that he may not see light. And on the day of the Great Judgment, he shall be cast into the fire and heal the earth which the angels have corrupted and proclaim the healing of the earth, that they may heal the plague, and that all the children of men may not perish through all the secret things that the Watchers have disclosed and have taught their sons.*"

The whole earth had been corrupted through the works that were taught by Azazel and to him ascribe all sin on the face of the earth.

The Most High turned and said to Gabriel, *"Proceed against the bastards and the reprobates, and against the children of fornication, and destroy the children of fornication and the children of the Watchers from amongst men and cause them to go forth and send them one against the other that they may destroy each other in battle. For the length of days shall they not have and no request that they, their fathers, make of them shall be granted unto their fathers on their behalf. For they will hope to live an eternal life and that each one of them will live five hundred years."*

The Most High turned and said to Michael, *"Go and bind Semjaza and his associates who have united themselves with women so as to have defiled themselves with them in all their uncleanness. For when their sons have slain one another in battle and they have seen the destruction of their beloved ones, bind them fast for seventy generations in the valleys of the earth, till the day of their judgment and of their consummation, till the judgment that is for ever and ever is consummated."*

"For in those days, they shall be led off to the abyss of fire and to the torment and the prison in which they shall be confined for ever. Whosoever shall be condemned and destroyed will from thenceforth be bound together with them to the end of all generations. Destroy the spirits of the reprobate and the children of the Watchers, because they have wronged mankind. Destroy all wrong from the face of the earth and let every evil work come to an end and let the plant of righteousness and truth appear, for it shall prove a blessing. The works of righteousness and

truth shall be planted in truth and joy for evermore."

"And then shall all the righteous escape and shall live till they beget thousands of children and all the days of their youth and their old age shall they complete in peace. Then shall the whole earth be tilled in righteousness and shall be planted with trees and will be full of blessing and all desirable trees shall be planted on it and they shall plant vines on it and the vine which they plant thereon shall yield wine in abundance and as for all the seed which is sown thereon each measure of it shall bear a thousand and each measure of olives shall yield ten presses of oil."

"Cleanse the earth from all oppression and from all unrighteousness and from all sin and from all godlessness and all the uncleanness that is wrought upon the earth to destroy from all the earth and all the children of men shall become righteous and all the nations shall offer adoration and shall praise Me and shall worship Me. The earth shall be cleansed from all defilement and from all sin and from all punishment and from all torment and I will never again send them upon it from generation to generation and for ever."

"In those days I will open the store chambers of blessing which are in the Shamayim, so as to send them down upon the earth over the work and labor of the children of men. Truth and peace shall be associated together throughout all the days of the world and throughout all the generations of men."

Behold, all these things Chanokh was hidden and no one of the children of men knew where he was hidden and where he abodes and what had become of him. As his activities had to do with the Watchers and his days were with the holy ones.

<u>IN THE DAYS OF DORE</u>

These days were unlike the days of Adam and Eve, the days of the Lawless One's rebellious act against the Father. Unlike the days of Qayin and Hevel and Seth, the days of Queen Alyssa and the rise and fall of her kingdom known as Bashemath, unlike the days of Chanokh, who walked with the Most High, unlike the days of Harold, who watched the clash between the Dark Gods and Cosmics as the Most High chose him to create a tablet to lock away the Dark God known as Negiter until the End Days where he would be released.

During the days of Dore, known in his time as the Mariner or the One Who Prophesized the Deluge, were truly terrible times. When Dore would enter the sinful cities of Tubal-Qayin and the old remaining cities of Bashemath, the old kingdom of Queen Alyssa, which was destroyed by The Most High for its sinful indulges. Dore would enter the city and begin prophesizing to anyone who would hear him. He spoke loudly about the Deluge that was on its way in a matter of time. The people laughed at Dore, calling him a lunatic, a fool, a weak-minded vessel, a lost spirit.

"He continues to prophesize and yet there hasn't been a drop of rain fall from the sky in three months span." A bystander says to his fellow city people. "This man is a fool and shows it without being shameful."

"You proceed to call me a fool today, yet, when the deluge comes, who will be the fool on that day." Dore said. "Who do you believe will be saved when the waters of the earth rise up and consume the land that you stand upon. Who will the Elohim of this earth protect from the waters that he sent and created to cleanse the earth of the foul beings that sit upon it."

The man would return to his tent, holding his head down in shame as the other bystanders would turn and laugh at him instead of Dore. Dore would continue his preaching before leaving the city.

Dore would ignore those types of comments and continue with his preaching. He would leave the city after preaching, returning to his home out in the wilderness with his wife, Emzarah, and their three sons, Adad, Samael, and Mordecai. The city people were unaware that Dore was building a large vessel to protect himself and his family from the Deluge. Uriel the Archangel would come by and watch as Dore would continue to build nonstop.

While Dore continued building, the city people were celebrating marriages, parties, feasts, and indulging in fornications, orgies, and human sacrifices. After many years of warnings from Dore, the people continued to ignore him and kept their lives going to the fullest. Dore was known as the stranger or the lost one when he would appear into the cities and prophesize.

Dore was never overshadowed by fear of the people or fear of their words and actions. Tubal-Qayin would speak to his people, saying, "Listen not to this stranger that appears among us. For he is a lost one, a child searching for his parents, an animal clinging to its prey's bones." Tubal-Qayin ruled much of the land during the days of Dore, he is also a descendent of a judge that once had a position of power in Queen Alyssa's days.

As the years began to go by, all three hundred and sixty-four days, Dore was coming closer to finishing the colossal vessel, Uriel the Archangel would appear and continue to watch as Dore and his sons were building the vessel.

"He continues, and it shows his faith." Uriel the Archangel had said.

Within the cities, the people began more ruthless and primitive than years' past. The Nephilim that were on the earth in those days, began to slaughter and consume mankind. They would also slaughter the animals and drink their blood. Mankind itself began to rape and murder women, kill the men, and sacrifice the children to their gods known as Negiter and the Dark Gods of old. The Most High grieved in the days of Dore.

"I will send a deluge upon the earth. Cleansing it of all corruption that mankind has created. Saving only Dore and his family." Saith יהוה thy Elohim.

The city people kept up their partying and marriages. Tubal-Qayin never took part in his people's festivities as he only watched them and always looked above at the sky for a sign of the deluge that Dore continued to prophesize about.

"If Dore is right and a deluge is coming, I must speak to him and him alone." Tubal-Qayin said to himself.

Tubal-Qayin had met with Dore a few short days later. They spoke about the deluge as Dore told him of what was coming. Tubal-Qayin believed him, yet were only interested in saving himself and a few of his close allied compensations. He even stated that he would come when the deluge would arrive and bring damsels with him, so he could go into them while inside the vessel. Dore declined that Tubal-Qayin do such a thing, causing a large rift between the two men.

"I hope you're aware of your days, Dore, son of Miykael." Tubal-Qayin said. "For it is only a matter of days that you will be killed and sacrificed before the Dark Gods."

"I will not be a sacrifice to your false gods that lie dormant in the darkness." Dore said. "Me and my family will be protected from your harm and affliction as long as we keep our obedience."

"You talk of obedience and yet you won't allow me and my

people to enter into your vessel. Remember, son of Miykael, I am a king on this land and I have an army at my disposal. You only have your family. A wife and three young boys. How would they fare against an army lead by me and me alone?"

"Because we're not alone. He is watching over us as the angels are as well."

Tubal-Qayin shook off the warnings of Dore and himself stood watch for the deluge. The Nephilim had killed off each other in a civil war that was started by Gabriel the Archangel under the Most High's command. After the civil war and the final destruction of the Nephilim, Dore knew that it was time.

When the deluge arrived, Dore and his family were already prepared and sealed in the vessel along with the clean and unclean animals of the earth as the Most High had clarified.

The waters rose up from the seas and burst from the earth, swallowing the city people who were stranded on the ground. Tubal-Qayin had attempted to climb aboard the vessel, but a giant wave knocked him off and dragged him deep under the water where he would drown to death.

Dore and his family survived the deluge and lived long lives of prosperity and happiness. Though, as it is said, *"As it was in the Days of Dore, so shall it become again in the days of the Son of Man."*

<u>DEATH OF A KING</u>

In an ancient kingdom in time past, there was a king of great power and a stature unlike those in the outside kingdoms. The King had fought many battles during his youth until his time of old age. His father and grandfather before him were mighty kings of the lands. They made warfare and combat against any opposing forces that would seek to overthrow the kingdom completely. Some have vowed to witness the end of the kingdom, but have met their own end at the end of the King's sword.

The King's grandfather had one wife that guided him and supported him during his reign. The King's father had two wives, both of whom had supported him during his reign as king. The King during his youth possessed a wife and later a second wife when he became King over the lands.

"I have chosen a second wife, father." The young King said.

"A second wife?" The Father said. "Are you sure you can handle the pressure of two compared to one?"

"If I am able to become your successor in full, father, I must follow in your footsteps."

The father chuckled at his son's words, but understood them completely and he knew how similar they were to his own words to his own father when he became king.

"What is this second wife's name?"

"Her name is Deborah. She lives near the creek in the outskirts of the kingdom."

"The outskirts? So, she's an outsider?"

"An outsider that has vast knowledge of royalty and how a king should rule his kingdom."

"Explain to me, how would this outsider wife of yours know much about ruling a kingdom?"

"She said she had a dream about a righteous king and how he ruled over his kingdom where there was everlasting peace and security."

"Everlasting peace, huh. I would've loved that during my reign as king."

"Do you believe I can give it a shot?"

"I believe you'll take good care of this kingdom, son. Only make sure that no one spits into your ears false ideals and techniques that would see your downfall."

"I will make sure of that, father. I will."

The young King brought Deborah into his chambers and went into her and she became his second wife. Through her, he begat a daughter and from his first wife, two sons.

Several years after the wars amongst the neighboring kingdoms concerning the ways of livestock and ideals, the young King, now in his middle ages sought out a woman from one of the neighboring kingdoms, lost and frightened. Dirty from the ground she walked on. Her face almost unrecognizable from the amount of dirt that covered her face and body. He comforted her and was told that her husband was killed in battle against his army.

"Come back to my kingdom, my lady." The middle age King said. "I will take good care of you there."

"Thank you, your majesty."

He took the woman back to his kingdom and she entered his castle, seeing the amount of treasures that they won through the spoils of war surrounding the castle grounds.

"This place isn't as filthy as the kingdoms in Lelat." The woman said. "What do you do with them, if I may ask of you?"

"We keep them as memories of the wars we've come to face. It reminds us of why we're still walking upright in our days upon this earth."

The maidservants of the King's two wives took the woman to a guest chamber of her own where she cleaned up herself and dressed in modest apparel similar to the maidservants. The King would visit her during the days to see how she was feeling and doing.

"I never got to know your name." The King said.

"My name is Amana."

"Integrity and truth your name stands for."

"How did you know that?"

"Because I can see it in your eyes and hear it in your voice."

"I take it you know of the meaning of names as well."

"I did some learning in my youth. Still learning more as I go about this life."

"You're a different king that the ones that came before."

"So, I've been told."

A few months later, the middle-aged King married Amana and she became his third wife. Through her, he had one son and two daughters. The son looked up to his older half-brothers and the daughters sat at the feet of the mother and their stepmothers, learning the ways of being a woman in life within the kingdom walls.

Several years had passed and another war was waged between the Kingdom and the neighboring kingdoms. The neighboring kingdom brought along men of great stature with them and they stood nearly the height of the trees outside of the kingdom walls. The middle-aged King and his first two sons went into battle with his army and slaughtered the opposing kingdoms within the span of five days. The men of great stature were slain, and their weapons were taken as trophies of the war.

Time slowly began to catch up to the middle-aged King, his body beginning to slow down on him. His great feats on the battlefield were slowly withering away. Near becoming an old man, his first two sons lead the kingdom's army into the battles that came their way. Defeating the likes of the kingdoms of Lelat and Ostacre.

The two sons were later killed in their middle ages, after having sons of their own. The near old King wept at the news of his eldest sons' deaths.

"My sons. I know you are in a better land now. With your grandfather and great-grandfather. You're among the family of the dead now. Soon, I will join you and see your faces again once more."

The now old man King had witnessed the death of his first wife and his second wife. Only his third wife remained at his side when he became bedridden.

"Amana, command some of the soldiers, tell them to take me to the trees near the waters. Also call for my daughters to meet me there."

"I will." A middle-aged Amana said.

The soldiers came and took the old King to the tress near the waters, where Amana and his three daughters came to sit with him as he looked out and witnessed the sun setting. His youngest daughter began to weep as she knew what was about to take place. The old King looked at her and grabbed her hand.

"Do not cry over me leaving this world. I am going to a place far better and far peaceful than what this world knows."

The old King looked to Amana with a small tear in his eye. She read the Book of King Liam to him, a king that was a man made after The Most High's own heart. When she finished reading the book to him. He looked out toward the waters and could see two angels standing before him with their hands held out to him.

"It is time." The Angel said.

The King nodded and kissed Amana and said goodbye to his three daughters as he gave up the ghost and entered the spirit world. The King whose name was *Magdiel,* meaning the chosen fruit of The Most High, passed on from the natural world and was engraved in the Book of Rulers for future generations to learn from.

THE HORSEMEN COMETH

The signs have been shown and the world around us having been revealing a large amount of revelations across itself. From the wars, the famines, the pestilence, and the deaths that has consumed this world ever since the Fall of Man. These four occurrences are controlled and ruled by what the world calls the Four Horsemen of the Apocalypse. The ones from the outer depths of space call them the Four Riders of the Universe. The Elect know them as the Four Horsemen of the Forbidden. They have come to this planet to reveal the End Days' arrival and preparation for Abaddon the Antichrist and the return of the Messiah, the One and Only Christ.

There was a series of events that took place within the world, where many witnessed the Horsemen themselves with their own eyes. Some have said their arrival is like a cometh or a presence. They can be felt before they're seen by anyone living within the physical world. They have aided events that have held wars of profound numbers, famines of great losses, pestilences of dire consequences, and deaths of an unspeakable and uncountable number.

The Horsemen of the Forbidden already possess the knowledge of their intended purposes and seek out to fulfill them at any cost, whether anyone living or dead gets in between them and their purpose. The Horsemen guard the field known as the Land of the Forbidden. The Land of the Forbidden is a sacred land where it is said to hold the Final Battle between the Most High Yah and the

Lawless One.

From the time of its inception and purpose, no living human has ever entered into the land and had yet to come out alive only to have their bodies found fully turned to dust. It is documented that only one man made it through the land with some injuries to go along with it. He is known to Us, the Elect as Kenari Clark.

The Horsemen each possess and individual name for themselves. A horse of their kind, a weapon of their choice, and a source of power that they may command at any moment that benefits their purpose. They are sent by the Most High to fulfill his ultimate purpose.

The first Horsemen is known to Us as Bane. Known as the Holder of Pestilence. He is seen wearing an all-white shrugged uniform with a tunic and a cape that both appear to be ripping apart from his body. His face is covered by his white mask, though his cold eyes can be seen. He possesses the weapon known to Us as the Endemic, a bow and arrow that he uses to slaughter the people and bring the diseases into the world. His horse possesses a white hide that many can see within the dark, for hardly no darkness of any kind can cover up the horse. Bane's power is known to go forth into conquest and to conquer by any means necessary. Bane is the first Horsemen of the Forbidden.

The second Horsemen is known to Us as War. Known as the Possessor of Wars. He is seen wearing all armor equipped with black cloth and a blood red cape and hood. The armor has the appearance of looking aged and used for centuries. The cloth is covered with dried blood as the cape and hood have ripped marks and tears across it. He possesses the weapon known to Us as the Redeemer, a longed medium sized blade that can cut and pierce through any form on

Earth. His horse possesses a black hide and its mane glistened like the flames of the sun. War's horse can be unseen in the darkness, until its fiery mane makes itself known to the darkness. War's power is known to take peace from the earth and to make the men of the world kill each other in fierce combat to spread their blood across the body and soil of the earth. Their primary task is to kill with the sword that they possess. The modern-day sword would be known as the gun. War is the second Horsemen of the Forbidden.

The third Horsemen is known to Us as Rage. Known as the Bringer of Famines. He is seen wearing gray armor with a helmet with two ram horns on each side. His eyes are seen glowing through the helmet with furious heat. He possesses the weapon known to Us as the *Vehemencer*. A double-sided war hammer used for destruction and fury. A hammer that possesses the double amount of force of an ordinary mortal war hammer that's used for combat. His horse possesses a deep black hide to where not even the darkness itself can find the animal as it buries itself deep within the darkness. Rage's power is known to bring fury upon the earth and to kill with intense torture. Rage is also responsible for the famines of both food and spirit across the earth. Rage is the third Horsemen of the Forbidden.

The fourth and last Horsemen is known to Us as the Reaper. Known as the Entropy of Death. He is seen wearing an all-black cloak with a hood. His face appears as a human skull, though with his white pierced eyes and shivering voice that emit from it. He possesses the weapon known to Us as the Collector, his large scythe with the bladed end that stretches six feet in length from the tip of the blade to the staff it was attached to. The Collector is used to take the souls of the earth and bring them into the spirit world, where they will be judged for their earthy actions and decisions. His horse possesses a pale hide that which many who see the animal shiver and freeze in fear of its appearance. For it appears as a ghost to them that see it and brings them the feeling of death. When his horse appears, people know that many will indeed die. Reaper's power is known to be followed by the powers of Hell, to kill with the scythe that he possesses in his grasps, with famines, diseases, and the beasts that scatter upon the earth. Those are his tools of destruction and desolation to the earth. Reaper is the fourth and final Horsemen of the Forbidden.

The Horsemen are currently guarding the Land of the Forbidden to the time of the Final Battle to take place. The Most High will gather his armies of angels to take battle with the Lawless One and his armies of angels to take battle. It is not sure if the Horsemen themselves will take part in the Final Battle to come, but they will be there to witness it unfold.

VISITATION TO THE ABYSS

There was a time where the entity called by the spiritual realm, Darkous traveled down into the first heaven on Earth. The atmosphere below the second heaven that is outer space or the universe. Darkous had visited Earth on several occasions, whether it was for a small council meeting, bounties, or being a messenger between the Light and the Dark. Darkous understood his role in the spiritual realm and his role within the boundaries of the physical realm.

Darkous had worn his traditional dark violet and black trench coat, though he didn't place the hood of the coat over his head as it laid against the back of the coat.

When Darkous walked down the large hallway that seemed to have no walls on either side except a fall into a bottomless pit into Sheol, which lead toward the entrance door into the atmospheric Abyss, he saw the head of the ha-Satan. Darkous stopped and stood still while facing him as he watched Darkous over the entrance door. The entrance doors themselves were surrounded by demonic spirits and had engraved pentagrams on its front. The ha-Satan's appearance seemed to indicate that he became much taller than he was in previous times, simply indicating that the wickedness taking place in the physical realm is making him much stronger and powerful as the days go by.

"Welcome to my present kingdom, Darkous." ha-Satan said. "I've been expecting your presence here."

"I'm only here on orders, ha-Satan. Not on a friend request. Its business that I speak to you."

"Very well. Enter at will, Darkous."

The large doors opened and flames burst from the doors and slowly moved toward the side as Darkous walked through them and into the main area of Satan's earthly kingdom. While inside he could see and smell the burning of human flesh as he witnessed people burning and screaming in the flame of eternal torment down in Sheol, each spirit having a traumatizing remembrance of their sins that occurred in their earthly lives. The screaming of the spirits was loud enough to cause a human to go insane and possibly would injure their ear drums.

"Please help me!!!!" A female spirit yelled toward Darkous.

"Sir, please!!! Let me tell my family about this place of torment! Let me warn them." A male spirit yelled.

Darkous stopped and looked at the spirit, seeing it was a male and he was in great torment.

"They have the writings of *Mosheh* and the Prophets." Darkous said to the spirit. "They even have the letters of the apostles. That should be enough."

"They won't believe them!!!!"

"Very well, if someone were to rise out of the grave and the pit of Hell, they wouldn't believe them either. I'm truly sorry for your natural family."

Darkous walked past them as he approached ha-Satan standing before him, a figure that stood at the approximate height of eighteen to twenty-three feet. He still possessed a form of his wings and had a burned look upon his body as it once shined brightly. Ha-Satan grinned at Darkous while rubbing his hands together.

"Don't get any ideas in here." Darkous said. "You know what will happen."

"You know I won't, believe you me. Now, let's discuss this business that you spoke of at the entrance door."

"The business that I speak of is about what's currently taking place on this planet Earth. You of all angels know how this place operates and how much wickedness and darkness consumes it because of your rebellion."

"I chose to rebel for a purpose that neither you or any of the angels could understand. I want to be like the Most High and I shall become like the Most High."

Darkous laughed quietly to himself as he listened to ha-Satan speak.

"Do you hear yourself, Lucifer? You already know the outcome. You already have control of the earth until the end of this Sixth Day."

"Silence your tongue! Don't speak of the day when my kingdom will fall. Of course, I know that I will be defeated and bind by chains into the eternal darkness that awaits me. You, Darkous are unlike the other entities that appeared after my rebellious act. You were only created by Him to have watchful eyes and ears over the darkness in the cosmos. Five days have passed since my rebellion and we're approaching the end of the six. I dread the Seventh Day and what it will bring toward me."

"Because you understand that during the Seventh Day, you will be in darkness for one thousand years in time and space."

"So, you say, though it will feel like twelve to twenty-four hours to me and I will be released yet again before my final end."

Darkous glanced down at the ground of earth. He could see the humans dwelling on it in mass. From his view, he could see nearly an entire continent if not two and the people living on them. He could also look further down at the tormented spirits of Sheol that scream in agony in the eternal lake of fire. Ha-Satan rubs his chin as he sits back in his throne chair made of molten rock and burned flesh.

"You never spoke of the business you claim here to make."

"The business I came to discuss involves this planet Earth and the humans that live upon it."

"What of them? You want me to stop the violence and desolation? I will not do such a thing, Darkous. The violence and desolation have a purpose of being on this planet because the humans put it there"

"By your deceitful speech toward Eve when you led her through temptation to sin and cause the Fall of Man to take place by the hand of Adam. I witnessed it happen along with the angels above."

Ha-Satan laughs off Darkous' sentence and shakes his head

while laughing hysterically. Darkous only stared at the ha-Satan with his arms crossed.

"You got me on that one, Darkous. I can give you that one for once. But, you know I will not cease those actions, so why bother asking me about them."

"I know you will not. You're doing what you chose to do. I speak of the humans that are fighting and destroying your kingdom on earth."

"Those saints of the Most High. I have them on my list to deceive and destroy in due time."

"How can you destroy them when they are protected by Elohim? You know you cannot and it drives you mad at times doesn't it. You want the Elect to transgress the Law, so it can open the door for you to enter and bring destruction upon them and boast in yourself at doing so."

"Sometimes you sound like Michael to me."

"At least he doesn't go around and boast about himself and what he did and what he can do. He could've rebuked you about the body of Mosheh, yet he did not."

"Just like you boast in your victories whether they're against your mystical adversaries or your successes on the humankind front."

"At least few of humankind is aiding us in destroying your kingdom until Elohim takes care of it in full."

"All in good time. But, from what I can understand and take curiously from your last mission, my servant Kabra surely did a move on you and your precious Beauty. Though, that Malach HaMavet proved to be a worthy foe against my kingdom. Though their deaths will not come yet, but it surely will take place by my command."

"Kabra will receive what he deserves and so will Mazakala and Desolation. While you sit by at times and watch what's ongoing, I and my allies, both on the spiritual and physical sides will continue to destroy your kingdom and end your wickedness."

"Sit by?! You've gone mad, Darkous! I roam the earth to and fro and walk up and down in it. I roamed the earth when Adam and Eve left the Garden of Eden and I continue to roam this day. I stand where my servants do their work and justify it to themselves in order to please me.”

“Well, contact me when you do show up on the earthly grounds again. Because I want to see you there and maybe I and the Elect can show you what we’re capable of on earthly grounds.”

“Don’t worry yourself and get anxious, Darkous. You will see me on the earth in due time and it will be at the right time.”

“I look forward to seeing you around, ha-Satan.”

“I want you to see me around, Darkous or Doctor Dark, as humankind calls you. I will look forward to murdering you and your allies and leaving your blood on the ground for the earth to drink as it did Abel.”

Darkous walked away and looked back at the ha-Satan and gave him a smile.

“I’m sure you want to see that. Funny how neither one of us know when it will take place and that makes it interesting to meditate on.”

Darkous walks out of the atmospheric kingdom of Satan as the entrance doors closed behind him, sounding like an earthquake had gone through the air. The ha-Satan stayed sitting on his throne, smirking.

“In due time, Darkous. All in due time.”

<u>INSTINCTS ARE A CALLING</u>

Preston Maddox, a homicide detective and Marshal of the United States goes into a mission that concerns the rise of Satanism. Maddox studied the case alongside his partner, Emily Weston. Both of whom, sit inside the office of their Chief, Eldon Ross, discussing the case and reading over the files.

"I didn't know it went this far." Emily said.

"It was meant to come." Preston said. "Just the question is how far it will go before it consumes all of the world."

"I believe it already has accomplished that, Preston." Eldon said as he walked into his office.

Eldon sat behind his desk as they talked about the case.

"Now, Preston I know you love this kind of stuff deep down, ever since your encounter with the Spirit after being shot. So, you will go on this case."

"I certainly will, and Emily has decided to tag along with me on it."

Eldon turned over to Emily. Discerning her facial expression, seeing how she's thrilled, but concerned about her well-being of being out in that area.

"You'll be fine, Emily. Trust me, Preston's got your back. Especially on a case like this he should."

Preston grabbed his coat and turns to Emily, who places the file back on Eldon's desk. She looked at him with a cautious face, Preston only smiled back toward her.

"You're ready for this?" Preston said to Emily.

"Ready when you are."

Preston and Emily had left the office and traveled through New Haven, Connecticut to find the newly built Satanic Church. The church is known for having secret human and animal sacrifices taking place in an underground area that the church itself is built over. Preston speeds down the street, as if he's racing to get to the church first.

"You ever heard of slowing down?" Emily said.

"This is an important case, Emily." Preston said. "Not just for us, but for everyone in the world. This kind of stuff can't be left alone to continue."

After a few stops and turns, they arrived at the Satanic Church. They exited the car and started walking up the stairs of the church that appeared to be made of burnt stone, possibly stones from an erupted volcano.

"These steps look as if they've been burnt by something." Emily said. "What do you think, Preston?"

"Its just something they had to build up the suspense of the damn place."

Upon reaching the top step and facing the front entrance, they noticed a variety of small statues that stood in front of the church. The statues consist of gargoyles, dragons, serpents, and a small bronze statue of Baphomet. Preston glanced upon them and spat on them.

"I hope no one saw what you just did." Emily said.

"Who gives a shit."

They opened the doors and entered the church. Inside the church, it appeared to be any ordinary church. Pews on both sides with a podium in the front at the center, though behind the podium was a large bronze statue of Baphomet that its height nearly reached the ceiling of the church. Preston stared with disgust brewing in him.

"This kind of stuff is sick I tell you."

Emily notices a priest, wearing a black and scarlet robe walking toward them. Emily grab Preston's attention as the priest approached them and they stood in front of the podium that sat in front of the statue of Baphomet.

"Welcome to our church." The priest said. "May I ask why you are here this day?"

"Preston Maddox, United States Marshal and Homicide Detective. This is my partner, Emily Weston, United States Marshal and Homicide Detective. We're here to speak with a Mr. Vernon Lance."

"Ah, our top priest. Well, he is here, but he's downstairs at the moment. Whatever you have to tell him, tell me and I will pass it along over to him."

"We need to speak with him in person, if you don't mind." Emily said. "Just call him up and we'll be out of your hair soon enough."

"Very well then, Marshals."

The priest walked back behind the back doors and Preston noticed he went down a flight of stairs. Emily glanced over to see what Preston was looking at.

"What do you see?"

"He just went down some stairs. I take it we'll be seeing Mr. Lance soon enough."

"Hopefully, because I can't stand being in this place. Something just doesn't feel right." Emily said.

"I understand what you're saying." Preston said. "I mean, who in the hell, no pun intended, would sit in a place where there's a statue of that caliber sitting and facing you."

"Most churches have statues facing them. Made either from wood or stone."

"Idolatry at its finest."

They hear some voices coming from the back of the church doors. They recognize one to be the voice of the priest, though the second one doesn't sound familiar to them. They see the back doors opening and the priest coming out first and behind him another man, with long wavy black hair that surpassed his shoulders, he wore a black trench coat that went down near his ankles, and he wore all black clothing with black fingernails. His pupils were the color of fire purging.

"What in the hell are we dealing with here." Preston said.

"We're about to find out."

The Priest and the man confront Preston and Emily. They stand their ground while facing the two individuals.

"Here's Mr. Vernon Lance, detectives." The priest said. "I will leave him to you."

The priest walked away, leaving Lance facing Preston and Emily. Lance let out a smile and extended his hand toward them.

"Excuse my manners, I am Vernon Lance. The Satanic Church's High Priest."

Preston shook his hand and stared Lance in the eyes intensely. Emily continued to watch on as the two started for about a minute.

"Preston Maddox, United States Marshal and Homicide Detective."

"I know who you are, and I know your partner as well. Ms. Emily Weston to be exact. I know a lot about the people of this city and the people of the world."

"If you don't mind me asking, Mr. Lance. But, are you the Satanic Priest that was talked about being discovered in an old abandoned church by a Dr. Galen Donovan and that Spirit-Seeker guy?"

"I cannot say. I would never forget of having a confrontation with Mr. Travis Vail. Though, if I did, I do not remember the event."

"We'll look into it for more information." Emily said.

"I'm sure you will, my lady. Now, why are the two of you here today?"

"We're here to discuss information that concerning of animal and human sacrifices taking place underneath this church."

"Sacrifices you speak of." Lance said. "If we were doing those things, we would obviously send out invitations for people to come and see and if need be, partake in them."

"What kind of person would say something like that?" Emily said.

"A greater kind."

"What kind of "greater kind" are you talking about, Mr.

Lance?" Preston said. "I'm just curious about what you're saying."

"All will be revealed in good time, but there are no sacrifices taking place here. I can assure you of that."

Lance glanced down at his watch and faced Preston and Emily.

"Now if you'll both excuse me, I have a meeting I need to get back to in my office. Nice speaking with you both. I hope to see you two sooner than later."

"We're sure, Mr. Lance." Preston said. "Twisted ass clown."

Preston and Emily left the church and returned to the Marshal office. They spoke with Eldon about what they saw and what Lance had told them. Eldon was still curious about the place and was uncertain of Lance's actions.

"You two can decide if you want further investigation on this case. If not, I'll just send Leon and Darius on it." Eldon said.

"We can take this case, Chief." Preston said. "You can count on it."

"Alright then, Preston. Hope you do the job well and not cause any casualties this time."

"Unless its necessary."

"Pretty much." Eldon said. "You're right on that."

Preston and Emily left the office. As they exited the elevator downstairs, Preston felt uncertainty entering into his mind. Emily noticed it by how Preston moved and walked.

"What's wrong?" Emily said.

"I feel there's something much greater taking place at that church and it won't bring any good."

"Maybe your instincts are calling out to you about the place and it doesn't seem to look good."

Later that night at the church, underground, Lance and five other priests are conducting an animal sacrifice with a goat. Lance reads from a book, where he later slashes the goat's through as it blood drained down a line which entered into a statue of *Baphomet*. The statue's eyes light up like fire, releasing a low toned growl as Lance smiles and bows before it.

"Take this offer, my master." Lance said. "For we here, serve you and your kingdom of eternal hell."

THE NEW AGE
AND
<u>FUTURE KINGDOM</u>

The time we are all living in is the End Time. The Sixth Day of the Seven. Wickedness is growing at a constant rate across the world. Morality is vanishing amongst humanity. Good is called evil and evil is called good. The faith of many are falling away, returning to a life of sin and unbelief. The confederate leaders of the world are preparing for the Man of Sin to make his grand entrance and proclaim himself to be God reincarnated.

The entire world will be pulled into the lying signs and wonders performed by the Man of Sin and will ultimately believe he is God. He will cause all both great and small to receive a mark on their forehead or their right hand. During his reign, the world will love what he presents. The Saints of The Most High will stay amongst themselves, away from those of the world. The Dragon, Satan himself, embodied in the flesh as the Man of Sin will make every attempt at finding the Saints, who are in hiding from the world in a prepared place in the wilderness.

The prophets of Old proclaimed these events to take place and they will take place. The signs of their coming have already presented themselves to the people of the world and many refuse to look and accept it for what it is. Riotous living will continue to grow as many become stacked up in the population centers called cities. Woe to the women who are with children or pregnant during these coming days. The coming days we live in are the ones the prophets wished to witness. The return of Egypt and Sodom in spirit.

During those days, the angels will blow their trumpets in sevens. Two witnesses will appear and prophesy a thousand two hundred and sixty days. They will stand upright as of two olive trees and candlesticks. The people who attempt to harm them will be consumed with fire from their mouths, which will devour them. They will possess the power to shut heaven, blocking the rain coming from the filled clouds in those days. They will possess the power to turn water into blood and smite the earth with the plagues that derived from the time of the Exodus in Moses' day.

In their final days of prophesy, the Beast, Satan himself will make war against them and he will overcome them and kill them. Their dead bodies will not be buried and will remain in the streets of the trodden down Jerusalem, where Jesus was crucified on a tree. Those days will the people of the world celebrate with gifts and rejoicings. They rejoiced because the two prophets had tormented them in those days on the earth. When three days and a half pass by, the Spirit of Life will enter them and they will rise up on their feet and great fear will fall onto the people of the world that witnessed their prophesying.

"Come up here." A voice from heaven will say to them.

The two witnesses will ascend to heaven in a cloud and their enemies will watch this all take place before their very eyes. The world will witness this event take place. Within that same hour, a great earthquake will tremble the earth and a tenth portion of the city will fall. the earthquake will take the lives of seven thousand people. The remnant of The Most High will be frightened and will give glory and praise to The Most High.

That will be the second woe passing away and the third woe will come quickly after that.

The nations of the world will make war with The Most High and his remnant with Satan as their leader. They will make way to Harmegiddo, the land where they declare war against The Most High and his remnant. The Returning Messiah will come down and kill the armies of the nations with the Word of The Most High and will destroy their city of Babylon within one hour. For within that one hour, the kings of the nations and their partakers all lost everything.

Babylon, the great harlot and mother of harlots and the abominations of the earth will fall by the hand of The Most High and His remnant will rejoice over her defeat. After the Great Tribulation, the Messiah will return from out of the clouds with a white horse and a vesture dipped in blood. His eyes were like the flame of fire. On his head were many crowns and a name that only Himself knew. The armies of heaven that followed him will be dressed in white linen, white and clean, and will be riding on white horses.

From His mouth will go a sharp sword, which will be use to smite the nations of the world and he will rule over them with a rod of iron. On his vesture and thigh will be a name written that says, King of Kings and Master of Masters. His name is called The Word of Yah. Satan will be bound in the abyss for one thousand years during the reining of the Messiah. The remnant that did not bow to the Beast nor received his mark will live and reign with the Messiah in the New Kingdom for a thousand years.

Within the Kingdom, the remnant will have ruler ship over the nations and the nations will be their servants and wine dressers. They will lick the dust from the remnant's feet. The people will visit the Messiah three times in a year during His feast days. Within the end of those thousand years, Satan will be released to cause more to fall way from The Most High and after the thousand years are completed, Satan himself will be placed into the eternal flames of hell along with his angels that sided with him in the beginning. The old heaven and the old earth will pass away and The Most High will create the new heaven and new earth in their place to remain for all the righteous to dwell for all eternity.

We are nearer today than the prophets were thousands of years ago. The end of the Sixth Day is at hand and the Seventh Day is approaching faster than many will come to notice. Repent of your sins and be transformed by the renewing of your mind. Separate yourselves from the world to determine what is of The Most High and become one of the few that will enter New Jerusalem.

THE VIRTUOUS AND THE WICKED

Throughout the centuries of the world's existence, there have been women of those that were considered virtuous and those that were considered wicked. Here, will be a small discussion on the lives of those that were virtuous and those that were of the wicked. From Hawwah, the second wife of Adam to Yessica, we receive those of the virtuous. From Lilith, the proposed first wife of Adam to Carissa, we receive those of the wicked.

The first of this brief document will be the wicked ones. Starting with Lilith, the proposed first wife of Adam. Little is known Lilith, it is said that she was created alongside Adam during the days of Creation by the Most High, Yahweh. It is said that Lilith didn't agree with Adam for being on the bottom during sexual intercourse and she yelled the secret name of Yahweh and vanished into the atmosphere where she is still roaming to this day with her ally and possible husband in theory, the ha-Satan.

The second in this brief document is Queen Alyssa, the dominant queen of the queendom she called Bashemath. The daughter of Qayin and Awan. Alyssa was physically beautiful and seductive toward men and women through the flesh. She became queen during her days of leading both men and women astray as she commanded them to build her a kingdom of her own, where she could rule over those who would appear and would see fit to live there. Alyssa knew of the existence of Yahweh due to her father receiving the Mark. Alyssa grew with a respect and honor toward the

Most High until her queendom was built and she began to see herself as a goddess amongst man of the earth.

It wasn't until she committed secret sodomy with a whore named Seba, that she was frequently visited by Uriel the Archangel, who gave Alyssa warnings to turn from her wicked ways and start focusing her whole attention on Yahweh by first banishing a homosexual from the queendom.

Alyssa agreed and started to do so until impatience took its course over the years and her heart was hardened. Her people began to worship her and even built monuments and images in her image. She later took place in many murders during the final years of her queendom until she had one more visit from Uriel, who told her that her queendom's demise would take place the next day and it did. Fire rained down from the heavens upon Bashemath, killing all who remained in the city. Alyssa was last to escape as she watched her queendom burn and turn into ash. The rise and fall of Queen Alyssa took place within a time span of thirty years. Alyssa later died in the wilderness at the age of seventy years old.

The third one that will be spoken of in brief detail is Ivah. The first wife of Dore during his younger years. The name Ivah means *iniquity* and that is what she brought upon him. They had no children together due to Ivah being barren, which hardened her heart toward Dore and toward Yahweh. Dore eventually sent Ivah away and nothing else is known of her till this day beside her actions toward Dore and Yah and the origin of her name.

The next wicked one to come across the earth was Jezebel, the wife of Ahab, who was the King of Israel during his day. The rebellious and stubborn woman who adorn makeup to attract those by the lust of the flesh. Jezebel continued to manipulate her weak husband into doing things her way, including to kill Elijah. After time made its course, Jezebel was killed when she was tossed out of a window and consumed by the dogs that awaited her fall.

The following wicked one is Queen Zimmah, the forceful queen who over through Queen Diana of her kingdom and took over it for a period of twenty-seven years until Diana's daughter, Yisabelle took back the kingdom by killing Zimmah and her daughter, Zimmariah. Queen Zimmah was known for being a queen that desired to over through King Liam of his kingdom, known in spirit as Israel. She is also known for trying to search what was beyond the steep hill until her army fell at the hands of a supernatural power beyond earthly comprehension.

There is one wicked woman to come in the latter days and she is only known as Death. Referred to by some as the Hallucination of Sin and the Seductive Princess, nothing much is known of Death besides being the sister of Negiter, the dark god. She has played a frequent role on earth and will play even a larger part that concerns a man who is one of Us and who is the one to carry the Sword of the Elohim at this time. He and Death will be known throughout eternity as archenemies. A yin to a yang.

One of the final wicked ones to come across in the near future will be named Carissa, derived from Queen Alyssa and will be her successor in the future days ahead. Carissa will be a queen over a kingdom not yet given and her power will surpass the other nations in that period. Her rule will be like a lion stalking its prey until it has it by the jaws with blood pouring out to satisfy its hunger.

Carissa is a woman who will look pleasurable after the flesh, but rotten in the spirit as her ambition will always be to please the ha-Satan. Her ultimate goal will be to convince the entire world to love Satan and to cause them to receive his mark in order to live in this earth. Carissa has an opponent in the last days known as Yessica who will be spoken about in the virtuous section of this document.

Now, we head into those of the virtuous. Starting with Hawwah, the second wife of Adam. Hawwah, known as Eve to many became the wife of Adam after Yahweh had taken the rib from Adam and formed her from it, thus the woman became the help meet of the man in this earth for its existence. Even though Hawwah is responsible for eating the forbidden fruit first before Adam, the woman is known as the weaker vessel or the meekness and gentleness of Yah. Therefore, was the serpent able to easily manipulate her into doing so and in convincing Adam to eat thereof and bring sin from the outside world into the physical realm. After a while, hardly much is spoken of about Hawwah besides giving birth to her three sons Qayin, Hevel, and Seth and her two daughters Awan and Aclima.

Emzarah is the next virtuous woman to be spoken of in this document. The second wife of Dore during his middle years. Dore married Emzarah when he was five hundred years old and they had three sons together. Adad, Samael, and Mordecai. Emzarah was later greatly helpful in helping her sons find themselves wives before the deluge would come upon the earth and drown it. After the deluge and the chaos that followed, Emzarah lived a happy life with Dore and she died in her old age.

The next woman is Moriah, the wife of Adad, elder son of Dore and Emzarah. Moriah was chosen to be Adad's wife by Dore and Emzarah during the search for wives for their three sons. Moriah showed great character and humility toward them that they knew she was the one for Adad. Moriah married Adad and after the deluge they had children of their own, which the seed of the righteous had later come through into the world.

The woman Stephanie is another virtuous woman who endured patience of over seven years for Yah to send her a husband worthy of her submissiveness and humility. During the seven years,

Stephanie had sought guidance and counsel from her grandmother, Merith. After which one man came to her and was discovered to be the wrong kind of man for her and within a short time, Lebbeus came into her life and they were married and had a son named Luke, who later became a warrior for Yah and His People.

The next woman is Beth, who had a somewhat situation similar to Stephanie's own. Beth was an attractive woman who had come from another nation where she had searched across the various nations of the earth at that time to find a husband to cover her. After a few years, Beth was led by the widow Naomi into the nation of Yah's People where she met her husband and married. After certain number of years, they had three children named Samael, Andro, and Krutis.

Yisabelle is the next one in this lineup who was deemed virtuous by her character and her actions toward Yah and His People. The mother of Yisabelle, Queen Diana had no where to look for guidance during the sacking of her nation by Queen Zimmah. Yisabelle sought to seek guidance from King Liam, where she later found herself being tested, proven, and tried by not only Liam, but of Yah as well. Yisabelle overcame the trials and tests where she confronted Zimmah with the aid of Liam as she defeated Zimmah and Zimmariah in combat to win back her mother's nation. Yisabelle later moved from her mother's nation and moved into Liam's nation where she remained until her death.

Zora is one virtuous woman who will appear into the world during the days when the United States loses its democracy and becomes a third-world country. Zora will grow up in a dictatorial United States with Lucef Lukas as its leader and who was the one to have killed Zora's father, Theos. Zora will come to her true purpose on this earth and over through Lukas to bring back some prosperity into the people's hearts.

The final woman to be spoken of in this document is Yessica, highly called, the Virtuous Woman. Yessica will be the antithesis of Carissa, the Wicked Woman. Unlike Carissa, who will grow up with the ambition to please Satan, Yessica will have the ambition to please Yah as she will live in the world. It will not be a long one before Yessica and Carissa cross paths as they will battle to the death in the days of the Great Tribulation with Yessica defeating Carissa and killing her.

"These are primary a few of the important ones of the Virtuous and the Wicked. There are countless others on both sides that have lived in times past and will exist in times future. For the young women living today on this side of glory, I, Michael Ledford ask of you to take a look at your life and what you're currently trying to seek and to make sure that you're on the right path and that path is the strait and narrow way into the Kingdom of Heaven."

SINGLENESS

Many call themselves single to feel more preserved about their own well-being. The society that we currently live in has an uncanny ability to look down on those that have no mate. Whether man or woman, they are looked down upon. Some are even caused names because of their singleness. Yet, when you see those individuals' lifestyles and how they treat their mate, it becomes clear that they desire to have your place in the life of singleness rather than being cling to someone they have no love towards.

The tale of singleness goes far beyond the years before this present moment. Many have lived in this world without a mate, later find one and fall asleep, returning to the earth as they were formed. Some goes through the earth with a mate and create a family amongst themselves, seeking and hoping their offspring enter the same form of agreement when they come to the age of knowing. You also have the ones who were assigned to be with certain mates. Depending on how the relationship is started and built in the process, one cannot fully tell how it will turn out. Some spit out their theories and emotions on another one's relationship, only to have destroyed it with their foul tongues.

For the Elect know that the tongue is an unruly evil and filled with deadly poison and holds life and death in one's mouth when they speak of others and amongst others. The tongue is almost equal to the heart of a person. For no one knows the heart, for it is also evil and neither one man nor woman on earth knows their own heart to discern it. When it comes to this subject, people automatically throw out their own feelings and emotions without even concerning the one who is either with a mate or potentially going to be with one.

For not everyone is destined a mate, nor are they destined to have offspring. There are those parents that have the possessive dream of their offspring creating their own children, granting them grandchildren. There are barren women that walk among us and are mocked because of their symptom. There are men who are unable to produce enough seed to create an offspring, yet, they are mocked as well amongst the barren women, but with greater feeling.

They say that men are programmed to crave an offspring at certain ages in their lifespan. There are those that crave it at an early age, those that crave it once they reach adulthood, and those who will never crave it. There are those today who constantly crave a child and yet have no sustainability to take care of it, let alone take care of themselves to have a child. They never take heed the warnings that are given to them by elders and friends and end up having the child and witness their lives turning into a living hell.

"Yet, who's to blame but the one that didn't take heed. For they mocked and scalded the ones who warned them and now they suffer greatly."

Some live their lives and continue with their mates. Living a prosperous life. Some end with death, with separation, with fornication, with adultery. Yet, today, these are taken as extras into what the world calls marriage. Yea, they have no knowledge and understanding when they become married and are granted a marriage license by their government. Not realizing that they have entered into a third-party agreement with the State.

"For why should one possess a piece of paper to proclaim their marriage to another. For it is nonsensical to one's eye such as mine."

The ones that are currently single and trying to discover their purpose in the world. Continue to do so. Do not bother with the poison that people will spit at you to cause you to have doubts and conjure up depressive thoughts and feelings to make you feel bad because they want you in something that they can't possess themselves. Though, there will be those who will speak kind words of encouragement and will not try to shove you into their perception of reality of how to live and breathe on this side of glory.

"If one should speak kindly to another, it will give them great inspiration and thought of how they should go out and do what they intend to do."

There is this notion of a Gift of Singleness that has been said to exist. Containing the notion of singleness grants an individual the ability to focus on more important things rather than their own personal lives. Be it selfish or selfless, they have the knowledge of working on bigger things than themselves and are humble enough to admit it to themselves and to others.

What these people should do is stay focus on achieving the bigger tasks at hand in this earth. For many have lived this life single and have had a greater purpose. Jeremiah was directly told by the Most High that he should remain single for his purpose on earth. Daniel was single due to his incredible hold on his faith toward the Most High. The apostle, Paul was single and wished that every man would be like him when it came to singleness. Because it gave him more time and energy to do the work of the Most High through the Messiah. Even the Messiah himself was a single man when he was on this earth.

"There will be those who marry, because they work better as a team rather than individuals. There will be those who do not marry, and work better because of their individuality."

The ones that marry, will marry and a few of them will live a long and prosperous life. The others will end up in chaos and separate from one another, hoping the next one will be the "One" for them. There will be those who will marry, and the Angel of Death will have come and taken their mate, leaving them a widow on the earth. There will be those who will never marry, because of symptoms or their individuality. Either way, they know their purpose.

"For if one knows they should marry, marry so that you can be happy. For those that know they should remain single, for their work is a greater task than having a mate, continue on with your work, for it will help many along the way and inspire those who are going through these circumstances."

The Gift of Singleness is given to those who possess the ability to achieve great tasks and are able to have more time to give thanks to the Most High and do the work of Him to spread it across the earth for the Elect to see and hear.

ONE SOUL

The fortune of knowing one's soul is very distant and unconscious to the conscious mind of society. Many in this present hour neither seek or find what one's soul truly is and how it could bring prosperity to someone life. Even their own lives if they desired to seek it. How can the people today study how a soul works if they don't have the desire to seek it themselves? In this current time space, people no longer have the belief in a soul. They only believe in a flesh body walking on top of concrete, dirt, grass, and whatever else lies beneath their feet.

If one should go out into a public location and ask the question, "Do souls exist and do we possess one soul?", the majority of the people would be astonished by the words that were spoken in the question and secondly, they wouldn't know how to answer. You'll get some yes answers, no answers, and those indifferent ones that only gravitate towards another's answer to fit in amongst the crowd. If you're currently reading this text amongst the other text in this Book of the Elect, you're sure to find more later on as you go in life until your time on this side of glory ends.

In this book, you've read the accounts of many who have in reality, lived centuries before this time period and some who are currently living amongst us still in their human bodies. The ones of the past centuries, such as Stephanie, Lebbeus, Luke, the Old Man, Ahab, Jezebel, Abishag, Dore, Paul, and amongst the others have gone onto the other side beyond this realm we currently inhabit. The ones who are living amongst us today in this realm are Dolph, Clark Zyack, Levi, Preston Maddox, the father who read to his son about the Unheard-Of, as well as those whose name appeared briefly in the other texts are still living amongst us and yet, you're probably wondering where do you fit in all of this.

The answer is really simple. You fit amongst all of us in this realm. There are those such as the Elect who are the Most High's chosen people and are currently scattered abroad the world and will be reunited with each other in full when the Messiah returns and places his Kingdom on this earth to rule for one thousand years. For one to know their place and where they fit in this colossal universe, you just simply follow the Most High's laws, statutes, and commandments and obey his Word above all things. If you choose not to follow him, enjoy your life here in this realm and be happy with it and try to bring as much happiness in your life as you can.

Sometimes, people like me wonder about those who have come in the past and have left, where are they and what are they currently doing in the other realms. Both Shamayim and Geyhinnom, as some would call them, Heaven and Hell or Sheol. What could they possibly be doing. They have no earthly body of any kind, nor the thoughts that they conjured while they were here. Its best that you protect your soul at all cost. Guard your heart and mind greatly from the corruptions in this realm.

For we, the Elect know that we do not fight against flesh and blood, but the principalities, the rulers, and the darkness of this decadent world. For we know that the Unheard-Of or the ha-Satan is the god of this world and his image is shown before the world in monuments, stickers, logos, and anything that can be thought of as an image. As the Bible says in *2 Timothy 2:15*, Study and show yourself approved unto Yah. By doing that you will have a sense of reality in your mind about how you should operate before jumping on others for their characteristics and lifestyle.

We must stand strong and fight the battle that is currently taking place all around us. For angels are battling demons on a daily basis and yet we have no sight of it, because the fight is taking place in the spiritual realm and in the near future it will be in the physical realm, where we will all see it unfold. The battle between good and evil in all its detail. Many will be frightened of the tribulation unfolding and yet they should build up faith in the Most High to protect them and shield them from His wrath upon the earth.

For we the Elect understand that we have only one soul and we determine where that soul will go once we leave this side of glory. We determine if we will be dwelling with the Most High in his Kingdom of peace and love or if we will be dwelling with the Unheard-Of in his kingdom of fire and sulfur. For those who will understand this small text, hopefully they will get the full picture soon as possible, with obedience to the Father and studying his Word.

I am aware that standing up for the Most High that I will have a slew of enemies from all sides of the earth and they will do whatever in their power to tear us down and annihilate us from this earth. Yet, as the ones of old such as Chanokh, Harold Vosloo, Dore, the Old Man, and those who live today, Levi, Maddox, Zyack, we understand that in the end of all of this, we will prevail. For we obey the Father and keep his commandments and laws.

Before this is finished, I must say that there is an age coming of perpetual revelations that will be unfolded for the world to witness. Those living today and those being born today are going to witness events that the ancients have not yet seen. For those who truly believe will see the signs around them and those who do not believe, will continue to live their lives happily as they can. I end this with a final statement. We all have one soul and it is up to us to determine our fate in this life and the next.

763

My name is Thomas Bradford and I say to you. *Shalom.*

AGE OF REVELATIONS

Allow me to properly introduce myself
My name is the Dragon of the Wilderness
I understand something apparently
Since I have existed on this earth
I have done some horrible things to many people

There is an event upon the horizon
An event that has reached afar in the minds
Of many in the world
The event has legendary proportions from its prophecies
The Age of Revelations

Humans, have you ever taken the time to see me for how I really am?
I am the Way into the cities of Babylon
I am the Way into eternal pleasure and pain
I am the Way to go among the lost beyond the time
I STAND!

I see the fire, I see the will
I can look into your own spirit
And I can honestly say
you honestly believe you can defeat Me
At Har Megiddo

Liar. Liar! You are a liar!
You built this Kingdom all around us
And your foolish pride allows you to prey upon the weak
And fill them up with all this… hope. But the hope is dead.
As will be your Kingdom

YOU should have been more careful of what you've wished
for

When I take center at Har Megiddo, you then will realize
That I am the most powerful entity
That has ever stepped foot
On this earth

Just remember this.
You're the one with everything to lose
When I come through and destroy
Who will be there for you
When I take it all away?!

You've sealed your own fate
When you decided to rebel and destroy
There's no escaping what will happen at Har Megiddo
You will be desolated
You will be punished

I have broken Your Saints.
I HAVE BROKEN YOUR SAINTS!!!
My sword has left a scar on their souls
A scar so deep and open
That can never heal

But you listen to Me now

The eternal flames after Har Megiddo
For you, your angels, and your nations
Will be the eternal punishment
For you all

You know this
Just as much as the angels in Shamayim
Just as much as your saints
Just as much as my kingdoms of the earth
I am already punished

The pain waiting on you after Har Megiddo
Will last for eternity as you,
Your angels, your nations
And your kingdoms
Will be the most pain of all

Humans, wake up, wake up,
WAKE UP!
Wake yourselves up and take a look around
Look at this world you're living in
Look at this world you're living in Man

I will open up the gates of Shamayim
And I will unleash a fury
A fury of which no mortal man
Throughout all of earth's history
Has never been seen

At Har Megiddo
Is the time and the place

Among your creations
Your beautiful creation of all
Is when reality sets itself in

At Har Megiddo
You will be defeated
You will be left alone
You will be judged
You will be rebuked and punished

Open your eyes, generations of Man.

<u>YAH is ONE</u>

A word by Kenari Clark

O' Yah
Save your remnant from this untoward generation
We await your coming with patience
With fear and tremble we stand
We await

Abba Father,
Be merciful toward your children
We may fall at times in this life
But we get back up to continue moving forward
Be merciful

O' Yah
Throughout all the days of my life
Will I worship and praise you
You brought me out of the world
And showed me your marvelous light

I thank you for your mercy
You formed me before I was in the womb
You knew me before the earth was created
You know all of us better than we know ourselves
We praise Your Name

You showed us the way of truth and life

Through your son, Jesus Christ
Who sacrificed himself for us
To wash away our sins
To cleanse us for a better day

We are becoming new
The old man is passing away
And the new man is being born
The new man will praise you
The new man will worship you

We renew our minds
We learn Your ways and abandon our ways
We guard Your Law with our hearts
We keep it within us to be in remembrance
We remember your promises

When Noah built the ark
He was counted as righteous
When Abraham had walked in faith
He was considered righteous
We strive for righteousness

With righteousness
We inherit your Kingdom
A Kingdom made by Your power
A Kingdom that will come down from the sky
A New Jerusalem

O' Yah
We know the day is near
We know the time is close

We see the prophecies coming to pass
We know to prepare

Both our hearts and minds
We are to prepare
Our enemies will seek to stumble us
But, we will stand firm
We will trust You

We will have faith in You
We seek Your Kingdom
As this earth passes away
And everything that dwells upon it
We strive

YOU ARE ONE

ABOUT THE BOOKS AND SHORT STORIES

BATTLE FOR ASTOLAT: A CONFLICT OF THE HAUNTED CITY

The Warslingers of the Heptad come to the city of Astolat after receiving a distress signal from Elaine, the princess of a city being attacked by a mystical army led by an unknown leader. The Warslingers come to the city of Astolat and learn more than what they were informed.

(Only available in this book and as a KOBO e-book exclusive)

THE LEGENDARY WARSLINGER: THE HAUNTED CITY I

The deserts roam the western world as the green, lush land has consumed the eastern world. Follow Randolph Henrich, a Warslinger of the Heptad. A group of holy knights who protect those from the malevolent entities roaming within and without the worlds. On his journey toward the cryptic Haunted City, Henrich meets both allies and enemies who will make his journey one to remember.

(Available now in paperback, e-book, and Special Edition hardcover.)

REDEMPTION OF THE LOST: THE HAUNTED CITY II

The Legendary Warslinger, Randolph Henrich continues his journey to The Haunted City with his associates Cody Landon and Beth Grasslands at his side. The Three fight off the dark forces of both man and spirit that encompass the ruined lands as they uncover a secret world where they realize that it's best to seek for the old paths.

(Available now in hardcover. Coming soon to paperback and e-book)

LOST IN SHADOWS: REMASTERED

U.S. Marshals and Homicide Detectives, Preston Maddox and Emily Weston are charged with a task to solve a series of murders which have conjured up in New Haven, Connecticut. Preston has a lead on who may be the cause of the murders, upon the moment where his childhood friend, Hoyt Bennett makes his return to New Haven from prison, along with old enemies reappearing from the past, triggering a turn for the worst when Preston and Emily find themselves lost in shadows.

(Available in hardcover. Coming soon to paperback and e-book)

<u>*THE PLEASURED KILLING: AN INSTINCTS SHORT STORY*</u>
A short story set after the events of *Lost in Shadows: Remastered.*
Following U.S. Marshal and homicide detective Brant Harper on a
case to find the mysterious Pleasure Man within the bounds of Point
Hope, Connecticut. The Sister City to New Haven. A small town
where strange matters dwell.

<u>*ACCOUNTS OF THE DEAD DAYS*</u>
Living in a world filled with the coming of the Undead has come
and with these three stories, enter the world of an estranged
zombie apocalypse. An apocalypse which began in secret, yet in
the open. These three stories reveal alternative looks at the
outbreak and those who fought their way through it and those
who lost.

(Available in paperback and Kindle e-book)

<u>*SYMBOLUM VENATORES: THE GABRIEL KANE COLLECTION*</u>
From Dracula, The Invisible Man, Phantom of the Opera, Zombies in
Feudal Japan, and UFOs during the American Civil War, one man was
there for them all. This collection features ten stories throughout points
in history where Gabriel Kane was present. from his youth and middle-
age, these accounts were his duty and his purpose.

(Available in paperback and Kindle e-book)

<u>*HOD*</u>
A story of dark fantasy, mystery, suspense, and supernatural.
Follow Mr. Hod on a case to uncover the events in which set up a
strange and macabre murder. A murder where only animalistic
footsteps remained aside of a deceased stranger.

(Available in paperback and Kindle e-book)

<u>*THE PASSOVER: A SHORT STORY*</u>
A story of to do and not to do.
A story of sowing and reaping.
A story of the past, the present, and the future.

ABOUT THE AUTHOR

Ty'Ron W. C. Robinson II is the author of several works of fiction. Including the *Dark Titan Universe Saga* series (*Dark Titan Knights, The Resistance Protocol, Tales of the Scattered, Tales of the Numinous, Day of Octagon*) and *The Haunted City Saga* series. Also of other books (*Lost in Shadows, Hod, The Book of The Elect, Symbolum Venatores, etc.*) and One-Shot short stories More information pertaining to the author and stories can be found at darktitanentertainment.com.

FOLLOW THE AUTHOR
Twitter: @TyRonRobinsonII
Instagram: @tyronrobinsonii

FOLLOW DARK TITAN ENTERTAINMENT
Twitter: @DarkTitan_
Instagram: @darktitanentertainment
Facebook: @darktitanent
Pinterest: @darktitanentertainment